The Meaning of Night

Also by Michael Cox

BIOGRAPHY

M. R. James: An Informal Portrait

ANTHOLOGIES

The Oxford Book of English Ghost Stories
(with R. A. Gilbert)

The Oxford Book of Victorian Ghost Stories
(with R. A. Gilbert)

The Oxford Book of Victorian Detective Stories

The Oxford Book of Spy Stories

EDITOR

M. R. James: 'Casting the Runes' and Other Ghost Stories
(Oxford World's Classics)

COMPILER

The Oxford Chronology of English Literature

The MEANING *of* NIGHT

· A CONFESSION ·

MICHAEL COX

W. W. NORTON & COMPANY
NEW YORK LONDON

Book design by Abbate Design
Production manager: Anna Oler

ISBN-13: 978-0-7394-7968-1

W. W. Norton & Company, Inc.
500 Fifth Avenue, New York, N.Y. 10110

For Dizzy. For everything.

THE MEANING OF NIGHT

A Confession

EDITED BY J. J. ANTROBUS

PROFESSOR *of Post-Authentic*

VICTORIAN FICTION,

University of Cambridge

CONTENTS

Editor's Preface

THE FOLLOWING WORK, PRINTED HERE FOR THE FIRST TIME, IS ONE OF the lost curiosities of nineteenth-century literature. It is a strange concoction, being a kind of confession, often shocking in its frank, conscienceless brutality and explicit sexuality, that also has a strongly novelistic flavour; indeed it appears in the hand-list that accompanies the Duport papers in the Cambridge University Library with the annotation '(Fiction?)'. Many of the presented facts – names, places, events (including the unprovoked murder of Lucas Trendle) – that I have been able to check are verifiable; others appear dubious at best or have been deliberately falsified, distorted, or simply invented. Real people move briefly in and out of the narrative, others remain unidentified – or unidentifiable – or are perhaps pseudonymous. As the author himself says, 'The boundaries of this world are forever shifting – from day to night, joy to sorrow, love to hate, and from life itself to death.' And, he might have added, from fact to fiction.

As to the author, despite his desire to confess all to posterity, his own identity remains a tantalizing mystery. His name as given here, Edward Charles Glyver, does not appear in the Eton Lists of the period, and I have been unable to trace it or any of his pseudonyms in any other source, including the London Post-office Directories for the relevant years. Perhaps, after we have read these confessions, this should not surprise us; yet it is strange that someone who wished to lay his soul bare in this way chose not to reveal his real name. I simply do not know how to account for this, but note the anomaly in the hope that further research, perhaps by other scholars, may unravel the mystery.

His adversary Phoebus Daunt, on the other hand, is real enough. The main events of his life may be traced in various contemporary sources. He may be found, for instance, in both the Eton Lists and in Venn's *Alumni Cantabrigienses*, and is mentioned in several literary memoirs of the period – though on his supposed criminal career the historical record is silent. On the other hand, his now (deservedly) forgotten literary works, consisting principally of turgid historical and mythological epics and a few slight volumes of poems and poetic translations, once enjoyed a fleeting popularity. They may still be sought out by the curious in specialist libraries and booksellers' catalogues (as can his father's edition of Catullus, mentioned in the text), and perhaps may yet furnish some industrious PhD student with a dissertation subject.

The text has been transcribed, more or less verbatim, from the unique holograph manuscript now held in the Cambridge University Library. The manuscript came to the CUL in 1948 as part of an anonymous bequest, with other papers and books relating to the Duport family of Evenwood in Northamptonshire. It is written, for the most part, in a clear and confident hand on large-quarto lined sheets, the whole being bound in dark-red morocco (by R. Riviere, Great Queen Street) with the Duport arms blocked in gold on the front. Despite a few passages where the author's hand deteriorates, apparently under psychological duress, or perhaps as a result of his opium habit, there are relatively few deletions, additions, or other amendments. In addition to the author's narrative there are several interpolated documents and extracts by other hands.

I have made a number of silent emendments in matters of orthography, punctuation, and so on; and because the MS lacks a title, I have used a phrase, appropriately enough, from the pen of

P. Rainsford Daunt himself, quoted by the author. I have also supplied titles for each of the five parts, and for the five sections of the so-called Intermezzo.

The sometimes enigmatic Latin titles to the forty-seven sections or chapters have been retained (their idiosyncrasy seemed typical of the author), though I have provided translations. On the first leaf of the manuscript are a dozen or so quotations from Owen Fellt-ham's *Resolves*, some of which I have used as epigraphs to each of the five parts. Throughout the text, my own editorial interpolations and footnotes are given within square brackets.

J. J. ANTROBUS
Professor of Post-Authentic
Victorian Fiction
University of Cambridge
October 2005

The words of his mouth were smoother than butter,
but war was in his heart:
his words were softer than oil,
yet were they drawn swords.

—PSALM 55: 21

I find, to him that the tale is told,
belief only makes the difference betwixt a truth, and a lie.

—OWEN FELLTHAM, *Resolves or, Excogitations. A Second Centurie* (1628),
iv ('Of Lies and Untruths')

For Death is the meaning of night;
The eternal shadow
Into which all lives must fall,
All hopes expire.

—P. RAINSFORD DAUNT, 'From the Persian',
Rosa Mundi; and Other Poems (1854)

TO MY UNKNOWN READER.

Ask not Pilate's question.
For I have sought, not truth, but meaning.

E.G.

Part the First

Death of a Stranger

October–November 1854

What a skein of ruffled silk
is the uncomposed man.

—Owen Felltham, *Resolves* (1623),
ii, 'Of Resolution'

· 1 ·

*Exordium**

AFTER KILLING THE RED-HAIRED MAN, I TOOK MYSELF OFF TO QUINN'S† for an oyster supper.

It had been surprisingly – almost laughably – easy. I had followed him for some distance, after first observing him in Threadneedle-street. I cannot say why I decided it should be him, and not one of the others on whom my searching eye had alighted that evening. I had been walking for an hour or more in the vicinity with one purpose: to find someone to kill. Then I saw him, outside the entrance to the Bank, amongst a huddle of pedestrians waiting for the crossing-sweeper to do his work. Somehow he seemed to stand out from the crowd of identically dressed clerks and City men streaming forth from the premises. He stood regarding the milling scene around him, as if turning something over in his mind. I thought for a moment that he was about to retrace his steps; instead, he pulled on his gloves, moved away from the crossing point, and set off briskly. A few seconds later, I began to follow him.

We proceeded steadily westwards through the raw October cold and the thickening mist. After descending Ludgate-hill and crossing over into Fleet-street, we continued on our course for some distance until, at length, and after having refreshed himself at a coffee-house, my man turned into a narrow court that cut

*[An introduction to a treatise or discourse. *Ed.*]

†[A shell fishmonger and supper-house at 40 Haymarket. *Ed.*]

through to the Strand, not much more than a passage, flanked on either side by high windowless walls. I glanced up at the discoloured sign – 'Cain-court' – then stopped for a moment, to remove my gloves, and take out the long-bladed knife from the inside pocket of my great-coat.

My victim, all unsuspecting, continued on his way; but before he had time to reach the steps at the far end, I had caught up with him noiselessly and had sunk my weapon deep into his neck.

I had expected him to fall instantly forwards with the force of the blow; but, curiously, he dropped to his knees, with a soft gasp, his arms by his side, his stick clattering to the floor, and remained in that position for some seconds, like an enraptured devotee before a shrine.

As I withdrew the knife, I moved forwards slightly. It was then I noticed for the first time that his hair, where it showed beneath his hat, was, like his neatly trimmed whiskers, a distinct shade of red. For a brief moment, before he gently collapsed sideways, he looked at me: not only looked at me, but – I swear – smiled, though in truth I now suppose it was the consequence of some involuntary spasm brought about by the withdrawal of the blade.

He lay, illuminated by a narrow shaft of pale yellow light flung out by the gas-lamp at the top of the passage steps, in a slowly widening pool of dark blood that contrasted oddly with the carrotty hue of his hair and whiskers. He was dead for certain.

I stood for a moment, looking about me. A sound, perhaps, somewhere behind me in the dark recesses of the court? Had I been observed? No; all was still. Putting on my gloves once more, I dropped the knife down a grating and walked smartly away, down the dimly lit steps, and into the enfolding, anonymous bustle of the Strand.

. . .

Now I knew that I could do it; but it gave me no pleasure. The poor fellow had done me no harm. Luck had simply been against him – together with the colour of his hair, which, I now saw, had been his fatal distinction. His way that night, inauspiciously coinciding with mine in Threadneedle-street, had made him the unwitting object of my irrevocable intention to kill someone; but had it not been him, it must have been someone else.

Until the very moment in which the blow had been struck, I had not known definitively that I was capable of such a terrible act, and it was absolutely necessary to put the matter beyond all doubt. For the despatching of the red-haired man was in the nature of a trial, or experiment, to prove to myself that I could indeed take another human life, and escape the consequences. When I next raised my hand in anger, it must be with the same swift and sure determination; but this time it would be directed, not at a stranger, but at the man I call my enemy.

And I must not fail.

The first word I ever heard used to describe myself was: 'resourceful'.

It was said by Tom Grexby, my dear old schoolmaster, to my mother. They were standing beneath the ancient chestnut tree that shaded the little path that led up to our house. I was tucked away out of view above them, nestled snugly in a cradle of branches I called my crow's-nest. From here I could look out across the cliff-top to the sea beyond, dreaming for long hours of sailing away one day to find out what lay beyond the great arc of the horizon.

On this particular day – hot, still, and silent – I watched my mother as she walked down the path towards the gate, a little lace parasol laid open against her shoulder. Tom was panting up the hill from the church as she reached the gate. I had not long commenced under his tutelage, and supposed that my mother had seen him from the house, and had come out expressly to speak to him about my progress.

'He is,' I heard him say, in reply to her enquiry, 'a most resourceful young man.'

Later, I asked her what 'resourceful' meant.

'It means you know how to get things done,' she said, and I felt pleased that this appeared to be a quality approved of in the adult world.

'Was Papa resourceful?' I asked.

She did not reply, but instead told me to run along and play, as she must return to her work.

When I was very young, I was often told – gently but firmly – by my mother to 'run along', and consequently spent many hours amusing myself. In summer, I would dream amongst the branches of the chestnut tree or, accompanied by Beth, our maid-of-all-work, explore along the shore-line beneath the cliff; in winter, wrapped up in an old tartan shawl on the window-seat in my bedroom, I would dream over Wanley's *Wonders of the Little World,** *Gulliver's Travels,* or *Pilgrim's Progress* (for which I cherished an inordinate fondness and fascination) until my head ached, looking out betimes across the drear waters, and wondering how far beyond the horizon, and in which direction, lay the Country of the Houyhnhnms, or the City of Destruction, and whether it would be possible to take a packet boat from Weymouth to see them for myself. Why the City of Destruction should have

*[Nathaniel Wanley (1634–80). The book was first published in 1678. The subtitle reads: 'A general history of man: In six books. Wherein by many thousands of examples is shewed what man hath been from the first ages of the world to these times ... Collected from the writings of the most approved historians, philosophers, physicians, philologists and others.' *Ed.*]

sounded so enticing to me, I cannot imagine, for I was terrified by Christian's premonition that it was about to be burned with fire from heaven, and often imagined that the same fate might befall our little village. I was also haunted throughout my childhood, though again I could not say why, by the Pilgrim's words to Evangelist: 'I am condemned to die, and after that to come to judgment; and I find that I am not willing to do the first, nor able to do the second.' Puzzling though they were, I knew that the words expressed a terrible truth, and I would repeat them to myself over and again, like some occult incantation, as I lay in my cradle of branches or in my bed, or as I wandered the windy shore beneath the cliff-top.

I dreamed, too, of another place, equally fantastic and beyond possession, and yet – strangely – having the distinctness of somewhere experienced and remembered, like a taste that stays on the tongue. I would find myself standing before a great building, part castle and part palace, the home of some ancient race, as I thought, bristling with ornamented spires and battlemented turrets, and wondrous grey towers, topped with curious dome-like structures, that soared into the sky – so high that they seemed to pierce the very vault of heaven. And in my dreams it was always summer – perfect, endless summer, and there were white birds, and a great dark fish-pond surrounded by high walls. This magical place had no name, and no location, real or imagined. I had not found it described in any book, or in any story told to me. Who lived there – whether some king or caliph – I knew not. Yet I was sure that it existed somewhere on the earth, and that one day I would see it with my own eyes.

My mother was constantly working, for her literary efforts were our only means of support, my father having died soon after I was born. The picture that always comes to mind, when thinking of her, is of spindles of grey-flecked dark hair escaping from beneath her cap and falling over her cheek, as she sat bent over the large square work-table that was set before the parlour window. There she would sit for hours at a time, sometimes well into the night, furiously scratching away. As soon as one tottering pile of paper was complete and despatched to the publisher, she would immediately begin to lay down another. Her works (beginning with *Edith; or, The Last of the Fitzalans,* of 1826) are now quite unremembered – it would be disloyal to her memory if I say deservedly so; but in their day they enjoyed a certain vogue; at least they found sufficient readers for Mr Colburn* to continue accepting her productions (mostly issued anonymously, or sometimes under the *nom de plume* 'A Lady of the West') year in and year out until her death.

Yet though she worked so long, and so hard, she would always break off to be with me for a while, before I went to sleep. Sitting on the end of my bed, with a tired smile on her sweet elfin face, she would listen while I solemnly read out some favourite passages from my precious translation of Monsieur Galland's *Les mille et une nuits;*† or she might tell me little stories that she had made up, or perhaps recount memories of her own childhood in the West Country, which I especially loved to hear. Sometimes, on fine summer nights, we would walk, hand in hand, out onto the cliff-top to watch the sunset; and then we would stand together in silence, listening to the lonely cry of the gulls and the soft murmur of the waves below, and gaze out across the glowing waters to the mysterious far horizon.

*[Henry Colburn (d. 1855), the publisher and founder of the *Literary Gazette. Ed.*]

†[The French orientalist Antoine Galland (1646–1715) made the first Western translation of *The Thousand and One Nights,* published in twelve volumes between 1704 and 1717 as *Les Mille et une nuits.* It was a great success and was followed by several other European translations, including the first English rendering of Galland's text, published anonymously 1706–8 and known as the 'Grub Street version'. This is undoubtedly the version referred to by the narrator. The translation was both defective and dull, but it inspired successive generations of English readers, up to and including the Romantic poets. *Ed.*]

'Over there is France, Eddie,' I remember her saying once. 'It is a large and beautiful country.'

'And are there Houyhnhnms there, Mamma?' I asked.

She gave a little laugh.

'No, dear,' she said. 'Only people, like you and me.'

'And have you been to France ever?' was my next question.

'I have been there once,' came the reply. Then she sighed. 'And I shall never go there again.'

When I looked up at her, I saw to my astonishment that she was crying, which I had never seen her do before; but then she clapped her hands and, saying it was time that I was in my bed, bundled me back into the house. At the bottom of the stairs, she kissed me, and told me I would always be her best boy. Then she turned away, leaving me on the bottom stair, and I watched her go back into the parlour, sit down at her work-table, and dip her pen into the ink once more.

The memory of that evening was awakened many years later, and has ever since remained strong. I thought of it now, as I puffed slowly on my cigar in Quinn's, musing on the strange connectedness of things; on the thin, but unbreakable, threads of causality that linked – for they did so link – my mother labouring at her writing all those years ago with the red-haired man who now lay dead not half a mile away in Cain-court.

WALKING DOWN TOWARDS THE RIVER, I FELT INTOXICATED BY THE thought that I had escaped discovery. But then, whilst paying my half-penny to the toll-keeper on Waterloo Bridge, I noticed that my hands were shaking and that, despite my recent refreshment at Quinn's, my mouth was dry as tinder. Beneath a flickering gas-lamp, I leaned against the parapet for a moment, feeling suddenly dizzy. The fog lay heavy on the black water below, which lapped and slopped against the piers of the great echoing arches, making a most dismal music. Then, out of the swirling fog, a thin young woman appeared, carrying a baby. She stood for a few moments, obliviously staring down into the blackness. I clearly saw the blank despair on her face, and instantly sensed that she was about to make a jump of it; but as I moved towards her, she looked at me wildly, clutched the child tightly to her breast, and ran off, leaving me to watch her poor phantom figure dissolve into the fog once more.* A life saved, I hoped, if only for a time; but something, perhaps, to set against what I had done that night.

For you must understand that I am not a murderer by nature, only by temporary design and necessity – a justified sinner. There was no need to repeat this experimental act of killing. I had proved what I had set out to prove: the capacity of my will to carry out such a deed. The blameless red-haired stranger had fulfilled his purpose, and I was ready for what now lay ahead.

I walked to the Surrey side of the bridge, turned round, and walked back again. Then, on a sudden impulse, as I passed once more through the turnstile, I decided to retrace my steps along the Strand instead of returning to my rooms. At the foot of the steps leading down from Cain-court, which I had descended not two hours earlier, a crowd of people had gathered. I enquired of a flower-seller concerning the cause of the commotion.

'Murder, sir,' she replied. 'A poor gentleman has been most viciously done to death. They say the head was almost severed from the body.'

'Good heavens!' said I, with every expression of sudden shock. 'What a world we live in! Is anyone apprehended?'

*[Waterloo Bridge was known as the 'Bridge of Sighs' because of the number of suicides who had leaped to their deaths from it. *Ed.*]

My informant was uncertain on this point. A Chinese sailor had been seen running from the court a little time before the body had been discovered; but others had said that a woman carrying a bloody axe had been found standing in a daze a few streets away, and had been taken off by the officers.

I shook my head sadly, and continued on my way.

Of course it was most convenient that ignorant rumour was already weaving nets of obscurity and falsehood around the truth. For all I cared, either the Chinese sailor or the woman with the bloody axe, if, indeed, they existed, could swing for my deed and be damned. I was armoured against all suspicion. Certainly no one had observed me entering or leaving the dark and deserted court; I had been most particular on that point. The knife had been of a common type, purloined for the purpose from an inn across the river in Borough High-street, where I had never been before, and to which I would never return again. My nameless victim had been entirely unknown to me; nothing but cold Fate connected us. My clothes appeared to be unmarked by his blood; and night, villainy's true friend, had thrown its accomplice's cloak over all.

By the time I reached Chancery-lane, the clocks were striking eleven. Still feeling unwilling to return to my own solitary bed, I swung northwards, to Blithe Lodge, St John's Wood, with the intention of paying my compliments to Miss Isabella Gallini, of blessed memory.

AH, BELLA! BELLISSIMA BELLA! SHE WELCOMED ME IN HER CUSTOMARY way at the door of the respectable tree-fronted villa, cupping my face in her long-fingered, many-ringed hands and whispering, 'Eddie, darling Eddie, how wonderful,' as she kissed me gently on both cheeks.

'Is all quiet?' I asked.

'Perfectly. The last one went an hour ago, Charlie is asleep, and Mrs D. has not yet returned. We have the house to ourselves.'

Upstairs I lay back on her bed watching her disrobe, as I had done so many times before. I knew every inch of her body, every warm and secret place. Yet watching the last piece of clothing fall to the floor, and seeing her standing proudly before me, was like experiencing her for the first time in all her untasted glory.

'Say it,' she said.

I frowned in pretended ignorance.

'Say what?'

'You know very well, you tease. Say it.'

She walked towards me, her hair now released and flowing over her shoulders and down her back. Then, reaching the bed, she once again clasped my face in her hands and let that dark torrent of tresses tumble around me.

'Oh, my America,' I declaimed theatrically, 'my new-found land!'*

'Oh, Eddie,' she cooed delightedly, 'it does so thrill me when you say that! Am I really your America?'

'My America and more. You are my world.'

At which she threw herself upon me with a will and kissed me so hard that I could scarcely breathe.

The establishment of which Bella was the leading light was several cuts above the usual introducing house, so much so that it was known to the *cognoscenti* simply as 'The Academy', the definite article proclaiming that it was set apart from all other rival establishments, and alluding proudly to the superiority of its inmates, as well as to the services they offered. It was run along the lines of a

*[From John Donne, 'Elegie XIX: To his Mistris Going to Bed'. *Ed.*]

highly select club – a Boodle's or White's of the flesh* – and catered for the amorous needs of the most discerning patrons of means. Like its counterparts in St James's, it had strict rules on admission and behaviour. No person was allowed entry to this choice coterie without the unequivocal recommendation of an existing member, followed by a vote; blackballing was not infrequent, and if a recommendation proved wanting in any way, both applicant and proposer faced summary ejection, sometimes worse.

Mrs Kitty Daley, known to the members as Mrs D, was the *entrepreneuse* of this celebrated and highly profitable Cyprian† resort. She went to great lengths to maintain standards of social decency: no swearing, profanity, or drunkenness was tolerated, and any disrespect towards, or ill-treatment of, the young ladies themselves was punished with the utmost severity. Not only would the perpetrator find himself immediately barred and exposed to public scandal; he would also receive a call from Mr Herbert Braithwaite, a former pugilist of distinction, who had his own highly effective way of making delinquent patrons understand the error of their ways.

Signor Prospero Gallini, Bella's father, the impoverished scion of a noble Italian family, having fallen on hard times, had fled his creditors in his native land in the year 1830, and had made his way to England, where he set himself up as a fencing-master in London. He was now a widower, and an exile; but he was determined to give his only daughter every advantage that his limited means permitted, with the result that she could converse fluently in several European languages, played exceptionally well on the

*[Boodle's, a gentleman's club of a semi-political character at 28 St James's Street; White's (originally White's Chocolate House, established towards the end of the seventeenth century), was another celebrated club-house at 37 and 38 St James's Street. *Ed.*]

†[An adjective carrying the meaning of licentious or lewd, deriving from Cyprus, an island famed for the worship of Aphrodite. *Ed.*]

piano-forte, had a delightful singing voice, and was, in short, as accomplished as she was beautiful.

I had lodged briefly with Signor Gallini and his alluring daughter when I first came to London. After his death I maintained an occasional, but friendly, correspondence with Bella, feeling that it was my duty to watch over her, in a brotherly sort of way, in gratitude for the kindness that her father had shown to me. Signor Gallini had left her little enough, and it became necessary for her to leave the house in Camberwell, to which her father had retired, and take employment as companion to a lady in St John's Wood, whose acquaintance we have already made. She had answered an advertisement for this position, which was Mrs D's way of recruiting new blood for her stable of thoroughbreds. Very few who applied found favour in Mrs D's discerning eye; but Bella had instantly charmed her, and was not in the least shocked when the true nature of her employment was revealed to her. Although she began her career as the most junior citizen in The Academy's little state, she quickly rose through the ranks, being exceptionally beautiful, talented, discreet, and as accommodating as any gentleman could wish. If there is such a thing as a vocation in this line of work, then Bella Gallini may be said to have possessed one.

Our intermittent correspondence continued for some years after she took up residence at Blithe Lodge. I would send a brief note every few months, to enquire how she did, and whether she was in need of anything, and she would always say that she was going on very well, that her employer was kindness itself, and that she wanted for nothing. Then one day, in the early months of 1853, I happened to be in the vicinity of St John's Wood and thought I would call on her, to see for myself that all was well, and (I confess) to satisfy my curiosity that she was still as beautiful as I remembered her.

I was admitted to an elegant drawing-room, displaying both

taste and means. The door opened; but it was not Bella. Two giggling young ladies, unaware that a visitor was within, burst into the room. On seeing me, they halted, looked me up and down, and then looked at each other. They were a most ravishing pair, one blonde, the other dark; and both had an unmistakable look about them. I had seen it a hundred times, though rarely in such sumptuous surroundings.

They begged my pardon (unnecessarily: I would have forgiven them any liberty they had chosen to take), and were about to withdraw when another figure appeared in the doorway.

She *was* as beautiful as I remembered her; dressed to the highest point of fashion, coiffured and bejewelled, but still possessed of a natural grace of carriage, and displaying that warm and open expression with which she had greeted me when I had first come to her father's house. After her fair companions had departed, we walked out into the garden and talked away, like the old friends we were, until a female servant came across from the house to tell Bella that she had another visitor.

'Will you call again?' she asked. 'I seem to have spoken only of myself, and would so like to hear more about what you have been doing with your life, and what you intend to do in the future.'

I needed no further hint, and said that I would come again the following day, if it was convenient.

Neither of us had said anything concerning the true character of Blithe Lodge; there was no need. She saw, by my look and tone of voice, that I was not in the least shocked or disgusted by what she had chosen to become; and for my part, I could see that – as she had told me so often – she wanted for nothing, and that her professed contentment with her lot was unfeigned.

I returned the next day, when I was introduced to Mrs D herself; and the following week attended a soirée, at which were assembled some of the most eminent and well-placed of the capital's fast men. Gradually, my visits increased in frequency, and soon brotherly solicitation began to transform into something more intimate. By special dispensation, I was not required to make any contribution to the domestic oeconomy of the house. 'You're most welcome here any time, my dear,' said Mrs D, with whom I had quickly become a great favourite, 'just as long as Bella ain't distracted from her professional duties.'

Mrs D being a widow with no dependants, it had long been settled that Bella, who had become like a daughter to her, would in the course of time assume the reins of power in this thriving carnal kingdom. On this account, I would call her my little heiress, and she would smile contentedly as I pictured to her the days of ease that lay ahead once the inevitable mortal release of Mrs D, now in her sixty-first year, delivered the succession into her hands.

'I don't like to think of it too much,' she said, as we lay together in the dark after the incident in Cain-court, talking of Mrs D's impending retirement, 'seeing how fond I am of Kitty, and how kind she's always been to me. But, you know, I can't help feeling – well, a little satisfied at the prospect, though I'm sure I don't deserve it.'

I rebuked her gently for her scruples, telling her that it was folly – and worse – to believe that we do not merit our good fortune, especially if it is ours by right. She kissed me and pulled me close; but I felt suddenly abandoned and alone. For was I not also an heir, and to a far greater kingdom than hers? Yet *my* inheritance had been taken from me, and could never now be reclaimed. This was hard enough to bear; but, through a considered act of betrayal, I had sustained an even greater loss, which had left me bereft of all hope of recovery. It is trite to speak of a broken heart. Hearts are not broken; they continue to beat, the blood still courses, even in the bitter after-days of betrayal. But something *is* broken when pain beyond words is suffered; some connection that formerly existed with light and hope and bright mornings is severed, and can never be restored.

I longed to throw off the habit of deceit, and this smiling mask of carelessness I wore to conceal the rage that foamed and boiled beneath. But I could not tell Bella the truth about myself, nor why I had been driven to kill a stranger that night in Cain-court. For she had become the one sweet constant in my life through a storm of trouble and danger of which she had been unaware; yet she, too, had been betrayed, though she did not know it. I had already lost her; but still I could not let her go – not quite yet – nor confess to her what I am now confessing to you, my unknown reader.

Yet there is one person who knows what I cannot tell Bella. And soon he will also come to know how resourceful I can be.

· 2 ·

*Nominatim**

I HAD SLEPT FITFULLY, AWARE OF THE SOFT, WARM MASS OF BELLA'S body curled up against mine as I drifted in and out of wakefulness. Though pricked by occasional anxieties, I remained confident that no one could connect me to my victim, and that I had completed my experiment in murder undetected. Having consciously subdued all thought of the man I had killed *as* a man, I found I had attained to a kind of indifference to the enormity of the act that I had so recently committed. I was guilty, and yet I experienced no feeling of guilt. It was true that, when I allowed my eyes to close, images of the red-haired stranger would rise up before me; yet even in this twilight state, between sleeping and waking, when conscience may often call up horrors from the depths of our being, I continued to feel no revulsion at what I had done.

Later, it also struck me as odd that my mind did not keep returning to the fatal moment itself, when the knife had entered the yielding flesh of my victim. Instead, I would see myself following the man along a dark and deserted thoroughfare. From time to time we would emerge into a ring of sickly yellow light thrown out from an open door set in a tall windowless building. Then we would proceed once more into darkness. Over and again, when uncertain sleep came, I would find myself in this perpetual proces-

*['By name'. *Ed.*]

sion through black and nameless streets. Not once did I see his face; his back was always towards me as we walked slowly from one oasis of jaundiced light to another. Then, just before daybreak, as I fell back once more into half-sleep, I saw him again.

We were in a small skiff, which he was rowing lazily down a placid river on a silent, heat-heavy afternoon. I lay in the rear of the vessel, my eyes fixed on the muscles of his back as they flexed beneath his coat with each pull on the oars. Incongruously, on such a day, his clothes were those he wore on that cold October evening, including his muffler and tall black hat. As we entered a narrow channel, he let the oars rest on the surface of the water, turned to face me, and smiled.

But it was not the face of my anonymous victim. It was the face of Phoebus Rainsford Daunt, the man whose life I was studying so assiduously to extinguish.

LEAVING BELLA ASLEEP, AND PLACING, AS I ALWAYS DID ON SUCH occasions, a gentle kiss on her flushed cheek by way of good-bye, I made my way to my rooms. The sky was beginning to lighten over the waking city, and the sounds of Great Leviathan stirring were all about me: the rattle of milk cans; a moaning drove of bullocks being driven through the empty street; the early cries of 'Fresh watercress!' as I approached Farringdon-market. As the church clocks struck six, I stopped at a coffee-stall near the market entrance to warm my hands, for it was a sharp morning; the man looked at me indignantly, but I faced him down, and he retired mumbling deprecations.

On reaching Temple Bar I considered strolling over once again to the scene of my late encounter with the red-haired man, to satisfy myself that all was well; instead I chose breakfast and a change of linen. At the corner of Temple-street, Whitefriars, I mounted the narrow flight of dark stairs that led up from the street to the top floor of the house in which I lodged, from there entering a long, wainscoted sitting-room under the eaves.

I lived alone, my only visitor being the woman, Mrs Grainger, who came from time to time to undertake some modest domestic chores. My work-table was littered with papers and note-books; a once handsome, but now faded, Turkey carpet covered most of the floor, and about the room were scattered several items of furniture brought from my mother's house in Dorset. From this apartment a door led off, first to a narrow bedroom lit by a small skylight, and then, beyond, to an even smaller space – really no more than a closet – that served as both wardrobe and wash-room.

The face that greeted me in the little cracked mirror that stood on a shelf above the wash-stand in this cubicle did not seem, to my objective gaze, to be the face of a cold-blooded murderer. The eyes looked back genially, and with calm intensity. Here was a face to trust, to confide in; yet I had despatched another human being with almost as little thought as I might crush an insect. Was I, then, some dissimulating devil in human form? No. I was but a man, a good man at heart, if the truth be told, driven to set right the wrong that had been done to me, absolved – even of murder – by the implacable fatalities to which I was then convinced my life had been subject. To me, this power was the Iron Master, forever forging the chains that bound me to actions I *must* take. My destiny, I believed, was to take back what was rightfully mine, whatever the consequences.

I peered a little closer into the mirror. A long lean face, with large, heavy-lidded dark eyes; olive-coloured skin; a nose perhaps a little skewed, but still finely shaped; a mouth that carried the merest hint of a smile, even in repose; black hair swept back from the forehead, innocent of Macassar oil and abundant at the sides, but, I confess, receding fast, and greying a little at the temples. Fine moustachios. Very fine. Taken all in all, I believe that I stood before the world as a moderately handsome fellow.

But what was this? I moved my face closer to the grimy glass. There, on the very tip of my shirt collar, was a splash of dull red.

I stood for a moment, bending towards the mirror, gripped by a sudden fascinated fear. This dumb, yet still eloquent, witness to the night's activities in Cain-court took me completely by surprise. Its pursuit of me seemed like a violation, and I quickly reviewed the dangerous possibilities that it presented.

Had it been enough to betray me? Had one of the waiters in Quinn's noticed it when it had still been vivid and unequivocal, or the flower-seller when I had returned – foolishly, as it might now prove – to the scene of my crime? Had Bella observed it, despite the haste of passion? Any of these, on reading or hearing of the murder, might recall the presence of blood on my shirt, and suspicion might thence be aroused. I looked more closely at the incriminating relic of my experiment.

It was insignificant enough in itself, certainly, though it constituted a very world of meaning. Here was a remnant of the life-blood of the stranger I had happened upon in Threadneedle-street as he went about his business, all unknowing of what was to befall him. Had he been returning home to his wife and children after a day in the City, or on his way to join a company of friends for dinner? What was his name, and who would mourn him? How had he seen his life ending? (Not in a pool of gore in a public thoroughfare, I warrant.) Did he have parents still alive whose hearts would break at the terrible demise of their dear son? Like a soldier in battle, I had ignored such questions in the heat of action, as being irrelevant to the task in hand; but now, as I stared at the little spot of dried blood on my collar, I could not prevent them rushing insistently into my mind.

My newly purchased gloves were, I knew, unsullied. But were there other traces of the crime that I had failed to notice? I hastily took my great-coat from its peg and hurried into the sitting-room to spread it out on my work-table, snatching up an eye-glass from beneath a pile of papers as I did so.

By the strengthening light of morning, I pored over every inch of the garment, turning the material methodically, occasionally bringing a piece up close to my eye-glass, like a jeweller eagerly examining some object of great worth. Then I removed my jacket and trousers, then my waistcoat, shirt and neck-tie: all were subjected to the same frantic scrutiny. Finally, I inspected my hat and placed my boots on the table, bathed now in pale sunlight. I went meticulously over the upper surfaces and soles of each boot with a dampened handkerchief, using slow circular movements and stopping every few seconds to see whether the white linen had taken up any incriminating residue of blood.

Having satisfied myself that I could find no other physical traces that could link me to my victim, I returned to the wash-room, where I diligently soaked my shirt collar in cold water to remove the bloodstain. In a few minutes, washed, shaved, and combed, and with a clean shirt on my back, I prepared to face the day.

It was the 25th of October 1854 – St Crispin's Day. Far away in the Crimea, though we in England did not yet know it, Lord Cardigan's heroic Light Brigade was charging the Russian guns at Balaclava. For me, the day passed quietly. In the morning, I occupied myself with the subject to which I have now devoted my whole being: the destruction of my enemy. Of him, you shall learn more – much more – in the course of these pages; for now, you must take it on trust that certain events had made it impossible that he should be allowed to live. The trial of my will that had its culmination last evening in Cain-court had demonstrated to my satisfaction that I was capable of doing what it was necessary to do; and the time was fast approaching when my enemy and I would meet face to face for the last time. But until then, I must think, and plan, and wait.

In the afternoon I had a little business to attend to, and did not return to my rooms until late, with evening coming on. There was a copy of *The Times* on my work-table that had been left earlier by Mrs Grainger. I can still see myself idly turning the pages of the news-paper until my attention was suddenly arrested by an announcement, and my heart began to thump. Hands shaking slightly, I walked over to the window, for the light was fading fast, and began to read:

> *Last evening at about 6 o'clock . . . Cain-court, Strand . . . Mr Lucas Trendle, First Assistant to the Chief Cashier of the Bank of England . . . Stoke Newington . . . savagely done to death . . . distinguished public servant . . . Elm-lane Chapel . . . many charitable works . . . horror of his many friends . . . authorities confident of success . . .*

He had been on his way to a meeting in Exeter Hall of some charitable enterprise dedicated to providing copies of Holy Scripture and serviceable footwear to the Africans. I now recalled a throng of clerical gentlemen in subfusc gathered outside the grand Corinthian portico of the Hall as I had passed down the Strand after leaving Cain-court. It was clear from the report that the police could discern no obvious motive to explain the crime, for nothing had been taken from the victim. I drank in the details of his respectable and blameless life; but only one thing held me, and holds me still. He was no longer the red-haired man. He had a name.

On first reading the report, I had paced about the room somewhat in a sulk, unexpectedly vexed by this knowledge. I had wanted him to remain eternally immured in his former anonymity; now I could not prevent myself from picturing the possibilities of his revealed individuality. I began to find the confinement of my attic room intolerable. At last, I could stand no more. In these moods, I needed to have the raw taste of London on my tongue.

With rain beginning to patter against the skylight of my little bedroom, I threw on my great-coat and ran down the stairs into the gathering night.

And a merciless rain it soon became, pouring in thick frothy streams from water-spouts and ledges, tumbling in vertical sheets from roofs and spires and parapets high above the teeming city, turning streets and thoroughfares into evil-smelling streams of filth and liquid refuse. I found my old companion, Willoughby Le Grice, lounging, as I knew he would be at this hour, at the Ship and Turtle in Leadenhall-street.

Le Grice and I had been chums since our schooldays, though we were as different as could be. Whether he had ever read a book through in his life, I beg to doubt; he did not care for books, or music, or paintings – as I most certainly did; as for more advanced pursuits, I believe that he considered philosophy to be actively pernicious, whilst the mention of metaphysics made him quite mad. Le Grice was a sportsman to his size-twelve boots: taller even than I; thick tow-coloured hair above a four-square manly gaze, the neck and shoulders of a young bull, and a luxuriant arc of curled hair above his top lip that made him look a very Caractacus. A true Briton, and a good man to have by you in a dangerous corner, though an innocent for all that. A strange pair, we must have made; but I could have wanted for no better friend.

We ate the grilled fowl (Indian style) for which the house was celebrated, washed down with gin-punch; then, ever biddable as he was on such occasions, Le Grice allowed me to take him across the river to the Victoria Theatre,* just in time for the nine o'clock performance.

There is no better place than the Victoria to watch the lower orders of the city taking their pleasure; to me, it was a constantly fascinating sight, like lifting a stone and observing the insect life beneath. Le Grice was not so charmed as I of such things; but he kept his counsel and sat back in his seat, a cheroot – as always – clenched grimly between his teeth, whilst I leaned forward eagerly. Below our box, the coarse deal benches were packed to overflowing: costers, navvies, lightermen, hackney-coach drivers, coal-heavers, and every sort of disreputable female. A ferocious, sweating, stinking herd. Only the louder shouts of the pigstrotter woman and the porter men who patrolled the aisles and stairways could be heard above the tumult of whistles and yells. Then, at last, the curtain rose, the master of ceremonies finally subdued the mob, and the performance – sublime in its vulgarity – began.

Afterwards, out in the New Cut, the rain had begun to ease, leaving the streets awash with mud and debris brought down from roofs and gutters. Degraded humanity, with its attendant stench, was everywhere: congregating on corners, or squatting beneath dripping archways; sitting on doorsteps, hanging out of windows, or huddling in the mouths of alleyways. Faces, hideously painted by the satanic light of the lamps and flares, and by the glow of the

*[Built in 1816, it opened in May 1818 'under the patronage of H.R.H. Prince Leopold of Saxe-Coburg', and was consequently known as the Royal Coburg Theatre. In July 1833 it was formally renamed the Royal Victoria Theatre. It was situated in Waterloo Bridge Road, Lambeth. *Ed.*]

baked-chestnut stoves that lit up the street stalls and public-houses, passed by us like a parade of the damned.

As we crossed back over the river, I suggested that we might drop into Quinn's. I wished especially to go to Quinn's. On the excuse of attempting to locate a lost pocket-book, I sought out the waiter who had served me the previous evening. It soon became perfectly clear that he had no recollection of me; and so I returned, with a lighter heart, to Le Grice, and we set about the consumption of oysters and champagne with a will. But eating oysters, Le Grice declared, only made him hungrier. He required meat and strong liquor, which, at this time of night, only Evans's could supply. And so, a little before midnight, we arrived in King-street, Covent Garden.

The parallel lines of tables, laid out like a college hall, were still packed with boisterous supper-goers. The air was cloudy with the smoke of cigars (pipes being sensibly prohibited) and heavy with the aroma of grog and roasted meat. Adding to the convivial din of conversation and laughter, a group of singers on the stage was lustily delivering a six-part glee, their strong and splendid voices rising in a resonant crescendo above the incessant clatter of plates and the rattle of cutlery. All about us, the tables were piled high with steaming sausages, sizzling cayenned kidneys, leathery baked potatoes, and dozens of glistening fried eggs, like so many miniature suns. We called for peppered chops and bitter beer, but no sooner had they arrived than Le Grice was persuaded by some of the other fellows to sing a comic song.

As he made his way tipsily towards the stage, to raucous applause, I slipped quietly away. The rain was falling with renewed intent; but London, brilliant and beautifully vile, and the undemanding company of dear old Le Grice, had done their work.

I was myself again.

· 3 ·

*Praemonitus, praemunitus**

THE FOLLOWING DAY, BELLA AND I WALKED OUT IN THE REGENT'S Park. It was an unusually fine afternoon for October in London; and so, after looking at the elephants in the Zoological Gardens, we sat for some time by the ornamental water, talking and laughing in the pale autumn sunshine. Towards four o'clock, as the air began to grow chill, we made our way back towards the gates that led out into York-terrace.

Near the entrance to the gardens of the Toxophilite Society,† Bella stopped and turned to me.

'Kitty wishes me to go with her to Dieppe tomorrow.'

'Dieppe? Whatever for?'

'Dearest, I have told you before. It is where her mother was born, and she has determined to retire there. There is a house she has coveted this past year, and it is now for sale. She wishes me to go with her to view it.'

'And you will go?'

'But of course.' She laid a gloved finger gently across my cheek. 'You don't mind, do you, dear? Say you don't – it will only be for a day or so.'

*['Forewarned, forearmed'. *Ed.*]

†[The society, founded by Sir Ashton Lever in 1781, was at the forefront of the revival of archery at the end of the eighteenth century. It obtained a lease from the Crown to establish its grounds in the Inner Circle of Regent's Park in 1833. *Ed.*]

Now even though the thought of not having the comfort of her dear person near me at this time of crisis unsettled me badly, I told her I did not mind in the least; but this, of course, was exactly what I should *not* have said, and I saw that she had taken exception to my feigned indifference, for she instantly removed her hand from my cheek and looked at me sternly.

'Well, then', she replied, 'I may as well stay on in Dieppe a little longer, as Kitty wishes me to. I'm sure there will be gentlemen aplenty who will be glad to entertain me.'

Now it is curious, but it had never before troubled me that Bella's profession required her to be, shall we say, companionable to other fellows; what services she performed for Kitty Daley's select circle of gentlemen had concerned me little. But my accommodating attitude, I already knew, had begun to irk her somewhat, and from time to time she had tried to arouse in me some spark of jealousy – which I believe ladies often interpret as a form of flattery. Her present attempt was transparent enough; but tonight, wrought to such a pitch by recent events, I *was* suddenly jealous of others enjoying that sweet body; and yet, in my confusion of mind, I found myself saying entirely the wrong thing.

'You must do as you please,' I told her, in a hard, careless tone. 'I have no hold over you.'

'Very well,' said Bella, 'I shall indeed please myself.'

With which she gathered up her skirts and walked angrily away.

Now this I could not allow, for I hated to see her upset and vexed; and so I called after her.

She turned. Her cheeks were reddened, and I saw clearly that I had hurt her.

I am not a monster. I could kill a stranger, but I could not bear to see Bella distressed, even though I had not treated her as she deserved. And so I folded her in my arms – it was growing dark, and we were alone on the stretch of path that led out of the Park – and kissed her tenderly.

'Oh, Eddie,' she said, tears welling up in her eyes, 'do you not like me any more?'

'Like you?' I cried. 'Of course I like you. More than – more than I can say.'

'Truly?'

'Truly,' I replied. I told her I hated myself for upsetting her so, that of course I would miss her while she was away, and that I would count the hours until she returned. My effusion brought forth a chiding laugh.

'Now, now,' she said in mock admonishment, 'don't come the poet with me, sir. An occasional thought in the course of the day will be quite sufficient.'

We kissed once more, but as she withdrew her lips from mine I saw again that look of seriousness in her eyes.

'What is it, Bella?' I asked. 'Is something wrong?'

She hesitated for a moment. 'No, not exactly wrong.'

'You are not —'

'No – by no means – no.' She reached into her pocket. 'I have received this. It came yesterday morning, after you left.'

She handed me a folded piece of paper.

'I must go. Kitty is expecting me. I hope you will call when we are back.'

I watched her walk away, waiting until she was out of sight before I unfolded and read what she had handed to me.

It was a short note, written in a small neat hand:

> *I write to you as a true friend.*
> *Beware of <u>Edward Glapthorn</u>. He is not what he seems. As you value your happiness, you would do well to sever all connexion with him immediately. <u>I know of what I speak.</u>*
> *Take heed.*

The note was signed 'Veritas' and was addressed simply to 'Miss Gallini', with no direction, suggesting that it had been delivered by hand.

Here was a thing, and I own that it knocked me back for a moment or two. I read the note again; but as the light was now nearly gone, I decided to go straight back to Temple-street and take stock.

I was, no doubt, in a somewhat nervous state, for as I was proceeding past the Diorama, in Park-square, I thought I felt a soft tap on my shoulder. But when I turned round, there was no one to be seen. The street was deserted, except for a single carriage, making its way back through the fading light towards the Park. This would not do. I grasped my stick with determination, and walked on.

BACK IN MY ROOMS, I LIT THE LAMP AND SPREAD THE NOTE OUT ON my table.

The hand had something familiar about it – some trace of

memory seemed to cling to it; but, try as I might, I could not bring its associations to mind.

I investigated the paper closely with my glass, held it up to the light, even sniffed it. Then I examined every character in turn, pondered the choice and order of the words, and why the author had underlined the name Edward Glapthorn. I studied the flourishes of the signature, and sought to tease out what lay behind the choice of the pseudonym 'Veritas'. As I write this, I am amazed by my obtuseness, by my inability immediately to grasp the truth; but there it is. The deed that I had so lately committed in Cain-court had, no doubt, produced confusion of mind, and dulled my usually acute powers of perception. In those dark autumn weeks, convulsed by the most terrible of betrayals, and in increasing fear of my own life, I was already in the grip of a kind of madness, unable to see that which was plainly before my eyes, and which will, in due course, be laid before yours. The consequence was, I spent an hour or more trying – with mounting frustration – to force the note to yield up its secret; but it defeated me. Except in this one thing: I knew, with utter conviction, that, though addressed to Bella, it had been meant *for me.* And so it proved.

Who? Who knew? Though I had never killed before, I was well used to living on the night-side of things. As I shall later relate, my work had hardened me to violence and danger, and I had trained myself in all the arts of the paid spy. I had therefore taken every precaution, deployed all my acquired skills, to ensure that my victim and I had entered Cain-court unobserved; but now it was clear, beyond a doubt, that I had been careless. Someone had followed us. *Someone had seen us.*

I paced the room, pounding my knuckles against my head, trying to recall every second of those fateful minutes.

I could remember glancing back towards the entrance to the

court, soon after striking the fatal blow, and again as I had slid the knife down the grating. Memory could give me back nothing to indicate that I had been observed. Except . . . Yes, the slightest of sounds, though no sign of movement. A rat, I had thought at the time. But was it possible that someone had been silently watching my victim and me from the deep shadows that lay in the angles of the walls?

This thought now instantly took hold, and then led to another. How had the presumed observer identified me? The answer must be that he already knew me. Perhaps he had been watching my movements for some time and had followed me in my peregrinations that night, then tracked me to Blithe Lodge. But why, with the information he possessed, had he not already denounced me to the authorities? Why had he written to Bella in such a fashion?

I could discern only one motive: blackmail. With that conclusion came a kind of relief. I knew how to deal with such a situation. All that I required was to gain some quick advantage over my pursuer. Then I would have him. Yet it was not altogether clear to me how such an advantage could be obtained; and still I could not understand why the blackmailer had revealed his hand to Bella first. Perhaps he merely wished to torment me a little before administering the *coup de grâce.*

He – it must be a man, and an educated one – was clever. I was prepared to grant him that. The note had been subtly conceived. To Bella, who knew nothing of what had happened in Cain-court, it hinted at dark possibilities that might alarm any woman, even a demi-mondaine: '*He is not what he seems . . .*' Women instantly distrust the unspecific, and their imaginations soon begin to transform hints and suggestions into solid fact. What would Bella's fancy conjure up from these vague but troubling insinuations? Nothing to my advantage, certainly, and much to her disquiet. But to me, the note sent a different message: a threat to reveal to Bella what I had done if I did not come to an accommodation. This was the cleverness of it: it was intended to put us individually on the rack; and by mischievously sowing doubt and alarm in the innocent Bella, it inflicted a double punishment on me.

I RETURNED TO MY TABLE AND PICKED UP THE NOTE AGAIN. THIS TIME I held it up to the light of my lamp and went carefully over every inch with my eye-glass, searching furiously for some clue to the identity of the sender, something that would set *me* on *his* trail. I was on the point of giving up in angry frustration when I noticed a row of small holes pricked into the paper, just below the signature.

On closer examination, I saw that these had been deliberately arranged in groups, separated by spaces. It did not take long to discern the simplest of codes: each group of holes represented a number, which in turn stood for a letter. With little trouble I deciphered the message: ez/vii/vi. Reaching for my Bible, I quickly found the verse from Ezekiel to which the message referred: 'An end is come, the end is come: it watcheth for thee; behold, it is come.'

Here was a serious setback to my plans, something that I could not have anticipated, but to the resolution of which I must now divert some of my energy. *Watcheth,* I perceived, was a word the sender particularly intended me to take to heart. I could do nothing, for the time being, to set aside whatever fears the note had raised in Bella; but I felt sure that I would receive a further communication before long, and this, I hoped, would afford me some opportunity to begin turning the tables on the blackmailer.

I SAT UP BEFORE THE FIRE FOR HALF AN HOUR SMOKING A CIGAR, THEN went to bed in a state of suppressed anxiety. Images came crowding in upon me: the dying smile of Lucas Trendle, elephants, Bella laughing in the autumn sunshine, a carriage making its way up a deserted street.

Then, when sleep eventually took hold, came a dream, which haunts me still.

I am walking through an unimaginably vast subterranean chamber, the echoes of my footsteps receding into endless depths of shadow on either side of what seems like an aisle or nave of titanic stone columns. In my hand is a candle, which burns with a steady flame, revealing an open space beyond the columns. Into this space, the boundaries of which are indiscernible, I now pass.

I walk on for some time, feeling a vast and oppressive emptiness pushing in all around me. I stop, and the reverberating echoes of my footsteps slowly die away in a sickening *diminuendo* into the surrounding immensity. The candle's flame reveals only darkness, limitless, entire; but then, suddenly, I know that I am not alone, and a choking terror begins to take hold. There is something fearsome here, invisible but present. All is silence; I have heard no sound of footsteps other than my own; and yet I know that danger is near. Then, with inconceivable horror, I feel a gentle tap on my shoulder and warm breath on my cheek and hear the faint hiss of exhaled air. Someone – some thing – standing just behind me softly blows out the candle. I drop the extinguished flame, and collapse in utter helplessness and revulsion.

I awoke three or four times from this nightmare in a sweat, my heart thumping, clutching at tangled sheets. Finally, at first light, I arose with a parched mouth and a ferocious headache. As soon as I entered my sitting-room I saw it: a rectangle of white paper, slipped under the door as I had slept.

It was a black-bordered card, written in the same hand as the note that had been sent to Bella. It seemed to confirm all my fears.

Mr. Edward Glapthorn is cordially invited
to the interment of Mr. Lucas Trendle,
late of the Bank of England,
at 3 p.m. on the 3rd of November, 1854,
Abney Cemetery, Stoke Newington.

"In the midst of life we are in death"

The quotation from the Burial Service at first seemed merely apt; but, as I considered it further, the words began to call to mind some other time and place – a face, already receding into the shadows of memory; a place of sorrow; rain and solemn music. It puzzled me, and worried me, though I could not say why. Then I concluded that I was seeing significance where there was none, and threw the card aside.

Seven days. There was time to prepare myself. I did not expect any further communication; the blackmailer's next move would no doubt come – presumably in person – on the day of the funeral. And if not in person, then he would have to reveal something more of himself in another communication in order to attain his objective; and that might allow me the advantage that I was seeking. In the meantime I resolved to try to put all thought of this business out of my mind, as far as I could. I had other pressing matters to attend to. For the time of reckoning with my enemy, Phoebus Daunt, was nigh.

· 4 ·

*Ab incunabulis**

On the evening after Bella returned from Dieppe, the 2nd of November 1854, I took her to dinner at the Clarendon Hotel.† Mrs D had been enchanted by the house they had viewed and had stayed on in France to begin arrangements for its purchase.

'She means to retire there as soon as circumstances permit,' said Bella, 'which of course means that my own position will change sooner than anticipated.'

She did her best to maintain her old easiness of manner, but I could see the effort that it was causing her. At length, she set aside all pretence.

'You have read the note?'

I nodded.

'What does it mean, Eddie? I must know the truth.'

'The truth of what?' I cried angrily. 'The truth of a lie? The truth of some vague and baseless slander? There is no truth here, none, I can assure you.'

'But who has sent me this?'

'Someone who wishes me harm for a reason that I cannot imagine, someone whose resentment of me – or perhaps of you . . . '

She was taken aback by the suggestion.

'Of me? What can you mean?'

'Think, my love: is there any member of The Academy who

*['From the cradle'. *Ed.*]

†[In Bond Street. *Ed.*]

might have a reason to cause you harm? Someone, perhaps, who has received a visit from Mr Braithwaite on your behalf?' I asked the question in the full knowledge that this matter had nothing to do with The Academy.

'No, none.' She thought for a moment. 'Sir Meredith Gore – you remember? – was lately ejected, but I was not the only one to complain of him. He is presently travelling on the Continent, and is not expected to return for some time, so I do not think it can be him. Besides, what possible benefit could he gain from this? And do you know the gentleman?'

I had to concede that Sir Meredith and I had enjoyed no personal contact, other than a chance meeting on the stairs at Blithe Lodge one evening; but, persisting to lay this false trail, I pointed out that it would be perfectly possible for him to invent some calumny against me without personal knowledge, to gain revenge on her for his expulsion.

'No, no,' said Bella, shaking her head vigorously, 'it's too implausible – impossible. No, it cannot be Sir Meredith.' She paused as the waiter came up with more champagne.

'You say,' she continued, toying with the stem of her glass, 'that the implied accusations are baseless. But how can I be sure? There must, after all, be some reason why the note was written to me. I know that your father died before you were born, and that your mother, whom you have told me you loved dearly, was an authoress; and you have spoken often of your years abroad. But are there things in your past – important things, perhaps – that you have deliberately withheld from me, to which the note may refer? If so, I beg you to tell me now.'

'I thought you were content to like me just as I am, the present here-and-now me,' I said sulkily.

'Circumstances have changed,' she replied, leaning back in her chair. 'When Kitty retires to Dieppe, I shall be required to take her place at The Academy, and that will allow me to give up my gentlemen.' She rested her steady gaze on me. 'It is important to me, Eddie, under these new circumstances, to know everything about the man I have fallen in love with.'

It was her first outright declaration of what she felt for me; the first time that the word love had been spoken. I could see that she was waiting for some reciprocal response. But how could I tell her what she wished to hear, when my heart still ached for another, whom I could never now possess?

'Do you have nothing to say?' she asked.

'Only that you are my dearest friend in the world, as I have often told you,' I replied, 'and that I cannot bear to see you distressed.'

'So do you like me – love me, even – merely as a friend?'

'*Merely* as a friend? Is that not enough?'

'Well, I see that you are now starting to play the philosopher with me, so I suppose I have my answer.'

I reached out and took her hand.

'Bella, dearest, forgive me. If you wish to call my feelings for you "love", then so be it. I am more than content for you to do so. For myself, I am devoted to you as the dearest, sweetest friend a man could have. If this is love, then I love you. And if it is love to feel safe and comfortable in your presence, then I love you. And if it is love to know that I am never happier than when you take my face in your hands and kiss me, then I love you. And if . . .' And so I went on, until I could obfuscate no more.

I smiled, in what I hoped was my most winning manner, and was rewarded by the sight of a faint animation of her lips.

'Then I suppose, Mr Edward Glapthorn, that your many ingenious definitions of love must suffice – for now.' She removed her hand from mine as she spoke. 'But for the sake of all we have been together, and for all we may be, you must set my mind at rest – completely at rest. The note — '

'Is false.' I looked at her steadily. 'False as hell – written by someone who wishes to do me – us – harm, for some reason we cannot yet know. But we shall defeat them, dearest Bella. I promise you shall know all about me, and then they shall have no hold over us. We shall be safe.'

If only it could be so. She was, as I had sincerely maintained, my dearest friend in the world; and perhaps what I felt for her was a kind of love. But in order to spare her from hurt and scandal, and perhaps for her own safety, I could not tell her that I had just killed one man in preparation for killing a second, or that I was not who I claimed to be, and that my heart would always be enslaved to another. But she deserved to know something more about me, to set her mind at rest until such time as I could unmask the blackmailer, and put the danger from us permanently. And then? Even when I had vanquished my enemy at last, and revenged myself for what he had done to me, could she ever replace what I had lost, dear to me though she was?

The Clarendon was a respectable hotel, and we had no luggage; but the manager was an old acquaintance of mine and discreetly secured us a room.

We sat up late into the night. This, in summary, is what I told her.

My mother's family, the Mores of Church Langton, were West Country farmers of long standing. Her uncle, Mr Byam More, was land-agent for Sir Robert Fairmile, of Langton Court near Taunton, whose only daughter, Laura, was nearly of an age with my mother. The two little girls grew up together and became the closest of friends, their friendship continuing when Laura married and moved to a Midlands county.

Within a month or so, my mother also married, though hers was a much less grand match than her friend's. Laura Fairmile had become Lady Tansor, of Evenwood in Northamptonshire, one of the most enchanting houses in England, and the seat of an ancient and distinguished line; my mother became the wife of a wastrel half-pay officer in the Hussars.

My father – always known as 'the Captain' – served inconspicuously in the 11th Regiment of Light Dragoons, the celebrated 'Cherrypickers', which later became famous, as the 11th Prince Albert's Own Hussars, under the command of Lord Cardigan, though the Captain was long dead before the regiment's immortal action in the Russian War. He left the regiment after sustaining injury in the Peninsula, and was promoted to half-pay; but his leisure was productive of nothing except a renewed dedication to a long-held love of strong liquor, which he pursued vigorously, to the exclusion of all other occupations. He spent little time with his wife, could settle at nothing, and, when he was not engaged with his local companions at the Bell and Book in Church Langton, was away visiting old regimental comrades, and partaking of the usual lively debauchery that such occasions afford. The birth of a daughter, it appears, did not encourage him to mend his ways, and on the evening of her untimely death, at only five days old, he was to be found in his usual corner at the Bell and Book. He compounded his iniquity by being absent – I know not where, but I can guess why – on the day of the poor child's funeral.

My mother and the Captain, on the latter's insistence, left Church Langton soon afterwards for Sandchurch, in Dorset, where remnants of the Captain's family resided. The change brought no improvement in his behaviour; he merely exchanged the Bell and Book in Church Langton for the King's Head in Sandchurch. I have said enough, I hope, to demonstrate the Captain's execrable character, and his utter contempt for the duties of a husband and father.

In the summer of 1819, my mother accompanied her friend, Laura Tansor, to France, where she stayed for several months. I was born there, in March of the following year, in the Breton city of Rennes. Some weeks later, the two companions travelled together to Dinan, where they took lodgings near the Tour de l'Horloge. Lady Tansor then departed for Paris whilst my mother remained in Dinan for several more days. But just as she was preparing to leave for St-Malo, she received terrible news from England.

The Captain, returning home late one pitch-black night from the King's Head in an extreme state of inebriation, had wandered off the path, missed his footing, and tumbled over the cliff not twelve yards from his door. Tom Grexby, the village schoolmaster, found him the next morning, his neck quite broken.

The Captain appears to have been perfectly content to let his wife gad off to France with her friend. He found it not in the least inconvenient to have the house to himself, and to be able to spend his leisure unencumbered by even the few domestic duties required of him when his wife was at home. And so he died, a miserable mediocrity.

On a June evening in the year 1820, my mother brought me home to Dorset, tucked up in a plaid blanket and laid on her lap, up the long dusty road that leads from the church to the little white-painted house on the cliff-top. Naturally, she received heartfelt sympathy from her friends and neighbours in Sandchurch. To return husbandless, and with a fatherless child! All about the village, heads could not stop shaking in disbelief at the double calamity. The general commiseration was received by my mother with genuine gratitude, for the sudden death of the Captain had been a severe shock to her, despite his inadequacies as a husband.

All these things I came to know much later, after my mother's death. I pass now to my own memories of my childhood at Sandchurch.

We lived quietly enough – my mother and I, Beth, and Billick, a grizzled old salt, who chopped wood, tended the garden, and drove the trap. The house faced south across a stretch of soft turf towards the Channel, and from my earliest years the strongest memory I have is of the sound of waves and wind, as I lay in my cradle under the apple-tree in the front garden, or in my room, with its little round window set above the porch.

We had few visitors. Mr Byam More, my mother's uncle, would come down from Somerset two or three times a year. I also have a clear memory of a pale, sad-eyed lady called Miss Lamb, who sat talking quietly with my mother whilst I played on the rug before the parlour fire, and who reached down to stroke my hair, and ran her fingers across my cheek, in a most gentle and affecting way. I can recall it still.

For a period of my childhood, my mother suffered from severe depression of spirits, which I now know was caused by the death of her childhood friend, Laura, Lady Tansor, whose name was also unknown to me until after my mother's death. Her Ladyship (as I later learned) had discreetly supported my mother with little gifts of her own money, and other considerations. But when she died, these payments ceased, and things went hard for Mamma, the Captain's paltry legacy to her having long since been exhausted; but she determined that she would do all in her power to maintain us both, for as long as possible, in the house at Sandchurch.

And so it came about that the publisher, Mr Colburn, received on his desk in New Burlington-street a brown-paper package containing *Edith; or, The Last of the Fitzalans,* the first work of fiction from the pen of a lady living on the Dorset coast. The covering letter sent Mr Colburn her very best compliments, and requested a professional opinion on the work.

Mr Colburn duly replied to the lady with a courteous two-page critique of its merits and demerits, and concluded by saying that he would be happy to arrange for publication, though on terms that provided for my mother's contributing towards the costs. This proposal she accepted, using money with which she could ill afford to speculate; but the venture was successful, and Mr Colburn came back gratifyingly quickly with a request for a successor, on much improved terms.

So began my mother's literary career, which continued uninterruptedly for over ten years, until her death. Though the income derived from her literary efforts kept us safe and secure, the effort involved was prodigious, and the effects on my mother's constitution were only too apparent to me as I grew older and observed her slight hunched form forever bent over the big square table that served her for a desk. Sometimes, when I entered the room, she would not even look up, but would speak gently to me as she continued to write, her face close to the paper. 'What is it, Eddie? Tell Mamma quickly, dear.' And I would say what I wanted, and she would tell me to ask Beth – and off I would go, back to the concerns of my own world, leaving her to scratch away in hers.

At the age of six, or thereabouts, I was put into the pedagogic care of Thomas Grexby. When I joined it, Tom's little school consisted of himself, a plump, blank-faced boy called Cooper, who appeared to find even the most elementary branches of learning deeply mystifying, and me. Master Cooper was set exercises in basic schooling that required him to pass long hours on his own in strenuous concentration, tongue lolling out with the effort, leaving Tom and me to read and talk together. I made rapid progress, for Tom was an excellent teacher, and I was exceedingly eager to learn.

Under Tom's care I quickly mastered my reading, writing, and numbers; and, on the firm foundations thus laid down, he encouraged me to build according to my own inclinations. Every subject, and every topic within every subject, to which Tom introduced me assailed me with a keen hunger to know more. In this way, my mind began to fill up with prodigious amounts of undigested information on every conceivable topic, from the principles of Archimedes to the date of the creation of the world according to Archbishop Ussher.*

Gradually, however, Tom began to impose some rigour on this habit of mental acquisitiveness. I settled down to gain a thorough mastery of the Greek and Latin tongues, as well as a solid grounding in history, and the main vernacular literatures of Europe. Tom was also a dedicated bibliophile, though his attempts to assemble a collection of fine editions of his own were severely curtailed by his always limited means. Still, his knowledge and connoisseurship in this area were considerable, and it was from him that I learned about incunabula and colophons, bindings and dentelles, editions and issues, and all the other minutiae beloved of the bibliographical scholar.

And so things went on until I reached the age of twelve, at which point my life changed.

On the day of my twelfth birthday, in March 1832, I came down to breakfast to find my mother sitting at her work-table with a wooden box in her hands.

'Happy birthday, Eddie.' She smiled. 'Come and kiss me.'

I did so most willingly, for I had seen little of her in recent days as she struggled to finish yet another work for Mr Colburn and his increasingly demanding deadlines.

*[James Ussher (1581–1656), archbishop of Armagh. He is best known for his *Annales veteris testamenti* (1650–4), in which he established a long-accepted chronology of Scripture and in which he computed the date of the Creation as occurring in 4004 BC. *Ed.*]

'This is for you, Eddie,' she said quietly, holding out the box.

It was deep, hinged, about nine inches square, and made of a rich dark wood, with a band of lighter wood running round an inch or so above the base. The lid had raised angled sides and was inlaid on one of the faces with a coat of arms. Two little brass handles were set on each side, and on the front face was a shield-shaped escutcheon. For several years it stood on my mantel-piece in Temple-street.

'Open it,' my mother said gently.

Inside nestled two soft leather purses, each containing a large quantity of gold coins. I tumbled them out onto the table. They amounted to two hundred sovereigns.*

Naturally, I could not comprehend how so much money could suddenly find its way to us in this way, when my mother's poor drawn face told so eloquently of what necessity required her to do, constantly and with no prospect of cessation, in order to keep our little family safe from want.

'Where has all this money come from?' I asked in astonishment. 'Mamma, is it yours?'

'No, my love,' my mother replied, 'it is yours, to do with as you like. A present from an old, old friend, who loved you very much, but who will never see you again. She wished for this to be given to you, so that you may know that she will think of you always.'

Now, the only friend of my mother's that I could think of was sad-eyed Miss Lamb; and so for some years I cherished the belief, never contradicted by my mother, that *she* had been my benefac-

*[A former gold English coin worth twenty shillings (i.e. one pound sterling). It is notoriously difficult to estimate comparative values; but using the indexes and formulas provided by J. O'Donoghue, L. Goulding, and G. Allen in *Consumer Price Inflation Since 1750* (Office for National Statistics, 2004), in 1832 the value of the two hundred coins was roughly equivalent to £14,000 in today's money. The coins would have carried the head of William IV (d. 1837). *Ed.*]

tress. Unsure though I was of the source of my good fortune, however, the weight of the coins, as they lay in my cupped hands, had a powerful effect, for I instantly saw that they would allow me to set my mother free from her literary labours. But she refused to countenance such a thing, and with an affronted resoluteness that I had never seen in her before. After some discussion, it was agreed that the money, except for fifty sovereigns, which I insisted that she must have, would be placed into the hands of her Uncle More, for investment in such a way as he would see fit to produce profit on the sum, until I attained my majority.

'There is more, Eddie,' she said.

I was to go to school – to a real school, away from Sandchurch. This special friend of my mother's, who had loved me very much, had wished for me to be educated as a foundation boy at Eton College on reaching the age of twelve, and had made arrangements to this effect. That time had now arrived. When the summer was over, and the leaves had fallen from the chestnut-tree by the front gate, if I had succeeded in the examination, I would become a Scholar of the King's College of Our Lady of Eton Beside Windsor, founded by that most devout and unworldly of English monarchs, Henry VI. At first, I did not well know how I should contemplate this momentous change, either for good or ill; but Tom Grexby soon put me right. It was the very best thing that could have happened, he said, and he knew – no one better – that it would be the making of me.

'Hold fast, Ned,' he said, 'to what we have done together, and go forward to greater things. Your life, your true life, is not here,' – he pointed to his breast and the heart beating within it – 'but here,' pointing now to his head. '*There* is your kingdom,' he said, 'and it is yours to extend and enrich as you please, to the ends of the earth.'

The scholarship examination, taken that July, held no terrors for me, and a letter came soon afterwards with the gratifying intelligence that I had been placed first on the list. Tom and I spent the remainder of the summer reading hard together, and taking long walks along the cliffs in deep conversation about the subjects we both loved. And then the day came; Billick brought the trap round to the front gate, my cases were stowed, and I climbed up beside him. Tom had walked up from the village to see me off and give me a gift to take with me: a fine copy of Glanvill's *Saducismus Triumphatus.** I stared in disbelieving delight to hold in my hands a volume that I had longed to read ever since Tom had set me to consider Hamlet's celebrated contention to Horatio, on witnessing the appearance of his father's ghost, that heaven and earth contain more things than we can dream of.†

'A little addition to your philosophical library,' he said, smiling. 'But don't tell your mamma – she might think I am corrupting your young mind. And be prepared, now, to be tested on it when you come home.' At which he took my hand and shook it hard – the first time anyone had done such a thing. It impressed me strongly that I was no longer a child, but had become a man amongst men.

When all was ready, we waited in the bright and windy sunshine for my mother to come out from the house. When she did, I noticed that she was carrying something, which I soon saw was

*[*Saducismus Triumphatus; or, Full and Plain Evidence Concerning Witches and Apparitions*, by Joseph Glanvill (1636–80), an attempt to convince sceptics that such things were real. It was in fact an enlarged and posthumous edition (with additions by Henry More) of Glanvill's *A Philosophical Endeavour Towards a Defence of the Being of Witches and Apparitions*, published in 1666, most of the copies of which were destroyed in the Great Fire of London. Glanvill's position was that disbelief in demons and witches would inevitably lead to disbelief in God and the immortality of the soul. It is now regarded as one of the most important and influential of all English works on the subject. The first edition of *Saducismus Triumphatus* was published for S. Lownds in 1681. *Ed.*]

†['There are more things in heaven and earth, Horatio,/Than are dreamt of in your philosophy.' *Hamlet*, I. v. 174–75. *Ed.*]

the box that had contained the two hundred sovereigns from her friend.

'Take this, Eddie, to remind you of the dear lady who has made this possible. I know you will not let her down, and that you will work hard at your lessons, and become a very great scholar. You will write, won't you, as soon as you can? And always remember that you are your mamma's best boy.'

And then she took my hand, but she did not shake it, as Tom had done, but drew it to her lips and kissed it.

To Bella, I now told the story of my time as an Eton Colleger; but as it is necessary for the reader of these confessions to be apprised, in some detail, of the events relating to my time at the school, in particular the manner of my leaving it, I propose to describe them at a more suitable place in my narrative, together with the story of my life in the immediately succeeding years.

Bella listened attentively, occasionally getting up to walk over to the window as I spoke. When I had finished, she sat in thought for a moment.

'You have said little concerning your present employment,' she said suddenly. 'Perhaps the answer lies there. I confess that I have never been quite clear in my mind what your duties are at Tredgolds.'

'As I have said before, I work in a private capacity for the Senior Partner.'

'You will forgive me, Eddie, if I say that your answer seems a little evasive.'

'Dearest, you must understand that there are professional confidences involved, which do not permit me to say more. But I assure you that the firm is highly respected, and that my duties there – purely of an advisory nature – can have no bearing on the present matter.'

'But how can you be sure?'

Her persistence gave me the opportunity that I had been looking for. I got up and began to walk around, as if gripped by some sudden realization.

'Perhaps you are right,' I said at last. 'It may be that I have overlooked the possibility of some antagonism arising from my work.'

I continued to pace the floor, until at last she came over to where I was standing.

'Eddie, what is the matter? You look so strangely.'

She gripped my hand imploringly.

It was cruel of me to let her suffer in this way; but as I could not tell her the truth, I had no choice but to let her think that the cause of the note lay in some matter connected with my employment. And so I resorted to the lie direct.

'There is a man,' I said at last, 'a client of the firm's, who blames me for the failure of a case he has recently brought, on which the firm advised.'

'And do you think this man could have written the note?'

'It is possible.'

'But for what purpose? And the note itself – why was it sent to me? And why does it say that you are not what you seem?'

I told her that the man I suspected of writing the note was rich and powerful, but of notorious reputation; that he might have no other design than to sow discord between us, to pay me back for my perceived part in the failure of his suit. She considered this for a moment, and then shook her head.

'It was sent to *me*! How did he know about me, or where I lived?'

'Perhaps he has set someone to follow me,' I ventured. At this, her whole body stiffened, and she gave a little gasp.

'Am I in danger, then?'

This, I said, was very unlikely, though I begged her not to go out again without the protection of Mr Braithwaite.

We continued to talk, as midnight came and went. I promised Bella that I would find out the truth and, if my suspicions proved correct, bring charges against the man, assuring her over and over that the implications of the note were false. But she remained visibly agitated, and it was plain that I had succeeded only in making the situation worse by my clumsy fabrication. We lay together on the bed, fully clothed, for an hour or so, saying nothing. Then, just before first light, she asked me to take her back to St John's Wood.

We slipped out of the side door of the Clarendon into a bitter yellow fog, walking through the almost deserted streets in silence, each of us wrapped in our own thoughts.

Arriving at Blithe Lodge, I asked whether I might call on Sunday.

'If you wish,' she said flatly, taking out a key from her reticule and opening the door.

She did not turn to kiss me.

· 5 ·

*Mors certa**

I RETURNED TO TEMPLE-STREET, BUT COULD NOT SETTLE. SLEEP WAS impossible; and I had no taste for reading, or for anything else for that matter. I could not even bring myself to take down my much-thumbed copy of Donne's sermons, which, like a cold bath, would usually invigorate my faculties and set me back on the path of action. I simply sat, sunk in gloomy reflection, before the empty fireplace.

I deeply regretted lying to Bella; but deceit had become a constant companion: I had already betrayed her in fact, and continued to do so in my heart. I lived for another, hungered for another, dreamed only of possessing another, though she was now lost to me beyond recall. How, then, could I tell Bella the truth? I could only lie to her. It was the lesser evil.

By the faint gleam of the staircase lamp below my window I could see the fog clinging and oozing against the glass. A dreary mood slid into me irresistibly, like a knife. Harder, deeper, it bit. I knew where it would end. I tried, as always, to hold it at bay, but to no avail. The blood began to thump in my temples until I could stand it no more; and so, submitting to my demons, I threw on my great-coat again and descended the stairs. Great Leviathan's unsleeping, inviting maw beckoned.

*['Death is certain'. *Ed.*]

I FOUND HER WHERE I KNEW I WOULD, WHERE THEY COULD ALWAYS BE found while a fragment of night remained – returning home from the West-end.

I caught up with her on the corner of Mount-street. A few words, and the bargain was secured.

The house was kept by a Jewess, who even at this late hour opened the door to the girl's knock, and stood regarding us suspiciously as we ascended three cramped flights of stairs to a long low chamber on the third floor.

The place was sparsely but decently furnished, and moderately clean. At the far end of the room, beneath a boarded-up window, a ginger kitten slept in a box festooned with bright red ribbons and with his name, 'Tyger', written in crude letters on the side; on a table close by lay a pile of unfinished needlework, the arm of a thick velvet dress hanging down towards the floor like a dead thing. At the other end of the room, alongside a half-curtained window that gave onto the street, stood a single French bed-stead draped with a patched and faded cover, too short for concealing the unemptied chamber-pot beneath.

'Do you have a name?' she asked.

'Geddington,' I replied, smiling. 'Ernest Geddington. General footman. And what do they call you?'

'*You* may call me Lady Jane,' came her answer, in a tone of strained jocularity. 'And now, Mr Ernest Geddington, general footman, I suppose you must be ready to judge the quality of the goods on offer.'

She was a slight, auburn-haired girl of about twenty years of age and spoke with a quiet Cockney intonation roughened by her life in smoke-filled places. Her attempt at levity was hollow. Her eyes were tired, the smile forced. I noticed her red knuckles, her thin white legs, and that she coughed quietly every few seconds. Swaying uneasily on her tired and swollen feet, she began undressing until she stood before me, shivering slightly, in just her chemise and drawers.

She led me backwards towards the bed-stead, and sat down.

'Your carriage awaits you, Mr Geddington,' she said, the exhaustion now plain in a barely withheld yawn.

'Oh no, my lady,' said I, turning her round as I spoke. 'I know my place. I'll take the back stairs, if you please.'

AND SO TO BLUEGATE-FIELDS, DANGEROUS AND DEADLY. A BLACK GASH of damp stone leads up from a narrow court, and into another kind of fog, dry and burning, which hurts the eyes as it curls and drifts about the room. A Lascar is huddled on the dirty, rain-stained floor, another attenuated figure mumbles in a far corner, and an empty divan awaits.

I lie down, am handed the instrument of dreams, loaded with its potent freight, and the dissolution begins. Clouds, piercing sunlight, the shining peaks of eternal mountains, and a cold green sea. An elephant gazes at me with a look of ineffable compassion in its small dark eyes. A man with red hair whose face I cannot see.

THE BOUNDARIES OF THIS WORLD ARE FOREVER SHIFTING – FROM DAY to night, joy to sorrow, love to hate, and from life itself to death; and who can say at what moment we may suddenly cross over the border, from one state of existence to another, like heat applied to some flammable substance? I have been given my own ever-changing margins, across which I move, continually and hungrily, like a migrating animal. Now civilized, now untamed; now responsive to decency and human concern, now viciously attuned to the darkest of desires.

I admit these degradations because they are true, as true as anything else in this confession; as true as the killing of Lucas

Trendle and my hatred of Phoebus Daunt; and as true as the cursed love I hold, and will always hold, for her whom I cannot yet name. If these acts disgust you, then it must be so. I do not – cannot – seek to excuse them, or explain them; for the terrible itching urge to wander perpetually, like some poor Ahasuerus,* between light and darkness, will stay with me, driving me under its goad, until the day of my death.

A reviving cigar and I return to the fog-weighted streets. Once again, I wearily climb the stairs to my rooms in Temple-street as the day struggles into life.

ON REACHING MY SITTING-ROOM, I SLUMPED HEAVILY INTO THE CHAIR by the fireplace I had left some hours before and fell into a deep untroubled sleep.

I awoke with a start a little before noon, thinking of Jukes.

Fordyce Jukes was my neighbour on the ground floor. I loathed his greasy, cunning look and insinuating manners: '*So* nice to see you, Mr Glapthorn. *Always* a pleasure, Mr Glapthorn. A touch cold today, Mr Glapthorn.' I learned to expect the opportune opening of his door as I passed up or down the stairs; the glutinous smile of greeting; and always the infallible sense of a watching eye at my back.

It was Jukes! I was sure of it. I should have seen it immediately. He had followed me that night to Cain-court. He knew it all.

He was a clerk in the offices of Tredgold, Tredgold & Orr, solicitors, of Paternoster-row, where I was also employed, and of which I shall have occasion to speak more fully hereafter. Clever enough, certainly; educated enough, with sufficient knowledge of my comings and goings to ensnare me. Yes, it must be Jukes. Under the

*[The Wandering Jew of legend. *Ed.*]

pretence of civility, his eye was always upon me, as if he half knew that I was not what I seemed. And he had recently had the opportunity to snoop amongst my papers, as I shall later relate. We had never spoken of Bella, it was true; our conversations had been scrupulously neutral on all personal matters; but he had watched me, followed me, and had found her out.

What had begun it? I knew him to be a damned inquisitive meddler; my nocturnal ramblings were frequent, and the stairs would have creaked out my exits to his always receptive ears. An urge one night – impossible for him to resist – to follow me out, to see where I went and what I did, was repeated on other nights until a habit was formed. How many shadows had welcomed his watching eye; how many doorways, how many dark and secret places?

Then, one night in late October, he followed me again, a little earlier than usual, puzzled by the apparent lack of any specific intent or objective, as I made my way to Threadneedle-street. He could not see Lucas Trendle standing outside the Bank: only I could see him. But he continued to watch, still puzzled, as I proceeded westwards towards the Strand.

He could not know why I committed the deed that he witnessed, but he knew that I did it. *He knew.*

The revelation galvanized me. After splashing my face with cold water, I descended the stairs. Jukes's door stayed closed, and there was no sound from within, for these were of course his usual hours at Tredgolds. But I knew that he must have contrived to be absent from the office for the afternoon in order to carry out his intention to confront me at Stoke Newington, or at least to satisfy himself that I had accepted his invitation to pay my last respects to Lucas Trendle. All the same, I stopped at the foot of the staircase and contemplated forcing an entrance to his chambers, in order to secure confirmation that the hand responsible for the two anonymous notes was his. But this, I decided, was both foolhardy and unnecessary; so I stepped out into the street, to execute the plan I had formed.

I WAS IN CHANCERY-LANE IN TIME FOR THE HALF-PAST TWELVE OMNIBUS to Stoke Newington, for it was now November the 3rd, and Mr Lucas Trendle was to be buried. The omnibus came and left without me – I did not intend to take any chances. I therefore held back, observing every face that passed along the street, every stationary or loitering figure. Then I moved to the back of the queue for the next green 'Favourite', which I boarded, immediately descending as it pulled away. Satisfied that I had not been followed, I finally took my place on the one o'clock vehicle, and arrived at last at my destination.

THROUGH THE PORTALS OF DEATH,* SURMOUNTED BY HIEROGLYPHS announcing 'The Gates of the Abode of the Mortal Part of Man', I walked into Abney Cemetery, in the quiet village of Stoke Newington. London lay behind me, beneath a louring and obscuring red-yellow pall interposed between earth and sky, the progeny of a million chimneys. Here the air was clear, the day dull, but with a promise of brightness.

It wanted an hour until the time. I wandered, as a casual visitor might, amongst the spacious lawns and Lebanon cedars, observing the monuments of granite and marble – some striking, most of a becoming simplicity, for this was a resting-place for Non-Conformist mortality; the petrified angels; the columns and draped urns. I examined the small Gothic Chapel, and then made

*[The monumental gates, in the Egyptian style, that lead into the cemetery. *Ed.*]

my way over to a fenced-off spot, around a large and venerable chestnut-tree, that marked the favourite place of retirement of Dr Watts,* friend of the former Lady Abney, and tutor to her daughters.

Lingering there, I looked about me, taking in the patterns of paths and walkways, and trying to picture to myself how events might unfold.

Would Jukes risk a direct approach in such a place? Would he take me quietly aside and put some proposal to me for the maintenance of his silence? I could not feel in the least physically threatened by him – a stunted, weaselly fellow – and was, in any case, well prepared for that eventuality. I would take the initiative and suggest a civilized discussion of the matter, gentleman to gentleman. He would be appreciative of my consideration; no need for unpleasantness, no need at all. Simply a little matter of business. A stroll, perhaps, towards the Chapel, and a further meeting arranged – at some mutually convenient place and time in town – in order to conclude matters. Then I would secure my advantage, complete and final.

Thus I imagined as I continued to stroll slowly up and down the path, as if in sober contemplation of my surroundings. I took out my watch. A few moments later the church clock tolled three.

I turned back towards the gates to see a hearse pulled by four horses – ostrich-plumed and richly caparisoned – enter the grounds, followed by two mourning coaches, and a number of smaller carriages swathed in rich black velvet. I counted four mutes in their gowns, and a little group of perhaps half a dozen pages. A moderately expensive affair, I reflected, in spite of Mr Trendle's plain theology.

*[Isaac Watts (1674–1748), the Dissenting divine, poet, and hymn-writer. The cemetery, laid out on the former Fleetwood-Abney estate, had been opened in May 1840. *Ed.*]

A small knot of villagers, not of the family party, followed the procession a little way behind. I scanned this group closely, moving nearer, and as quickly as I dared, to try to make out my man.

The cortège entered through one of the arches of the Chapel; the coffin was removed by the bearers and taken inside; the mourners descended and followed the doleful burden.

I had stationed myself a short distance off. His mother – there – for sure; a slight figure holding for support the arm of a tall younger gentleman, perhaps his brother. I did not detect a wife or children, for which I was grateful. But the sight of his poor mother unnerved me momentarily, as I saw again in memory the rictus smile that her son had given me as I had withdrawn the knife from his neck.

As the members of the family party took their places in the Chapel, I surveyed the accompanying group for a second time. Jukes must surely be amongst them, though his distinctive squat figure was not apparent to me. Then the thought struck me that he might have sent an agent; unlikely as it seemed, I swept my eye once more over the onlookers, and moved closer, until I became a part of the little crowd.

'Were you acquainted with Mr Trendle, sir?'

The plaintive enquirer was a little person of some rotundity, who gazed up at me through pale grey-green eyes from behind a pair of gold spectacles.

'Slightly, ma'am,' I replied.

My companion shook her head slowly from side to side. 'Such a wonderful man – wonderful. So good and generous, so adoring of his mamma. You know Mrs Trendle, I dare say?'

'Slightly.'

'But perhaps not her late husband?'

'No, indeed.'

I did not wish to keep up the conversation, but she came back again.

'You are of the Chapel, perhaps?'

I replied that I had known the deceased only through business.

'Ah, business. I do not understand business. But Mr Trendle did. Such a clever man! What the dear people in Africa will do without him, I cannot think.'

She continued her lament for some time, expounding in particular, with a curious kind of wistful relish, upon the wickedness and certain damnation of the person who had thus deprived the Africans of their great champion.

Eventually, unencouraged by any response from me, she smiled faintly and waddled away, her fluttering mourning clothes making her seem like a great aggregated ball of soot that had escaped from the prison of fog that still lay in a dark looming bar across the murmuring city at our back, pressing down on the poor souls beneath like the weight of sin itself.

No sign. Nothing. I moved about the crowd, anxious to be part of it, but wary of any individual contact. When would he come? *Would* he come?

In due course, the Chapel bell tolled out, and the coffin, followed by the mourners and their attendants, was carried back out to the awaiting hearse. Slowly, the procession wound its way to the place that had been prepared.

The ceremony of interment was duly performed by an elderly white-haired clergyman, accompanied by the usual displays of grief. I found myself unwillingly regarding the coffin as it was lowered gently into the receiving earth, the last mortal home of the unfortunate Lucas Trendle, late of the Bank of England. For I had put him there, and for nothing he had done to me.

The party began to disperse. I looked once more at his mother, and at the gentleman I had seen accompanying her earlier. From beneath the rim of his hat peeked a narrow curtain of red hair.

Eventually, I was left alone at the graveside with the diggers and their assistants. Of Fordyce Jukes there was not a trace.

I waited for nearly an hour, and then made my way back towards the Egyptian portals, with darkness coming on. The gatekeeper tipped his hat as he let me through a smaller side entrance. I took a deep breath. The wretched Jukes had played me for a fool, sending me all the way out here as a prank, for which he would pay dearly when the moment of reckoning came.

But then, just as I was passing beneath the deeply shadowed arch into the outer world, I felt a tap on my shoulder as a person – a man – pushed past me. I had instinctively swung to the left, towards the shoulder on which I had received the tap; but he had gone to the right, quickly becoming absorbed in a remaining group of mourners standing just outside the gates, and disappearing into the deepening gloom.

It had not been Jukes. He was taller, broader, quick on his feet. *It had not been Jukes.*

I RETURNED TO TEMPLE-STREET, DEJECTED AND CONFUSED. AS I PASSED through the staircase entrance, the door of the ground-floor chamber opened.

'Good evening, Mr Glapthorn,' said Fordyce Jukes. 'I trust you've had a pleasant day?'

· 6 ·

*Vocat**

THE CONVICTION THAT FORDYCE JUKES WAS MY BLACKMAILER WOULD not leave me; and yet he had not been at Stoke Newington, nor had any attempt been made by any other person or persons to make themselves known to me – except for that tap on the shoulder, that unsettling sense of gentle but firm pressure deliberately applied. An accidental brush by a hastily departing stranger, no doubt. But not the first such 'accident' – I still thought of the incident outside the Diorama. And not the last.

Why had Jukes sent me out to Stoke Newington, if he had not intended to reveal himself to me there? I could reach no other conclusion but that he was biding his time; that the second note, summoning me to the interment of my victim, had been designed to apply a little additional twist of the knife, which I would repay with compound interest. Two communications had been received. Perhaps a third would bring matters to a head.

I kept a close eye on Jukes from that moment on. From my sitting-room window, if I placed my face close against the glass, I could just see down to where the staircase gave onto the street. I observed him carrying in his provisions, or passing the time of day with the occupants of neighbouring chambers, sometimes taking his mangy little dog out for a walk by the river. His work hours were regular, his private activities innocent.

Nothing happened. The expected third communication did

*['He calls'. The significance of the title of this section is not altogether clear. *Ed.*]

not come; there was no soft knock on the door, and no indication of an unravelling plan. Slowly, over the following days, I began to gain ground on my enfeebled self, and, with returning strength and concentration, emerged one morning after a sound night's sleep – the first for a week or more – to rededicate myself to the destruction of my enemy.

Of *his* history and character you shall know more – much more – as this narrative continues. He was ever in my mind. I breathed him in every day, for his fate was anchored to mine. 'And I shall cover his head with the mountains of my wrath, and press him down,/And he shall be forgotten by men.' This is an untypically fine line from the epic pen of P. Rainsford Daunt (*The Maid of Minsk*, Book III); but there is a finer by Mr Tennyson, which I had constantly before my mental eye: 'I was *born* to other things.'*

On the Sunday following the interment of Lucas Trendle, I called at Blithe Lodge, as arranged, and was shown into the back parlour by Charlotte, the Scottish housemaid. I waited for some little time until, at last, I heard the sound of Bella's distinctive tripping tread on the stairs.

'How are you, Eddie?' she asked. She did not take my hand, or kiss me spontaneously, as she might once have done, or even proffer her own cheek to be kissed.

We exchanged the usual pleasantries as she sat down on a chaise-longue by the tall sash-window that looked down over the dark garden below.

'Well, then,' she said, 'tell me what you've been doing. Things

*[The line is from *In Memoriam* (1850), cxx: 'Let him, the wiser man who springs/Hereafter, up from childhood shape/His action like the greater ape,/But I was *born* to other things'. *Ed.*]

have been so busy here. So much to do, and so many things to think about! And with Mary leaving – you know of course that Captain Patrick Davenport is going to marry her! Such excitement – and so brave of him! But she deserves it, the dear girl, and he does love her so. Kitty has a new girl coming tomorrow, but of course we never know how these things will work out, and then Kitty herself has gone back to France, and so it falls to me to conduct the interview, as well as everything else, and you know that Charlie is to go to Scotland for her sister's confinement . . . '

She twittered on in this inconsequential way for some minutes, laughing from time to time, and curling her fingers around in her lap as she spoke. But the old light in her eyes had gone. I saw and felt the change. I did not have to ask the reason. I could see that she had considered, in the cold light of day, what I had told her at the Clarendon Hotel, and had found it wanting – fatally so. A tale told to a child; a demeaning, absurd fantasy of a paste-board villain and his mysterious henchman – one of my mother's stories, perhaps, dusted down for the purpose. All to hide the truth – whatever hideous truth it was – about Edward Glapthorn, who was not what he seemed. It was only too apparent that she had taken 'Veritas' at his word.

Charlotte brought us tea, and Bella continued with her trivial banter – I sitting silently, smiling and nodding from time to time as she went on – until a knocking on the front door announced the arrival of some member of The Academy to whom she had to attend.

We stood up; I shook her unlingering hand and left by the garden door. She had been a dear friend and companion to me; but I had not loved her as she had wished me to do. I had sought, out of deep regard, to protect her from hurt; and, if my fate had been otherwise, would have married her gladly, and been content to give myself to her alone. But my heart was no longer mine to bestow on whom I pleased; it had been ripped from me by a greater power and given to another, against my will, and would now remain in *her* possession, a poor forgotten prisoner, for all eternity.

THE NEXT DAY, FEELING TETCHY AND OUT OF SORTS FOLLOWING THE previous evening's conversation with Bella, I sent a note over to Le Grice proposing a spin in the skiff that I kept at the Temple Pier, to which he immediately agreed. Our plan was to row up to the Hungerford Passenger Bridge, take a little lunch at his club, and then row back. The morning had broken fair, though with a brisk wind, and I sallied forth to meet him with a lust for exertion.

At the bottom of the stairs, the door to Jukes's room stood ajar. I stopped, unable to help myself.

Across the street I saw the distinctive figure of my neighbour, his rounded back towards me, disappearing towards the Temple Gardens with his little dog in tow. He had not meant to leave his door open, of that I was sure, a careful, crafty fellow like that. But it *was* open, and it was an irresistible invitation to me.

The sitting-room was a large, panelled apartment, with a little arched door in the far corner leading to the sleeping area and wash-room. It was comfortably furnished, with evidence of taste and discernment that seemed to sit ill with the walking, breathing Fordyce Jukes. I had often wondered, as I gazed down on his comings and goings from my room in the eaves, what mental world the funny little creature inhabited; to see such wholly unsuspected illustrations of that world palpably adorning the walls and shelves momentarily distracted me from my immediate purpose.

Adjacent to the door of his bedchamber stood an elegant glass-fronted cabinet containing several exquisite items: miniatures from the Tudor period (a Hilliard?), little painted boxes of the highest-quality workmanship, Chinese ivory carvings of the greatest delicacy, Delftware, Bohemian goblets; a dazzling miscellany of objects linked only by the refinement of taste – and sufficiency of income – that had assembled them. On the walls, carefully mounted and displayed, were equally startling indications of the unexpected character of Fordyce Jukes's interests. Works by Altdorfer, Dürer, Hollar, and Baldung. Books, too, which drew my especial attention. I gazed in wonderment at the first edition of Thomas Netter's *Sacramentalia* (folio, Paris, François Regnault, 1523),* which I had long wished to own, and at other sweetly choice items that stood arranged in glowing ranks in another locked cabinet beside the desk.

My amazement was complete. That such a man as Jukes could have assembled this collection of rarities, beneath my very nose, as it were, seemed inconceivable. How had he come by it all? Where had he acquired the taste and knowledge? And where the money to dispose on these treasures?

I began to consider the idea that blackmail and extortion might be Jukes's real trade, his secret profession, slyly exercised away from the workaday light of his duties at Tredgolds, though with a success that I could hardly credit. Taste and knowledge can be acquired; money, if it be not naturally to hand, demands other skills to amass. Perhaps his talent, for which his employment at Tredgolds would place him in a helpful position, was to extort

*[Thomas Netter (*c.*1375–1430), born in Saffron Walden in Essex (thus known in religion as Thomas Waldensis), was a Carmelite theologian and controversialist and a confessor to Henry V. He played a prominent part in the prosecution of Wycliffites and Lollards. The *Sacramentalia* is the third volume of the author's *Doctrinale antiquitatum fidei ecclesiae catholicae,* a complete apologia of Catholic dogma and ritual intended to counter the attacks of Wycliff and others. On the face of it, it is a strange work for the narrator to covet. *Ed.*]

money from clients of the firm who had something to hide from the world at large.

It seemed fanciful at first, but the more I thought on it, the more it seemed to constitute a sort of possibility, an explanation for what I had found in this treasure cave that had lain, unremarked, for so long beneath my feet. Was I, then, merely the most recent of his victims? Did he suppose that I had the means to satisfy his demands, and so enable him to acquire one more rare and beautiful item for his walls and cabinets? But I would be no victim of Fordyce Jukes's, or of any man's. From these thoughts, I recalled myself to my present task and turned towards the desk, which, like mine three floors above, stood before the window looking out into the street.

The polished surface bore nothing except a fine silver inkstand. The drawers were fast locked. I looked about me. Another locked cupboard in the corner. No papers. No note-books. Nothing to show me the character of Jukes's hand for comparison with the notes Bella and I had received. Another sign, I thought, that my renewed suspicions were well founded. A man who had acquired so much through extortion would not be so careless as to leave such evidence easily open to view.

Then, on a small side table by the fireplace, I noticed an open book. Approaching nearer, I saw that it was an octavo Bible of the seventeenth century, though of no especial beauty or rarity. The title-words of the opened recto met my astonished gaze: 'The Book of the Prophet EZEKIEL'

I had found no evidence of the creature's handwriting, but this seemed to provide the proof I needed that Jukes was the blackmailer.

I turned to leave, standing at the half-open door for a moment to see whether he was returning; but the street was clear, so I stepped out, and headed down towards Temple Pier.

· 7 ·

*In dubio**

I FOUND LE GRICE WAITING FOR ME, LOUNGING AGAINST A WALL, cheroot in mouth, in the feeble but welcome sun.

'God damn you, G,' he cursed, good-humouredly, as I approached. 'Been waitin' for you for fifteen minutes or more. Where the devil have you been? The tide will be out before we get off.'

We pulled the skiff down to the water, stowed our coats in the stern, rolled up our sleeves, and pushed off into the inky-brown water.

Behind us were the myriad masts of the Docks, London Bridge, dense with its morning traffic, and the looming dome of St Paul's; before us, the distant line of Waterloo Bridge, and the slow curve of the broad stream down towards Hungerford Market. All around were vessels of every type and size, plying up and down, and on each bank the city bristled in silhouette against the pearly grey light, brushed over with the always present haze that the metropolis exuded. Past vistas of dark lanes opening out towards the river's edge we went, past the crazy lines of chimney pots and jagged tenements etched against the sky, and the nobler outlines of spires and battlements, past watermen's stairs and landing stages, warehouses and gardens. All about us gulls wheeled and circled, their raucous cries mingling with the river sounds of waves

*['In doubt'. *Ed.*]

slapping against moored hulls, the flap of sails and pennants, the distant toot of a steam-tug.

We rowed on steadily, saying nothing, each enjoying the sensation of pulling against the mighty stream, glad to be out on the open water – even foul Thames water on a November day. For my part, I felt sweet release from the many nights that I had spent staring at the skylight above my bed. In front of me, the muscles of Le Grice's great back wrenched and stretched the oyster-coloured silk of his waistcoat almost to bursting, and for a moment my mind started back to my former dream of rowing down a hot summer river behind the muffled form of Lucas Trendle. But the image passed, and I pulled on.

Just below Essex Wharf, a woman dressed in tattered and filthy clothes, a hamper suspended by her side from a leather strap about her shoulders, the remnant of a ragged bonnet on her head, was prodding and poking along the shore, serenely seeking objects of value in the ooze and foetid slime of the river's margin. She looked up and, ankle-deep in the mud, stood watching us, her hand shielding her eyes against the strengthening sun, as we rowed past.

After tying up below Hungerford Stairs, I reached into the stern to retrieve our coats. On doing so I noticed, some way behind us, a single figure in a small rowing boat, oars down in the water. He had clearly been proceeding upstream on a similar course to ours, but now, like us, he had come to a rest, though he remained some distance out from the shore.

'Did you not see him?' asked Le Grice, twisting his great neck back towards me and looking over at the solitary figure. 'He joined us soon after we saw the woman at Essex Wharf. Friend of yours?'

No friend of mine, I thought. He presented a threatening silhouette, his tall hat standing up starkly black against the light that was now breaking westwards down the channel of the river.

Then it struck me. I had been a fool to believe that Fordyce Jukes would think of following me himself, knowing that I would instantly have recognized him. He must have some accomplice – and here he was, the man in the boat, grimly biding his time; the man, perhaps, who had tapped me on the shoulder outside the Diorama; and the man who had pushed past me under the Egyptian portals at Abney Cemetery. No longer invisible; no longer shadow-hidden: he was here, in full daylight, though still out of reach. But sweet relief washed over me on seeing him; for now, I hoped, I could begin to turn the tables. *Come a little closer,* I whispered to myself, *just a little closer. Let me see your face.*

'What's that you say?' Le Grice was reaching back for me to hand him his coat.

'I said nothing. Here.'

I threw his coat at him, and then turned again to look back at our pursuer. If I could lure him from the safety of his boat on to dry land, then I might contrive an opportunity to confront him. I pulled on my coat, feeling the reassuring weight of the pocket-pistols I always carried with me. Then I gave one more look astern, to fix in my mind the distant figure of the watcher.

He was exceptionally tall, with broad shoulders – even broader, perhaps, than Le Grice's; clean shaven, as far as I could tell, though his upturned coat collar might conceal whiskers; and his large ungloved hands gripped the oars purposefully as he contended with the current to maintain his stationary position. But the more I scrutinized him, the more anxious I became. A formidable opponent, doubtless; but I am also a big man, and was confident that I could give a good account of myself, if it came to it. Why, then, this anxiety? What was it about this bobbing figure that discomfited me?

. . .

WE GAINED THE STREET, AND PROCEEDED TO LE GRICE'S CLUB, THE United Service. Le Grice had been kicking around for some years with no fixed prospect in view; but being a soldier's son, the opening of hostilities in the East earlier in the year, and the despatch of the expeditionary force to the Crimea, had suddenly stirred him to buy into the Guards, though he had yet to take up his duties. He talked excitedly of his impending military career. Like everyone at that time, his head was full of the great events in the Russian campaign, especially of the Light Brigade's heroic charge at Balaclava, soon to be so memorably evoked in Mr Tennyson's great ode.* For my part, I was happy to let him talk on, for my mind was occupied with our friend from the river. I had expected to catch sight of him by now, but, to my surprise, no one appeared to be following us.

We reached the steps of the Club, crowded with arriving members, without incident. Luncheon was excellent in every respect. Le Grice, in fine form, called for a second bottle of champagne, and then another; but I wished to stay alert, thinking still of our pursuer, and so let him have the lion's share. After an hour or so had passed, it became apparent that my companion was in no fit state to row back with me; and so, after putting him into a hansom, I returned to the river alone.

Stopping every few yards to make sure I was not being tracked, I finally arrived at Hungerford Steps, retrieved the skiff, and prepared to row back. My head was racing. Where was he? I set off, turning my head from time to time, expecting he would be there, but I could see nothing. Arriving at Temple Pier, I stood up to moor the craft, lost my balance, and fell back into the river. As I sat there, in two feet of cold stinking water, the amused

*['The Charge of the Light Brigade' was published in *The Examiner* on 9 December 1854. The poem was reprinted in *Maud, and Other Poems* (1855). *Ed.*]

object of attention of a number of passers-by on the embankment above, I saw the dark figure of the solitary rower. Once more he had stopped his craft mid-stream, laid back his oars, and sat looking straight ahead with ominous concentration. Again, no features were discernible, simply this alarming attitude of acute attentiveness.

Cursing under my breath, I slopped and splashed my way back to Temple-street. At each corner I stopped and looked back, to see if the mysterious rower had disembarked his craft and was following me, but there was no sign of him. Unable to bear the water in my boots any longer, I tore them off in frustrated fury and walked the last few yards to the staircase of my chambers in just my stockinged feet.

And so it was, my sodden stockings muffling the sound of my footsteps on the stairs, that I came upon Fordyce Jukes bending down at my door, preparing to slip something underneath it.

HE SCREAMED LIKE A STUCK PIG AS, THROWING MY DRIPPING BOOTS ON the stairs, I grabbed him by his miserable neck and hurled him to the floor.

Holding him still by the scruff, like the cur he was, I unlocked the door, and kicked him inside.

He cowered in the corner, his hand across his face.

'Mr Glapthorn! Mr Glapthorn!' he whimpered, calling me by the name by which I was known in the firm, 'whatever is the matter? It is me, your neighbour Fordyce Jukes. Do you not know me?'

'Know you?' I snarled back. 'Oh yes, I know you. I know you very well for the villain you are.'

He leaned back a little into the corner, letting his hand drop away from his face to reveal a look of genuine alarm. I had him now.

'Villain? What can you mean? What villainy have I done to you?'

I advanced towards him, as he frantically forced himself back yet further into the corner, the heels of his boots scraping noisily on the boards, in a futile attempt to escape the beating that I was now preparing to administer. But something held me back.

'Well, let us see now,' said I. 'Perhaps this will serve as an instance.'

I turned away from him and went back to the door, picked up the paper he had been pushing under it when I had arrived unnoticed behind him, and began to read it.

It was written in a highly distinctive hand; but it was the distinctiveness of the professional scribe, the practised hand of a solicitor's clerk. It bore no resemblance at all to either of the notes that Bella and I had received. And the message it contained? An invitation for Mr Edward Glapthorn to join Mr Fordyce Jukes, and a few other friends, at a dinner to celebrate his birthday, at the Albion Tavern, on Saturday evening, the 12th of November.

I stood in silent befuddlement.

What on earth could be happening? I had caught the rogue red-handed, or so I had thought; and now – this! Was it some kind of diabolical variation on his usual game to throw me off the scent? And then, as I considered the matter, the clearer became the possibility that I might have been mistaken – dangerously mistaken – about the identity of the blackmailer. But if not Jukes, then who?

My stomach knotted as the threatening figure of the solitary rower rose up before my mind's eye. The anxiety that I had earlier experienced returned; but the truth had not yet begun to form itself, and I could not see what I should have seen, when I had tried to force the blackmail note to give up the identity of its author.

Still Jukes cowered in the corner, but he had seen my discomposure on reading the invitation, and his attitude had relaxed somewhat.

'Mr Glapthorn, please. Allow me to stand.'

I said nothing, but walked instead over to my armchair by the fire and threw myself down, still clutching the piece of paper.

I heard him pick himself up from the floor, dust himself down, and walk across to where I was sitting.

'Mr Glapthorn, please, I meant no harm, no harm at all. Perhaps coming on me like that – it is quite dark on your landing, is it not? – I can see – that is, I expect you mistook me for some house-thief or such. A shock, I'm sure, to find someone here. But no harm intended, sir, no harm at all, no, none at all . . .'

And so he went on, repeating the same sentiments over and over, and wringing his fat little hands to emphasize his contrition and regret at the trouble caused.

I took a deep breath, rose from my chair, and faced my neighbour.

'Mr Jukes, I apologize. Sincerely and completely. It is *I* who have done *you* wrong. Much wrong. You are right. In the gloom of the landing I thought that someone was attempting to break into my rooms. I have been on the river, you see, and am a little fatigued and dizzy from the exertion. I did not recognize you. Unforgivable.'

I screwed up all my will-power and held out my hand.

He limply reciprocated, at which I immediately withdrew myself to my work-table and sat down again.

'I thought that we see so little of each these days, Mr Glapthorn,' I heard him say, though my mind was already far away from the stunted figure in old-fashioned breeches and tailcoat, standing on my Turkey rug, still wringing his hands, and looking about him nervously. 'You are so rarely in the office now, and I used to so enjoy our little chats. Not that we have ever been friends as such, I realize, but we are neighbours, and neighbours, you know, should be neighbourly. And so I thought, perhaps Mr

Glapthorn is in need of some company? And then I thought, couldn't I bring together a few friends to partake in a little celebratory dinner – it being my birthday on Saturday – and invite Mr Glapthorn— '

He had paused.

'I'm afraid I am not free on Saturday, Mr Jukes, but I thank you for your invitation.'

'Of course. I understand, Mr Glapthorn. You are a busy man, I'm sure.'

He edged a little towards the door.

'Well,' he said, in an effort to brighten his tone, 'I shall take my leave.'

I was preparing to apologize again for my rough behaviour, but he forestalled me with a rapid shake of his head. 'Pray, say no more, Mr Glapthorn. All a mistake. No harm done, none at all.'

I nodded. Then a thought struck me. Perhaps I might be wrong in acquitting him.

'A moment, Mr Jukes.'

He looked up.

'Are you a religious man?'

'Religious?' he said, evidently surprised at my question. 'Well, I suppose I am as observant in that way as most. I was brought up strictly, though perhaps I have relaxed a little in my ways. But I attend the Temple Church every Sunday morning, and read my Bible every day, sir – every day.' He raised his head as he spoke the last words, and pulled his shoulders back in a little gesture of defiance, as if to say, 'There now. Here is villainy!'

'Every day?' I said, quizzically.

'Every day. Regular as clockwork, a few pages before I take Little Fordyce for his walk. It is surprising how much one gets through. I am coming towards the end of the Old Testament for the second time this twelvemonth.'

'Well,' I said, 'that is excellent. Excellent. Good day, Mr Jukes, and— '

He held up his hand again. 'No need, sir, no need at all.' With which he turned, smiled wanly, and closed the door.

I sat, still in my dripping clothes, looking out of my little dormer window at rags of clouds, drifting like smoke over a battlefield, until I heard him descend the stairs and bang his own door shut.

· 8 ·

Amicus verus[*]

THE FOLLOWING MORNING, A NOTE CAME FROM LE GRICE APOLOGIZING for his over-consumption of champagne the previous day, and announcing that he would be at the Ship and Turtle at his usual hour that evening, if I cared to join him.

He was in voluble mood, and I happily let him regale me with reports of what this fellow or that had been up to, who had said what at the Club, and where so-and-so had been, the gossip supplemented by an excited account of all the business upon which he was then engaged, preparatory to leaving for the war. I was sorry that he was going, and was of course anxious for his safety; but it was impossible not to become caught up in his enthusiasm, to the extent that I almost began to regret that I had never thought of going for a soldier myself.

We parted just before midnight. He was heading back to his rooms in Albany[†] when he suddenly stopped short.

'By the by,' he called back, 'I almost forgot. This was sent to me at the Club. It's for you.' Reaching into the inside pocket of his great-coat, he handed me a small wrapped package, obviously containing a book.

*['A true friend'. *Ed.*]

†[On the north side of Piccadilly, almost opposite Fortnum & Mason. Formerly Melbourne House, built in 1770, it was converted into sixty-nine elegant bachelor apartments in 1802 by Henry Holland. The author properly refers to it as 'Albany' (without the definite article). *Ed.*]

'You'll never guess who it's from.'

I looked at him blankly.

'That fearful tug* Daunt. You'll remember him, of course. Pretty thick at school, weren't you, for a time? Scribbles poetry for a living now. Sends his compliments to me with a request to pass this on to you. Haven't written back yet, of course. Thought I'd speak to you first.'

He instantly saw that his words, and the package, had produced an effect, and he reddened.

'I say, G, is anything the matter? You look a little upset.'

I delayed my reply as I turned the package over in my hands.

'Has he written to you before?'

'First time, old boy. Not quite my sort. Never expected to hear from him again after going down from the Varsity. Damned unpleasant blighter, always putting on airs. Little sign, by all accounts, that he's changed for the better.'

When I did not reply, Le Grice took a step closer and looked me straight in the eye.

'Look here,' he said, 'there's something going on, I can see. Wouldn't dream of pressing you, of course, but glad to help, if I can.'

'You can tell him I'm travelling abroad,' I replied. 'Present whereabouts, unknown. Date of return, uncertain.'

'Right-oh. Nothing easier. Consider it done.' He coughed nervously and made to go; but he had only taken a few steps when he suddenly stopped and swung round to face me again.

'There's another thing. You can tell me to go and boil my head, but answer me this, if you can. Why was that fellow follow-

*[Now obsolete Eton slang for a boy on the foundation (King's Scholar or Colleger), from the Latin *togati*, or 'wearers of gowns'. *Ed.*]

ing us on the river yesterday? It's no use saying he wasn't, so why not come out with it straight?'

I could have hugged the dear old bear. For weeks I had been living on my nerves, desperately engaged night and day in mental combat with my enemy, my spirit broken by betrayal, racked by rage and despair, but unable to confide in any living soul. I had believed that I had no ally, no strength other than my own with which to contest the great battle of my life; but here was dear old Le Grice, bull-headed in friendship, obstinately loyal, offering me his hand. And if I took it? There was no one more trustworthy than him, no one more willing to fight by your side to the last breath, no one more forgiving of a friend's sins. Yes, but if I took it? He would need to be told the secrets that I had been living with for so long. Would he then keep faith with me, stand by me in the final contention, and forgive me? Then he spoke again.

'You and me, G – chalk and cheese. But you're the best friend I have. Do anything for you, don't you know, anything at all. Not good at this sort of thing, so you'll just have to take it as it comes. You're in trouble – no point trying to deny it. It's been written on your face for weeks past. Whether it's to do with Daunt, or with this fellow on the river, I can't say. But something's wrong, even though you've tried to pretend all's well. But it isn't, so why not spill it, and let's see what can be done about it?'

There are times in a man's life when he must put his immediate fate into the hands of another, regardless of the risk. In a moment, though doubts remained, I had decided. I would spill it.

'Dinner at Mivart's,* tomorrow night,' I said.

*[At 51 Brook Street, Berkeley Square. Opened in 1812 by James Mivart, it is now better known as Claridge's. *Ed.*]

And then we shook hands.

I RETURNED HOME IN MEDITATIVE MOOD, QUESTIONING THE WISDOM of confiding in Le Grice, but still determined to go through with it. I shrank, though, from the prospect of confessing what had been done to Lucas Trendle in Cain-court, and what I was planning to do, now that I had proved myself capable of murder. I was sure, when I had revealed my true history to Le Grice, and set before him the calculated viciousness of our mutual acquaintance, Phoebus Daunt, that I would secure his full-hearted sympathy and support. But would even his staunch soul be put to the test by the knowledge of what I had been driven to do? And could I, even in the name of friendship, ask him to share this burden? Musing thus, I arrived in Temple-street and mounted the stairs.

Once in my rooms, I unwrapped the package Le Grice had given to me. As I had guessed, it contained a book – a small octavo in dark green cloth, untrimmed, bearing the title *Rosa Mundi.* Taking up my paper-knife, I slowly began to cut away the edges, and opened out the title-page.*

*[The volume was published in December 1854, post-dated 1855. The Latin motto from Horace reads: 'Mix with your wise counsels some brief folly./In due place to forget one's wisdom is sweet.' *Ed.*]

ROSA MUNDI;

and

Other Poems

P. RAINSFORD DAUNT

Misce stultitiam consiliis brevem:

Dulce est desipere in loco. Hor. Odes, iv. viii

London: Edward Moxon, Dover-street.

MDCCC-LV

The fly-leaf had been inscribed by the author: 'To my friend, E.G., with fondest memories of old times, and hope of early reunion.' Beneath the inscription was a couplet, 'When all is known, and naught remains,/But Truth released from falsehood's chains,' which I later discovered was a quotation from one of the poems printed in the volume. If there was meaning in it, I could see none.

I threw the book down in disgust, but could not help staring at the open fly-leaf. To see that hand again, after so many years! It had not changed a great deal; I recognized the idiosyncratic flourish of the initial 'T' of 'Truth', the intricate descenders (the bane of his teachers at school), the fussiness of it. But what memory had been aroused by it? Of Latin Alcaics and hexameters, exchanged and criticized? Or of something else?

. . .

The next evening, as arranged, I met Le Grice at Mivart's.

He was awkward and ill at ease, coughing nervously, and constantly running his finger around the inside of his shirt collar, as if it were too tight. As we lit our cigars, I asked him whether he was still willing to hear what I had come to tell him.

'Absolutely, old boy. Ready and waiting. Fire away.'

'Of course I may count on your complete – your complete, mind – discretion?'

He laid down his cigar, positively bristling with indignation.

'When I give my word to some fellow at the Club,' he said, with impressive seriousness, 'then he may expect me to keep it, no questions asked. When I give my word to *you*, therefore, there can be not the slightest doubt – not the slightest – that I shall be inclined, under any provocation, to betray whatever confidence you may honour me with. Hope I've made myself clear.' Having delivered himself of this short, but emphatic, speech, he picked up his cigar again and sent me a look that plainly said, 'There, I've said what needed to be said; now contradict me, if you dare.'

No, he would never betray me, as others had done; he would be true to his word. But I had resolved that there would be a limit to what I would tell him – not because I distrusted him, or even that I feared he might repudiate our friendship when he learned what I had done, and what was now in my mind to do; but because there was mortal danger in knowing all, to which I would not expose him for all the world.

Calling for another bottle, I began to tell him, in outline, what I now propose to tell you, my unknown reader, in full and complete form – the extraordinary circumstances of my birth; the character and designs of my enemy; and the futile passion that has made it impossible that I can ever love again.

. . .

If it is true, as the ancient sage averred, that confession of our faults is the next thing to innocency,* then I hope this narrative will weigh something in my favour with those who may read it.

I began with my name. When 'Veritas' warned Bella that Edward Glapthorn was not what he seems, he lived up to his pseudonym. To Bella, to my employer, to my neighbours in Temple-street, and to others with whom you will soon become acquainted, I was Edward Glapthorn. But I was born Edward Charles Glyver – the name by which I had been known at Eton, when I first met Willoughby Le Grice, and by which, shortened to 'G', he has known me ever since. Yet even this was not my true name, and Captain and Mrs Edward Glyver of Sandchurch, Dorset, were not my parents. It all began, you see, in deceit; and only when the truth is told at last will expiation be made and the poor unquiet soul, from whom all these troubles have flowed, find peace at last.

You have already learned something of the early history of Edward Glapthorn, which, though incomplete, was also a true account of the upbringing of Edward Glyver. I shall return to that history, and its continuance, in due course. But let us first put a little flesh on the bones of Phoebus Rainsford Daunt, my illustrious but as yet shadowy enemy, whose name has already graced the pages of this narrative.

He will already be known to many of you, of course, through his literary works. No doubt, in due course, for the delectation of posterity, some enterprising drudge will assemble an anodyne *Life and Letters* (in three fat, unreadable volumes), which will reveal nothing whatsoever concerning the true character and proclivities

*[Pubilius Syrus (42 BC), *Maxims. Ed.*]

of its subject.* Until then, let me be your guide instead – like Virgil leading Dante through the descending circles of Hell.

By what authority do I presume to take on such a role? My own. I have become the detective of his life, seeking, over many years, to learn everything I could about my enemy. You will find this strange. No doubt it is. The scholar's temperament, however, which I possess in abundance, is not content with facile generalities, or with unsubstantiated testimony, still less with the distortions of self-promotion. The scholar, like the lawyer, requires corroboration, verification, and firm documentary evidence, of a primary character; he sifts, and weighs, and patiently accumulates; he analyses, compares, and combines; he applies the nicest of discrimination to separate fact from fabrication, and possibility from probability. Using such methods, I have devoted myself to many objects of study in the course of my life, as I shall describe; but to none of these have I given so much of my time and care as to this pre-eminent subject. Luck, too, has played its part; for my enemy has attained celebrity, and this always loosens tongues. 'Ah yes, I knew him when he was a boy.' 'Phoebus Daunt – the poet? Indeed I remember him.' 'You should speak to so-and-so. He knows a good deal more about the family than I.' And so it proceeds, piece by piece, memory by memory, until, at last, a picture begins to emerge, rich and detailed.

It is all there for the picking, if you know how. The principal sources on which I have drawn are as follows: the fragmentary rec-

*[An attempt was begun by J.R. Wildgoose (1831–89) in 1874 but was abandoned. A fragmentary biographical assessment of Daunt, based on Wildgoose's researches, appeared in the latter's *Adventures in Literature* (1884). Wildgoose was himself a minor poet and author of a short life of Daunt's contemporary, Mortimer Findlay (1812–78). As far as I am aware, no further attempts have been made to memorialize Daunt's life and work. *Ed.*]

ollections of Daunt's time at Eton, which appeared in the *Saturday Review* of 10th October 1848; a fuller memoir of his childhood, adolescence, and literary career, punctuated throughout with little droppings of maudlin verse, and published in 1852 as *Scenes of Early Life*; the personal testimony of Dr T—, the physician who attended Daunt's mother before and immediately after her son's birth; extracts from the unpublished journal of Dr A.B. Daunt, his father (which, I regret to say, came into my hands by unorthodox means); and the recollections of friends and neighbours, as well as those of numerous servants and other attendants.

Why I began on this biographical quest will soon be told. But now Phoebus – the radiant one – attends us. Let us not keep him waiting.

Part the Second

PHOEBUS RISING

1819–1848

I have never yet found Pride in a noble nature:
nor humility in an unworthy mind.

—Owen Felltham, *Resolves* (1623),
vi, 'Of Arrogancy'

· 9 ·

*Ora et labora**

HE WAS BORN – ACCORDING TO HIS OWN ACCOUNT PUBLISHED IN *Scenes of Early Life* – on the last stroke of midnight, as heralded by a venerable long-case clock that stood on the landing outside his mother's room, on the last day of the year 1819, in the industrial town of Millhead, in Lancashire.

A year or so before this great event, his father had been presented to the living of Millhead by his College, when his Fellowship there was forfeited by marriage. At Cambridge, as a young Fellow of Trinity who had already taken the degree of Doctor of Divinity and, by way of diversion from theological dispute, had produced an admirable edition of Catullus, the Reverend Achilles Daunt had acquired the reputation of a man who had much to do in the world of learning, and meant to do it. Certainly his many friends expected much of him, and but for his sudden – and, to some, inexplicable – decision to marry, his abilities would, by common consent, have carried him with little effort to high College and University office.

It was at least widely acknowledged that he had married for love, which is a noble thing for a man of ambition and limited personal means to do. The lady in question, though undeniably a beauty and of acceptable parentage, was of delicate constitution, and had no fortune. Yet love is its own justification, and of course is irresistible.

*['Pray and labour' (St Benedict). *Ed.*]

When Dr Daunt conveyed his decision to the Master of his College, that placid gentleman did his kindly best to dissuade him from a step that would certainly delay, if it did not actually curtail, his University career. For the fact was that the College just then had only one vacant living of which to dispose. Dr Passingham spoke frankly: he did not think that this living would do for a man of Daunt's temper and standing. The stipend was small, barely enough for a single man; the parish was poor, and the work hard, with no curate to lend his aid.

And then the place itself: an utterly unlovely spot, scarred by long-established mine workings and, in latter years, by numerous foundries, workshops, and other manufactories, around which had grown up a waste of smoke-blackened brick. Dr Passingham did not say so, but he considered Millhead, which he had visited only once, to be the kind of place with which no gentleman would wish willingly to be associated.

After some minutes of attempting quiet persuasion, it began to vex the Master somewhat that Dr Daunt did not respond to his well-meant words in the way that he had hoped, persisting instead in a desire to accept the living, and its attendant hardships, at all costs. At last, Dr Passingham had no choice but to shake his head sadly and agree to put the arrangements in hand with all speed.

AND SO, ON A COLD DAY IN DECEMBER 1818, THE REVEREND ACHILLES Daunt took up residence, with his new wife, at Millhead Vicarage. The house – which I have personally visited and inspected – stands, squat and dismal, with its back to a desolate tract of moor, facing a gloomy view of tall black chimneys and ugly, close-packed dwellings in the valley below. Here, indeed, was a change for Dr Daunt. Gone were the lawns and groves and mellow stone courts of the ancient University. To his daily contemplation now lay a very different prospect, peopled by a very different humanity.

But the new incumbent of Millhead Vicarage was determined to work hard for his Northern flock; and certainly it could not be denied that in this, his first, ministry he performed his duties with unswerving diligence. He became especially celebrated in the district for his well-prepared sermons, delivered with intellectual passion and dramatic power, which soon began to draw large congregations to St Symphorian's of a Sunday.

In appearance, he matched the heroic Christian name that his parents had seen fit to bestow upon him: a tall and confident figure, broad-shouldered, deep-voiced, bearded like a prophet. As he tramped the wet and dirty streets of Millhead, he exuded an intimidating air of conscious merit. To the world at large, he seemed a rock and a rampart, a citadel against which nothing could prevail. Yet, by degrees, he began to find that great things were not easy to accomplish in this place of toil, where kindred spirits were few. His work amongst the working poor of the town began to depress him more than he felt it ought to have done; nor did preferment and removal from Millhead come quickly, as he had hoped it would. In short, Dr Daunt became something of a disappointed man.

The imminent birth of his first child did a little to lift his spirits; but, alas, the arrival in the world of baby Phoebus brought tragedy in its wake. Within three days of presenting Dr Daunt with his son and heir, his pretty little wife was dead, and he was left alone, save for the perpetually howling infant, in the dreary house on the hill, with no prospect that he could see of ever being able to leave.

The extremity of his grief brought him to the brink of despair. Great silences descended on the house when, for days on end, the Vicar would shun all human contact. During this black period, solicitous friends from their little circle came to offer succour to him in his bewilderment. Amongst the most attentive was Miss Caroline Petrie, one of those who had sat admiringly before Dr Daunt's pulpit at St Symphorian's. Gradually, Miss Petrie became established as the chief agent of the Vicar's recuperation; she concluded matters most satisfactorily by becoming the second Mrs Daunt in the autumn of 1821.

Of the transition from a state of spiritual and mental annihilation to another of restituted faith and confidence, Dr Daunt never spoke; one can only guess at the compromises that he had to make with both soul and conscience. But make them he did, with some advantage to himself, and grave disadvantage to me.

THE FORMIDABLE MISS CAROLINE PETRIE, WHO BROUGHT WITH HER to Millhead Vicarage a small but welcome annuity, was as different from the first Mrs Daunt as could be. She exhibited strength – of mind, as well as body – at every point. Her bearing was what one would naturally call regal, conveying a dignity of form and expression that immediately commanded attention in both high and low. Partly this was due to her unusual height (she was fully a head taller even than Dr Daunt, and had the advantage of literally looking down upon practically everyone to whom she spoke); partly it arose from her striking physiognomy.

At this time she was nine-and-twenty, and had been living quietly with her uncle for several years, both her parents having died some time before. She was no beauty in the conventional sense, as the first Mrs Daunt had been, the impression created by her features being rather of tribulation vanquished – indeed she carried the visible signature of suffering overcome in the disfiguring etchings of small-pox.

Yet any poet worth his laurels, or painter hungry for inspiration, would have flown instantly into a fine frenzy at first sight of that imperious face. It seemed always set in an austere intensity of expression, as though she had at that very moment looked up from the absorbed perusal of some improving work of irresistible interest – though such works were in fact largely unknown to her. But there was a mitigating softness, too, a yielding about the mouth and eyes that, as one became aware of it, transposed the whole effect of her countenance from the minor to the major key. Besides which she had spirit, the most charming manners when she wished, and blunt good sense. Furthermore, she had ambition, as events were soon to show.

With the money she brought to the marriage, a nurse – Mrs Tackley by name – was employed to watch over the infant Phoebus, which she did most capably until the boy was two years old, when his step-mamma assumed full responsibility for his upbringing and welfare. As a consequence, the boy's character grew to resemble hers in many points, particularly with regard to her worldly outlook, which stood in distinct contrast to the longing of her husband to take up the life of the cloistered scholar once again. It was extraordinary how close they became, and how often Dr Daunt would encounter them locked closely together in conversation, like two conspirators. Though the Vicar was still, of course, responsible for the boy's formal education, in all other respects it seemed that his second wife had taken over from him as the dominant influence on his son's life; and even here, in the study, his authority was frequently undermined. The boy generally applied himself well to his lessons; but if he wished at any time to go and ride his pony, or fish in the stream at the bottom of the garden, instead of getting declensions into his head, then he only had to appeal to his step-mamma and he would be instantly released from his labours. On other occasions, too, the Vicar would find his wishes thwarted, and his orders countermanded. One day, he required the boy to accompany him to one of the worst parts of the town, where utter poverty and hopelessness were starkly manifest on every corner, feeling no doubt that the experience would be useful in awakening in his son some compassion for the plight of those so much less fortunate than himself. But they were intercepted at the front door by his furious wife, who proclaimed that under no circumstances was dear Phoebus to be exposed to such disgusting and dangerous sights. The Vicar protested; but argument was useless. He went down into the town alone, and never again attempted to take his son with him. From these and other instances of the second Mrs Daunt's ascendancy, it is impossible not to conclude that, gradually, and by means that he was unable to resist, Dr Daunt's son was being taken away from him.

By an evil chance, or, as I once believed, as a consequence of that fatality which had shaped my history, the Vicar's wife was the second cousin of Julius Verney Duport, 25th Baron Tansor, of Evenwood Park in the County of Northamptonshire – whose first wife has already been briefly mentioned in connexion with my mother. Several comfortable livings in Northamptonshire lay in the gift of Mrs Daunt's noble relative, and that of Evenwood itself fell vacant in the early summer of 1830. On learning of this, with fire in her eyes, Mrs Daunt instantly flew south to press her new husband's claims with his Lordship.

Already, however, something more than wifely duty appears to have been animating this redoubtable lady. Accounts concur that she had often expressed a wish to remove herself and her husband – and particularly her dear boy, Phoebus – from Millhead, which she detested; and it was doubtless kind of her to offer to lay Dr Daunt's abilities before Lord Tansor. Her husband, I am sure, was touched by his wife's selfless alacrity in this matter. I suspect, however, that selflessness was not her guiding principle, and that in rushing south, with such demonstrable urgency, she was in fact obeying the urgings of her own ambitious heart. For if her suit was successful, she would no longer be a distant and forgotten relation existing in the outer darkness of Millhead; she would instead be counted amongst the Duports of Evenwood – and who knew where that might lead?

I have no records of the meeting between Mrs Daunt and Lord Tansor; but, from Mrs Daunt's point of view, it must have been accounted a success. An invitation to join her was speedily sent back to Dr Daunt in the North; the boy Phoebus was packed off to relations in Suffolk; and the outcome was that Dr and Mrs Daunt returned together from Northamptonshire two weeks later in high spirits.

There followed an anxious wait; but Lord Tansor did not disappoint. Barely another fortnight had passed before a letter – tremendous in its condescension – arrived, confirming Dr Daunt as the new Rector of St Michael and All Angels, Evenwood.

According to one of my informants, on the day after his return from his Suffolk relations, the boy Phoebus was called before his step-mother. Sitting in a small button-backed chair set in front of the drawing-room window – that same chair in which the first Mrs Daunt had often sat, looking forlornly out across the remnant of moor that lay between the Vicarage and the encroaching town – she was heard to impress upon the boy the significance of his father's translation to Evenwood, and what it would mean for them all. I am told that she addressed him in deep melodious tones as her 'dear child', and tenderly stroked his hair.

Then she told him something of their relations and patrons, Lord and Lady Tansor; how great was their standing in the county, and in the country at large; how they also had a grand house in London, which he might see in due course if he was very good; and how he was to call them Uncle and Aunt Tansor.

'You know, don't you, that your Uncle Tansor does not have a little boy of his own any more,' she said, taking his hand and walking him to the window. 'If you are very good, as I know you will be, I am sure your uncle will be especially kind to you, for he misses having a son dreadfully, you know, and it would be such a considerate thing if you were to pretend sometimes to be his very own boy. Could you do that, Phoebus dear? You will always be your papa's boy, of course – and mine, too. It is only a sort of game, you know. But think what it would mean to poor Uncle Tansor, who has no son of his own, as your papa does, to have you constantly by him, and to be able to show you things, and perhaps take you to places. You would like that, wouldn't you? To be taken to nice places?'

And the boy, of course, said that he would. And then she told him of all the wonders of Evenwood.

'Are there chimneys at Evenwood?' the boy asked.

'Why, yes, my dear, but they are not like Millhead chimneys, all dirty and horrid.'

'And is my Uncle Tansor a very great man?'

'Yes indeed,' she said reflectively, looking out across the black valley, 'a very great man.'

At the appointed time, the family's belongings and household goods were despatched south, and the Vicarage at last stood shuttered and empty. As the fly rattled away from the gloomy windswept house, I picture Dr Daunt leaning back against the seat, closing his eyes, and offering up a silent prayer of thanks to his God. His deliverance had come at last.

· 10 ·

*In Arcadia**

THUS CAME THE DAUNT FAMILY TO EVENWOOD, THE PLACE ON WHICH all my hopes and ambitions once rested.

His new situation suited Dr Daunt completely. With four hundred pounds a year from his stipend, and another hundred from his glebe lands, he was now able to keep a carriage and a good table, and generally assume a position of some consequence in the neighbourhood. No longer beset by the adversities of his Millhead living, Dr Daunt lay becalmed and contented in the sunlit harbour of Evenwood.

Light and spacious, the Rectory – a former prebendal manor-house – was set amidst well-tended gardens, beyond which was a sweet prospect of sloping meadows and, across the river, the inviting darkness of close-set woodland. Much of the Rector's work – such as it was in this small and prosperous country parish – could be easily delegated to his curate, Mr Samuel Tidy, a fidgety young man who stood deeply in awe of Dr Daunt (and even more of his wife). Lord Tansor laid infrequent demands on his Rector, and those few duties required of him were painlessly fulfilled. Soon the Rector found himself with ample time, and more than sufficient income, to pursue at his leisure those intellectual and antiquarian interests to which he had clung so desperately at Millhead, and he saw no reason why he should not do so.

It was not long before his wife set to work forging as close a

*[The idealized pastoral world evoked by Virgil's *Eclogues*. *Ed.*]

bond as possible between the Rectory and the great house. Her kinship with the Duport family undoubtedly gave her a degree of privilege, which she adroitly used to her advantage. To Lord Tansor, she quickly made herself indispensable, much as she had done to her husband after the death of his first wife. Nothing was too much trouble. She would not hear of his Lordship being incommoded in any way whatsoever, no matter how small the circumstance. Naturally, she did not undertake any menial tasks herself, displaying instead a winning ability to get them done by other people. She soon became possessed of a thorough knowledge of the house's domestic arrangements, and began to exert a degree of control over them that was wonderful to behold. She did all this, moreover, without a word of complaint from the below-stairs population, who – to a man and woman, even including Cranshaw, his Lordship's long-serving butler – deferred to her commands like old campaigners to the orders of a much-loved general. Indeed, she insinuated herself into all the doings of the household with such tact, combined with effortless charm, that no one appeared in the least affronted by what otherwise might have been seen as rank impudence.

Lord Tansor was delighted by the active deference and domestic assistance of his relative, whom he had barely known before her marriage to the Rector, but whom he now regarded as a signal adornment to the society of Evenwood. Mrs Daunt's diplomatic skills were also put to work on mild Lady Tansor, who, far from feeling injured or indignant at the former's swift assumption of dominance in her house, was touchingly grateful to be relieved of duties which, in truth, she was only too glad to relinquish.

So it was that Dr Daunt and his wife attained to an enviable measure of prosperity and eminence in the country round about Evenwood. It would surely have been forgivable if Mrs Daunt, surveying her work, privately allowed herself the merest smile of satisfaction. But in accomplishing her ends, she had opened a veritable Pandora's Box, with consequences that she could not possibly have foreseen.

I SOMETIMES LIKE TO IMAGINE DR DAUNT, FOR WHOM I HAVE ALWAYS had a sincere regard, coming into his study of a morning – say a bright August morning in the year 1830 – and throwing open the windows to a nascent and glittering world, in a conscious gesture of satisfaction at his lot.

Observe him now, on this imagined morning. It is early, the sun new risen, and not even the servants yet about. The Rector is in high good humour, and hums a merry tune quietly to himself as the sweet cool air flows gently in from the garden. He turns from the window, and looks about him with pleasure and pride.

As I have seen for myself, his books are arranged methodically from floor to ceiling on every wall; uniform note-books (carefully categorized and labelled) and papers (sorted and docketed) are stacked neatly to hand, together with a plentiful supply of writing materials, upon a large square table, on which also stands a seasonal posy, renewed daily by his wife. All is order, comfort, and convenience – exactly as he likes it.

He stands by his desk, affectionately surveying his library. In an alcove on the far wall are the works of the Church Fathers – his eye picks out the familiar presence of his Eusebius, St Ambrose (a particularly choice edition: Paris, 1586), Irenaeus, Tertullian, and St John Chrysostom. By the door, in an ornate case, are his biblical commentaries, the writings of the Continental reformers, and a cherished edition of the Antwerp Polyglot, whilst on either side of the fireplace are ranged the classical authors that are his enduring passion.

But this is no ordinary morning. It is, in every sense, a new dawn; for a task now lies before him which, God willing, may vindicate at last his decision to quit the University.

Late the previous afternoon, a message had come from Lord Tansor asking whether the Rector would be good enough to step up to the house as soon as was convenient. It was, as it happened, rather *in*convenient just then, for Dr Daunt had earlier ridden into Peterborough on business and, on the way back, had been forced to walk the final four miles when his horse had lost a shoe. He had arrived at the Rectory hot, uncomfortable, and ill tempered, and had barely had time to remove his boots when Lord Tansor's man knocked at the front door. But no request from the great house could easily be refused – least of all because of sore feet and an unbecoming sweat.

He was admitted to the house, and conducted through a succession of formal reception rooms, towards the terrace that runs the length of the West Front. Here he found his Lordship seated in a wicker chair in the purple evening light, his spaniel by his side. He was smoking a cigar, and contemplating the sun setting over Molesey Woods, which marked the boundary of his property on its western side.

A word or two concerning Dr Daunt's patron. In person, he was of no more than middling height; but he carried himself like a guardsman, his ramrod back making him seem far taller than he really was. His world was circumscribed by his principal seat, Evenwood, his town-house in Park-lane, the Carlton Club, and the House of Peers. He rarely travelled abroad. His acquaintances were many, his friends few.

One did not trifle with his Lordship. It took very little for him to suspect presumption. The only thing to do with Lord Tansor was to defer to him. On that simple principle was the world of Evenwood, and all its dominions, maintained. The inheritor of an immense fortune, which he had already significantly augmented, he was a naturally accomplished politician, with influence at the highest levels. When the Duport interest demanded action, his Lordship had only to whisper quietly in the ear of Government, and it was done. By nature he was an implacable opponent of reform in every sphere; but he knew – none better – that publicly articulated principles, of whatever complexion, can gravely incommode the man of affairs; and thus he was careful so to frame his views as to remain always at the pivot of power. His opinion was sought by men from all sides. It was of no consequence who was in, and who was out: his sagacity was valued by all. Lord Tansor, in a word, mattered.

A summons from his Lordship, therefore, was always something to heed, and perhaps to be anxious about. Whether Dr Daunt was definitely anxious when he approached his patron, I cannot say; but he would certainly have been curious to know why he had been called up to the house so urgently on a Thursday afternoon.

On becoming aware of his visitor, Lord Tansor rose, stiffly proffered his hand, and gestured to his visitor to sit beside him. I have obtained a résumé of their conversation (from a most reliable source: John Hooper, one of his Lordship's long-serving footmen, whom I later befriended), which forms the basis of the following elaboration.

'Dr Daunt, I'm obliged to you.'

'Good evening, Lord Tansor. I came as soon as I could. There is nothing wrong, I hope?'

'Wrong?' barked his Lordship. 'By no means.' Then he stood up, dropping the butt of his still-smoking cigar into a nearby urn as he did so. 'Dr Daunt, I was lately in Cambridge, dining with my friend Passingham.'

'Dr Passingham? Of Trinity?'

Disdaining the question, his Lordship continued.

'You are well remembered there, sir, very well remembered. Cambridge is not a place that I have ever cared much for, though of course it may have changed since my time. But Passingham is a sound fellow, and he spoke highly of your abilities.'

'I am flattered to hear you say so.'

'I do not say it to flatter you, Dr Daunt. I will be frank. I deliberately sought Passingham's opinion of your competence as a scholar. I believe, from his testimony, that you once stood pretty high in the estimate of the best men there?'

'I had some small reputation, certainly,' replied Dr Daunt, with increasing wonderment at the course that his interrogation was taking.

'And you have, as I understand, kept up your learning – reading, writing articles, and what not.'

'Certainly I have endeavoured to do so.'

'Well, then, the case is this. I am satisfied from my enquiries that your talents recommend you for a commission of the highest importance to me. I hope I can rely on your acceptance.'

'By all means, if it is within my power . . . ' Dr Daunt felt rather acutely that this qualification was redundant. He knew that he had no choice in the matter. The realization was irksome to his still doughty self-esteem; but he had learned discretion. His education in humility since coming to Evenwood from Millhead had been swift, spurred on by necessity and by the exhortations of his wife, who was ever eager to oblige the Duports whenever an opportunity presented itself.

Lord Tansor turned and, followed by his dog, walked towards a pair of imposing French-windows, leaving Dr Daunt to make the assumption that he intended him to follow.

On the other side of the windows lay the Library, a magnificent apartment of noble proportions, decorated in white and gold, with a sumptuous painted ceiling by Verrio.* Lord Tansor's grandfather, the 23rd Baron, had been a gentleman of various, though somewhat contradictory, talents. Like his father and grandfather before him, this gentleman had possessed a cool head for business and had shrewdly extended the family's interests, before retiring at an early age to Evenwood. There he sat to Gainsborough with his plump wife and two rosy-cheeked boys, planted a great number of trees, bred pigs, and – to the complete indifference of his wife – entertained numerous lady admirers (his Lordship being both handsome and famously virile) in a secluded tower situated in the far reaches of the Park.

From these activities he would turn, in a moment, to his other great passion: his books. His Lordship was one of the great collectors of his day, paying frequent trips each year to Paris, Cologne, Utrecht, and other Continental cities, where he purchased liberally, and with discernment, amongst the booksellers and collectors of those places. The consequence, at his death, was a collection of over forty thousand books and manuscripts, for the housing of which he had caused the former ballroom on the West Front of Evenwood to be transformed into the Library in which his grandson and Dr Daunt now stood.

The present Lord Tansor had not, in the slightest degree, inherited his grandsire's bibliographical enthusiasms. His reading matter was confined, on the whole, to the *Morning Post*, *The Times*, his accounts, and an occasional foray into the novels (never the poetry) of Sir Walter Scott; but he was aware – no one could be

*[Antonio Verrio (*c.*1639–1707), Italian decorative painter who settled in England in the early 1670s. He enjoyed much royal patronage, being employed at Windsor Castle, Whitehall Palace, and Hampton Court. He also worked at a number of great houses, including, besides Evenwood, Chatsworth and Burghley. *Ed.*]

more so – that the volumes in his custody represented a considerable material asset, if it were ever to be realized, as well as a visible demonstration of the family's talent for augmenting its physical possessions generation by generation. For the intangible significance of the collection, he cared not a jot. He wished instead to establish exactly what he owned and its approximate value in pounds, shillings and pence, though it was not in these mercenary terms that he presented Dr Daunt with the task of preparing a *catalogue raisonnée* of the entire collection.

As they entered the Library, a man, small of stature and wearing a pair of round spectacles, looked up from an escritoire at the far end of the room, where he had been busily engaged with a pile of documents.

'Do not mind us, Mr Carteret,' said Lord Tansor to his secretary. The man returned quietly to his work, though Dr Daunt noticed that he would now and again look surreptitiously across to where they stood, returning to the perusal of the documents that lay upon the desk with an exaggerated expression of concentration.

'It would be a service to me to know what I have here,' continued Lord Tansor to Dr Daunt, looking about him coldly at the ranks of volumes packed tightly behind their gilded metal grilles.

'A service also to learning,' said the Rector, lost for a moment in delighted consideration of the task that had been laid before him.

'Quite so.'

Here was an undertaking of great usefulness and, for Dr Daunt, of surpassing interest. He could not imagine a more congenial assignment, or one more suited to his talents and inclinations. The scale of the project did not dismay him in the least; indeed he welcomed it as making its accomplishment all the more worthy of applause. He also saw how he might revive his lapsed reputation as a scholar, for in preparing a catalogue of the collection, he had already determined to produce extensive commentaries and annotations to the most important volumes, which in themselves would be of lasting value to generations of scholars and collectors to come. It is unlikely that Lord Tansor guessed the Rector's unspoken aims. His own design, as a man of business, was simply to have an accurate inventory of his stock, and this Dr Daunt appeared to be both willing and capable of supplying.

It was speedily agreed that the preliminary work would start the very next day. Dr Daunt would come up to the house every morning, excepting of course Sundays, to work in the Library. Everything needful would be placed at his disposal – Carteret would see to it all; and, said Lord Tansor magnanimously, Dr Daunt might have the temporary use of one of his own grey cobs for the daily journey across the Park.

THEY RETRACED THEIR STEPS TO THE TERRACE. THERE WAS A SLIGHT sunset wind moving through the avenue of limes that led away from the formal gardens to the lake. The rustle of its passing only served to deepen the sense of descending silence. Lord Tansor and Dr Daunt stood for a moment looking out across the flower-beds and the criss-cross of clipped grass paths.

'There is another matter I wished to put before you, Dr Daunt,' said Lord Tansor. 'It would please me to see your boy do well in life. I have often had occasion to observe him of late, and I discern in him qualities that a father could be proud of. Do you intend that he should take Orders?'

Dr Daunt hesitated slightly. 'That has always been . . . understood.' He did not say that he had already sensed a distinct animosity in his only son towards the prospect of ordination.

'It is gratifying, of course,' continued Lord Tansor, 'that the young man's inclinations concur with your own wishes. Perhaps you may live to see him made a Bishop.'

To his surprise, Dr Daunt saw that Lord Tansor's expression had formed into something approaching a stiff smile.

'As you know,' he resumed, 'your wife has been kind enough to bring your son to visit us here often, and I have become fond of the boy.' Gravity had resettled his Lordship's features. 'I think I may even say that I envy you. Our children are a sort of immortality, are they not?'

The Rector had never before heard his patron speak with such frankness, and did not well know what to say in reply. He was aware, naturally, that Lord Tansor's son, Henry Hereward Duport, had died only a few months before he and his family had been led out of Millhead through the exertions of his second wife. On first coming into the great vestibule, the visitor to Evenwood was confronted with a large family group by Sir Thomas Lawrence – his Lordship and his first wife, holding their baby son in her arms – illuminated in daylight hours by a glazed Gothic lantern high above, and at night by six large candles set in a semi-circle of ornate sconces.

The premature death of his son, at the age of seven years, had left Lord Tansor cruelly exposed to the thing that he dreaded most. Though he was generally accounted to be a proud man, his pride was of a peculiar character. Having inherited enough – and more than enough – to satisfy the most acquisitive and prodigal nature, he nevertheless continued to accumulate wealth and influence, not simply for his own aggrandizement, but in order to bequeath an augmented, inviolable inheritance to his children, as his immediate forebears had done. But when his longed-for son had been taken from him, compounding the loss of his first wife, he had been confronted by the terrible prospect of having to forfeit all that he held most dear; for, without a direct heir, there was every likelihood that the title, along with Evenwood and the other entailed property, would fall into the hands of his collateral relatives – to which Lord Tansor was violently, though perhaps irrationally, opposed.

'Returning to the matter of your boy,' he said after a moment or two. 'Is it still the case that you intend to prepare him for the University yourself?'

Dr Daunt replied that he saw no particular advantage in sending his son to school. 'It would be unwise,' he continued, 'to expose him to circumstances which might well be injurious to him. He is able in many ways, but weak and easily led. It is better for him that he should remain here, under my care, until such time as he attains more discretion and application than he presently possesses.'

'You are, perhaps, a little hard on him, sir,' said Lord Tansor, stiffening slightly. 'And you will permit me to say that I do not altogether concur with your plan. It is a bad thing for a boy to be shut up at home. A boy needs early exposure to the world, or it will go badly for him when he has to make his way in it – as your boy certainly must. It is my view, Dr Daunt, my *decided* view,' he added, with slow emphasis, 'that he should be sent to school as soon as possible.'

'Of course I respect your Lordship's opinion on this matter,' said the Rector, insinuating as much assertion as he dared into his smiling response, 'but you will allow, perhaps, that a father's wishes on such a point must count for a great deal.'

He felt uneasy at even so hesitant a display of defiance towards his patron, and reflected to himself that the years had wrought much change in him, dulling his once fiery temper, and rendering him diplomatic where once he would have relished confrontation.

Lord Tansor allowed one of his threatening silences to

descend on the conversation, and turned his eyes towards the dark outline of trees, now standing out blackly against the afterlight of the setting sun. With his hands clasped behind his back, and continuing to stare into the gathering darkness, he waited for a second or two before resuming.

'Naturally, I could not insist upon usurping your wishes in respect of your son. You have the advantage of me as far as that goes.' He meant Dr Daunt to take the point that he had no son of his own, and the rebuke that it implied. 'Permit me to observe, however, that your new duties here will leave you little time to devote to the instruction of your son. Mr Tidy is able to do much of your work about the parish; but Sundays remain' – it was his Lordship's strict requirement that the Rector took all the Sunday services, and delivered the morning sermon – 'and I am surprised that you are able to contemplate no reduction in your other occupations to accommodate the task – the not inconsiderable task – that you have so kindly agreed to undertake.'

Dr Daunt realized where he was being led and, remembering that a patron can take away as well as bestow, conceded that some rearrangement of his responsibilities would be necessary.

'I am glad we are in agreement,' returned Lord Tansor, looking now straight into the Rector's eye. 'That being so, and having the interests of your son equally in mind, which I have recently had the pleasure of discussing with your wife, I venture to suggest that you might do worse than to put the boy up for Eton.'

It needed no elaboration from Lord Tansor for Dr Daunt to recognize that a decree had been pronounced. He made no further attempt to argue his case and, after some further discussion on the practical arrangements, finally assented to the proposal, with as much good grace as he could muster. Young Master Phoebus, then, would go to Eton, with which the Duport family had a long connexion.

The matter being settled, Lord Tansor wished Dr Daunt good-night, and a safe journey home.

A Dream of the Iron Master.

December, MDCCCXLVIII.*

Links, always links; forged slowly in the mould, accumulating, entwining more subtly and stronger still under the Iron Master's hand; growing ever longer and heavier until the chain of Fate – strong enough to hold even Great Leviathan down – becomes unbreakable. A casual act, a fortuitous occurrence, an unlooked-for consequence: they come together in a random dance, and then conjoin into adamantine permanence.

Down comes the great unstoppable hammer. Clang! Clang!
The links are forged; the chain runs out a little further.
Closer, ever closer, until we are fast bound together.

We are born within months of each other, like millions of others. We take our first breath and open our eyes for the first time on the world, like millions of others. In our separate ways, and under our separate influences of instruction and example, we grow and are nourished, we learn and think, like millions of others. We should have remained immured in our separateness and disconnexion. But we two have been singled out by the Iron

*[These paragraphs, written in darker ink than the rest, have been pasted in to the text at this point. *Ed.*]

Master. We will be engineered and stamped with his mark that we may know each other, and the links will be coiled tight around us.

Out of a hard, dark northern place he came, with his papa and step-mamma, to settle – without the right of blood – into the paradise that should be mine; from the south, honey-warm in memory, I was brought back to England; and now we are to meet for the first time.

· 11 ·

*Floreat**

THE DAYS OF DR DAUNT'S DEPENDENCE ON SURPLICE FEES TO PAY FOR occasional luxuries might now be over; but since Lord Tansor had not felt it necessary to offer any degree of financial assistance in the furtherance of his desire that young Phoebus should be sent to Eton – merely furnishing a recommendation, not easily refused, to the Provost and Fellows that the boy should be found a place – it was impossible that the Rector's son could be supported there as an Oppidan.† He must therefore be entered for a scholarship, despite the lowly standing of those who lived on the foundation. But the young man acquitted himself well, as was to be expected of one who had been so ably and constantly tutored, and in the year 1832 – when all was reformed‡ – became Daunt, K.S., the most junior of the band of scholars provided for by the bounty of King Henry VI.

Thus the Iron Master threw us together, with fatal consequences for us both. On the very same day that Phoebus Daunt made his way south to Eton from Evenwood to begin his schooling, Edward Glyver travelled north from Sandchurch to commence his. Here, perhaps, I may give my faculties rest and quote directly from the recollections compiled by Daunt for the *Saturday Review.* They

*['Let it flourish', alluding to the Eton school motto 'Floreat Etona'. *Ed.*]

†[A boy who was not a King's Scholar (KS for short). Oppidans boarded in Dames' houses in the town, their upkeep being paid for by their families. *Ed.*]

‡[An allusion to the Reform Bill of that year, intermingled with personal overtones. *Ed.*]

are typically maundering and self-regarding in character, but I flatter myself that their introduction into this narrative will not be uninteresting to those readers who have persevered so far.*

Memories of Eton

by

P. Rainsford Daunt

I went to Eton, as a Scholar, in the year 1832, at the behest of my father's patron, Lord T—. My first few days were, I confess, miserable enough, for I was homesick and knew no one at the School. We Collegers also had to endure the venerable hardships of Long Chamber – now swept away – and I have the dubious distinction of being amongst the last witnesses of its ancient brutalities.

My closest friend and companion during my time at the School was a boy of my own Election,† whom I shall call G—.

I see him now, striding across School Yard on the day of my arrival, like some messenger of Fate. I had made the journey to Eton alone – my father having important diocesan business, and my step-mother being indisposed – and was standing beneath the Founder's statue, admiring the noble proportions of the Chapel, when I noticed a tall figure detach itself from a knot of boys at the entrance to Long Chamber. He approached with purpose in his dark eyes, clasped my hands warmly, and introduced himself as my new neighbour. Within a moment, the formalities were

*[Several printed pages from the *Saturday Review* of 10 October 1848 are interpolated here. *Ed.*]

†[i.e. of the same year's intake of Scholars. *Ed.*]

concluded, and I found myself caught up in a dazzling stream of talk.

His long pale face, and the refinement of his features, gave him a rather delicate, almost girlish look; but the effect was countered by the broadness of his shoulders, and by massive square hands that seemed somehow to have made their way to the ends of his arms from some other and coarser body. He appeared, from the first, to possess the experience and wisdom of a more senior boy, and it was he who tutored me in the customs of College life, and elucidated its mysterious *patois*.

And so my thraldom began. I never thought to reflect on why G— had taken such complete charge of me, with whom he had enjoyed no previous acquaintance. But I was a docile young fellow then and, all unthinking of my dignity, was content enough to trot behind in G—'s shadow. Because he seemed indubitably marked out for greatness in some sphere or other, it was by no means disadvantageous for me to be known as his friend, and I was spared from the worst of the torments reserved for new tugs as a consequence of the association.

He possessed a formidable precocity of intellect and understanding, which elevated him far above the common herd. He was our Varro,* having a vast store – almost a superfluity – of obscure knowledge, though it lay tangled and unsorted in his mind, and would spill out constantly in rambling effusions. This made him a kind of magus in our eyes, and bestowed upon him an aura of brilliance and genius. I had been coached by my father, and knew by his

*[Marcus Terentius Varro, poet, satirist, antiquarian, jurist, geographer, scientist, and philosopher, called by Quintilian 'the most learned of Romans'. *Ed.*]

example how to recognize the lineaments of the true scholar. G— was no such thing. He hoarded knowledge greedily, but indiscriminately; yet there was something marvellous about it all. His memory was so prodigious, and the exercising of it so expressive and captivating, that he overwhelmed the pedant in me.

My education under my father had been thorough but conventional and, like others, I was dazzled by G—'s displays of learning, and struggled hard to keep up with him in the schoolroom. He would even compose Latin Alcaics and Greek Iambics aloud on our Sunday walks, whilst I would labour long over my verses and drive myself nearly mad.

We had our differences, naturally. But, particularly when we reached the Fifth Form, there were golden times, of which I still like to think. Summer afternoons on the river, when we would swing down to Skindle's, past the murmuring woods of Cliveden, then back for a plunge in the cool waters of Boveney Weir; and then I like to recall slow autumn saunters back and forth along the Slough Road, kicking through carpets of elm leaves, whilst G— discoursed torrentially – on what Avicenna had to say about the sophic mercury, or the manner of St Livinus' martyrdom – before returning to Long Chamber for tea and Genoa cake round the fire.

Of his home and family G— never spoke, except to discourage further enquiry. Consequently, no invitations to visit him during the holidays were ever issued; and when I once blushingly suggested that he might care to pass part of the summer with me, I was coldly rebuffed. I remember the incident well, for it coincided with the beginning of a change in our relations. Over the course of a few weeks, he became ever more solitary and aloof, and at times seemed clearly disdainful of my company.

I saw him for the last time one perfect autumn evening. We were returning from Windsor, after attending Evensong in St George's Chapel – whither we and a group of like-minded companions would often resort to feed G—'s passion for the old Church music. G— was in high spirits, and it began to seem as if our progress towards estrangement had been halted. Just as we crossed Barnes Pool Bridge we were met by his fag. G— had been urgently summoned to see the Head Master.

As I watched his departing figure, I heard the distant chimes from Lupton's Tower. Carried on the still evening air, the sound spoke to me with such dolesome import as I stood there – beneath shadowy gables in the empty street – that I felt suddenly bewildered and helpless. It soon became clear that he had left Eton. He never returned.

I do not wish to dwell on the reason for the sudden nature of his premature departure from the School. It is as painful for me, his closest friend, to recall the circumstances, as it must be for him.

After his departure, G— soon passed into legend. In time, new tugs were regaled with stories of his prowess at the Wall* or on the river, and of how he confounded his masters with his learning. But I thought only of the flesh-

*[A reference to the Eton Wall Game, a unique form of football, played on 30 November, St Andrew's Day. The first recorded game, played between Collegers and Oppidans, was in 1766. It takes place on a narrow strip of grass against a brick wall, built in 1717, some 110 metres end to end. Though the rules are complex, essentially each side attempts to get the ball (without handling it) down to the far end of the wall, and then to score. It is a highly physical game as each player attempts to make headway through a seemingly impenetrable mass of opponents. *Ed.*]

and-blood G—: of the little tricks of speech and gesture; and of the warm-hearted patronage so freely bestowed on his undeserving companion. Life had become a poor dull thing indeed without his enlivening presence.

A touching account, is it not? And I am naturally sensible of the encomia that he has seen fit to bestow on me. We were friends for a time: I acknowledge it. But he comes the *littérateur* too much – seeing significance where none existed, making much of nothing, dramatizing the mundane: the usual faults of the professional scribbler. This is memory scrubbed and dressed up for public consumption. Worse, he exaggerates our intimacy, and his claims on the matter of our respective intellectual characters are also false, for I was the careful scholar, he the gifted dabbler. I had many other friends in College besides him, and amongst the Oppidans too – Le Grice in particular; and so I was very far from depending solely on Master Phoebus Daunt for company. A dull dog, indeed, I would have been, had that been the case! Finally, he omits to say – though perhaps this is understandable in the light of what happened – that the friendship we enjoyed when we were first neighbours in Long Chamber had, by the end of our time at Eton, through his perfidy, crumbled to dust.

Yet this was the estimation of my character and abilities that Phoebus Daunt claims to have formed after our first meeting in School Yard, and which he saw fit to lay before the British reading public in the pages of the *Saturday Review*. But what was *my* estimation of *him*; and what was the true nature of our relation? Let me now place the truth before you.

My old schoolmaster, Tom Grexby, had accompanied me from Sandchurch to Windsor. He saw me down to the School, and then put himself up at the Christopher* for the night. I was glad to know that the dear fellow was close by, though he left early for Dorset the next day, and I did not see him again until the end of the Half.

I did not feel in the least non-plussed by my new surroundings, unlike several of the other new inmates of College whom I encountered standing or nervously scuffing around their allotted places in Long Chamber, some looking pale and withdrawn, others with affected swaggers that only served to show up their discomfort. I was strong in both body and mind, and knew that I would not be intimidated or hounded by any boy – or master, come to that.

The bed next to mine was empty, but a valise and canvas bag stood on the floor. Naturally, I bent down to look at the handwritten label pasted on the side of the former.

P. R. Daunt
Evenwood Rectory
Evenwood, Nthants

The name of Evenwood, though not of my as yet unseen neighbour, was instantly familiar to me. 'Miss Lamb has come from Evenwood to see your mamma'; 'Miss Lamb wishes to kiss you, Eddie, before she leaves for Evenwood'; 'Miss Lamb says you must come to Evenwood one day to see the deer'. The echoes came ringing back across the years, faint but clear, of the lady in grey silk who had visited my mother when I was young, and who had

*[The Christopher Inn (now Hotel), in Eton High Street. *Ed.*]

looked down so sadly and sweetly at me, and had stroked my cheek with her long fingers. I found that I had not thought about her all this time, until the name of this place – Evenwood – had brought her misty image to my mind. Miss Lamb. I smiled fondly at the memory of her name.

Despite my sequestered upbringing at Sandchurch, without many friends to speak of, beyond a few desultory playmates amongst the local boys, I had, and have, a natural gregariousness, though I rarely exercise it. I soon made the acquaintance of my new neighbours in Long Chamber, and accounted for their names and places; together, we then clattered down to take the air in School Yard before dinner.

I saw him immediately, slouching disconsolately beside the Founder's statue, and knew that it was my new neighbour in Long Chamber. He stood, hands in pockets, occasionally kicking the ground, and looking about him purposelessly. He was a little shorter than me, but a well-formed boy, with dark hair, like mine. None of the other boys had noticed him, and no one seemed inclined to go over to him. So I did. He was my neighbour, after all; and, as Fordyce Jukes was to point out to me many years later, neighbours should be neighbourly.

And so it was in this friendly spirit that I walked towards him with outstretched hand.

'Are you Daunt?'

He looked at me suspiciously from beneath the crown of a new hat that allowed a little too much for future growth.

'And if I am?' he said, with a surly pout.

'Well then,' said I, cheerfully, still holding out my hand, 'we are to be neighbours – friends too, I hope.'

He accepted the proffered greeting at last, but still said nothing. I encouraged him to come over and join the others, but he was unwilling to leave the little patch of territory beneath the statue of King Henry in his Garter robes that he appeared to feel he had secured for his private use. But by now it was time for dinner in Hall and, gracelessly, he finally relinquished his place, dragging himself along beside me like some reprimanded but still defiant puppy.

Over our first meal together, I coaxed some hesitant conversation out of him. I learned that he had been taught at home by his father; that his mamma was dead, though he had a step-mamma who had been very kind to him; and that he did not much like his new surroundings. I ventured to say that I supposed he was naturally a little homesick, like several of the other new boys. At this, something like a spark of life arose in his pale blue eyes.

'Yes,' he said, with a curious sigh, 'I do miss Evenwood.'

'Do you know Miss Lamb?' I asked.

He thought for a moment. 'I know a Miss Fox,' he replied, 'but not a Miss Lamb.' At which he giggled.

This exchange seemed to encourage him to greater intimacy, for he leaned forward and, lowering his voice to a whisper, said: 'I say, Glyver. Have you ever kissed a girl?'

Well, the truth was, that I had known very few girls of my own age, let alone any whom I might have wanted to kiss.

'What a question!' I replied. 'Have you?'

'Oh yes. Many times – I mean I've kissed the same girl many times. I believe she is the most beautiful girl in the world, and I intend to marry her one day.'

He went on to describe the incomparable virtues of his 'little princess', whom I gathered was a neighbour of his at Evenwood; and soon the sulky reticence that he had earlier displayed had been replaced by excited volubility, as he spoke of how he intended to be a famous writer and make a great deal of money, and live at Evenwood with his princess for ever and a day.

'And Uncle Tansor is so kind to me,' he said, as we made our way from Hall back to Long Chamber, in which Collegers were then shut up for the night. 'Mamma says that I am almost like a son to him. He is a very great man, you know.'

A little later he came and stood by my bed.

'What's that you have there, Glyver?' he asked.

I was holding the rosewood box in which my sovereigns had been placed, and which my mother had insisted I take with me to Eton to remind myself of my benefactress, whom I continued to believe had been Miss Lamb.

'It's nothing,' I replied. 'Just a box.'

'I've seen that before,' he said, pointing to the lid. 'What is it?'

'A coat of arms,' I replied. 'It's only a decoration, nothing more.'

He continued to stare at the box for some moments before returning to his own bed. Later, in the darkness he whispered:

'I say, Glyver, have you ever been to Evenwood?'

'Of course not,' I whispered back crossly. 'Go to sleep. I'm tired.'

THUS I BECAME THE FRIEND AND ALLY OF PHOEBUS RAINSFORD Daunt – his only friend and ally, indeed, for he showed no inclination to seek out any other. For the whole of our first Half at Eton, we ate together, sat at our lessons together, and took our leisure together. I must do the memory of those early times justice. He was the first real friend I had ever known – having, as I say, few companions in Sandchurch, and none that I could call friend. When I returned home, I found myself feeling lonely for the first time in my life, and looked forward to returning to school, and my new friend, with the greatest anticipation.

Yet, even from the start, it was an unequal partnership. The ways of the School appeared to mystify and disgust him in equal measure, making him the inevitable target of the natural vindictiveness of his fellows. He should have been well able to withstand such assaults, being, as I say, a well-made boy, even strong in his way; but he was completely disinclined to offer up any physical resistance to his tormentors whatsoever, and it often fell to me to rescue him from real harm, as when he was set upon, soon after our arrival in Long Chamber, and assailed with pins in the initiatory operation known as 'Pricking for Sheriff'. New Collegers were expected to display cheerfulness and equanimity in the face of such ordeals, and even to embrace them merrily. But I fear that Daunt, K.S., was somewhat girlishly vocal in his complaints, in consequence of which he attracted even more unwelcome attention from that class of boy who is ever ready and eager to make the lives of his compatriots thoroughly miserable. I myself was never subjected to such troubles after I shut the head of one of the chief tormentors, a grinning oaf by the name of Shillito, in the door to Long Chamber, refusing to release him until his face had near turned blue. I had declined to take part in some piece of horseplay, and he had tipped a jug of cold water over me. He did not do it again. Mine is not a forgiving nature.

Daunt calls it 'thraldom', this friendship of ours; but it was a strange kind of slavery in which no submission was asked of the enslaved. As time went by, his dependence on me became an increasing irritation. He was free to do what he wished, make friends with whom he chose; but he did not. He seemed willingly to embrace his dependent state, though I would encourage him to find wings of his own. Despite this adhesiveness, I found him an able and lively debater on topics of which I was surprised he had any knowledge at all, and soon I began to discover an elasticity of mind and comprehension, and also a sort of energetic cunning, that sat strangely with the strain of moping dullness that so often characterized his company.

I saw, too, the solid academic grounding that he had received under his father; but with this went a fatal inability to fix the mental eye steadily on its object. He would garner quickly and move on. I, too, was hungry to learn whatever I could of man and the world, but my haste was not self-defeating speed. He assembled bright impressive surfaces of knowledge admirably, but the inner structures that would keep the building in place were flimsy, and constantly shifting. He was adaptable, fluid, accommodating; always absorbent, never certain or definitive. I sought to know and to comprehend; he sought only to acquire. His genius – for such I account it – consisted in an ability to reflect back the brilliance of others, but in a way that, by some alchemical transmutation, served to illuminate and enlarge himself. These qualities did not hold him back in his work: he was generally accounted one of the School's best scholars; but they showed me – gifted, as I like to think, with finer instincts, like his own father – his true measure.

And so we proceeded together through the School, and began to attain a measure of seniority. He seemed to have thrown off many of his former timidities, and now often distinguished himself on the Playing-fields and on the river. Though I had acquired a large circle of other friends, he and I continued to enjoy a special intimacy arising from our first meeting. But then he began to show signs of a return to his former ways, by expressing renewed disapproval of some of my new friends. He would appear at all times of the day to suggest some activity or other, when often I was most disinclined to participate, or when he knew I was definitely engaged elsewhere. It was as if he wished to possess my company completely, to the exclusion of all others. He simply would not leave me be, and his dogged clinging to my coat-tails, to the detriment of my other friendships, began at last to arouse real annoyance in me, though I fought hard against showing it.

Then things got to such a pitch that, one day, as we were

returning from a walk down the Slough Road, he angered me so much by his insistence that I must stop going around with a number of fellows, of whom he disapproved, that I was forced to tell him to his face that I found his company wearisome, and that I had other friends whom I liked better. I immediately regretted my harsh words, and apologized for them. This exchange, I suppose, accounts for the accusation of 'coldness' from me, though I continued – against my better judgment – to give freely of my time to him when I could, even when I was racking myself hard with a view to gaining the Newcastle* on leaving the School.

But then, not long after this incident, came an event that showed me Phoebus Rainsford Daunt in his true colours, and brought about my departure from the School. He mentions this crisis, briefly, and with estimable tact, in the account quoted earlier. I laughed out loud when I read it. Judge for yourself the trustworthiness of our hero as I now set matters before you in their true light.

*[The Duke of Newcastle Scholarship, Eton's premier academic award, which would have financed Glyver's time at King's College, Cambridge, the school's sister foundation. *Ed.*]

· 12 ·

*Pulvis et umbra**

One Wednesday afternoon, in the autumn of 1836, as I was returning from Windsor with a small group of companions, to which Daunt had unwelcomly attached himself, I was summoned to see the Head Master, Dr Hawtrey, in Upper School.†

'I believe that you have been given exceptional permission to use the Fellows' Library?' he asked.

The Library was strictly out of bounds to all boys; but I confirmed that I had been given the key by one of the Fellows, the Reverend Thomas Carter, whose pupil I had been when he was Lower Master. Mr Carter, having read several papers that I had written, was sympathetic to my enthusiastic interest in bibliographical matters, and so had allowed me the unusual, though only temporary, freedom of the Library to gather material for a new paper that I was writing on the history and character of the collection.

'And you have made use of this privilege recently?'

I began to feel uncomfortable at the questioning, but as I knew that I had committed no misdemeanour, and because I also knew that Dr Hawtrey was a distinguished bibliophile, I unhesitatingly

*['Dust and shadow'. *Ed.*]

†[Edward Craven Hawtrey (1789–1862), who had succeeded the infamous flogger Dr Keate as Head Master only two years earlier. He was, as Glyver notes, a great bibliophile himself and was a member of the premier association for bibliographical scholars, the Roxburghe Club. *Ed.*]

said that I had been there the previous afternoon, making notes on Gesner's *Bibliotheca Universalis* (Zurich, 1545).

'And you were alone?'

'Quite alone.'

'And when did you return the key?'

I replied that normally I would have taken the key straight back to Mr Carter, but that yesterday I had gone out on the river with Le Grice, leaving the key in his boarding-house – in which I also had use of a room – until we returned.

'So when you came off the river, you took the key back to Mr Carter?'

'Yes, sir.'

'Mr Glyver, I have to tell you that I have received a serious allegation against you. According to information I have been given, I have reason to believe that you have taken a most valuable item from the Library without permission, with the intention of keeping it.'

I could hardly believe my ears, and my utter surprise must have been only too evident to the Head Master, for he signalled me to sit down, and waited until I had composed myself before speaking again.

'The item in question is the Udall. You know it, perhaps?'

Naturally I knew it: the unique copy, *circa* 1566, of *Ralph Roister Doister*, one of the earliest of English comedies, by Nicholas Udall, a former Head Master of the School. I had examined it only recently, in the course of my researches. A volume of exceptional rarity and value.

'We know that it was in the library on Tuesday morning, because it was seen by one of the Fellows. It is not there now.'

'I assure you, sir, I know nothing of this. I cannot understand— '

'Then you will have no objection if we examine your belongings?'

I replied in the affirmative without hesitation, and was soon following Dr Hawtrey's gowned figure down the stairs and out into School Yard. A few minutes later we were in the room in Le Grice's boarding-house, where I kept my personal effects and took my breakfast. On opening my trunk, I immediately saw that it was not as I had left it. Beneath a jumble of clothes could plainly be seen the brown calf binding of the missing book.

'Do you still profess ignorance of this matter, Mr Glyver?'

Before I could reply, Dr Hawtrey had retrieved the book, and ordered me to follow him back to Upper School, where I found Mr Carter and the Vice-Provost – the Provost being absent on business in London – awaiting us.

I was questioned at some length for over half an hour, during which I felt my anger rising. It was clear that I had been the victim of some mean conspiracy to destroy my reputation, and bring shame and worse – the loss of my scholarship and consequent expulsion – upon my head. Was it possible? They had called me 'the learned boy' when I had first come to the School, whilst my prowess at the Wall had been the object of general acclaim. Was I not liked and admired by everyone, boys and masters alike? Yet someone had set out to bring me down – jealous, no doubt, of my abilities and my standing.

I could hear the blood beating louder and louder in my ears as rage welled up, like some scalding volcanic plume, from the depths of my being. At last I could stand it no longer. 'Sir,' I cried out, breaking in on the questioning. 'I have not deserved this, indeed I have not! Can you not see how ridiculous, how risible, this charge is, how worthy of your contempt? I beg you to consider: what possible reason could I have for perpetrating such an act? It would have been the height of folly. Do you suppose that I am such a fool as to attempt to steal so celebrated an item? Only an ignoramus would believe that a book of this rarity could be easily disposed of – and by a mere schoolboy – without suspicion being aroused. Or perhaps you think that I intended to keep the book for myself, which is equally absurd. Discovery would have been inevitable. No, you have been gravely deceived, gentlemen, and I have been the object of a vicious calumny.'

I must have made an alarming, even intimidating, figure as I fumed and ranted, heedless of the consequences. But the genuineness of my passion was only too evident, and I thought that I could see in Dr Hawtrey's face that the tide might be turning in my favour.

For some minutes more, I continued to protest my innocence most vehemently, as well as deriding the ludicrous nature of the charge. At last, Dr Hawtrey signed for me to resume my seat, whilst he held a whispered consultation with his two colleagues.

'If you are innocent, as you claim,' he said at last, 'then it follows that someone else was responsible for removing the Udall quarto from the Library, and for attempting to implicate you as the thief. You say the key was in your room. How long were you on the river?'

'No more than an hour. The wind was exceptionally keen.'

There was more consultation between my interrogators.

'We shall make further enquiries,' said Dr Hawtrey, gravely. 'For the moment, you are free to go. You will not, however, be allowed to use the Library, and you are forbidden to go up town until further notice. Is that clear?'

THE NEXT MORNING, I WAS AGAIN SUMMONED TO SEE DR HAWTREY. He immediately informed me that a witness had now come forward, who swore that he had seen me placing the book in my trunk.

There have been few times in my life when I have been lost for words; but on this occasion, I was momentarily struck dumb, utterly unable to believe what was being said to me. When I came back to myself, I angrily asked for the name of the witness.

'You cannot expect me to give you that,' said Dr Hawtrey.

'Whoever this witness is, he is lying!' I cried. 'As I said before, I have been the victim of some plot. It is obvious, surely, that your witness must also be the thief.'

Dr Hawtrey shook his head.

'The witness is of impeccable character. Furthermore, his testimony has now been corroborated by another boy.'

Knowing the impossibility that any witness, let alone two, could exist to a crime that I did not commit, I continued to argue as fiercely as I could for my innocence, and for what I considered to be the true state of the case: that I had been the object of a deliberate and vicious conspiracy. But it was useless. Motive and opportunity were already against me; and now came corroborated testimony, sealing my fate. My arguments were dismissed, and the verdict pronounced. My scholarship was to be terminated and I was requested to leave the School immediately, using any public pretence I wished. If I went without protest, then no further action would be taken against me, and the matter would be closed. If not, then I would face formal expulsion and public disgrace.

I thought of my poor mother, alone in the parlour at home, filling page after page for Mr Colburn; and then of Miss Lamb, my presumed benefactress, whose generosity had brought me here. For their sakes, I saw that I must go quietly, though I knew that I was innocent. And so I capitulated, though with a heavy heart, and with rage still boiling and bubbling inside me. Dr Hawtrey was kind enough to say how sorry he was to see me leave under such distressing circumstances, for he regarded me as one of the School's best scholars, and certain to gain a Fellowship at the University in due course. He also tried to mitigate the immediate effects of my sentence by kindly suggesting that I should stay with one of the Fellows, who had a house a few miles from Eton, until my mother was informed, and arrangements could be made for me to be fetched. But I said that I did not wish him to write to my mother, requesting instead that I be allowed to give her my own account of why I would not be returning to Eton. After some thought, Dr Hawtrey agreed. We shook hands, without speaking, and my school days were over. Worse than this, there was now no chance that I would proceed to Cambridge, and my dream of a Fellowship there would remain forever unrealized.

As I was making my way to Le Grice's boarding-house, I came upon Daunt in School Yard, standing with one of his new companions – none other than Shillito, whose fat head I had once shut in the door. (You will observe that, in his published recollections, Daunt stated, quite categorically, that he never saw me again after the evening we returned from attending Evensong in St George's Chapel. That was a deliberate falsehood, as I shall now reveal.)

'Been to see the Head Master again?' he called. Shillito gave a little sneer, and I saw straightaway how things were. Daunt had contrived to take the key from Le Grice's boarding-house and remove the book from the Library; he had then come forward as an unwilling witness – I expect that he put on a good show, playing also, no doubt, on his father's acquaintance with the Head Master – before enlisting the help of Shillito in his plot. It was also clear why Dr Hawtrey had been so confident in the probity of his main witness. He thought that we were still friends, you see; that we were still the inseparable companions we had once been. He was not aware that I had broken away from Daunt, and so of course he could not believe that my best friend in the School could possibly bear false witness against me.

'Glyver's a great one for getting his nose into old books,' I heard Daunt say to Shillito, as if he were speaking on my behalf. 'My pa's the same. He and the Head belong to a club for such people.* I expect Glyver's been talking to the Head about some old book or other. Isn't that right, Glyver?'

He looked at me, coolly, insolently, and in that look was concentrated all the petty envy that he harboured against me, and the spiteful desire to make me pay for turning my back on him in favour of other, more congenial, companions. It was all written on his face, and in the attitude of casual defiance that he had adopted, like one who believes that he has unequivocally demonstrated his power over another.

'Care for a walk up town?' he then asked. Shillito threw me another contemptuous grin.

'Not today,' I replied, with a smile. 'I have work to do.'

My apparent collectedness appeared to unsettle him, and I saw that his mouth had tightened.

'Is that all you can say?' he asked, blinking a little.

'Nothing else occurs to me. But wait. There *is* something.' I drew closer, interposing myself between Daunt and his acolyte. 'Revenge has a long memory,' I whispered into his ear. 'A maxim you might wish to ponder. Good-bye, Daunt.'

In a moment, I had gone. I did not need to look back. I knew that I would see him again.

WHEN I RECOUNTED THIS EPISODE TO LE GRICE, OVER TWENTY YEARS later in the comfort of Mivart's, I experienced again the maddening anger that had consumed me on that day.

*[The Roxburghe Club. *Ed.*]

'So it was Daunt,' said Le Grice, after giving a little whistle of surprise. 'You've kept that damned close. Why did you never tell me?' He seemed rather put out that I had not confided in him; and in truth it now seemed absurd to me that I had never thought to do so.

'I should have done,' I conceded. 'I see that now. I'd lost everything: my scholarship, my reputation; above all, my future. And it was all because of Daunt. I wished to make him pay, but in my own time and in my own way. But then one thing happened, then another, and the opportunity never came. And once you get into the habit of secrecy, it becomes harder and harder to break it – even for your closest friend.'

'But why the devil is he trying so hard to find you now?' asked Le Grice, a little pacified by my words. 'Unless, perhaps, he wishes to make amends . . .'

I gave a hollow little laugh.

'A little dinner *à deux*? Contrite apologies and regret for blackening my name and destroying my prospects? I hardly think so. But you must know a little more about our old school-fellow before you can understand why I do not think that remorse for what he did is the reason for Daunt's present desire to find me.'

'In that case,' said Le Grice, 'let's settle up and decamp to Albany. We can put our feet up, and you can talk away till dawn if you want.'

Once ensconced in Le Grice's comfortable sitting-roon, before a blazing fire, I continued with my story.

THE JOURNEY HOME TO SANDCHURCH WAS MADE IN THE COMPANY OF Tom Grexby, who had travelled up to Eton instantly on receipt of my letter. I met him at the Christopher, but, before I had a chance to speak, he had taken me aside to give me grave news: my mother had been taken ill, and it was not expected that she would recover.

Shock had been piled on shock, heaping Pelion on Ossa.* To lose so much, in so brief a space! I did not weep – I could not weep. I could only stare, wordlessly, as if I had suddenly found myself in some strange desert landscape, devoid of any familiar landmark. Taking my arm, Tom led me out into the yard, from where we walked slowly down the High Street to Barnes Pool Bridge.

In my letter to him, I had held back the circumstances that had necessitated my leaving Eton; but as we reached the bridge, having walked most of the way from the Christopher in silence, I laid the matter out before him, though without revealing that I knew the name of the person who had betrayed me.

'My dear fellow!' he cried. 'This cannot stand. You are innocent. No, no, this must not be allowed.'

'But I cannot prove my innocence,' I said, still in a kind of daze, 'and both circumstance and testimony appear to prove my guilt. No, Tom. I must accept it, and I beg you to do the same.'

At last he reluctantly agreed that he would take no steps on my behalf, and we walked back to prepare for our jouney to Sandchurch. To my relief, Le Grice was on the river, and so I was able to remove my belongings from his boarding-house without the need to lie about why I was leaving so suddenly, or why I would not be returning. When all was safely aboard, Tom climbed up

*[Meaning one huge event piled on another, alluding to the giants, the Aloadae, in Greek mythology who attempted to reach the abode of the gods by placing Mount Pelion upon Mount Ossa, two peaks in Thessaly (*Odyssey*, XI, 315). The narrator is also doubtless alluding to Laertes' words on the death of Ophelia: 'Now pile your dust upon the quick and the dead/Till of this flat a mountain you have made/To o'ertop old Pelion' (*Hamlet*, V. i. 247). *Ed.*]

beside me and the coach drove off towards Barnes Pool Bridge, taking me away from Eton for ever.

When we arrived at the little house on the cliff-top, late that evening, we were met by the village doctor. 'I'm afraid you've come too late, Edward,' said Dr Penny. 'She's gone.'

I stood in the hall looking blankly at all the old familiar things – the brass clock by the door, ticking away as I had always remembered it; the silhouette portrait of my grandfather, Mr John More of Church Langton; the tall cylindrical pot, decorated with dragons and chrysanthemums, containing my mother's umbrella – and breathing in the comfortable smell of beeswax polish (my mother had been a tyrant for cleanliness). The parlour door was open, revealing her work-table piled high with paper. The curtains were drawn, though it was broad day outside. A burned-out candle, in its pewter holder, stood precariously on a little stack of books nearby, a mute witness to the final night hours of drudgery.

I ascended the stairs, oppressed by the insidious presence of death, and opened the door to her room.

Her last book, *Petrus*, had only recently been published, and she was preparing to embark on yet another romance for Mr Colburn – the first few pages still lay on the floor by her bed, where they had fallen from her hand. The years of unremitting toil had finally taken their toll, and I could not help feeling glad that her labours were over. Her once beautiful heart-shaped face was lined and sunken, and her hair – of which she had been so proud in her youth – was now thin and grey, though she was but forty years old. Thin, too, were her careworn fingers, stained still with the ink she had expended on meeting her obligations to her publisher. I placed a parting kiss on her cold forehead, and then sat by her side until morning, wrapped in the suffocating silence of death and despair.

She had been my only parent, and my sole provider until the

generosity of my benefactress brought some relief to our circumstances; yet even then she had continued to write, with the same determination, day after day. What had driven her, if not love? What had sustained her, if not love? My dearest mother – no, more than a mother: the best of friends and the wisest of counsellors.

I would see her no more, bent over her work-table; nor sit with her, excitedly unwrapping her latest production before we placed it proudly on the shelf – made by Billick from the timbers of a French man-of-war shattered at Trafalgar – with all the others. She would tell me no more stories, and would never listen again, with that sweet half-smile, as I read to her from my translation of *Les mille et une nuits*. She had gone, and the world seemed as cold and dark as the room in which she now lay.

We buried her in the church-yard overlooking the sea at Sandchurch, next to her errant husband, the little-lamented Captain. Tom was by my side; and I was never more glad to have him there. At my request, to the sound of gulls and the distant pounding of the waves, Mr March, the incumbent of Sandchurch, read out a passage from John Donne; and then she was gone for ever, beyond sight and touch and hearing, a withered flower in her shroud of flinty earth.

My mother's death provided a reason for my returning home from school that no one questioned; and the same excuse was conveyed by letter to Le Grice and my other friends at Eton. Only Tom knew the truth, and to him I now turned.

Mr Byam More, my sole surviving relative, offered to become my guardian; but, as I was firmly disinclined to remove to Somerset, it was agreed that Tom would temporarily stand *in loco parentis*, and that I would be placed under his educational care once again, whilst remaining – alone but for Beth and old Billick – in the house at Sandchurch, which had been left to me by my mother. The fifty sovereigns that I had insisted that she should keep as her own had been laid out on a number of unavoidable expenses; and so it became necessary to apply to Mr More, as my trustee, to release some of my remaining capital in order to maintain the household oeconomy.

In the meantime, I sought to accustom myself to the unexpected sensation of being master in my own house, at the age of sixteen. To be there alone, without my mother, gave me the most curious sensation at first, as if I half expected to meet her on the stairs, or see her walking down the garden path when I looked out from my bedroom window. Sometimes, at night, I became certain that I could hear her moving around in the parlour. I would hold my breath, heart beating fast, straining to make out what I had heard – whether it was, indeed, the sound of her poor ghost, unable to find rest from pressing pen to paper, pulling up her chair to the great work-table to take up some eternally unfinished work, or simply the timbers of the old house, creaking and straining as the wind howled in from the sea.

I lived at Sandchurch, tutored by Tom, and under his informal guardianship, until the autumn of 1838. My former schoolfellows, including Phoebus Daunt, were preparing to leave Eton for the Varsity, and I too wished to continue my studies at some suitable seat of learning. Thus it was that, at Tom's suggestion, I went to Heidelberg, where I enrolled at the University to take a number of classes, and indulged myself to the full in the pursuit of my many interests. My intellectual ambitions had been frustrated by having had to leave school prematurely, thus forfeiting the chance of proceeding to Cambridge and a Fellowship there; and so, though I did not intend to take a degree, I determined to use the time as well as I could.

I attended lectures and read like a perfect fiend, by day and by night: philosophy, ethics, jurisprudence, rhetoric, logic, cosmology – I fairly guzzled them down, like a man dying of thirst. Then

I would run furiously back to the favourite subjects of my early youth – the old alchemical texts, the Rosicrucian teachings, and the ancient Greek Mysteries – and, through one of the Professors at the University, I imbibed a new passion for the archaeology of the ancient seats of civilization, Assyria, Babylonia, and Chaldea. Then I would be eager to search out paintings by the old German Masters in lonely forest-wrapped castles, or would travel on a whim all over the region to hear some local virtuoso play Buxtehude on an early eighteenth-century organ, or a village choir singing old German hymns in a white-painted country church. I would haunt the bookshops of the old German towns, unearthing glowing rarities – prayer-books, missals, illuminated manuscripts from the court of Burgundy, and other bibliographical treasures of which I had knowledge but, until now, had never seen. For I was mad to see, to hear, to *know*!

That was my golden time (Phoebus Daunt is welcome to his): in particular, the bliss of tracing the track of the Philosophenweg* with an armful of books on a bright summer's morning; to find my private spot high above the Neckar, from where I could gaze down on the Heiliggeist Church and the Old Bridge through the clear new air; and then to lie back on soft grass, sun seeping through the branches, with my books and my dreams, with swallows wheeling against clouds that might have been painted by Poussin, an infinity of blue above me.

*[The famous 'Philosopher's Path' that leads up to the northern bank of the Neckar. *Ed.*]

· 13 ·

*Omnia mutantur**

A MAN OF KNOWLEDGE INCREASETH STRENGTH, SAYS THE PROVERB;[†] and this saying I proved to be true, as I daily enlarged my store of understanding in the subjects to which I applied myself. I experienced a dizzying feeling of expanding power in my mental and physical capabilities, until I could conceive of no subject too abstruse for my apprehension to grasp, and no task too great for my ability to accomplish.

And yet I suffered continually from bouts of gnawing rage, which often threatened to undermine this swelling self-confidence. A fearful black humour would descend upon me without warning, even on the brightest of days, when the world about me was alive with life and hope. And then I would shut out the light, and pace about my room like a caged beast, for hours on end, eaten up by only one thought.

How would I be revenged? I turned the question over and over in my mind, imagining the ways in which Phoebus Daunt might be made to feel what I had felt, and envisioning the means by which *his* hopes could be destroyed. He was at Cambridge now, as I knew from Le Grice, both having taken their places at King's College. Daunt, as expected, had secured the Newcastle, and was received at King's with that expectation that naturally surrounds the holder of such a prize. Certainly he continued to display real ability in his

*['Everything changes'. *Ed.*]

†[Proverbs 24: 5. *Ed.*]

studies, but again with that tendency to indiscipline that would have aroused the severe displeasure of his meticulous father. The Rector's old friend, Dr Passingham of Trinity, did his best to maintain a paternalistic eye on the young man's doings and would, from time to time, communicate discreet pastoral reports on his progress back to Northamptonshire. It was not long before such reports became troublesome to Dr Daunt.

From Le Grice, I received accounts of a number of incidents witnessed by him that testified to a distinct shabbiness of character, and which luridly corroborated the more sober notes of concern that flowed, with increasing frequency, between the Master's Lodge at Trinity and Evenwood Rectory.

The first might, perhaps, be seen as an undergraduate prank (though it was not so construed by his father when it was reported to him). On being good-humouredly reprimanded by the Dean of the College for some trivial misdemeanour, young Daunt placed a game hamper before that gentleman's door, directed to him 'With Mr Daunt's compliments'. When opened, the hamper was found to contain a dead cat, with an escort of five skinned rats. On being arraigned and questioned, Daunt coolly maintained his innocence, arguing that he would hardly have affixed his own name to the hamper had he been the culprit. And so he was released with due apology.

The second incident is more substantial, with respect to Daunt's developing character.

He had been invited to a dinner given by the Provost. At the head of the table, Dr Okes* sat in earnest discussion with the College's Visitor, Bishop Kaye, whilst on either side a dozen or so men conversed at their ease. Daunt, one of three freshmen present, found himself sitting next to Le Grice; on the other side of

*[Dr Richard Okes (1797–1888), Provost of King's. *Ed.*]

the table sat a senior Fellow of the College, Dr George Maxton, a gentleman well advanced in years and of much-impaired hearing.

Towards the conclusion of the meal, Daunt leaned forward and, with a fixed smile, spoke to this venerable figure.

'Well, Dr Maxton, and how are you enjoying yourself?'

The good gentleman, seeing himself addressed, but hearing nothing above the surrounding chatter, merely smiled back and nodded.

'You think it a pretty fair spread, do you, you old fool?' Another nod.

Daunt continued, still smiling.

'The oysters were barely tolerable, the hock execrable, the conversation tiresome, and yet you have found it all perfectly to your taste. What a rattlepate you are.'

Daunt persisted in this impertinent and insulting vein for some minutes, making the most uncomplimentary remarks to the poor deaf gentleman across the table as though he were discoursing on the most common topics. All the while, Dr Maxton, unaware of what was really being said to him, received the young man's impudence with mute gestures of touching courtesy; and still Daunt continued to derogate his fellow guest, smiling as he did so. This, as Le Grice observed, was behaviour most unbecoming to a gentleman.

There were other – indeed, numerous – instances of such behaviour during Daunt's time at the Varsity, all of them displaying an innate viciousness and egotism. I eagerly read Le Grice's reports, which formed the beginnings of what was to become an extensive repository of information concerning the history and character of Phoebus Daunt.

I would be revenged on him. This became an article of faith with me. But I must first come to know him as I knew myself: his family, his friends and acquaintances, his places of resort – all the externalities of his life; and then the internal impulsions: his hopes and fears, his uncertainties and desires, his ambitions, and all the secret corners of his heart. Only when the subject of Phoebus Rainsford Daunt had been completely mastered would I know where the blow should fall that would bring catastrophe upon him. For the moment, I must bide my time, until I returned to England, to begin setting my plans in motion.

AT EVENWOOD, DR DAUNT'S GREAT WORK ON THE DUPORT LIBRARY was drawing to its triumphant close after nearly eight years' labour. It had become a famous enterprise, with articles on its progress appearing regularly in the periodical press, and the publication of the final catalogue, with its attendant notes and commentaries, was eagerly awaited by the community of scholars and collectors, both in England and on the Continent. The Rector had written and received hundreds of letters during the course of his work, to the extent that Lord Tansor had agreed to hire an amanuensis to assist him in the completion of the great task. His own private secretary, Mr Paul Carteret, had also been seconded to help the Rector when required; and so, aided by this little team, and driven daily by his own unbounded eagerness and energy, the end was now in sight.

Mr Carteret's assistance had proved invaluable, especially his extensive knowledge of the Duport family, of which he was himself a member. His familiarity with the family papers, stored in the Muniments Room at Evenwood, enabled Dr Daunt to establish where, when, and from whom the 23rd Baron Tansor had purchased particular items, as well as the provenance of some of the books in the collection that had been acquired in earlier times. To Mr Carteret was also delegated the important and demanding task of listing and describing the manuscript holdings, which were a particular interest of his.

Lord Tansor had wanted a superior kind of inventory of his goods; but he was not so much the Philistine that he did not feel satisfied by the true nature of his asset, nor take pride in what had been laid down by his grandfather for the benefit of posterity. Its material value proved, in the end, difficult to calculate, except that it was almost beyond price; but its worth in other terms had been indubitably confirmed by Dr Daunt's work, and it now stood to the world as one of the most important collections of its kind in Europe. For this confirmation alone, and the great renown thrown on his name by the publication of the catalogue, Lord Tansor was well pleased.

The intellectual and artistic glories of the Duport Collection had come to him from his grandfather through his father. To whom would they now pass? How could they be transmitted, intact, to the next generation, and to the next, and to their heirs and descendants, and thus become a living symbol of the continuity that his soul craved? For still no heir had been vouchsafed to his union with the second Lady Tansor. In his Lordship's mind, the completion of Dr Daunt's work merely served to underscore his precarious dynastic position. His wife was now a poor stick of a woman, who meekly followed her husband around, in town and country, forlorn and ineffectual. There was, it seemed, no hope.

It was just at this time that Lord Tansor – egged on, I suspect, by his relative, Mrs Daunt – began to lavish signs of especial favour on the Rector's son. What follows is based on information I obtained some years after the events described.

During the Long Vacation of 1839, Lord Tansor began to express the opinion that it would be good for his Rector's son if he 'ran around a little', by which his Lordship meant to imply that a period of harmless leisure would not go amiss, even for so accomplished a scholar. He suggested that a few weeks spent at his house in Park-lane, whither he was himself about to repair with Lady Tansor, would be productive of useful amusement for the young man. The young man's step-mamma fairly purred with delight to hear Lord Tansor expatiating so enthusiastically on what might be done for her step-son by way of a social education.

As to his future, once his time at the Varsity was over, the young man himself expressed a certain open-mindedness on the subject, which, doubtless, alarmed his father, but which may not have been displeasing to Lord Tansor, whose nods of tacit approval as the lad held forth on the various possibilities that might lie before him after taking his degree – none of which involved ordination, and one of which, a career in letters, went completely against his father's inclinations – were observed and inwardly deplored by the helpless Rector.

That summer, Phoebus Daunt duly 'ran around a little' under the watchful eye of Lord Tansor. The debauchery was not excessive. A succession of tedious dinners in Park-lane, at which Cabinet ministers, political journalists of the more serious persuasion, distinguished ecclesiastics, military and naval magnates, and other public men, predominated; for light relief, an afternoon concert in the Park, or an expedition to the races (which he particularly enjoyed). Then to Cowes for some sailing and a round of dull parties. Lord Tansor would hold the flat of his right hand out stiffly, fingers and thumb closed tight together, arm bent at the elbow, just behind the boy's back, as he introduced him. 'Phoebus, my boy' – he had taken to calling him 'my boy' – 'this is Lord Cotterstock, my neighbour. He would like to meet you.' 'Phoebus, my boy, have you made the acquaintance yet of Mrs Gough-Palmer, wife of the Ambassador?' 'The Prime Minister will be down tomorrow, my boy, and I should like you to meet him.'

And Phoebus would meet them, and charm them, and generally reflect the rays of Lord Tansor's good opinion of him like a mirror until everyone was convinced that he was the very best fellow alive.

And so it went on, for the rest of the vacation. On his return to Evenwood in September, he seemed quite the man about town: a little taller, with a gloss and a swagger about his manner that he had completely lacked as a schoolboy only a short time before. There was now a gloss, too, about his appearance, for Uncle Tansor had sent him off to his tailor and hatter, and his stepmamma quite caught her breath at the sight of the elegantly clad figure – in bright-blue frock-coat, checked trousers, chimney-pot hat, and sumptuous waistcoat, together with incipient Dundreary whiskers – that descended from his Lordship's coach.

From then on, whenever he returned to Evenwood, the undergraduate would find himself immediately invited up to the great house to regale his patron with an account of how he had comported himself during the previous term. It was gratifying to his Lordship to hear how well the boy was regarded by his tutors, and what a great mark he was making on the University. A Fellowship surely beckoned, he told Uncle Tansor, though, speaking for himself, he did not feel that such a course quite accorded with his talents. Lord Tansor concurred. He had little time for University men in general, and would prefer to see the lad make his way in the great world of the metropolis. The lad himself could only agree.

Of the making of Phoebus Rainsford Daunt there seemed to be no end. With each passing month, Lord Tansor devised new ways to raise the young man up in the world, losing no opportunity to insinuate him into the best circles, and to put him in the way of meeting people who, like Lord Tansor himself, *mattered.*

On the last day of December 1840, in the midst of his final year at the University, Daunt attained his majority, and his Lordship saw fit to arrange a dinner party in his honour. It was a most dazzling affair. The dinner itself consisted of soups and fish, six *entrées*, turtle heads, roasts, capons, poulards and turkeys, pigeons and snipes, garnishes of truffles, mushrooms, crawfish and American asparagus; desserts and ices; even several bottles of the 1784 claret laid down by Lord Tansor's father, all attended by footmen and waiters brought in especially – to the consternation of the existing domestic staff – to dispense *service à la française.*

The guests, some thirty or so in number, had included, for the principal guest's benefit, several literary figures; for Lord Tansor, a little against an innate prejudice towards the profession of writing, had been impressed by the dedication to literature that the young man was beginning to display. He would often come across the lad tucked away in a corner of the Library (in which he seemed to pass a great deal of his time when he was home), in rapt perusal of some volume or other. On several occasions he had even found him absorbed in one of Mr Southey's turgid epics, and it would amaze Lord Tansor, on returning to the same spot an hour later, to discover the young man still engrossed – it being unaccountable to his Lordship that so much time and attention could be devoted to something so unutterably tedious. (He had once ventured to look into a volume of the Laureate's,* and had sensibly determined never to do so again.) But there it was. Further, the boy had displayed some talent of his own in this department, having had a simpering ode in the style of Gray published in the *Eton College Chronicle*, and another in the *Stamford Mercury*. Lord Tansor was no judge, of course, but he thought that these poetic ambitions might be encouraged, as being both harmless and, if successful, conducive to a new kind of respect devolving upon him as the young genius's patron.

*[Robert Southey was Poet Laureate from 1813 until his death in 1843. *Ed.*]

So up they had trotted to Evenwood, at Lord Tansor's summons: Mr Horne, Mr Montgomery, Mr de Vere, and Mr Heraud,* and a few others of their ilk. They were not, it must be admitted, first-division talents; but Lord Tansor had been much satisfied, both by their presence and by their expressions of encouragement when Master Phoebus was persuaded to bring out one or two of his own effusions for their perusal. The literary gentlemen appeared to think that the young man had the mind and ear – indeed, the vocation – of the born bard, which gratifyingly confirmed Lord Tansor's view that he had been right to allow the young man his head in respect of a possible career. The author himself was also flattered by the kind attentions of Mr Henry Drago,† the distinguished reviewer and leading contributor to *Fraser's* and the *Quarterly*, who gave him his card and offered to act on his behalf to find a publisher for his poems. Two weeks later, a letter came from this gentleman to say that Mr Moxon,‡ a particular friend of his, had been so taken by the verses that the critic had placed before him that he had expressed an urgent wish to meet the young genius as soon as may be, with a view to a publishing proposal.

Before Daunt had finished his studies at Cambridge, he had completed *Ithaca: A Lyrical Drama*, which, with a few other sundry effusions, was duly published by Mr Moxon in the autumn of 1841. Thus was launched the literary career of P. Rainsford Daunt.

Mrs Daunt, now established as the *de facto* chatelaine of Evenwood, naturally watched these developments with a warm glow of satisfaction; it was most pleasant to observe that her plans

*[The poets Richard Hengist Horne (1803–84), Robert Montgomery (1807–55), Aubrey Thomas de Vere (1814–1902), John Abraham Heraud (1799–1887). *Ed.*]

†[Henry Samborne Drago (1810–72), poet and critic. *Ed.*]

‡[The publisher Edward Moxon (1801–58), whose authors at this time included Elizabeth Barrett Barrett, her future husband Robert Browning, and Tennyson. *Ed.*]

for ingratiating her step-son with Lord Tansor were succeeding so well. Her husband, with more discernment, felt a good deal of disquiet at the palpably hollow lionization of his son when the boy had done nothing, in his view, to deserve the plaudits that he was receiving, other than to have fallen under the capacious wing of his Lordship's patronage. With the end in sight of his labours on his catalogue, the Rector now felt able to turn his full gaze on the character and future prospects of his son. But his position was weak in respect of Lord Tansor's growing dominion over his only child. What could be done? Give up his comfortable living in this place of beauty and contentment and risk removal to another Millhead? That was out of the question.

And yet he felt impelled to do his utmost to retrieve his son, and put him back on a path more consonant with his upbringing and antecedents. It might not be possible to bring him to ordination – the Rector's dearest hope – but it might be possible to dilute the effects of Lord Tansor's increasingly prodigal attentions.

The Rector thought that he might have a solution to the problem. Removing his son from Evenwood and the influence of Lord Tansor for an extended period might have the effect of somewhat loosening his patron's grip on his son. He had therefore quietly arranged through a cousin, Archdeacon Septimus Daunt of Dublin, for the boy to spend a further year of study at Trinity College. It now only remained for him to acquaint his son, and Lord Tansor, of his decision.

· 14 ·

*Post nubila, Phoebus**

A WEEK AFTER ATTAINING HIS MAJORITY, P. RAINSFORD DAUNT, PLAINLY agitated and with a rather high colour, could have been seen leaving the Rectory at Evenwood, mounting his father's borrowed grey cob, and making his way up towards the great house, where he was received as a matter of urgency by a concerned Lord Tansor.

The Rector had summoned his son early in order to present him with his decision that he should further his studies in Dublin, after taking his degree. Words were spoken – I do not have an exact transcript – and things were said, perhaps on both sides, which made compromise on the matter impossible. The Rector certainly told the boy, coolly and frankly, that if he did not fall in with the arrangement he would himself go to Lord Tansor to request that he intervene on his behalf.

Poor man. He had no conception that it was already too late; that he had lost every chance of influence over his son's future; and that Lord Tansor would do nothing to support his wishes in the case.

'I do not, of course, say that it is a bad plan,' Lord Tansor opined when, that afternoon, the Rector stood before him, 'for the young man to go to Ireland – that, of course, must be a matter for you to settle with him yourself. I only say that travel in general is overrated, and that people – especially young people – would be better advised to stay at home and look to their

*['After clouds, the sun'. Phoebus was the sun god. *Ed.*]

prospects there. As for Ireland, there can, I think, be few places on earth in which an English gentleman could feel less at home, or where the natural comforts and amenities of a gentleman's condition are less susceptible of being supplied.'

After more barking pronouncements of this sort, delivered in Lord Tansor's best baritone manner, Dr Daunt saw how things lay, and was dismayed. His son did not go to Dublin.

PHOEBUS DAUNT TOOK HIS DEGREE THAT SUMMER, AND SO RETURNED again to Evenwood, on a fine warm day, to ponder his future.

A fictional fragment, part of an uncompleted prose romance entitled *Marchmont; or, The Last of the FitzArthurs*,* undoubtedly describes that return, though transposed from summer to autumn for dramatic effect. I append part of it here:

FRAGMENT FROM 'MARCHMONT'

by

P. Rainsford Daunt

BEYOND THE TOWN the road dips steeply away from the eminence on which the little town of E— is situated, to wind its tree-lined way down towards the river. Gregorius always delighted in this road; but today the sensation of a progressive descent beneath a vault of bare branches, through which sunlight was now slanting, was especially delicious to him after the tedium and discomfort of the journey from Paulborough, sitting with his trunks on the back of the carrier's cart.

*[It was published in Daunt's *Scenes of Early Life* (1852). *Ed.*]

At the bottom of the hill, the road divided. Instead of crossing the river at the bridge by the mill, he turned north to take the longer route, along a road that ran through thick woodland, with the aim of entering the Park through its Western Gates. He had in mind to sit a while in the Grecian Temple, which stood on a terraced mound just inside the gates, from where he would be able to see his favourite prospect of the great house across the intervening space of rolling parkland.

The woods were chill and damp in this dying part of the year, and he was glad to gain the wicket-gate in the wall that gave onto the Park and pass out into weak sunlight once more. A few yards took him onto a stony path that ran off from the carriage-drive up towards the Temple, built on a steep rise, and surrounded on three sides by a plantation of good-sized trees. He walked with his eyes deliberately fixed on the gravel path, wishing to give himself the sudden rush of pleasure that he knew he would feel on seeing the house from his intended vantage point.

But before he was halfway along the path, he was aware of the sound of a vehicle entering the Park behind him from the western entrance. He was but a little way off the road, and so turned to see who was approaching. A carriage and pair were rattling up the little incline from the gates. Within a moment or two the carriage had drawn level with the spur of the path on which he was standing. As it passed, a face looked out at him. The glimpse had been fleeting, but the image held steady in his mind as he watched the carriage crest the incline and descend towards the house.

He remained staring intently after the carriage for several moments after it had disappeared from view, puzzled, in a peculiarly keen way, that he had not immediately resumed his way towards the Temple. That pale and lovely face still hung before his mind's eye, like a star in a cold dark sky.

Despite the crude attempt to disguise the location ('Paulborough' for 'Peterborough'), and himself (as 'Gregorius'), wrapped up and prettified though it all is, the place and source of the author's lyrical remembrance are easily explicated and dated. On the 6th of June 1841, the day Phoebus Daunt came down from Cambridge for the last time, at approximately three o'clock in the afternoon, Miss Emily Carteret, the daughter of Lord Tansor's secretary, returned to Evenwood after spending two years abroad.

MISS CARTERET WAS AT THAT SWEETEST OF AGES – JUST TURNED seventeen. She had been residing with her late mother's younger sister in Paris, and had now come back to Evenwood to settle permanently with her father at the Dower House. Their nearest neighbours were the Daunts, just on the other side of the Park wall, and she and the Rector's son had each grown up with a decided view of the other's character and temperament.

Little Miss Carteret had been a serious young lady from an early age, with a serious mind and serious expectations of others. Her young neighbour, though capable of seriousness when he pleased, found her meditative disposition galling, when all he wanted to do was tumble down a slope with her, or climb a tree, or chase the chickens; for she would *think* about everything, and for so long at a time, that he would give up coaxing her in exasperation and leave her alone, still thinking, while he attended to his pleasures. For her part, the young lady sometimes thought him uncouth and frightful in his antics, though she knew that he could be kind to her and that he was by no means a stupid boy.

It would have been strange indeed had not the boy found that her reticence towards him only increased her fascination. Though his junior by four years, Miss Carteret appeared to rule him with the wisdom of ages; and as they grew older, her sovereignty over him became complete. In time, of course, he asked for a kiss. She demurred. He asked again, and she considered a little longer. But at length she capitulated. On his eleventh birthday she knocked at the Rectory door with a present in her hand. 'You may kiss me now,' she said. And so he did. He began to call her his Princess.

To him, she was Dulcinea and Guinevere, every aloof and unattainable heroine of legend, every Rosalind and Celia, and every fairy-tale princess of whom he had ever read or dreamed; for she had a serious and haunting beauty, as well as a serious mind. Her father, Mr Paul Carteret, had observed only too plainly which way the wind blew in the mind of Phoebus Daunt with regard to his daughter, even before she had left for the Continent. Now two years of travel and education, as well as some exposure to the best Parisian society, had rendered her allure irresistible.

The fact was that Mr Carteret, in the face of received opinion at Evenwood, unaccountably failed to regard Phoebus Rainsford Daunt as a precocious specimen of British manhood. He had always found the Rector's son ingratiating, plausible, slippery, cleverly insinuating himself into favour where he could, and ingeniously spiteful in revenge where he could not. It may therefore be supposed that he did not relish the prospect of his daughter's return to Evenwood, and to the attentions of P.R. Daunt, at a time when that young gentleman's star was on its seemingly irresistible rise. To put the matter frankly, Mr Carteret disliked and distrusted Lord Tansor's *protégé*. On more than one occasion he had come across him in the Muniments Room, where he had no obvious business, rummaging through the documents and deeds that were stored there; and he was sure that he had surreptitiously perused his Lordship's correspondence as it lay on the secretary's desk.

But, like that of his neighbour, the Rector, Mr Carteret's position was also dependent on Lord Tansor's good opinion. It was thus perplexing to Mr Carteret as to how he ought to proceed if and when – as seemed possible – the young man confided to his patron the nature of his feelings for his daughter. Could he actively forbid any amorous advances, especially if they were made with his Lordship's approval, without the likelihood of severe consequences to his own interests? For the moment, he had no choice but to watch, and hope.

At their first encounter after her return from France, in the presence of her father, Miss Carteret received the young man with courteous reserve. She asked him politely how he had been, agreed that he had changed a good deal since their last meeting, and accepted an early copy of *Ithaca*, signed by the author. She had grown quite beautiful in her French clothes and bonnet *à la mode*, with its delicately shaded, pointed ribbons and little bouquet of pale roses, violets, and primroses; but her father was greatly relieved to observe that her character was as thoughtful, and her behaviour as obedient, as before. Gratifyingly, during the many subsequent occasions on which they were obliged to meet over the course of the summer, Miss Carteret studiously continued to maintain the same air of calm and courteous detachment towards her former playfellow.

As the year 1841 drew to a close, P. Rainsford Daunt, B.A., set his mind to conquering the world of letters. The following spring, Lord Tansor arranged for his portrait to be painted, and there was intense excitement in the bosom of Mrs Daunt when an invitation addressed to the young gentleman arrived at the Rectory requesting the pleasure of his presence at Her Majesty's *bal masqué* at Buckingham Palace, at which the Court of Edward III and Queen

Philippa was re-created in astonishing magnificence. A week later, he was formally presented at Court, at a levee at St James's Palace, absurdly resplendent in knee breeches, buckle shoes, and a sword.

His saddened father, meanwhile, retreated to his study to correct the proofs of his catalogue; his Lordship spent a good deal of time in town closeted with his legal man, Mr Christopher Tredgold; and I had set my feet on the path that would eventually lead to Cain-court, Strand.

· 15 ·

*Apocalypsis**

I LEFT HEIDELBERG IN FEBRUARY 1841, TRAVELLING FIRST TO BERLIN and thence to France. I arrived in Paris two days before my twenty-first birthday, and settled myself in the Hôtel des Princes† – perhaps a little expensive, but not more than I thought I could afford. As I had reached my majority, the residue of my capital, which had been entrusted to Mr Byam More, was now mine. Inspired by this happy thought, I allowed myself to draw deeply on my reserves, in anticipation of their being very soon replenished, and abandoned myself to the infinitely various pleasures that Paris can offer a young man of tolerable looks, a lively imagination, and a good opinion of himself. But there must be an end to all pleasure, and soon the nagging apprehension that I must soon settle on a way to earn my living began to intrude most unwelcomingly on my days and nights. Reluctantly, after six highly entertaining weeks, I began to make my preparations for returning to England.

Then, on the morning before my intended departure, I ran across Le Grice in Galignani's Reading Room,‡ which had been my daily place of resort during my stay. We spent a delightful evening recounting the separate courses that our lives had taken over the five years since we had last seen each other. Of course he

*['Revelation', *Ed.*]

†[In the Rue de Richelieu. *Ed.*]

‡[In the Rue Vivienne: 'a great resource to the Englishman in Paris', according to Murray's *Hand-Book for Travellers in France* (New Edition, 1844). *Ed.*]

had news of several old school-fellows, Daunt amongst them. I listened politely, but changed the subject as soon as I decently could. I had no need to be reminded of Phoebus Daunt; he was constantly in my thoughts, and the desire to execute effectual vengeance on him for what he had done to me still burned with a bright and steady flame.

Le Grice was *en route* to Italy, with no particular purpose in view other than to pass some time in pleasant surroundings and congenial company whilst he considered what to do with himself. Given my own uncertainty on this subject, it did not take much persuasion on his part for me to abandon my plan of returning to Sandchurch, and join him on his ramblings. I immediately wrote to Mr More, requesting him to transfer the balance of my capital to my London account, and sent word to Tom that I would be remaining on the Continent for a little longer. The next morning, Le Grice and I began our journey south.

AFTER MANY LEISURELY DETOURS, WE ARRIVED AT LENGTH IN Marseilles, from whence we proceeded along the Ligurian coast to Pisa, before finally setting ourselves up, in some splendour, in a noble Florentine palazzo, close to the Duomo. Here we remained for some weeks, indolently indulging ourselves, until the heat of the summer drove us to the cooler air of the mountains and, in due course, to Ancona, on the Adriatic coast.

By the end of August, having made our way north to Venice, Le Grice was beginning to show signs of restlessness. I could not get my fill of churches, and paintings, and sculpture; but these were not at all in Le Grice's line. One church, he would say wearily, looked very like another, and he expressed similar sentiments when confronted with a succession of Crucifixions and Nativities. At last, in the second week of September, we finally took our leave of each other, promising that we should meet again in London as soon as our circumstances allowed.

Le Grice departed for Trieste to take ship to England, whilst I, after a few days on my own in Venice, headed south again. For the next year or so, with Murray's *Hand-book to Asia Minor* as my guide,* I wandered through Greece and the Levant, reaching as far as Damascus, before sailing back through the Cyclades to Brindisi. After sojourns in Naples and Rome, I found myself in Florence once more, in the late summer of 1842.

On our first visit to the city of the Medici, we had met an American couple, a Mr and Mrs Forrester. Once back in Florence, I presented myself at the Forresters' residence and, finding that the position of tutor to their two boys had become vacant, owing to the unsuitability of the previous incumbent, I immediately offered my services. I remained in the well-paid and undemanding employment of Mr and Mrs Forrester for the next three and a half years, during which time I grew lazy and, in my idleness, neglected my own studies grievously. I thought often of my former life in England, and how I must one day return; this, however, would always call up the shade of Phoebus Daunt, and the unfinished business that lay between us. (Even in Florence I had been unable to escape him: on my twenty-third birthday I was presented with a copy of his latest volume, *The Tartar-King: A Story in XII Cantos*, by Mrs Forrester, a notable bluestocking. 'I *doat* on Mr Daunt,' she had sighed, wiltingly. '*Such* a genius, and *so* young!')

It was from this time that I began to form certain habits that have occasionally threatened to nullify irrevocably any vestige of the higher talents with which I have been blessed. My lapses were modest then, though I began to hate both myself and the life I was

*[*A Hand-book for Travellers in the Ionian Islands, Greece, Turkey, Asia Minor and Constantinople* (John Murray, 1840). *Ed.*]

leading. At length, following an unfortunate incident concerning the daughter of a city official, I made my apologies to the Forresters and left Florence in some haste.

I still had no desire to return home, and so I set my course northwards. In Milan, I fell in with an English gentleman, a Mr Bryce Furnivall, from the Department of Printed Books at the British Museum, who was about to depart for St Petersburg. My conversations with Mr Furnivall had rekindled my old bibliographical passions; and when he asked whether I had a mind to accompany him into Russia, I readily agreed.

In St Petersburg we were kindly received by the celebrated bibliographer V.S. Sopikov, whose shop in Gostiny Dvor became my daily place of resort.* Then, after a week or so, my companion, Mr Furnivall, was obliged to return to London, but I chose to remain. For I was bewitched by this extraordinary city of white and gold, entranced by its great public buildings and palaces, its wide vistas, its canals and churches. I found a set of rooms close to Nevsky Prospekt, began to learn the Russian language, and even embraced the fearsome winters with a kind of delight. Bundled in furs, I would often wander the streets at night, with the snow falling all about me, to stand contemplatively on the Lion Bridge by the Griboedova Canal, or watch the ice floating downstream on the mighty Neva.

Nearly a year passed before I began to set my sights homeward at last. Before departing, Mr Furnivall had requested, with some warmth, that I should come to see him at the Museum on my return, to discuss the possibility of my filling a vacancy in the Department that had recently arisen. As I had no other career in view, it began to seem like an attractive prospect. I had been an

*[Vasily Stepanovich Sopikov, book dealer and author of a standard essay on Russian bibliography. *Ed.*]

exile from my native country for too long. It was time to make something of myself. And so, in February, 1847, I quit St Petersburg, travelling leisurely westwards, occasionally deviating from my route as the fancy took me, and arriving at last in Portsmouth at the beginning of June.

BILLICK BROUGHT THE TRAP TO MEET ME OFF THE PORTSMOUTH COACH at Wareham. Having heartily slapped each other on the back for a second or two on first seeing each other, we travelled back for two hours and more in complete silence, save for the sound of my companion's incessant chewing on an old piece of tobacco, to our mutual satisfaction, until we arrived at Sandchurch.

'Drop me here, Billick,' I said, as the trap passed the church.

As he continued on his way up the hill, I knocked on the door of the little leaning cottage next to the church-yard.

Tom opened the door, spectacles in hand, a book that he had been reading tucked under his arm.

He smiled and held out his hand, letting the book fall to the ground.

'The traveller returns,' he said. 'Come on in, old chap, and make yourself at home.'

And a second home it had once been to me, this low, dusty room tumbled from floor to ceiling, and up the stairs from ground to roof, with books of every shape and size. Its dear familiarity – the three-legged dresser supported by a groaning stack of mouldering leather folios, the fishing rods crossed above the fireplace, the discoloured marble bust of Napoleon on a little shelf by the door – was both poignant and painful. Tom, too, his long lined face shining in the fire-glow, his great ears with grey tufts growing out of them, his lilting Norfolk accent, brought a sense of childhood rushing in on me.

'Tom,' I said, 'I believe you've lost what little hair you had when I last saw you.'

And we laughed, and there was an end of silence for the night.

On we talked, hour after hour, about what I had done and seen during my time on the Continent, as well as reminiscing over old times, until at last, the clock striking midnight, Tom said that he would get the lantern and walk up the hill with me to see me safe home. He left me at the gate beneath the chestnut-tree, and I entered the silent house.

After nearly nine years of wandering, I lay down that night in my own bed again, and closed my eyes once more to the eternal music of sea meeting shore.

THE SUMMER PASSED QUIETLY. I BUSIED MYSELF AS BEST I COULD, reading a good deal, and attempting a little work about the house and garden. But as autumn came on, I began to feel restless and dissatisfied. Tom would come and sit with me most days, and I saw plainly that he was troubled by my indolence.

'What will you do, Ned?' he asked at last.

'I suppose I shall have to earn a living,' I sighed. 'I have used up nearly all my capital, the house is in a very bad state of repair, and now Mr More has written to say that my mother borrowed a hundred pounds from him before she died of which he now has need.'

'If you still have nothing definite in view,' Tom said after a pause, 'I might venture to suggest something.'

Whilst travelling in the Levant, I had written to him of my new passion for the ancient civilizations of Asia Minor. Apprised of my imminent return to England, and unaware that I was considering the position at the British Museum, he had acted on my behalf to make some tentative enquiries concerning the possibility of my joining an expedition just then assembling to excavate the monuments at Nimrud.

'It would be an experience, Ned, and a little money in your hands, and you could start to make a name for yourself in a growing field.'

I said it was a splendid idea, and thanked him heartily for putting me in the way of it, though in truth I had some reservations about the plan. The gentleman leading the expedition, known to Tom through a relation, lived in Oxford; it was soon agreed that Tom would write to him immediately, to suggest he and I go up there at the Professor's earliest convenience.

IT WAS SEVERAL WEEKS BEFORE AN ANSWER CAME, BUT THEN, ONE bright and windy autumn morning, Tom called to say that he had received a reply from Professor S— in Oxford,* who had expressed interest in receiving me in New College to talk over my candidature for the expedition.

The Professor's rooms were crammed full of casts and fragments of bas-relief, inscriptions covered in the mysterious cuneiform writing I had read about in Rawlinson's account of his travels in Susiana and Kurdistân,† and carvings of muscular winged bulls in glowering black basalt. Maps and plans lay all about the floor, or were draped over tables and the backs of chairs; and on an easel in the centre of the room stood what I at first took to be a monochrome painting of an immense crowned

*[I have not been able to identify 'Professor S—' and am unable to say why the author chose to respect his anonymity. He seems to have been involved in some rival enterprise to the expeditions to Nimrud of Austin Henry Layard (1817–94) that did not materialize. *Ed.*]

†[The accounts of tours undertaken in 1836 and 1838 and written for the Royal Geographical Society by Henry Creswicke Rawlinson (1810–95). *Ed.*]

king, bearded and braided and omnipotent in attitude, beneath whose feet crouched a captive enemy or rebel, frozen in abject surrender to the might of the conqueror.

On closer inspection, I saw that it was not a painting at all, but what the Professor, seeing my interest, described as a photogenic drawing – a technique invented by Mr Talbot,* a fellow student of the cuneiform texts. I stood amazed at the sight; for the image of the king – a gargantuan and looming stone presence standing in a waste of desert sand – had been made, not by some transient agent devised by man, but by eternal light itself. The light of the world; the sun that had once shone on ancient Babylon, and now struggled to light up the dreary October streets of Oxford in the nineteenth century, had been captured and held, like the slave beneath the king's feet, and made permanent.

I tell you all this because the moment was a significant one in my life, as shall appear. Up until then, I had followed the familiar paths of knowledge that wound out from the safe harbour of the Liberal Arts. Now I saw that science, somewhat neglected in my education, held open possibilities of which I had not dreamed.

The Professor smelled a little overripe in the close confinement of his attic rooms, and seemed to think that standing very close to someone and talking loudly into their faces was the most convenient way of conducting an interview. He questioned me closely on my knowledge of Mesopotamia and the Babylonian kings, and on a variety of congeneric questions, whilst Tom hovered some distance off with a hopeful smile on his face.

It may well be that I passed muster. Indeed, I know it to be the

*[William Fox Talbot (1800–77), British pioneer of photography. He had been working on producing 'photogenic drawings' since 1835. A paper on his photogenic techniques was read to the Royal Society on 31 January 1839. He patented his improved 'calotype' or 'talbotype' process for making negatives in 1841. *Ed.*]

case, for a few days after our return to Sandchurch, the Professor wrote to communicate his desire that I should return to Oxford as soon as it could be so arranged, in order to make the acquaintance of the other members of the proposed expedition.

But by then my heart had found a new desire. That glorious imprisonment of light and shadow, which I had observed in the photogenic image of the great stone king, began to consume me, and all thought of digging with my finger-nails in the heat and dust of the Mesopotamian desert was driven out. And besides, I had had enough of travelling. I wished to settle, find some congenial employment, and master the photographic art, which perhaps might one day furnish a means of earning my living.

To Tom I said nothing, but I skilfully contrived excuses for not returning to New College, as requested by the Professor, and, by feigning a slight but temporarily debilitating sickness, managed to keep myself close in the house for several days.

ON THE FIRST DAY OF MY PRETENDED ILLNESS, THE RAIN CAME DOWN hard from the south, and remained beating in from the Channel until darkness edged across the cliff-top and enveloped the house. In the morning, I had settled down with Buckingham's *Travels in Assyria*,* lying back in the parlour window-seat that looked out to sea, in a vain attempt to assuage my conscience at deceiving Tom; but by the time Beth came in with my luncheon I had grown weary of Buckingham, and turned instead to my dear old copy of Donne's sermons, in which I lost myself for the rest of the afternoon.

After supper, I began to think about practicalities. There was

*[*Travels in Assyria, Media and Persia* (1830) by James Silk Buckingham (1786–1855). *Ed.*]

much that I needed to do in order to establish myself in a firm and permanent way of success, lacking, as I did, a University degree. Until Tom's intervention on my behalf, I had determined to sell the house and move to London, to see what I could try there in the way of some work that would draw on my capacity for intellectual application. I had planned, first of all, to take up the invitation of Mr Bryce Furnivall to put myself forward for the vacancy in the Department of Printed Books at the British Museum. It remained a congenial prospect; the bibliographical fire burned strong within me, and I knew that a whole life of useful work could be found in this – for me – absorbing study.

Whichever way I went – to Mesopotamia or Great Russell-street – I should need ready money to support myself in the beginning. A start would also have to be made on reviewing and arranging my mother's papers, for I had been lax in this regard, and they had lain for the past eleven years, undisturbed and reproachful, in bound heaps on her work-table. That task, at least, could now be commenced. I therefore proposed to myself that I would begin looking over them first thing in the morning, lit up a cigar (a bad habit that I had acquired in Germany), pulled my chair close to the fire, and prepared to take my evening's ease with a neat little edition of Lord Rochester's poems.

But as the flames flickered, and the rain continued to hammer against the window, I put the book down and began to stare at the yellow and curling piles of paper on the work-table.

On the wall flanking the table was the set of shelves, made by Billick, housing my mother's published works, in two and three volumes, dark-green or blue cloth, their spines and blocked titles gleaming in the firelight, assembled in strict order of publication, from *Edith* to *Petrus; or, The Noble Slave*, her somewhat half-hearted attempt at the historical mode published in the year of her death. Below this library was the arena of her labours itself – the great square work-table, fully eight feet across, that would later stand in my rooms in Temple-street.

It was a landscape of paper, with little peaks and shadowed troughs, tottering sheer-sided gorges, and here and there the aftermaths of little earthquakes, where a crust of curling sheets had slid across the face of its fellows beneath, and now leaned crazily against them. The mass of paper that lay before me contained, I knew, working drafts and fragments of novels, as well as accounts and other items relating to the running of the household. My mother's curious system had been to parcel up little battalions of sheets and other pieces relating to a particular category, before binding them together with string or ribbon or thin strips of taffeta. Then she would stack them up, unlabelled, roughly in the order in which they had been created, one on top of the other. The effect, where it remained intact, was rather like a model of the battlefield of Pharsalus* that I had once seen, with massed and opposing squares and echelons. Nestling in the midst, surrounded on three sides by the encroaching walls of paper, was the space, no wider than a piece of foolscap, in which she had worked.

There were, too, a number of small, perfectly square note-books with hard, shiny black covers, each closed up by delicate silk ribbons of the same hue, which used to draw my fascinated eye as a child because of their resemblance to slabs of the darkest chocolate. In these my mother would commit her thoughts by bending even closer to the page than she was wont to do when engaged on her literary work, for the leaves were small – no more than three or four inches square, requiring her to adopt a miniscule hand for the purpose. Why she had chosen willingly to put herself to so much trouble – the note-books were made especially for her by a

*[In Thessaly, northern Greece, at which Julius Caesar defeated the Senatorial forces of Pompey in 48 BC. *Ed.*]

stationer in Weymouth, which seemed a most uncharacteristic luxury – I never knew. A dozen or more of these miniature volumes now stood, line astern, on one side of the working space, held in formation at the edge of the table by the rosewood box that had once contained my two hundred sovereigns.

On a whim, I thought I would just look into one of these diminutive black books before retiring. I had never before known what they contained, and a rather anxious curiosity – I cannot account for the slight tingle of nervous anticipation that I felt as I walked over to the table – began to rouse me from the drowsiness that had begun to come over me as I had sat by the dying fire reading Lord Rochester's eloquent bawdy.

I took the first of the note-books from its place and undid its silk ribbon. Placing it beneath the candle's light, I opened the hard black cover, and began to read the tiny characters that had been pressed onto the page from top to bottom with so much care and deliberation. They told of my mother's last weeks at Church Langton before she and the Captain moved to Sandchurch. Intrigued, I read on for a few more pages, then closed the volume and picked up another. I continued thus, looking into one of the tiny books, and then moving on to its fellows, for near an hour. It was approaching eleven o'clock when I thought that I would put my nose into just one more volume before I went to bed.

The first two pale yellow leaves contained little of particular interest, consisting mainly of brief and inconsequential *résumés* of daily activities. I was on the point of closing the volume and picking up another when, flicking forward, my eye lighted on the following passage:

> That this is folly, sheer fatal folly, I know only too well. All my feelings revolt against it, everything that I hold sacred is appalled by the prospect. And yet – it is asked of me, & I

cannot dash the cup from my lips. My nature is not my own, it seems, but must be press'd into shape by another's hand – not God's! We spoke at length yesterday. L was tearful at times, at others angry and threatening of worse than even what is proposed. Can there be worse? Yes! And she is capable of it. He wd not be home that night & this wd give us more time. After dinner L came to my room again and we cried together. But then her resolve return'd & she was all steel & fire once more, cursing him with a vehemence that was horrible to behold. She did not depart until first light, leaving me exhausted by her rage so that I did not return from E— to here until pm today. The Captain not in evidence and so made no mention of my lateness.

The passage bore a date: '25. vi. 19'.

To gaze so fixedly upon my mother's private journal seemed a gross intrusion; but I found I could not bring myself to secure the silk ribbon again and confine the contents to obscurity. For, being a journal or personal chronicle of some kind, then it must contain something of truth about her, something hidden but authentic about the little hunched and distracted figure, constantly writing, of my childhood memory. I felt impelled to uncover what lay behind the words that I had just read, even if it led to the postponement of my own plans to begin making my way in the world.

But what truth informed this enigmatic passage eluded me completely. For this was not simply a record of events, as earlier entries had been, but of some impending crisis, speaking of deep inward searching, the roots of which, it seemed, were as yet impossible to conjecture. A subsequent passage, dated a few days later, whilst clearer in its detail, appeared equally impenetrable to immediate interpretation:

L's appearance today, so wild & unexpected, at the door, was a great disturbance, made worse by Beth coming down the stairs just as she arrived, to hear her knocking furiously like the Devil himself. Beth asked if the lady was ill but I sent her off to fetch a drink as soon as I got L. into the parlour & when she return'd L was as composed & gracious as you like. He had come back but had refus'd her again – & this time something more (and terrible) had happened that she wd not say but which had open'd up a new chasm between them. I saw the rage begin again and urged her with much tender anxiety to quieten herself – which she did in a little while. She had come all this way to tell me – trusting nothing but her own whispered words as she always does – that Mme de Q was to be in Town next Mon. & Tues. & that I shd expect to hear something more quite soon thereafter.

Who was 'L'? Who was the man so clearly referred to: the Captain, or someone else? And what of 'Mme de Q'? I was now wide awake, held in an iron grip by what I had read. I tried to connect the memory of my mother's quiet and industrious life to these clear intimations of some looming climacteric, in which she had become involved; but I quickly gave up, and began to read on, urgently scanning the tiny yellow pages, to see whether some light could be shed on this mystery.

And so it began. I opened another little black book, then another, in a kind of dazed concentration, alive to the strangeness of what I was reading but transfixed, until my eyes were wearied. At last, looking up as the second or third candle I had lit began to gutter, I saw that a pink arc of light was creeping above the line of horizon beyond the parlour window. A new day had broken, for the world beyond, and for me.

· 16 ·

*Labor vincit**

Later that morning, I heard Tom's knock on the front door. When I opened it to him, I did not have to feign exhaustion.

'My dear fellow,' he said stepping in and helping me back to my chair by the fireplace, where I had fallen asleep, fully clothed, only an hour before. 'What is the matter? Shall I call for Dr Penny?'

'No, Tom,' I replied, 'no need for that. I shall be right as rain soon, I'm sure. A temporary indisposition only.'

He sat with me for a while as I took a little breakfast. Then, noticing the copy of Buckingham's book lying on the window-seat, he asked whether I had thought more about the expedition to Mesopotamia. He could see from the evasiveness of my reply that my interest in the project had lessened, but was friend enough to say that he expected I would see things differently when the indisposition had passed. But I could not let him think so, and told him straight out that I had definitely fixed against joining Professor S— in Nimrud.

'I'm sorry to hear it, Ned,' he said, 'for I think it was a promising opening, with much to gain in all respects. Perhaps you have other possibilities in view for earning a living?'

I had not often seen Tom angry with me, but I could not blame him for feeling somewhat put out. The prospect of adventure and advancement in the field of archaeology had only been a tempo-

*['Labour conquers'. *Ed.*]

rary passion, and I should have squashed it firmly underfoot at the start, in fairness to Tom. I tried to mend the mood by saying that I was also considering an opening at the British Museum, but then spoilt it by adding that this, too, might not be quite suitable for me at the present time.

'Well, then,' said Tom, standing up to go, 'I shall write to the Professor. Good morning, Ned. I hope to see you improved soon.'

I took the unspoken reprimand in his parting words without reply, and stood at the window gloomily watching him make his way back down the path to the village.

I should never now see Mesopotamia, and Great Russell-street would have to get on without me. For I was being drawn irresistibly back to the little black books that now lay scattered across my mother's work-table. The urge to discover the meaning of what my mother had written was to grow ever stronger, and soon became all-consuming, leading inexorably to ends of which I could not then have conceived.

THE DECIPHERMENT OF MY MOTHER'S JOURNALS AND PAPERS – FOR that, in effect, is what it became – began in earnest the next day, and continued in its first phase almost unabated for two or three months. Tom had departed to spend some time with a cousin in Norwich, feeling no doubt that it was best, for both of us, to leave any further discussions concerning my future to some later date. And so I remained indoors, alone and undisturbed, except for brief daily visits from Beth, and devoted myself night and day to my task, only occasionally leaving the house for a day or so to hunt out information that I needed to explain, or to confirm some reference or other.

Besides assiduously committing her private thoughts to her journals, it had been my mother's habit, in all her practical dealings, never to throw anything away; accordingly, there were innumerable items – bills, receipts, tickets, odd scribbled notes, lists, correspondence, drafts, memoranda – all bound together in bundles on that battlefield of paper. Through these I now also began to pick, piece by piece, day by day, night by night. I sifted, collated, sorted, categorized, deploying all the skills of scholarship, and all the gifts of intellectual application and assimilation at my disposal, to reduce the mass to order, to bring the light of understanding and fixity to bear on the fleeting, fluid shadows in which the full truth still lay hidden.

Gradually, a story began to emerge from the shadows; or, rather, the fragmentary and incomplete elements of a story. As if extracting broken shards from the imprisoning earth, I painstakingly gathered the fragments together, and laid them out, piece by piece, seeking the linking pattern, the design that would bring the whole into view.

One word gave me the vital clue. One word. The name of a place that echoed faintly in my memory at first, but which began to ring out more clearly, bringing with it two seemingly unconnected images: one of a lady in grey silk; the other of a bag, an ordinary valise, carrying a label with the owner's name and address written on it.

P. R. Daunt
Evenwood Rectory
Evenwood, Nthants

Evenwood. In a journal entry of July, 1820, my mother – inadvertently, I supposed – had written out the name in full. Prior to this entry, and subsequently, it appeared simply as 'E—' and, in this form, I had stupidly failed to identify it. But once I had this name, links began to form: Miss Lamb had lived at Evenwood; Phoebus Daunt had come from a place with the same name. But was there perhaps more than one Evenwood? My mother had amassed a large working library, to assist her in her work, and Bell's *Gazetteer* and Cobbett's *Dictionary** quickly supplied the answer. No, there was only one: Northamptonshire; Easton, four miles; Peterborough, twelve miles; Evenwood Park – the seat of Julius Verney Duport, 25th Baron Tansor.

That first night at Eton, in Long Chamber, I had asked Daunt if he knew Miss Lamb, and, later, he had enquired whether I had ever been to Evenwood. We had both answered in the negative, and I had thought no more about the coincidence. But, as I recalled it for the first time in fifteen years, his question seemed odd; or, rather, the guarded, almost suspicious tone in which it had been posed now struck me as being significant in some way. Yet what could Daunt have to do with all this?

I next considered the identity of 'L', the character at the centre of the mystery. Could it be Miss Lamb? For days I searched through piles of letters and other documents, in an attempt to establish that her Christian name, like her surname, began with the letter 'L'; but, to my amazement, I could find not a single piece of correspondence from this person, nor, indeed, any mention of her. Yet this lady had visited us as my mother's friend, and, as I thought, had showed extraordinary generosity towards me.

*[James Bell (1769–1833), *A New and Comprehensive Gazetteer of England and Wales* (1833–4). William Cobbett (1763–1835), *A Geographical Dictionary of England and Wales* (1832). *Ed.*]

Frustrated and perplexed, I had retreated to the one certainty I had: the place that connected Miss Lamb, Phoebus Daunt, and my mother. Taking down the 1830 edition of Burke's *Heraldic Dictionary*,* I turned to the epitome of the Tansor Barony:

> **The Baron Tansor** (Julius Verney Duport), of Evenwood Park, co. Northampton in England, *b.* 15th Oct. 1790, *s.* his father Frederic James Duport 1814 as 25th holder of the title; *educ.* Eton Coll., Trinity Coll., Cambridge; *m.* 1stly, 5 Dec., 1817, Laura Rose Fairmile (who *d.* 8 Feb., 1824), only dau. of Sir Robert Fairmile, of Langton Court, Taunton, Somerset, and had issue,
>
> Henry Hereward, *b.* 17 Nov., 1822, and *d.* 21 Nov., 1829.
>
> He *m.* 2ndly, 16 May, 1827, Hester Mary Trevalyn, 2nd dau. of John David Trevalyn, of Ford Hill, Ardingly, Sussex . . .

I read the paragraph over again, dwelling particularly on Lord Tansor's first wife, the daughter of Sir Robert Fairmile, of Langton Court. Now this latter was a name I knew well: he had been the employer of Mr Byam More, my mother's uncle and my former trustee. My heart began to beat a little faster as I wrote down the date of the first Lady Tansor's death. Then, opening one of the little black volumes, I turned to the entry dated the 11th of February, 1824, which I now read for the first time:

> A letter from Miss E telling me that the end came on Friday evening. A light has passed from the world, and from my

*[John Burke (1787–1848), *A General and Heraldic Dictionary of the Peerage and Baronetage of the British Empire*, first published by Henry Colburn in 1826, and now generally known as *Burke's Peerage*. The 1830 edition was the third. *Ed.*]

life, and I must now walk on through the twilight of my days until I too am called. In her letters L had seemed distracted and wildered of late, and I had begun to fear for her mind. But Miss E says the end was peaceful, with no preceding agonies, for which comfort I thank God. I had not seen her since she came here with the box for little E and to tell me what arrangements she had prepared for the time he should go to school. She was much changed, and I almost wept to see her thin face and hands. I remember E was playing at her feet all the time she was here, and oh! the pitiful look in her sweet eyes! He is such a fine, spirited young fellow, any mother would be proud of him. But she knew he would never know her, or that she had given him life, and it was a deadly pain to her. I marvelled at the persistence of her will, and told her so; for even at that moment, if she had been resolved at last to undo all that had been done, I would have surrendered him, though I love him like my own. But L was as fixed in her determination, though by now dreadfully oppressed by it, as she had been when she first recruited me to her cause, and I saw that nothing would ever move her. 'He is yours now,' she said softly before she left, and I wept to hear it. If she had been unfaithful to her marriage vows, then the case would perhaps be a little less dreadful. But he was lawfully conceived, and his father must now live out his days in ignorance of his son's existence. She came to feel most keenly the wrong she has done him; but nothing would persuade her to undo that wrong. Such is the curse of a passionate nature.

We embraced and I walked with her up the path to where her carriage was waiting, with Miss E inside, beneath the chestnut-tree by the gate. I watched them descend the

> hill from the cliff-top to the village. Almost at the bottom, just as the carriage was turning through the bend in the road, a limp black-gloved hand appeared out of the window and waved a forlorn farewell. I shall never see that hand again. I go now to pray for her soul, that she may find, in eternity, the peace that her restless and impetuous heart was denied on this earth.

'Miss E' had been mentioned before, but I gave no thought to her; for it had quickly become apparent that references to 'L' began to decrease in succeeding entries until, in April 1824, they ceased altogether. There could be no doubt: Lady Duport, Lady Tansor, was 'L'.

Yet solving this little puzzle had revealed an altogether greater mystery, the core of which seemed to be alluded to in this extraordinary passage, which fairly floored me when I first read it. I will not weary you further with how I came, by dint of much labour, to understand the implications of what my mother had written, and the identity of the person referred to as 'little E'. When I did, finally, fit the last fragment of the truth into place, what did I feel? A hideous sense of desolation. An agony too deep for tears. I sat – for how long? An hour? Two hours? – staring out of the window towards the chestnut-tree by the gate, and beyond towards the restless sea. At last, with darkness falling, I rose and made my way down to the beach, where I stood at the water's edge, and wept until I could weep no more.

MISS LAMB HAD NEVER EXISTED, OTHER THAN AS A NAME ASSUMED BY Lady Tansor when she visited us – my mother, and I. Now I knew why the lady in grey had looked upon me with such sadness as I had sat and played at her feet; why she had stroked my cheek so tenderly; why she had given me the box of sovereigns on my twelfth birthday; and why I had been sent to Eton at her behest. She had done these things because she was the woman who had given me life. Lady Tansor was my mother.

'*He is yours now.*' Disbelief quickly changed to angry incomprehension. Riddle me this: the mother I had loved was not my mother; my real mother had abandoned me; and yet it seemed that both had loved me. Whose child, then, was I? How my head ached in trying to disentangle it all!

The bare bones of the plot, at least, were now clear to me: my mother and her friend, Laura Tansor, who was in the early stages of pregnancy, had gone to France together; I had been born there, and had been brought back to England as the son of Simona Glyver, not of Lady Tansor. But the motives and passions that lay behind this simple sequence of events were still hidden from me, in an unknown number of secret places. How could they now be brought into the light?

Towards her who had sat on my bed every night as a child, who had walked with me on the cliff-top to watch the sun setting, and who had been the axis on which my little world had revolved, I felt both bitterness and pity: bitterness for keeping the truth from me; pity for what she must have suffered to maintain her friend's secret. Her actions had been a kind of betrayal, for which I must censure her; and yet what better mother could I have had?

There was still so much to discover, but, slowly, I came to an acceptance: I was not the son of Captain and Mrs Edward Glyver. My blood was not theirs. It connected me instead to other places and times, and to another name – an ancient and distinguished name. I had nothing of the man I had thought was my father in me, nothing of the woman I had called my mother. The eyes that were reflected in my mirror on rising every day were not her eyes, as I had always liked to think. But whose were they? Whom did I resemble – my real father, my real mother, or my dead brother? *Who was I?*

The questions went round and round in my head, day and night. I would wake from fitful sleep in a state of extreme agitation, as if the ground had been cut away from under my feet and I was falling through infinite space. I would then get up and wander the silent house, sometimes for hours on end, trying to repudiate this dreadful feeling of abandonment. But I could not. I did not belong here, in this place I had previously called home, where the past no longer seemed to hold any meaning.

Little by little, I began to examine my situation with a clearer and cooler eye. I did not know yet why this thing had been done – *that* knowledge would only come later, and gradually; but if what I had deduced from my mother's journals were true, then a simple fact, of extraordinary consequence, would follow: *I was the heir, lawfully conceived, to one of the most ancient and powerful families in England.*

It seemed absurd. Surely there must be some other explanation? But, after returning again and again to the journals, I could reach no other conclusion. Yet what use was the knowledge that I was convinced I now possessed? Who else would believe that what my mother – I still could not call her by any other name – had written was the honest truth, and not some fantastic fiction? Even if believed, how could it be proved? Unsubstantiated imputations, uncorroborated possibilities – nothing more. Such, surely, would be the immediate verdict if I went to law. But where was the substantiation? Where the corroboration? The questions began to multiply once more, hammering insistently in my brain until I thought I would go quite mad.

I looked again at the synoptic account of the Tansor peerage in Burke's *Dictionary*. Four densely packed columns contained the names and pedigrees of people of whom I had never before heard, but who I must now call my ancestors. Maldwin Duport, the 1st Baron Tansor, summoned to Parliament in 1264; Edmund Duport, the 7th Baron, made an Earl under Henry IV, but who died without issue; Humfrey Duport, the 10th Baron, attainted and executed for treason in 1461; Charles Duport, the 20th Baron, who turned Papist and went into exile with James II;* and then my nearer relatives – William Duport, the 23rd Baron and founder of the great Library at Evenwood; and at last my father, Julius Duport, the 25th Baron, who had succeeded to the title because of the death of his older brother; and my own deceased brother, Henry Hereward. I began to fill a note-book with their names, the dates of their births and deaths, and with every fact concerning their lives that I could glean from Burke, or from other authorities to which I then had access.

How strange it was, how infinitely strange, to consider myself as a member of this ancient line! But would I ever be given a place in some future epitome? Would a curious heraldic scholar, a hundred years hence, look into Burke and read of Edward Charles Duport, born on the 9th of March, 1820, in Rennes, Ille-et-Vilaine, France? Only if I could find some source of unequivocal and incontrovertible proof to supplement the indirect and oblique testimony of my mother's journals. Only then.

Concluding the entry in Burke were the following notes on the Tansor peerage:

Creation—By writ of summons, 49 HEN. III, 14 Dec. 1264.

Arms—Quarterly, 1st and 4th Or three piles enarched

*[Charles Duport (1648–1711) was created a Duke in the Jacobite peerage – a title without legal existence in England. His son Robert (1679–1741), a stout Protestant, inherited only the Barony. *Ed.*]

throughout issuant from the dexter base gules; 2nd, Per pale indented ermine and ermines on a chevron per pale indented or and argent five roses gules barbed and seeded proper; 3rd, Argent gutty d'huile a lion's rear gamb erased azure and transfixed through the thigh by a sword in bend sinister proper hilted pommelled and quilloned or. *Crest*—A demi man crowned royally proper crined and bearded argent vested in a robe gules lined ermine holding in his dexter hand a sceptre and in his sinister an orb gold. *Supporters*—Two lion-sagittarii each drawing a bow and arrow proper and banded about the temples with a fillet azure. *Motto*—FORTITUDINE VINCIMUS.*

The Tansor arms were illustrated at the head of the entry. Contemplating the unusual device of the lion-sagittarii,† I knew, with redoubled certainty, that what I had inferred from my mother's journals was the truth. On the wooden box that had once contained my two hundred sovereigns were displayed the same arms.

Fortitudine Vincimus was the Tansor motto. It would now be mine.

FROM TIME TO TIME, TOM WOULD CALL AND WE WOULD TALK desultorily for half and hour or so. But I could see his dismay as he surveyed the sea of paper spreading across the work-table and spilling over onto the floor; and I also saw that he had observed the darting look of wild absorption in my eyes, which all too obviously signalled an eagerness to return to my work – to which I

*['By endurance, we conquer'. *Ed.*]

†[i.e. sagittarius-lions, half-men, half-lions. *Ed.*]

never attached any specific character – as quickly as possible. He had not entirely forgiven me for passing over the opportunity to go to Mesopotamia with Professor S—, and was concerned, I could see, that I was making no attempt to secure any other form of employment. My capital had diminished more quickly than I had anticipated, largely as a result of my years abroad; debts left by my mother, which she had been keeping at bay with her writing, had also been paid out of it, and it was now becoming imperative for me to find a source of regular income.

'What's happening to you, Ned?' Tom asked one March morning, as I was walking him to the door. 'It pains me to see you like this, shut up here day after day, with no firm prospect in view.'

I could not tell him that I had in fact formed the clearest possible ambition. Instead, I prevaricated by saying that I planned to go to London to find some suitable temporary position until a permanent course of action presented itself.

He looked at me doubtfully. 'That is not a plan, Ned,' he said, 'but you must do what you think best. London, certainly, will offer many more opportunities than Sandchurch, and I would urge you to make your move soon. The longer you stay cooped up here, the harder it will be for you to break away.'

The following week, he called again and insisted that I leave the house and take some air, for in truth I had not stepped outside for several days.

We walked along the undercliff, and then down to the smooth area of wet sand washed by the waves. The sky was a perfect blue – the blue of my Heidelberg memories – and the sun shone in brilliant majesty, throwing down glancing points of light onto the ever-swelling wave-tops, as if God himself were casting a myriad new-born stars across the face of the waters.

We walked some distance in silence.

'Are you happy, Ned?' Tom suddenly asked.

We stopped, and I looked out across the dancing waves to where the vault of heaven met the shimmering horizon.

'No, Tom,' I replied, 'I am not happy and, indeed cannot say where happiness can be found in my life. But I *am* resolved.' I turned to him and smiled. 'This has done me good, Tom, as you knew very well that it would. You are right. I have immured myself here for too long. I have another life to lead.'

'I'm glad to hear you say so,' he said, grasping my hand. 'I shall miss you, God knows. The best pupil I ever had – and the best friend. But it would grieve me more if you were to waste away here, and make no mark upon the world.'

'Oh, I intend to make a mark on the world, Tom, have no fear. From this moment I am reborn.'

It was true. I had felt a surge of energy as I gazed out at the mighty rolling ocean, alive with sunlight – a new consciousness that my life now had purpose and definition. I had made my decision. I would go to London, and from there I would begin my great enterprise.

My restoration.

· 17 ·

*Alea iacta est**

THE ONLY PERSON WHOM I KNEW IN LONDON WAS MY OLD SCHOOL-friend and travelling companion, Willoughby Le Grice, to whom I immediately wrote to ask whether he could recommend suitable lodgings. He replied by return to say that a fellow at his Club had suggested I should write to a Signor Prospero Gallini, a former fencing master, who, by all accounts, now kept a good house in Camberwell.

I had taken the decision to abandon my given name of Glyver, except of course with respect to those few, like Le Grice and Tom Grexby, who already knew me. It was not mine by birth but was a kind of alias, imposed on me, without my knowledge or consent, by others. What loyalty did I owe the name of Glyver? None. Captain Glyver was not my father. Why, then, should I bear his name? I was who I was, whatever I chose to call myself; and so, until I could redeem my rightful name and title, I would put on whatever pseudonym suited my present purposes. My whole life would be a disguise, a daily change of dress and character. I would inhabit a costumed world, entering now as one character, now as another, as circumstance demanded. I would be *Incognitus*. Unknown.

There were, besides, practical considerations. In making enquiries concerning my true self, carrying the name of Glyver might be disadvantageous to my cause. Concerning the plot hatched by

*['The die is cast'. *Ed.*]

Lady Tansor, there were undoubtedly many aspects of which I was as yet unaware; and to use my mother's married name would immediately reveal my interest and connexion to the protagonists. No, for the time being, it was better to work in the shadows.

I therefore wrote to Signor Gallini as Edward Glapthorn – the name by which I now became generally known in my new life. The following week, after receiving a satisfactory reply, I took coach from Southampton to make arrangements with my new landlord, whom I found to be exactly as Le Grice's friend had described him: tall, courteous, and quietly spoken, but with a melancholy patrician bearing, like an exiled Roman emperor.

The village of Camberwell – despite the growing proximity of the metropolis – was charming, with open fields and market gardens all around, and pleasant walks through woods and lanes to nearby Dulwich and its picture gallery. Signor Gallini's house stood in a quiet street close to the Green – not far, as I later discovered, from the birthplace of Mr Browning, the poet.* I was offered two rooms on the first floor – a good-sized sitting-room with a small bedchamber adjoining – at a most reasonable rent, which I instantly agreed to take.

Just as I was leaving, our business having been concluded satisfactorily with a glass of wine and a cigar, both of excellent quality, the front door opened and in walked the most beautiful girl I thought I had ever seen. Already, I liked to fancy myself as a pretty hard-nosed young dog when it came to the female sex; but I confess that I felt like a callow schoolboy when I saw those lustrous black eyes, and the voluptuous figure that her light-blue morning dress and short lace-collared cape did little to conceal.

'May I introduce my daughter, Isabella?' said Signor Gallini.

*[Robert Browning was born at 6 Southampton Street, Camberwell, on 7 May 1812. *Ed.*]

'This, my dear, is the gentleman who has been recommended to us. I am glad to say that he has consented to take the rooms.'

His English was perfect, though spoken with the still-detectable accent of his native country. Miss Gallini smiled, held out her hand, and said that she hoped I would like Camberwell, to which I could only reply that I believed I would like it very well indeed. So began my connexion with Isabella Gallini, my beautiful Bella.

The time had now come to leave Sandchurch behind me. I set about packing my mother's journals and papers into three sturdy trunks, and instructing Mr Gosling, her former lawyer, to sell the house. It was hard to let Beth go, for she had been part of the household for as long as I could remember, and had continued to cook and clean for me since my return from the Continent; but it had been agreed that she would perform the same domestic duties for Tom, which eased my conscience a little. Billick took the news of my departure in his usual taciturn fashion: he pursed his lips, nodded his head slowly, as if in silent recognition of the inevitable, and shook me by the hand, most vigorously. 'Thankee, sir,' he said, receiving the small bag of coins that I had held out; whereupon he spat out a piece of tobacco, and walked off down the path to the village, whistling as he went. That was the last I ever saw of him.

I was not embarking on my new life entirely without some plan as to what I should do with myself. Ever since the moment that I had gazed upon the photogenic drawing of the great stone king in Professor S—'s rooms in Oxford, the idea had been growing in me that the production of such images might perhaps furnish a means of making a living, or at least of supplementing my income. I had not mentioned this to Tom, fearing that it would produce another disagreement between us, but I had quietly taken steps to acquaint myself more fully with the possibilities and techniques of this wonderful new medium. I flatter myself that I was amongst its pioneers and, but for the subsequent course of my life, I think I might have made my name in the field, and have been remembered by posterity for it, along with Mr Talbot and Monsieur Daguerre.*

I had always been fascinated by the camera obscura and its ability to throw fleeting images onto paper, the creations of an instant, which then, just as rapidly, faded away when the camera was removed. Tom – to my utter delight – possessed one, and as a boy I would often harangue him, once our lessons were done on a fine summer evening, to go out into his little garden and let me look into 'the magic mirror'. Those memories had been instantly revived by the photogenic drawing displayed in the Professor's rooms, and I now determined to learn for myself how to catch and hold light and shadow in perpetuity.

To this end, a few weeks earlier, I had written to Mr Talbot, and he had kindly agreed to receive me at his house at Lacock,† where I was inducted into the art of producing photogenic drawings of the kind I had seen in New College, and into all the mysteries of sciagraphs,‡ developers, and exposure. I was even given one of Mr Talbot's own cameras, dozens of which had lain all about the house and grounds. They were perfect little miracles: simply small wooden boxes – some of them no more than two or three inches square (Mrs Talbot called them 'mousetraps') – made to Mr Talbot's design by a local carpenter, with a brass lens affixed to the front; and yet what wonders they produced! I had returned home to Sandchurch, afire with enthusiasm for my new hobby, and eager to begin taking my own photographs as soon as possible.

*[Louis-Jacques Mandé Daguerre (1787–1851), French photographic pioneer and inventor of the Daguerreotype process. *Ed*]

†[Lacock Abbey, near Chippenham in Wiltshire. *Ed.*]

‡[What Sir John Herschel later called 'negatives', the term we still use. *Ed.*]

Then came the hot July day when I closed behind me the front door of the house on the cliff-top for what I thought would be the last time. I paused for a moment, beneath the chestnut-tree by the gate, to look back at the place that I had formerly called home. The memories could not be restrained. I saw myself playing in the front garden, eagerly climbing the tree above me to look out from my crow's-nest across the ever-changing waters of the Channel, and trudging up and down the path, in every season and all weathers, to and from Tom's school. I recalled how I would stand watching my mother through the parlour window, doubled over her work for hour after hour, never looking up. And I remembered the sound of wind off the sea, the cry of sea-birds as I woke every morning, the ever-present descant of waves breaking on the shore below the cliff, thundering in rough weather like the sound of distant cannon. But they were Edward Glyver's memories, not mine. I had merely borrowed them, and now he could have them back. It was time for my new self to begin making memories of its own.

DURING MY FIRST FEW WEEKS IN CAMBERWELL, I MADE SEVERAL TRIPS to town in search of employment. All proved fruitless, and, soon, with my little store of money diminishing fast, I began to fear that I should have to fall back on tutoring again – a most uncongenial prospect. Perhaps if I had possessed a degree, my way might have been made easier; but I did not. Phoebus Daunt had put paid to that.

The summer began to pass, and, determined I would not subside into idleness, I turned again to my mother's journals. It was then that I made a great discovery.

My eye had happened to fall on an entry dated '31. vii. 19': 'To Mr AT yesterday: L not present, but he kindly put me at my ease & explained what was required.' 'L' was, of course, Laura Tansor;

but the identity of 'Mr AT' was unknown to me. On an impulse, I searched out a tied bundle of miscellaneous documents, all of which dated from 1819. It did not take long to extract a receipt for a night's stay, on the 30th of July of that year, at Fendalls Hotel, Palace Yard. Adhering to the back was a card:

ANSON TREDGOLD, ESQ.
SENIOR PARTNER

TREDGOLD, TREDGOLD, & ORR

17, PATERNOSTER-ROW, CITY

'Mr AT', I thought, could now be identified, tentatively, as Mr Anson Tredgold, solicitor. This now explained an earlier entry: 'L has agreed to my request & will speak to her legal man. She understands that I fear discovery & require an instrument that will absolve me of blame, if such a thing can be contrived.' It seemed clear from this that some form of legal document or agreement had been drawn up, to which both women had been signatories. Of such an agreement I had found no trace amongst my mother's papers; but, seeing its likely importance to my case, I began there and then to devise a way of getting my hands on a copy of it. My great enterprise had begun.

The next day I wrote to the firm of Tredgolds in a disguised hand, and using the name Edward Glapthorn. I described myself as secretary and amanuensis to Mr Edward Charles Glyver, son of the late Mrs Simona Glyver, of Sandchurch, Dorset, and requested the pleasure of an interview with Mr Anson Tredgold, on a confidential matter concerning the aforementioned lady. I waited anxiously for a reply, but none came. The tedious weeks dragged by, during which I continued to make a number of enquiries concerning employment, without success. August came and went, and I began to despair of ever receiving a reply to my enquiry to Mr Anson Tredgold. It was not until the first week of September that a short note arrived informing me that a Mr Christopher Tredgold would be pleased to receive me privately (the word was underlined) on the following Sunday.

THE DISTINGUISHED FIRM OF TREDGOLD, TREDGOLD & ORR HAS already been mentioned in this narrative, in connexion with my neighbour Fordyce Jukes, and as the legal advisers of Lord Tansor. Their offices were in Paternoster-row,* in the shadow of St Paul's: a little island of the legal world set in a sea of publishers and booksellers, whose activities have made the street proverbial amongst those of a literary inclination. The firm occupied a handsome detached house, on the other side of the street from the Chapter coffee-house; as I was soon to discover, part of the building, unlike many in the City, was still used by the present Senior Partner, Mr Christopher Tredgold, as his private residence. The ground floor formed the clerks' offices, above which, on the first floor, were the chambers of the Senior Partner and his junior colleagues; above these, occupying the second and third floors, were Mr Tredgold's private rooms. One peculiarity of the building's arrangement was that the residential floors could also be reached from the street via two side staircases, each with its own entrance that gave onto two narrow alleys running down either side of the house.

It was a fine morning, bright and dry, though with a distinct feeling of impending autumn in the air, when I first saw the premises of Tredgold, Tredgold & Orr, which were soon to become so

*[Paternoster Row was completely destroyed during the Blitz, on December 1940. *Ed.*]

familiar to me. The street was unusually quiet, but for the dying chimes of a nearby church clock and the rustle of a few newly fallen leaves drifting along the pavement and gathering beside me in a little twirling heap.

A manservant showed me up to the second floor, where Mr Christopher Tredgold received me in his drawing-room, a well-proportioned apartment whose two tall windows, looking down on the street, were swathed and swagged in plush curtains of the most exquisite pale yellow, to which the sunlight streaming in from outside added its own soft lustre.

All, indeed, was shine and softness. The carpet, in a delicate pattern of pink and pale blue, had a deep springy pile, reminding me of the turf against which I had lain in my little nook above the Philosophenweg. The furniture – sparse but of the finest quality, and much against the present ponderous taste – gleamed; light danced off brilliantly polished silver, brass fittings, and shimmering glass. The the long sofa and tête-à-tête chair,* in matching blue-and-gold upholstery, that were set around the elegant Adam fireplace – each item also enclosing an abundance of perfectly plumped cushions of Berlin-work – were deep and inviting. In the space between the two windows, beneath a fine classical medallion, stood a violincello on an ornate wrought-brass stand, whilst on a little Chippendale table beside it was laid open the score of one of the divine Bach works for that peerless instrument.

Mr Christopher Tredgold was a gentleman of some fifty years or so. He was of middling height, clean shaven, with a full head of feathery grey hair, a fine square jaw, and eyes of the most piercing blue, set widely in his broad, tanned face. He was dressed immaculately in dove-grey trousers and shining pumps, and held in his left hand an eye-glass on a dark-blue silk ribbon attached to his

*[A double chair, on which two people could sit side by side. *Ed.*]

waistcoat, the lens of which, during the course of our interview, he would polish incessantly with a red silk handkerchief kept constantly by him for this purpose. In all the time of our subsequent acquaintance, however, I never once saw him raise the glass to his eye.

Dulcis was the word that impressed itself on my mind when I met Mr Christopher Tredgold for the first time. Pleasant, soft, charming, mellifluous, refined: all these intangible impressions of character seemed to mix with the atmosphere of the room, its elegance and fragrance, to produce a sensation of sweet and dreamy ease.

Mr Tredgold rose from the seat he was occupying by the window, shook my hand, and invited me to make myself comfortable on the tête-à-tête chair, whilst he (somewhat to my relief) took a seat on the sofa. He smiled seraphically, and continued to beam as he spoke.

'When your letter was passed to me – Mr . . . Glapthorn . . . ' – he hesitated for a moment as he glanced down at a little sheaf of notes he was holding – 'I thought it would be more convenient for us both if we conducted this interview in a private capacity.'

'I am grateful to you, Mr Tredgold,' I replied, 'for giving up your time in this way.'

'Not at all. Not at all. You see, Mr Glapthorn, your letter intrigued me. Yes, I may say that I was intrigued.'

He beamed again.

'And when I am intrigued,' he continued, 'I can be sure that the matter in hand is out of the ordinary. It is a remarkable instinct I have. It has happened time and again. I am intrigued; I investigate the matter in a private capacity, carefully, quietly, and at my leisure; and then – it always happens – I find something extraordinary at the bottom of it all. The ordinary I can leave to others. The *extra*ordinary I like to keep for myself.'

This statement was delivered in the smoothest of tenor tones, and with slow precision of enunciation, which gave it a chant-like quality. Before I could reply, he had consulted his notes again, polished his eye-glass, and had proceeded with what was evidently some sort of prepared introduction to our meeting.

'In your letter, Mr Glapthorn, I find mention of Mr Edward Glyver and his late mother, Mrs Simona Glyver. May I ask what your relationship is to either of these two persons?'

'As I stated in my letter, I have been engaged by Mr Edward Glyver as a confidential secretary, to assist him in the ordering and final disposal of his late mother's papers.'

'Ah,' beamed Mr Tredgold, 'the authoress.'

'You know her work?'

'By reputation.'

It did not strike me as odd then, though it did later, that Mr Tredgold was aware of the identity that lay behind the anonymous and pseudonymous works of my mother. He nodded at me to continue.

'Mr Glyver is presently residing on the Continent and wishes to conclude his mother's affairs as quickly as possible. As it is impossible for him to take on the whole task himself, he has delegated the business side of things to me.'

'Ah,' said Mr Tredgold, 'the business side. Indeed.' Another polish of the eye-glass. 'May I ask, Mr Glapthorn, you will excuse me, whether you have some authority on which we may proceed?'

I had come prepared for this, and reached into my coat.

'A letter from Mr Edward Glyver,' I said, 'granting me temporary power of agency over his affairs.'

'I see,' he replied, taking the document and looking over it. 'A little irregular perhaps, but this all looks to be in order, although of course I have not had the pleasure of meeting Mr Glyver, and I do not think we hold any correspondence from him.'

Again I was prepared.

'A corroborating signature, perhaps?' I asked.

'Certainly that might suffice,' said Mr Tredgold, and I handed him a receipt, signed of course by myself, for the supplying of a handsome pocket translation of Plato by Ficino (Lyons, 1550, in a pretty French binding) by Field & Co., Regent's Quadrangle. This appeared to satisfy the Senior Partner, who, having polished his glass once more, leaned back and responded with a further question.

'You spoke of a confidential matter in respect of the late distinguished authoress, Mr Glyver's mother. May I know what it concerns?'

His cerulean eyes widened a little as he tilted his head to one side and stroked back a delicate feather of hair from his forehead.

'I have found mention in Mrs Glyver's papers of an agreement between herself and a certain lady, whom I have inferred must be a client of your firm's. The late Laura, Lady Tansor?'

Mr Tredgold said nothing.

'Unfortunately, Mrs Glyver does not seem to have retained a copy of this agreement, and her son is naturally concerned that it might contain some undertaking that he is obliged to discharge on her behalf.'

'Most commendable,' said Mr Tredgold. He rose from his chair, walked over to a little French writing-desk, opened a drawer, and took out a piece of paper.

'This, I think, is the document you seek.'

· 18 ·

*Hinc illae lacrimae**

I WAS AMAZED. I HAD EXPECTED LAWYERLY EVASION AND PROCRASTI-nation from Mr Tredgold, a firm rebuff even; but not such an easy and rapid capitulation to my request.

It was a simple enough arrangement.

> I Laura Rose Duport of Evenwood in the county of Northamptonshire do hereby solemnly and irrevocably absolve Simona Frances Glyver of Sandchurch in the County of Dorset from all accountability charge blame censure prosecution or crimination in law in relation to any private arrangement concerning my personal affairs that the said Simona Frances Glyver and I Laura Rose Duport may agree to or undertake and do further instruct that the said Simona Frances Glyver be exculpated and remitted from any prosecution or crimination in law *in toto* and in all respects from any consequences whatsoever and whenever that may arise from the said arrangement and that further and finally the provisions contained herein shall be incorporated at the proper time and place into those of my last will and testament.

The document had been signed by both parties and dated: '30th July 1819'.

*['Hence these tears' (Terence, *Andria*). *Ed.*]

'This was drawn up by—?'

'Mr Anson Tredgold, my late father. An old gentlemen then, I fear,' replied his son, shaking his head.

I did not ask whether such an agreement would ever have held in law if challenged; for I saw that it did not matter. It had been a gesture merely, a willing acquiescence on Lady Tansor's part to her friend's natural desire to possess an illusion of protection, if all failed, from the clearly dangerous confederacy upon which they had been engaged.

'I believe,' Mr Tredgold went on, 'that Mr Edward Glyver can be assured that nothing in this arrangement can now devolve upon him in any way at all. It remains – well, I should say it remains an unexecuted curiosity. As I said before, something extraordinary.'

He beamed.

'Do you – did your father – have knowledge of the nature of the private arrangement referred to in this document?'

'I'm glad you have asked me that, Mr Glapthorn,' he replied, after a discernible pause. 'I, of course, was not party to the drawing up of the document, having only recently joined the firm. My father was Lord Tansor's legal adviser, and so it was natural that her Ladyship should have come to him to put her arrangements in hand. But after receiving your letter, I did undertake a little delving. My father was a methodical and prudent man, as we lawyers of course must be; but on this occasion he was, I fear, a little lax in his dealings with Lady Tansor. For I do not find he left any note or other sort of memorandum on the matter. He was, as I say, an elderly gentleman . . .'

'And do you know whether Lord Tansor himself was aware that his wife had consulted your father on this matter?'

Mr Tredgold cleaned his eye-glass.

'As to that, I think I can say with certainty that he did not. I can also say that the agreement you have in your hand was *not* finally incorporated into her Ladyship's will, for she came to me some time later, with Lord Tansor's full knowledge this time, specifically to prescribe new testamentary provisions following the birth of her son, Henry Hereward Duport.'

I had one final matter to raise with the Senior Partner.

'Mrs Glyver . . .'

'Yes?'

'I believe certain arrangements were put in place, of a practical nature?'

'That is so: a monthly remittance, which this office disposed through Dimsdale & Co.'

'And that arrangement ceased . . .?'

'On the death of Lady Tansor, in the year 1824.'

'I see. Well, then, Mr Tredgold, I need detain you no further. The business appears to have been concluded to the satisfaction of all concerned, and I think I can report to Mr Edward Glyver that he need have no further disquiet regarding this matter.'

I rose to go, but Mr Tredgold suddenly sprang up from his chair, with a speed that surprised me.

'By no means, Mr Glapthorn,' he said, taking my arm. 'I shall not hear of it! You shall stay to luncheon – it is all ready.'

And with this wholly unanticipated expression of civility towards me, I was escorted to an adjoining room, where a substantial cold collation had been laid out. We chatted easily for an hour or more over what was a really excellent repast – prepared and brought in for Mr Tredgold by a *protégé* of no less a person than M. Brillat-Savarin* himself. We soon discovered that the Senior Partner had spent some time in Heidelberg as a student, which precipitated

*[Jean-Anthelme Brillat-Savarin (1755–1825), whose most celebrated work, *Physiologie du gout*, was published in 1825. *Ed.*]

some mutually happy memories of the town and its environs.

'The receipt that you showed me earlier, Mr Glapthorn,' he said at length. 'Do you perhaps share Mr Glyver's bibliographical interests?'

I replied that I had made some study of the subject.

'Perhaps, then, you would give me your opinion on something?'

Whereupon he went to a glass-fronted case in the far corner of the room and took out a volume to show me – Battista Marino's *Epithalami* (Paris, 1616 – the first collected edition, and the only edition printed outside Italy).*

'Very fine,' I said admiringly.

Mr Tredgold's remarks on the character, provenance, and rarity of the volume were accurate and judicious, and although his knowledge of the field in general was inferior to my own, he nevertheless impressed me with the extent of his expertise. He affected to defer immediately to what he kindly claimed was my obviously superior judgment on such matters, and ventured to suggest that we might arrange another visit, at which he could show me more of his collection at leisure.

So it was that I charmed Mr Christopher Tredgold.

I left by one of the side entrances, escorted down to the street door by the serving man who had let me in a few hours before. Just as we reached the bottom, Mr Tredgold shouted down:

'Come again, next Sunday.'

AND I DID; AND THE NEXT SUNDAY, AND THE FOLLOWING. BY MY FIFTH visit to Paternoster-row, in early October, I had formed a plan that

*[Giambattista Marino (1569–1625), Italian Baroque poet, whose extravagant and sensuous images had an influence on the English poet Richard Crashaw. *Ed.*]

I hoped would take advantage of my increasingly friendly connexion with the Senior Partner.

'I fear, Mr Tredgold,' I said, as I was about to depart for Camberwell, 'that this may have to be the last of our pleasant Sundays.'

He looked up, and for once the beam had vanished.

'What? Why do you say so?'

'My employment with Mr Glyver was, as you know, only temporary. It will be over as soon as he returns from the Continent in the next few days and I can discharge the final portions of my duty to him in person.'

'But what will you do then?' asked Mr Tredgold, with every appearance of genuine concern.

I shook my head and said that I had no immediate prospect of further employment.

'Why, then,' he beamed, 'I can give you one.'

It had fallen out even better than I had dared hope. I had envisaged the possibility of finding a way to join the firm in some junior or even menial capacity; but instead, here was Mr Tredgold offering to employ me as his assistant. In addition, he offered to introduce me to Sir Ephraim Gadd, QC, the recipient of many of Tredgolds' most lucrative briefs, who was at that moment seeking someone to act as tutor in the classical languages to those applying for admission to the Inner Temple who had not taken a degree.

'But I have no degree either,' said I.

Mr Tredgold smiled – seraphically – once more.

'That, I can assure you, will be no bar. Sir Ephraim is always ready to take the advice of Tredgold, Tredgold & Orr.'

With my new position came a good salary of a hundred and fifty pounds *per annum,** and a set of top-floor rooms in Temple-

*[About £12,500. *Ed.*]

street, in a building owned by the firm, for which only a modest rent was requested. It was agreed that I would begin my employment – the precise nature of which remained almost deliberately vague – on the first day of November, in a little over four weeks' time, when the rooms I had been given were vacated by their present temporary occupant.

I returned to Camberwell elated by my triumph, but saddened at having to leave my comfortable lodgings. Signor Gallini, from whom I had received many kindnesses and attentions in the short time we had been acquainted, was the first new friend I made in London, and it was a real sadness to leave his quiet little house, not to mention the charms of the delectable Miss Bella, and move into the teeming heart of the city. But leave I did, and duly left Camberwell for Temple-street at the end of October. Now settled on this new course, I celebrated Christmas 1848 in the Temple Church, singing my heart out alongside the devout amongst my new neighbours, in a mood of genuine thanksgiving.

THE FIRST LETTER THAT I RECEIVED IN MY NEW HOME WAS FROM Signor Gallini and Bella (with whom I had determined I should not lose contact), wishing me the compliments of the season and sending their very best hopes that I would prosper in my new career. A few days after Christmas, two more letters were delivered, this time to the accommodation address I had taken in Upper Thames-street, hard by, in order to receive correspondence directed to Edward Glyver.

One was from Mr Gosling, my mother's legal man in Weymouth, advising me that the house at Sandchurch had been sold but indicating that, owing to its somewhat parlous condition, we had not achieved the price we had anticipated. The proceeds had been disposed according to my instructions: the money owed to Mr More had been remitted to him, and this, on top of other necessary disbursements, had left a balance of £107 4*s.* and 6*d.* This was far less than I had expected, but at least I now had employment, and a roof over my head.

The other letter was from Dr Penny, the physician who had attended my mother in her last illness.

Sandchurch, Dorset

4th January, 1849

My Dear Edward, —

It is with very great sorrow that I have to inform you that poor Tom Grexby passed away last evening. The end was swift and painless, I am glad to say, though quite unexpected.

I had seen him only the day before and he seemed quite well. He was taken ill during the afternoon. I was called, but he was unconscious when I arrived and I could do nothing for him. He died, quite peacefully, just after eight o'clock.

The funeral is today week, the 11th. I am sorry to be the bearer of such mournful news.

I remain,
yours very sincerely,
Matthew Penny.

A week later, on a bitter January afternoon, I returned to Sandchurch, for the last time in my life, to see my dear friend and former schoolmaster laid to rest in the little church-yard overlooking the grey waters of the Channel. A keen wind was coming in from the east, and the ground was flint-hard underfoot from several days' hard frost. I remained alone in the church-yard after everyone else had departed, watching the last vestiges of day succumb to the onset of darkness, until it became impossible to distinguish where the sky ended and the heaving expanse of black water began.

I felt utterly alone, bereft now of Tom's sympathetic companionship; for he had been the only person in my life who had truly understood my intellectual passions. During my time as his pupil, by generously and selflessly putting his own extensive knowledge at my complete disposal, and by encouraging me in every possible way, he had given me the means to rise far above the common level of attainment. Eschewing the dead hand of an inflexible system, he had showed me how to *think*, how to analyse and assimilate, how to impose my will on a subject, and make it my own. All these mental strengths I would need for what lay ahead, and all these I owed to Tom Grexby.

I stood by the grave until I was fairly numb with cold, thinking over the days of my boyhood spent with Tom in his dusty house of books. Though I could not comfort myself with the pious certainties of Christianity, for I had already lost whatever allegiance I might have had to that faith, I remained susceptible to its poetical power, and could not help saying aloud the glorious words of John Donne, which had also been spoken at my mother's funeral:

> And into that gate they shall enter, and in that house they shall dwell, where there shall be no Cloud nor Sun, no darknesse nor dazling, but one equall light, no noyse nor silence, but one equall musick, no fears nor hopes, but one equal possession, no foes nor friends, but one equall com-

munion and Identity, no ends nor beginnings; but one equall eternity.*

Desperately cold, and with a heavy heart, I left the church-yard, eager now to seek the warmth and comfort of the King's Head. Yet, despite my discomfort, I could not help first walking up the cliff path, to take one final look at the old house.

It stood in the freezing gloom, dark and shuttered, the garden untended, the little white fence blown over in the late gales. I do not know what I felt as I regarded the creeping desolation, whether grief for what had been lost, or guilty sorrow for having abandoned my childhood home. Above me, the bare branches of the chestnut-tree, in which I had built my crow's-nest, creaked and cracked in the bitter wind. I would never again clamber up to my old vantage point, to look out across the ever-changing sea and dream of Scheherazade's eyes, or of walking with Sindbad through the Valley of Diamonds.† But to the inevitability of change, all things must submit; and so I turned my back on the past and set my face into the east wind, which quickly dried my tears. I had a great work to accomplish, but I trusted, at the last, to come into that gate, and into that house, where all would be well; where, as Donne the preacher had said, fear and hope would be banished forever, in one equal possession.

Death took another friend that cold January: Prospero Gallini, who died of a broken neck after falling down the stairs.

*['A Sermon Preached at White-hall. February 29. 1627'. In *XXVI Sermons* (1660). *Ed.*]

†[Described in the Second Voyage of Sindbad the Sailor, in *The Thousand and One Nights. Ed.*]

Bella wrote to tell me the terrible news, and of course I immediately went down to Camberwell to be with her.

'I do not know yet what I shall do,' she said, as we walked back from the church after the interment, 'but I must leave here, that is for sure. There are debts to be paid, and the house must be sold. I shall go to London and find a position as soon as I can.'

I told her that she must not fail to inform me when she was settled, and begged her to regard me as her friend and protector in London. As I was leaving, she gave me a charming little edition of Dante's *Vita Nuova* that had belonged to her father.

'This is for my kind and considerate friend,' she said, 'whom I shall always think of with affection.'

'You promise to write to me?'

'I do.'

Some weeks later, a letter arrived to tell me that she had found a position as companion to a Mrs Daley in St John's Wood. I was glad of it, for her father's sake, and determined that I would thereafter do my best, through regular correspondence, to watch over her. This I did, though it was to be three years until we met again.

THE GREAT TABLE AT WHICH MY MOTHER HAD SPENT SO MANY WEARY hours was now set before the window in my new rooms in Temple-street, Whitefriars. On it, the journals that had revealed my lost self were arranged in order, girded round, as at Sandchurch, by yellowing bundles of paper, dozens of them, each bundle now sorted into chronological order, and carrying a label denoting its contents. Blank note-books, fresh from the stationers, were stacked up in readiness; pencils had been sharpened; ink and nibs laid in. I was ready to embark on my great work, to prove my true identity to the world.

I had made an excellent beginning. The agreement drawn up

between my mother and Lady Tansor, which lent its circumstantial weight to my claim, was now in my possession; and, by an unexpected stroke of luck, I had secured employment at Tredgolds, Lord Tansor's legal advisers. What might come of this situation, I could not foresee. But some advantage, surely, would present itself, if I could gain the complete confidence of Mr Christopher Tredgold.

And an advantage, however small, is everything to the resourceful man.

MY FIRST VISITOR TO TEMPLE-STREET HAD BEEN LE GRICE, WHO arrived unannounced, late one snowy afternoon, a few days after I had returned from Tom's funeral. His thundering ascent of the wooden stairs, and the three tremendous raps on the door that followed, were unmistakable.

'Hail, Great King!' he bellowed, pulling me towards him and slapping me on the back with the flat of his huge hand. He stamped the snow from his boots and then, removing his hat and taking a step back, surveyed my new kingdom.

'Snug,' he nodded approvingly, 'very snug. But who's that awful little tick on the ground floor? Poked his horrid nose round the door and asked whether I was looking for Mr Glapthorn. Told him, politely, to mind his own business. And who's Glapthorn, when he's at home?'

'The tick goes by the name of Fordyce Jukes,' I said. 'Mr Glapthorn is yours truly.'

Naturally, this information produced a look of surprise in my visitor.

'Glapthorn?'

'Yes. Does it bother you that I've adopted a new name?'

'Not in the least, old boy,' he replied. 'Got your reasons, I expect. Creditors pressing, perhaps? Irate husband, pistol in hand, searching high and low for E. Glyver?'

I could not help giving a little laugh.

'Either, or both, will do,' I said.

'Well, I won't press you. If a friend wants to change his name, and that same friend wishes to keep his reasons to himself, then let him change it, I say. Luckily, I can continue to call you "G" in either case. But if assistance is required, ask away. Always ready and eager to oblige.'

I assured him that I needed no assistance, financial or otherwise, requesting only that any correspondence sent to Temple-street, or to my employer's, should be directed to Mr E. Glapthorn.

'I say,' he said suddenly, 'you're not working for the Government, in some secret capacity, I suppose?'

'No,' I said, 'nothing like that.'

He seemed disappointed, but was true to his word and did not press me further. Then he reached into his pocket and drew out a folded copy of the *Saturday Review*.

'By the way, I came across this at the Club. It's a few months old now. Did you see it? Page twenty-two.'

I had not seen it, for it was not a periodical that I often read. I looked at the date on the cover: 10th October 1848. On the page in question was an article entitled 'Memories of Eton. By P. Rainsford Daunt', from which I have previously quoted.

'Seems to be a good deal about you in it,' said Le Grice

So many years had gone by since Daunt had betrayed me; but my desire to make him pay for it was as strong as ever. I had already begun to assemble information on him, which I kept in a tin box under my bed: reviews and critical appreciations of his work, articles that he had written for the literary press, notes on his father from public sources, and my own descriptive impressions of his first home, Millhead, which I had visited the previous November. The archives were small as yet, but would grow as I searched for some aspect of his history and character that I could use against him.

'I shall read it later,' I said, throwing the magazine onto my work-table. 'I'm hungry and wish to eat – copiously. Where shall we go?'

'The Ship and Turtle! Where else?' exclaimed Le Grice, throwing open the door. 'My treat, old boy. London awaits. Take up your coat and hat, *Mr Glapthorn*, for I shall be your guide.'

IN NOVEMBER 1854, SETTLED BEFORE A ROARING FIRE IN LE GRICE'S rooms in Albany, with a glass of brandy in my hand, I found it hard to believe that only six years had passed since I had left Sandchurch for London. It seemed as if a whole lifetime had gone by – so many memories crowding in, so much rosy hope, and so much bleak despair! Faces in the flames; the smell of a September morning; death and desire: impressions and remembrances floated before my eyes, coalesced, and separated again, a multitude of ghosts in an eternal dance.

'I've never told anyone, you know,' Le Grice was saying quietly, head thrown back, watching the smoke from his cigar curl upwards towards the ceiling, deep in shadow. 'Never said a word, about this life you've been living. Whenever one of the fellows asks, I always say you're travelling, or that I haven't heard from you. That's right, isn't it? That's what you wanted?'

He lifted his head and looked directly at me, but I did not reply.

'I don't know where all this is leading, G, but if what you say is true . . .'

'It's all true. Every word.'

'Then of course I understand. You weren't Edward Glyver, so you may as well be Edward Glapthorn. I thought you must have the money-lenders on your tail, or some such, though you wouldn't admit it. But you had to keep things close, I see that, until everything could be made right. But what a story, G! I won't say I can't believe it, because I must believe it, if you tell me it's true. There's more to come, though, that's clear, and I'm all ears, old boy. But do you want to go on now, or sleep here and carry on in the morning?'

I glanced at the clock. Ten minutes to two.

'No sleep tonight,' I said. 'And now, let me tell you a little more about Mr Tredgold.'

· Intermezzo ·

1849–1853

· I ·

Mr Tredgold's Cabinet

MR CHRISTOPHER TREDGOLD HAD BEEN AS GOOD AS HIS WORD, AND had duly advised that shining ornament of the legal profession, Sir Ephraim Gadd, QC, that he could do worse than engage my pedagogic services to dispense linguistic knowledge to candidates requiring admission to the Inner Temple who lacked the necessary University qualifications, over which persons Sir Ephraim exercised authority as a Bencher.* These duties were not in the least arduous to me, and I fulfilled them easily alongside my daily employment at Tredgolds, of which I shall speak presently.

The marked partiality that Mr Tredgold had shown towards me at our first meeting had again been apparent on the first day of my employment. On my arrival in Paternoster-row, I was immediately taken up to his private office on the first floor by Fordyce Jukes. The latter was one of the longest-serving of Tredgolds' clerks, and occupied an exalted position behind a high desk by the front door of the establishment, where, as the house's gatekeeper, he would welcome clients, and conduct them up to one or other of the partners.

His admiration of the Senior Partner knew no bounds; but soon his professions of regard for me, whom he barely knew, became hardly less immoderate. He was continually obliging, ever affable, looking up eagerly from his work to smile, or nod 'good-day', as I passed.

*[One of the senior members of the Inns of Court. *Ed.*]

I disliked him from the first, with his bull neck and thick flat nose. He wore his hair short, like a workhouse terrier crop, brushing it up at the front into a crown of little black spikes. The straightness of the line where the hair met the flesh of his neck, and around his ears and temples, made the whole arrangement appear like some strange cap or hat that he had placed over a perfectly normal head of hair. I hated too his moth-eaten little dog, his puce, clean-shaven face, and the leering quality of his look. He was always clicking his fingers, shaking his head, or scratching his crown of spikes, whilst in his small green eyes one detected a flickering, unquiet energy, which would never quite show itself plain, but perpetually hid and ducked, like some pursuing assassin melting into doorways and alleys to baffle his victim. All this rendered him repulsive in my eyes.

Before long, so insistent had his attentions become, whenever I appeared at the office of a morning, that I took to avoiding the front door altogether, and instead would gain my room by means of the side stairs; but still I would often encounter him, at the end of a day, hovering in the street, waiting for me. 'There you are, Mr Glapthorn,' he would say, in his strange high-pitched voice. 'I thought we might walk back together. A little company and a friendly chat at the end of the day, so pleasant.'

Jukes's most unwelcome interest in me had begun on my very first morning in Paternoster-row. As I entered through the front door, he jumped down from his desk and began bowing obsequiously.

'Honoured to make your acquaintance, Mr Glapthorn,' he said, shaking my hand furiously as he spoke, '*honoured.* I hope we may see much of each other, in a social as well as a business capacity. Neighbours, you know. New blood always welcome, sir – lubrication for the great Tredgold engine, eh? We must move forward, mustn't we, Mr Glapthorn? Yes, indeed. So clever of the SP to bring you to us, but then we expect no less of the SP.'

He went on in this vein until we reached the door of Mr Tredgold's office. He conducted me into the room, giving yet another oily obeisance, and then, with reiterated bobbings of his head, closed the door softly behind him.

The Senior Partner rose from his desk, beaming.

'Welcome, welcome, Mr Glapthorn!' he said, shaking me warmly by the hand. 'Please sit down, sir. Now, is there anything you require? Shall I ring for some tea? It is a little cold this morning, is it not? Would you like to move nearer to the fire?'

He continued in this warmly considerate manner for some minutes, until I convinced him at last that I was not in the least bit cold, and that I did not require any warming beverage to fortify me. I then asked him what duties I would be expected to undertake at the firm.

'Duties? Yes, of course. There are certainly duties.' He gave his eye-glass a little polish, and beamed.

'Might I ask, Mr Tredgold, what those duties might be?'

'Of course you may. But first, Mr Glapthorn, you ought to know something of my colleagues. We are called Tredgold, Tredgold, and Orr, but there is only one Tredgold now – myself. Mr Donald Orr is the Junior Partner; and then there is Mr Thomas Ingrams. There are six clerks, including Mr Jukes, who is the most senior of their number. It is a varied practice. Criminal work, divorce, bankruptcy and insolvency (the particular interest of Mr Donald Orr), probate, the management of estates and properties, and so on; and of course we represent the interests of a large number of distinguished persons.'

'Such as Lord Tansor?'

'Indeed.'

'And in which particular area of the practice will my duties lie?'

'You are a great one for duty, I see, Mr Glapthorn, and it is apparent you are keen to be at it.'

'At what, Mr Tredgold?'

'Well, now, let me see. I thought, to begin with, you might wish to cast your eye over some papers relating to a bankruptcy case that we recently conducted. Would that please you?'

'I am not here to be pleased, Mr Tredgold,' I replied, 'I am here to please you, and to earn a living.'

'But I *am* pleased,' he cried, 'and will be even more so if you will kindly consent to look over these papers.'

'May I enquire whether you require me to do anything other than read the documents?'

'Not at this time. Come!'

And with that, he took me by the arm and ushered me down the corridor and into a dark little room, with a large desk in the centre, and a cheerfully crackling fire.

'Wait here, if you please,' he said. A few minutes later he returned with a large bundle of papers, and set them down on the desk.

'Will you be comfortable here?'

'Perfectly.'

'Then I shall leave you to your labours. I shall be out of the office today. Leave when you wish. Good-day, Mr Glapthorn.'

I duly applied myself to the documents that Mr Tredgold had given me. When I had finished reading them, having nothing else to occupy me, I returned to Temple-street. For the remainder of the week, I would come into my little room every morning to find another bundle of papers waiting for me, which I would diligently read through, to no apparent purpose, and then return home. On Friday, as I was about to depart, the door of Mr Tredgold's office opened.

'An excellent week's work, Mr Glapthorn. May I have the pleasure of your company on Sunday, at the usual time?'

Once again, I found myself in Mr Tredgold's private residence, enjoying a most appetizing collation. Afterwards, as always, we fell into talking about books. As I was being conducted down the side stairs by the man, Harrigan, he handed me a key.

'Please to use this, sir, at Mr Tredgold's request, when you next come. No need to knock.'

Astonished at this sign of my standing with the Senior Partner, I looked at Harrigan for a moment, but his face showed no expression. As I did so I noticed, just behind him, a woman of about my own age, regarding me with a similar impassivity. These two persons – whom I had been told were husband and wife, Albert and Rebecca Harrigan by name – were the only other inhabitants of the building on the Sundays when I was entertained by Mr Tredgold. I would catch glimpses of them from time to time, going about their duties silently, and never saying a word to each other.

Another week passed. Every day I walked from Temple-street to Paternoster-row, read carefully through whatever papers Mr Tredgold had left on my desk, and then walked home. As I was leaving my room on the second Friday afternoon, a beaming Mr Tredgold issued another invitation to join him on Sunday in his private residence. This time, I had my key, and let myself in by the side door.

After luncheon was over, and we had settled ourselves on the ottomans in front of the fire, the conversation soon turned towards books. During our bibliographic chats, Mr Tredgold would often get up to pick out some volume from his collection to make a point, or to ask my further opinion on some matter of typography or provenance. On this occasion, he had been speaking of some of the unusual testamentary provisions that the firm had occasionally been asked to prepare, which led me to mention the mock last will and testament drawn up by Aretino* for Pope Leo X's pet elephant, Hanno, in which the poet solemnly bequeathed the beast's private parts to one of His Holiness's Cardinals.

'Ah, Aretino,' said Mr Tredgold, beaming and polishing his eye-glass. 'The infamous Sixteen Postures.'

Now having become something of a connoisseur in the history of warm literature during my time in Heidelberg (and possessing, as I did, good editions of Rochester and Cleland,† as well as rare examples of the genre from earlier periods), I was instantly familiar with the reference, but taken aback somewhat by my host's unabashed mention of this celebrated masterpiece of the erotic imagination.

'Mr Glapthorn.' He put down his red silk handkerchief and looked steadily at me. 'Would you mind giving me your opinion on this?'

He stood up and walked over to a large walnut-fronted cabinet that I had often noticed, standing between the two doors that gave access to the room. Taking out a key on a delicate gold chain from his waistcoat pocket, Mr Tredgold unlocked this cabinet to reveal six or eight shelves of tightly packed books, as well as a number of slim, dark-green wooden boxes. Taking down one of the volumes, he re-locked the cabinet, and returned to his seat.

To my astonishment, it was the exquisitely rare 1798 Paris (P. Didot) edition of Aretino's sonnets, with engravings by Coiny after Carrache, something I had never seen before in all my bibliographic searchings.

*[Pietro Aretino (1492–1556), Italian poet. In 1524 he wrote accompanying sonnets to sixteen pornographic drawings by Giulio Romano, pupil of Raphael. *Ed.*]
†[John Cleland (1709–89), author of the infamous *Memoirs of a Woman of Pleasure* (1749), otherwise known as *Fanny Hill. Ed.*]

'I have presumed, Mr Glapthorn,' he said, 'that such a work is interesting to you – as a scholar and collector. I hope I have not offended in any way?'

'By no means,' I replied, turning over the volume slowly in my hands to admire the binding. With the content of the illustrations, as well as the accompanying verses, I was naturally familiar: the muscular bodies, fiercely entwined limbs, and tumescent members, the urgent couplings against tasselled cushions beneath great canopied beds. That my employer should also be familiar with them, however, was wholly unexpected.

The production of the volume led to a more general discussion of the field as a whole, and it soon became clear that, in this department of bibliography at least, Mr Tredgold's knowledge was considerably in advance even of my own. He invited me back over to the cabinet, unlocked the doors again, and we spent a pleasant hour or so admiring together the gems of venereal literature that he had collected over the course of some twenty years.

'These, too, may perhaps interest you,' he said, taking out and opening one of the slim green boxes that I had noticed earlier.

It contained a complete collection, laid lovingly on a bed of soft embossed paper, of those prints by Rowlandson in which the artist had depicted various accommodating ladies in the act of revealing their charms to the fervid male gaze. The other boxes held prints and drawings of a similar nature, by some of the finest practitioners.

My amazement was now complete.

'It appears, sir,' I said, smiling, 'that you have hidden depths.'

'Well, well,' he replied, beaming back at me. 'The law, you know, can be a dreary business. A little harmless diversion is certainly required, from time to time. As a corrective.'

The conversation went on pleasantly over tea as we discussed various rarities in the field of voluptuous literature that we were each keen to locate. Mr Tredgold was particularly eager to augment his collection with a copy of *The Cabinet of Venus,* the partial, anonymous translation put out in 1658 of the celebrated *Geneanthropeia* of Sinibaldi. I made a mental note of this, believing that I might know where I could lay my hands on a copy, and thinking that its acquisition would ingratiate me even further with my employer.

At about five o'clock, much later than my usual hour for departing, I rose to take my leave. But before I could say anything, Mr Tredgold had jumped to his feet and had taken me by the hand.

'May I say, Edward – I hope you will not mind if I presume to address you by your first name – that I have been extremely satisfied by your work.' One of his hands continued to hold mine tightly, whilst the other he placed gently on my shoulder.

'I am glad to hear it, Mr Tredgold, though I do not know in what way I can possibly have rendered satisfaction.'

'You have done what I asked of you, have you not?' he asked.

'Of course.'

'And you have done it to the best of your ability, diligently, without shirking?'

'I believe so.'

'So do I. And if I were to ask you a question concerning any of the documents you have read, do you think you would be able to answer it?'

'Yes – if you would allow me to consult my note-book.'

'You took notes! Capital! But perhaps you found the task a little irksome? No need to answer. Of course you did. A man of your talents should not be confined. I wish to liberate your talents, Edward. Will you allow me to do that?'

Not knowing how to reply to this curious question, I said nothing, which Mr Tredgold appeared to take as assent.

'Well then, Edward, your probationary days are over. Come to my office tomorrow, at ten. I have a little problem that I wish to discuss with you.'

So saying, he wished me a pleasant evening, beamed, and retired to his study.

· II ·

Madame Mathilde

The next morning, as requested, I presented myself at Mr Tredgold's private office. When I left, an hour later, it was as the Senior Partner's confidential assistant, a post which, as he was at pains to emphasize, would involve undertaking a variety of duties 'of a discreet and private kind'. These duties, to which only Mr Tredgold and I were privy, I undertook for the next five years, with, I think I may say, some success.

It may be imagined that a distinguished, and successful, solicitor such as Mr Tredgold often needed to lay his hand on information essential for a case that was not – shall we say – readily obtainable through the usual channels. On such occasions, when it was best that he remain in ignorance of the sources of such information, as well as the means by which it came to him, Mr Tredgold would summon me, and suggest a turn or two round the Temple Gardens. A problem of particular concern for the firm would be set out – theoretically, of course – and discussed (in the abstract).

'I wonder,' he would say, 'whether anything might be done about this?'

Nothing further would be said, and we would make our leisurely return to Paternoster-row, discoursing on nothing in particular.

No formal instructions were issued, no records of conversations kept. But when something needed doing – of a discreet and private kind – it became my task at Tredgold, Tredgold & Orr to ensure that it was done.

The first 'little problem' that Mr Tredgold placed before me, for theoretical consideration, concerned a Mrs Bonner-Childs, and may be taken as typical of the work that I subsequently undertook.

This lady had been a patron of an establishment in Regent-street called the Abode of Beauty, run by a certain Sarah Bunce, alias Madame Mathilde.* Here, Madame enticed gullible females dedicated to the pursuit of eternal beauty (a not inconsiderable market, one would suppose) into parting with their – or more often their husbands' – money by dispensing ingenious preparations with exotic names (to effect the complete and permanent removal of wrinkles, or to preserve a youthful complexion in perpetuity) at twenty guineas a time. The establishment also offered a room sumptuously fitted out as an Arabian Bath. The unfortunate Mrs Bonner-Childs, having been tempted to partake of this last amenity, had come back to her clothes to find that her diamond ring and earrings had vanished. Upon confronting Madame Mathilde, she was informed by the proprietress that if she made a fuss over the loss, then Madame would inform Mrs Bonner-Childs' husband – Assistant Secretary at the India Board, no less – that his wife had been using the Bath for immoral assignations.

The success of Madame Mathilde's establishment – like Kitty Daley's Academy – depended on the fatal spectre of public scandal doing its work on those unfortunates who succumbed to this and to other similar ruses; but in this case, Mrs Bonner-Childs immediately informed her husband of what had happened, and he, trusting completely in his wife's innocence in the matter, instantly consulted Mr Christopher Tredgold.

My employer and I duly took a turn round the Temple

*[This lady appears to have been a precursor of the more famous Rachel Leverson, extortionist and thief, who was prosecuted in 1868 and sentenced to five years' penal servitude for exactly the same activities as Madame Mathilde. *Ed.*]

Gardens. Mr Bonner-Childs was ready to prosecute if it came to it, but had expressed the hope that Mr Tredgold might be able to suggest a way by which this might be avoided, and his wife's jewels returned. Either way, the question of the firm's fee – at whatever level it might be set – was immaterial.

'I wonder whether anything might be done about this?' mused Mr Tredgold aloud, whereupon we returned to Paternoster-row, conversing as usual about nothing in particular.

The next day I set about observing the daily round of entrances and exits at the Abode of Beauty. In due course, I saw what I was looking for.

The late-morning drizzle had slowly thickened into rain. All around, the city thundered and roared. At every level of human existence, from the barest subsistence to luxurious indolence, its inhabitants crossed and re-crossed the clogged and dirty arteries of the great unsleeping beast, each according to his station – trudging through the murk and mud, insulated in curtained carriages, swaying knee to knee in crowded omnibuses, or perched precariously on rumbling high-piled carts – all engrossed by their own private purposes.

Though it was not yet midday, the light seemed already to be failing, and lamps were burning in the windows of houses and shops. It is a dark world, as I have often heard preachers say, and on that day the metaphor was made flesh.

I had been standing in Regent-street for some time, and was somewhat aimlessly glancing into the window of Messrs Johnson & Co.,* thinking that perhaps I might make a present to myself of a new hat, when I saw the reflected image of a woman in the glass. She was about thirty years of age and, passing just behind me, had stopped before the Abode to look up at the luridly painted sign

*[Hatters to the Queen. *Ed.*]

above the door. She hesitated, and then proceeded on her way; but she had taken only a few steps when she stopped again, and then returned to the door of the establishment.

She had an open honest face, and was wearing a fine pair of emerald earrings. I immediately stepped forward to prevent her entering. She looked momentarily shocked, but I swiftly persuaded her to move away from the door. This was my first lesson in boldness, and I learned it well. I also found, to my surprise, that I possessed a natural persuasiveness in such situations and quickly gained the confidence of the lady, who agreed, after we had retired a little way down the street to discuss the matter, to fall in with my plans.

A few minutes later, she re-entered the establishment and immediately requested a bath, taking off her clothes and jewellery in an adjoining room, as Mrs Bonner-Childs had done. Having observed that Madame Mathilde was the sole person within the premises at that moment, I had entered behind my accomplice and, waiting a few moments for her to enter the bath chamber, had the satisfaction of surprising Madame in the act of helping herself to the lady's emerald earrings.

We exchanged a few words, with the result that Madame appeared to see the error of her ways. She lived exceptionally well from the Abode of Beauty, and could not risk prosecution, which I assured her would now be a simple matter to accomplish.

'A mistake, sir, a simple mistake,' she said, plaintively. 'I was just on the point of puttin' them away for safety – like the girl did with the other lady's, only I wasn't aware at the time that she'd done so . . .'

And so on until, at last, she produced Mrs Bonner-Childs' jewellery, with much self-pitying hand-wringing and fervent promises to send the girl packing who had been so thoughtless as to hide away the items without telling anyone.

Mr Tredgold expressed great satisfaction that the matter had been resolved so quickly and quietly, without recourse to public prosecution, and Mr Bonner-Childs promptly settled a substantial bill from the firm for services rendered, a satisfactory portion of which was remitted to my account at Coutts & Co.

I must also mention, briefly, the later case of Josiah Pluckrose, as being illustrative of the more unpleasant side of the work I undertook for Mr Tredgold, and for other reasons, which will later become clear.

He was a common sort of man, this Pluckrose; a butcher from a long line of butchers, who had managed to amass a good deal of capital by means that Mr Tredgold described, in a whisper, as 'dubious'. He had given up the art of butchery at the age of twenty-four, had done a little boxing, had worked as a waterman and as a brush-maker, and had then, miraculously as it seemed, emerged from the mire as a *pseudo*-gentleman, with a house in Weymouth-street, and more than a few pennies to his name.

Tall and thick-set, with reptilian eyes and a livid scar across one cheek, Pluckrose had a wife who had previously been in service at some great house or other, and whom he had treated abominably during the short period they had been married. One day, in the autumn of 1849, this poor lady was found dead – beaten around the head in a most terrible way – and Pluckrose was arrested for her murder. He had previously engaged Tredgolds on a number of business matters, and so the firm was naturally retained as the instructing solicitors for his defence. 'An unpleasant necessity,' Mr Tredgold confided, 'which, as he has introduced a number of clients to the firm, I do not think I can avoid. He protests his innocence, of course, but still it is all a little distasteful.' He then asked me whether I could possibly see any way round this particular 'little problem'.

To be short, I did find a way – and, for the first time since I began such work, it went a little against my conscience. The details need not detain us here; the case came on in January 1850; Pluckrose was duly acquitted of the murder of his wife; and an innocent man later went to the gallows. I am not proud of this, but I discharged my office so well that no one – not even Mr Tredgold – ever suspected the truth. Good riddance to the odious Pluckrose, then.

Or so I thought.

WITH THE BUSINESS OF MADAME MATHILDE, IN FEBRUARY 1849, began a life of which I could have had no conception only six months earlier, so alien was it to my former pursuits and interests. I soon discovered that I had a distinct talent for the work that I was called upon to undertake for Mr Tredgold – indeed, I took to it with a degree of proficiency that surprised even my self-assured nature. I gathered information, establishing a network of connexions amongst both high and low in the capital; I uncovered little indiscretions, secured fugitive evidence, watched, followed, warned, cajoled, sometimes threatened. Extortion, embezzlement, crim. con.,* even murder – the nature of the case mattered not. I became adept in seeking out its weak points, and then supplying the means by which the foundations of an action against a client could be fatally undermined. My especial talent, I found, was sniffing out simple human frailty – those little seeds of baseness and self-interest which, when brought to the light and well watered, turn into self-destruction. And so the firm would prosper, and Mr Tredgold's seraphic beam would grow all the broader.

London itself became my workshop, my manufactory, my *study*, to which I devoted all my talents of application and assimilation. I

*[i.e. 'criminal conversation' – adultery. *Ed.*]

sought to master it intellectually, as I had mastered every subject to which I had turned my mind in the past; to tame and throw a leash round the neck of what I came to picture as the Great Leviathan, the never-sleeping monster in whose expanding coils I now dwelled.

From the heights to the depths, from brilliant civility and refinement to the sinks of barbarity, from Mayfair and Belgravia to Rosemary-lane and Bluegate-fields, I quickly discerned its lineaments, its many intertwining natures, its myriad distinctions and gradations. I watched the toolers and dippers,[*] and all the other divisions of the swell mob, do their work in the crowded affluence of the West-end by day, and the rampsmen[†] at their brutal work as the shadows closed in. I observed, too, with particular attention, the taxonomy of vice: the silken courtesans brazenly hanging on the arms of their lords and gentlemen; the common tails and judies, and every other class of gay[‡] female. Each day I added to my store of knowledge; each day, too, I extended my own experience of what this place – unique on God's earth – could offer a man of passion and imagination.

I have no intention of laying before you my many amorous adventures; such things are tedious at best. But one encounter I must mention. The female in question was of that type known as a dress-lodger.[§] It was not long after the affair of Madame Mathilde, and I had returned to Regent-street to look again at the wares of Messrs Johnson & Co. She was about to cross the street when she caught my eye: well dressed, petite, with a dimpled chin

[*] [Types of pickpockets. *Ed.*]
[†] [Violent street robbers. *Ed.*]
[‡] [Used in the contemporary sense of 'immoral', not in the modern sense. *Ed.*]
[§] [A prostitute who was provided with expensive-looking clothes by her keeper. *Ed.*]

and delicate little ears. It was a dull, damp morning, and I was close enough to see tiny jewels of moisture clinging to her ringlets. She was about to join a small group of pedestrians on a swept passage across the street. On reaching the opposite pavement she stopped, and half turned, fingering an errant lock of hair nervously. It was then that I saw an elderly woman, crossing the roadway a few yards behind her. This, I knew by now, was her watcher, paid by the girl's bawd to ensure that she did not abscond with the outfits provided for her. Girls such as she were too poor to deck themselves out in the finery required to hook in custom, like the sharp bobtails of the theatre porticos and the Café Royal.

I began to follow her. She walked with quick steps through the crowds, sure of her way. In Long Acre, I drew level with her. The business was swiftly concluded, her watcher retired to a nearby public-house, whilst the girl and I entered a house on the corner of Endell-street.

Her name was Dorrie, short for Dorothy. She had become what she was, she said afterwards, to support her widowed mother, who could now find no regular employment of her own. We talked for some time, and I found my heart begin to go out to the girl. At my request, she took me, with her watcher still a few paces behind us, to a cramped and damp chamber in a dreary court hard by. Her mother, I guessed, was only some forty years of age herself, but she was bent and frail, with a harsh wheezing cough. When I saw the evident signs of perpetual struggle and weariness on her face, I was immediately put in mind – though the cases were very different – of my own mother's constant labours, and the toll that they had taken on her.

Almost without thought on my part, an arrangement was made. I never regretted it. For several years, until circumstances intervened, Mrs Grainger came two or three times a week to

Temple-street, to sweep my room, take my washing away, and empty my slops.

As she entered of a morning, I would say: 'Good-morning, Mrs Grainger. How is Dorrie?'

'She is well, sir, thank you. A good girl still.' And that is all we would ever say.

Thus I became a kind of benefactor to Dorrie Grainger and her mother. Yet even this unpremeditated act of charity on my part was to become a connective strand in that fatal web of circumstance that was already closing round me.

Great leviathan.

On waking, February, mdcccl*

O City! Deep and wide!
Womb of all things!

This Sun, this Moon, these stars – I touch and feel them.
I burn. I freeze.
These mountains I grind to powder under my hand.
These torrents I consume, these forests I devour.

*[As with the passage on the Iron Master (p. 125), these lines have been pasted on to the page at this point. The reason for their inclusion here is not immediately obvious, though they were clearly of significance to the author, and we may perhaps further conjecture that they were written under the influence of opium. *Ed.*]

I live in all things, in light and air, and music unheard.
O City of blood and bone and flesh!
Of muscle and sinew, of tooth and eye!

Theatre of all vanity, the hell for which I yearn:
Wild and raging beneath my feet.
My life. My death.

· III ·

Evenwood

After taking up residence in Temple-street, and commencing my employment at Tredgolds, my photographic ambitions had languished for a while, though I continued to correspond with Mr Talbot. But, once settled, I constructed a little dark-room within a curtained-off space in my sitting-room. Here also I kept my cameras (recently purchased from Horne and Thornethwaite),* along with my lamps, gauze, pans and bowls, trays and soft brushes, fixing and developing solutions, beakers, glasses, quires of paper, syringes and dippers, and all the other necessary paraphernalia of the art. I worked hard to familiarize myself with the necessary chemical and technical processes, and on summer evenings would take my camera down to the river, or to picturesque corners of the nearby Inns of Court, to practise my compositional techniques. In this way, I began to build up my experience and knowledge, as well as amassing a good many examples of my own photographic work.

The satisfaction of close and concentrated observation; the need to perceive minute gradations of light and shadow, and to select the correct angle and elevation; the patient scrutiny of backdrop and setting – these things I found gave me intense fulfilment, and transported me to another realm, far away from my often sordid duties at Tredgolds. My principal partiality, artistically

*[Opticians, 'chemical and philosophical instrument makers', and also a leading supplier of photographic equipment, at 121 and 123 Newgate Street. *Ed.*]

speaking – the seed planted by seeing a photogenic drawing that Mr Talbot had made of Lacock Abbey – was to seek to capture the spirit or mood that certain buildings evoke. London offered such a variety of subjects – ancient palaces, domestic dwellings of every type and age, the river and its bridges, great public buildings – that I soon developed a keen eye for architectural line and form, shadow and sky, texture and profile.

One Sunday, in June 1850, feeling I had attained to a good level of competence, I decided I would show Mr Tredgold some examples of my photographic work.

'These are really excellent, Edward,' he said, turning over a number of mounted prints that I had made of Pump-court, and of Sir Ephraim Gadd's chambers in King's Bench-walk. 'You have an exceptional eye. Quite exceptional.' He suddenly looked up, as if struck by a thought. 'Do you know, I think I could secure a commission for you. What would you say to that?'

I replied, of course, that I would be very happy for him to do so.

'Excellent. I am obliged to pay a visit to an important client next week, and, seeing what you have done here, it occurs to me that this gentleman might wish to have some photographic representations of his country property, to provide an indelible record for posterity. The property in question would certainly afford the most ravishing possibilities for your camera.'

'Then I shall be even more willing to agree to the proposal. Where is the property?'

'Evenwood, in Northamptonshire. The home of our most important client, Lord Tansor.'

Whether Mr Tredgold saw my surprise, I cannot say. He was beaming at me, in his usual way, but his eyes had a guarded look about them, as if in anticipation of some disagreeable response. He cleared his throat.

'I thought,' he went on, 'that you might also be curious to see the former home of Lady Tansor – I allude, of course, to her friendship with your last employer's late mother, Mrs Simona Glyver. But if this proposal is against your inclinations . . .'

I raised my hand.

'By no means. I can assure you that I have no objections at all to such an expedition.'

'Good. Then it is settled. I shall write to Lord Tansor immediately.'

How could I possibly have refused to go along with Mr Tredgold's adventitious proposal, when Evenwood was the one place on earth I wished to see? I was already familiar, from various published accounts, with the history of the great house, the disposition of the buildings, and the topography of the extensive Park. Now I had been given the opportunity to experience, in my waking being, what I had so often fashioned in imagination.

Since commencing my employment at Tredgolds, I had made little progress in my pursuit of some piece of objective evidence that would confirm what I had read in my mother's journals. I had suggestions and hints, providing strong and, to me, compelling testimony to the truth concerning my birth; but they were not indubitable, and shed no light on the causes of the conspiracy between my mother and Lord Tansor's first wife, or on how their plan had been accomplished. By now, I had read every word of my mother's journals several times over, as well as making copious notes on them, and had begun to re-examine and index every scrap of paper she had left behind, from bills and receipts to letters and lists (my mother, I discovered, had been an inveterate list-maker; there were scores of them). I hoped to find some fragment of the truth that I might have overlooked; but it was becoming clear to me that little more could be gleaned from the documents in my possession, and that I would achieve nothing by remaining in my rooms, and brooding on my lost inheritance. If that inheritance was to be recovered, I must begin to widen my view; and what better way to start than by seeing my ancestral home for myself?

A few days later, Mr Tredgold informed me that Lord Tansor was happy for me to accompany him to Evenwood, where I would be given liberty to roam as I pleased. Next morning, both of us feeling relieved to be escaping the heat and dust of London, we took the train northwards to Peterborough.

ONCE WE HAD BOARDED OUR TRAIN, MR TREDGOLD AND I IMMEDIATELY fell into our customary bookish talk, which we kept up all the way to Peterborough, despite several attempts on my part to encourage my employer to speak of Evenwood and its principal residents. Having arrived in Easton, some four miles from Evenwood, Mr Tredgold went on ahead to the great house, leaving me to accompany the trunk containing my travelling equipment in the carrier's cart. At the gate-house, just beyond the village of Evenwood, I got out, leaving the cart to trundle off. It was approaching two o'clock when I ascended the long incline that carries the road from the gates, and rested at the top to look down over the river towards the vista spread out before my hungry eyes.

And now, at last, I am to show you Evenwood, which I first beheld on that perfect June afternoon in 1850 – an afternoon, perhaps, like the one that had seen the arrival of Dr Daunt and his family twenty years earlier. I see it again in memory, as clearly as on that day.

The village lies, in quiet seclusion, close to a slow-moving tributary of the River Nene, the Even, commonly called the Evenbrook by the local inhabitants, which winds through the Park to join the main river a few miles to the east. A church and adjoining rectory, a noble Dower House of the late seventeenth century, clusters of picturesque cottages, some outlying farms, and then the great house itself: similar compositions can be found all over England; but Evenwood is like no other place on earth.

The always-sighing reed beds and the overarching willows in the water-meadows, the pale stone houses with their roofs of thatch or Collyweston stone,* the undulating Park with its lake and ancient trees, and, in the midst, the faery splendour of Lord Tansor's residence, are sources of deep and abiding solace for those weary of the quotidian world. The whole place seems to be somehow beyond time, shut in and protected from the meanness of existence by the meandering river, and the gently wooded slopes on either side, which, on a fine day, dissolve into long soft swathes of grey-green.

If you consult Verekker's dull but dependable *Guide to the County of Northamptonshire* (a copy of the augmented 1812 edition is now before me as I write),† you will read of Lord Tansor's seat being 'pleasantly situated in a well-wooded Park of many acres, planted with noble stands of oak, ash, and elm, and watered by the Even, or Evenbrook. The house, or manor, is built of brick and freestone. The accretions of centuries have bestowed upon the house a pleasing irregularity of form, at once imposing and romantic.' You will also learn from Verekker the bare architectural facts concerning the house: the licence to crenellate granted in 1330; the Elizabethan extensions to the fortified mediaeval dwelling; the Jacobean refinements; the remodelling by Talman early in the last century; and the improvements lately effected in the Classical style by Henry Holland, who also worked on another of the county's great houses, Althorp.

*[The famous stone roofing slates of northern Northamptonshire. *Ed.*]

†[Conrad Verekker (1770–1836). The first edition of his guide was published in 1809. *Ed.*]

What you will not find in Verekker, or in any other guide, is an anatomy of Evenwood's power to bewitch both soul and sense. Possibly, it is beyond human art to convey the sense of something lost, but eternally present, that such places inspire. In every light, and in every season, it possesses a transcendent beauty; but in summer it is very paradise. Approach it if you can – as I first did – from the south, on a mid-summer afternoon. On entering the Park, you ascend the incline that I have mentioned, at the summit of which you will certainly pause, as I did, to catch your first sight of the great house. To your left, over the low boundary wall, light dances on the river curving gently westwards; and then you glimpse the church – its delicate spire on such a day set against a cloudless sky of deepening blue – facing the ivy-covered Rectory on the far side of a little field of graves.

Proceed a little further. The carriage-drive descends towards the river, crosses it by a fine balustraded bridge, then turns to the right, levelling out to give a fuller view of the house and the swaying haze of trees behind; then it divides, to sweep either side of a perfect oval of lawn, with a fine Classical group – Poseidon with Tritons – at its centre, before passing through a pair of massive iron gates into an enclosed and gravelled entrance court.

Always your eye is drawn upwards, to a riot of gables and fluted chimneys, and, dominating all, six soaring towers topped with arched, intricately leaded cupolas. Behind the formality of Holland's frontage, the remains of earlier ages ramble in picturesque confusion: cobbled alleys between high walls, a vaulted cloister opening on to gardens. Tudor brick mingles with smooth ashlar; oriels and battlements oppose classical columns and pediments. And, in the midst, a sequestered mediaeval courtyard filled with urns and statuary, heavy in summer with the scent of lavender and lilies, and echoing always to the sound of birds and trickling water.

Evenwood. I had wandered its corridors and great rooms in dreams, collected representations of it, greedily hoarded every published account of its history and character, no matter how trite and inconsequential, from William Camden to the pamphlet published in 1825 by Dr Daunt's predecessor as Rector. For years it had been, not a built thing of stone and timber and glass, which could be touched and gazed upon under the light of sun and moon, but a misty dream-place of unattainable perfection, like the great Pavilion of the Caliphat described so perfectly by Mr Tennyson.*

Now it was spread out before me. No dream, it stood planted deep in the earth that my own feet were treading, washed by the rain of centuries, warmed and illuminated by countless dawns, raised and shaped by dead generations of mortal men.

I was overwhelmed, almost choked by tears at the first sight of the place that I had seen only with the interior eye. And then – it was almost like the sensation of physical pain – I became certain that I had seen it before; not in books and paintings, not in fancy, but with my own eyes. I said to myself: I have been *here*. I have breathed *this* air, heard *these* sounds of wind through the trees, and the music of distant waters. In an instant, I was a child again, dreaming of a great building, half palace, half fortress, with soaring spires and towers reaching to the sky. But how could these things be? The name of this place held dim childhood associations, but no recollection of ever having been brought here. Whence came, then, this certainty of re-acquaintance?

In a kind of daze, confused by the confluence of the real and the unreal, I walked a little further, and the perspective began to shift. Shadows and angles emerged to soften or delineate; defini-

*[In 'Recollections of the Arabian Nights', first published in *Poems, Chiefly Lyrical* (1830). *Ed.*]

tions hardened, elevations extended and attenuated. A dog barked, and I saw rooks wheeling and cawing about the towers and chimneys, and white doves fluttering. Between high enclosing walls was a fish-pond, dark and still, overlooked by two little pavilions of pale stone. As I drew nearer still, details of ordinary human activity began to emerge: planted things, a broom leaning against a wall, window-curtains moving in the warm breeze, smoke drifting up from a chimney stack, a water pail set down in a gateway.

We know, from the account of his life published in the *Saturday Review*, that Evenwood burst upon young Phoebus Daunt like Paul's vision. It seemed – they were his words – 'almost as if I had not lived before'.

I do not blame the boy Phoebus for feeling thus on encountering the beauty of Evenwood for the first time. No one with eyes to see, or a heart to feel, could be unmoved by the place. I, too, felt as he did when I first caught sight of its cupolas and battlements, rising up through the summer haze; and with greater familiarity came greater attachment, until, even in memory, Evenwood assumed such a power to enthral that it sometimes made me sick with a desire to spend my life within its bounds, and to possess it utterly.

If Phoebus Daunt truly experienced such an epiphany on his first coming upon Evenwood, then I freely absolve him. Remove it from the tally, with my blessing. But if he believed the words that he wrote in his public recollections, that Evenwood was 'an Eden made for me alone', he was culpably wrong.

It had been made for *me.*

MY TRAVELLING CHEST, CONTAINING MY CAMERA, TRIPOD, AND OTHER necessary equipment, had been placed on a trolley in a narrow yard leading off the entrance court. The footman who assisted me in the task, one John Hooper, was a pleasant, amenable fellow, and we chatted easily as he helped pull the trolley to the first location. In due course, I would have occasion to apply to him, discreetly, for information concerning certain matters connected with Evenwood, which he was happy to supply.

I had brought with me a dozen dark slides containing negatives prepared according to the process recently introduced by Monsieur Blanquart-Evrard.* For three hours I worked away, and was satisfied that Lord Tansor would be well pleased with the results.

I had just finished taking several views of the Orangery and was stepping through a little gate set in an ancient fragment of flint wall when I was brought up short by the sound of someone laughing. Before me was a broad sweep of close-cut grass on which four figures, two ladies, and two gentlemen, were engaged in a game of croquet.

I would not have been aware of his presence had he not laughed; but as soon as I heard that distinctive note, and the concluding snort, I knew it was him.

He seemed to have grown taller, and was broader in the shoulder than I remembered; and now he had a dark beard, which, with the silk handkerchief that he had tied round his head, gave him a distinctly piratical air. There he was, in the flesh: P. Rainsford Daunt, the celebrated poet, whose latest volume, *The Conquest of Peru*, had just been published, to great acclaim.

*[Louis Désiré Blanquart-Evrard (1802–72), a cloth-maker from Lille. He developed an improved version of the Calotype process that allowed paper negatives to be prepared in advance and developed hours or even days after exposure. The negatives also had greater sensitivity to light, and thus had shorter exposure times. In 1850 Blanquart-Evrard introduced the albumen paper print process, which became the primary print medium until gelatine paper became available in the 1890s. *Ed.*]

I stood spellbound. To see him here, leaning on his mallet, and to hear his voice paying gallant compliments to his partner, a strikingly tall young lady with dark hair, seemed to twist the knife into the wound that had been festering within me for so long. I considered for a moment whether I should make myself known to him; but then, looking down at my dusty boots, I noticed that I had a tear in the knee of my trousers where I had kneeled down on the gravel of the entrance court to adjust my tripod. Altogether I made a rather sorry sight, with my dirty hands and high colour, for it had been warm work, pulling the trolley from one location to the next. Daunt, by contrast, stood elegantly at his ease on the new-mown lawn, waistcoat shimmering in the sunlight, unaware of his former friend concealed in the shadow of a large laurel bush.

I confess that I could not help feeling envious of him, which gave the knife yet another little turn. He looked so assured, so settled in comfort. If I had known then the full extent of his good fortune, I might have been tempted into some rash deed. But, in my ignorance, I simply stood observing him, thinking of when we had last spoken together in School Yard, and wondering whether he still remembered what I had whispered to him. I doubted it. He looked like a man who slept well. It seemed almost a pity to disturb his peaceful slumbers; but one day my words would come back to him.

And then he would remember.

I REMAINED OUT OF SIGHT BEHIND THE LAUREL BUSH FOR A QUARTER of an hour or more, until Daunt and his companions picked up their mallets, and returned to a small shaded terrace, where tea had been laid out for them. He strolled back with the tall young lady, whilst the other two followed behind, chatting and laughing.

It was now a little before five o'clock, and so I returned to the entrance court. I was beginning to pack up my things when Mr Tredgold appeared on the steps.

'Edward, there you are. I trust you have had a productive afternoon? Very good. My business with his Lordship is concluded, but there is one more thing you might do before we leave.'

'Certainly. What is it?'

He gave a little cough.

'I have persuaded his Lordship that it would be a great thing, for his posterity, to have a photographic likeness of himself made. I urged him to consider what it would mean for his descendants to have an unmediated image of him as he really is, at this very time. I said it would be as if he lived again in their eyes. I hope it will not be too much trouble for you? His Lordship is waiting for us on the Library Terrace.'

The Library Terrace was on the west side of the house; Daunt and his friends were taking tea on the south. I quickly weighed up the risks of our meeting each other, and decided that they were small. Besides, the opportunity to study the man whom I believed to be my father was irresistible; and if Daunt did appear, I was confident that my recently acquired moustachios would prevent discovery.

'Not in the least,' I replied, as calmly as I could. 'I have two negatives left, and will be very glad to oblige his Lordship. If you will allow me a moment to gather up my things . . .'

When we arrived at the terrace, Lord Tansor was pacing up and down, the silver ferrule of his stick clattering on the stones, the sunlight glinting off his immaculate silk hat.

'Your Lordship,' said Mr Tredgold, advancing towards him. 'This is Mr Glapthorn.'

'Glapthorn. How d'ye do. You have all your instruments, cameras, and what not, I see. A travelling chest? Everything to hand, what? Very good. That's the way. Now then, let's get on.'

I began to set up my tripod as Lord Tansor continued to walk up and down, conversing with Mr Tredgold. But I found that I could not take my eyes off him.

Now in his fifty-ninth year, he was a smaller man than I had expected, but with a straight back and strong shoulders. I became immediately fascinated by his little mannerisms: the left hand placed behind him as he walked; the way he tilted his head back when he spoke; the gruff, staccato phrases and the barking interrogatives with which his speech was punctuated; the impatient tic in his left eye when Mr Tredgold directed some observation to him, as if his toleration were about to expire at any second.

Above all, my attention was held by the complete absence of either humour or vulnerability in the heavy-lidded, close-set eyes, and especially in the small, almost lipless mouth. I noticed the curious fact that one rarely saw Lord Tansor's teeth. His mouth appeared to be permanently fixed shut, even when he spoke, which naturally conveyed the impression that here was a man in whom disapproval and suspicion of his fellow human beings was instinctive and irreversible. Everything about him was tight, ordered, contained. There was so much concentrated potency and will in the way that he looked you up and down, and in the stance of purposeful readiness that he habitually adopted – shoulders pulled sharply back, feet slightly apart – that you quickly forgot the shortness of his stature. I have met many impressive men, but few have impressed me with the completeness of their self-possession, born of the long exercise of personal and political authority, as he did. I have strong arms and a strong body, and am a giant compared to him; but as he approached to ask whether all was ready, I could hardly look him in the eye.

Yet I believed he was my father! Could it be true? Or had I been deluding myself? Say that he *was* my father, standing next to me in the bright June sunshine, and seeing only a stranger busying himself with his camera and tripod. Would the day ever come when I would turn and face him as my true self?

The sun had moved westwards, and was now illuminating the far end of the terrace, beyond which was a raised pavement, with a half-glazed door set in the return. We stepped down to a gravel path, and Lord Tansor – grasping his stick firmly in his right hand, and holding his left arm straight to his side – positioned himself a foot or two in front of this pavement, with the door behind his left shoulder. Through the lens of my camera, each individual detail of his appearance increased in clarity and definition: his square-toed boots, brightly polished as always; the surmounting gaiters, grey like his trousers and waistcoat; his black four-button coat and black stock; his gleaming hat. He stood straight and still, tight-lipped, white side-whiskers trimmed to perfection, small black eyes gazing out over bright pleasure-grounds and sunlit parkland, and beyond to the distant prospect of farms and pasture, rivers and lakes, woods and quiet hamlets. Lord of all he surveyed. The 25th Baron Tansor.

My hands were shaking as I completed the exposure, but at last it was done. I was about to begin preparations to expose the last negative, but his Lordship informed me that he did not wish to detain me any longer. In a moment he had thanked me brusquely for my time, and was gone.

MR TREDGOLD AND I PASSED THE NIGHT IN PETERBOROUGH, RETURNING to London the next morning. We left Evenwood without catching further sight of Phoebus Daunt; but I could not rid myself of the fixed image that I now had of him: standing in the sun, laughing, gay and self-assured, without a care in the world.

We had both been too tired the previous evening to discuss the events of the day, and during the homeward journey, on the following morning, my employer seemed no more inclined to talk. He had settled himself into his seat immediately on boarding the train, and had taken out the latest number of *David Copperfield*,* with the deliberate air of someone who does not wish to be disturbed. But as we were approaching the London terminus, he looked up from his reading and regarded me inquisitively.

'Did you form a favourable impression of Evenwood, Edward?'

'Yes, extremely favourable. It is, as you said, a most ravishing place.'

'Ravishing. Yes. It is the word I always use to describe it. It transports one, does it not, almost forcibly, carrying one rapturously away, to another and better world. What it would be to live there! One would never wish to leave.'

'I suppose you have been there frequently,' I said, 'in the course of business.'

'Yes, on many occasions, though not so often now as formerly, when the first Lady Tansor was alive.'

'You knew Lady Tansor?' I heard myself asking the question somewhat eagerly.

'Oh yes,' said Mr Tredgold, looking out of the carriage window as we entered under the canopy of the terminus. 'I knew her well. And now, here we are. Home again.'

*[Dickens' novel was published in monthly parts from May 1849 to November 1850, and in book form in November 1850. Mr Tredgold would therefore have taken out the second number, for June. *Ed.*]

· IV ·

The Pursuit of Truth

I did not see Mr Tredgold again for several weeks. He left London the next day to visit his brother in Canterbury, and I was just then embarked on investigating a case of fraud, which obliged me to be out of the office a good deal. It was not until a month after we returned from Evenwood that I received an invitation to spend a Sunday with the Senior Partner.

We quickly resumed our old bibliological ways; but it appeared to me that there was not that unalloyed surrender by my employer to our shared enthusiasm for book-lore as before. He beamed; he polished his eye-glass; he brushed his feathery hair away from his face; and his hospitality was as warm as ever. But there was a change in him, detectable and troubling.

The negatives exposed at Evenwood had been developed, fixed, and printed, and all the views, with the exception of the portrait of Lord Tansor, had been mounted, at my own expense, in an elegant album, embossed with the Duport arms. The portrait, which I had mounted separately in a morocco case, would have been a fine piece of work, had it not been spoiled by the face of an inquisitive servant, whom I had failed to notice, peeping through the glazed door just behind where Lord Tansor had been standing. But Mr Tredgold complimented me on the work, and said that he would arrange for the album and the portrait to be sent to Evenwood.

'His Lordship will be happy to remunerate you,' he said, 'if you would care to let him have a note of your charges.'

'No, no,' I replied, 'I shall not hear of it. If his Lordship is satisfied with the results, then I am well rewarded.'

'You have a generous nature, Edward,' said Mr Tredgold, closing the album. 'To have worked so hard, and then to refuse reward.'

'I did not expect to be rewarded.'

'No, I'm sure you did not. It is my belief, however, that good deeds will always be rewarded, in this life or the next. This accords with another belief of mine, that what has been taken from us will one day be restored by a loving providence.'

'Those are comforting convictions.'

'I find them so. To believe otherwise, that goodness will receive no recompense in some better place, and that loss – real loss – is irreversible, would be the death of all hope for me.'

I had never before heard Mr Tredgold speak in so serious and reflective a manner. Nothing more was said for a moment or two, as he sat contemplating the portrait of Lord Tansor.

'You know, Edward,' he said at last, 'it seems to me that there is a kind of correspondence between these convictions of mine and the photographic process. Here you have captured and fixed a living person, permanently imprisoning light and form and all the outward individualities of that person. Perhaps the lineaments of our souls, and of our moral characters, are similarly imprinted on the mind of God, for His eternal contemplation.'

'Then woe to all sinners,' I said, smiling.

'But none of us is wholly bad, Edward.'

'Nor wholly good, either.'

'No,' he said slowly, still looking down at Lord Tansor's portrait, 'nor wholly good.' Then, more brightly: 'But what an age we live in – to have the power to seize the evanescent moment, and fix it on paper for all to see! It is quite extraordinary. Where will it all lead? And yet how one wishes that some earlier age had made these wonderful discoveries. Imagine looking upon the face of Cleopatra, or gazing into the eyes – the very eyes – of Shakespeare! To see things as they were, long ago, which we can now only dream of – that would be wonderful indeed, would it not? And not only to look upon the dead of ages past, but also upon those we have recently lost, whom we yearn to see in their living forms again, as those who come after us will now be able to see Lord Tansor when he is no more. Our friends who died before this great miracle was discovered can never now be rendered permanently visible to our eyes, in the full flower of their lives, as his Lordship has been rendered, here in this photographic portrait. They must live only in our imperfect and inconstant memories. Do you not find that affecting?'

He looked at me and, for a moment, I thought his eyes were moist with tears. But then he jumped up, and went over to his cabinet to retrieve some item that he wished to show me. We talked for another half-hour, when Mr Tredgold said that he had a slight headache, and begged me to excuse him.

As I was leaving, he asked me whether I had many friends in London.

'I can claim one good friend,' I replied, 'which I find sufficient for my needs. And then of course I have you, Mr Tredgold.'

'Do you think of me as a friend, then?'

'Most certainly.'

'Then, speaking as a friend, I hope you will always come to me, if you are in any difficulty. My door is always open to you, Edward. Always. You will not forget that, will you?'

Touched by his tone of genuine solicitation, I said that I would remember his words, and thanked him for his kindness.

'No need to thank me, Edward,' he said, beaming broadly. 'You are an extraordinary young man. I consider it a duty – a most pleasant duty – to offer you every assistance, whenever you may feel it needful. And, besides, as I told you when we first met, the ordinary I can leave to others; the *extra*ordinary I like to keep for myself.'

So my life proceeded for the next three years. On Mondays and Tuesdays I would be engaged on my work as Mr Tredgold's confidential assistant – sometimes in the office, but more frequently following some investigatory trail that might take me to every corner of London, and occasionally beyond. On Wednesdays, I took the pupils sent to me for instruction by Sir Ephraim Gadd, whilst on Thursdays and Fridays I resumed my duties at Tredgolds. I took my lunch at Dolly's, and my dinner at the London Restaurant, day in, day out.*

My free time, except for occasional Sunday visits to the Senior Partner's private residence, was devoted to a renewed study of my mother's papers. To facilitate the work, I had begun to acquaint myself with shorthand, using Mr Pitman's system,† which I used to make notes on each item or document. These were then indexed and arranged in a specially constructed set of small compartmentalized drawers, somewhat like an apothecary's chest. But in all the mass of paper through which I had wandered, like some primaeval discoverer on an unknown ocean, I could still find nothing to supplement or advance my original discovery. Time and Death had also done their work: Laura Tansor was no more, and could not now be cross-examined; and her companion, whom I had

*[Dolly's Chop-House, Queen's Head Passage, Paternoster Row. The London Restaurant was in Chancery Lane. *Ed.*]

†[Isaac Pitman's *Stenographic Sound-Hand* was first published in 1837. *Ed.*]

called Mother, had followed her into eternal silence. My work at Tredgolds, however, had made me wiser in the art of detection, and I now commenced on several new lines of enquiry.

Gradually, through surviving receipts and other documents, I began to trace my mother's movements during the summer of 1819, visiting several inns and hotels where she had stayed, and seeking out anyone in those places who might have remembered her. I met with no success until I was directed to an elderly man in Folkestone, who had been the Captain of the packet that had taken my mother and her friend to Boulogne, in August 1819. He distinctly remembered the two ladies – one, small of stature and of rather nervous appearance; the other, tall and dark, who 'bore herself like a queen', as he said, and who had paid him a substantial consideration so that she and her companion could spend the crossing undisturbed in his cabin.

I then travelled to the West Country, to make enquiries concerning Lady Tansor's family, the Fairmiles, of Langton Court, a handsome house of Elizabeth's reign situated a few miles from where my mother was born. In due course, I discovered a voluble old lady, Miss Sykes by name, who was able to tell me something concerning the former Laura Fairmile. Of particular interest to me was what she had to say about Miss Fairmile's aunt on her mother's side. This lady, Miss Harriet Gilman, had married the *ci-devant* Marquis de Québriac, who had resided in England, visibly impecunious, since the days of the Terror. After the Amiens Peace had been struck,* the couple returned to the Marquis' ancestral château, which stood a few miles outside the city of Rennes. But the gentleman died soon after, and the chateau was

*[The Peace of Amiens, 27 March 1802, between France and its allies, on the one hand, and Great Britain, on the other. It is generally seen as marking the end of the French Revolutionary Wars. *Ed.*]

placed in the hands of his creditors, leaving his widow to decamp to a small house in the city, in the Rue du Chapitre, belonging to her late husband's family. It was to this house that Lady Tansor and her companion later came.

At last the references in my mother's journals to 'Mme de Q' were satisfactorily explained, and so in September 1850, on the basis of this new intelligence, I travelled to France, having obtained permission from Mr Tredgold to take a short holiday.

The house in the Rue du Chapitre was boarded up, but I found an old priest at the Church of St-Sauveur who was able to tell me that Madame de Québriac had died some twenty years since. He also recalled the time when Madame's niece, accompanied by a friend, had resided with her for several months, and that a baby had been born, though he could not recall to which lady, or whether it had been a boy or a girl. The priest directed me to a Dr Pascal, who also lived in the Rue du Chapitre; but he, too, proved to be an old man, with few useful memories, and these added little to what the priest had already told me. The doctor did, however, inform me of an ancient retainer of Madame de Québriac's who was still living, he thought, just outside the city. I arrived at the place in high hopes, only to learn that the old man had died a few weeks earlier.

Interesting though they were, however, such little discoveries as I was able to make whilst in France served only to show me how far I was from my goal. All my efforts had increased my store of plausible inferences, hypotheses, and suggestive possibilities; but I was no closer to uncovering the independent proof that I required, which would confirm, beyond disputation, that I was Lord Tansor's lost heir, the son for whom he longed.

As for Phoebus Daunt, my endeavours to gather information on him, with the aim of conceiving some effective means of revenge, had been somewhat more successful, and were spurred on by the recent sight of him at Evenwood. Years had passed since my enforced departure from Eton, but my anger at his perfidy was undiminished. He had prospered; he had made his mark on the world, as I had once hoped to do; but *my* prospects had been blighted because of him. Perhaps I might have been a great figure at the University by now, with even greater distinctions in view. But all that had gone, stolen from me by his treachery.

SINCE MAKING THE ACQUAINTANCE OF DR T—, DURING MY EARLIER visit to Millhead, I had been regularly regaled with lengthy epistles from that brazenly indiscreet gentleman on the history of Dr Daunt and his family during their time in Lancashire. The information thus obtained was of only slight significance, though it served to show me how much influence the second Mrs Daunt had wielded, and perhaps wielded still, over her step-son.

Then, one day in Piccadilly, I happened to encounter an old school-fellow, who, over an expensive dinner at Grillon's,* which I could ill afford, was happy to supply me with some tittle-tattle concerning our mutual acquaintance. According to my informant, Daunt had lately enjoyed a little dalliance with a French ballet-dancer, and was rumoured to have proposed to Miss Eloise Dinever, the banking heiress, but had supposedly been refused. He dined at his club, the Athenaeum, of an evening when in London, kept a box at Her Majesty's,† and could be seen riding out in Rotten-row‡ on most Saturdays, between five and seven, during the Season. He had a good house, in Mecklenburgh-

*[A hotel in Albemarle Street. *Ed.*]

†[i.e. owned an opera-box at Her Majesty's Theatre in the Haymarket. *Ed.*]

‡[A roadway for saddle-horses on the south side of Hyde Park, crowded during the Season with the most fashionable riders. *Ed.*]

square, and was generally a figure in fashionable, as well as literary, society.

'But where does he get his money from?' I asked in surprise, knowing well the cost of maintaining such a life in London, and strongly suspecting that the writing of poetic epics would hardly keep him in dinners, let alone a box at the Opera.

'Bit of a mystery,' said my informant, lowering his voice. 'But there's plenty of it.'

Now, a mystery was exactly what I was looking for; it spoke to me of something concealed from public gaze that Daunt might not wish to be known – a secret which, once unlocked, could perhaps be used against him. It might prove to be nothing at all; but, where money is in the case, my experience always inclines me to adopt a sceptical view of things. Yet even with all the means at my disposal, having by now begun to accumulate quite a little army of agents and scouts about the capital, I failed to locate the source of Daunt's evident wealth.

Time went on, but no new information on Daunt came to light, and I had made no further progress in my search for the evidence that would prove my true identity. Weeks came and went; months passed, and slowly I began to sink into an enfeebling gloom that I could not shake off. This was a black time indeed. I was perpetually on edge, eaten up by frustrated rage. To ease my spirits, I passed long oblivious hours in Bluegate-fields, under the deft ministrations of Chi Ki, my customary opium-master. And then, night after night, I would wander the streets, taking my accustomed way from the West-end via London-bridge, along Thames-street, past the Tower, and so on to St Katharine's-dock and the fearful lanes and courts around and about the Ratcliffe-highway, in order to observe the underside of London in all its horror. It was on such excursions, pushing my way through dirty crowds of Lascars and Jews, Malays and Swedes, and every form of our British human scum, that I became truly acquainted with the character of our great metropolis, and learned to trust my ability to frequent its most deadly quarters with impunity.

Whilst I languished thus in my dull sublunary life, pulled hither and thither by my demons, the rise of Daunt's literary star had been ceaseless. The world, I concluded, had gone quite mad. I could hardly open a news-paper or a magazine without coming across some piece of eulogistic clap-trap extolling the genius of P. Rainsford Daunt. The volumes had flowed thick and fast from his prodigal pen, an unstoppable torrent of drivel in rhyming couplets and blank verse. In 1846 had come that ever-memorable monstrosity, *The Cave of Merlin*, in which the poet out-Southey-ed Southey at his most execrable, but which the *British Critic* unaccountably considered to be 'sublime in conception', averring that 'Mr Phoebus Daunt is without equal, a master of the poetic epic, the Virgil of the nineteenth century'. This production was followed, in tedious succession, by *The Pharaoh's Child* in 1848, then *Montezuma* in 1849, and, the following year, by *The Conquest of Peru*. With every publication, more inflated estimates of the poet's *oeuvre* would greet me as I idly perused *Blackwood's* or *Fraser's*, whilst paragraphs would rise up before my affronted eyes in *The Times*, informing his eager and adoring public that Mr Phoebus Daunt, 'the celebrated poet', was presently in town, and then proceeding to enumerate his doings in tedious detail. In this way, I learned that he had been to Gore House to sit to the pencil of the Count d'Orsay,* who also later modelled in plaster a fetching bust of the young genius. Naturally, his inclusion with other notables at the ceremonial opening of the Great Exhibition† had excited no

*[Count Alfred Guillaume Gabriel d'Orsay (1801–52), wit, dandy, and artist, who was a prominent member of Lady Blessington's social and artistic circle at Gore House. *Ed.*]

†[In May 1851. *Ed.*]

little interest amongst a certain impressionable section of society. I recall opening the *Illustrated London News* over breakfast in the spring of 1851 and being greeted by a preposterous engraving of the poet – dressed in dark *paletôt,* light trousers strapped under the instep, embroidered waistcoat, and stove-pipe hat – together with his noble patron, Lord Tansor, standing proudly with the Queen and the Prince Consort, beside the gilded cage containing the Koh-i-Noor diamond.*

With the rest of the world, I had also attended the Exhibition, drawn there by a desire to view the latest photographic advances. Accompanying me had been Rebecca Harrigan, Mr Tredgold's housekeeper, with whom I had struck up a kind of friendship. On more than one occasion, I had caught her looking at me in an interested way. She had a fine little figure, and was pretty enough; but, as I quickly discovered, after engaging her in a little conversation, she also possessed a sharp mind, and a pleasingly audacious spirit. I soon began to take quite a fancy to her.

One evening, in St Paul's Church-yard, I encountered her sheltering under the portico of the Cathedral from a shower of rain. We chatted inconsequentially until the rain began to ease, and then I asked her if she might care to take some dinner with me. 'If your husband wouldn't mind,' I added, believing that she and Mr Tredgold's manservant, Albert, were man and wife.

'Oh, 'e ain't my 'usband,' she said, looking at me as cool as you like.

'Not your husband?'

'Not 'im.'

'Then . . .'

'I'll tell you what Mr Glapthorn,' she butted in, giving me a

*[One of the many attractions of the Great Exhibition. The cage had been made by Messrs Chubb. *Ed.*]

quite delightfully sly little smile, 'you take me to dinner, and I'll come clean.'

She was respectably and soberly dressed in blue taffeta, with a matching stole and bonnet, an ensemble which, with her delicate little reticule, made her look like a vicar's daughter. So, after walking a little way, I hailed a hansom in Fleet-street and took her off to Limmer's,* where I asked the waiter to find a table for myself and my sister.

Over the course of the evening, Rebecca recounted something of her history. Her real name was Dickson. Orphaned at the age of nine, she had been obliged to fend for herself on the unforgiving streets of Bermondsey. But – like me – she was resourceful and had quickly found a protector, a noted cracksman,† for whom, as she said, she 'thieved like a good 'un' in return for food and a roof over her head. In due course, she graduated to whoring; but then, through the good offices of one of her customers, she succeeded in gaining a place in service, as a maid in the house of a Director of the East India Company. It was there that she had met Albert Harrigan, a servant in the same establishment. She and this Harrigan soon formed an attachment, even though her paramour (whose real name was Albert Parker) had an abandoned wife and child somewhere in Yorkshire. All went along nicely until their employer lost all his money in a failed railway speculation, and committed suicide. His legal adviser had been none other than Mr Christopher Tredgold, who happened just then to be in need of a manservant for his private residence. Harrigan was duly taken on, to be joined after a few weeks by his supposed wife. But their relationship had quickly soured, and now only convenience kept them together.

*[A respectable first-class hotel in Conduit Street. *Ed.*]
†[A burglar; safe-breaker. *Ed.*]

She told me all this – peppering her account with several anecdotes of questionable propriety – with all the gusto of a tavern raconteur; but as soon as the waiter arrived with each course, the wily little slut instantly assumed an expression of the most perfect demureness, smiling sweetly and turning the conversation, without once dropping her aitches, to some topic of unimpeachable dullness.

In the weeks following, Rebecca and I found occasion to promote our friendship, in ways that I am sure I do not need to describe. If Harrigan guessed how things lay between us, then it did not appear to trouble him. As for Rebecca, her good humour and healthy natural appetites, together with that optimistic artfulness that comes from having successfully made the most of a very bad lot, soon began to have a beneficial effect on me; and, as she had no wish to put a rope round my neck and lead me to the altar, we got on very well, meeting when the inclination took us, and pursuing our own interests whenever we wished.

This, then, was my life, from 1849 to 1853. And so things would perhaps have continued, but for two events.

The first occurred in March of the latter year. I found myself in St John's Wood, on Mr Tredgold's business, and had just turned into a pleasant tree-lined street when the name on the gate-piers of a large white-painted villa, half hidden behind a screen of shrubs, brought me up short. Blithe Lodge – where the beauteous Isabella Gallini had lived for the past four years – stood before me. I have already written of how I renewed my acquaintance with Bella and how, under the auspices of Mrs Kitty Daley, she became my mistress. Until the great events of the autumn of that same year broke upon me, I discovered that I was able to remain faithful to Bella, saving a few minor and quite meaningless indiscretions, which I confess here for honesty's sake. Rebecca, however, I did give up. She received the news with little emotion.

'Well,' she said, 'that don't matter. I've still got Albert, such as 'e is. An' I reckon we'll stay friends, you an' me. You're a chancer, Edward Glapthorn, for all you're a gennelmun, and so am I. An' that makes us equals in a way, don't it? Friends an' equals. So, gimme a kiss, and let's 'ear no more about it.'

The second event was of a very different character, and of far more moment.

It was the morning of the 12th of October 1853 – a date indelibly impressed on my memory. I was just leaving my room at Tredgolds, and was on the point of descending to the clerks' room, when I saw Jukes leap up from his desk at the sound of the front bell. I could not see who the visitor was, but in a moment Jukes was hurrying up the stairs towards me.

'Lord Tansor himself,' he whispered excitedly as he passed.

I leaned back against the wall and gazed down.

He was sitting bolt upright, both hands clasping his cane before him. The office, before his arrival, had been quietly going about its business, with just the usual rustle of papers and scraping of pens, and the occasional sound of subdued conversation between the clerks breaking the silence. But in his presence, the atmosphere seemed suddenly charged, somehow put on alert, and a blanket of strained silence instantly descended. All conversation ceased; the clerks moved about the room with concentrated deliberation, opening their drawers with the utmost care, or silently closing doors behind them. I watched this phenomenon closely, and observed that several of the clerks would look up from their work from time to time, and direct apprehensive glances over towards the seated figure, as if, sitting there tapping his foot impatiently as he waited for Jukes to return, he was about to weigh the feather of truth in the scales of justice against their sinful hearts.

In a few moments, Jukes hurried past me again, heading back

down the stairs to where the visitor sat. I stepped back into my room as his Lordship followed the clerk to the door of Mr Tredgold's private office. As Lord Tansor entered, I heard the Senior Partner's effusive welcome.

Jukes closed the office door and began to make his way back to his position.

'Lord Tansor,' he said again, seeing me as he came past my door. He stopped, and leaned his head towards me in a confidential manner. 'There are firms,' he said, 'that would give a great deal – a *very* great deal – to have such a client. But the SP keeps him tight with us. Oh yes, he's Tredgolds' as long as the SP is with us. A great man. One of the first men in the kingdom, you know, though who has heard of him? And he's ours.'

He delivered this little speech in a rapid whisper, looking back and forth to the door of Mr Tredgold's office as he did so. Then he nodded quickly, and scampered back down the stairs, scratching his head with one hand, and clicking his fingers with the other.

I walked back to my desk, leaving my door slightly ajar. At length, I heard the Senior Partner's door open, and the muffled sound of conversation as the two men passed along the passage to the head of the stairs.

'I'm obliged, Tredgold.'

'Not at all, your Lordship,' I heard Mr Tredgold reply. 'Your instructions in this matter are much appreciated, and shall be acted upon without delay.'

I sprang from my desk and went out into the passage.

'Oh, pardon me,' I said to the Senior Partner. 'I did not realize.'

Mr Tredgold beamed at me. Lord Tansor's face was expressionless at first, but then he began to regard me more closely.

'You seem familiar to me,' he barked.

'This is Mr Edward Glapthorn,' prompted Mr Tredgold. 'The photographer.'

'Ah, the photographer. Very good. Excellent work, Glapthorn. Excellent.' Then he turned to the Senior Partner, nodded his good-bye, and immediately descended the stairs with short rapid steps. In the next moment he was gone.

'I notice it is a fine day outside, Edward,' said Mr Tredgold, smiling radiantly. 'Perhaps you might like to join me for a little stroll in the Temple Gardens?'

· V ·

In the Temple Gardens

ONCE AWAY FROM THE OFFICE, AND HAVING ENTERED THE TEMPLE Gardens, Mr Tredgold began to outline, in his usual circuitous and abstract way, a 'little problem' with which he had been presented.

'Tell me, Edward,' he began, 'how extensive is your genealogical knowledge?'

'I have some slight acquaintance with the subject,' I replied.

'I find, my dear Edward, that you have some slight acquaintance with most subjects.'

He beamed, took out his red silk handkerchief, and proceeded to polish his eye-glass as we walked.

'Baronies by Writ, for instance. What can you tell me about them?'

'I believe that such dignities are so called because they describe the old practice of summoning men of distinction to sit in the King's Parliament by the issuing of a writ.'*

*[Baronies by Writ are, in fact, a legal fiction. As a result of decisions made in the House of Lords and elsewhere, between the early seventeenth century and the early nineteenth, a doctrine – now considered indefensible – grew up that, where a man had been directly summoned to attend one of a specific list of mediaeval parliaments, and there was evidence that he had done so, and that he was not the eldest son of a peer or another person also summoned to such a parliament, then he could be taken as thereby honoured with a barony, in the modern sense of a peerage. It was further construed (as Mr Tredgold rightly says) that such titles were heritable by heirs general of the first baron, though no mediaeval writ deals with the matter of succession, for the simple reason that they were not then conceived as creating an hereditary title of honour. However, by the mid-nineteenth century the legal doctrine of heritable Baronies by Writ held full sway. *Ed.*]

'Correct!' exclaimed Mr Tredgold. 'Now, by several statements of law laid down since Stuart times, these Baronies are held to be heritable by heirs general – that is to say, through females as well as males. The present Lord Tansor's peerage is just such a Barony. Perhaps,' he continued, 'it would be interesting to you, from an antiquarian point of view, to have a brief account of Lord Tansor's noble line?'

I said that nothing would give me greater pleasure, and begged him to proceed.

'Very well – pray stop me if any of this is familiar to you. In the reign of Henry III, Lord Maldwin Duport was a person of power and influence. Of Breton extraction, an ancestor having come over with the Conqueror, he was memorably described in one of the chronicles as "a man of iyrn and blud". A dangerous and belligerent man, we may perhaps assume, but one whose services were much in demand in those uncertain and violent times. He was a great landowner, already a baron by tenure, holding lands in Buckinghamshire, Bedfordshire, Warwickshire, and Northamptonshire, in addition to other properties in the North and the West Country.

'In December 1264, Maldwin was summoned to attend the rebel Parliament called by Simon de Montfort in the King's name – Henry himself, along with his son, Prince Edward, being then under lock and key following the Battle of Lewes. Maldwin was subsequently summoned to Parliament in 1283, 1290, and 1295, and his successors continued to be called into the next century and beyond. In the course of time, their constant presence in Parliament was interpreted as constituting a peerage dignity deriving from the 1264 Parliament, thus giving the Barony senior precedence, along with those of Despencer and de Ros, in the English peerage.

'The Lord Maldwin's principal estate, or *caput*, was the castle of Tansor, in Northamptonshire – a few miles to the south of the present Lord Tansor's seat of Evenwood – and so he was summoned to Parliament as *Malduino Portuensi de Tansor.* Of course the family has suffered many vicissitudes of fortune – especially during the Commonwealth; but the Duports have generally married judiciously, and by the time of George, the 22nd Baron, at the beginning of the last century, they had risen to that position of eminence and influence that they continue to enjoy.

'This position, however, is now under threat – at least, that is how the present Lord Tansor interprets matters. The absence of an heir – I mean of a lineal heir, whether male or female – has caused him great concern; and it is this lack, and the consequences that may flow from it, that he feels may signal a decline in the family's fortunes. His fear is that the title and property could pass to a branch of the family in which, to put things in his own terms, the qualities that have been so conspicuously demonstrated by successive generations of his ancestors are lacking. His Lordship has certainly been singularly unlucky. As you may know, the only son from his first marriage died when still a child, and his present union has so far been without issue.'

Mr Tredgold had taken out his handkerchief; but, rather than cleaning his eye-glass, he was using it instead to mop his forehead. I noticed that he had coloured a little, and so asked whether he would prefer to move out of the sun, which, though low in the sky, was unusually intense for the time of year.

'By no means,' he replied. 'I like to feel the light of heaven on my face. Now then, where was I? Yes. In a word, then, it appears that there is, at present, ahem, no male heir of the direct line, which raises the distinct possibility that the title will pass to a member of one of the collateral branches of the family, an outcome to which his Lordship is deeply opposed.'

'There are legitimate collateral claimants, then?' I asked.

'Oh yes,' said Mr Tredgold. 'His cousin and secretary, Mr Paul

Carteret,* and, in due course, Mr Carteret's daughter. But, as I say, his Lordship's aversion to collateral succession is – well, entrenched and immovable. It is perhaps irrational, because the Barony has reverted to collateral relatives on a number of occasions in its history, but there it is. Come, I am a little tired of walking. Let us sit.'

Taking my arm, Mr Tredgold drew me to a bench in the corner of the Gardens.

'There may yet, of course, be time for a satisfactory outcome to Lord Tansor's predicament in the normal course of events, as it were. His physician considers it possible that her Ladyship might still be capable of conceiving an heir. I believe these things have been known. But his Lordship is not prepared to put his trust in Nature, and, after considering the matter carefully for several years, has finally come to a decision. He has wisely rejected divorce, against which I strongly advised, there being no grounds other than the lack of an heir, and it would go hard on his Lordship's standing and reputation to behave like some Eastern potentate and take such a step. He understands this, and so has taken an alternative course.'

Pausing once again, he looked up at the radiant blue of the sky through the branches of the tree under which we were seated, and shielded his eyes with his hand against the sun.

'An alternative course?'

'Indeed. A somewhat unusual one. The adoption of an heir of his own choosing.'

I CANNOT DESCRIBE WHAT I FELT ON HEARING THESE WORDS. AN HEIR of his own choosing? But *I* was Lord Tansor's heir! Struggling hard

*[The younger son of Sophia Mary Carteret, *née* Duport (1765–1836), Lord Tansor's aunt. *Ed.*]

to maintain some appearance of composure, I began to experience the most peculiar sensation, as if I were falling through great darkness into infinite space.

'Are you well, Edward? You look a little pale.'

'Perfectly well, thank you,' I replied. 'Please go on.'

But I was far from being perfectly well. I thought my heart would burst from my chest, so assailed was I by panic at this entirely unexpected turn of events. Then I began to see that this was not the end of all my hopes; whatever such a course might mean in practice, I would still be able to claim my rightful place in the succession, if I could discover corroborative proof of my identity. All was not lost. Not just yet.

'The firm,' Mr Tredgold was saying, 'has been charged with the task of modifying the provisions of Lord Tansor's will, by the addition of a codicil. The baronial title, of course, is a separate matter; it must go whither the law dictates, to the next heir in line of succession, whether direct or collateral; which of course means that Mr Paul Carteret, through his Duport mother, may, as things presently stand, become the 26th Baron Tansor. I hope I am not being too abstruse?'

'Not at all.'

'Good. I wish you to be aware of the situation, as it pertains to his Lordship's present intentions. You do understand, don't you, Edward?'

It was such a curious question that I did not well know how to answer, but simply nodded mutely.

'Good again. The title, then, is not in Lord Tansor's gift. But what his Lordship possesses materially – including Evenwood, the greatest and noblest of all his possessions – is his to bestow, subject to certain legal procedures, on whomsoever he wishes – as is, in a specific sense, the Duport name. He has therefore taken a decision of great consequence. He has separated the baronial dignity, conferred by the writ that summoned Lord Maldwin Duport to Parliament in 1264, from the material interests that the family has subsequently garnered to itself, resolving that the future title-holder will inherit little but the dignity. His Lordship desires that all the entailed property that he himself inherited, as well as those possessions specifically bequeathed to him by his father, should be left to his nominated heir.'

'And has Lord Tansor made his nomination?'

'He has.'

Mr Tredgold paused. His china-blue eyes met mine.

'It is to be Mr Phoebus Rainsford Daunt, the poet. You may have seen the reviews of his new volume.* It has, I believe, been very well received.'

A TERRIBLE HELPLESSNESS BEGAN TO GRIP ME, SUCH AS THOSE MUST feel who see their doom approaching, but are powerless to resist it. This moment I shall always count as one of the most significant of my life; for now I became absolutely convinced that I had been driven forwards, and was still being driven, by a fatality from which I could never escape. In his recollections of how we had first met, in School Yard at Eton, Daunt had likened me to some messenger of Fate, as if he knew, as I now did, that our destinies were inextricably entwined. Had the consequences of his youthful treachery been merely the precursor of this greater loss, of which he had been made the agent? This terrible possibility was like a knife of ice to my heart. But, once again, I was saved from despair by the thought that neither of us could know the end towards which we were being impelled. Who was fated to receive the final prize? The true heir, or the false? Until that question could be answered

*[*Penelope: A Tragedy, in Verse* (Bell & Daldy, 1853). *Ed.*]

beyond all doubt, I must continue to hope and believe that I would come at last into the life that I had been born to live. Yet I remained mesmerized by the bitter humour of it all, and could not suppress a mirthless smile.

'Is something amusing you, Edward?' asked Mr Tredgold.

'By no means,' I replied, quickly assuming an expression of concern, which indeed I did not need to manufacture.

'As I was saying, Lord Tansor intends, by breaking the entail, that Mr Daunt will succeed to the possession of Evenwood, and of all the other property that his Lordship inherited from his father, on condition of Mr Daunt's assuming the Duport name and arms on his Lordship's death.'

'And is it in Lord Tansor's power to do all this?'

'Assuredly. The property he inherited from his father is his to dispose of as he wishes. It will be be necessary for his Lordship to sign a deed of recovery for the entailed property, and to enrol it in Chancery, before he can bequeath this portion of his inheritance to Mr Daunt; but this is a relatively straightforward procedure, and is, indeed, already in hand.'*

THE AIR HAD TAKEN ON A SLIGHT CHILL AS THE MID-AFTERNOON SUN began to wane.

We had been nearly an hour in the Gardens – an hour that had changed my life for ever.

'Mr Phoebus Daunt's prospects are rosy indeed,' I said, as care-

*[This process would have 'barred', or rendered ineffective, the entailed property – i.e. the oldest part of the Tansor inheritance, which included Evenwood and the other principal estates that had been settled 'in tail general' on all heirs inheriting the title of Baron Tansor. As entailed property, it could not in the normal way be disposed of by any one possessor as absolute owner; but by breaking the entail, Lord Tansor would be free to bequeath this property to his nominated heir. *Ed.*]

lessly as I could, though I was burning inside. 'A most fortunate young man. Already a distinguished poet, and with expectations before too long of succeeding to Lord Tansor's wealth and possessions, and to Evenwood itself.'

'Expectations, yes,' said Mr Tredgold, 'though one might perhaps wish to qualify them. *Pro tempore*, and until the codicil is executed, Mr Daunt remains the prospective heir of his Lordship's property. But Lord Tansor is fit and robust, his present union may yet be productive of a child; and of course the birth of an heir of the blood, unlikely though that is, would change everything, and would then bring about a revocation of the proposed provisions. Besides, who knows what the future may hold? Nothing is certain.'

For a moment or two we sat looking at each other in awkward silence. Then he stood up and smiled.

'But you are right, of course. As things presently stand, you may certainly say that Mr Phoebus Daunt is a most fortunate young man. He has already received ample demonstrations of Lord Tansor's regard for him, and soon he is to be formally anointed, if I may so put it, as his Lordship's legal heir. When the day comes, Mr Phoebus Daunt, or should I say Mr Phoebus Duport, though he will not be the 26th Baron Tansor, will be a very powerful man indeed.'

We left the Gardens, and began to make our way back to Paternoster-row.

'Forgive me, Mr Tredgold,' I said, after we had walked some way in silence, 'I am unclear as to what part in the proceedings that you have outlined you expect me to play. This is a legal matter, but I am no lawyer. The case is far removed from the Abode of Beauty. '

Mr Tredgold smiled at the reference to my first success for the firm.

'Indeed it is,' he said, taking my arm. 'Well, Edward, here it is.

There is what I may call an additional element, of which Lord Tansor is as yet unaware, and which must remain strictly confidential for the time being. I have received a communication – a private communication – from his Lordship's secretary, Mr Paul Carteret. The circumstances whereby he has come to be employed by his relative are interesting, but need not concern us now. It appears that Mr Carteret – whom I have known and liked for many years – has been troubled for some time by a little discovery that he has made. He has not seen fit to vouchsafe its full nature to me, but his letter appears to suggest that it has a direct and fundamental bearing on the matters that we have just been discussing. In short, Mr Carteret seems to raise the possibility, if my inference is correct, that, unknown to his Lordship, a legitimate and direct heir of the blood exists. This, then, is the little problem that I would like your assistance in resolving. And now, I think I should like some tea. Will you join me?'

THE CLOCK ON LE GRICE'S MANTELPIECE STRUCK THREE O'CLOCK.

He had said nothing after I had finished telling him of my conversation with Mr Tredgold in the Temple Gardens. Behind him, in the shadows, towered a portrait of his father, Brigadier-General Sir Hastings Le Grice, of the 22nd Foot, who famously distinguished himself with Napier at the Battle of Meeanee.* Stretched out below, his long legs resting on the brass fender, the general's

*[The Battle of Meeanee (or Miani), a few miles north of Hyderabad in present-day Pakistan, was fought on 17 February 1843, during the Sind War of that year. A British force of under three thousand men, commanded by Sir Charles Napier (1782–1853), defeated the emirs of Sind, whose army numbered over twenty thousand. Sind was subsequently annexed by Britain. *Ed.*]

son sat gazing at the ceiling, ruminatively twirling the end of his moustache.

'This is a tangled tale, G,' he said at last, grasping a poker and leaning forward to stir the dying embers of the fire, ' so let me see if I've got things straight. Old Tansor has taken it into his head to leave everything to Daunt, except his title, which isn't his to give. You believe you're Tansor's heir, but can't prove it. Now this chap Carteret has come along with a little secret to impart, which may, or may not, have a bearing on the case. So far, so good. But, look here: it's all very well, you know, to make Daunt pay for what he did to you at school. It's a long time to bear a grudge, but that's your business, and I can't say I mightn't have felt the same myself. But, hang it, G, you can't blame Daunt if old Tansor has taken a fancy to him. It's rum that it should be Daunt, I'll grant; dashed bad luck actually, but . . .'

'Luck?' I cried. 'Not luck, not chance, not coincidence! Can't you see? There's a fatality at work here, between him and me. It had to be Daunt! It could have been no one else. And there's worse to come. Much worse.'

'Well, then,' said Le Grice, calmly, 'you'd better push on, as quickly as you can, and tell me the rest. The regiment leaves in three weeks, and if I'm to perish valiantly for Queen and Country, then I must know that all's well with you before I go. So, speed on, Great King, and let's hear all about Carteret and his mysterious discovery.'

He refilled his glass and leaned back in his chair once more, whilst I, taking my cue, lit another cigar, and began to tell him of Mr Carteret's letter, in which, though I did not yet know it, the seeds of an even greater betrayal had been sown.

Part the Third

Into the Shadow

October 1853

I will take heed both of a speedy friend,
and a slow enemy.

—Owen Felltham, *Resolves* (1623),
iii, 'A Friend and Enemy, When Most Dangerous'

· 19 ·

*Fide, sed cui vide**

Back in my rooms, after the discussion with Mr Tredgold in the Temple Gardens, I considered the new prospect that now lay before me.

My position had appeared fatally threatened by the revelation that Lord Tansor had determined to make Daunt his heir; but now Mr Tredgold seemed to offer the startling possibility of a resolution in my favour, if his inference concerning Mr Carteret's discovery was correct. Did Lord Tansor's secretary indeed possess the proof that I needed?

This is the letter that Mr Tredgold had received, and which he had given to me when we parted with the words, 'Read this, Edward, and tell me what you think should be done.'

The Dower House, Evenwood Park
Evenwood, Northamptonshire

Wednesday, 5th October 1853

My Dear Tredgold, —

I write to you in a strictly private & confidential *capacity, in the full knowledge that your own rectitude & respect for my position here will ensure that no word or hint of this communication will be given to any third party, especially to my employer. We have had many occasions to cor-*

*['Trust, but be careful in whom'. *Ed.*]

respond over the years in a professional capacity, and it has been my pleasure also to welcome you to Evenwood as a much esteemed guest – and friend. I therefore hope and believe that the sincerity of my regard for you will be more than sufficient to bind you to this undertaking.

What I wish to say to you, most urgently, cannot be set down in writing but must be conveyed to you in person, for it goes to the heart of the present matter. *I am aware – acutely aware – that my position is a delicate one, since my own interests are involved. But you will know that I speak God's truth when I say that I have always had the sincerest desire to serve my employer to the best of my ability, regardless of my personal interests.*

I have been troubled for some little time by a matter that has presented itself to me, quite unexpectedly, in the course of my work here, relating to the question that is of most concern to my employer, and which he is now seeking to resolve by the means of which we are both aware. The consequences are momentous for his Lordship, and have their origins in the actions of a certain person, now deceased, for whom you and I once cherished an exceptional regard. But I cannot say more in writing.

I am unable to come up to town for some weeks, and so you would oblige me greatly if you could suggest some arrangement for us to meet in the country in private. *I would not wish to anticipate any plan you may have, beyond saying that I usually find myself in Stamford of a Tuesday morning, & that I also find the tap-room of the George Hotel a convenient place to take some refreshment at around midday.*

I cannot impress upon you enough the need for absolute discretion.

Please direct reply via Post-office, Peterborough.

I have the honour to be,
Yours very sincerely,
P. Carteret.

The next morning, Mr Tredgold and I laid our plans. Feeling that he could not risk undertaking such a clandestine meeting himself, he suggested that I might go to meet Mr Carteret in his stead. To this I readily agreed, and so he replied immediately requesting Mr Carteret's permission to send a trusted agent. Two days later a letter came back. The secretary was unwilling to sanction such an arrangement, saying that he would speak only to Mr Tredgold in person. But a further exchange of letters produced a slight softening in his attitude, and it was arranged that I, as Mr Tredgold's surrogate, should travel to Stamford to meet Mr Carteret the following Tuesday, the 25th of October, though I decided I would go a day earlier and settle myself in the George Hotel in readiness.

The day prior to my departure happening to be a Sunday, Mr Tredgold invited me to spend the afternoon with him in his private residence.

'I think perhaps we should forgo our usual bibliological entertainment,' he said after we had taken our lunch and were sitting before the fire in his sitting-room, 'and speak a little about the matter of Mr Carteret – if you do not mind?'

'Of course. I am entirely at your disposal.'

'As you always are, Edward,' he beamed. 'Well, then, no doubt you find Mr Carteret's letter puzzling enough – as I do also – with respect to the matter he wishes to disclose. It may be that Mr Carteret exaggerates the importance of what he has discovered; but I suspect, knowing him to be a gentleman of careful judgment, that he would not have written to me in this way unless it was of the greatest possible moment. Whether Mr Carteret will choose to reveal the matter to you in person, I cannot say. Whatever happens, I hope you will be kind enough to keep me closely informed. I'm sure I do not need to impress on you the necessity for absolute discretion.'

'I understand completely.'

'That is one of your most valuable qualities, Edward,' said Mr

Tredgold. 'You instinctively understand what is required in any given situation. Is there anything else I can tell you?'

'Mr Carteret, you have said, is Lord Tansor's cousin.'

'That is correct. He is the younger son of his Lordship's late aunt. His father, Mr Paul Carteret Senior, fell into pecuniary difficulties, leaving his two sons with no alternative but to earn a living. Mr Lawrence Carteret, now deceased, entered the diplomatic service; Mr Paul Carteret Junior was offered employment by his noble relative.'

'A generous gesture,' I observed.

'Generous? Yes, you may say that, although the offer was perhaps made more out of duty towards Mrs Sophia Carteret, his Lordship's aunt.'

'You also mentioned, I think, during our talk in the Gardens, that Mr Carteret will inherit the Tansor title.'

'He will – assuming of course that his Lordship's position regarding an heir of his own remains as it is at present.'

Mr Tredgold took out his red handkerchief and began to polish his eye-glass.

'You should be aware,' he continued, 'that Lord Tansor's resolve to bequeath the major portion of his property to Mr Phoebus Daunt has been strengthened by a history of ill-feeling between the two branches of the family. A financial disagreement between Lord Tansor's father and Mr Paul Carteret Senior has, alas, coloured his Lordship's relationship with his cousin. The Carteret line, in his opinion, is also tainted by mental impairment.'

He lowered his voice and leaned towards me.

'Mr Carteret Senior's mother died insane, though there is not the slightest indication that his son has inherited the malady. Indeed, Mr Carteret Junior is one of the sanest men I know; and his daughter, too, is decidedly free of any imputation of mental feebleness, being a fiercely intelligent and capable young woman – and a beautiful one, too. Lord Tansor, however, is prey to an acute sensitivity on this subject, deriving, I believe, from the fact that his Lordship's elder brother, Vortigern Duport, died of an epileptic seizure. More tea?'

We sipped silently, Mr Tredgold appearing to take keen interest in an area of the ceiling just above my head.

'Do you wish me to say something about Mr Phoebus Daunt?' he suddenly asked.

'Mr Daunt?'

'Yes. To better understand the circumstances that have led to the present situation.'

'By all means.'

Whereupon Mr Tredgold began to give me a full and detailed account of how Dr Daunt and his family had come to Evenwood as a result of his second wife's connexion with Lord Tansor, and of how the Rector's son had been taken into his Lordship's favour through his step-mother's influence – much of what he told me has been incorporated into an earlier section of this narrative.

'It cannot be denied,' Mr Tredgold was saying, 'that the young man is highly gifted. His literary genius is well known, and Lord Tansor takes pleasure in it as far as it goes. But he has also displayed a rather extraordinary talent for business, which is much more to his Lordship's taste. I think it is certain that this has played no little part in Lord Tansor's wish to see him succeed to his property, in preference to Mr Carteret and his successors.'

Now this was a completely new, and unexpected, view of my enemy, of which I was eager to hear more. According to Mr Tredgold, Daunt had been given two hundred pounds by Lord Tansor on his twenty-first birthday. Not six months later, the young man had requested an interview with his patron, at which he confessed, with a solemn face, that he had committed the whole sum to a railway speculation recommended to him by an old college acquaintance.

Lord Tansor was not pleased. He had expected better. A foolhardy railway speculation! Why, better that the boy had lost it all on the tables at Crockford's* – after all, a few salutary sacrifices to the goddess of chance were to be expected of gilded youth (not that *he* had ever been so irresponsible). But this straight-faced confession was merely in the nature of a calculated *lever de rideau*;† for, seeing Lord Tansor's face darken with disapproval, Daunt, no doubt grinning in self-satisfaction, then proudly announced that the speculation had been sound, and that it had paid out a handsome profit, which he had now realized; his original investment, it seemed, had all but doubled.

Lord Tansor, though gratified to hear this, was nonetheless inclined to think that the lad had been prodigiously lucky. Imagine his surprise, therefore, when, at a further interview some months later, he learned that the profit from the first venture had been invested in a second, with similar satisfactory results. He began to think that the boy might have a nose for these things – he had known such people; and, in the course of time, after further demonstrations of Daunt's financial instincts, he decided to place some of his own money into the young man's hands. No doubt he awaited the outcome with not a little anxiety.

But he was not disappointed. His investment was returned to him within three months, together with a substantial profit. There was, as Mr Tredgold had suggested, no better way for Daunt to have recommended himself to Lord Tansor. Reading the many laudatory reviews of his work was one thing; but this new talent

*[The celebrated gambling house in St James's. *Ed.*]

†[A curtain-raiser. *Ed.*]

was of a different order altogether. It impressed Lord Tansor, the consummate man of affairs, as no number of blank-verse epics could have done. Gradually, and with due diligence, his Lordship began to delegate little matters of business to Daunt, until, by the time of which I now write, his *protégé* had his fingers in a number of exceedingly large Duport pies.

I made the observation that Mr Phoebus Daunt must now be a man of some means.

'It would appear so,' Mr Tredgold replied guardedly. 'However, he has received nothing from Lord Tansor, as far as I know, other than the two hundred pounds that I have mentioned; nor, I think, has Dr Daunt contributed to his son's upkeep. Whatever he has made of that principal sum, by way of speculation and investment, must have supported him in the life that he presently leads.'

I thought to myself that he must be a genius indeed, to make such a sum go so far.

'Mr Phoebus Daunt is away from Evenwood at present,' said Mr Tredgold, brushing a speck from his lapel. 'He is in the West Country, inspecting a property recently acquired by Lord Tansor. But there will be other opportunities, I am sure, for you to make his acquaintance. And so, Edward, I think I have said all I intended to say, and now I wish you *bon voyage*. I shall await your report, whether written or in person, with the greatest interest.'

We shook hands, and I turned to go; but as I did so, I felt Mr Tredgold's hand on my shoulder.

'Take care, Edward,' he said quietly.

I had expected to see his usual beaming smile. But it was not there.

THAT EVENING I WENT TO BLITHE LODGE. BELLA WAS IN CAPTIVATING mood, and I was utterly charmed by her, as we sat by the fire in

Kitty Daley's private sitting-room, talking of this and that, and laughing at tid-bits of Academy gossip.

'You are such a dear,' I said, feeling a sudden uprush of affection for her as she sat in the firelight, gazing dreamily into the flames.

'Am I?' she asked, smiling. Then she leaned forward, cupping my face between her long fingers so that I felt the gentle impress of her rings on my skin, and kissing me tenderly.

'An absolute, utter, and complete dear.'

'You are quite sentimental tonight,' she said, stroking my hair. 'It is very pleasant. I hope you don't have a guilty conscience.'

'Why should I have a guilty conscience?'

'You ask me that!' she laughed. 'Every man who comes here has one, whether they admit it or not. Why shouldn't you?'

'That is rather hard, when all I wished to do was to pay you a compliment.'

'Men are such martyrs,' she said, giving my nose a mischievous little tweak. Then she sat down at my feet, placed her head on my lap, and gazed into the fire once again. Outside, the rain began to lash against the front windows of the house.

'Isn't it delicious,' she said, looking up, 'to hear the rain and the wind, while we are so snug and safe?' Then, resting her head on my lap once again, she whispered: 'Will I always be dear to you, Mr Edward Glapthorn?'

I bent down and kissed her perfumed hair.

'Always.'

THE FOLLOWING AFTERNOON, THE 24TH OF OCTOBER, 1853, A YEAR TO the very day before my chance meeting with Lucas Trendle, I took an express train northwards to Stamford, arriving at the George Hotel just before dark.

I awoke the next morning to find that the day had broken grey, wet, and cold. As it was market day, the town was full of local farmers and labourers; and by noon, the hotel was overflowing with a noisy bustling herd of muddy-booted, red-cheeked gentlemen, all eager to partake of the establishment's amenities.

In the tap-room, thick clouds of pungent pipe smoke mingled with the appetizing aromas of roast meats and strong ale. The press of burly country bodies, and waiters rushing hither and thither, made it impossible at first to make out whether anyone there appeared to be waiting for me. After a few moments, however, a space in the *mêlée* cleared temporarily and I saw a man, seated on a settle in front of the window that looked out onto the long cobbled yard round which the hotel was built. He was occupied in reading a news-paper, from the perusal of which he occasionally looked about him with a slightly anxious air. I knew immediately that it was Mr Paul Carteret.

In appearance, he was a series of rounds. A round face, from which sprouted a closely clipped black-and-silver beard, like a well-kept lawn; large round eyes behind round spectacles; round ears, a perfectly round button nose above a cherubic round mouth, all set upon a small round body – not corpulent, simply round. You instantly saw a natural disposition towards goodness, his roundness seeming appropriately indicative of a corresponding completeness of character: that enviable, unaffected integration of feeling and temperament in which there is excess neither of preening self-regard, nor impatience with the failings of others.

'Have I the honour of addressing Mr Paul Carteret?'

He looked up from his paper and smiled.

'Mr Edward Glapthorn, I think. Yes. Mr Glapthorn it is, I am sure. I am very pleased to meet you, sir.'

He rose from his seat, though his lack of height still caused him to look up at me as he did so, and held out his hand, with which he gripped mine with remarkable firmness. He then called over a waiter, and we commenced on some pleasant preliminaries before, at last, he looked hard at me and said:

'It is rather close in here, Mr Glapthorn. Shall we walk?'

WE LEFT THE DIN AND SMOKE OF THE TAP-ROOM AND PROCEEDED OVER the Town Bridge and up towards the soaring spire of St Mary's Church, which looked back from atop its little hill towards the River Welland. Mr Carteret set a brisk pace, turning round every now and again as if he expected to see someone following close behind. We had not gone far when it began to rain hard again. He clapped me on the shoulder and hurried me up the remaining part of the hill.

'Here,' he said.

Quickly ascending a short but steep flight of steps, we ran through a cramped little graveyard into the porch of the church, to take shelter from the rapidly intensifying downpour.

Seating himself on one of the rough stone benches hewn out of the inside walls on either side, he signalled to me to take my place opposite. The floor of the porch was still muddied over following a recent interment – the newly filled grave was just within my view beyond the porch opening – and our shelter was lit by two Gothic windows; but they were unglazed and the rain, blown in by strong gusts of wind, soon began to pound against the back of my coat. Mr Carteret, however, seemed not to notice the discomfort, and sat smiling at me, his round hands gripping his parted knees, and looking as settled and comfortable as if he had been sitting before a blazing fire.

'May I ask, Mr Glapthorn,' he began, leaning forward a little across the wet and muddy flagstones, 'how my letter was received in Paternoster-row?'

'Mr Tredgold was, of course, concerned by its implications.'

He did not reply immediately, and I noticed for the first time a look of weariness in his large round eyes, which regarded me intently from behind his thick round spectacles.

'You come here, Mr Glapthorn, as I understand, with the full authority and confidence of Mr Christopher Tredgold, whom I have had the pleasure of knowing these many years past. I am perfectly happy, as a consequence, to put my complete trust in Mr Tredgold's choice of a surrogate.'

I said that I appreciated his sentiments, and assured him that I had been charged with no other task than to listen, note, and report back to my principal. He nodded approvingly, but said nothing; and so we sat in silence for some moments.

'Your letter mentioned a discovery,' I ventured at last.

'A discovery? Yes, certainly.'

'I am at your service, sir, should you wish to inform me further concerning its nature.' I took out my note-book and a pencil, and regarded him expectantly.

Very well,' he said, whereupon he leaned back a little and began to tell me something of his history.

'I WAS FIRST EMPLOYED,' HE SAID, 'BY MY COUSIN, LORD TANSOR, AS his confidential private secretary over thirty years ago. My dear and much-lamented mother was alive then, but my father had recently died. A good man, but I fear an irresponsible one, like his father before him. He left us with debt and discredit, the consequences of foolish and reckless investments in concerns about which he knew nothing.

'After my father's death, Lord Tansor was kind enough to allow my late wife and me, together with my mother, to take up residence with his step-mother in the Dower House at Evenwood, which he refurbished at his own expense. He also offered me employment as his secretary.

'For my cousin's treatment of me, when my brother and I were left almost destitute, I shall always feel the deepest gratitude. While I live as his employee, I intend to serve him as well as I can, with no other end in view than to earn my salary to the best of my ability.

'Mr Tredgold will, I'm sure, have told you that Lord Tansor has no heir. His only son, Henry Hereward, died when still quite a boy, not long after his seventh birthday. The shock to my cousin was beyond words, for he loved the child to excess. The loss of his son was terrible enough; the loss of his only direct heir compounded his grief dreadfully.

'The continuation of his line has been the dominant – I may say the animating – principle of my cousin's life. Nothing else matters to him. He had received much from his father, who had received much from *his* father before him; and Lord Tansor intended that his son should receive much from him, in a cycle of giving and receiving, the maintenance of which he held to be a trust and duty of the highest order.

'But when that cycle was broken – when the golden chain was snapped, so to speak – the effect on him was almost catastrophic, and for several weeks after the death of Henry Hereward he locked himself away, refusing to see anyone, hardly eating, and coming out only at night to wander the rooms and corridors of Evenwood like some tormented spirit.

'Gradually, he recovered himself. His dear son was gone, but time, he realized, was still on his side and could yet furnish him with an heir, for he was only then in his thirty-ninth year.

'This, I'm sure, will all be familiar to you, Mr Glapthorn, but you must hear it all again from me for this reason. I do not look upon his Lordship as most people do, who see him as cold and aloof, concerned only with his own affairs. I know he has a heart, a feeling heart, a generous heart even, though it has only been revealed *in extremis*. It is there, nonetheless.'

I LET HIM TALK ON, AND STILL THE RAIN CAME DOWN.

By-and-by he said: 'It does not improve, and we are getting a little wet here. Let us walk in.' So we stood up and moved towards the great black studded door of the church, only to find it was shut fast.

'Oh well,' he sighed, 'we must stay where we are.'

'A metaphor of Fate, perhaps,' said I.

He smiled as he took his seat again, this time tucking himself tightly into the corner of the porch away from the window, beneath an already blackening memorial tablet erected to Thomas Stevenson and his wife Margaret, deceased three months apart (also their daughter Margaret, *ob.* 1827, *aet.* 17).

'I knew Tom Stevenson,' he said, observing me looking up at the memorial. 'His poor daughter drowned, down by the bridge there.'

He was silent for a moment.

'I shared Lord Tansor's sorrow, you see, for our first-born child had been taken from us the year before poor Henry Hereward. Drowned, if you will believe it, like Tom Stevenson's girl, but in the Evenbrook, which runs through Evenwood Park. She was walking along the top of the carriage-road bridge, in the way that children love to do. Her nursemaid had turned back to retrieve something she had dropped. All over in a moment. Six years old. Just six.' He sighed, and leaned his round head back against the cold stone. 'The ever-flowing stream that took her has gone to its own unknown ends. But the heart's lacerations, Mr Glapthorn: they remain.'

He gave another deep sigh, and then continued.

'The death of a child, Mr Glapthorn, is the saddest thing. Tom Stevenson was mercifully spared knowledge of his poor daughter's fate – he predeceased her, as you see from the dates. But it was not given to Lord Tansor to be so spared, nor to me. We both suffered the keenest pangs of grief and loss. Prince or pauper, all of us must endure such trials alone. In this, Lord Tansor was – is – no different to you or I, or to any other human soul. He occupies a privileged station in life, but there are burdens, too, mighty ones. But I expect that you are not persuaded. Perhaps you perceive the servility of the old retainer in me?'

I said that I was very far from possessing the natural temperament of the *sans culotte*,* and that I was quite happy for Lord Tansor to enjoy what had been given to him by a kind Fate.

'Well, we can agree on that,' said Mr Carteret, smiling. 'These are democratic and progressive times, I know – my daughter constantly tells me so.' He sighed. 'Lord Tansor does not see it – I mean the inevitability of it all, that it *will* all end one day, which is perhaps not too far distant. He believes in a perpetual, self-sustaining order. It is not hubris, you know, but a kind of tragic innocence.'

And then he apologized for inflicting what he called his usual homily on me, and went on to speak of the present Lady Tansor, and of his Lordship's increasing desperation, over the years following his marriage to her, that no heir had been forthcoming.

After a while, he fell silent and sat, hands on knees, regarding me as if in anticipation of my making some remark.

'Mr Carteret, forgive me.'

'Yes, Mr Glapthorn?'

'I am here to listen, not to question you. But will you allow me

*[A member of the working classes during the French Revolution, who wore trousers as opposed to the knee-breeches of the aristocracy. *Ed.*]

to ask this one thing, concerning Mr Phoebus Daunt? He has been mentioned to me, by Mr Tredgold, as a person who enjoys Lord Tansor's particular favour. Are you at liberty to say now, or when we next meet, whether this gentleman's position, in respect to his Lordship, is in any way germane to the concerns that you voiced in your letter?'

'Well, that is a very lawyerly way of putting it, Mr Glapthorn. If you mean, has Mr Phoebus Daunt become the object of Lord Tansor's ambitions to secure an heir, then I can of course answer immediately in the affirmative. I am sure, in fact, that Mr Tredgold must have told you as much. Do I blame my cousin for the action he wishes to take with respect to Mr Daunt? No. Do I feel slighted by it? No. Lord Tansor's possessions are his to dispose of as he wishes. Even if I should succeed to the title, it would be an empty dignity, a name only; and I truly do not desire it – full or empty. However, the matter that I wished to place before Mr Tredgold, and which I am now to place before you, does not concern Mr Daunt directly, though indirectly it certainly bears – rather critically – on his future prospects. But if I am to say more, then I think perhaps it will be best to do so at our next meeting. I see the rain eases a little. Shall we go back?'

I WAITED IN THE DOORWAY OF THE TAP-ROOM WHILE MR CARTERET retrieved a battered leather bag from the hall-porter and spent some few minutes in conversation with him. Out of the corner of my eye, I observed him hand over a small package, and then speak a few more words to the man. He rejoined me, and we walked out together into the stable-yard, where he girded his little round body in a capacious riding-coat, slapped a battered old hat on his head, and secured the bag tightly across his chest.

'Will you reach home before dark?' I asked.

'If I press on now. And I have the comfortable prospect of tea, and the welcome of my dear daughter, to light my way.'

We shook hands, and I waited in the yard while he mounted a stocky black horse.

'Come to tea tomorrow,' he said. 'About four o'clock. Dower House, Evenwood. Just by the Park gates. South side.'

He was about to pass through the archway at the far end of the cobbled yard when he turned, and shouted back.

'Bring your bags and stay the night.'

AFTER DINNER, I RETIRED TO MY ROOM TO WRITE A BRIEF ACCOUNT for Mr Tredgold of my first meeting with Mr Carteret, which I sent down to the desk to be despatched by the early post the next morning. Then, overcome with tiredness, and feeling no need of my usual opiate cordial, I went to bed, and quickly fell into a deep and dreamless sleep.

After some time, I was conscious of being gradually drawn back into wakefulness by an insistent tapping against my window. I rose from my bed to investigate, just as the nearby bell of St Martin's Church chimed one o'clock.

It was nothing more than a loose tendril of ivy moving in the wind; but then I happened to glance down into the stable-yard.

Under the archway at the far end was what appeared to be a single red eye. Slowly, the darkness around it began to coalesce into a darker shape, enabling me to discern the figure of a man, half lit by the light of the street lamp on the other side of the archway. He was smoking – I could now make out the glow of his cigar expanding and contracting as he drew in and released the smoke. He remained motionless for some minutes; then he suddenly turned and disappeared into the shadows of the archway.

I thought nothing of this at the time. A late dinner guest on his way home, perhaps, or one of the hotel staff. I shuffled back to bed, and fell fast asleep once more.

THE NEXT AFTERNOON, I SET OFF ON ONE OF THE HOTEL'S HORSES TO Evenwood, reaching the village just before three o'clock.

In the main street of the village, I pulled up my horse to look about me. There was St Michael and All Angels, with its soaring spire, a little beyond which stood the creeper-covered Rectory, home of the Reverend Achilles Daunt and his family. A great stillness had descended, broken only by the faint sound of a breeze passing through the trees that lined both sides of the lane that led down to the church. I moved off, following the line of the Park wall until I reached the towered gate-house – put up in the gloomy Scottish style by Lord Tansor in 1817, in a temporary fit of enthusiasm after reading Scott's *Waverley*. Once in the Park, the main carriage-drive began to ascend, for the great house was hidden from here, a pleasure cunningly deferred by 'Capability' Brown when he remodelled the Park; but a building could be glimpsed to the left, through an area of thickly planted trees.

A spur from the main driveway passed through the plantation and brought me to a gravelled space. From here, it bisected an area of well-tended lawn, and led up to the main entrance of the Dower House – a fine three-storeyed building of creamy Barnack stone, built in the second year of King William and Queen Mary,* as proclaimed by the incised numbers on the semi-circular pediment above the shallow portico. It struck me as looking like a beautiful doll's house for some giant's child, perfect both in its simple proportions and in the well-mannered taste of its construction. A flight of half a dozen or so steps led up to the pillared por-

*[i.e. 1690. *Ed.*]

tico. I dismounted, ascended the steps, and knocked at the tall unglazed double doors; but no one came to my knock. Then I heard the sound of a woman crying, somewhere at the back of the house.

I tethered my mount and followed the sound through a gate and down a short flight of steps into a walled garden, lying now in the shadows of late afternoon, then towards an open door in the rear of the residence.

A young serving girl was sitting on a chair by the door being comforted by an older lady in cap and apron.

'There, there, Mary,' the older lady was saying, stroking the girl's hair and attempting to brush away her tears with the hem of her apron. 'Try to be strong, my dear, for Missie's sake.'

She looked up and saw me.

'Forgive me,' I said. 'I have been knocking at the front door.'

'Oh, sir, there is no one here – Samuel and John are up at the great house with his Lordship. We are all at sixes and sevens, you see. Oh sir, such a terrible thing . . . '

She continued in this, to me, incomprehensible way for some moments until I interrupted her.

'Madam, perhaps there is some misunderstanding. I am here by appointment to see Mr Paul Carteret.'

'No, no, sir,' she said, as Mary began to wail with renewed force, 'Mr Carteret is dead. Killed on his road back here from Stamford last evening, and we are all at sixes and sevens.'

· 20 ·

*Vae victis!**

I PRIDE MYSELF ON MY COOLNESS UNDER DURESS – A NECESSARY quality for my work at Tredgolds. But I simply could not disguise my shock, my complete shock, at this news.

'Dead?' I cried, almost frantically. 'Dead? What are you saying? It cannot be.'

'But it is true, sir,' said the lady, 'only too true. And what will Miss Emily do now?'

Leaving Mary to her tears, the lady, who introduced herself as Mrs Rowthorn, the Carterets' housekeeper, escorted me through the kitchen and up a short flight of stairs, from which we emerged at the rear of the vestibule.

As was my custom, I quickly sought to fix the details of my new surroundings in my mind. A floor of black-and-white tiles; two windows flanking the front door, which was secured by two bolts, top and bottom, and a sturdy central mortice. Pale-green walls with fine stucco work, equally fine plasterwork on the ceiling, and a plain white marble fireplace. A staircase with an elegant wrought-iron handrail leading to the first floor. Four doors leading off, two at the front, two at the rear; a further door leading back into the garden.

Out of one of the front rooms, a young woman now emerged.

She was tall, unusually so for her sex, nearly indeed my own height, and was dressed in a black gown with a matching cap that was almost indistinguishable from her jet hair.

*['Woe to the conquered!' A phrase from Livy. *Ed.*]

As I looked upon her extraordinary face, I thought that I had not known what human beauty was until that moment. The beauty that I thought I had known, even Bella's, now seemed delusive and figmental, a half-realized dream of beauty, moulded by invention and desire. But now beauty stood in plain sight, real and unmediated, like starlight, or sunrise over a snow-covered land.

She stood, in the diminishing afternoon light, with her hands folded in front of her, regarding me calmly. I had expected a homely, round person, like Mr Carteret; a welcoming domestic angel. She wore spectacles, like her father, but the resemblance went no further; and, far from detracting from the uncommon loveliness of her face, they seemed only to heighten it – a phenomenon I have often observed.

She possessed the exaggerated prettiness of a doll, but somehow elevated and made noble. Her heavy-lidded eyes – almond-shaped, and cool black, like her hair – were exceptionally large, and dominated her face, as pale as a November moon. Her nose was perhaps a little long, her upper lip perhaps a little short; and the mole on her left cheek might have been considered by some to be a blemish. But hers was not a perfection of individual features; her beauty seemed greater by far than the sum of its parts, as music played transcends the written notes.

I desired Miss Emily Carteret from that very first moment, as I had desired no other woman. Her soul seemed to beckon to mine, and I had no choice but to follow where she led. Yet, if my true identity could be proved, we were cousins, with Duport blood in common. The thought was thrilling, and seemed to make my desire for her all the keener.

My reveries were interrupted by Mrs Rowthorn.

'Oh, Miss,' she said, with evident agitation, 'here's a gentleman been knocking to see your poor father.'

'Thank you, Susan,' replied Miss Carteret calmly. 'Please bring some tea into the drawing-room – and tell Mary that she may go home if she wishes.'

Mrs Rowthorn dropped a slight curtsey and hurried back down the stairs to the kitchen.

'Mr Glapthorn, I think. Won't you come in?'

Her voice was warm and low, laced with a caressing but distant musical quality that somehow put me in mind of a viola played in an empty room.

I followed her into the apartment from which she had just emerged. The blinds had been drawn, and lamps had been lit. She stood with her back to the window while motioning me with a slow wave of her hand to take a seat on a small upholstered chair in front of her.

'Miss Carteret,' I began, looking up at her, 'I hardly know what to say. This is the most appalling news. If I can— '

She interrupted the little speech of condolence that I had planned to give. 'Thank you, Mr Glapthorn, but I neither desire nor need your support at this time – for that, I think, is what you were about to offer me. My uncle, Lord Tansor, has put everything necessary in hand.'

'Miss Carteret,' I said, 'you know my name, and I infer you also know that I had arranged to see your father here today on a confidential matter.'

I paused, but she said nothing in response, and so I continued.

'I came here with the authority of Mr Christopher Tredgold, of Tredgold, Tredgold & Orr, whose name, I also infer, is not unfamiliar to you.'

Still she stood, silently attentive.

'I undertook to keep Mr Tredgold fully informed of my time here, and that undertaking I must of course honour. May I ask – are you able to tell me – how this dreadful thing happened?'

She did not answer for a moment but instead turned away,

looking at the blank surface of the window-blind. Then, with her back still towards me, she began to recount, in a level, matter-of-fact tone, how her father's horse – the little black horse that I had seen him mount in the yard of the George – had been found trotting riderless through the Park at about six o'clock the previous evening, on the track that led down from Molesey Woods. A search party had been sent out. They soon found him, just inside the line of trees, close to where the road entered the Park from the Odstock Road. He was alive but unconscious, fearfully beaten about the face and head, and had been taken on a cart back to the great house, where his body still lay. Lord Tansor had immediately been informed, and had sent to Peterborough for his own local physician; but before the medical gentleman arrived, Mr Carteret had died.

'They believe he had been followed from Stamford,' she said, now turning away from the window, and fixing her gaze on me.

It appeared that there had been a number of such attacks over the past few months, carried out by a gang of four or five ruffians, whose ploy was to follow farmers and others who appeared likely to be returning home from market with money in their bags. A farmer from Bulwick had been badly assaulted only the week before, though until now there had been no fatalities. The attacks had caused outrage in the vicinity, and had been the subject of furious calls for action to be taken in the pages of the *Stamford Mercury*.

She stood looking down at me, as I sat awkwardly, like some scolded schoolboy, in my little chair.

She had the most extraordinary unblinking stare that I have ever seen. Her dark, fathomless eyes revealed nothing of herself, seeming instead like perfect mechanical devices. They immediately put me in mind of the lenses of my cameras: hard, penetrative, all-seeing; impassively absorbing, capturing and registering every detail and nuance of any object that came into view, but giving nothing back. The discomfort of that gaze, its disconcerting combination of impenetrability and *knowingness,* affected me intensely, producing a kind of paralysis of will. I felt that she knew me instantly for what I was, and for who I was, in all my disguises. It appeared to me that those eyes had taken in all the degradations of my life, and recorded all my doings committed beneath the light of heaven, or the cloak of night; that they saw, too, what I was capable of, and what, with time and opportunity, I would do. I suddenly felt unaccountably afraid of her; for I knew then that I would have no choice but to love her, with nothing given back.

At that moment we were interrupted by Mrs Rowthorn, bringing in a tray of tea. For the first time since our interview began, Miss Carteret moved away from the window, and took a seat opposite me. She poured out the beverage, which we drank in silence.

'Miss Carteret,' I said at length, 'this is difficult for me to ask, but it will, as I say, be necessary for me to give Mr Tredgold as full a report as possible of the recent terrible events. I shall therefore need to inform myself, as far as I can, of the precise circumstances of your father's death. It is possible, indeed probable, that I was the last person to see him alive, other than his attackers, and that likelihood in itself involves me in the tragedy. But I would also beg you to think of me as your friend – and your father's also – for though I only met him for the first time yesterday, I had already grown to like and respect him.'

She put down her cup.

'You are a stranger to me, Mr Glapthorn,' she replied. 'All I know of you is that you are Mr Tredgold's representative, that my father left here yesterday to meet you in Stamford, and that you were likely to be returning here today to continue your discussions. My father instructed that a room should be prepared for you, and you are of course welcome to stay for as long as you require, in order to compose your report to Mr Tredgold. I am sure, once that is done, that you will wish to return to London as soon as possible. Mrs Rowthorn will show you to your room.' At which she rose and rang for the housekeeper.

'Good-bye, Mr Glapthorn. You must ask Mrs Rowthorn if there is anything you require.'

'Miss Carteret, I cannot express my sorrow— '

'It is not for you to be sorry at what has happened,' she interrupted. 'You are kind, but I do not need your sympathy. It does not help me. Nothing can help me.'

Mrs Rowthorn soon appeared at the door (I knew enough of housekeepers to suppose that the speed of her arrival signified that she had been eavesdropping on our conversation). I made a slight bow to Miss Carteret, and followed the housekeeper back out into the vestibule.

Minutes later, I was being shown into a small but welcoming room on the second storey of the house. Raising the blind of one of the two windows, I saw that the room looked out across the front lawn and its screen of trees towards the South Gates. I then lay on the bed, closed my eyes, and tried to think.

But my head was full of Miss Carteret, and whenever I attempted to direct my thoughts towards the business of her father's letter to Mr Tredgold, I could see only her great black eyes under their hooded lids. I tried to think of Bella instead, but found that I could not. At last, I took out paper, pen, and ink, lit a cigar, and began to compose a report to my employer on the circumstances of Mr Carteret's death, as they had been told to me.

DUSK HAD FALLEN BY THE TIME I HAD COMPLETED MY TASK AND TAKEN some supper, which Mrs Rowthorn brought up on a tray. I had just opened the window, feeling the need to take a draught of the cold evening air, when the silence was broken by the sound of a pianoforte.

The delicate melody and its ravishing harmonies, the affecting shifts from the major to the minor mode, and from *pianissimo* to *forte*, took hold of my heart and wrung it dry. Such pathos, such grief-laden beauty, I had never experienced in my life. I did not immediately recognize the piece – though I know now that it was by the late Monsieur Chopin – but I guessed the player. How could it be anyone else but her? It seemed clear that she was playing for her father, articulating through her instrument, and the composer's perfect arrangement of tones and rhythm, the agony she could not, or would not, reveal to a stranger.

I listened, spellbound, imagining her long fingers moving over the keys, her eyes washed with tears, her head bowed in the desolation of her grief. But as suddenly as it had begun, the playing stopped, and there came the sound of the lid of the instrument being banged shut. I returned to the window, and looked down into the garden to see her walking quickly across the lawn. Just before reaching the Plantation, she stopped, looked back towards the house, and then moved a little closer towards the trees. Then I saw him, a darker form, emerge from the shadows, and enfold her in his arms.

They remained in a silent embrace for some minutes before she suddenly drew back and began to speak to him in evident animation, shaking her head violently, and twisting around from time to time to look back at the house. Gone was the reserve and cold restraint that I had witnessed earlier; instead I saw a woman gripped by irresistible emotion. She made to leave, but the man caught her by the arm and pulled her back towards him. They continued to converse, their heads close together, for some minutes; then she broke away once more and appeared to remonstrate with him, pointing from time to time into the shadows behind him. At last she turned and ran back to the house, leaving the man standing with empty outstretched arms for a moment or two. I watched her disappear under the portico and heard the sound of the front door closing. When I looked back towards the Plantation, the man had gone.

So she had a lover. It could not of course be Daunt, for Mr Tredgold had told me before I left that he was in the West Country, on Lord Tansor's business; he had also mentioned, in passing, that Daunt's former amorous designs on Miss Carteret had been firmly discouraged by the young lady, in deference to her papa's thorough dislike and disapproval of his neighbour's son, and that they now maintained a civil but unencumbered friendship. But she was beautiful, and unattached, and must have many admirers amongst the county's bachelors. Doubtless I had witnessed an assignation with some local buck. But the more I considered the dumb-show that had been played out before me, the more puzzling it seemed. One might expect a man who comes a-courting to step up to the front door, and announce himself boldly, not skulk in the shadows; nor did it seem to me that this had been a lovers' tiff, but something of far greater moment. There was, it appeared, far more to beautiful Miss Carteret than met the eye.

There was a knock at the door, and the housekeeper came in to remove my tray.

'Mrs Rowthorn,' I asked, as she was about to leave, 'these attacks that have taken place recently: how many have there been?'

'Well, sir, let me see. Mr Burton, who has a farm of Lord Cotterstock's over at Bulwick – he was the last, poor man. And then there was Squire Emsley's man, and I believe there was another gentleman from Fotheringhay, but I can't recall. The poor master would be the third or fourth, I think.'

'And were they all carrying money?'

'I believe so – except for the master.'

'What do you mean?'

'I mean, sir, that the others had all been about their business in Stamford, it being market day when they were attacked. Mr Burton had near fifty pounds taken. But the master keeps his money at the bank in Peterborough, though I don't know how much he had about him in the normal way of things.'

'Why, then, did he go to Stamford yesterday?'

'To meet you, sir, and to go to the bank.'

'The bank? To withdraw money, perhaps?'

'Oh no, sir,' she replied. 'I believe it was to bring back some papers they'd been holding safe for him. Before he left here, he came to ask me where he could find something big enough to put them in, and I found him an old leather bag of Mr Earl's – who used to be his Lordship's gamekeeper – that has been hanging on the back of the pantry door these two years . . .'

I remembered the item distinctly, and how Mr Carteret had strapped it tightly over his riding-coat in the stable-yard of the hotel.

'And where is the bag now?' I asked.

She paused for a moment.

'Now there's a thing,' she said. 'I don't seem to recall seeing it when they . . . excuse me, sir, I do beg your pardon . . . '

She put the tray down to fumble for her handkerchief, and I apologized for my thoughtlessness. When she had composed herself, and after a few consolatory words, she picked up the tray again and wished me good-night.

I was certain now that Mr Carteret had not been tracked and set upon by this supposed gang for the money that they believed he might be carrying. This was no crime of opportunity. Mr Carteret had been attacked for a clear and specific purpose; and had I been a betting man, I would have put money on its involving the contents of the missing bag. But it puzzled me to surmise what Mr Carteret had been carrying, if not money, and what could have been so valuable that cold-blooded, brutal murder was no bar to obtaining it.

This quiet place, standing in elegant seclusion within the walls of Evenwood Park, had suddenly become a place of conspiracy and violent death. Slowly, but insistently, a conviction began to form in me of some link between the death of Mr Carteret and the letter that he had written to Mr Tredgold. By and by, I concluded that such a conviction was groundless. Yet Mr Tredgold had told me to take care. I began to wonder whether his words had been anything more than a conventional farewell.

I sat up for another hour or more, turning matters over in my mind, contending with vague fears and unfounded suspicions, until I could stand no more and blew out my candle. Then I lay, open-eyed, in the darkness, listening to the call of an owl in the Plantation, and watching shadows cast by the trees playing on the white-washed ceiling. How long I lay there, I do not know; but at last I sank into a fitful sleep, pulled down into dreams that were haunted by the face of Miss Emily Carteret.

· 21 ·

*Requiescat**

RISING EARLY, I AND MADE MY WAY DOWN THROUGH THE SILENT HOUSE to find the front door locked and bolted, making it necessary to take the back stairs down to the kitchen. There I encountered the servant girl, Mary Baker, at work at a great stone sink. She turned on hearing my footsteps and curtsied.

'Oh, sir, is anything the matter? Did you ring?'

'No, no, Mary,' I replied. 'I am going for a walk, but the front door is locked.'

She looked up at a clock hanging above the range. It told just a little before half past five.

'The master would always come down himself with the keys, at six sharp,' she said. 'Every morning, without fail.'

'I suppose Miss Carteret has the keys now,' I said.

'I can't say, sir. I was that upset yesterday evening that Mrs Rowthorn said I might go home, which I did, though I made sure I was here early this morning.'

'And do you live in the village, Mary?'

'All my life, sir.'

'I imagine this has been a terrible shock. So senseless and unexpected.'

'Oh sir, the poor dear master . . . such a good man, so good to us all.' Whereupon her voice began to falter, and I saw that tears were not far off.

*['May he rest [in peace]'. *Ed.*]

'You must be strong, Mary,' I said, 'for your mistress's sake.'

'Yes, sir, I shall try. Thank you, sir.'

As I was about to leave, a thought struck me.

'Tell me, Mary, if it does not upset you too much, who found Mr Carteret?'

'John Brine, sir.'

'And who is John Brine?'

She described him as Mr Carteret's man, by which I understood her to mean his general factotum.

'And how many other servants are there here, besides John Brine?'

'Well, Mrs Rowthorn, of course, and myself. I mostly help Mrs Barnes, the cook, and do the cleaning, though Mr Tidy's girl comes in three times a week to help me with that. Then, besides John Brine, there's his sister Lizzie – Miss Emily's maid – and Sam Edwards, the gardener.'

She turned from the sink, and began rubbing her hands on her apron. It appeared that John Brine had been on some errand to the great house when Mr Carteret's horse was first seen trotting riderless through the Park. Brine, together with two of Lord Tansor's grooms, Robert Tindall and William Hunt, had immediately set off to look for Mr Carteret, the two grooms taking the main road to the gates that stood on the southern side of the Park, Brine following the smaller track that led through a swathe of woods to the western gateway on the Odstock Road.

'So Mr Carteret was found by John Brine alone, then?' I asked.

'I believe so, sir. He rode back straight away to find the others, and then they all went there together.'

'And where can I find John Brine?'

. . .

MARY DIRECTED ME TO A YARD LEADING OFF THE GARDEN, ONE SIDE OF which consisted of a range containing two or three stables and a tack-room. Here I found a stocky young man of about thirty, with light sandy hair and beard. He looked up from his work as I entered, but said nothing.

'John Brine?'

'I am,' he replied, in a suspicious tone, drawing himself up and straightening his back.

'Then I would like to ask you a few questions concerning the attack on Mr Carteret. I am—'

'I know your name, Mr Glapthorn,' he said. 'We were told to expect you. But I don't know why you feel it is appropriate to question me. I've told everything I know to Lord Tansor, and I don't think, beggin' your pardon, sir, that his Lordship would consider it proper that I repeat myself to a stranger. I hope you understand my position, sir. If you'll excuse me.'

At which he returned to his work. But I would not be brushed off so easily by such as he.

'Just a minute, Brine. You should know that I am remaining here for a day or so with the express permission of Miss Carteret. It is incumbent upon me, in my professional capacity, for reasons I need not trouble you with, to inform myself as fully as possible with all the circumstances surrounding this terrible event. You will oblige me greatly, Mr Brine, if you could see your way to giving me your account, in your own words, of how you found Mr Carteret. I would not wish to rely on hearsay or rumour, which might distort or contradict the truth I know that I shall hear from your own lips.'

He looked at me for a moment, trying no doubt to gauge the sincerity of my little speech. Then he appeared to relax his stance somewhat, nodded to me to take a seat on an old wheel-backed chair that stood by the door, and began to tell me his story.

In outline, it confirmed what I had already heard from Mary.

He had been at the great house when one of the gardener's boys had run into the stable-yard to say that Mr Carteret's black mare was trotting through the Park, but that there was no sign of its rider. With darkness now coming on, Brine and the two grooms had at once mounted up and ridden out, the grooms heading towards the South Gates, Brine veering west towards the woods.

Brine had found him lying face down amongst the trees, a little way off the track, not far from the Western Gates.

'Had he fallen where he was attacked, do you think?' I asked.

'No,' said Brine, 'I don't think so. The track bends sharply at that point, just before the gates. I believe they were waiting for him on the far side of the bend, just within the trees. He wouldn't have seen them until it was too late. After he'd fallen, I suppose they'd sent the horse off and then dragged him into the trees – you could see the flattened grass. He was still breathing when I found him, but I couldn't rouse him.'

'And his bag?'

'Bag?'

'The bag he had across his chest.'

'There was no bag.'

I then asked him where they had taken Mr Carteret.

'William Hunt rode back to the great house and they brought up a cart. We took him back on that.'

'To the great house, not here?'

'Yes. Lord Tansor insisted. He said he should be kept as quiet as possible until Dr Vyse could be brought from Peterborough. Robert Tindall was sent straight away.'

'What time was this?'

'Around eight o'clock.'

'But Mr Carteret died before the doctor arrived?'

'At about half past nine, or thereabouts. Miss Carteret was with him, and Lord and Lady Tansor.'

I held out my hand, which he took after a little hesitation. I was determined to get the fellow on my side, though he seemed somewhat dull-witted and morose.

'Thank you, Brine. I am grateful to you. Oh, Brine,' I said, as I was about to leave, 'where is Mr Carteret now?'

'In the chapel at the great house. Lord Tansor thought it would be best.'

I nodded. 'Indeed. Yes. Thank you, Brine. Oh, by the way, could you arrange for this to get to Peterborough, in time for the midday railway mail?' I handed him the second account that I had written for Mr Tredgold, describing the reported circumstances of the fatal attack on Mr Carteret.

'You will need some money,' I added, taking out some coins. 'This should suffice.'

He made no reply, but merely nodded as he took the proffered money.

I retraced my steps to the garden, and then walked across the lawn to the gate-house. As I stepped out onto the roadway, I noticed something dark lying on the ground and stooped down to examine it more closely. It was the remains of a half-smoked cigar, sufficient for me – by now a seasoned connoisseur – to recognize one of the premier Havana brands, Ramón Allones no less. Miss Carteret's lover was a man of discernment. I threw the stump on the ground, and proceeded on my way.

A LITTLE BEFORE GAINING THE POINT AT THE SUMMIT OF THE LONG incline from where the great house could be seen, I stopped and turned to look back. Below and behind me were the turrets of the gate-house; to the right, the Plantation, with a glimpse of the Dower House beyond. Further to the right was the boundary wall, on the other side of which could be seen the roof of the Rectory and the spire of St Michael's and All Angels. The irresistible swell and spread of pure fresh morning light was breaking along the distant line of the river; to the west, the great arc of woodland that clothed the higher ground towards Molesey and Easton stood in silent half-shadow.

I turned and resumed my trudge up the remainder of the long slope. The road here begins to swing through a gentle curve, flanked on either side by a short avenue of oaks, and then levels out before descending to cross an arched bridge across the Evenbrook, which can be seen making its sinuous way eastwards through the Park. I emerged from the trees and stopped.

The house was spread out below, its magical splendour even more dizzyingly captivating in the misty October light than I remembered it from my first visit in high summer. I proceeded down the slope, across the bridge, and at last found myself standing in the inner courtyard. Before me were the main doors to the house, on each side of which two elegant Doric columns supported a pediment carrying the Tansor arms and an inscription: 'What thing so Fair but Time will not Pare. Anno 1560'. A little further off, to left and right, abutting into the forecourt, two of the many cupola-topped towers for which Evenwood is celebrated soared into the brightening air; a little way beyond the southernmost of these was a small archway, through which I could discern a cobbled courtyard.

I did not stop to consider what I would say or do if I encountered anyone. I had laid no plans, had no alibi or excuse prepared. Without thinking, I found myself walking through the archway and into the courtyard beyond, heedless of the possible consequences. I was simply intoxicated by the grave beauty of the building, which seemed to drive away all calculated and rational thought.

I had entered one of the oldest parts of the house. Three sides of the court consisted of open-arched cloisters, unchanged since the Middle Ages; the fourth, forming the outer wall at this point and containing the chapel, was a closed-in range, altered in the last century, with four rectangular windows of painted glass, two on each side of an ogee-arched door standing at the top of a little semi-circular flight of steps. Surmounting the roof of this range was a magnificent clock of brightly coloured wood within an intricate Gothic housing, the gilded panels of which were now catching the first gleams of the early morning sun.

As I ascended the steps, the bell of this instrument tolled the half-hour. I looked at my pocket-watch: half-past six. The household would already be about its business, but still I paid no heed to the prospect of being discovered while creeping uninvited about the building. I pushed open the door and entered.

The interior of the Chapel, wainscoted in dark wood and paved in white marble, was cool and silent. I noted, with approval, the pretty little three-manual pipe-organ of the last century, which I knew from my researches had been made by Snetzler.* On either side of a central aisle, three or four rows of ornately carved chairs stood facing a simple railed-off altar, above which hung a painting of the Sacrifice of Isaac. Before the altar, placed on trestles and lit by four tall candles in massive golden holders, stood the open coffin of Mr Paul Carteret.

The upper part of his body had been covered by a white cloth. I gently pulled it back and looked down at the man I had last seen trotting out of the George Hotel in Stamford, anticipating a good tea and the company of his daughter.

Death had not been kind to him. His jaw had been temporarily bound; but the rest of his poor round face showed all too clearly the violence that had been meted out to him. The right eye

*[John Snetzler (1710–85), the German-born organ builder to George III. *Ed.*]

was closed and undamaged, but the left had gone completely, reduced to a horrifying mess of bone and pulp, along with much of that side of the face. I had seen such injuries before, on many dangerous midnights in London, and knew with cold certainty that whoever had visited this violence upon him had done so with truly murderous intent, having, I guessed, something of overwhelming moment to lose if their victim survived the attack. I was now sure that Mr Carteret had been doomed from the moment he took horse from Stamford: he had been carrying his own death warrant in the bag that he had strapped round him, and which had now disappeared.

Though I went to church dutifully throughout my childhood, I had retained little of what is generally called religion, except for a visceral conviction that our lives are controlled by some universal mechanism that is greater than ourselves. Perhaps that was what others called God. Perhaps not. At any rate, it was not reducible to forms and rituals, and required only stoical assent and resignation, since I considered mediation or intervention to be useless. Yet, after pulling the cloth back over Mr Carteret's face, I found myself bowing my head nonetheless – not in prayer, for I had no listening deity to whom to pray, but in common human sympathy.

It was as I stood in this apparent attitude of reverential supplication that I heard the door to the chapel open.

A TALL, WHITE-BEARDED FIGURE IN CLERICAL GARB STOOD FRAMED IN the doorway. He had removed his hat, revealing two wings of white hair swept back on either side of a broad highway of pink flesh. It could be no other than the Reverend Achilles Brabazon Daunt, Rector of Evenwood.

'I beg your pardon,' I heard him say, in deep plangent tones. 'I had not expected to find anyone here at this hour.'

He did not leave, however, but closed the door behind him, and walked down the aisle towards me.

'I do not think I have had the pleasure of your acquaintance.'

There was no help for it now, so I told him my name and the simple truth: that I had come up to meet Mr Carteret on a matter of business; that he had invited me to stay on for a day or so; and that it had only been on my arrival at the Dower House, the previous day, that I had learned the terrible news.

We exchanged the usual pieties, dwelled a little on the iniquity of men, and discussed the likelihood of the attackers being apprehended.

'This must not stand,' he said, shaking his head slowly, 'indeed it must not. These wretches will certainly be discovered, I have no doubt on that score. Such a crime cannot stay hidden. God sees all – and so do men's neighbours, I have found. Lord Tansor is placing an advertisement in the *Mercury*, offering a substantial reward for any information that leads to a successful prosecution. That, I think, may loosen a few tongues. Such atrocities are common, I believe, in London, but not here; no, not here.'

'It is in the power of every hand to destroy us,' I said.

A smile broke across his broad face.

'Sir Thomas Browne!' he cried, with evident delight. '"And we are beholding unto everyone we meet he doth not kill us." There is always something in good Sir Thomas – a kind of *sortes Homericae*.* I often use him thus. Open him anywhere, and wisdom pours from his page.'

We stood in silent contemplation of the coffin for a moment or two. Then he turned to me again.

*[A form of divination that consisted of taking the first passage from Homer, or, later, Virgil, that the eye fell upon as an indication of future events. The Bible was also so used. *Ed.*]

'Will you join me in a prayer, Mr Glapthorn?' he asked.

Mirabile dictu! Behold me now, kneeling beside the coffin of Mr Paul Carteret, with the Reverend Achilles Daunt, the father of my enemy, at my right hand, intoning a prayer for the peace of the poor victim's soul, and swift retribution to be visited on the heads of his murderers – to which last sentiment I was only too happy to add my 'Amen'.

We rose and went out once more into the courtyard.

'Shall we walk back together?' he asked, and so we set off.

'You are not a complete stranger to me, Dr Daunt,' I said, as we were descending the Chapel steps. 'I have had occasion to consult your great catalogue,* and am delighted, on that score alone, to have made your acquaintance.'

'You have an interest in such things, then?' he asked with a sudden eagerness.

And so I began to reel him in, just as I had done with Mr Tredgold. It was the bibliophilic temperament, you see; its possessors constitute a kind of freemasonry, ever disposed to treat those blessed with a similar passion for books as if they were blood brothers. It did not take me long to demonstrate my familiarity both with the study of books in general, and with the character of the Duport Collection in particular. By the time we had begun to ascend the slope back towards the South Gates we were in deep discussion on whether the 1472 Macrobius (Venice: N. Jenson) or the 1772 folio of Cripo's *Conjuracion de Catalina* (Madrid: J. Ibarra), with its rare signed binding by Richard Wier, was the most perfect example of the typographer's art in the collection.

*[*Bibliotheca Duportiana. A Descriptive Catalogue of the Library Established by William Perceval Duport, 23rd Baron Tansor, by the Reverend A.B. Daunt, M.A. (Cantab). With an Annotated Handlist of Manuscripts in the Duport Collection by P.A.B. Carteret* (privately printed, 4 vols, 1841). *Ed.*]

He spoke at length, too, of Mr Carteret, whom Dr Daunt had known since first coming to Evenwood as Rector. After Lord Tansor had volunteered his secretary's services as the Rector's assistant in the preparation of the great catalogue, their acquaintance had deepened into friendship. Mr Carteret had been especially helpful with regard to the manuscript holdings, which, though not extensive in comparison with the printed books, contained several important items.

'He was not a trained scholar,' said Dr Daunt, 'but he was extremely well informed on the manuscripts acquired by his Lordship's grandfather, and had already prepared some commendably accurate descriptions and summaries, which spared me a great deal of labour.'

By now we had reached the point at which the path to the Dower House led off the main carriage-road.

'Perhaps, Mr Glapthorn, if you have no duties that you need to attend to, you might wish to take some tea at the Rectory this afternoon? My own collection is modest, but there are one or two items that I think will interest you. I would invite you for a spot of breakfast now, but I have to call on my neighbour, Dr Stark, at Blatherwycke, and then go on to Peterborough. But I shall be back in good time for tea. Shall we say three o'clock?'

· 22 ·

*Locus delicti**

After leaving Dr Daunt, I was admitted to the Dower House by Mrs Rowthorn. As I was ambling towards the stair-case, I noticed that one of the doors leading off the vestibule was ajar.

Now I cannot resist a half-opened door – just as I am unable to stop myself from peeping into a lighted and uncurtained window as I pass it on a dark night. The desired privacy proclaimed by a deliberately closed door I can respect; but not if it is half open. That, for me, is an invitation that I will always accept. This one was especially tempting, for I knew that it must lead into the room in which Miss Carteret had been playing the piano-forte the previous evening.

I continued on my way, but waited on the first-floor landing for a moment or two until I was sure that the housekeeper had returned to the lower regions of the house, then quickly descended the stairs again, and entered the room.

The atmosphere was close, heavy, and silent. The instrument I had heard – a fine Broadwood six-octave grand – stood before the far window. On it, opened, as if ready to be played, was a piece of music: an *Étude* by Chopin. I turned over the pages, but it was not the piece that I had heard the night before. I looked about me. The pale blinds had been drawn down, and through them the morning sun cast a muted silver light about the room. My eye picked out three or four dark-velvet ottomans and matching

*['The scene of the crime'. *Ed.*]

chairs, with coloured cushions of Berlin-work scattered upon them; the walls, hung with a rich red self-patterned wall-paper, were covered with a profusion of portraits, prints, and silhouettes. A number of round tables, covered in chenille cloths and laden with a variety of japanned and *papier-mâché* boxes, pottery ornaments, and bronze figurines, were placed here and there amongst the chairs and ottomans, whilst above the fireplace, to the right of the door, hung an umbrageous seventeenth-century depiction of Evenwood.

The comfortable but unremarkable character of the room left me feeling a little cheated until I noticed, lying under the pianoforte, two or three half-torn sheets of music, which appeared to have been violently ripped out of a larger compilation. I walked over to the instrument, and bent down to pick up the remnants.

'Do you play, Mr Glapthorn?'

Miss Emily Carteret stood in the doorway, looking at me as I was picking up the ripped sheets to place them on the piano-stool.

'Not as well as you, I fear,' I said, truthfully, though the note sounded false, a pathetic attempt at gallantry. But my words had an effect on her nonetheless, for she began to look at me with a strange concentration of expression, as if she were waiting for me to confess some mean action.

'You heard me playing last evening, I suppose. I hope I did not disturb you.'

'Not in the least. I found it extremely affecting. A most satisfying accompaniment to the close contemplation of a twilit garden.'

I meant her to know that I had not only heard her playing, but had also witnessed the rendezvous with her lover in the Plantation; but she simply remarked, in a flat, vacant tone, that I did not give the impression of possessing a contemplative disposition.

I immediately regretted the cynical tone that I had adopted, for I saw now that her face was drawn, with dark rings around the eyes that betokened long hours of sleeplessness. Her manner had less of the frigidity of our first encounter, although I remained wary of the way that her eyes slowly but constantly scrutinized my person with judicial intensity, like a prosecuting counsel cross-examining a hostile witness. But the burden of her grief was now apparent. She was human, after all; and what could have prepared her for this, the senseless slaughter of her father? It was not in her nature to speak her misery – I saw that clearly; but the o'er-fraught heart* must somehow find expression, or it will break.

She picked up the torn pieces of music that I had placed on the piano-stool.

'A favourite piece of my father's,' she said, though offering no explanation as to why the sheets had been spoiled in this way. 'Are you an admirer of Chopin, Mr Glapthorn?'

'In general, I prefer the music of earlier times – the elder Bach, for instance; but I attended Monsieur Chopin's concert at Lord Falmouth's . . .'

'July forty-eight,' she broke in. 'But I was there, too!'

At this, I recounted how I'd found myself in London in the summer of that year, soon after taking up residence in Camberwell, and had happened to see an advertisement for the recital. The coincidence of our both being present that evening to hear the maestro play produced a distinct change in her. Her look softened somewhat, and as we talked about our separate recollections of the evening, a faint smile would occasionally moderate the severity of her expression.

'Miss Carteret,' I said softly, as I was taking my leave, 'I hope you will not think it presumptuous of me if I beg you – once more – to see me as a friend, for I truly wish to be so. You have told me

*[The phrase is from *Macbeth*, IV. iii. 210. *Ed.*]

that you neither want nor need my sympathy, but I fear I must presume to give it to you, whether you will or no. Please will you let me?'

She said nothing, but at least she did not rebuff me, as formerly; and so, emboldened, I pressed on.

'I have despatched my report to Mr Tredgold, and so shall return to Stamford this evening, and take train to London tomorrow. But, if I may, I hope you will allow me to return for your father's funeral. I shall not, of course, presume on your hospitality . . .'

'Of course you may return, Mr Glapthorn,' she interrupted, 'and I shall not hear of your staying anywhere tonight but here. You will forgive me, I hope, for being so cold with you before. It is my nature, I fear, to let very few people into my confidence. To my disadvantage, I have nothing of my father's outgoing nature.'

I thanked her for her generosity, and then we spoke a little further of the arrangements that had been put in hand. The inquest was to take place on the following Monday in Easton, the nearest town to Evenwood, under Mr Rickman Godlee, coroner for the district; the interment, at St Michael's and All Angels, would be tomorrow week.

'By the way, Mr Glapthorn,' she said, 'I am required to speak with some police-officers from Peterborough this afternoon. I have already indicated to the authorities that you would be happy to put yourself at their disposal. I trust that you do not object?'

I replied that, naturally, as the representative of Tredgold, Tredgold & Orr, and perhaps as the last person to have seen her father alive, I would do everything possible to assist those responsible for identifying Mr Carteret's assailants.

She expressed her gratitude, and informed me that the officers would be arriving at two o'clock, if that would be convenient for me. As this would still give me an hour before I was due at the

Rectory, I said that I would return at the appointed time and turned to go.

'I hope, Miss Carteret,' I said at the door, 'that you have friends hereabouts and that you will not be too much alone in the coming days?'

'Friends? Of course. But I do not mind being alone. I grew up more or less on my own – after my poor sister died. Solitude holds no terrors for me, I can assure you.'

'And you are fortunate to have good neighbours too, I think?'

'You are referring to Dr and Mrs Daunt, perhaps?'

I briefly recounted my meeting with the Rector, and my decidedly favourable impressions of that gentleman.

'Dr Daunt is certainly a good neighbour,' she said. 'I could wish for no better.'

'And Mr Phoebus Daunt must be a welcome addition to any society,' I continued, as disingenuously as I could, for I was determined that my liking for Miss Carteret would not deflect me from learning as much as I could about my enemy.

'Are you acquainted with Mr Phoebus Daunt?'

Her mouth perceptibly tightened, and I noticed that she passed her hand over her forehead as she spoke, though her eyes held me fast in their gaze.

'His literary reputation precedes him,' I replied. 'Who has not read and admired *Ithaca*?'

'Do you mock my distinguished neighbour, Mr Glapthorn?'

I sought, but could not quite find, something in her face that would confirm that her literary estimation of P. Rainsford Daunt coincided with my own.

'Not at all. It is a very great thing to be a poet, and to be able to write so much poetry at a time is surely enviable.'

'Now I know that you are being unkind.'

She looked me straight in the eye, and then she laughed – a

clear spontaneous laugh, which instantly produced a similar response in me. The action briefly transformed her face into something even more wonderful, and for a moment or two she stood swaying from side to side in a most charming, child-like manner. Then she sought to check herself, looking away slightly, and affecting to tidy up some flower petals that had fallen from a display on a nearby table-top.

'I must tell you, Mr Glapthorn, what perhaps you already know, that I grew up with Mr Daunt, and that it is very cruel of you to deride the literary efforts of my childhood companion.'

'Oh, I do not deride them, Miss Carteret,' I replied. 'I do not pay them any heed at all.'

By now she appeared to have collected herself, and turned from the table to hold out her hand.

'Well, Mr Glapthorn,' she said, 'perhaps we shall be friends after all. I do not know how you have made me laugh at such a time as this, but I am glad you have done so, though I must caution you not to underestimate Mr Daunt. He is exceptional in many ways – and not a little like you.'

'Like me? How so?'

'For one thing, he is determined to make his mark on the world – as, I believe, from our brief acquaintance, that you are also. For another, I think he would make a dangerous enemy – as you would.'

'Well, then,' I replied, 'I must be sure to keep my opinions concerning his literary productions to myself. It would never do to antagonize so dangerous a man.'

I could not help delivering these words in a swaggering manner, which I immediately regretted when I saw the smile fade from Miss Carteret's face.

'Well,' she said, 'I have warned you. I know him well, as well as anyone, I think, and I say again that he is not a man to be crossed.

But perhaps you already know the gentleman as well as his works?'

Of course I lied, and said that I had not yet had the pleasure of meeting him in person, but that I hoped to rectify this as soon as possible.

She moved towards the window to raise up the blind. 'It is such a beautiful morning,' she said. 'Shall we take a turn round the garden?'

And so round we went, several times, at first in silence but then, in answer to my questions, she began to speak of her childhood at Evenwood, and of how she had once become lost in the great house, and thought she would never be found again; then, at my gentle prompting, she told me something of the terrible day that her sister died, which she recalled even now in all its heartbreaking detail, though she had only been four years old when they brought the bedraggled little body back to the Dower House. She fell silent again, the painful memory of that loss no doubt compounding the grief that she felt at the brutal slaying of her father. So, to change the subject, I asked her about her time abroad, and how she had liked Paris, and because she said that she adored the French language, I suggested that we should converse in that tongue, which we proceeded to do until, somewhat overawed by her fluency, I stumbled over a word, and she laughed at my embarrassment.

'I see you are not used to being laughed at, Mr Glapthorn,' she said. 'I suspect few people get the better of you, and when they do, you take it hard. Is it not so?'

I admitted that she was right in general, but that, with regard to my spoken French, I humbly deferred to her superior proficiency, and – which was true – was happy to be laughed at. At length, after we had taken several turns of the garden, we sat down to rest on a little stone bench, where we remained, saying nothing, for some minutes.

The autumn sun was warm on our faces, and when I turned to speak to her I saw that her eyes were closed. How exquisitely beautiful she was! She had left her spectacles in the house, and her pale skin, framed and intensified by the stark black of her hair, was bathed in the clear October light, bestowing on it a strangely numinous, unearthly quality. She sat perfectly still, her head tilted upwards, her lips slightly parted. It was the most enchanting composition, and I wished so much to have my camera to capture the fleeting moment, and fix it for ever. Then she opened her eyes and looked straight at me.

'Your business with my father,' she said. 'Are you at liberty to say what it concerned?'

'I'm afraid that must remain confidential.'

'Do you not trust me?' she asked.

There was a hard look in her eye that matched her tone of voice. I struggled to find a suitable answer, but could only prevaricate.

'Miss Carteret, it is not a question of trust between you and me, but between my employer and myself.'

She thought for a moment and then stood up, blocking out the sun.

'Well, then,' she said, 'there is nothing more to be said. I had begun to hope that we might perhaps become friends, but without trust—'

'I assure you, Miss Carteret,' I began, but she held up her hand to stop me from speaking further.

'No assurances, Mr Glapthorn,' she said, with terrible emphasis. 'I do not care for assurances. They are given all too lightly, I find.'

And then she turned, and began walking back towards the house, leaving me to follow her. Just as I caught up with her, a tall thin gentleman with a lugubrious expression, and wearing trousers that appeared to belong to a much shorter person, appeared on the path that led from the gate-house through the Plantation. He bowed obsequiously on seeing Miss Carteret. At once her demeanour changed.

'Mr Gutteridge,' she whispered, keeping her eyes on the visitor. 'The undertaker. I'm afraid we must continue our conversation another time. Good-morning, Mr Glapthorn.'

And with that she left me.

For the next hour or so, I passed the time by making an exploration of the Park and considering, as I walked, my last conversation with Miss Carteret.

I naturally regretted having discomposed her during this time of mourning; but her late father had bound Mr Tredgold to strict confidentiality, and I, as Mr Tredgold's agent, was subject to the same obligation. Yet I was forced to acknowledge that duty was even now under threat from desire, and I did not know whether I would have the strength to refuse her again. Like a half-conscious somnambulist, I felt I was stumbling towards – I knew not what; and, compounding this sudden wilful folly, all my once sincere intentions towards Bella were being driven from my mind, so blinded was I by Miss Carteret's beauty, and so deaf to the quiet urgings of conscience.

I had taken a branch of the main carriage-road that led towards the Temple of the Winds, the Grecian folly built by Lord Tansor's great-grandfather in 1726. From here, I made my way up through the woods that formed the western boundary of the Park, and then descended again, through silent ranks of oak and ash and fluttering showers of leaves, to emerge before the West Front of the great house.

The sight of its walls and towers wrenched me back to the task in hand. If I achieved my purpose, then this wondrous place would be mine by right of succession. I could not allow what might be only a temporary infatuation to lure me from the path on which my feet had been set. What though Miss Carteret was beautiful? Bella was beautiful, and kind, and clever, and as affectionate a companion as any man could wish for. I knew nothing of Miss Emily Carteret, except that she was proud and self-possessed, and that her heart might already belong to another. But Bella I knew to be open-hearted, and warm, and devoted to me alone. What had I to do with cold Miss Carteret? I concluded that I had suffered from some temporary perturbation of the emotional faculties, brought about by the terrible death of Mr Carteret. After standing for some time contemplating my situation, I began to believe that I had reasoned myself out of my silly fancy, as a fool in love will sometimes do. And so I set off back to the Dower House, certain that when I next saw Miss Carteret, the spell she had cast would have been broken by brisk walking and fresh October air.

INSPECTOR GEORGE GULLY, ACCOMPANIED BY A CONSTABLE WAS waiting for me in the drawing-room. I settled myself in an armchair and took out a cigar.

The interrogation, though lengthy, was not of the subtlest, and the Inspector seemed satisfied with the perfectly truthful account – truthful, that is, as far as it went – that I gave him of my meeting with Mr Carteret in Stamford.

'You have been most obliging, Mr Glapthorn,' he said at last, closing his note-book. 'I do not think, you being a stranger hereabouts, that we shall need to trouble you further. But if we do have occasion to speak to you again—'

'Of course.' I handed him a card carrying the address of Tredgold, Tredgold & Orr.

'Just the ticket, sir. Thank you. As I said, merely a precaution. We won't be intruding on you further, I'm sure. We'll be on to these rogues soon enough, you mark my words.'

'You believe them to be local, then?'

'Not a doubt of it,' replied the Inspector. 'Not the first such outrage in this vicinity of late, I regret to say, though the first fatality. But we already have our suspicions . . . I shall say no more.'

He gave me a look that seemed to say, 'You see what we are made of here in the shires!'

'Well, Inspector,' I said, getting to my feet, 'I shall report to my principal that, in my opinion, the investigation could not be in better hands. And if there is anything further I can do to assist your enquiries, please do not hesitate to inform me. And now, if you will excuse me.'

This oaf would never discover who killed Mr Paul Carteret. His death was bound up with a far greater mystery, which was beyond the ability of Inspector George Gully and his minions to unravel.

· 23 ·

*Materfamilias**

HALF AN HOUR LATER, AT A LITTLE BEFORE THREE O'CLOCK, I PRESENTED myself as arranged at the Rectory, where Dr Daunt received me in his study. We passed a pleasant hour or so, perusing his extensive collection of biblical and theological texts. This is not a field in which I have any great expertise, and I was content to let the Rector pick out volumes of particular rarity or importance and expatiate on them at some length, occasionally contributing a comment or two of my own, where I could. Then a first edition of Bunyan's *Pilgrim's Progress* (Ponder, 1678) caught my eye.

'Ah, Bunyan!' I cried, seizing on the volume. 'I read him often as a child.'

'Did you, though?' said Dr Daunt, with evident approval. 'I applaud your young taste, Mr Glapthorn. I never could get my son to like the book, though I would read it to him when he was a boy. I fear that allegory held no appeal for him.' He sighed. 'But he was an imaginative child – and I suppose he is imaginative still, though now it is in what I may call a professional capacity.'

'I think Mr Carteret mentioned to me that your son was born in the North?'

Dr Daunt seemed disposed to talk, and I was eager to let him.

'Yes, indeed. I had taken a living in Lancashire on my marriage – my first marriage, I mean. I am sorry to say that my dear wife –

*['The mother of a household'. *Ed.*]

my first wife, you understand – was taken from us soon after Phoebus was born.'

He sighed again and turned away, and I saw him glance up at a small portrait in oils that hung in an alcove between the bookshelves. It showed a slight, fragile figure in a pale mauve gown and a neat cap, with misty blue eyes and clusters of airy curls at her neck. It was plain enough that his love for his first wife was still strong. Clearing his throat and brushing down his beard, he was about to speak again when the door opened, and a tall figure in rustling black silk swept into the room.

'Oh! Forgive me. Achilles, I was not aware that we had a visitor.'

'My dear,' said Dr Daunt, with the air of someone who has been caught in a guilty act, 'may I introduce Mr Edward Glapthorn?'

She gazed at me imperiously, and held out her hand. I think that she was expecting me to kiss it humbly, like a queen's; but instead I touched the ends of her outstretched fingers in the briefest of gestures, and bowed stiffly.

'I am honoured to meet you, Mrs Daunt,' I said, and withdrew a few steps.

Well, she was a deuced handsome woman, I will say that. I could easily see how her good looks, together with a spirited and capable character, would have made it – let us not say easy, but perhaps less difficult for Dr Daunt, in his grief at the loss of his first wife, and entombed alive as he had been in Millhead, to succumb to her charms. She had brought life and hope to that dismal place, and I supposed he had been glad of it. But he had never loved her; that was plain.

'Mr Glapthorn,' the Rector ventured, 'is staying at the Dower House.'

'Indeed,' came the frosty reply. 'Are you a friend of the Carterets, Mr Glapthorn?'

'I came up from London to see Mr Carteret on a matter of business,' I replied, intending to dispense as little information concerning my visit as possible. She had seated herself next to her husband, placing her hand protectively over his whilst we spoke about the shocking events of recent days, and how the placid community of Evenwood had been riven by what had happened to their well-liked neighbour.

'Mr Paul Carteret was my second cousin,' intoned Mrs Daunt, 'and so, naturally, this terrible crime affects me particularly closely— '

'Not, perhaps, as closely as his daughter,' I interjected.

She shot me a look that was intended, no doubt, to crush my impudence.

'One must of course suppose that Miss Emily Carteret feels the loss of her father deeply, especially under such dreadful circumstances. Do you know Miss Carteret?'

'We have only recently met.'

She smiled and nodded, as if to signify her complete comprehension of the matter.

'And do you work in some professional capacity, Mr Glapthorn?'

'I am a private scholar.'

'A private scholar? How interesting. And is that a line of business?'

'I beg your pardon?'

'You said just now that you had come to see Mr Carteret on a matter of business.'

'In a manner of speaking.'

'In a manner of speaking. I see.'

Dr Daunt, looking a little uncomfortable, then broke in.

'Mr Glapthorn has been so kind as to compliment me on my bibliographic labours, my dear. It is always pleasant for us poor scholars to receive the approval of a discriminating intellect.'

He was looking at me, in anticipation, I supposed, of some pertinent remark or other; but before I could say anything, Mrs Daunt had spoken again.

'My husband's catalogue has been widely approved, by some of the most eminent authorities,' she said, intimating no doubt that my own praise of Dr Daunt's labours was poor enough by comparison. 'And have you published anything in the bibliographical line yourself, Mr Glapthorn?'

Of course I had to admit that I had not.

'My husband's son is also a published author,' she continued. 'He is, as you may know, a poet of some distinction. He has always had a remarkable gift for literary expression, has he not, Achilles?'

The Rector smiled helplessly.

'Of course, his genius was immediately discerned by Lord Tansor, who has been like a second father to Phoebus. Achilles, I'm sure Mr Glapthorn would be interested to see Phoebus's new volume. The reviews have been most gratifying, you know,' she said, watching her husband as he walked over to his desk to pick up the latest production from the pen of P. Rainsford Daunt – *Penelope: A Tragedy, in Verse.*

I dutifully flicked through the volume, stopping occasionally to read a line or two, and nodding as if in sage appreciation of the beauties contained therein. It was, of course, stuffed full of his usual hectic and overblown versifying.

'Remarkable,' I said, 'quite remarkable. Your son has several such volumes to his credit, I believe?'

'Indeed he has,' replied Mrs Daunt. 'And they have all been extremely well received. Achilles, fetch Mr Glapthorn that copy of the *New Monthly* . . .'

'Pray don't trouble yourself, Dr Daunt,' I said hastily. 'I believe that I have read the article in question. What a thing, though, to have a poet in the family! Of course his celebrity precedes him, and I confess that I was hoping to have the pleasure of meeting your son while I was in Northamptonshire.'

'I'm afraid he is away. Phoebus enjoys the particular confidence of my noble relative,' said Mrs Daunt. 'His Lordship, having been a little unwell of late, has asked Phoebus to undertake a business engagement on his behalf.'

'It will be a great shock for your son when he learns of the attack on Mr Carteret,' I said.

'It will most certainly prostrate him,' replied Mrs Daunt, with solemn emphasis. 'His is a most feeling and compassionate nature, and of course he has known Mr Carteret, and his daughter, since he was a little boy.'

After a moment or two's silence, I turned to the Rector.

'I suppose, Dr Daunt, that your son's rise in the world now precludes him from following in your footsteps?'

It was a mischievous question, I own, but it was intended for his wife, not for him; and indeed, before he had time to speak, Mrs Daunt was already answering it.

'Our lot here is an extremely fortunate one. We are not rich, but we live in the hand of a most loving and generous master.'

'You allude to God, perhaps?'

'I allude, Mr Glapthorn, to the beneficence bestowed on us by Lord Tansor. If Phoebus had no other prospects, then I am sure the Church would be a most suitable channel for his talents. But of course he has great prospects, very great prospects, both as an author and . . . ' She hesitated for a moment. I looked at her, eyebrows raised in expectation. But before she could resume, there was a knock at the door and a maid entered with a tray of tea things.

This fortuitous diversion allowed Mrs Daunt quickly to change the subject, and, as she poured out and passed around the tea, she began to ask me a number of questions about myself – Had I lived in London all my life? Was I a Cambridge man, like her step-son? Was this my first visit to Evenwood? How long had I known Mr Carteret? Was I a member of the Roxburghe Club, like her husband, and had I known the late Mr Dibdin,* whom they had often had the honour of entertaining at Evenwood? I answered all her questions politely, but as briefly as I could. Of course she perceived my evasion, and countered by throwing out still more questions. So we continued in our dance – Dr Daunt sitting all the while in silence. Then she asked me whether I had inspected the great house. I told her that I had visited the Chapel briefly that morning, to pay my respects to Mr Carteret, but that I hoped to enjoy a fuller acquaintance with Lord Tansor's residence in the very near future.

'But you must at least see the Library before you go,' cried Dr Daunt suddenly.

'I'm afraid I must return to London tomorrow.'

'But we could go now, if that would be convenient.'

Nothing could have been more to my liking, and so I eagerly assented to the proposal. We quickly finished our tea, and Mrs Daunt rose to leave.

'Good-bye, Mr Glapthorn. I do hope we shall have the pleasure of seeing you again soon. Perhaps when you next visit Evenwood, Fate will look more kindly on us and allow us to introduce you to my step-son.'

I said that that would be a pleasure which, I hoped, would not be long deferred.

She had drawn herself up to her full height and I found myself gazing into her grey eyes. How old was she now? Fifty-three or fifty-

*[The Roxburghe Club was founded in 1812, at the height of the bibliomania craze, by the bibliophile and bibliographer Thomas Frognall Dibdin (1776–1847). *Ed.*]

four?* I could not remember. Whatever her age, she still had about her a fascinating look of practised coquetry. I began to see how she had managed matters with Lord Tansor in respect of her step-son: her undeniable beauty and charm, in concert with her commanding personality, had no doubt been deployed to the full on his behalf. As she looked at me with those winning eyes – it was but for the most fleeting of moments – I felt sure that she had divined that, in some way that she could not yet comprehend, I was a threat to her prosperous condition, and to that of her precious Phoebus. In short, she disliked and distrusted me, as I did her.

Left to ourselves once more, Dr Daunt and I soon reverted to an earlier discussion concerning the Neoplatonic philosophy, with particular reference to Taylor the Platonist's† translations of Plotinus and Proclus. The Rector was discoursing on Taylor's paraphrastic rendering of Porphyry's *De antro nympharum*,‡ which led us on to other equally engaging topics concerning the theologies of the ancient world, a subject in which each of us professed both interest and expertise.

'Mr Glapthorn,' said Dr Daunt at length. 'I wonder whether I might ask a favour of you?'

'By all means,' I returned. 'Name it.'

'It is just this. Though I am an admirer of Mr Taylor in general, his philological and linguistic skills do not always match his enthu-

*[Mrs Daunt was born in April 1797, so she was 56 when the narrator first encountered her in October 1853. *Ed.*]

†[Thomas Taylor, 'the English pagan' (1758–1835), who devoted himself to translating and expounding the philosophy of Plato, Aristotle, the Neoplatonists, and the Pythagoreans. He was an important influence on William Blake and on the Romantic poets (Shelley in particular), and much later on W.B. Yeats. *Ed.*]

‡['Concerning the Cave of the Nymphs', an allegorizing interpretation of the Cave of the Nymphs on the island of Ithaca, described by Homer in the *Odyssey*, Book XIII. *Ed.*]

siastic advocacy of these important subjects. His translation of Iamblichus is a case in point. I have therefore presumed to prepare a new rendering of the *De mysteriis*,* the first part of which is to be published in the *Classical Journal*.† The piece is now in proof and is being looked over by my friend, Professor Lucian Slake, of Barnack. Perhaps you are familiar with Professor Slake's work on Euhemerus?‡ The Professor's knowledge of Iamblichus is sound, but not so complete, I think, as yours. The favour that I would wish very much to ask of you, therefore, is this: would you do me the greatest kindness by agreeing to cast your eye also over the proofs, before the piece goes to press?'

Now this, I thought, was an opportunity to establish a closer relationship with Dr Daunt, which, in turn, might eventually open up an advantageous position with respect to his son. I therefore told him that I would be pleased and honoured to review the work; and so it was settled that Dr Daunt would immediately send word to Professor Slake, asking him to direct the proofs to me at the George Hotel before my departure for London.

'And now,' he said brightly, 'let us be off.'

THE COLLECTION OF BOOKS ASSEMBLED BY WILLIAM DUPORT, THE 23rd Baron Tansor, soon after the Revolution in France, bore

*[Taylor's translation of *Iamblichus on the Mysteries of the Egyptians, Chaldeans, and Assyrians*, which dealt with such matters as theurgy and divination, was published in 1821. Iamblichus (*c.*AD 245–*c.*325), born in Syria, was a Neoplatonist philosopher. *Ed.*]

†[Despite extensive searching, I cannot find that Dr Daunt's translation and commentary were ever published in the *Classical Journal*, even though they apparently reached proof stage. *Ed.*]

‡[A native of Messene, perhaps active as late as 280 BC. He wrote an influential fantasy travel novel, the *Hiera anagraphï*, known mainly through fragments in the work of Diodorus Siculus; it was also quoted by the Christian apologist Lactantius. *Ed.*]

comparison with the libraries established by the 2nd Earl Spencer at Althorp, and by the 3rd Duke of Roxburghe. The 23rd Baron had inherited some three thousand volumes, assembled haphazardly by his forebears over the centuries. Shortly after succeeding to the title, he added to this stock by acquiring the entire library of a Hungarian nobleman – around five thousand items, and particularly notable for containing many hundreds of the first printed editions of the Greek and Roman Classics, as well as many outstanding examples of the *de luxe* printers of the seventeenth and eighteenth centuries, such as Baskerville and Foulis. He then set about augmenting his collection by methodical – and occasionally unconventional – means, travelling widely in order to seek out early editions of those Classical authors that had eluded Count Laczkó, and gathering along the way a large number of early Bibles, fifteeners,* and – a particular interest of his – examples of Early English literature. By the time of his death, in 1799, the collection had grown to over forty thousand volumes.

The original library at Evenwood had been housed in a dark and rather damp chamber of the Elizabethan period, on the north side of the building, which was soon overflowing with his Lordship's acquisitions. And so in, 1792, as I have previously described, he wisely determined to refurbish the large ballroom on the West Front, with its famous ceiling by Verrio, into a place fit to hold his rapidly growing collection. The work took but twelve months to complete, at enormous expense, and in the summer of 1793 the books amassed to that date were transferred to their present home, where they were soon joined by many thousands more.

I saw this wonderful room for the first time, in the company of the Reverend Achilles Daunt, on the afternoon of the 27th of

*[i.e. what are now termed 'incunabula' (from the Latin 'things in the cradle'), meaning books produced in the infancy of printing in the late fifteenth century. *Ed.*]

October 1853. We had walked through the Park from the Rectory, with the declining sun in our eyes, talking of Mr Carteret.

Away from his wife, Dr Daunt was an altogether different man – voluble, energetic, and enthusiastically companionable. In her presence he had seemed somehow lessened, and unwilling to set his own strong character against hers. Now, in the open air, as we strode together down the hill towards the river, he appeared renewed. We spoke of various matters relating to the *Bibliotheca Duportiana*, and I congratulated him again on his great achievement – it was, in my view, a work that would keep its compiler's name alive amongst scholars of the printed book for generations to come.

'The labour, of course, was very great,' he said, 'for the books had not been properly catalogued before, and were in some disorder. There was, to be sure, Dr Burstall's hand-list of the seventeenth-century English books, which he drew up in – when was it, now? Eighteen ten, or thereabouts. Burstall,* as you perhaps know from his little book on Plantin, was a most careful scholar, and I was able to use many of his descriptions virtually *verbatim*. Yes, he saved me a good deal of work, though his hand-list also brought to light a little mystery.'

'Mystery?'

'I allude to the disappearance of the *editio princeps* of that minor but most noble work, Felltham's *Resolves*.† The book, listed unequivocally in Burstall's list, simply could not be found. I

*[John Burstall (1774–1840) was a close contemporary of the celebrated bibliographer Thomas Frognall Dibdin and a Fellow of Corpus Christi College, Cambridge. In 1818 he published *Plantin of Antwerp*, a pioneering study of Christophe Plantin (1514–89), the French-born bookbinder and printer. *Ed.*]

†[Owen Felltham or Feltham (1602?–68), essayist and poet. The first edition, or century, of his famous collection of moral essays and maxims was published *c.*1623. It proved extremely popular and went through twelve editions by 1709. *Ed.*]

searched high and low for it. The collection contained later editions, of course, but not the first. It was impossible that Dr Burstall had included it in his list in error, and I was sure it had not been sold. I expended many hours, looking through the records of disposals, which have been most meticulously maintained over the years. The curious thing was that when I mentioned this to Mr Carteret, he distinctly remembered seeing this edition of the work – indeed, he knew that it had been read by Lord Tansor's first wife, some time before her unfortunate death. It is hard to believe it was stolen; a wonderful little book, of course, but not especially valuable. Mr Carteret searched her Ladyship's apartments most assiduously, in case it had not been returned to the Library; but it was nowhere to be found. It has not been found to this day.'

'Speaking of Mr Carteret,' I said, as we approached the great iron gates of the Front Court, 'I suppose that Lord Tansor will be obliged to find another secretary.'

'Yes, I think that will certainly be necessary. His Lordship's affairs are many and various, and Mr Carteret was a most conscientious and industrious gentleman. It will not be easy to replace him – he was no mere amanuensis. It may fairly be said that he performed the work of several men, for besides dealing with Lord Tansor's business and estate correspondence, which is extensive, he was also the *de facto* keeper of the Muniments Room, librarian, and accomptant. There is an agent for the farms and woods, of course – Captain Tallis; but Mr Carteret was, in all other respects, the steward of Evenwood – although he was not always treated by his Lordship with that gratitude owed to a good and faithful servant.'

'And you tell me that he was a good scholar besides?'

'Yes, indeed,' replied Dr Daunt. 'I believe he missed his true calling there, excellent though his other abilities were. Mr Carteret's hand-list of the manuscript collection exhibits a knowledgeable and discerning intellect. With very little amendment, I was able to incorporate it in its entirety as an appendix to my catalogue. Alas, it will be his only monument, though a noble one. If only he had lived to complete his great work. That would have been a monument indeed.'

'His great work?' I asked.

'His history of the Duport family, from the days of the 1st Baron. A mighty undertaking, on which he had been engaged for nigh on twenty-five years. In the course of his duties, he naturally had access to the family papers stored in the Muniments Room – a collection of voluminous extent, stretching back some five hundred years – and it was on the examination of these that his history was to be based. I fear it is unlikely now that anyone else will be found with the requisite talents and capacity for industry to finish what he had started, which I deem a great loss to the world, for the story is a rich and fascinating one. Well now, here we are at last.'

· 24 ·

*Littera scripta manet**

We were standing before the great West Front, with its prospect of carefully tended pleasure-gardens, and the distant mass of Molesey Woods. A paved terrace, balustraded and lined with great urns – that same terrace where I had made the photographic portrait of Lord Tansor – stretched the length of this western range.

As we entered the Library, the late-afternoon sun, streaming through the line of tall arched windows, transformed the interior of the great room into a dazzling confection of white and gold. Above us, Verrio's ceiling was a misty swirl of colour; around us, rising from floor to ceiling on three sides of the huge space, was a glorious vista of white-painted book-cases, arranged in tall colonnaded bays. My eyes gorged on the sight that lay before me: row upon row of books of every type – folios, quartos, octavos, duodecimos, eighteenmos – exhibiting every facet of the printer's and binder's art.

Taking a pair of white cotton gloves from his pocket, and drawing them carefully over his hands, Dr Daunt walked over to one of the bays, and reached up to remove a thick folio.

'What do you think of this?' he asked, gently laying the volume down on an elaborately carved giltwood table.

It was a perfect copy of Jacobus de Voragine's *Legenda Aurea,* translated and printed by Caxton at Westminster in 1483: a vol-

*['The written word remains'. *Ed.*]

ume of superlative rarity and importance. Dr Daunt procured another pair of cotton gloves from the drawer of the table and offered them to me. My hands were shaking slightly as I opened the massive folio, and gazed in awe at the noble black-letter printing.

'The *Golden Legend*,' said the Rector, in hushed tones. 'The most widely read book in late mediaeval Christendom after the Bible.'

Reverently, I turned over the huge leaves, lingering for some moments on an arresting woodcut of the Saints in Glory, before my eye was caught by a passage in the 'Lyf of Adam':

> God had planted in the begynnynge Paradyse a place of desyre and delytes . . .

A place of desire and delights. No better description of Evenwood could be found. And this paradise would one day be mine, when all was accomplished at last. I would breathe its air, wander its rooms and corridors, and take my ease in its courtyards and gardens. But greater than all these delights would be the possession of this wondrous library for my own use and pleasure. What more could my bibliophile's soul ask for? Here were marvels without end, treasures beyond knowing. You have seen the worst of me in these confessions. Here, then, let me throw into the opposite side of the balance, what I truly believe is the best of me: my devotion to the mental life, to those truly divine faculties of intellect and imagination which, when exercised to the utmost, can make gods of us all.

'This,' said Dr Daunt, laying his hand on the great folio that had so entranced my soul, 'was the first volume for which I wrote a description. I remember it as if it were yesterday. August, 1830. The twenty-ninth day – a day of wind and rain, as I recall, and so dark, if you will believe it for that time of the year, that you could hardly see beyond the terrace. We had the lamps burning in here all day long. The book was not in its proper place – you will observe that the bays in this section of the library are arranged in alphabetical order by author – and I thought at first to remove it to where it belonged, and make my acquaintance with it at some later date; but then, on a whim, I decided to deal with it then and there. And so it has retained a special place in my heart.'

He was smiling to himself as he stroked his long beard and gazed fondly at the open folio. I felt a great closeness to the dear old fellow in that moment, and caught myself wishing that I had had such a man as my father.

He returned the book to its place, and then took down another: Capgrave's *Nova Legenda Angliae*, printed by Wynkyn de Worde in 1516. As he left me to pore over this, he strode over to another bay and brought back the first printing of Walter Hylton's great mystical treatise, the *Scala Perfectionis*, the Ladder of Perfection, printed again by de Worde in 1494, and the first book to which he put his name. I had hardly begun to examine it when he hurried back with yet another treasure – Pynson's reprint of the *Ars Moriendi*. Then off he went again, returning this time with St Jerome's *Vitas Patrum*, Caxton's translation, completed on the last day of his life, and exquisitely printed in folio by de Worde in 1496.

And so it went on, until darkness began to fall, and a servant appeared to bring us lights. At length, while the Rector was replacing a particularly fine copy of Barclay's Sallust, I began to make my own perambulation of the room.

In a recess between two of the arched windows that gave onto the terrace I stopped to look into a little glass-topped display case, containing a curious piece of vellum, dirty and browned, a few inches wide and two or three inches from top to bottom, placed on a piece of blue velvet. It had plainly been folded up for a long period of time but had now been opened out for display, held down at each corner by round brass weights, each of which had been stamped with the Duport coat of arms.

It was crammed with tiny writing, elegantly executed, and peppered with many little flourishes and curlicues, contractions, and abbreviations. A magnifying-glass lay on top of the cabinet, and with this I slowly began to make out the opening words: 'HENRICUS *Dei gratia Rex Angliae Dominus Hyberniae et Dux Aquitaniae dilecto et fideli suo Malduino Portuensi de Tansor militi salutem.*'*

As I mouthed the words to myself, I realized that it was the original writ, sent out by Simon de Montfort in the name of King Henry III, summoning Sir Maldwin Duport to attend Parliament in 1264 – a document of exceptional rarity, and probably unique of its kind. How it had survived seemed little short of miraculous.

I was momentarily transfixed, both by the rarity of the document, and by what it signified. Knowing now that I was descended from Sir Maldwin Duport, what qualities of character, I wondered, had I inherited from this man of iron and blood? Courage, I hoped, and a bold, enduring will; a spirit not easily cowed; resolve above the common; and the strength to contend until all opposition failed. For I, too, had been summoned, like my ancestor – not by the will of some earthly monarch, but called by Fate to reclaim my birthright. And who can deny what the Iron Master has ordained?

I laid down the magnifying-glass, and continued my inspection of the Library. At the far end was a half-open door, which, as my

*['HENRY by the grace of God King of England Lord of Ireland Duke of Aquitaine to his well-beloved liegeman Maldwin Duport of Tansor, knight, Greeting.' The writ, which is of great historical interest, is now in the Northampton Record Office. The Latin text was printed in full in *Northamptonshire History*, vol. xiv (July 1974), with a translation and commentary by Professor J.F. Burton. *Ed.*]

readers will already know, I am unable to resist. And so I put my head round it.

The chamber beyond was small, and appeared to be windowless, although on closer examination I made out, high up, a row of curious glazed apertures, triangular in shape, that admitted just enough light for me to be able to discern its general character and contents. Picking up one of the lighted candles left earlier by the servant, I entered.

From its shape, I realized that this must be the ground floor of the squat octagonal tower, of Gothic design, that I had noticed abutting the south end of the terrace. Standing against one of the angled walls was a bureau overflowing with papers; the rest of the room was fitted out with shelves and cupboards, the former stacked with labelled bundles of documents that reminded me irresistibly of those on my mother's work-table at Sandchurch. Tucked away in the far corner was a little arched door, behind which, I surmised, must be a staircase leading to an upper floor.

But what had instantly caught my attention on entering the chamber was a portrait that hung above the bureau. I raised the candle to observe it more closely.

It showed a lady, full length, in a flowing black dress of Spanish style. Her dark hair, crowned with a cap of black lace rather like a mantilla, was drawn back from her face, and fell about her bare shoulders in two long ringlets. A band of black velvet encircled her lovely throat. She was looking away, as if something had caught her attention; the long fingers of her left hand rested on a large silver brooch attached to the bodice of her dress, whilst her right hand, in which she held a fan, dangled languorously by her side. The artist had depicted her leaning against a piece of ancient stonework, beyond which a bright moon could be seen peeping out from behind an angry mass of dark clouds.

It was altogether an arresting composition. But her face! She had the most strikingly large eyes, with intense black pupils, and pencil-thin black eyebrows; striking, too, was her long but slender *retroussé* nose, and her delicately moulded mouth. The effect of her physical loveliness, combined with the expression of wilfulness in repose, which the artist had so skilfully caught, was utterly enchanting.

I held the candle closer, and discerned an inscription: 'R.S.B. *fecit.* 1819.' I knew then, without a doubt, that this was Lord Tansor's first wife – my beautiful wayward mother. I tried to reconcile this surpassing beauty with the memories that I still had of sad, faded Miss Lamb, but could not. The artist had painted her in her prime, at the pinnacle of her beauty and pride – in the very moment before she took the fateful step that was to change her life, and mine, for ever.

There was a noise behind me. Dr Daunt was standing in the doorway, a book in his gloved hands.

'Here you are,' he said. 'I thought you would like to see this.'

He handed me a copy of Sir Thomas Browne's *Pseudodoxia Epidemica*, the first edition of 1646.

I smiled, thanked him, and began to examine the book, another constant companion of mine, but my mind was elsewhere.

'So you have found your way into Mr Carteret's sanctum. It seems strange to be here and not see him sitting in his customary place.' He gestured towards the bureau. 'But I see you have also found my Lady. Of course I did not know her – she died before we came to Evenwood; but people still remember and speak of her. She was, by all accounts, an extraordinary woman. The portrait is unfinished, as you will have noticed, which is why it hangs here. Goodness me, is that the time?'

The clock in the library had struck the hour of six.

'I'm afraid I must return to the Rectory. My wife will be expecting me. Well, then, Mr Glapthorn, I hope the afternoon has not been too unpleasant for you?'

WE PARTED AT THE HEAD OF THE PATH THAT LED THROUGH A GATE IN the Park wall, past the Dower House, to the Rectory.

The Rector paused for a moment, looking towards the lights of the Dower House.

'That poor girl,' he said.

'Miss Carteret?'

'She is alone in the world now, the fate above all others that her poor father feared. But she has a strong spirit, and has been brought up well.'

'Perhaps she may marry,' I said.

'Marry? Perhaps she may, though I wonder who would have her. My son had some hopes once in that direction, and my wife – I mean my wife and me, of course – would not have been against the match. But she would not have him; and I fear also that her father was not fond of him. Mr Carteret was not a rich man, you know, and his daughter will now be dependent on Lord Tansor's generosity. And then she has such decided opinions on matters that really ought not to concern a young lady. I suppose that comes from her time abroad. I myself have never left these shores, and hope I never have to do so. My son, though, has expressed a wish to go to America, of all places. Well, we shall see. And now, Mr Glapthorn, I must bid you a very good evening, and hope we may have the pleasure of seeing each other again very soon.'

As he made to leave, my eyes strayed towards the baronial towers of the South Gates, and something that I had been half conscious of all day suddenly rose to the surface.

'Dr Daunt, if you don't mind my asking, why do you suppose Mr Carteret rode home through the woods? Surely the quicker route from Easton to the Dower House is through the village.'

'Well, yes, now you come to mention it, that would indeed have been the quickest way,' he replied. 'The only reason to come into the Park through the Western Gates from the Odstock Road would be if there were a need for Mr Carteret to go up to the great house, which is much closer to that entrance than to this.'

'And was there such a need, do you know?'

'I cannot say. Perhaps he had some business with Lord Tansor before he returned home. And so, Mr Glapthorn, I'll wish you another good-evening.'

With that, we shook hands and I stood watching him as he walked off towards the gate in the wall. As he passed through, he turned and waved. And then he was gone.

I TOOK THE PATH THAT LED INTO THE STABLE-YARD. THERE I ENCOUNTERED Mary Baker, the kitchen-maid, lantern in hand.

'Good-evening, Mary,' I said. 'I hope you're feeling a little better than when last I saw you.'

'Oh, yes, thank you, sir, you're very kind. I'm sorry you had to see me like that. It took me hard, that's the truth. The master had been so kind to me – so kind to us all. Such a dear man, as I'm sure you know. And then it brought to mind, in such a terrible way, what happened to my poor sister.'

'Your sister?'

'My only sister, sir – Agnes Baker as was. A little older than me, and a mother to me, too, after our own mother died when we were still little. She worked in the kitchen up at the great house, under Mrs Bamford, until that brute came and took her away.'

She hesitated, as if in the grip of some strong emotion.

'I'm sorry, sir, I'm sure you don't wish to hear all this. I'll say good-evening, sir.'

She turned to go, but I called out to her to stop. Something was stirring in a dark, unvisited corner of my memory.

'Mary, don't go, please. Sit down a moment, and tell me about your sister.'

With a little more gentle persuasion, she agreed to postpone the task that she had been engaged upon, and we sat down in the fading light on a roughly made bench constructed around the thick, gnarled trunk of an old apple-tree.

'You mentioned a brute, Mary. What did you mean?'

'I meant that murdering villain who took my sister away, and killed her.'

'Killed her? You don't say so!'

'I should say I do! Killed her, in cold blood. Married her, then killed her. As soon as I saw him, I knew he was a bad 'un, but Agnes wouldn't hear of it. It was the only time we ever argued. But I was right. He was a bad 'un, for all he charmed her.'

'Go on, Mary.'

'Well, sir, he called himself a gentleman – dressed like one, I'll grant you. Even spoke a bit like one. But he weren't no gentleman. Not him. Why, he weren't hardly more than a servant when he first came to Evenwood.'

'And how did your sister meet him?'

'He'd come up from London, with Mr Daunt.'

'Mr Daunt?' I said, incredulously. 'The Rector?'

'Oh no, sir, Mr Phoebus Daunt, his son. He'd come up with Mr Phoebus and another gent, for a great dinner, on the occasion of his Lordship's birthday. I was by the gates when they went past. But he wasn't invited to the dinner, just Mr Phoebus and the other gentleman. He seemed like he was a serving-man, or some such, for he was driving the carriage that they all came in, and yet he dressed so well, and thought so much of himself, and seemed to be on easy terms with the other two gentlemen. Anyways, that's when he met Agnes, that evening, in the yard by the ice-house. Oh, he was a sly one. He wheedled and cooed, and she, poor fool, took it all in, and thought he was such a great man, taking notice of such as she. But he was no better than her – no, he was a lot worse. We were decent folk, well brought up. But he'd come from nothing, and made his money, Lord knows how. Why Mr Phoebus took up with him, who could say? He came back a week later, but not with Mr Phoebus, nor to see him neither. And then – what do you think? Agnes comes down the next day and says, "Well, congratulate me, Mary, for I'm to be married, and here's the proof," and she holds out her hand to show me the ring he'd given her. After a week! There was nothing anyone could say. She just shut her ears and shook her head. And off she went, poor lamb. And, if you'll believe me, sir, that was the last I saw of her. My poor dear sister, who'd been my closest and dearest friend in the whole world.'

'What happened then, Mary?' I asked, feeling increasingly certain that I knew where her story was leading.

'Well, sir, I had a letter from her a month later to say he'd been as good as his word and had married her, and that she was set up in fine style in London. And so of course my mind was eased a little, though I still couldn't see how this was to end in anything but trouble for her, being tied to such as he. I waited and waited, longing to hear from her again, but no letter came. Six months passed, sir, six whole months, and I was going quite mad with worry – you ask Mrs Rowthorn if I weren't. So John Brine, to set my troubled mind at rest, says he would go down to London and find her and send word back. Oh, sir, how I trembled when his letter came – and weren't I right to tremble! I couldn't open it, so I gave it to Mrs Rowthorn and she read it to me.

'It was the worst news that there could be: my poor sister had been murdered by that brute – savagely beaten, so bad, they said, that you could hardly recognize her darling face. But *he* had been taken, and would stand trial, and so I took some comfort that he would be hanged for his evil deed, though that was too good for him. But even that comfort was denied me, for some villainous lawyer got the jury to find another man guilty. They said that this other man had been her lover! My Agnes! She'd never do such a thing, never. So her husband was set free to murder again, and the other man was hanged – though Lord knows he was as innocent as my poor dear sister.'

She ceased, tears beginning to well up in her pretty brown eyes. I laid my hand on hers, to offer some comfort before asking my final question.

'What was the name of your sister's husband, Mary?'

'Pluckrose, sir. Josiah Pluckrose.'

· 25 ·

*In limine**

PLUCKROSE.

I remembered the cynical smile of contempt he had given the jury when he was acquitted of the murder of his wife, Mary Baker's sister, Agnes. 'You fools,' he seemed to be saying. 'You know I did it, but we've been too clever for you.' And he had me to thank – me! – for escaping the noose.

He was a beast of a man, tall and heavy, though quick on his feet, with shoulders even broader than Le Grice's, and huge hands – one of which, the right, was lacking an index finger, amputated accidentally during his butchering career. Now, I am afraid of no man; but there was something about Josiah Pluckrose that I did not care to confront: an intimation in those narrow eyes of a raw, unbridled capacity for purposeless and terrible violence, rendered all the more unsettling by the suavity of his dress and manner. If you met him casually in the street, by his appearance you would almost think him a gentleman – almost. He had long ago scrubbed the gore of Smithfield from his fingers, but the butcher was in him still.

Everything about him proclaimed Josiah Pluckrose to be guilty of the remorseless murder of his poor wife following some trivial domestic disagreement; and yet, because of me, he had cheated the bells of St Sepulchre's,† and lived to murder again. After his

*['On the threshold'. *Ed.*]

†[The bells of the church opposite Newgate Prison, which tolled to announce impending executions. *Ed.*]

acquittal, he had returned to his house in Weymouth-street, in defiance of his neighbours and opinion generally, as if nothing had happened. Of course Mr Tredgold had never expressed any wish to know how the trick had been done. I had seen the excellent M. Robert-Houdin* perform in Paris, and had witnessed for myself the effect of the art of illusion, when practised by a master, on those who wish to believe in the impossible. I could not use mirrors, or the power of electricity, to produce the impression of guilt that would condemn an innocent man, and deny Calcraft,† or some other nubbing cove,‡ the pleasure of stretching Pluckrose's miserable neck. Nevertheless, I had other well-tried means at my disposal, just as productive of complete persuasion in my audience: documents, apparently in his own hand, setting forth the unfortunate dupe's guilty association with Mrs Agnes Pluckrose, *née* Baker, and witnesses – some ready to swear to the furious temper of the man, and the fact of his being in the house on the fateful afternoon, and others to affirm the presence of Pluckrose in a public-house in Shadwell at the time of the murder. Having done their work, the witnesses – carefully chosen, exhaustively coached, and extremely well paid – had then sunk back into the deeps of London.

And so it was that, following the conclusion of a new investigation, Mr William Cracknell, chemist's assistant, of Bedford-row, Bloomsbury, stepped out of the Debtors' Door at Newgate, one cold December morning, to keep his appointment with Mr Calcraft, whilst Josiah Pluckrose, swinging the heavy silver-headed stick with which he had smashed his poor wife's skull, and wearing

*[Jean-Eugène Robert-Houdin (1805–71), a former watchmaker from Blois who became one of the greatest stage magicians of the nineteenth century. *Ed.*]

†[William Calcraft (1800–79), the most prolific of all English executioners, who carried out over four hundred hangings between 1829 and 1874. *Ed.*]

‡[Slang term for hangman. *Ed.*]

the boots that had crushed her ribs as she lay dying, sauntered forth that same morning with a view to taking the air on Hampstead-heath. After the trial, I was not in the least inclined to congratulate myself on my triumph, and neither I nor Mr Tredgold felt any satisfaction that our client had gone free. And so Pluckrose had been forgotten.

After Mary had gone, and I was walking about the stable-yard, I could not help recalling the evidence of Mr Henry Whitmore, surgeon and apothecary of Coldbath-square, Clerkenwell, concerning the violence done to the person of Agnes Pluckrose. Overcome by rage, I left the yard in a kind of daze, walking at a furious pace out into the darkness.

Mary's tale of her sister's seduction by this brute had moved me more than I would have thought possible. But there was more than Pluckrose to consider: there was Phoebus Daunt – again! He seemed to haunt me at every turn, a jarring, discordant *basso continuo* to my life. I was completely baffled by the association revealed by Mary. What common interest, I wondered in bewilderment, could possibly unite this murderer and the son of the Rector of Evenwood?

After wandering aimlessly, in this morbid state, for an hour or more through the Park, I found myself at the foot of a steep track that wound its way up to the Temple of the Winds. Feeling disinclined to go back to the Dower House just yet, I followed the track up the artificial mound on which the Temple was built, eventually reaching a short flight of steps leading up to a terrace. Here I turned for a moment to look back across the Park to the twinkling lights of the great house.

I was about to make my way back down the steps when I

noticed that the door of the Temple's North Portico was open. On an impuse, I decided to look inside.

The building – partly modelled, like the more famous version at Castle Howard, on Palladio's Villa Rotonda in Vicenza – was in the form of a domed cube, with four glazed porticos set at each point of the compass.* The interior, which, even in the deepening gloom, I could see was decorated in superb scagliola work, smelled of damp and decay, and as I entered I could feel myself treading on fragments of plaster that had fallen from the ceiling. In the midst of the space stood a round marble-topped table, and two wrought-iron chairs; a third chair lay on its back some distance away. On the table stood a stub of candle in a pewter holder.

I placed my hat and stick on the table, took out a lucifer† from my waistcoat pocket, and proceeded to light what remained of the candle, followed by a cigar to cheer my dismal and unsettled mood. The flickering light revealed the quality of the Temple's internal decoration, though it was plain that the place had been in a state of disrepair for some years. Several of the panes in the glazed door of the North Portico were smashed – fragments of dirty glass still littered the floor – and black dust-filled nets of spiders' webs, undulating eerily in the dank air, hung all about like discarded grave-clothes.

Leaving the candle on the table, I walked over to the upturned chair and set it back on its feet. As I was doing so, I noticed a small dark form on the floor, just discernible amongst the shadows cast by the candle stub. My curiosity aroused, I kneeled down.

It was a blackbird – the poor creature must have flown in through the open door of the Temple and dashed itself against a

*[The Temple was finally demolished in 1919, by which time it was virtually a ruin. *Ed.*]
†[A friction match. *Ed.*]

large gilt-framed looking-glass, cracked and mottled, that hung on the wall above where it now lay. Its wings were outstretched, as though frozen in flight. From one staring but sightless eye flowed a jagged stream of viscous black liquid, staining the dusty floor; the other eye was closed in peaceful death.

It somehow affronted me that it lay here, in this gloomy place, in plain sight, away from the warm enshrouding earth. Gently, I picked the bird up by the tip of one wing, with the intention of conveying it solemnly to some suitable resting-place outside the Temple. But the act of lifting it up from the dirty floor revealed something curious.

Beneath it, previously hidden by one of the bird's outstretched wings, was a small piece of battered brown leather, some three inches square, with a hole punched in one corner. I took my discovery over to the candle, now nearly burned down, and saw then what it was – a label, apparently, bearing a name in faded gold letters: 'J. Earl.'

I recognized the name, but could not for the moment recall how or where I had heard it. It seemed strangely imperative, however, to bring its significance to mind, and so I stood for a minute or more in some perplexity, racking my brains for a clue as to its associations.

At length, I seemed to hear the voice of Mrs Rowthorn, Mr Carteret's housekeeper. Something that she had said – a trivial fact that I had half heard, and then forgotten. But nothing is ever really forgotten, and slowly the vaults of memory began to open and yield up their dead.

'*I found him an old leather bag of Mr Earl's – who used to be his Lordship's gamekeeper – that has been hanging on the back of the pantry door these two years . . .*'

This rough square of leather that I now held in my hand had been attached to Mr Carteret's bag. I was sure of it. From this deduction quickly followed another: the bag itself must surely have been here, in the Temple of the Winds. But that posed a problem. Had Mr Carteret been here also? It seemed impossible. The testimonies of those who had found him made it certain that he had been attacked soon after he entered the Park through the Western Gates. No, he had not come to the Temple, but the bag had certainly been here.

I looked about me, and began to picture what might have happened. A chair had been overturned, and this piece of leather had somehow become separated from the bag. And then – the following day, perhaps – a bird had flown into the Temple and, in its fear and turmoil, had mistaken a dirty reflection of the outside world for the living freedom of the open sky, dashed itself against the looking-glass, and fallen to the ground, just where the piece of leather lay. And there the bird, and the object beneath it, might have stayed, perhaps for weeks or months, perhaps for years, had I not, on a whim, and in a fury at Mary's story of the murderous villain Pluckrose, taken the path up to the Temple of the Winds.

Of course it had been no whim. I believed then that I was in the Iron Master's hands, and that he had pulled me hither for the deliberate purpose of finding this thing. But what did it signify? I sat down at the table, dropped my still-smoking cigar on the floor, and buried my head in my hands.

This much I was still absolutely sure of: Mr Carteret had died because of what he had been carrying. I was certain, too, that he had been intending to place the bag's contents before me at our next meeting, and that he had been attacked by a single assailant who knew their worth and importance.

I began to wonder why the bag had been brought to the Temple after the attack. Had Mr Carteret's murderer been *un homme de main*,* acting on someone else's orders? Perhaps he had

*[A hired hand. *Ed.*]

been instructed to bring the bag and its contents here, to the Temple, where it was to be examined by his employer. Somehow, the little leather label had become separated from the bag.

All this seemed perfectly plausible, probable even; but I could go no further. What had been carried in Mr Carteret's bag, and the identities of both the murderer and his master, were mysteries that – as yet – I had no means of unravelling. Until more light could be shed on them, there was nothing else to do but stumble on through the darkness a little longer.

I placed the leather label in my coat pocket, and turned back towards where the dead bird still lay, intending to carry it outside, and then make my way back to the Dower House. In that instant, the guttering candle on the table finally went out and, in the sudden enveloping blackness, I was aware of another presence. There was a figure in the doorway, a dark form against the clear, star-filled sky.

SHE DID NOT SPEAK, BUT WALKED SLOWLY TOWARDS ME, A SMALL lantern held in her left hand, until her face was close to mine, so close indeed that I could feel and smell her warm breath.

'Good-evening, Mr Glapthorn. What on earth brings you here at this time?'

Her voice had a delicious, inviting softness about it that made my blood race with desire, but her inexpressive stare told another story. I tried to strip that gaze of its disconcerting power by looking full into her dark eyes; but I knew that I was done for. It was all over with me. A great iron door had come down, separating me from the life I had lived before. Henceforth, I knew, my heart would be hers to command, for good or ill.

'I might wonder the same about you, Miss Carteret,' I replied.

'Oh, but I often come to the Temple. It was a favourite resort of my father's. He would sometimes bring his writing-case and work here. And it was here that I last saw him alive. So, you see, I have reason enough. But what are your reasons, I wonder?'

She continued to look at me, standing stock-still in her mourning clothes; but then she smiled – a sad, child-like, half-smile – and once again she uncovered, for the merest instant, a touching vulnerability.

'Would you believe me if I said that I had no reason at all for coming here; that I had no other object in view but to take the air, and that I found myself here quite by chance?'

'Why should I not believe you? Really, Mr Glapthorn, your conscience seems rather too eager to protest the innocence of your motives. I merely wondered what brought you here. I'm sure I did not mean to suggest that you were not perfectly entitled to prowl around this damp place in the dark if you wished to do so. You have no need to answer to me – or to anyone, I dare say.'

All this was spoken in a sweet, low, confiding tone, quite at odds with her teasing words. I said nothing in reply as she turned and walked back to the door but picked up my hat and stick, and followed her.

She was standing on the steps leading down to a narrow terrace, below which the ground fell away steeply towards the main carriage-road. Where the track from the Temple joined the road, I could see two lights twinkling in the darkness.

'You have not come alone, then,' I said.

'No, John Brine brought me up in the landau.'

She seemed suddenly disinclined to talk, and took a few more steps down towards the terrace. Then, holding her lamp up close to her face, and with a troubled expression, she turned and said: 'My father believed that everything we do in this life will be judged in the next. Do you believe that, Mr Glapthorn? Please tell me whether you do.'

I said that I feared Mr Carteret and I would have disagreed on this point, and that I favoured a rather more fatalistic theology.

At this, her face assumed a strange look of concentration.

'So you do not believe in the parable of the sheep and the goats? That those who do good will see Heaven, and those who do evil will burn in the eternal fire?'

'That was what I was brought up to believe,' I replied, 'but as I have been deficient in perfection from an early age, it has never seemed to me a comfortable philosophy. It is so ridiculously easy, don't you think, to fall into sin? I prefer to believe that I was predestined for grace. It accords far more closely to my own estimation of myself, and of course it relieves one of the tedious necessity of always having to do good.'

I was smiling as I said the words, for I had meant them – partly – as an attempt at levity. But she had become strangely agitated, and began to walk quickly hither and thither about the terrace, apparently talking to herself in a mumbled undertone, her little lamp swinging by her side, until at last she stopped at the top of the steps that led down to the path, and stood staring out into the darkness.

The sudden change in her manner was dramatic and alarming, and I could see no immediate reason for it. But then I concluded that the grief that she had been holding back had begun at last to assert its natural ascendancy over her spirits, through being in a place that had such strong associations with her recently deceased father. I was about to tell her, as tenderly as I could, that there was no shame in mourning her poor papa; but I had hardly stepped down to the terrace when she looked up at me and, in an anxious voice, said she must return to the Dower House, whereat she began running down the path towards where John Brine was waiting with the landau.

I was determined not to run after her, like some panting

Touchstone after his Audrey,* but instead set off as coolly as I could, though with long urgent strides, following the bobbing lamp down the path. By the time I caught up with her, she was sitting back in the landau, pulling a rug across her lap.

And then, to my astonishment, she held out her hand and bestowed upon me the most delicious smile.

'If you have quite finished taking the air, Mr Glapthorn, perhaps you would accompany me back to the Dower House. I'm sure you have walked quite far enough tonight. John, will you take us back, please.'

As we drove along, she began to speak reminiscently about her father – how he had taken her to the coronation of the present Queen,† on the day after her fourteenth birthday, and how, at Lord Tansor's instigation, Lady Adelaide Paget, one of the trainbearers, had introduced her to the new monarch, then of course not much more than a girl herself. From this recollection she turned to Mr Carteret's inordinate fondness for anchovies (which *she* could not abide), his passion for Delftware (numerous fine examples of which I had noted on display in various parts of the Dower House), and the close relationship that he had enjoyed with his mother. How or why these things were connected in her mind, I cannot say; but she continued in this frantic recollective vein, running from one hurried memory of her father's tastes and character to another in quick succession.

I looked out to see the looming mass of the many-towered house, rearing up against the paler backdrop of the early night sky, and studded here and there with little points of light. My attention was arrested by a fleeting glimpse of the Chapel win-

*[Audrey was the country wench wooed by Touchstone in Shakespeare's *As You Like It. Ed.*]

†[On 28 June 1838. *Ed.*]

dows, a subdued flickering glow of ruby-red and azure, illuminated from within by the candles set around Mr Carteret's coffin. In that moment, the bells of Evenwood began to toll the hour of nine, and I became aware that my companion had fallen silent. When she spoke again, her manner and tone showed clearly that her thoughts had been brought back to the contemplation of her poor father's fate, and to the trials of the coming days.

'May I ask, Mr Glapthorn, whether your parents are still living?'

'My mother is dead,' I replied. 'I never knew my father.'

I said the words without thinking, then instantly reflected on the singularity of my situation. For whom did I speak? For the orphaned Edward Glyver, with a dead mother and a father who had died before he was born? Or Edward Glapthorn, whom I had conjured into existence on learning the truth about my birth, and who was the possessor of two fathers and two mothers? Or the future Edward Duport, whose mother was indeed dead, but whose father still lived and breathed, here, in this great house, not a quarter of a mile from where we now were?

'I am sorry for you, truly,' she said. 'Every child needs a father's guiding presence.'

'Not every father, perhaps,' I observed, thinking of the execrable Captain Glyver, 'can be considered fit for such a task. But I believe, Miss Carteret, from my brief acquaintance with him, that you may count yourself fortunate that yours was exceptional in that regard.'

'But then some children, perhaps, are unworthy of their parents.'

She had turned her face away, and I saw her raise her hand to her face.

'Miss Carteret, forgive me, is anything the matter?'

'Nothing is the matter, I assure you.' But she continued to look out into the darkness with unseeing eyes, her hand resting against her cheek. I saw that she was suffering, and so I thought I would make another attempt at encouraging her to give expression to her anguish.

'Will you allow me to observe, Miss Carteret, as someone who has your interests most sincerely at heart, that grief should not be denied. It is— '

But I was unable to finish my clumsy peroration, for she instantly turned an affronted face upon me.

'Do not presume, sir, to lecture me on grief. I will take no lessons on that subject from any person, least of all from someone who is little more than a stranger to me and mine!'

I attempted to apologize for my forwardness; but she silenced me with another terrible look, followed by some further strong words, which together induced me to sit back, somewhat nonplussed, and to hold my tongue for the remainder of our journey.

In this awkward state, we turned in through the Plantation and drew up at last before the Dower House. As the landau came to a halt, I observed that her face had once again reverted to its accustomed look of passionless abstraction. Without saying a word, or even bestowing the slightest glance in my direction, she slowly removed the rug from her lap and, assisted by John Brine, descended from the vehicle.

'Thank you, John,' she said. 'That will be all for tonight.' Then she turned her head and looked at me, with infinite sadness in her eyes.

'I believe that my father was right,' she said, almost in a whisper. She seemed to be looking straight through me, as if talking to some unseen distant presence. 'We shall be judged for what we do. And so, there is no hope for me.' And with that, she was gone.

I watched her walk the short distance to the house. She stood for a moment beneath the portico lamp, and I longed for her to turn and retrace her steps; but then I saw Mrs Rowthorn open the front door, and say a few words to her that I could not catch, whereupon she instantly picked up her skirts and ran inside.

· 26 ·

*Gradatim vincimus**

I ACCOSTED JOHN BRINE IN THE STABLE-YARD, AS HE WAS UNHITCHING the horses from the landau.

'Brine, I have found something.'

He said nothing in reply, but looked at me in that dour, threatening way of his.

Reaching into my pocket, I held out the little square of leather that I had discovered in the Temple. He took it from me, and began to examine it by the light over the tack-room door.

'James Earl,' he said. 'Gamekeeper here some years past. May I ask, sir, where you found this?'

'In the Temple,' I answered, eyeing him closely. 'Not a much-frequented place, I think.'

'Not since the youngster died.'

'Youngster?'

'His Lordship's only boy, Master Henry. He went up there on his pony. He would not be told, that boy, and his Lordship could do nothing but indulge him. It was his birthday, you see, and the pony had been his father's gift.'

'And can you tell me what happened?'

He thought for a moment, and then nodded me towards the open door of the tack-room.

'Perhaps you'd like to wait in there, sir,' he said as he led the horses away to their stalls. A few minutes later he returned. There

*['We win by degrees'. *Ed.*]

was still a distrusting look about him, but he appeared inclined to resume his story.

'There'd been a hard frost. We'd ridden all over the Park . . . '

'Excuse me,' I interjected, 'do you mean that you accompanied the boy?'

'I was only a lad myself, and my old father, who was his Lordship's groom, was ill that day and said I should go with them instead – the boy and his Lordship – to make sure all was well. But after we came down through the woods, the boy took off on his own. Headstrong, you see, like his mother.

'Well, we set off after him, of course, but my horse picked up a stone and I couldn't keep up. He'd taken the path that goes up to the Temple – you've seen it yourself, sir: steep, uneven, dangerous, even for an experienced horseman. And, as I say, there'd been a hard frost. His Lordship dismounted, and called the boy back. But that was a mistake, for as he tried to turn the pony round, the beast slipped, and threw the boy off. I never thought to see that man cry, and I ain't seen it since. But cry he did, most dreadful to behold, and I don't ever want to hear such a sound again. It fair tore your heart out to, with the poor little chap lying there at his feet so pale and still.

'And so they buried him, Lord Tansor's only boy, and since that day his Lordship has never set foot in the Temple, and few others go up there.'

'But someone *has* been there,' I said, 'and recently. Someone who knows a good deal more about the attack on Mr Carteret than we do.'

I did not know how far I could trust the man; but then I thought how he had taken it upon himself to go to London, on Mary Baker's behalf, to search for news concerning her sister, the doomed Mrs Agnes Pluckrose. That action spoke of a generous and courageous spirit, and, with Mr Carteret dead, there might be a question as to how he would earn his daily bread; and so, having already recognized the need to find a means of informing myself on the doings of Evenwood and its residents, I decided to risk taking Brine into my confidence a little.

'Brine, I believe you to be an honest man, and a faithful servant to your former master. But you have no master now, and Miss Carteret's future, I venture to say, is far from certain. My acquaintance with your late master was short, but I know him to have been an excellent gentleman who did not deserve his fate. More than this, his death has thrown the outcome of our business together into jeopardy, and that must be rectified. I cannot say more on this point. But will you now trust me and help me, as you are able, to seek out those responsible for this dreadful act, and in so doing assist me to conclude the matter that brought me here?'

Brine said nothing in reply, but I could see a glint of interest in his eyes at the question.

'Our arrangement must be on a strictly confidential basis,' I continued. 'I'm sure you understand me. And it would involve no risk to yourself. I simply wish to be informed on what happens here, who comes, who goes, what is said amongst the servants concerning the late Mr Carteret, that sort of thing. I shall pay you well for your loyalty and discretion, and shall ensure that it will never be a matter of regret to you that you assisted me in this matter. And so here's my hand, John Brine. Will you take it?'

He hesitated, as I expected he would, and looked me square in the eye, without speaking, for some seconds. But whatever he saw therein appeared to decide him. He gripped my hand, like the sturdy fellow he was, and shook it hard.

But then he appeared to hold back a little, and I thought at first that he had repented of his decision.

'What is it, Brine?'

'Well, sir, I was thinking . . . '

'Yes?'

'My sister Lizzie, sir, who is maid to Miss Carteret. She's a canny girl, my sister, and a deal smarter than me in knowing what's what, if you take my meaning. And so I was thinking, sir, if I can put this to you straight, whether you might feel your interests would be even better served if you was to extend the arrangement you have so kindly offered me to her as well. You won't find better than her for the work. She's with her mistress privily every day, and comes and goes as she pleases to Miss's room. Yes, sir, she knows what's what round here, and she'll keep it all as tight as you'd ever want. If you'd like to meet her for yourself, sir, she's but a step or two down the road.'

I considered the proposition for a moment. Through my employment at Tredgolds, I had acquired long experience of recruiting such as Brine to serve my purposes; but it was often the case that a certain sort of woman proved more adept, and more subtle, at the work than the men.

'I will see your sister,' I said at last. 'Lead on.'

WE WALKED A LITTLE WAY INTO THE VILLAGE, TO A COTTAGE ON THE corner of the lane that led down to the church.

'I'll go in first, sir,' said Brine at the door, 'if you don't mind.'

I nodded and he entered through the low doorway, leaving me in the roadway to walk up and down. At length, the door opened again, and he ushered me inside.

His sister was standing by the blazing hearth, a book in her hand, which she placed on a table as I walked in. I saw that it was a volume of poems by Mrs Hemans,* and, on looking round the simply furnished room, I noted a set of Miss Austen's works, a recent novel by Mr Kingsley, and a volume or two by Miss Martineau,† together with a number of other modern works, which indicated that Miss Brine possessed literary tastes far superior to those of most people of her class and occupation.

She appeared to be in her late twenties, and had her brother's sandy hair and pale freckly skin, but was shorter and slighter, with darting green eyes, and having – as her brother had accurately described her – the unmistakable look of someone who knew what was what. Yes, she was a sharp one all right. I thought she might do very well.

'Your brother has explained to you the nature of the proposed arrangement, Miss Brine?'

'He has, sir.'

'And what do you say to it?'

'I'm very happy to oblige you, sir.'

'And do neither of you feel disquiet at what I am asking you to do?'

They looked at each other. Then the sister spoke.

'If I may speak for my brother, sir, I will say that no such arrangement would have been possible, or considered by us, if our dear master was alive. But now he is gone, God bless his soul, we

*[The poet Felicia Dorothea Hemans (1793–1835), author of *Tales and Historic Scenes in Verse* (1819), *The Forest Sanctuary, and Other Poems* (1825), *Records of Women, with Other Poems* (1828), *Songs of the Affections, with Other Poems* (1830), and many other works. She also published translations of the sixteenth-century Portuguese poet Luís Vaz de Camões. *Ed.*]

†[Harriet Martineau (1802–76), social reformer and woman of letters. Her works included *Letters on Mesmerism* (1845), *Eastern Life, Present and Past* (1848), *Household Education* and her radical *History of the Thirty Years' Peace* (both 1849), and her novel *Deerbrook* (1839). *Ed.*]

are somewhat anxious concerning our future prospects here. Who knows but that my mistress will not take it in her head to flit back to France, where she always says she was so happy. If she does, she won't take me, that's for sure. She's told me as much in the past. And maybe she'd stay there, and then what would we do?'

'Perhaps she might marry and still live here, though,' I said.

'She might,' she replied. 'But it would suit us, sir, to prepare for the former eventuality. To put a little money by against the day, if it should come, would be a great comfort to us. And we would give good service.'

'I'm sure you would.'

I plainly saw that Lizzie would be the more useful member of the partnership, and that she would also keep her brother in line.

'So you do not feel the same loyalty to your mistress as you did to her father?'

She shrugged.

'You might say that, sir, though I would not,' Lizzie replied. 'But it is true that, circumstances having changed so suddenly, we must look to ourselves a little more than we used.'

'Tell me, Lizzie, do you like your mistress? Is she kind to you?'

The question caused her brother to look at her a little asquint, as if in anticipation of her reply, which did not come immediately.

'I do not complain,' she said at last. 'That would not be my place. I am sure, as my mistress has often told me, that I am slow and clumsy, and that I do not have the delicate manners of the French girl who looked after her in Paris, and who she is always setting up as an example to me. It may be, too, that I am stupid, for of course I would not expect a lady possessed of such accomplishments as Miss Carteret to think much of a poor girl like me.'

She glanced in a deliberate way towards the volume of poetry lying on the table.

I thanked her for her frankness, and after a few more words, took my leave.

Outside the cottage door, the arrangements were concluded with a handshake. And so it was that John Brine, formerly Mr Paul Carteret's man, together with his sister Lizzie, Miss Carteret's maid, became my eyes and ears in and around the Dower House at Evenwood.

As John Brine and I walked back, I had one other matter that I particularly wished to set before my new agent.

'Brine, I wish you'd tell me about Josiah Pluckrose.'

The effect of my words was extraordinary.

'Pluckrose!' he roared, his face colouring. 'What have you to do with that murdering devil? Tell me, or by God I'll knock you down where you stand, agreement or no!'

Naturally, under normal circumstances, I would not for a moment have tolerated such insolence from a common fellow like John Brine; even as things were, I was within an inch of teaching him a lesson that he would not forget, for I was easily his match in height and weight, and I knew, perhaps better than he, how to conduct myself in such situations. But I drew back; for, after all, what difference of opinion could possibly exist between us regarding Josiah Pluckrose?

'I have only one aim in view with respect to that gentleman,' I said, 'and that is to send him as speedily as possible, with my very best regards, to the deepest pit of hell.' Whereupon Brine's face took on a more compliant expression and he began to apologize, in a fumbling embarrassed sort of way, for his outburst; but I stopped him and told him straightaway of my conversation with the housemaid Mary Baker, though of course I did not go so far as to divulge my prior acquaintance with friend Pluckrose.

And then he told me, in a quiet, feeling way, which almost endeared me to the fellow, that he had once entertained what he termed a 'fondness' for Agnes Baker, which it was left to me to interpret how I would.

'Well, Brine,' I said, as we walked under the gate-house arch, 'I see there is common ground between us on the matter of Josiah Pluckrose. But what I would particularly like to know,' I continued, feeling the need for another cigar, but having no more about me, 'is how such a man came to be associated with Mr Phoebus Daunt. I cannot be alone in observing the incompatibility of the relationship. Can you tell me, for instance, how Mr Carteret viewed the matter?'

'Like any right-thinking gentleman would,' said Brine, a little evasively. 'I know, because I heard him telling Miss Emily.'

'Telling him what, Brine? Speak up, if you please, for there must be no secrets now between us.'

'I'm sorry, sir, but it just don't seem right, that's all, speaking of what was said privately.'

I damned the fellow for his scruples. A fine spy he was going to make! I reminded him, rather pointedly, of the terms of our engagement and, after a moment or two, though still somewhat unwillingly, he began to recount the substance of the conversation that he had overheard between Mr Carteret and his daughter.

'His Lordship had given a dinner for his birthday, and afterwards it fell to me to bring the master and Miss Emily back from the great house in the landau. It's an old thing that belonged to Mr Carteret's mother, but it gives good service and— '

'Brine. The facts, if you please.'

'To be sure, sir. Well, sir, as I say, I went up to fetch the master and the young miss back in the landau, and I saw straightaway that something was up. Black as thunder her face was as I helped her in, and Mr Carteret looking nearly as bad.'

'Go on.'

'There was a fair old wind that night – I remember that very well – and we had a rough time of it on our way back, I can tell you, especially coming up from the river, battered and buffeted and I don't know what. But though the wind was hard in my face, there were times when I could still catch what Master and Miss were saying.'

'And that's when Mr Carteret spoke of Pluckrose?'

'Not by name, though I knew it was him the master was speaking of. He'd driven a carriage up that evening with Mr Phoebus Daunt and another gentleman – it was that same cursed evening that he first spied Agnes. There'd been some trouble in the servants' hall – Pluckrose had been given his supper there while t'other two gents were upstairs with the quality, and he'd threatened his Lordship's butler, Mr Cranshaw. I heard all about the rumpus from John Hooper, who saw it all. Well, we got home and I handed her out – Miss Emily, I mean – and blow me, she fair stormed into the house, with her father following, and calling to her to stop. And so I brought the landau round to the yard, and stabled the horses, like tonight, and then went along to the kitchen, for 'twas a rare old night, as I say, and Susan Rowthorn would always have a little something waiting for me, in the way of refreshment, as I might say, on such a night. "Well," says she when I open the door, "here's a to-do. Master and Miss are going at it hammer and tongs." Those were her exact words: hammer and tongs. Now Miss has a temper – we all knows that. But Susan says she'd never heard the like, doors slamming and I don't know what.'

'And what was the cause of the upset, do you suppose?'

'Oh, I don't suppose, sir. I had everything pat and in apple-pie order from Susan. She'd heard everything and noted everything, just as it happened, as is her way. I don't know, sir, as you hadn't ought to have brought her into your employ rather than me.'

He smiled a stupid smile, and, once again, I silently damned him, and his feeble attempt at humour.

'Get to it, Brine, and quickly,' I said impatiently. 'What did the woman tell you?'

Now, to spare you any more of John Brine's ramblings, I intend to present my own account of what happened on that fateful evening, when Josiah Pluckrose came to Evenwood in the company of Phoebus Daunt, and Mr Carteret and his daughter fell out with each other for the first time in their lives. It draws directly on the recollections of the Carterets' housekeeper, Mrs Susan Rowthorn, and of John and Lizzie Brine.

ONCE RETURNED TO THE DOWER HOUSE, HAVING BEEN BUMPED AND blown all the way, Miss Carteret ran inside, with her father calling after her, and went straight up to her room, slamming the door behind her. She had barely had time to ring for her maid, Lizzie Brine, when there was a short knock at the door, and her father entered, still in his great-coat, and still in an extremely agitated state.

'Now this will not do, Emily. Really it won't. You must tell me all, or you and I shall never be friends again. And that's the long and the short of it.'

'How can I tell you all when there is nothing to tell?'

She was standing before the window, her travelling cloak over her arm, her hair disarranged from the wind, which continued to howl all around the house. Dismayed and still angered by the turn of events, and feeling that she had been humiliated by her father, she was in no mood for conciliation.

'Nothing to tell! You can say that? Very well. Here it is. You will have nothing further to do with that man, do you hear? We must of course observe the decencies of social intercourse with our neighbours, but there must be nothing more. I hope I make myself clear.'

'No, you do not, sir.' Her anger was now uncontained. 'May I ask of whom you speak?'

'Why, Mr Phoebus Daunt, of course, as I said before.'

'But that is absurd! I have known Mr Phoebus Daunt since I was six years old, and his father is one of your most valued and devoted friends. I know that you do not esteem Phoebus as others do, but I own myself amazed that you should take against him so.'

'But I saw you, at dinner. He leaned towards you, in a distinctly . . . ' He paused. 'In a distinctly intimate manner. Ah! You say nothing. But why should you? That's your way, I see, to let me think one thing while you are doing another.'

'*He leaned towards me?* Is that your accusation?'

'So you deny, do you, that you have been secretly encouraging his . . . his attentions?'

He had placed his hands in his pockets and was rocking back and forth on his heels, as though to say, 'There! Deny it if you can!'

But deny it she did, and with a kind of cold fury in her voice, though turning her head away as she spoke.

'I do not know why you treat me so,' she went on, angrily throwing her cloak on the bed. 'I have, I hope, been ever attentive to your wishes. I am of age, and you know that I could leave here tomorrow, and marry anyone I pleased.'

'But not him, not him!' said Mr Carteret, almost in a moan, passing his hand through his hair as he did so.

'Why not him, if I so chose?'

'I beg you again to judge him by the company he keeps.'

She stood for a moment, waiting to see whether her father

intended at last to elaborate further on his statement. Just then came another knock at the door. It was Lizzie Brine, who found her mistress and Mr Carteret facing each other in silence.

'Is anything the matter, Miss?'

She looked at her mistress, then at Mr Carteret. Of course she had heard the door slamming, and the sound of angry voices. Indeed, she had been lingering in the passage for some time before making her presence known. And she was not alone, for the housekeeper, Susan Rowthorn, assiduous as ever in her duties, had already found a pressing reason to climb the stairs as quickly as her short legs would carry her, in order to inspect the room adjacent to Miss Carteret's, which contained a connecting door, against the key-hole of which Mrs Rowthorn felt obliged – no doubt for good housekeeping reasons – to place her eye.

'No, nothing is the matter, Lizzie,' said Miss Carteret. 'I shall not need you tonight after all. You may go home. But be here sharp in the morning.'

And so Lizzie bobbed and departed, slowly closing the door behind her. But she did not go home immediately. Instead she tiptoed into the adjacent chamber to join Mrs Rowthorn, who, crouching down by the connecting door, turned and placed a finger on her lips as she entered.

Left alone once more (or so they thought), father and daughter stood awkwardly for a moment or two, saying nothing. It was Miss Carteret who spoke first.

'Father, as you love me, I must ask you to be plain with me. What company is Mr Phoebus Daunt keeping that appears to be so abhorrent to you? Surely you do not refer to Mr Pettingale?'

'No, not Mr Pettingale. Though I do not know that gentleman, I have no reason to believe anything ill of him.'

'Then whom do you mean?'

'I mean the other . . . person. A more loathsome, villainous creature I have never seen. And he calls himself an associate of Mr Phoebus Daunt's! You see! This swaggering brute, this . . . this Moloch in human form, comes here, to Evenwood, in the company of Mr Daunt. There now: what do you say to that?'

'What can I say?' she asked. She was calm now, standing framed by the curtained window in that characteristic pose of hers, hands crossed in front of her, her head tilted slightly back and to one side, her face devoid of all expression. 'I do not know the person you describe. If he is, indeed, an associate of Mr Phoebus Daunt's, well then, that is Mr Daunt's affair, not ours. There may be perfectly good reasons why it is necessary for him, perhaps temporarily, to have dealings with the person you describe. You must see that we are not in a position to judge on this point. As for Mr Daunt himself, I can assure you, on my dear mother's life, and before Heaven, that I can find no reason – no reason at all – to rebuke myself for any dereliction of the duty that a daughter owes to a father.'

Though she had said nothing very specific, her attitude, and the emphatic tone in which she had delivered the words, appeared to have a composing effect on Mr Carteret, who ceased continually removing his spectacles, and now replaced his handkerchief in his pocket.

'And am I truly wrong, then, my dear?' The question was asked quietly, almost plaintively.

'Wrong, father?'

'Wrong to think that you cherish a secret regard for Mr Phoebus Daunt.'

'Dearest father . . .' Here she reached forward, and took his hand in hers. 'I feel for him as I have always done. He is our neighbour, and my childhood friend. That is all. And if you force me to be direct, then I will say that I do not like Mr Daunt, though I will always be civil to him, for his father's sake. If you have mistaken civility for affection, then I am sorry, but I really cannot be blamed.'

She was smiling now, and what father could have resisted such a smile? And so Mr Carteret kissed his daughter, and said that he was a foolish old man to think that she could ever go against him.

Then a thought seemed to strike him.

'But, my dear,' he asked anxiously, 'you will want to get married, I suppose, some not very distant day?'

'Perhaps I shall,' she said gently. 'But not yet, Papa, not yet.'

'And not to him, my dear.'

'No, Papa. Not to him.'

He nodded, kissed her again, and wished her good-night. As he turned the corner of the passage that led to his bedchamber, Mrs Rowthorn, with Lizzie Brine in tow, quietly returned to the kitchen.

This, then, is a true and accurate record, or as true and accurate as I am able to make it, of what passed that night between Mr Paul Carteret and his daughter.

But was anything left unsaid? And were there secrets in each heart that neither could tell to the other?

· 27 ·

*Sub rosa**

After walking back to the stable-yard, I entered the Dower House by the kitchen door. There I came upon Susan Rowthorn deep in conversation with the cook, Mrs Barnes. In my professional work I always like to cultivate servants; and here was just the opportunity that I had been seeking.

'Will you take some food in your room, sir?' asked the housekeeper.

'I'll take some food, certainly,' I replied, 'but I'll take it here with you, if I may.'

My gallantry having produced its desired effect, I left the two women to their preparations, while I returned to my room to replenish the supply of cigars that I usually keep about my person.

At the foot of the staircase, I stopped.

Just inside the front door stood a black leather imperial,† together with three or four smaller bags. Was someone leaving? Or someone visiting? I noted the initials on the lid of the trunk: 'M-MB'. A visitor, I concluded. Another question for Mrs Rowthorn.

Having re-supplied myself with cigars from my bag, I returned to the kitchen, noticing *en route* that the drawing-room door, which had been shut when I was examining the trunk, was now open. Naturally I peeped inside, but the room was empty,

*[Literally, 'under the rose' – i.e., secretly, in secret. *Ed.*]

†[A case or trunk adapted for the roof of a coach or carriage. *Ed.*]

although my nose, which is sensitive to such things, caught a faint and intriguing scent of lavender lingering on the air.

The meal prepared by Mrs Barnes was a hearty one and, after my excursion to the Temple and the ride back in the landau with Miss Carteret, most welcome. I sat by the fire, allowing Mrs Rowthorn full rein, for an hour or more. What she told me, as I tucked into a chop with two broiled kidneys, lubricated with a generous go of gin-punch and followed up by a slice of most excellent apple pie, I have incorporated into the preceding account. One question only remained.

'I suppose Miss Carteret is engaged with her visitors?'

'Oh, only one visitor, sir,' offered Mrs Rowthorn. 'Miss Buisson.'

'Ah, yes. A relative, perhaps?'

'No, sir, a friend. From her Paris days. John Brine has just gone to take her things up to her room. What a shock for her, poor lamb, to get here at last and find us all in such a state.'

I asked whether Miss Buisson had known Mr Carteret well, to which Mrs Rowthorn replied that the young lady had paid many visits to England, and that she had been a particular favourite of her late master's.

'I suppose Miss Carteret must have many friends of her own sex in the neighbourhood,' I ventured.

'Friends?' came the answer. 'Well, yes, you could say so. Miss Langham, and Sir Granville Lorimer's girl; but, strange to say, no one like Miss Buisson.'

'How so?'

'Inseparable, sir. That is the word I should use. Like sisters, they are when together, though of course so unlike in looks and character.' She shook her head. 'No. Miss has no other friend like Miss Buisson.'

As I was about to leave, John Brine came down the hall stairs. He coloured slightly on seeing me, but I quickly diverted the women's attention by knocking over my third (or was it fourth?) glass of gin-punch. Apologizing for my clumsiness, I made good my escape.

Back in my room, I lit another cigar, kicked off my boots, and lay down on my bed.

I felt sick and uneasy. A surfeit of gin-punch, and too many cigars, no doubt. Though I was exhausted, my mind was unquiet, harassed with commotion, and sleep seemed impossible. Tomorrow I would return to London, no wiser concerning the nature of Mr Carteret's discovery than when I came to Northamptonshire, but certain that it had brought about his death. And if the Tansor succession was at the heart of the business, then this could mean that I, too, was caught up in the plot that had led to his murder.

I tried to force myself to think of other things – of Bella, and what she would be doing. Tonight, I knew, there was to have been a dinner at Blithe Lodge for one of the most distinguished members of The Academy, the Earl of B—. The best silver would be out, and Mrs D would be resplendent in garnet and pearls, and sporting the remarkable peacock-feathered headdress that she always wore on such occasions, as signifying her supreme position in the body politic of The Academy. I imagined Bella wearing her blue silk dress, her favourite Castellani necklace* encircling her wonderful neck, a wreath of white artificial rose-buds nestling in her abundant black hair. The company would ask her to play and sing, and of course she would charm every man there. Some would even half believe they were in love with her.

*[The Italian jeweller Fortunato Pio Castellani (1793–1865), who specialized in making pieces that emulated the work of the ancient Etruscan goldsmiths. *Ed.*]

I closed my eyes, but still the sleep that I craved eluded me. I remained in this state for perhaps an hour, half awake, half dozing, until the striking of the gate-house clock roused me. Now fully alert, and as far from sleep as ever, I was considering what to do with myself when my ears caught a strange sound. I thought perhaps it might be the wind, but on looking out of the window again, I could see that the branches of the trees in the Plantation were barely moving. Silence descended once more, but in a few moments it came again – an urgent whimpering, such as I have heard dogs make in their sleep.

I rose and put my boots on. Candle in hand, I opened the door.

The passage outside my room was dark, the house deathly silent. To my right was the main staircase leading down to the vestibule; ahead, the passage ran almost the length of the house. On my left I made out two doors, leading, I presumed, to rooms that, like mine, overlooked the front lawn; another room opposite – which I later learned was Mr Carteret's study – clearly gave onto the gardens at the rear. As I proceeded slowly down the passage I saw that, at the far end, it made a turn to the right, towards the back of the house.

For a few moments I stood listening intently, but there was no sound to be heard, and so I began to retrace my steps a little more rapidly. To prevent the flickering flame from being extinguished, I cupped my hand around the candle, which immediately produced huge shadow-fingers that slid silently across the walls and doors on either side as I passed. Then, as I reached the second of the doors on the front side of the house, I heard it again, like a soft, involuntary moan. Placing the candle-holder on the floor, I kneeled down, my boots creaking slightly. The key-hole had a little brass cover but it was fixed fast; and so I put my ear to the door.

Silence. I waited, hardly daring to draw breath. What was that?

A rustling noise, like a silken garment falling to the floor; a moment later, I began to catch what sounded like fragments of a whispered conversation. I strained to hear what was being said, pressing my ear closer to the door, and squinting my eyes in concentration; but I could make nothing out until—

'*Mais il est mort. Mort!*'*

No longer a whisper, but an anguished cry – *her* cry! Then, tenderly urgent, came the reply from another voice:

'*Sois calme, mon ange! Personne sait.*'†

Again the conversation subsided to a whisper on both sides, and only occasionally, when one or the other of the speakers raised their voice a little, was I able to catch more than a word or two.

'*Il ne devrait pas s'être produit . . .*'

'*Qu'a-t-il dit ? . . .*'

'*Qu'est-ce que je pourrais faire? . . . Je ne pourrais pas lui dire la vérité . . .*'

'*Mais que fera-t-il ? . . .*'

'*Il dit qu'il lui trouvera . . .*'

'*Mon Dieu, qu'est-ce que c'est que ç'?*'‡

In moving my position a little way, to ease the cramp in my leg, I had knocked over the candle-holder, putting out the flame in the process. Instantly, I heard footsteps inside the room hurrying towards the door. There was no time to return to my own room, and so, hastily gathering up the candle-holder, I ran as quickly as

*['But he is dead. Dead!' *Ed.*]

†['Be calm, my angel! No one knows.' *Ed.*]

‡['It should not have happened . . .'
'What did he say? . . .'
'What could I do? . . . I could not tell him the truth . . .'
'But what will he do? . . .'
'He says that he will find him . . .'
'. . . My God, what was that?' *Ed.*]

I could back down the passage, reaching the point at the far end where it turned sharply towards the rear part of the house just as the door opened.

I could not see them, but I imagined two frightened faces peering out and anxiously looking up and down the passage. At length, I heard the door being closed, and a few moments later I ventured my head round the angle of the wall to confirm that the coast was clear.

Back in my room, I immediately sat down and wrote out as much of the conversation between Miss Carteret and her friend as I could remember. Like a scholar working on fragments of some ancient text, I sought to fill in the lacunae to make sense of what I had heard, but without success; my incomplete and disconnected transcriptions – set out above – refused to yield up their secrets. Convinced that I was seeing mystery and conspiracy where there was none, I walked to the window to look out once again on the moonlit garden.

Miss Carteret, Miss Carteret! I was completely, preposterously, bewitched by my beautiful cousin, though I hated myself for the absurdity of it all. It had happened in two days – only two days! It was mere infatuation, I told myself yet again. Forget her. You have Bella, who is everything you could want or need. Why expend precious time on this cold thing, time that ought to be given to the accomplishment of your great enterprise?

But whoever heeds the voice of reason when love whispers, softly persuasive, in the other ear?

I WAS AWOKEN EARLY BY MRS ROWTHORN KNOCKING AT MY DOOR with a tray of breakfast, as I had requested.

On descending to the vestibule half an hour later, I looked

into the dining-room, and then into the two reception rooms at the front of the house; but there was no sign of either Miss Carteret or her friend, Mademoiselle Buisson. A little French clock on the mantel-piece was chiming half past seven as I opened the front door, and stepped out into a cold, dull morning.

I was drawing deeply on my first cigar of the day, in the hope that strong tobacco would have the required stimulative effect on my sluggish faculties, when Brine brought my horse round from the stable-yard. He wished me a safe journey and I asked whether he had seen Miss Carteret that morning.

'No, sir,' he said. 'Not this morning. She gave orders to my sister that she would be late coming down, and that she was not to be disturbed.'

'Please give Miss Carteret my compliments.'

'I will, sir.'

'You have the address safe that I gave you?'

'Yes, sir.'

I mounted up, and was riding off under the dark echoing arch of the Scottish gate-house when I reined in my mount. Turning the horse, I galloped back into the Park.

Pushing on up the long incline, and through the avenue of oaks at its summit, I pulled up and looked down across the misty river to where Evenwood lay.

It was a day of lead-grey louring cloud, with a cold east wind sighing through the leafless trees; yet even on such a day, my heart was captivated by the beauty of the house – this place of desire and delights. When would the day come that I would enter it as Master, and my feet stand secure within its gates at last?

As I passed the Rectory, I saw Dr and Mrs Daunt, arm in arm, walking up the lane from the church. On seeing me, the Rector stopped and raised his hat in salute, which gesture I returned in kind. His wife, however, immediately disengaged her arm, and walked off alone down the lane.

In another moment I had left Evenwood, and Miss Emily Carteret, behind.

After a cold, damp ride, I turned into the High Street in Stamford at a little before nine o'clock. Returning my nag to the ostler at the George, I then arranged with the hall-porter for my bags to be carried across to the Town Station in time for the next train to Peterborough. The ride had cleared my head, lightened my mood, and sharpened my appetite; and so, having an hour in hand, I cheerily ordered up chops, bacon, and eggs, and a pot of strong coffee, and settled myself in a box by the fire in one of the public rooms to read the daily news-papers until it was time to stroll over to the station.

It wanted ten minutes to the time that the train was due to arrive when, as I was walking into the first-class waiting-room, something that Dr Daunt had said on our walk back from the Library returned to me. He had been speaking of an early ambition of his son's to follow a career in the law, in emulation of his closest friend at Cambridge. I had given no further thought to the Rector's words; but now, standing in the waiting-room of the Town Station in Stamford, they returned with a strange force.

Now I am a great believer in the instinctive powers – the ability to reach at truth without the aid of reason or deliberation. Mine are particularly acute; they have served me well, and I have learned to trust them whenever they have manifested their presence. You never know where they may lead you. Here was a case in point. I cannot say why, but I was instantly seized with the notion that I must find out the name of this companion of Daunt's at the University. Acting on this impulse, therefore, I immediately changed my plans and, after consulting my Bradshaw,* resolved upon a diversion to Cambridge.

By now the train for Yarmouth, which I was to take as far as Ely, had arrived. I was on the point of picking up my bag, when one of the tap-room servants from the George came puffing up to me, and thrust a thick envelope, almost a small package, into my hand.

'What is this?

'Beg pardon, sir, hall-porter says this has been directed to you.'

Ah, I thought. The proofs of Dr Daunt's translation of Iamblichus. They had been forwarded to me, as arranged, by Professor Slake. I had quite forgotten about them. As it was necessary for me to board the train immediately, I had no time to reprimand the stupid red-faced fellow for the hotel's failure to give me the package earlier; and so I brushed him aside without a word, stuffed the proofs into my great-coat pocket, and managed to take my seat just as the station-master was blowing his whistle.

To my consternation, the carriage that I had chosen was crowded almost to capacity, and I spent a most uncomfortable two and a quarter hours wedged between a stout and exceedingly truculent lady, a basket containing a spaniel puppy set precariously on her knees, and a fidgeting boy of about thirteen (much interested in the puppy), with my bag lying between my feet on account of the racks being full.

I disembarked, to my great relief, in Ely, and managed to catch a connecting train to Cambridge with seconds to spare. Arriving at my destination at last, I took a cab into the town, and was set down before the gates of St Catharine's College.

*[One of the monthly Railway Guides published by George Bradshaw (1801–53), the first volume of which, in what were to become their familiar yellow wrappers, was published in December 1841. *Ed.*]

· 28 ·

*Spectemur agendo**

IN THE YEAR 1846, THROUGH THE GOOD OFFICES OF MY FORMER travelling companion, Mr Bryce Furnivall, of the British Museum, I had begun a correspondence with Dr Simeon Shakeshaft, a Fellow of St Catharine's College, who was an authority on the literature of alchemy, in which I had developed a strong interest while studying at Heidelberg. We had continued to correspond, and Dr Shakeshaft had been instrumental in helping me assemble a small library of alchemical and hermetic texts. This gentleman, like the Rector of Evenwood, was a member of the Roxburghe Club, and I had recalled Dr Daunt mentioning that this mutual acquaintance had known his son during the latter's time at King's College.† Dr Shakeshaft had recently written to me, at my accommodation address, on the subject of Barrett's *Magus*,‡ a curious compendium of occult lore which I had wished to acquire; and so, as we had not yet had occasion to meet face to face, I would have the satisfaction of killing two birds with one stone.

Dr Shakeshaft's set was at the far end of the charming three-

*['Let us be judged by our actions'. *Ed.*]

†[King's is the neighbouring college to St Catharine's. *Ed.*]

‡[*The Magus* (1801) by Francis Barrett, born between 1770 and 1780, is a seminal work on the subject of magic and occult philosophy. The Preface states that it was written 'chiefly for the information of those who are curious and indefatigable in their enquiries into occult knowledge, we have, at a vast labour and expence, both of time and charges, collected whatsoever can be deemed curious and rare, in regard to the subject of our speculations in Natural Magic – the Cabala – Celestial and Ceremonial Magic – Alchymy – and Magnetism'. *Ed.*]

sided red-brick court that forms the principal feature of St Catharine's. Having ascended a narrow stair-case to the first floor, I was welcomed most cordially into Dr Shakeshaft's book-lined study. We talked for some time about a number of subjects of common interest, and my host brought out several superb items from his own collection of hermetic writings for my inspection. This was most pleasant, and it was a relief to expend mental energy on topics of such absorbing fascination after the difficult events of the past few days.

It was with some unwillingness, therefore, that I wrenched myself back to my purpose, and introduced the subject of Phoebus Daunt.

'Did Mr Daunt have a wide circle of acquaintance in his College?' I asked, as casually as I could.

Dr Shakeshaft pursed his lips in an effort to remember.

'Hmm. I would not say wide. He was not popular amongst the sporting men, and, as I remember, most of his friends, such as they were, came from other Houses.'

'Was there any particular friend or companion that you can recall?' was my next question. This time the response was instantaneous.

'Indeed there was. A Trinity man. They were very close, always going about together. I entertained them both myself – young Daunt's father and I, you know, are old friends. But wait a moment.' He thought for a moment. 'Yes, now I remember. There was some trouble.'

'Trouble?'

'Not involving Daunt. The other gentleman. Young Pettingale.'

I remembered the name from the accounts given to me by John and Lizzie Brine of the dinner given by Lord Tansor, following which Mr Carteret had accused his daughter of secretly encouraging the attentions of Phoebus Daunt. He had been Daunt's guest on that occasion, and they had been driven to Evenwood by Josiah Pluckrose.

'May I ask, if you are able to tell me, the nature of the trouble you speak of?'

'Ah,' replied Shakeshaft, 'you'd best talk to Maunder.'

And so I did.

Jacob Maunder, DD, of Trinity College, occupied a splendid ground-floor set in Great Court, with a fine view of Nevile's Fountain. Tall and stooping, with a lazy curling smile and a sardonic eye, he had occupied the position of Senior Proctor in the University for a period that coincided with Phoebus Daunt's time at King's College. The duties of a Proctor are of a disciplinary nature, and consequently expose the holders of this office to the more sordid and unpleasant propensities of those *in statu pupillari*.* 'When you perambulate the streets at night,' as the Provost of King's, Dr Okes, once memorably remarked to one of their number, 'you rarely see the constellation Virgo.' The post also required a stout heart, as the unfortunate Wale had famously discovered when he was pursued by a mob of undergraduates from the Senate House to the gates of his College.†

I could not imagine Jacob Maunder fleeing in the face of intimidation. He appeared to me fully to deserve his reputation, described to me in brief by Dr Shakeshaft, as a stern and unyielding upholder of University statute and procedure, and a less than merciful judge of the follies of youth. Did he, I asked, handing

*['Under guardianship or scholastic discipline'; i.e. undergraduates. *Ed.*]

†[Alexander Wale of St John's College, then Senior Proctor. The incident took place in April 1829. *Ed.*]

him a note of recommendation from Shakeshaft, recollect a gentleman by the name of Pettingale?

'This is a little irregular, Mr— '

'Glyver.' I felt no qualms about using the name by which Dr Shakeshaft knew me.

'Quite. I see here that Dr Shakeshaft speaks very highly of you. Were you up at the University yourself?'

I told him that I had done my studying in Germany, at which he looked up from his perusal of Shakeshaft's note.

'Heidelberg? Why, then, you will know Professor Pfannenschmidt, I dare say.'

Of course I knew Johannes Pfannenschmidt, with whom I had spent many a wonderful hour in deep conversation concerning the religious mysteries of the Ancients. This acknowledgement of an acquaintance with the Herr Professor produced a visible mitigation of Dr Maunder's raptorial demeanour, and appeared to remove any lingering scruples that he had concerning the propriety of answering my enquiry.

'Pettingale. Yes, I recollect that gentleman. And his friend.'

'Mr Phoebus Daunt?'

'The same. My old friend's son.'

'Dr Shakeshaft mentioned some trouble concerning Mr Pettingale. It would assist me greatly, in the prosecution of a highly confidential matter, if you were able to inform me, in a little more detail, of its nature and consequences.'

'Nicely put, Mr Glyver,' he said. 'I will not enquire further into your reasons for seeking this information. But insofar as the matter, in its general outline, is one of public record, I am willing to give you some account of the business.

'I first came across Mr Lewis Pettingale when I apprehended him in a house of ill-fame – a not uncommon occurrence, I am afraid to say, amongst the undergraduate population of this

University. Youth can be a little lax in point of moral resolve.' He smiled. 'He was disciplined, of course, and put on notice that, if it happened again, he would be rusticated.* But the affair that Dr Shakeshaft has in mind was altogether more serious, though its conclusion appeared to exonerate Mr Pettingale of any taint of guilt or censure.

'It began, from my point of view, when I was called upon, in my capacity as Senior Proctor, by a police inspector from London who wished to question Mr Pettingale in connexion with a serious case of forgery. It appears that the young man had gone to a firm of London solicitors – Pentecost and Visard, as I recall – for assistance in the matter of an outstanding debt. He had taken with him a promissory note for the amount of one hundred pounds, signed by a Mr Leonard Verdant. The solicitors undertook to write to this Mr Verdant forthwith, and demand payment of the sum in question, on pain of legal proceedings immediately being taken out against him. Within twenty-four hours, a messenger had appeared at the solicitors' office with the outstanding debt in cash, and a request from Mr Verdant for a signed receipt.

'On being informed that the debt had been paid, Mr Pettingale went again to the solicitors to receive his money, which was paid to him, at his request, with a cheque drawn on the firm's bankers – also my own, as it so happened, Dimsdale & Co., Cornhill. Well, the cheque was duly presented, and the matter was concluded to the satisfaction of all parties.

'But then, a week or so later, a clerk in the solicitors' office noticed that three cheques, to a total of eight hundred pounds, had been drawn on the firm's account without, it appeared, any record of the transactions having been made. The alarm was duly raised and the police were called in. A few days later, a man by the

*[i.e. sent down from the university for a specified time. *Ed.*]

name of Hensby was apprehended on the premises of the firm's bank attempting to present a further forged cheque, this time for seven hundred pounds.

'Now, for the fraud – for fraud it clearly was – to be brought off, two things were required: a specimen of the authorized signature, and a number of blank cheques. It was surmised by the police that the necessary signature might have been obtained from the receipt sent to this Mr Verdant, or even from the cheque paid to Mr Pettingale for the amount owed to him. It was recalled that Mr Pettingale had especially requested a cheque, rather than cash, and the police were also informed by the solicitors that no other cheques had been authorized since this one had been issued. The coincidence was obvious, and so both Mr Verdant and Mr Pettingale fell under suspicion. As far as Mr Pettingale was concerned, he could not deny, of course, that he had sought payment of the original debt from Mr Verdant, but he vehemently denied all knowledge of the subsequent forgeries, and, indeed, there was not a shred of evidence to connect him to them. When asked by the inspector why the money was owed to him, he replied that he had lent the money to this Verdant, whom he said he had met several times at the Newmarket races, for the settlement of a debt.'

'And was there any reason to doubt his account?' I asked.

Dr Maunder gave me a somewhat skeptical smile.

'None that the police, or I, could uncover. Mr Pettingale was required to go with the officers to London, and was called as a witness at the subsequent trial; but he could not be identified by the man Hensby, who claimed that he had been casually employed by a gentleman – not Mr Pettingale – whom he had met in a coffee-house in Change-alley, to run various errands, one of which was to present the forged cheques at Dimsdale & Co. and to bring the proceeds back, at a pre-arranged time, to the coffee-house.'

'This gentleman: was Hensby able to identify him?'

'Unfortunately, no. He provided only a rather indistinct description, which rendered identification of this person by the police virtually impossible. As for Mr Verdant, when the police called at his address in the Minories he had vanished, and was of course never seen again. The poor dupe Hensby, for such I deem him to have been, was prosecuted, found guilty, and transported for life. A travesty of justice, of course. The fellow could hardly write his name, let alone demonstrate the skill to carry out what were, by all accounts, most convincing forgeries of the authorized signature.'

He ceased, and looked at me as if in expectation of further questioning.

'From your most informative account, Dr Maunder, it certainly seems clear that the perpetrator was the mysterious Mr Verdant, perhaps working with others. Mr Pettingale appears to have been a perfectly innocent party in the business.'

'You might say so,' he replied, smiling. 'I questioned Mr Pettingale myself, of course, on behalf of the University authorities, and could only conclude, with the police, that he had played no part in the conspiracy – or, rather, that there was no substantive evidence that he had played any part.'

He smiled again, and I took my cue.

'May I ask, then, whether you entertained any personal doubts on the matter?'

'Well now, Mr Glyver, it would not be right, not right at all, you know, to bring my personal feelings into this. As I say, what I have told you is a matter of public record. Beyond that – well, I am sure you understand. It does not signify in the least, of course, that I am by nature of a rather doubting turn of mind. And besides, the affair did not lay too deep a stain on Mr Pettingale's character.

After going down from here, I believe he was called to the Bar by Gray's-Inn.'

'And Mr Pettingale's friend, Mr Phoebus Daunt?'

'There is no reason at all to believe that he was implicated in the crime in any way. He was certainly not asked to account for himself by the police, or, indeed, by the University. The only connexion I could establish, in the course of questioning Mr Pettingale, was that he had accompanied his friend to Newmarket on several occasions.'

I thought for a moment.

'Regarding the blank cheques, is it known how they were obtained? Was there, perhaps, an earlier break-in?'

'You are right,' said Dr Maunder. 'There *had* been a break-in, some days before Mr Pettingale sought legal help on the matter of the outstanding debt. One must presume that the cheques were stolen then. Again, suspicion fell on the mysterious Verdant. But as it proved impossible to find this gentleman, well, there the matter rested. And now, Mr Glyver, if you will excuse me, I have an appointment with the Master.'

I thanked him for his time, we shook hands, and he showed me to the door.

LEAVING TRINITY COLLEGE, I TOOK AN OMNIBUS FROM THE MARKET-square back to the station, and had only a few minutes to wait before the next train to London. As we rattled southwards, I felt a curious elation of spirits, as though a door – be it ever so small – had opened an inch or so, and let in a little gleam of precious light on the darkness through which I had been wandering.

Of Mr Lewis Pettingale's guilt in the clever conspiracy described to me by Dr Maunder, I had not the least doubt; but it was clear that he had not worked alone. This Leonard Verdant, now: he had been a co-conspirator I was sure, a conclusion indicated, I thought, by his possession of a most unlikely name, concealing – whom? I had my suspicions, but they could not yet be tested. And then there was Mr Phoebus Daunt. Ah, Phoebus, the radiant one, unsullied and incorrupt! There he stood, as ever, whistling innocently in the shadows. Was he as guilty as his friend Pettingale and the elusive Mr Verdant? If so, what other iniquities did he have to his credit? At last, I began to sense that I was gaining ground on my enemy; that I had been given something that might, perhaps, give me the means I needed to destroy him.

Yet with regard to more pressing matters, all this was of scant comfort. I was returning to London with no more knowledge of why Mr Carteret had written his letter to Mr Tredgold than when I had started out; and the expectations that I had cherished that the secretary might be in possession of information to support my cause had also been shattered by his death. The only certainty I had brought back was that what Mr Carteret knew concerning the Tansor succession had led, directly or indirectly, to this catastrophe. As for me, what a change had been wrought in the matter of a few days! I had left London believing that I might be falling in love with Bella. I returned the helpless slave of another, in whose presence I constantly burned to be, and for love of whom I must turn my back on the certainty of happiness.

Do not ask me why I loved Miss Carteret. How can such an instantaneous passion be explained? She seemed beautiful to my eyes, certainly, more beautiful than anyone I had known in my life. Though I knew little of her character and disposition, she seemed to possess a discerning, well-stocked mind, and I knew from direct experience that she could claim musical ability well above the common. These accomplishments – and no doubt others of which I was yet unaware – were worthy of admiration and respect, of course; but I did not love her for them. I loved her because – because I loved her; because I could not help succumbing to this irresistible contagion of the heart. I loved her because choice was denied me by some greater force. I loved her because it was my fate to do so.

Part the Fourth

THE BREAKING OF THE SEAL

October–November 1853

Nothing wraps a man in such a mist of errors,
as his own curiosity in searching things beyond him.

—Owen Felltham, *Resolves* (1623),
xxvii, 'Of Curiosity in Knowledge'

· 29 ·

*Suspicio**

THAT NIGHT, I TOOK MY SUPPER AT QUINN'S – OYSTERS, A LOBSTER, some dried sprats on the side, followed by a bottle of the peerless Clos Vougeot from the Hotel de Paris. It was still early, and the Haymarket had not yet put on its midnight face. Through the window I contemplated the usual metropolitan bustle, the familiar panorama of unremarkable people doing unremarkable things, which you may see out of any window in London at eight o'clock on a Friday evening. But in a few hours' time, after the crowds had poured out of the Theatre, taken their supper at Dubourg's or the Café de l'Europe, and made their laughing way home to warmth and comfort, this broad and glittering thoroughfare of shops, restaurants, and cigar-divans would take on a very different aspect, transformed then into a heaving, swollen river of the damned. What is your pleasure, sir? You may find it here, or hereabouts, with little trouble, at any hour of the night after St Martin's Church has tolled the final stroke of twelve. Liquor in which to drown; tobacco and song; boys or girls, or both – the choice is yours. Ah! How often have I thrown myself into that continually replenished stream!

Evenwood! Had I dreamed thee? Here, lying at my ease once more on the scaly back of Great Leviathan, feeling the monster's deep, slow breath beneath me, its rumbling pulsing heart beating in time with my own, the things that I had so recently seen and

*['Suspicion'. *Ed.*]

heard and touched now seemed as real in imagination, and as unreal in fact, as the palace of Schahriar.* And had I truly breathed the same air as Miss Emily Carteret, when I had stood so close to her that I could see the rise and fall of her breast, so close that I only had to stretch out my fingers to caress that pale flesh?

I loved her. That was the plain and simple truth. It had come upon me suddenly on swift wings, pitiless as death: inescapable, and undeniable. I felt no joy at my new condition, for how can the conquered slave be joyful? I loved her, without hope that she would ever return my love. I loved her, and it was bitter to me that I must break my dearest Bella's heart. For there is no mistress like Love. And what cares she for those who suffer when their dearest one betrays them for love of another? Love only smiles a conqueror's smile, to see her kingdom advanced.

A second bottle of the Clos Vougeot was perhaps a mistake, and at a little after ten o'clock I walked out into the street, somewhat unsteadily, with a light head and a heavy heart. It had begun to rain and, assailed by melancholy thoughts, and feeling a great need for company, I headed off to Leadenhall-street, in the hope of finding Le Grice taking his usual Friday supper at the Ship and Turtle. He had been there, as I had expected, but I had missed him by a matter of minutes, and no one could tell me where he had gone. Cursing, I found myself back in the street again. Normally, in such a mood of restless melancholy, I would have taken myself northwards, to Blithe Lodge; but I was too much of a coward to face Bella just yet. I would need a little time, to regain some composure, and to learn dissimulation.

Down to Trafalgar-square through the dirt and murk I wandered, and then eastwards along the Strand – aimlessly, as I

*[The Sultan to whom Scheherazade tells her stories in *The Arabian Nights' Entertainments. Ed.*]

thought; but before long I had passed St Stephen, Walbrook, and had begun to walk at a more purposeful pace.

WELCOME, WELCOME! I HAD BEEN GONE TOO LONG, THE OPIUM-MASTER said.

And so, bowing low, he led me through the kitchen, dark and vaporous, to a truckle-bed set against a greasy, dripping wall in the far room, where, curling myself up, I laid my head on a filthy bolster whilst the master, with many soothing words, plied me speedily with my means of transportation.

In Bluegate-fields I had a dream. And in my dream I lay on a cold mountain, with only the stars above me; but I could not move, for I was held down fast with heavy chains, about my legs and feet, around my chest and arms, and in a great loop around my neck. And I cried out for ease – from the bitter cold and from the pressing, suffocative weight of the chains – but no help came, and no voice returned my call, until at last I seemed to faint away.

A sleep within a sleep. A dream within a dream. I awake – from what? And my heart leaps, for now I stand in sunshine, warm and vivifying, in a secluded courtyard, where water plays and birds sing. 'Is she here?' I ask. 'She is,' comes the reply. And so I turn and see her, standing by the fountain, and smiling so sweetly that I think my heart will burst. In black mourning no more, but in a comely robe of dazzling white samite, with her dark hair flowing free, she holds out her hand to me: 'Will you come?'

She leads me through an arched door into a deserted candlelit ballroom; faint echoes of a strange music reach us from some unimaginable distance. She turns to me. 'Have you met Mr Verdant?' And then a sudden wind extinguishes all the lights, and I hear water lapping at my feet.

'I do apologize,' I hear her saying from somewhere in the

darkness. 'But I have forgotten your name.' She laughs. 'A liar needs a good memory.' And then she is gone, and I am left alone on a drear and lonely shore. I look out to see a heaving black ocean, with a pale yellow light suffusing the horizon. In the distance, something is bobbing on the waves. I strain my eyes; and then, with a fearful pang, I see what it is.

A blackbird, stiff and dead, its wings outstretched, drifting into eternity.

THE CARRIAGE-CLOCK THAT STOOD ON THE MANTEL-PIECE STRUCK half past five. It was now Sunday morning, and I had spent a second profitless night seeking oblivion in the company of my demons, returning home feeling sick and tired, and falling asleep in my chair.

When I awoke, the room was cold, and had a strangely desolate air about it, though it was full of familiar things: my mother's work-table, covered in papers as usual; next to it, the cabinet with its little drawers, overflowing with the notes I made; the curtained-off area at one end containing cameras and other photographic necessaries; the faded Turkey rug; the rows of books, each one a well-remembered old friend; the tripod-table on which I kept my travelling copy of Donne's sermons; the portrait of my mother, which used to hang over the fireplace in the best parlour at Sandchurch; and, on the mantel-piece, next to the clock, the rosewood box that had once held 'Miss Lamb's' two hundred sovereigns.

I sat staring into the empty hearth, still in my coat and boots. I was troubled in spirit, and once again, as it had done on my last night at Evenwood, the sleep my mind and body crave fled from me, like some taunting nymph.

What was happening to me? I had no happiness, no contentment, only restiveness and agitation. I was adrift on an ocean of mystery, like the blackbird in my dream – powerless, frozen. What dark creatures inhabited the unseen deeps beneath me? What landfall awaited me? Or was this my fate, to be forever pushed and pulled, now this way, now that, by the winds and currents of circumstance, without respite? The goal that I had once had constantly before me – simple and supreme – of proving my claim to be the lawfully begotten son of Lord Tansor, seemed to have become dismembered and dispersed, like a great imperial galleon full of treasure dashed to pieces on a rocky shore.

There was a piece of paper lying on the tripod-table beside me, a stub of pencil with it. Seizing both, I began to compose a hasty memorandum to myself, outlining the problems confronting me that were now demanding resolution.

I read over what I had written, three, four, five times, in mounting despair. These disjoined and yet, it seemed, inter-twined and co-essential conundrums swirled and chattered and roared around my head like Satan's legions, refusing utterly to coagulate into a single reasoned conclusion, until I could stand it no more.

As I stood up to throw off my great-coat, something fell out of the pocket, and landed on the hearth-rug. Looking down, I saw that it was the package containing the proofs of Dr Daunt's translation of Iamblichus, handed to me by the servant from the George as I was about to take train from Stamford. It was impossible to bend my mind to such work at present, and so I threw the package on my work-table, intending to open it when my mind was clearer.

I dozed for an hour or so. When I awoke, the idea of a chop and some hot coffee suddenly thrust itself forward for my consideration. I examined the proposal and found it excellent in every way. It was still early, but I knew of a place.

I stood up, rather shakily reaching for my great-coat, which was lying on the floor. Whoa there!

And then the floor-boards seemed to fall away beneath me and I was tumbling through the air, spinning round and round, descending ever deeper into a great yawning, roaring void.

I CAME ROUND TO FIND MRS GRAINGER DABBING MY FACE WITH A WET napkin.

'Lord, sir,' she said, 'I thought you was dead. Can you stand, sir? There now, a little more. I 'ave you, sir, don't you worry. Dorrie 'ere'll help. Look sharp, dear. Take Mr Glapthorn's arm. Gentle does it. That's it. All's well now.'

I had never heard her say so many words to me. Sitting back in my chair, with the wet napkin tied round my forehead, I was also surprised to see her daughter standing by her side. Then, to my complete astonishment, I learned that it was Monday morning, and that I had slept the clock round.

After I had recovered a little, I thanked them both, and asked the girl how she was.

'I am well, thank you, sir.'

'As you see, Mr Glapthorn,' said her mother, smiling weakly, 'she goes on very well. A good girl still, sir.'

Dorrie herself said nothing, but seemed, indeed, in fine fettle, with a bright expression on her face, dressed in a neat little outfit that showed off her figure extremely well, and altogether looking winsome and contented.

I said I was glad to hear, and to see for myself, that Dorrie appeared to be prospering, and felt not a little satisfaction that I had done some good by the simple expedient of employing her mother, and sending a little money to Dorrie every now and again.

'Prospering?' exclaimed Mrs Grainger, with a sly look at her daughter. 'Why, you may say so, sir. Go on, Dorrie, spill it.'

I looked quizzically at the girl, who blushed slightly before speaking.

'We have come to tell you, sir, that I am to be married, and to thank you for all you have done for us.'

She bobbed sweetly, giving me such a fond and modest look as she did so, that it fair made my heart melt.

'And who is your husband to be, Dorrie?' I asked.

'If you please, sir, his name is Martlemass, Geoffrey Martlemass.'

'A most excellent name. Mrs Geoffrey Martlemass. So far, so good. And what sort of a man is Mr Martlemass?'

'A good and kind man, sir,' she replied, unable to hold back a smile.

'Better yet. And what does good and kind Mr Geoffrey Martlemass do?'

'He is a clerk, sir, to Mr Gillory Piggott, of Gray's-Inn.'

'A legal gentleman! Mr Martlemass holds a pretty full hand, I see. Well, I congratulate you, Dorrie, on your good fortune in finding good, kind Mr Martlemass. But you must tell him that I shall expect no nonsense from him, and that if he does not love you as you deserve, he shall have me to answer to.'

A little more good-humoured raillery on my part followed, after which Dorrie ran off to fetch in some breakfast, Mrs Grainger set to with mop and bucket, and I repaired to my bed-chamber to wash my face and change my linen.

With breakfast over, and my chin shaved, I felt revived and ready for the day. Dorrie was off to meet her beau at Gray's-Inn, and that piece of information immediately settled the matter of what I would do with myself for the next few hours.

'If you will allow me, Dorrie,' I said gallantly, 'I'll escort you.'

I offered her my arm, an act that appeared to amaze Mrs Grainger greatly, and off we went.

. . .

IT WAS A CLEAR BRIGHT MORNING, THOUGH THERE WAS A STIFF BREEZE off the river. As we walked, Dorrie spoke a little more of Mr Geoffrey Martlemass, whom I began to conceive as a dependable sort of fellow, if a little serious in his outlook, an impression confirmed when we encountered a small man of notably anxious mien, distinguished by a pair of magnificently bushy mutton-chops,* standing by the entrance to Field-court.

'Dorothy, my love,' he cried, in an anguished tone, on seeing us. 'You are past your time. Whatever has happened?'

Dorrie, releasing her arm from mine and taking his, laughed and chided him gently that it was only a minute or two beyond the hour appointed and that he must not worry so about her.

'Worry? But naturally I worry,' he said, apparently distraught that he could ever be thought too solicitous for the welfare of one so precious. We were introduced, and Mr Martlemass, Dorrie's senior by some years, removed his hat (revealing an almost perfectly bald pate except for two little tufts of hair above each ear) and made a low bow, before grasping my hand and shaking it so vigorously that Dorrie had to tell him to stop.

'You, sir,' he said, with great solemnity, replacing his hat and throwing back his shoulders, 'have the appearance of a man, and yet I know you to be a saint. You amaze me, sir. I thought the age of miracles had passed; but here you are, a living, breathing saint, walking the streets of London.'

In this wise, Mr Martlemass began to heap praises upon my head for, as he put it, 'rescuing Dorothy and her estimable parent from certain death or worse'. I did not enquire of him what he conceived could be worse than death; but the warmth of his grat-

*[Side-whiskers, narrow at the ears, broad and rounded at the lower jaw. *Ed.*]

itude for the little I had done to remove Dorrie from the life in which I had first found her was most apparent, and rather affecting. I then learned that he was a member of a small philanthropical society that took an especial interest in the rescue and rehabilitation of fallen females, as well as being a churchwarden at St Bride's,* where he had first encountered Dorrie. Normally I cannot abide a treacly do-gooder, but there was a simple sincerity about Mr Martlemass that I could not help but admire.

I let the little man rattle on, which he seemed determined to do, but at last proclaimed that I must leave them, and so made to go.

'Oh, Mr Martlemass,' I said, turning back as though struck by an afterthought. 'I believe an old College friend of mine has chambers in Gray's-Inn. We have lost touch, and I would so like to see him again. I wonder whether you know him by any chance – Mr Lewis Pettingale?'

'Mr Pettingale? You don't say so! Why, certainly I know the gentleman. He has the set above my employer, Mr Gillory Piggott, QC. Mr Piggott is in Court today,' he added, lowering his voice somewhat, 'which is why I have been allowed to take an hour or so for an early fish ordinary at the Three Tuns† with my intended. Mr Piggott is a most considerate employer.'

He directed me to a black-painted door in a range of red-brick houses on the far side of the court. I thanked him, and said that I would try to call on Mr Pettingale the next day, as I had some urgent business to attend to in another part of town.

We parted, and I walked off towards Gray's-Inn-lane, dirty and dismal even on such a bright day. Stopping at a book-stall, I began

*[In Fleet Street. Designed by Wren and completed in 1703. *Ed.*]

†[The Three Tuns Tavern was in Billingsgate. Its celebrated fish 'ordinaries' – i.e. fixed price meals – were served at one and four o'clock; the charge was 1*s.* 6*d.*, including butcher's meat and cheese. *Ed.*]

idly turning over the mouldering tomes there displayed (ever hopeful, like all bibliophiles, of unearthing some great rarity). After five or ten minutes, I returned to Field-court.

The court was deserted, the love-birds had flown; and so through the black door I went, and up the stairs.

· 30 ·

*Noscitur e sociis**

IN MY WORK AS PRIVATE AGENT FOR MR TREDGOLD, I HAD LEARNED TO follow my nose. It has rarely let me down. There was a distinct smell about Mr Lewis Pettingale, though I knew nothing about him, only that he appeared to be a close associate of Daunt's. But this was enough for me to give up an hour or two of my time, with the object of making his acquaintance, and to see what might come of it. I had my opening planned. It might be instructive, I thought, to discuss the subject of forged cheques.

On the first floor, a painted name-plate greeted me: 'Mr L. J. Pettingale'. I put my ear to the door. Someone within coughs. An inner door closes. I knock softly – it wouldn't do simply to walk in – but no one answers. So I enter.

It is a large, well-appointed chamber, with oak panel-work, a stone fireplace, and a plaster ceiling of the Stuart period. To my left as I enter are two tall windows that give out onto the court below. A fire blazes pleasantly in the dog-grate† on the hearth, on either side of which two comfortable chairs are set. Above the fire-place hangs a painting of a bay horse, a terrier at its feet, standing in a park landscape. In the corner of the room, to my right, is another door, closed, through which I can hear the sound of

*['He is known by his companions'. *Ed.*]

†[A free-standing raised fire-basket of wrought iron, usually on ornamental legs and having a decorated backplate. *Ed.*]

someone attempting, in a thin tenor voice, a version of the aria *Il mio tesoro,** to the accompaniment of water splashing.

I decide to leave the singer to his ablutions, settle myself in one of the chairs, feet on the fender, and light up a cigar. I have almost finished smoking it when the door in the corner opens and a tall, thin man emerges, wearing an ornately fashioned brocade dressing-robe, Persian slippers, and a tasselled skull-cap made of red velvet, from beneath which a few meagre strands of straw-coloured hair descend almost to his shoulders. He is about my own age, but looks prematurely aged. His skin is sallow and papery, and from where I am sitting I am not sure that he possesses eyebrows.

'Good morning,' I say, smiling broadly and throwing my cigar butt into the fire.

He stands for a moment, disbelief on his skull-like face.

'Who the devil are you?'

His voice, like everything else about him, is thin, with a reedy, querulous tremor about it.

'Grafton, Edward Grafton. Pleased to meet you. Cigar? No? Oh well, bad habit, I'm sure.'

He is taken aback for a moment by my coolness, and then asks haughtily whether he knows me.

'Well, now, there's a question,' I reply. 'Are you of a philosophical turn? For we might spend a good few hours considering the nature of knowledge. It is a large subject. We might begin with Aquinas, who said that, for any knower, knowledge is after the fashion of his own nature; or, as St Augustine put it . . .'

But Mr Pettingale seems disinclined to enter into a discussion on this interesting question. He angrily stamps a slippered foot,

*[From Mozart's *Don Giovanni,* sung by Don Ottavio, Donna Anna's fiancé. Convinced that Don Giovanni has killed Anna's father, Don Ottavio swears to avenge her and to return 'as the messenger of punishment and death'. *Ed.*]

threatens to call for assistance if I do not leave at once, and grows quite red – almost replicating the colour of his skull-cap – with the exertion of it all. I tell him to calm himself; that I have merely come to seek a professional opinion; and that I knocked at the door but could not make myself heard. Somewhat calmer, he asks whether I am in the profession myself – an instructing solicitor, perhaps? Alas, no, I tell him; my interest is personal, though it is a matter of law on which I wish to consult him. I invite him, with a broad smile, to sit down, which he does, a little reluctantly, looking pleasingly foolish in his dandyish get-up. As he takes his seat, I vacate my own chair and stand with my back to one of the tall windows, through which soft sunshine is now pouring.

'Here it is, Mr Pettingale,' I say. 'I put a case to you. Some years ago, two rascals masquerading as gentlemen swindle a firm of solicitors out of a considerable amount of money – let us say, for the sake of argument, fifteen hundred pounds. The thing is done cleverly – one almost admires the cleverness – and the two scallywags come out the other end without a stain on their characters, but considerably richer than when they started. There is a third rascal, but we shall come to him in a moment. More than this, they so contrive matters that, when all is done, an innocent man is sent to the other side of the world, to toil his life out, on their behalf, in the wilderness of Van Diemen's Land.* Now, the question on which I wish to seek your professional opinion is this: knowing, as I believe I do, the identity of two of the three persons I have described, how may I best lay a charge against them, so that they can be brought at last to justice?'

The effect of my speech is most gratifying. His mouth falls open; he reddens even more, and begins to sweat.

'You say nothing, Mr Pettingale? A lawyer with nothing to say!

*[i.e. Tasmania. *Ed.*]

A most uncommon sight. But by your uncomfortable demeanour, I see you have perceived that I have been playing a little game with you. Well then; let us be more direct, shall we? What is done is done. Your secret is safe with me – for the time being, at least. I have no argument with you, Mr Pettingale. My real interest lies in your friend, the distinguished author. You know to whom I allude?'

He nods dumbly.

'I wish to know a little more about your association with this gentleman. I will not trouble you with my reasons.'

'Blackmail, I suppose,' says Pettingale mournfully, taking off his cap and using it to wipe his perspiring brow. 'Though how you come to know all about it is beyond me.'

'Blackmail? Why yes, you have it, Mr Pettingale. A palpable hit! You are a sharp one, I see. So: the floor is yours. Be quick, be bold, hold nothing back. I would particularly wish that you do not hold anything back. Let us be completely frank with one another. And, for good measure, you may throw in a few words concerning the third rascal. Again, I'm sure you know to whom I am referring?'

Once more he nods, but does not speak. I wait; but still he says nothing. He bites his lip, and his knuckles turn white with gripping the arms of the chair so hard. I begin to get a little impatient, and tell him so.

'I cannot,' he says at last, with a kind of faltering moan. 'They – they will – '

As he is speaking, I see him give a sudden darting glance towards the door, and in a flash he is on his feet. But I am ready for him. I throw him back into his chair and stand over him. I ask again for him to begin his recitation, but still he will not sing out. For the third and last time, I tell him to speak, taking out one of my pocket-pistols, and laying it with exaggerated deliberation on the table. He blanches, but shakes his head. I try another means of encouragement, and *voila*!

The prospect of having your fingers broken one by one appears to be a mighty incentive to do as you are told; and in no time at all he capitulates. Here, then, though a little more persuading was required as we went along, is what Mr Lewis Pettingale, of Gray's-Inn, told me on that October afternoon.

He had been introduced to Phoebus Daunt at the Varsity by a mutual friend, a Kingsman* by the name of Bennett. They had hit it off straight away, and quickly cemented their friendship by discovering a shared, though largely untested, enthusiasm for the turf. Off they would go to Newmarket, whenever occasion offered, where they got in with a rather dangerous set of men up from London. These flash coves knew what they were about, and they welcomed Daunt and Pettingale with open arms. Bets were placed by the pair and, in short order, money was lost. No matter; their new friends were more than willing to advance them a little credit; and then a little more. At last, with the touching optimism of youth, our heroes determined on a rather risky course: they would hazard all that they had – or, rather, all that they had been advanced – on a single race. If their choice came in, all would be well.

But it did not come in, and all was not well. However, their benefactors took a statesman-like view of the situation. If the gents would co-operate in a scheme that this company of obliging family men† had in view, then they would be pleased to consider the debt paid. There might even be a little something in it for them. If not . . . The offer was quickly taken up, and one of the gang, an impressive party with a prominent set of Newgate knockers,‡ was

*[i.e. a member of King's College. *Ed.*]

†[A slang term for the criminal classes. *Ed.*]

‡[Heavily greased side-whiskers, which swept back to, or over, the ears. *Ed.*]

deputed to assist the noviciates in the prosecution of a little well-planned fraud.

The two young scholars took to the business with a certain aptitude for what was required, particularly on the part of the Rector's son. I need not repeat what was told to me by Dr Maunder, about how the fraud was accomplished; I will only say that Pettingale revealed that the shadowy person who had employed the dupe, Hensby, had been Daunt, and that it was Daunt also who, after demonstrating to the gang a remarkable facility to replicate signatures, had actually carried out the forgeries.

'And who was Mr Verdant?' I asked. 'He was part of the dodge, wasn't he?'

'Certainly,' said Pettingale. 'A leading light in the little fraternity we got mixed up with at Newmarket. He was the one appointed to shepherd us through the business. Couldn't have done it without him. Burglary was his trade. None better than Verdant. He broke into the solicitor's office and got us the blank cheques.'

'Verdant, now,' I said. 'Uncommon name, that.'

'Pseudonymous,' Pettingale came back. 'Not his own, though few people knew his real one.'

'But you did, I think?'

'Oh, yes. His mother knew him as Pluckrose. Josiah Pluckrose.'

I said nothing on hearing Pluckrose's name, but inwardly exulted that the suspicions that I had been harbouring as to the identity of Mr Verdant had been proved correct. The origin of his pseudonym was nothing more than this. At Doncaster, in the year '38, he had put twenty stolen guineas on a rank outsider called Princess Verdant, who rewarded his faith in her by coming in at extremely favourable odds, though her victory may have been assisted by the fact – barely worth mentioning – that she was a four-year-old entered in a race for three-year-olds.* No matter. Thereafter, he was known as 'Mr Verdant' to his friends and associates amongst the capital's criminal fraternities.

After the dodge on the solicitors had been successfully brought off, Pluckrose fell out with his former colleagues over the division of the spoils and quit the gang in high dudgeon, vowing to be revenged on them all. And revenged he was. Not one of his confederates – five in number – lived to see the year out: one was found in the river at Wapping with his throat cut; another was bludgeoned to death as he left the Albion Tavern one evening;† the three that remained simply disappeared from the face of the earth and were never seen again. Pettingale could not conclusively say that Pluckrose had done for them all himself; but that he had signed their death warrants, as it were, seemed certain.

'The last to go was Isaac Gabb, the youngest member of the gang – elder brother kept the public-house down in Rotherhithe where the gang used to meet. Rather a decent fellow, young Gabb, despite his roguery. The brother took it hard, and takes it hard still, as I hear. He'd have come down on Pluckrose if he could, not a doubt of it, but he knew him only as Verdant, you see, and as such he'd disappeared, like Master Isaac, without a trace, and was never heard of again. Verdant was dead. Long live Pluckrose.'

Then Pettingale's story turned to the subject in which I was most interested. After making a little money from the original fraud, Phoebus Daunt developed a taste for criminality, and began to look upon himself as quite a captain of the swell mob. Having no clear idea of what he would do in the world when he had taken

*[A common method of rigging races, along with pulling favourites and doping. As Baron Alderson noted in his summing up of a case brought before the Court of Exchequer after the 1844 Derby, 'if gentlemen will condescend to race with blackguards they must expect to be cheated'. *Ed.*]
†[At 153 Aldersgate Street. *Ed.*]

his degree, though he might babble to Lord Tansor about the prospect of a Fellowship, and feeling that a man of his genius needed a certain minimum amount of capital with which to establish a position in society, which he could not at that moment lay his hands on, he conceived the practical, though by no means original, notion of taking what he needed from other people. To assist him in the enterprise, he enlisted his friend and fellow fraudster Pettingale, for his legal brain, and their erstwhile companion-in-arms Josiah Pluckrose, alias Verdant, for his brawn, as well as his his demonstrable skills with the jemmy and the other tools of the ken-cracker's art.*

I own that I could not have been more astonished if Pettingale had told me that Phoebus Daunt was none other than Spring-Heeled Jack himself.† But he had even more to tell.

The extraordinary head for business, which Lord Tansor believed that he had discovered in his favourite, was in reality nothing else but a low talent for devising schemes to relieve the gullible of their money. I might have regarded this as harmless enough, for a man must live, and there are a million deserving fools in the world ready and willing to be fleeced; but when he practised his deceits on my father, who was not in the least gullible, only properly trusting of someone to whom he had shown an uncommon degree of preference, and from whom he had a right to expect loyalty and deference – then the case was

*[Ken-cracker: slang term for house-breaker. *Ed.*]

†[A terrifying cloaked figure that began to terrorize London in 1837. His usual modus operandi was to pounce on unsuspecting passers-by, often women, and rip at their clothes with claw-like hands. He was sometimes said to breathe fire, had eyes that burned like hot coals, and was capable of leaping great heights over walls and fences. Whether Jack was real or imagined is still debated, though the attacks were widely reported in the press. *Ed.*]

very much altered. And it was all to ingratiate himself still further with his Lordship, with the object – duly attained – of insinuating himself ever more closely into the latter's affairs.

The 'speculations', to which he had freely confessed to Lord Tansor, were nothing but gimcrackery; the 'profits' that he returned to his protector were only the proceeds of various swindles and chicaneries. Some were epic in conception: imaginary gold-mines in Peru, a projected tunnel under the Swiss Alps, proposed railway lines that were never built. Others were more modest, or were merely confidence tricks performed on the unwary.

False documents of all kinds, concocted with superlative skill and aplomb by Daunt, were their principal weapons. Inventively convincing references and recommendations ascribed to men of known character and reputation; fictitious statements of assets from distinguished banking-houses and accomptants, counterfeit certificates of ownership, dexterously produced maps of non-existent tracts of land, grandiose plans for buildings that would never be built. Daunt, with help from the young lawyer Pettingale, began to attain a certain mastery of the spurious, whilst Pluckrose was retained to encourage the faint-hearted amongst those they preyed upon, and to discourage those inclined to squeal about their losses to the authorities. They chose their victims with infinite care, adopted clever disguises and aliases, hired premises, employed dupes like the unfortunate Hensby, and conducted themselves always with gravity and sobriety; and then, when all was done, they evaporated into thin air, leaving not a wrack behind.

Now I had the measure of Phoebus Rainsford Daunt indeed, and what a joy it was to have the truth revealed at last! The insolent and preening scribbler was also a deep-dyed sharp: a practised chizzler, no better than the macers on the Highway.* Mr Pettingale continued to sing out nicely. His colour had returned to its customary pastiness, and perspiration no longer stood out on his forehead. Indeed he seemed, to my eye, to be warming to his task, and I began to sense that all was not as it once had been between the lawyer and his literary friend.

'We don't see each other as much as we did,' he said at last, looking meditatively into the fire. 'All very well, you know, when we were younger. Difficult to explain – excites the mind greatly, this sort of work. And brings home the bacon. But it started to go against the grain a bit – some of the chaps we took were quite decent sorts of fellows, wives and families, etcetera, and we left them with nothing. Anyway, I told Daunt we couldn't go on for ever. Sooner or later we'd slip up. Didn't fancy following Hensby on the boat† – or worse. Came to a head when that unutterable blackguard Pluckrose did for his wife. Never understood why Daunt brought him in – and told him so. Capable of anything, Pluckrose. We knew that, of course. Bit of a flare-up, I'm afraid. Words said, and all that. Gulling a flat‡ one thing. Topping your wife quite another. Very bad business. Worst of it was that Pluckrose got off by some piece of trickery and some other cove paid his account in full and swung for what he'd done. Clever work, that, never seen better. Sir Ephraim Gadd, briefed by Tredgolds. Anyway, truth is, I thought it was time we threw over Pluckrose once and for all and went steady. Thought Daunt would

*[*Sharp*: someone constantly ready to deceive you; chizzler: slang term from *chizzle*, to cheat; *macers*: thieves or sharps ('Flash Dictionary', in *Sinks of London Laid Open*, 1848). By 'the Highway' the author means the Ratcliffe Highway, which ran from East Smithfield to Shadwell High Street. It was described by Watts Phillips in *The Wild Tribes of London* (1855) as 'the head-quarters of unbridled vice and drunken violence – of all that is dirty, disorderly, and debased'. *Ed.*]

†[i.e. transportation. *Ed.*]

‡[Slang term for a gullible victim. *Ed.*]

agree – in the public eye, toast of the literary world, and all that. He said I might do as I pleased, but *he* had only just got started, and that a new tack he was on would set him up for life.'

'New tack?'

'*Apropos* his uncle, as he called him. Lord Tansor. Powerful gent. Know the name, do you? Lost his own son, I believe, and thought he'd have Daunt instead. Very rum, but there it is. Old boy bit of a tartar, but rich as Croesus, and Daunt was comfortably situated, for he stood in a fair way to step into the old man's shoes in the course of time. But he couldn't wait. Thought he'd take a little bit here and there in advance. Ready cash first, slyly done, for he had Uncle Tansor's trust, you see. Then a little judicious forging of the old boy's signature – second nature to Daunt. Rather a genius in that way. Amazing to observe. Give him a minute and he'd produce you the signature of the Queen herself, and good enough to fool the Prince-Consort. Old boy as sharp as they come, but Daunt knew how to play him. Reeled him in nice as you like. Didn't suspect a thing. A dangerous game though – I told him so, but nothing would move him. Old boy's secretary got on the scent, keen old cove called Carteret. When Mr Secretary became suspicious of him, Daunt started on his new tack. We'd been working a sweet little turn, our first for some months, but Daunt went cold on it. Everything put in jeopardy. More words, I fear. Much said in anger. Not pleasant. He said he had something better.'

'And what was it?'

'Only this: the old boy has a very grand house in the country – been there myself. Said house in the country packed to the rafters with portable booty.'

'Booty?'

'Prints, porcelain, glassware, books – Daunt knew a bit about books. All cleverly and quietly done, of course, and everything now laid up safely in a repository – in case the old boy didn't come across, he said, or against some unseen occurrence. Worth a king's ransom.'

'And where is this repository?'

'Ah, if only I could tell you. He cut me out. Dissolved the partnership. Haven't seen him these twelve months.'

I had him now, had him tight in the palm of my hand! After all these years, I had been given the means to bring him down. His box at the Opera, his house in Mecklenburgh-square, his horses, and his dinners – all paid for by the proceeds of crime! I was almost delirious with joy at the prospect of my triumph. Why, I could now destroy him at a moment's notice; and, in the ensuing scandal, would Lord Tansor rush to his heir's defence? I think not.

'You'd speak out against him, of course,' I said to Pettingale.

'Speak out? What do you mean?'

'Publicly declare what you have just told me.'

'Now hang on a moment.' Pettingale made to get up out of his chair, but I pushed him back.

'Something wrong, Mr Pettingale?'

'Look here,' he said, 'I can't, you know. Implicate myself, and all that. And my life wouldn't be worth a sniff.'

'Don't take on so,' I said soothingly. 'I might only need you to testify privately to Lord Tansor. No repercussions. Just a quiet conversation with his Lordship. You could do that all right, couldn't you?'

He thought for a moment. To aid reflection, I picked up my pistol from the table.

At length, looking whiter and pastier than ever, he said that he supposed he could, if matters were so arranged that his identity was concealed from Lord Tansor.

'We'll need some evidence,' I said. 'Something unequivocal, in writing. Could you lay your hands on such a thing?'

He nodded, and bowed his head.

'Bravo, Pettingale,' I said with a smile, patting him on the shoulders. 'But remember this: if you tell your former associates of our conversation, or if you subsequently take it into your head to be unco-operative, you may be assured of paying a very high price. I hope we understand each other?'

He did not reply, so I repeated my question. He looked up at me, with such a weary and resigned look.

'Yes, Mr Grafton,' he said, closing his eyes and giving a great sigh. 'I understand you perfectly.'

· 31 ·

*Flamma fumo est proxima**

I LEFT FIELD-COURT IN THE HIGHEST OF SPIRITS. AT LAST I HAD THE means to destroy Daunt's reputation, as he had once destroyed mine. It was exhilarating to feel my power over my enemy, and to know that he was even now going about his business in ignorance of the Damoclean sword hanging over him. But still there was the question of when to draw on Pettingale's testimony, and on the evidence that he claimed he could provide concerning Daunt's criminal activities. To do so before I could prove to Lord Tansor that I was his son would be an incomplete revenge. How infinitely more tormenting it would be for Daunt if, at the very moment of his destruction, I could stand revealed as the true heir!

My thoughts now returned to Mr Carteret's murder, and to the question of his 'discovery'. He had said to me, during our meeting in Stamford, that the matter that he had wished to lay before Mr Tredgold had a critical bearing on Daunt's prospects. I was now absolutely certain that Mr Carteret had been in possession of information relating to the Tansor succession that would have helped me establish my identity; it might even have provided the unassailable proof that I had been seeking. It therefore followed that what was of the utmost value to me had also been of value to someone else.

Suspicions and hypotheses filled my head, but I could come to no clear conclusion. Back in my rooms, I wrote a long memoran-

*['Flame follows smoke' – i.e. there is no smoke without fire (Pliny). *Ed.*]

dum to Mr Tredgold in which I attempted to marshal under various heads all the various matters relating to recent events. Then I walked briskly to Paternoster-row, and knocked on the Senior Partner's door.

There was no reply. I knocked again. Then Rebecca appeared, coming down the internal stairs that led to Mr Tredgold's private apartments.

''E's not there,' she said. ''E left for Canterbury yesterday, to see 'is brother.'

'When will he be back?' I asked.

'Thursday,' she said.

Three days. I simply could not wait.

When I sat down at my desk I found an envelope containing a black-edged card, with the following communication printed in black-letter type:

> The family and friends of the late Mr Paul Carteret, M.A., F.R.S.A., request the favour of Mr Edward Glapthorn's company on Friday next, the 4th of November, 1853, to unite with them in paying the last tribute of respect to the deceased. Mourners are asked to assemble at 11 o'clock, at the DowerHouse, Evenwood, Northamptonshire, and then to proceed in the coaches provided to the church of St Michael and All Angels, Evenwood. An early reply to the undertaker, Mr P Gutteridge, Baxter's Yard, Easton, Northamptonshire, will oblige.

I duly sat down to write a formal note of acceptance to Mr Gutteridge, and a personal note to Miss Carteret, which I called for one of the clerks to take to the Post-office.

This business done, I determined at once to go down to Canterbury, to see my employer. I therefore instantly dashed off a note to Bella, whom I had been engaged to meet that evening, and then consulted my Bradshaw.

I ARRIVED IN CANTERBURY AT LAST TO FIND MYSELF STANDING BEFORE a tall, rather forbidding three-storey residence close by the Westgate. Marden House stood a little back from the road, separated from it by a narrow paved area and a low brick wall topped with railings.

I was admitted, and then shown into a downstairs room. A few moments later, Dr Jonathan Tredgold entered.

He was shorter and a little heavier than his brother, with the same feathery hair, though darker and in somewhat shorter supply. He held my card in his hand.

'Mr Edward Glapthorn, I believe?'

I gave a slight bow.

'I beg you to excuse this intrusion, Dr Tredgold,' I began, 'but I hoped it might be possible to speak with your brother.'

He pulled his shoulders back and looked at me as if I had said something insulting.

'My brother has been taken ill,' he said. 'Seriously ill.'

He saw the shock that his words had produced, and gestured to me to sit down.

'This is sad news, Dr Tredgold,' I began. 'Very sad. Is he—'

'A paralytic seizure, I am afraid. Completely unexpected.'

Dr Tredgold could not give me a categorical assurance, as things then stood, that his brother's paralysis would pass quickly, or that, even if it did abate, there would not be severe and permanent debilitation of his powers.

'I believe that my brother has spoken of you,' he said after a short space of silence. Then he suddenly slapped his knee and cried, 'I have it! You were amanuensis, secretary, or what not, to the son of the authoress.'

I struggled to conceal the effect of this wholly unexpected and astonishing reference to my foster-mother, but evidently without success.

'You are surprised at my powers of recall, no doubt. But I only have to be told something once, you see, and it can be brought to mind in perpetuity. My dear brother calls it a phenomenon. It was a matter of much amusement between us – a little game we would play whenever he came here. Christopher would always try to catch me out, but he never would, you know. He mentioned to me, some years ago now, I believe, that you had such a connexion with Mrs Glyver, who I believe was a client of the firm's and whose works of fiction he and I – and our sister – used greatly to admire; and of course I have never forgotten it. It is a gift I have; and, in addition to the harmless amusement that it affords my brother and me whenever we meet, it has had some practical use in my medical career.'

His words were delivered with a succession of deep sighs. It was apparent that a close bond united the two brothers, and I divined also that the doctor's expert knowledge made him less sanguine, with regard to the Senior Partner's prognosis, than he might have been without it.

'Dr Tredgold,' I ventured, 'I have come to regard your brother as more than an employer. Since I first came into his service, he has become, I might almost say, a kind of father to me; and his generosity towards me has been out of all proportion to my deserts. We have also shared many interests – of a specialist character. In short, he is a person I esteem highly, and it pains me greatly to hear this terrible news. I wonder, would it be at all presumptuous if—'

'You would like to see him?' Dr Tredgold broke in, anticipating my request. 'And then, perhaps, we might take a little supper together.'

I accompanied Dr Tredgold upstairs, to a bedchamber at the rear of the house. A nurse was sitting by the bed, whilst in a chair by the window sat a lady in black, reading. She looked up as we entered.

'Mr Edward Glapthorn, may I present my sister, Miss Rowena Tredgold. Mr Glapthorn is come from the office, my dear, on his own account, to ask after Christopher.'

I judged her to be some fifty years of age, and, with her prematurely silvered hair and blue eyes, she bore a most remarkable resemblance to her afflicted brother, who lay on the bed, deathly still, eyes closed, his mouth drawn down unnaturally to one side.

The introductions over, she returned to her book, though out of the tail of my eye I caught her looking at me intently as I stood, with Dr Tredgold, by the bedside.

The sight of my employer in such distress of body and mind was most painful to me. Dr Tredgold whispered that the paralysis had affected his brother's left side, that his vision was seriously impaired, and that it was presently almost impossible for him to speak. I asked again whether there was a chance of recuperation.

'He may recover. I have known it before. The swelling in the brain is still in the acute phase. We must watch him closely for any deterioration. If he begins to wake soon, then we may hope that, in time, he may regain motivity, and perhaps also some operative residue of his communicative faculties.'

'Was there any immediate cause?' I enquired. 'Some extreme excitation of feeling, or other catastrophe, that might have precipitated the attack?'

'Nothing discernible,' he replied. 'He arrived here last night in the best of spirits. When he did not come down at his usual hour this morning, my sister said I should go up to see whether all was well. He was in the grip of the seizure when I found him.'

I took supper with Dr Tredgold and his sister in a cold, high-ceilinged room, sparsely furnished except for a monstrous *faux*-Elizabethan buffet that took up nearly a whole wall. Miss Tredgold said little during the meal, which was as sparse as the furniture; but I felt her eye upon me more than once. Her look was one of strained concentration, as though she was attempting, unsuccessfully, to recall something from the depths of memory.

Suddenly, there was a loud knocking at the front door, and a moment or two later a servant came in to announce that Dr Tredgold was wanted urgently at the house of a neighbour who had been taken ill. I used the opportunity to take my leave of the doctor and his sister. Though they pressed me to stay the night, I preferred instead to take a room at the Royal Fountain Hotel. I wished to be alone with my thoughts; for now I had lost my only ally, the one person who could help me find a way through the labyrinth of supposition and speculation surrounding the death of Mr Carteret.

I secured my accommodation with little trouble. Having a headache, I took a few drops of laudanum,* and closed my eyes. But my sleep was troubled by a strange and disturbing dream.

I appear to be standing in a darkened place of great size. At first I am alone, but then, as if a light is slowly being let in from some unseen source, I discern the figure of Mr Tredgold. He is sitting in a chair with a book in his hands, slowly turning over the

*[A mixture of opium and alcohol. Legal restrictions on the use of opium did not come into force until 1868 and at this period laudanum was widely prescribed, and widely abused. Initially a drug for the poor, laudanum became a favoured means of pain relief for the middle classes: celebrated literary users included Coleridge, De Quincey, and Elizabeth Barrett Browning. The novelist Wilkie Collins became virtually dependent on it and confessed that much of *The Moonstone* (1868) had been written under its influence. 'Who is the man who invented laudanum?' asks Lydia Gwilt in Collins's *Armadale* (1866). 'I thank him from the bottom of my heart.' *Ed.*]

pages, and lingering every now and again on some point of interest. He looks up and sees me. His mouth is drawn down to one side, and he appears to be mouthing words and sentences, but no sound comes out. He beckons me over, and points to the book. I look down to see what he wishes to show me. It is a portrait of a lady in black. I look closer. It is the painting of Lady Tansor, which I had seen hanging in Mr Carteret's work-room at Evenwood. Then more light floods in, and behind Mr Tredgold I make out a figure on a black-draped dais, sitting behind a tall desk and writing in a great ledger. This person, too, is dressed in black, and seems to be wearing a grey full-bottomed wig, like a judge; but then I see that it is in fact Miss Rowena Tredgold, with her hair let loose around her shoulders. She stops writing and addresses me.

'Prisoner at the bar. You will give the court your name.'

I open my mouth to speak, but cannot. I am as dumb as Mr Tredgold. She asks me for my name again, but still I am unable to speak. Somewhere a bell tolls.

'Very well,' she says, 'since you will not tell the court who you are, the verdict of the court is that you shall be taken hence to a place of execution, there to be hanged by the neck until you are dead. Do you have anything to say?'

I fill my lungs with air, and try to scream out a protest at the top of my voice. But there is only silence.

Back in Temple-street the following day, I remained indoors, beset by a vacillating and porous state of mind in which nothing could be fixed or retained; and so, with the afternoon drawing to a close, I thought I would go down to the Temple Steps, and take my skiff out on the river for half an hour.

Later that evening, Bella received me at Blithe Lodge with her customary warmth, and with many demonstrations of amity.

It was our first meeting since I had made the acquaintance of Miss Carteret, and I was never more conscious of being 'a thing of sin and guilt'.* I sat a little way off and watched Bella as she sat by the fire in Kitty Daley's drawing-room with some of The Academy's junior nymphs. Whores, every one of them, of course, but a sweeter, kinder, and livelier bunch of girls you could not wish to meet; and Bella was the sweetest and kindest of them all. She looked so fresh and alive, discoursing easily and amusingly to the little sorority gathered all around her of Lord R—'s insistence, during a recent encounter with one of the absent nymphs, that she must dress herself up like the Queen, complete with a diadem of paste diamonds, and a pale blue sash across her bust, whilst he whispered warm encouragements into her ear, in a German accent, as they went to it.

Laughter filled the room; champagne was brought in; cigarettes were lit; Miss Nancy Blake trip to the piano-forte to extemporize, *con brio*, a spirited little waltz, whilst Miss Lilian Purkiss (a flame-haired Amazon) and Miss Tibby Taylor (petite, grey-eyed, and lusciously agile) cantered round and round and in and out of the furniture, giggling as they repeatedly bumped into chairs and tables. Bella, clapping her hands in time to the waltz, looked across to me from time to time and smiled. For though, as usual, she was at the centre of the gaiety, I knew that she never forgot me; in company, she would always seek me out, or would let me know, by a loving look or by gently pressing my arm as she passed, that I was the true and only occupier of her thoughts. Even when

*[Milton, *Comus*, in a passage describing Chastity: 'A thousand liveried angels lackey her,/Driving far off each thing of sin and guilt.' *Ed.*]

I left that evening, she would continue to think fondly of me, and to muse on what we had done together, and what we would do when I next returned to Blithe Lodge.

But what could I now offer her in return? Only neglect, inattention, and betrayal. I was a damned fool, I knew, and did not deserve the tender regard of such an excellent creature. But it was my fate, it seemed, wilfully to cast this treasure from me. She was vividly and gloriously present to my senses at that moment, there in Kitty Daley's drawing-room. I knew that I would give her but little thought when I once again saw the face of Miss Emily Carteret, whom I loved as I could never love Bella. But I could not bear to give Bella up – not yet. The plain fact was that my affection for her had not yet been quite snuffed out, or negated, by what I felt for Miss Carteret. It remained bright and true, though overshadowed by a greater and stranger force. As I looked at her, it was brought home to me that my heart would be broken, too, if I were to turn away from her now, and for nothing gained.

After the rest of the company had departed, she came over and sat next to me, placing a jewelled hand on mine, and looking smilingly into my eyes.

'You have been quiet tonight, Eddie. Has anything happened?'

No, I told her, running my finger-nail gently down her cheek, and then placing her hand to my lips. Nothing has happened.

· 32 ·

*Non omnis moriar**

It is Thursday, November the 3rd 1853. I have arrived back at the Town Station in Peterborough and took a coach to the Duport Arms in Easton. The town, which lies some four miles south-west of the great house belonging to the family from which this establishment takes it name, is, as far as I am aware, distinguished for nothing in particular, except for its antiquity (there has been a settlement here since the time of the Vikings), its quaint cobbled market-square, and the picturesqueness of its slate-roofed houses of mellowed limestone, many of which look out across the valley, from atop the gently sloping ridge upon which the town is built, to the village of Evenwood and the wooded boundaries of the great Park.

After I had settled myself in my room – a long low-beamed apartment overlooking the square – I opened my bag and took out a small black note-book, a remnant of my student days in Germany. Tearing out some notes that I had made on Bulwer's *Anthropometamorphosis*,† I wrote on the new first page the words: Journal of Edward Duport, November mdcccliii. I pondered this title for some time, and decided that it looked very well. But the sensation of forming the letters of my true name for the first time had engendered a *frisson* that was both exhilarating and produc-

*['Not all of me will die': Horace, *Odes*, III. xxx. 6. *Ed.*]

†[*Anthropometamorphosis: Man Transform'd; or, The Artificiall Changeling* (1650), a history of bodily adornments and mutilations, by the physician John Bulwer (fl. 1648–54). *Ed.*]

tive of a strange feeling of unease – as though, in some way that I could not comprehend, I had no right to possess what I knew to be rightfully mine.

I had decided, before leaving for Northamptonshire, that I would begin recording, in brief, the daily course of my life, partly in emulation of my foster-mother's habit, but with the additional purpose of providing myself, and perhaps posterity, with an accurate digest of events as I embarked on what I had become convinced would be a critical phase of my great project. Enough of irresolution and fluctuation. Not only had I forgotten who I was, and what I was capable of: I had also forgotten my destiny. But now I seemed to hear the Iron Master's hammer once more, like gathering thunder, rolling ever closer – the blows raining down faster and harder to fashion the unbreakable links, sparks flying up to the cold sky, the great chain tightening around me as I was dragged ever closer, and now more swiftly than ever, to meet the fate that he had reserved for me. For it is the afternoon of my life, and night approaches.

So I began to write in my new journal, and it is from this source that I have mainly drawn for the remainder of my confession.

TEN O'CLOCK. THE SQUARE WAS DESERTED. A THIN RAIN HAD BEEN falling for the past hour but was now pattering harder against my window, beneath which a creaking board carrying the ancient arms of my family – with the painted motto 'FORTITUDINE VINCIMUS' – swayed back and forth in the wind.

I took dinner in one of the public rooms, with only a sullen, lank-haired waiter for company.

Self: 'Quiet tonight.'

Waiter: 'Just you, sir, and Mr Green, up from London like yourself.'

Self. 'Regular?'

Waiter. 'Sir?'

Self. 'Mr Green: a regular here, perhaps?'

Waiter. 'Occasional. Another glass, sir?'

Back in my room I lay down on my bed, and took out an octavo volume of Donne's *Devotions,* which I had brought with me for its inclusion of the incomparable 'Deaths Duell' – Donne's own funeral sermon. The book was an old companion of mine, which I had purchased during my long sojourn on the Continent.* I contemplated the reproduction of the striking frontispiece to the 1634 edition, showing an effigy of the author in a niche wrapped in his winding sheet, and then mused for a moment on my youthful signature on the fly-leaf: 'Edward Charles Glyver'. Edward Glyver was gone; Edward Duport was to come. But in the here and now, Edward Glapthorn fell asleep over John Donne's great rolling periods, and woke up with a start to hear the church clock striking midnight.

I went over to the window. The square was lit by one gas-lamp on the far side. It was still raining hard. I noted a late wanderer in a long cloak and a slouch hat. My breath clouded the window-pane: when I wiped the glass clean with my sleeve, the wanderer had gone.

I laid my head back on the pillow and slept for an hour or more, but on a sudden I was clear awake. Something had roused me. I lit my candle – twenty minutes past one o'clock by my repeater.† There was no sound, except the rain against the window, and the creaking of the inn sign. Was that the sign swinging

*[This was probably the edition of *Devotions* published in octavo by William Pickering in 1840, which also included (as well as the reproduced frontispiece mentioned by Glyver and the famous 'Deaths Duell' sermon, preached before King Charles I, February 1631), Izaak Walton's *Life of Donne. Ed.*]

†[A repeating pocket watch. *Ed.*]

on its hinges? Or a footfall on the shrunken boards outside my door?

I sat up. There, again – and again! Not the sign swaying in the wind; but another sound. I reached for my pistol as the door handle slowly and silently turned.

But the door was locked and, just as slowly and silently, the handle was turned back. The floor-boards creaked once more, and then all was silence.

Pistol in hand, I carefully opened the door and looked out into the corridor; but there was no one to be seen. There were rooms on either side of mine, Numbers 1 and 3. Stairs led down to the tap-room, with another flight up to the next floor, on which were situated two more rooms. I had no way of knowing whether my unwelcome visitor was still on the premises, perhaps in one of these rooms; but I did not think he would return. I tip-toed to the first of the adjacent chambers: the door was unlocked, the room unoccupied. But the other door, at the head of the stairs, I found was shut fast.

I lay awake for another hour, pistol at the ready. But, as I expected, I was not disturbed again. I concluded at last that I was being foolish, that it was only a fellow guest – Mr Green, perhaps – mistaking my room for his.

And so I gave myself up to sleep.

I AWOKE TO WEAK SUNSHINE, BUT, LOOKING OUTSIDE, SAW THAT THE square was still wet from the night's rain, and that there was a threatening look to the eastern sky. Going downstairs, I asked the waiter from the previous evening whether my fellow guest, Mr Green, had come down yet. The waiter, still sullen, could not say; so I took my breakfast alone.

After concluding my meal, I returned to my room to prepare

myself. I had to take the greatest care to avoid being recognized by Phoebus Daunt, whom I presumed would certainly be present at the interment. I examined myself closely in the mirror. We had not seen each other, face to face, for seventeen years, not since our last meeting in School Yard in the autumn of 1836. Would he trace the lineaments of his old school-fellow in the face that now looked into the glass? I did not think so. My hair was longer and thicker, and, with the assistance of dye, blacker than formerly; altogether, I felt confident that the changes brought about by the passage of time, together with the luxuriant moustachios and side-whiskers that I had since acquired, and a pair of green-glass spectacles, would shield me from discovery. I donned my great-coat, procured an umbrella from the sullen waiter, who seemed to be the only servant in the whole establishment, and set off.

A pleasant walk along a steep tree-shaded road, the banks on each side smothered with glistening ivy, led me out of the town down to Odstock Mill. At the bottom of the hill, I took the way that veered eastwards towards Evenwood village. It wanted a quarter of an hour to eleven o'clock.

In the village, there were already people walking down the lane leading to the church – villagers, I perceived on getting a little closer, amongst whom I recognized Lizzie Brine, walking with another woman. She did not see me, for I was already taking care to intrude myself as little as possible on the scene, having determined not to present myself at the Dower House with the other invited mourners, but to stand back from the proceedings, and observe them from a distance.

I therefore waited until the little crowd had turned under the lych-gate and into the church-yard, and then positioned myself a little way off, behind the trunk of a large sycamore-tree. From here, I had a good view, both of the church and of the gravelled track that branched off to the Dower House. I was also shielded from the view of anyone else coming down the lane that led back to the village. To my left was St Michael and All Angels, a noble building, largely of the thirteenth century, dominated by its celebrated spire – tall and needle-pointed, resting on a slender tower, and crocketed up the angles. As I was gazing up at the golden cross placed on its tip, it began to rain. Before long, it had become a regular torrent, requiring me to open up my borrowed umbrella.

As the clock struck eleven, I heard the sound of footsteps on gravel, and looked out from my place of concealment to see the vanguard of the funeral procession coming down the narrow track from the Dower House ahead of the coaches – a large squadron of pall-bearers, feathermen,* pages, followed by bearded mutes carrying wands, all solemnly be-gowned, and all looking more melancholy than even their duties demanded on account of the heavy rain now soaking their hired finery.

A few moments later, the glass-sided hearse appeared, with its canopy of black ostrich feathers, and decorations of gilded skulls and cherubs, the coffin inside covered over with a dark-purple cloth. Following close behind was the main armada of six or seven funeral coaches. Then I saw Dr Daunt emerge from the porch of the church with his curate, Mr Tidy, at his side. As the first coach passed my vantage point, I noticed that one of the blinds was up, enabling me to catch a clear view of Lord Tansor. He sat, grim-faced, his mouth set tight shut. Then he was gone, but not before I had caught the briefest of glimpses of a tall bearded figure sitting at his right hand. I could not mistake the profile of my enemy.

The remaining coaches, all with their blinds closed, splashed past. Before the lych-gate was an open area, where the vehicles pulled up to discharge their occupants. Attendants rushed for-

*[Hired men carrying plumes of black feathers. *Ed.*]

ward with umbrellas to shepherd the mourners towards the shelter of the church porch; after the latter had entered into the building, the pall-bearers removed the coffin from the hearse and carried it through the rain down the tree-lined path to the church. Lord Tansor, straight-backed, his eyes fixed ahead of him, and looking the very image of proud authority, waved away the offer of an umbrella, and marched off purposefully through the downpour; but Daunt, a few steps behind his Lordship, haughtily signalled to the same servant to perform the service for *him* that his noble patron had refused.

Miss Carteret had been in the second coach, with Mrs Daunt and two other ladies, one of whom was unknown to me; the other, however, I thought must be her French visitor, Mademoiselle Buisson. She was slight of build and of middling height, but except for an impression of pale hair tucked up under her bonnet, her features were obscured by her veil. As Miss Carteret descended from the coach, she took her friend's arm and pulled her close; thus entwined, they made their way to the church, with John Brine following behind, holding a large umbrella over them.

Though Miss Carteret, too, was veiled, the poise and grace of her tall figure could not be disguised. Her back was towards me, but in my mind I could picture her face, as I had first seen it, in the light of a late October afternoon. I watched her, arm in arm with her companion, as she walked towards the church, thinking again of how, in a moment, I had seen in those commanding eyes everything that I had ever desired, and everything that I had ever feared. It was clear that she was suffering – I saw it in her bowed head, and the way she leaned on Mademoiselle Buisson for support; and I suffered for her, and longed to comfort her for the loss of the father she had loved.

When all the company had entered the church, and the organ had begun to play a solemn voluntary, I left my place beneath the dripping branches of the sycamore-tree. Inside the porch, I halted. The choir had begun to sing Purcell's divine 'In the midst of life we are in death',* with its anguished dissonances. The bitter-sweet sound, reverberating through the vaulted spaces of the church, tore at my heart in the most extraordinary way, and I felt angry tears welling up as I thought of the man whose blameless and useful life had been so violently cut down. Then came the resonant voice of Dr Daunt intoning the words of St John: 'I am the resurrection and the life, saith the Lord: he that believeth in me, though he were dead, yet shall he live: and whosoever liveth and believeth in me shall never die.'†

I remained in the porch as the congregation began to say together the words of Psalm 90, 'Domine, refugium', in which the Psalmist complains of the frailty and brevity of our life on earth, and of the suffering that is inseparable from our sinful nature; then, as the mourners came to the verses in which Moses speaks of God setting our misdeeds before Him, and our secret sins in the light of His countenance, I picked up my umbrella, turned away, and walked back out into the church-yard.

In due course came the sound of the church door being opened. The committal of Mr Carteret's body was soon to commence. I moved away, tucking myself in the recess of the west door, beneath the bell-tower, from where I was able to observe the mourning party and the various attendants, along with a number of villagers, and the household servants from the Dower House, follow the pall-bearers through the rain to where the pile of earth marked the last resting-place of Paul Stephen Carteret. Lord Tansor followed directly behind the coffin, oblivious, it seemed, to the unremitting rain; a few

*[From the Music for the Funeral of Queen Mary, performed in March 1695. The music was performed again at Purcell's own funeral in November 1695. *Ed.*]

†[John 11: 25–6. From the Order for the Burial of the Dead in the Book of Common Prayer. *Ed.*]

paces back, Phoebus Daunt, now with umbrella in hand, solemnly matched him step for step, like a soldier on parade. One by one, the company began to assemble themselves about the grave.

It was a most melancholy spectacle: the ladies in their bombazine and crape huddled together under umbrellas, the gentlemen, for the most part, standing unsheltered in the rain or beneath the yew-trees that grew about the church-yard, the black bands on their tall hats fluttering in the wind; the ranks of mutes and other mercenaries supplied by Mr Gutteridge – some a little the worse for liquor – forlornly holding up their batons and soaking plumes; and the simple wooden coffin being borne towards the terrible gaping gash in the wet earth, preceded by the imposing figure of Dr Daunt. Everything contributed to a bitter sense of the futility of the mortal condition. All was black, black, black, like the smoke-black angry sky above.

I found I could not take my eyes off the coffin, and saw again in imagination what pitiless brutality had done to the round and once genial face of Mr Carteret. And now he was to be consigned to a muddy hole in the ground. I never was so despairing and comfortless, to see what he had come to, and to what we all must come. I found I could not help but think of the deceased secretary as resembling Donne's private and retired man, who in life 'thought himselfe his owne for ever, and never came forth', but who, in death, had to suffer the indignity of his dust being 'published' – such an apt and terrible image – and 'mingled with the dust of every high way, and of every dunghill, and swallowed in every puddle and pond'. It was, as the preacher averred, 'the most inglorious and contemptible *vilification*, the most deadly and peremptory *nullification* of man, that we can consider'.* I did consider it. And it was indeed so.

*[From Donne's last sermon, the aforementioned 'Deaths Duell', (see p. 441). *Ed.*]

Miss Carteret had emerged from the church with Mademoiselle Buisson again by her side, and both ladies now stood next to Dr Daunt as he began to deliver the final part of the Order for the Burial of the Dead.

'Man that is born of a woman hath but a short time to live, and is full of misery. He cometh up, and is cutteth down like a flower; he fleeth as it were a shadow, and never continueth in one stay. In the midst of life we are in death . . .'

And so, with the rain beginning to lessen, they buried Paul Carteret at last, to the mournful tolling of a single church bell. *Requiescat in pace*, was all I could think. In small groups, the mourners – led by Lord Tansor, with Daunt close by his side – dispersed to their coaches, the mutes and the feathermen tramped off, and Dr Daunt returned to his church. Only Miss Carteret lingered by the grave, whilst Mademoiselle Buisson, with John Brine in attendance, began to walk back to her carriage. She turned her head as she reached the lych-gate, to see whether her friend were following; but Miss Carteret remained for some minutes at her station, looking down at the coffin. She appeared to show no external sign of grief – no tears, at least; but as she brushed aside the black silk ribbons of her bonnet, which a sudden breeze had blown across her face, I clearly saw that her hands were trembling. Then she nodded to the sexton and his assistant to do their work, and began to walk slowly back towards the church.

I stood alone, watching her tall figure until it reached the open ground beyond the lych-gate, where her companion was waiting for her. As she reached the door of the carriage, Mademoiselle Buisson took out a white handkerchief, gently wiped her friend's face, and kissed her on the cheek.

. . .

I waited until Miss Carteret's carriage had splashed its way up the lane towards the Dower House before leaving the churchyard to begin my walk back to Easton. I wished so much to see her again, to hear her voice, and to look once more into those extraordinary eyes; but, expecting that Daunt would be amongst the company gathered at the Dower House, I felt unsure of my ability to maintain my assumed identity in his presence. Yet as I reached the outskirts of the town, the desire to feed on her beauty once more overcame my misgivings. I turned on my heels and retraced my steps back to Evenwood.

As I reached the lane leading down to the Rectory, it occurred to me that I might leave a note for Dr Daunt, as a matter of courtesy, apologizing for not having read his proofs. When I knocked at the door, the girl informed me that the Rector and Mrs Daunt, as well as Mr Phoebus Daunt, were still at the Dower House, and so I requested pen and paper and was left alone in Dr Daunt's study to write my note. When I had finished, and was about to leave, I noticed three or four thick leather-bound note-books lying on the desk, each with a label carrying the words Daily Journal. It was wrong of me, I admit it, but I could not help myself from opening one of the volumes and reading it. In a moment, I had taken out my pocket-book and had begun frantically scribbling in shorthand; for the pages contained entries relating to the Rector's Millhead years. I expected the girl to return at any moment, but she did not; and so I continued in my task for as long as I decently could, before slipping out unseen. I had discovered nothing of great significance, except the satisfaction of knowing a little more concerning the upbringing and character of my enemy; but that, to me, had justified my actions.

Ten minutes later, I was standing within the Plantation, looking out across the lawn towards the Dower House.

Through the drawing-room window, the figure of Lord Tansor could be easily picked out, talking with Dr Daunt; behind him, I could see Mrs Daunt, with her step-son by her side. To gain a closer view of the proceedings, I moved stealthily through the dripping trees, taking up my station amongst a planting of shrubs close to one of the windows. The blind had been half drawn, but by crouching down I was able to see into the room.

Miss Carteret was standing by the fire, alone. Elsewhere, her guests – a dozen or so in all – had arranged themselves into quietly conversing groups. A young lady broke away from one of these and walked over to join her. She had blonde hair, of a most unusual paleness, which, with the unconsciously familiar way she took Miss Carteret's hand in hers, confirmed to me that she must be Mademoiselle Buisson.

They said nothing, but remained, hands clasped, for some moments until they saw Phoebus Daunt approach, at which they disengaged and stood side by side to greet him. He gave a little bow, in acknowledgement of which Miss Carteret inclined her head slightly, and spoke a few words. Her face remained expressionless, and she merely dipped her head again in response to whatever he had said. Bowing once more to Miss Carteret, and then to Mademoiselle Buisson, he took his leave. A few moments later, I saw him emerge through the front door and make his way back down the path to the Rectory.

All through this brief scene my heart had been pounding as I strained to see how Daunt would be received by Miss Carteret; but when it quickly became obvious that there was not the slightest spark of intimacy between them, I began to breathe more easily – the more so when, as Daunt had turned to go, I had seen Mademoiselle Buisson lean towards Miss Carteret and whisper something in her ear. This had produced an involuntary little smile, which she immediately sought to hide by placing her hand over her mouth. From the rather mischievous look on Mademoiselle Buisson's face, I made a guess that the remark had been in some way uncomplimentary to Daunt, and I was most satisfied to see how Miss Carteret had responded to her friend's comment, even at such a time.

Now that my enemy had gone, I thought that I might after all present myself to Miss Carteret, as I had been invited to do. Then I considered that I was wet, and a little dishevelled, and that my bag was at the Duport Arms; but yet I was expected, and she would think it strange if I did not come. I dithered and dawdled for several minutes until, at last, I got the better of my misgivings. I was on the point of quitting my place of concealment when the front door opened. Lord and Lady Tansor appeared, followed by Miss Carteret and her friend, and Dr and Mrs Daunt. The party proceeded down the steps and into two waiting carriages, which then moved away through the Plantation and into the Park.

Feeling tired and dejected, and with no reason to remain, I once more made my way back through the rain to Easton.

In the tap-room of the Duport Arms, my friend the sullen waiter was throwing fresh sawdust on the floor.

'Has Mr Green left?' I asked.

'Two hours since,' he said, without looking up from his work.

'Are there any more guests tonight?'

'None.'

The Peterborough coach was about to arrive, and so, dispensing with another solitary dinner, I sent the man upstairs for my bags whilst I fortified myself with a gin-and-water and a cigar. In ten minutes I had boarded the coach and was just settling myself inside, thankful that I was the sole occupant, when John Brine's face, red from exertion, appeared at the window.

'Mr Glapthorn, sir, I am glad to have caught you. Lizzie said I should tell you.' He paused for breath, and I heard the driver ask him whether he intended to get in.

'One minute, driver,' I shouted. Then, to Brine: 'Tell me what?'

'Miss Carteret and her friend are to leave for London next week. Lizzie said you'd wish to know.'

'And where will Miss Carteret be staying?'

'At the house of her aunt, Mrs Manners, in Wilton-crescent. Lizzie is to attend her.'

'Good work, Brine. Tell Lizzie to send word of Miss Carteret's movements to the address I gave you.' I leaned my head towards him and lowered my voice. 'I have reason to think that Miss Carteret may be in some danger, as a result of the attack on her father, and wish to keep a close eye on her, for her own protection.'

He gave a nod, as if to signify his complete comprehension of the matter, and I handed him a shilling so that he could refresh himself before returning to Evenwood. As the coach moved off, I drew the tattered silk curtain against the rain, and closed my eyes.

· 33 ·

*Periculum in mora**

'DO YOU REMEMBER THE LAST TIME WE WENT TO THE CREMORNE Gardens,'† I asked Le Grice.

It was now past three o'clock, and the fire had died quite down. I had been recounting the events subsequent to the violent death of Mr Paul Carteret.

Le Grice looked up and thought for a moment.

'Cremorne?' he said at last. 'Of course. We took the threepenny steamer. When would it have been?'

'November last year,' I said. 'A few days after I'd returned from Mr Carteret's funeral. We played bowls.'

'We did, and then we watched the Naval Fête. Yes, and I recall a little set-to as we were leaving. But what has this to do with anything?'

'Well, I shall tell you,' I said, 'while you throw another log on the fire and refill my glass.'

The night of Wednesday, the 9th of November 1853, remained clear in my mind. We had amused ourselves most satisfactorily for an hour or two. As eleven o'clock approached, and the lamp-lit arbours began to fill up with carmined whores and their tipsy swells, I had been game to continue our jollities elsewhere; but, unusually,

*['There is danger in delay' (Livy, *Ab urbe condita*). *Ed.*]

†[Celebrated pleasure gardens near Battersea Bridge. Regular entertainments included fireworks, dancing, concerts, and balloon ascents. It was open from three in the afternoon until midnight. After its respectable patrons had departed, it became an infamous haunt of prostitutes. It finally became so great an annoyance to its neighbours that in 1877 it was forced to close. *Ed.*]

Le Grice had expressed a strong wish to be in his bed. And so, at a few minutes before twelve, we had made our way out of the Gardens.

By the pay-box, at the King's-road entrance, we had come upon an altercation. A group of four or five women – whores every one, as I quickly judged – and a couple of fancy roughs were disputing in a rather bellicose fashion with a small man sporting a prominent pair of mutton-chop whiskers. As we approached nearer, one of the roughs grabbed the man by the collar and threw him to the ground. By the light of the large illuminated star above the pay-box, I immediately recognized the anxious face of Mr Geoffrey Martlemass, fiancé of Dorrie Grainger.

Our arrival had heated up the proceedings somewhat, but the roughs were quickly persuaded, by a brief demonstration of our combined force and determination, to leg it, while the whores swayed away into the darkness, shouting and jeering as they went.

'It's Mr Glapthorn, isn't it?' asked the little man, as I helped him to his feet. 'What an extraordinary coincidence!'

Much against the advice of his inamorata, the philanthropic Mr Martlemass had been on a mission that night to bring the light of Christ to the whores of Cremorne – a task that would have taxed St Paul himself. He was rather crestfallen at his failure, but seemed manfully inclined to dust himself off and attempt the task again. It was only after a good deal of persuasion that he consented to let the uncaring objects of his crusade abide in darkness for a little while longer and accepted our advice to return home.

'We took a hansom,' said Le Grice, 'and you dropped me off in Piccadilly. What happened then?'

After Le Grice had been deposited safely at the Piccadilly entrance to Albany, Mr Martlemass and I continued our way eastwards. 'The night has been a failure,' he said, shaking his head mournfully, as we passed through Temple Bar, 'but I am glad, at any rate, that our paths have crossed again. I wished to ask after your poor friend.'

I could not think to whom he was referring, whereupon, seeing my puzzlement, he enlarged upon his statement.

'Your friend Mr Pettingale. Of Gray's-Inn?'

'Ah, yes. Pettingale. Of course.'

'Are the injuries extensive?'

I had no idea what the little man was talking about; but my interest had of course been roused by the mention of Pettingale's name, and so I decided to feign comprehension of the matter.

'Extensive? Oh, moderately so, I believe.'

'All the members of the Society have expressed condemnation and concern – an attack upon a member in his chambers is an occurrence that is believed to be without precedent – and naturally my employer, Mr Gillory Piggott, as a near neighbour of Mr Pettingale's, feels the outrage particularly keenly.'

'Quite.'

A little subtle probing on my part soon elicited enough information for me to grasp the story in outline.

A few days after my interview with him, Mr Lewis Pettingale had returned to his chambers one evening at about eight o'clock. His neighbour, Mr Gillory Piggott, happening to come into Field Court half an hour later, noticed a large man leaving the staircase leading to Mr Pettingale's set. The next morning, as usual, a waiter from the coffee-house near Gray's-Inn-gate ascended those same stairs carrying Mr Pettingale's breakfast, but, on knocking at the lawyer's door, received no answer.

The door was found to be unlocked. On further investigation

by the waiter, the body of Mr Pettingale was discovered slumped across the corner of the hearth. He had been beaten, with some violence, about the face and head, but was still alive. A doctor had been called, and that afternoon the injured lawyer had been taken away in a coach to his house in Richmond, there to be attended by his own physician.

We had now reached the corner of Chancery-lane, and Mr Martlemass, insisting that he would not allow me to be taken out of my way, descended from the cab and, after shaking my hand with his customary vigour, marched briskly off towards his lodgings in Red Lion-square.

During the last leg of the journey to Temple-street, I mused on what the attack on Pettingale might signify; but, as so often of late, I felt as if I were groping blindfold in the dark. I could not say for certain that there was a connexion with the lawyer's former associate, Phoebus Daunt, though instinct strongly urged me to that conclusion. Perhaps Pettingale's criminal past had simply caught up with him. A trip to Richmond, I decided, might be both pleasant and instructive.

THE FOLLOWING MORNING I ROSE EARLY, AND WITH SMALL DIFFICULTY arrived in Richmond at a little after ten o'clock. I took a late breakfast at the Star and Garter, by the Park gates, where I began to enquire of the waiters whether they knew of a Mr Lewis Pettingale. At my third attempt, I was given the information I sought.

The house was on the Green, in Maids of Honour Row, a pretty terrace of three-storey brick houses.* It stood at the end of the row, fronted by a well-tended garden. I entered through a

*[Built in 1724 for the Maids of Honour of George II's wife, Caroline of Anspach. *Ed.*]

wrought-iron gate and proceeded down the path to the front door, which was opened to my knock by a whey-faced girl of about twenty.

'Will you give your master this? I shall wait.'

I handed her a note, but she looked at me blankly and thrust the note back at me.

'Mr Pettingale is here, is he not, recovering from his injuries?'

'No, sir,' she said, looking at me with staring eyes, as if I had come to murder her.

'Now then, what's this?'

The question was asked by a grim-looking man with a patch over one eye and a white spade beard.

'Is Mr Pettingale at home?' I asked again, in some irritation.

'I'm afraid not, sir,' said the man, assuming a protective position in front of the girl.

'Well then, where may I find him?' was my next question.

At this the girl began to play somewhat nervously with her pinafore, while casting anxious looks at the man.

'Phyllis,' he said, 'go inside.'

When she had gone, he turned to me, and threw his shoulders back, as if he might be preparing to stand his ground against my assault.

'Mr Pettingale,' he said at last, 'has left the country, which, if you were a true friend to him, you would already know.'

'I am not a friend of Mr Pettingale's,' I replied, 'but neither do I wish him any harm. I have only recently made his acquaintance, and so of course do not expect to be taken into his confidence. He has gone to the Continent, perhaps?'

'No, sir,' said the man, relaxing his stance a little. 'To Australia.'

. . .

PETTINGALE'S FLIGHT, AND THE REASONS FOR THE ASSAULT ON HIM, raised yet more perplexing questions; he had also robbed me of the means of exposing Phoebus Daunt to Lord Tansor, and to the world, for the thief and fraudster he was.

I returned gloomily to London. Every way I turned, my progress was blocked by unanswered questions, untested presumptions, and unsubstantiated suspicions. The murder of Mr Carteret held the key to the restitution of my birthright, of that I was certain. But how could that key be discovered? I found that I had not the least idea what to do next. Only one man could bring forth into the full light of understanding the weighty truth that so evidently lay behind Mr Carteret's letter to Mr Tredgold: the author himself; and the dead cannot speak.

On reaching Temple-street, in this depressed and frustrated state of mind, I took to my bed and immediately fell into a sound slumber, from which I was awoken by a loud knocking at the door.

When I answered the knock, I saw, to my surprise, one of the office boys from Tredgolds on the landing, holding out a brown-paper parcel.

'Please, sir, this has come for you, to the office. There is a letter as well.'

I perused the letter first, with some curiosity. It was a short note of apology from Dr Daunt's friend, Professor Lucian Slake, of Barnack:

Dear Sir,—

I am sorry to inform you that I have only just been told by the people at the George Hotel that the package I sent for your attention was mislaid, and has only now come to light. I have written a very strong letter of complaint to the manager, for the inconvenience this has caused to all concerned. But, as Dr Daunt took the precaution of giving me the address of your employer, I now send you the proofs of his partial translation of Iamblichus, as he requested. It is, in my opinion, a fine piece of work, a most necessary corrective to Taylor's rendering; but you will know better than I.

I am, sir,
yours most respectfully,
Lucian M. Slake.

This was puzzling. I immediately tore open the package, which did indeed contain the proofs of Dr Daunt's translation. What, then, was in the other package, the one that had been thrust into my hand by the serving-man from the George Hotel as I was preparing to take the train to Peterborough?

It still lay on my work-table, hidden under several old copies of *The Times*, and was addressed to 'E. Glapthorn, Esq., George Hotel'. I then noticed, for the first time, that it was marked 'Confidential'.

Inside were some thirty or forty sheets of unlined paper, folded like the leaves of a small quarto book, the first leaf being in the form of a title-page laid out in neatly formed capitals. Each of the remaining leaves was covered to the edges with small, close-packed writing – but in a different hand from the one that had inscribed the wrapper.

Intrigued, I put a match to the fire, pulled my chair a little closer to the hearth, and turned up the lamp. Holding the pages close to the light with shaking hands, I began to read.*

*[The author's narrative temporarily concludes on this page of the manuscript. The following account, transcribed in the author's hand, has been bound in at this point. *Ed.*]

Deposition of P. Carteret, Esq.

Concerning the Late Laura, Lady Tansor

To whom it may concern.

I.

Friday, 21st October 1853

I, Paul Stephen Carteret, of the Dower House, Evenwood, in the county of Northamptonshire, being of sound mind and in full possession of my faculties, do hereby solemnly swear that the following deposition is the truth, the whole truth, and nothing but the truth. So help me God.

I begin in this fashion because I wish to establish, from the outset, that I intend hereafter to assume the character and responsibilities of a witness to certain events, though I do not stand in any dock to deliver my evidence. Nevertheless, I beg most earnestly to be regarded as such a person by whomsoever may read this, taking my place – though in imagination only – before the bar of Blind Justice, with due solemnity, and delivering myself, as fully and as accurately as I can, of my testimony.

Crimes, like sin itself, are various both in form and in the severity of their effects; consequently, various are the punishments meted out to those who perpetrate them. But the crime I must herein expose – where does it stand amongst the divisions of wrong-doing, and what penalty does it deserve? That it *was* a crime, I have no doubt; but what to call it? Here lies my first difficulty.

I must leave it to sager minds than mine to deliver judgment on this point. But of this I am confident: the matter of which I shall speak was an active and considered act of moral harm against another person. And what does that signify, if not a crime? No material possessions were taken, and no blood spilled. And yet I say that it was theft – of a kind; and that it was murder – of a kind. In short, that it was a crime – of a kind.

There is a further difficulty: the perpetrator is dead, whilst the victim is ignorant of the outrage that has been visited upon him. Yet I persist in calling this a crime, and my conscience will not let me rest until I have set down the facts of the case, as far as they are known to me. I cannot yet see how it will all end; for though I know *something*, I do not know *all*. I write this, therefore, as a necessary preliminary to some future process whose outcome I cannot as yet foresee, and in which I myself may, or may not, play a part. For I believe that dangerous consequences have been set in motion by what I have uncovered, which cannot now be averted.

In four days' time, I am engaged to meet a representative of the firm of Tredgold, Tredgold and Orr, my employer's legal advisers. I am not acquainted with this gentleman, though I am assured he has the full trust of Mr Christopher Tredgold, whom I *have* known and respected, as a business correspondent and friend, these twenty-five years and more. I have undertaken to reveal in person to Mr Tredgold's agent a matter that has given me the greatest possible concern, since making certain discoveries in the course of my work.

To set things in their proper light, I must first say something about myself and my situation.

I BEGAN MY PRESENT EMPLOYMENT, AS SECRETARY TO MY COUSIN, THE 25th Baron Tansor, in February 1821. I had come down from Oxford three years earlier with little notion of what I would do in life, and for a time, I fear, idled most irresponsibly at home.

We lived then – my father and mother and I, my elder brother having by then secured a diplomatic position abroad – in a good deal of comfort, just across the river from Evenwood, at Ashby St John, in a fine old house that had been purchased by my paternal great-grandfather, the founder of the family's prosperity. But, as the younger son, I could not remain in a state of dependency on my father indefinitely; and, besides, I wished to marry – wished very much to marry – the eldest daughter of one of our neighbours, Miss Mariana Hunt-Graham. And so I resolved at last, after a little travelling, to follow my elder brother Lawrence into the Foreign Service, having at my disposal, besides a respectable degree and the good offices of my brother, a powerful recommendation from my cousin, Lord Tansor, to the then Foreign Secretary.* On the strength of this resolve, my father – albeit reluctantly – agreed to my proposing to Miss Hunt-Graham, and to providing us with a small allowance until I had established myself in my new career. She accepted me, and we were married in December 1820, on a day that I shall always regard as one of the happiest of my life.

But within a month of my marriage my father was taken ill and died; and with his death came ruin. Unknown to us all, even to my mother, the former Sophia Duport, he had committed all his capital to ruinous speculations, had borrowed most injudiciously, and, as a consequence, left us almost destitute. The house, of course, had to be sold, along with my father's prized collection of Roman coins; and there was no question now that my new wife and I could make a new life for ourselves in London. My poor mother suffered greatly with the shame of it all, and if it had not

*[Robert Stewart, Lord Castlereagh (1769–1822). He became Foreign Secretary in February 1812 and, suffering from a form of paranoia, committed suicide by cutting his throat with a penknife in August 1822. *Ed.*]

been for the generosity of her noble nephew, in immediately offering me a position as his private secretary, together with accommodation for us all with his step-mother in the Dower House at Evenwood, I do not well know what we should have done. I owe him everything.

At the time that I took up my employment, my cousin was married to his first wife, Laura, Lady Tansor, whose people, like my father's, were from the West Country. There had recently been a rift between Lord and Lady Tansor, apparently now healed, during which her Ladyship had left her husband to spend over a year in France. She returned from the Continent in late September 1820, a changed woman.

I cannot think of her Ladyship without affection. It is impossible. I acknowledge that her character was flawed, in many ways; but when I first knew her, in the early years of her marriage to my cousin, she seemed to my impressionable mind to be like Spenser's Cyprian goddess, 'newly borne of th' Oceans fruitfull froth'.* I was already in love with Miss Hunt-Graham, and had eyes for no one else; but I was flesh and blood, and no young man so composed could fail to admire Lady Tansor. She was all beauty, all grace, all spirit; lively, amusing, accomplished in so many ways; a soul, as I may say, so fully alive that it made those around her seem like dumb automata. The contrast with my cousin, her husband, could not have been greater, for he was by nature grave and reserved, and in every way the opposite of his vivacious wife; yet, for a time, they had seemed curiously suited to each other; each, as it were, neutralizing the excesses of the other's temperament.

I had almost daily opportunity to observe my cousin and his wife after the latter's return from France. I had been given a workroom adjoining the Library at Evenwood, on the ground floor of

*[Spenser, *Faerie Queene*, II. xii. 65. *Ed.*]

what is called Hamnet's Tower,* the upper storey of which comprised the Muniments Room, containing legal documents, accounts, estate and private correspondence, inventories, and so forth relating to the Duport family, and dating back to the time of the 1st Baron Tansor in the thirteenth century. To this work-room I would come every day to undertake my duties, which soon also began to encompass general stewardship of the Library – then uncatalogued – after I evinced an informed interest in the manuscript books, stored in the Muniments Room, which had been collected by our grandfather.

My first duty of the morning would be to call upon my cousin at eight o'clock to receive his instructions for the day. He would usually be taking breakfast with his wife in what was known as the Yellow Parlour, sitting at a small table set in a bow-window, looking out upon a secluded walled garden on the south side of the house. Lady Tansor had been back in England, and seemingly reconciled with her husband, for nearly a year when I began my employment at Evenwood. A portrait of her, begun before the rift of which I have just spoken, hung unfinished on one of the walls of this modest apartment, and provided a salutary daily reminder of the strange transformation of her physical appearance that had taken place since the artist had first begun to paint her – from the dazzling, captivating beauty of former times, with proud flashing eyes and abundant raven hair, to the gaunt and slightly stooped figure, her hair now prematurely flecked with grey, who sat opposite her husband each morning, come rain or shine, and whatever the season, silently staring out over his shoulder into the garden, whilst he, with his back to the window, read *The Times* and drank his coffee. Such a change! And so sad to see! As I entered the room each

*[Named after Hamnet Duport, 19th Baron Tansor (1608–70), who made extensive alterations to Evenwood in the 1650s. *Ed.*]

morning, she barely noticed my presence, and would take no part in my conversations with her husband. Sometimes she would rise absently from the table, letting her napkin drop to the floor, and, without a word, would drift from the room like some poor ghost.

She would spend days on end, especially during the dreary winter weeks, shut away in her rooms above the Library, and generally saw no one, except her maid and her companion, Miss Eames, and of course her husband at meal-times. But, as time went by, she would sometimes, and on a sudden, take it into her head to go up to Town, or to some other place, regardless of the weather and the state of the roads. Once, for instance, she insisted, with something of her old force, that she absolutely must go to see an old friend, and so off she went to the South Coast in the midst of a most ferocious downpour, accompanied only by Miss Eames, to the considerable disapproval of my cousin, and the consternation of those of us who loved her and fretted after her well-being. This, I think, was towards the close of the year 1821.

I remember the incident particularly because, after she returned from the coast, she appeared to have regained a little of her former spirit, almost as if a weight had been lifted from her. Little by little, she began to show her husband small considerations, and as I came into the Yellow Parlour of a morning I would sometimes even catch her smiling at some trifling pleasantry of Lord Tansor's – a slight, pained smile, to be sure; but it gladdened my heart to see it. Then, as spring came on, she began to busy herself a little – planning a new area of garden, replacing the window-curtains in her private sitting-room, arranging a weekend party for some of her husband's political associates, sometimes accompanying his Lordship to Town. And so a kind of contentment returned to my cousin's marriage, though things were not – nor ever would be – as they had been formerly, and my Lady's eyes never regained the radiant energy captured so well in the unfinished portrait that hung by the breakfast-table in the Yellow Parlour.

This partial restoration of happiness between my cousin and his wife, muted and delicate though it was, continued, culminating in an announcement, made to the general delight of their many friends, that her Ladyship was with child. Lord Tansor's joy at the news was plain for all to see, for it had been the cause of much distress and anxiety for my cousin that his union with Lady Tansor had, so far, denied him the thing he desired above all others: an heir of his own body.

The change in him was quite remarkable. I even remember hearing him whistle, something I had never heard him do before, as he was coming down the stairs one morning, a little later than usual, to take his breakfast. He became wonderfully solicitous towards his wife, showing her every attention she could have desired; so absorbed in her welfare did he become that he would often send me away of a morning, saying that he could not put his mind to business at such a time, or reprimanding me sharply for intruding when, as he said, I could see that her Ladyship was tired, or that her Ladyship needed his company that morning, or strongly conveying by word or look some other mark of his determination to do nothing else that day but devote himself to my Lady's service.

The object of his concern, however, received these unwonted demonstrations of partiality with little outward show of satisfaction; indeed, she appeared to regard them with an increasing irritation that seemed likely to throw into disarray the state of peace and equilibrium that had latterly been established between them. This did not in the least deflect her husband from his purpose, but it produced an uncomfortable atmosphere in which my cousin doggedly, and with unusual patience, sought even more ways of expressing his care for his wife's condition, whilst she became peevish and captious, brushing off his well-meant enquiries with a brusqueness that I fear he did not deserve. Once, when I was about to knock at the door of the Yellow Parlour as usual one morning, I heard her telling him sharply that she did not want to be molly-coddled so by him, that she neither desired it nor deserved it. I reflected afterwards on her words, concluding that some residual action of guilt for having abandoned her husband was responsible, in concert with the natural anxieties of impending motherhood, for her peppery behaviour.

So things went on until the 17th of November, in the year '22, when, at a little after three o'clock in the afternoon, my Lady gave birth to a son. The boy, who would be christened Henry Hereward, was a hale and hearty creature from the first; but his mother, grievously weakened by the exertion of bringing him into the world, sank into a deep decline that lasted several days. She lay, hardly breathing, lingering between life and death, in the great curtained bed, fashioned to a fantastic design by du Cerceau,* that had been brought to Evenwood by Lady Constantia Silk on her marriage to Lord Tansor's father. Gradually, she began to revive, take a little food, and sit up. A week to the day after the birth of her son, her husband, accompanied by the wet-nurse, brought the child to her for the first time; but she would not look at it. Propped up in the heavy-curtained bed, she closed her eyes and said only that she wished to sleep. My cousin remonstrated gently that she ought to make the acquaintance of their fine son and heir; but, with her eyes still shut, she told him, in a barely audible whisper, that she had no wish to see him.

'I have done my duty,' was all she would say when pressed by her husband to open her eyes just a little and look upon her son's

*[Jacques Androuet du Cerceau (*c.*1520–*c.*1584), French architect and engraver. *Ed.*]

face for the first time. She would not even consent to attend the boy's christening, which had been held off until she should have recovered sufficiently.

So Lord Tansor left her alone, and did not return. Thenceforth, he devoted himself to the nurture of his son, where formerly his wife had been his only care.

II.

Friday, 21st October 1853 (continued)

The winter of 1822 came on, damp and raw. Her Ladyship left her bed, but refused to dress, sitting instead wrapped up in a shawl in an arm-chair before the fire, which burned night and day, and sometimes falling asleep there until her maid came in to draw back the window-curtains in the morning. The weeks passed, but still she would not see her son or quit her apartments. Her reply, when urged by friends to rouse herself and take up the duties of motherhood, was always the same: 'I have done my duty. The debt is paid. There is no need to do more.'

One by one, she cut herself off from all visitors, even my late dear wife, of whom she had been particularly fond. Only her companion, Miss Julia Eames, was permitted to stay with her in the gloomy panelled chamber in which she spent most of her days. My cousin did not quite approve of Miss Eames, and had often questioned the necessity of her remaining in his house when his wife enjoyed such a wide acquaintance, both in the country and in town. But my Lady, alas, would not accede to his wishes, and it became a regular source of friction between them that she angrily refused to give up her companion.

It was to Miss Eames, and to her alone, that my Lady turned for comfort and companionship in the weeks and months following the birth of her son. I became particularly aware of the intimacy that existed between them when, one day, my Lady sent word that she wished me to bring up a copy of Felltham's *Resolves* from the Library. It pleased me a great deal to receive the request, thinking it betokened the beginning of a return to her former habits; for my Lady, though she had been a great one for dresses and jewels and other fripperies, had always been an earnest and discriminating reader – unlike my cousin, whose literary tastes were somewhat rudimentary and who, in this as in so many other aspects of my Lady's character and inclinations, found his wife's fondness for poetry and philosophy incomprehensible.

When I took the volume she had requested up to my Lady's sitting-room, I discovered her in close conversation with Miss Eames, heads together talking with quiet intensity, their chairs drawn round a small work-table on which, open to view, was an ebony writing-box containing a considerable number of letters and other papers. On seeing me enter, Lady Tansor slowly closed the box and sat back in her chair, whilst Miss Eames stood up and walked towards me, holding her hand out to receive the book I had brought, though it seemed to me that her action had also been intended to prevent me from drawing too close to the writing-box and its contents.

The incident may seem trifling, but it was to gain in significance retrospectively, as I shall shortly record.

And so to continue my deposition, and to conclude it as quickly as I may.

Still my Lady could not be persuaded to give up her self-imposed exile from society, and she absolutely refused to quit her apartment under any circumstance. But then, as the summer days began to shorten, her spirits gradually revived, and one bright cold day, at the beginning of October 1823, bundled up in her furs, she finally left her rooms, for the first time since the birth of her son – I observed her myself from the window of the Muniments Room taking the air on the Library Terrace, walking slowly up and down, arm in arm with Miss Eames. The next morning her son was brought by his nurse to be dandled for a minute or two on his Mamma's knee; the following morning, she began to take her breakfast again with her husband in the Yellow Parlour.

My cousin treated her return to domestic life with cold civility; for her part, she regarded him with utter indifference, though she ate her meals with him and sat with him of an evening, neither of them speaking the whole time, until each retired without a word of good-night to their own bedchambers at opposite ends of the house. She showed not much more interest in her son, though she raised no objection when my cousin brought up Sir Thomas Lawrence to paint the family portrait that now adorns the vestibule at Evenwood.

But then my Lady began to exhibit worrying signs of a severe nervous affection, slight at first, but increasing in frequency and intensity. In November 1823, as I noted in my journal, she repeatedly expressed a strong and intemperate desire to go and see the old friend she had previously visited on the south coast. Her husband sensibly prohibited such a thing; but her Ladyship contrived a means of leaving Evenwood when Lord Tansor was required to be in town on business. On her return, angry words were spoken; whereupon she locked herself in her room for two days and refused to come out, even when begged to do so by Miss Eames, until at last my cousin was obliged to order that the door be broken down. When his Lordship entered the apartment, to satisfy himself that she had not harmed herself in any way, she thrust a piece of paper into his hand, on which was a passage she had copied out of the edition of Felltham's *Resolves* that I had taken up to her some months before. This was what she had written:

> When thou shalt see the body put on death's sad and ashy countenance, in the dead age of night, when silent darkness does encompass the dim light of thy glimmering taper, and thou hearest a solemn bell tolled, to tell the world of it; which now, as it were, with this sound, is struck into a dumb attention: tell me if thou canst then find a thought of thine devoting thee to pleasure, and the fugitive toys of life.*

She had once been the brightest ornament of society, beautiful and carefree. Now her thoughts were all centred on the anguished contemplation of her inevitable demise. It pains me, even now, to speak of these last months, during which Lady Tansor became ever more unpredictable and distracted. My cousin had given instructions that, henceforth, his wife must never be left alone, and had arranged for a woman from the village, Mrs Marian Brine, to sleep in a truckle-bed next to my Lady's own bed, whilst during the day, even when Miss Eames was with her, a servant was required to sit outside the door of her apartments, the keys of which had been confiscated to prevent her from incarcerating herself again.

But these safeguards proved insufficient, and one night, dressed only in her shift, when a late frost had rendered the earth iron-hard, she slipped out of the house and was found wandering the next morning on the path near the Grecian Temple that stands on the western edge of the Park, dirty and dishevelled and wailing in

*[Felltham, *Resolves*, xlvii ('Of Death'). *Ed.*]

the most terrible fashion, her poor bare feet cut to pieces from walking through brambles and thorns.

They covered her, and she was brought back in the arms of Gabriel Brine, then his Lordship's groom, and husband of the woman who had been set to watch over her at night. Brine himself told me how she had continued to babble and moan as he had carried her, crying out over and over again, 'He is lost to me, my son, my son'; but when he attempted to comfort her by telling her that all was well, and that Master Henry was safe in his cradle, she became maddened, and began to shriek and kick and writhe, cursing him in the most dreadful manner until, coming into the Front Court at last and seeing her husband standing beneath the light of the portico lamp, anxiously awaiting her return, she quietened herself, closed her eyes, and sank back, her strength exhausted, into Brine's arms.

Lord Tansor stood for a moment, silently contemplating the destruction of his once beautiful wife. I, too, was there, just inside the door. I saw his Lordship nod to Brine, who proceeded to carry his pathetic burden upstairs, where she was laid in Lady Constantia's great carved bed, from which she was to rise never more.

She died peacefully on the 8th of February 1824, at a little after six o'clock in the evening, and was laid to rest three days later in the Mausoleum built by her husband's great-grandfather.

So ended the life of Laura Rose Duport, *née* Fairmile, wife of the 25th Baron Tansor. I now turn to the hidden consequences of that tragic life, and – at last – to the crime I that believe was committed against the closest interests of my cousin, for which I hope – constantly and most fervently – that the soul of the perpetrator has been forgiven by the grace of Him into whose hands we all must fall.

. . .

III.

Saturday, 22nd October 1853

Immediately after the interment of his wife, Lord Tansor called for Miss Eames, her Ladyship's former companion, and requested her to leave Evenwood at her earliest convenience. To what she was owed by way of remuneration, he added a generous additional payment, thanking her coldly for the services that she had rendered to his late wife. He hoped that she would have no cause to complain that she had been treated badly by him, to which she replied that he need have no fear on that score, and that she was properly grateful for the consideration she had received in his house.

He did not stop to ask, either Miss Eames or himself, whether she had a home to go to. As it happens, she did not; her father, a widower, had died soon after her Ladyship had absconded to France, and her other sisters were all married. One of these, however, lived in London, and to her, by means of a telegraphic message sent from Easton, Miss Eames now applied for temporary sanctuary.

Leaving Miss Eames to arrange her few possessions for departure, his Lordship then came to my work-room and instructed me to gather up all his late wife's private papers, and place them in the Muniments Room. Did he wish to peruse them himself after they had been collected? He did not. Did he wish me to examine or order them in any way? He did not. Were there any further instructions concerning her Ladyship's papers? There were not. Only one more thing was required: the unfinished painting of her Ladyship was to be removed from the Yellow Parlour and placed 'in a less conspicuous position'. Did his Lordship have a specific location in mind? He did not. Would there be any objection to my hanging it here, in my work-room? None whatsoever.

An hour or so later, there was another knock at my door. It was

Miss Eames, come to bid me farewell. She spoke most kindly of the little services that I had been happy to provide for her during the time I had been employed at Evenwood, and said that she would always think of me as a friend. Then she said something that struck me as very odd:

'You will always think well of me, won't you, Mr Carteret? I would not like it – I could not bear it – if you did not.'

I assured her that I could think of no circumstance that would alter my very high opinion of her, for, indeed, I regarded her as a very sensible and dependable soul, in whom resided a great deal – a very great deal – of natural goodness and sympathy; I told her as much, and also that no one could have served her late mistress better, or more faithfully. That alone would always command my admiration, the prosecution of one's duty to an employer or benefactor being, to my mind, a cardinal virtue.

'Then I am content,' she said, giving me a rather wan smile. 'We are both loyal servants, are we not?' And with that rather curious interrogative, she retired to ready herself for her journey. That was the last I saw of Miss Julia Eames.

THE NEXT MORNING, AFTER WAITING ON MY COUSIN AS USUAL, I BEGAN searching through my Lady's apartments for letters and other papers to remove to the Muniments Room, as I had been instructed. I collected a good many items from her green-lacquer desk that stood by the window in her sitting-room, and many more from various table-drawers and cabinets; but of the ebony writing-box that I had seen on several occasions, and which I particularly remembered from the time I had brought my Lady the copy of Felltham's *Resolves*, there was no sign. I searched most diligently, going through the contents of every cupboard and drawer two or three times over, and even getting down on my hands and knees to look underneath the great curtained bed; but without success. Somewhat puzzled as to the box's whereabouts, I placed my haul of documents in the portmanteau that I had brought with me, returned downstairs to my work-room, and ascended from thence to the Muniments Room.

It went against my nature simply to leave the papers in a disordered state; and so I thought that I would sort them roughly according to type, and then make a preliminary general inventory before storing them. This was quickly and easily done, and within an hour I had several separate bundles of receipts, bills, letters, sketch-books, notes and memoranda, correspondence, and drafts of letters from her Ladyship, and a number of miscellaneous items, principal amongst which were an autograph album, a commonplace-book with red silk wrappers inserted in a gilt steel cover, a note-book containing what appeared to be original poems and prose fragments, and an address book enclosed within an embossed calf wallet. I could not resist – who could? – looking over a number of the items as I placed them in their allotted pile, though I acknowledge that I did so a little guiltily, having received a specific instruction from my employer to leave the papers in an unclassified state.

The autograph album afforded an interesting record of friends and distinguished visitors, both to Evenwood and to his Lordship's town-house in Park-lane; and then I lingered for longer than I should have done over a book of delightful pen-and-ink drawings and pencil sketches made by my Lady over several years. A series of French scenes – a record, no doubt, of her Continental escapade – was particularly well done, for my Lady had been a skilled draughtswoman, with a keen eye for composition. Most were signed and dated 'LRD, 1819', and one or two carried descriptions. I particularly recall a most striking and romantic sketch, bearing the legend 'Rue du Chapitre, Rennes, evening', of an ancient and imposing half-timbered mansion with elaborately carved beams, and a canopied entrance half disclosing an interior courtyard. There were also a number of more finished views of the same location, all of them executed with remarkable feeling and care.

The striking of twelve noon from the Chapel clock roused me from my reveries, and I set about placing the separate bundles, which I had loosely tied together with string, in a small iron-bound chest that lay to hand, to which I affixed an identifying label. I was on the point of descending to my work-room when, on putting away my portmanteau, I noticed a single piece of paper that I had omitted to retrieve.

On examination, it appeared to be of little importance, simply a receipt, dated the 15th of September, 1823, for the construction of a rosewood box by Mr James Beach, carpenter, Church-hill, Easton. I do not well know why I make mention of it here, other than from an earnest desire to present as full and as accurate a statement of events as I can, and because it seemed odd to me that her Ladyship should have commissioned such an apparently valueless object on her own account from a man in the town, when Lord Tansor employed an excellent estate carpenter who could have made it for her in a moment. But there it was; I had no justification for spending any more of his Lordship's time on idle speculation, and had already dallied far too long on the task he had set me. And so I assigned the receipt to the proper bundle in the chest, shut the lid, and proceeded back down to my work-room.

I had no immediate reason of my own to consult Lady Tansor's private papers further, and received no request from my employer to do so. All financial and legal documents of importance, of course, had already passed under his Lordship's eye and hand during the course of his marriage, and were now in my custodial possession; consequently, over the course of the next few weeks, the contents of the little iron-bound chest began gradually to recede from my present view until, in time, they disappeared entirely.

I DID NOT HAVE CAUSE TO REMEMBER THE EXISTENCE OF MY LADY'S private papers for many years. During the intervening period, life, as it always does, brought us our share of fair weather and foul. Lord Tansor's step-mother, Anne Duport, with whom we shared the Dower House, departed this life in 1826. The following spring, my cousin had married the Honourable Hester Trevalyn, and it was expected – his Lordship being then only thirty-six years of age, and his new wife ten years his junior – that, in time, their union would be blessed with offspring that would secure the succession to the next generation.

After his first wife's death, his Lordship had given himself completely to the care and instruction of his son. I have no doubt that he mourned his first wife; but he did so, if I may so put it, in his own way. People called him unfeeling, particularly when, within a year or so of Lady Tansor's death, he began to set his sights on Miss Trevalyn; but that verdict, I think, arose from the habit of impermeable reticence that characterized his whole demeanour, and from a failure on the part of those who criticized him to comprehend the responsibilities of his position.

Towards his son, he displayed a fine and natural capacity for spontaneous affection. He adored the child. There is no other word for it. The boy bore a striking resemblance to his mother, with his large dark eyes and flowing black hair, and, as he grew up, he began to reveal also something of her Ladyship's character. He was heedless, argumentative, forever pulling at his father's sleeve and asking to be allowed to do this or that, and then running off in a howling rage when he was denied; and yet I never saw his father angered by these tantrums, for within a moment the boy would be back, afire with some other scheme that *was* allowed by his father, and off he would go skipping and whooping like a happy savage. He had such an air of abounding, irrepressible vigour about him – an abundant and entirely natural charm – that made him the favourite of everyone who met him.

And more than all these natural amiabilities, he was his father's heir. It is impossible to overstate the importance, in the eyes of my cousin, of the boy's status in this regard. No father wished more for his son; no father did more for his son. Imagine, then, the effect on my cousin when, one black day, death came softly knocking and took away, not only his child, but also his sole heir.

It was a catastrophe of the greatest possible magnitude, a gargantuan affront, an indignity my cousin could neither withstand nor comprehend: it was all these things, and more. He was a father, and felt like a father; but he was also Baron Tansor, the twenty-fifth of that name. Who now would be the twenty-sixth? It prostrated him utterly. He was lost to all comfort, all consolation; and for some weeks we feared – seriously feared – for his sanity.

It is hard for me to write of these things, for as Lord Tansor's cousin I had, and have, a place in the collateral succession to the Barony. I state here, most solemnly, that this potentiality never overruled the duty I felt I owed to my cousin: his interest was always my first care. What also makes it difficult for me is that the loss of Henry Hereward came upon my cousin just fifteen months after our own dear girl, Jane, had been so cruelly taken from us. Indeed, the two sweet babes often played together, and had been doing so on the afternoon our little angel fell from the bridge that carries the road from the South Gates across the river to the great house. Our lives were darkened irredeemably from that day.

But it is of my cousin that I write; and I have dwelt on his grief at the death of his only son for this reason: to demonstrate as clearly as I can the terrible nature of the crime I believe was wilfully visited upon him. In the light of what I have said concerning Lord Tansor's monomaniacal desire to secure an heir for his line (I do not say he was actually mad on this point, but the phrase, I maintain, is metaphorically apt), what would be the greatest harm, barring physical assault or murder, that could be done to such a man as this?

I leave the question unanswered *pro tempore*, and will now proceed with my deposition. I fear I have rambled somewhat, through trying my best to anticipate the questions and objections of an imagined interlocutor. Having put pen to paper, it has surprised me to find how difficult it has been to confine myself to the salient points: so many things push themselves forward in my mind for attention.

Well, then, to be as brief as I can. The death of his only son and heir might have been borne by my cousin, as far as such a thing can be borne by a sentient human soul, if his second marriage had been productive of other heirs; but it had not been, nor perhaps would ever be. As the years have passed, his Lordship has therefore been obliged to consider his position afresh; and now, in his sixty-third year, he has devised another method to secure his desires in respect of a successor. I shall return to this critical point in due course.

. . .

IV.

Sunday, 23rd October 1853

In the summer of 1830, our little circle received a most welcome augmentation when the Reverend Achilles Daunt, whom I am now proud to call my friend, was appointed to the living of Evenwood by my cousin. Dr Daunt, accompanied by his second wife and a son from his first marriage, came to us from a Northern parish with a high, and most deserved, reputation as a scholar. Evenwood offers many blessings, but I fear that men of real intellectual accomplishment are not many in number hereabouts, and the addition of Dr Daunt to our society was a great thing indeed for me, providing, as it did, a man of discernment and wide knowledge with whom to share and discuss my own historical and palaeographical interests. I had the honour of assisting my friend, in a modest way, in the preparation of his great catalogue of the Duport Library; and it was at his suggestion that I later took upon myself the task of collecting material towards a history of the Duport family, in which enterprise I am grateful to have been encouraged and supported by my cousin.

My friend's only son soon became a great favourite with Lord Transor, who was instrumental in sending the boy to Eton. It became of great concern to me to observe how my cousin began to look upon the Rector's son almost as his own. I watched this conspicuous liking for the boy grow over time into something other than mere partiality. It became a kind of covetousness that fed on itself, blinding my cousin to all other considerations. The boy was strong, healthy, lively, good at his books, and properly grateful for the attentions that he received from his father's noble patron; perhaps it was natural for Lord Transor to see in him a reflection, pale though it was to a less partial observer, of the lost heir. What did not seem natural to me (I hesitate to express criticism of my noble relation, but feel under a solemn obligation to state my opinion) was his Lordship's patent desire – expressed in countless material benefactions, personally audited by myself in my professional capacity – to possess the Rector's son as his own (if I may so put it). He could not, of course, buy him outright, like a horse of good stock, or a new carriage; but he could, and did, appropriate him gradually, binding the boy ever more closely to himself by the strongest of chains: self-interest. What young man, just down from the Varsity, could fail to feel flattered to the highest degree, and be mightily emboldened in his self-regard, at being treated with such extraordinary attention by one of the most powerful peers in the realm? Not Mr Phoebus Daunt, certainly.

The notion of adopting Mr Phoebus Daunt as his heir had first occurred to my cousin after the young man came down from Cambridge. As time has passed, it has gradually become fixed in his mind, and, at the time of writing, nothing, it seems, can now persuade his Lordship against pursuing this course of action. It is not for me to question the wisdom or propriety of my cousin's desire to leave the bulk of his property to this gentleman, on the single condition of his changing his name to that of his noble patron; I will only say that the choice of his heir perhaps does not demonstrate that acuity of judgment that his Lordship has usually displayed in his affairs; further, ever since the disclosure of his decision to the parties concerned, the effect on my friend's son has been pernicious, serving to magnify a number of deficiencies in his character. This little ceremony took place some three months since, at a private dinner at Evenwood to which only Dr and Mrs Daunt, and their son, were invited; and I may say that, when the news became generally known, it was remarked by many in our local society that, while the young man and his step-mother instantly began to put on airs, and behave in an altogether insufferable manner (I regret the candour of my remarks, but do not withdraw them), the Rector maintained a dignified silence on the matter – in fact, he appeared positively disinclined to speak of it.

I might say a good deal more concerning Mr Phoebus Daunt; but I am conscious that I digress from my immediate purpose.

To return to my projected history of my cousin's family (and, of course, of my own). I need not weary the reader of this statement by rehearsing in detail the progress of the work, the sources for which are extensive and requiring of careful and patient scrutiny. Year by year I continued to work, slowly but steadily, through the documents accumulated and stored by each successive generation, making notes thereon, and composing drafts.

In January of the present year, 1853, I was drafting an account of the perilous Civil War period, during which the family's fortunes stood in dire jeopardy. I happened to look up, as I often did, at the unfinished portrait of my cousin's first wife that now hung on the wall of my work-room. My secretary's duties were over for the day, and for the next hour or so the history of the family during the time of Charles I should have claimed my attention; but I was much wearied by my recent exertions and, as I contemplated the image of the beautiful face in the picture above me, suddenly wished very much – I cannot say why – to look again at the remnants of the life of Laura Tansor, which I had gathered together after her death. It was most unmethodical and, I may say, uncharacteristic of me to deviate from a logical course of action, for I had been proceeding with assembling material for my projected *Historia Duportiana* on a strictly chronological basis. But I succumbed to this sudden keen desire and, going upstairs to the Muniments Room, opened the little iron-bound chest in which I had placed my Lady's papers nearly thirty years earlier.

I looked again at her wonderful sketches and drawings, especially those executed during her time in France, and read for the first time poems and other effusions that immediately brought her back to mind, so passionate were they, so full of life and spirit. I then turned my attention to a large bundle of letters and, not wishing to put my time to waste, began to compose some brief notes thereon; but when I had finished, I was presented with a puzzle.

Her Ladyship's correspondence was extensive, dating back to letters written to her by my cousin during their courtship, and including a large number of communications from members of her family and friends from the West Country. Faced with such a large number of items, I usually commence by arranging them by date and sender; but when I had finished ordering them in this way, it was clear that a quantity of letters were missing, particularly those from a certain Simona More, later Glyver, who appeared to have been an old childhood friend of her Ladyship's. There was a sequence of communications – at least one a month, sometimes two or three – from this lady, beginning in August 1816, the year that her Ladyship first became acquainted with my cousin; but then, in July 1819, the letters ceased altogether, only resuming their previous frequency in October 1820. It was manifest, from her letters to Lady Tansor, that Miss More, or rather Mrs Glyver, as she soon became, had enjoyed an exceptionally intimate acquaintance with my cousin's first wife, which made the gap in the correspondence – a period of some fifteen months – all the more singular.

Some of the other categories of document – bills, receipts, &c. – showed similar chronological disruptions. After considering the matter for some little time, and going back to the Dower House to consult my own daily journal on the matter of dates, I concluded that a deliberate attempt had been made to remove, and perhaps destroy, any document, no matter how trivial, that dated from July 1819, just before her Ladyship left for France, until after she returned to her husband, at the end of September the following year.

I went to make discreet enquiries of my cousin as to whether any of his first wife's papers were still in his possession, but it seemed they were not. I even made another search of her former apartments, and other places where I thought perhaps they might be, but could find nothing. And so, baffled, I placed the letters back in the chest.

V.

Sunday, 23rd October 1853 (continued)

I see from my journal that it was on the 25th of March 1853, that I received the following communication:

Dear Mr Carteret, —

I regret to inform you that my sister, Miss Julia Eames, passed away on Thursday last, the 21st inst. Her family and many friends thank God that, though her sufferings have been great, her final hours were peaceful.

Before the end came, my dear sister had strength enough to request, most insistently, that I write you this note, to be sent after God had taken her, to tell you that there is something here she was most desirous for you to have, something placed into her keeping that she said must now pass to you.

I therefore hope that you will favour me with a reply at your earliest convenience, stating a day and a time that will suit you to visit us here, so that I may discharge this last duty to my dear departed sister.

I am, sir,
yours very sincerely,
C. McBryde (Mrs)

My cousin happened to be on the Isle of Wight just at that time, advising the Prince-Consort on some matter connected with Her Majesty's new residence,* and was not to return for some time; and so I immediately arranged with Mrs McBryde to call upon her on the following week.

I was received kindly by this lady, who bore a close resemblance to her late sister, at a well-appointed house in Hyde-Park-square, in that new residential district of London known as Tyburnia.† After the usual introductions and exchanges, during which I commiserated most sincerely with Mrs McBryde for her loss, I was offered tea, which I declined. She then walked over to a large cabinet in the corner of the room, which she proceeded to unlock.

'This is what my sister wished you to have.'

I had last seen it nearly thirty years ago, standing on a table in my Lady's sitting-room at Evenwood. A large ebony writing-box, bearing the initials 'LRD' in mother-of-pearl on the lid.

'There is this also.' She handed me a letter, addressed to myself.

After a few words more, I took my leave. As I had some further business in town the next day, I had taken a room at the Hummums Hotel;‡ and it was to this establishment that I now repaired.

*[Osborne House, built as a private retreat for Queen Victoria and Prince Albert on an estate overlooking the Solent of nearly three hundred and fifty acres, purchased from Lady Isabella Blachford. The work, begun in 1845 and supervised by the Prince Consort, was completed in 1851. *Ed.*]

†[The name, no longer in use, of the area of London roughly bounded by the Edgware Road on the east, Bayswater on the West, Hyde Park on the south, and Maida Hill on the north. It was inhabited mainly by professional men and City merchants. 'Ah, ladies!' writes Thackeray in Chapter LI of *Vanity Fair* (1848), 'ask the Reverend Mr Thurifer if Belgravia is not a sounding brass, and Tyburnia a tinkling cymbal. These are vanities. Even these will pass away.' *Ed.*]

‡[In Covent Garden. A relatively inexpensive establishment, its typical clientele were single gentlemen up from the country. *Ed.*]

I did not immediately investigate the contents of the box. Instead, I placed it on a table in my room and proceeded to open the letter.

It was, as I had surmised, from Miss Eames, written in an unsteady hand, and dated three days before her death. I transcribe it here.

My Dear Mr Carteret,—

I do not know how much longer I may have on this earth, only that my time is short. Not wishing to pass into the hands of Almighty God without discharging my last duty to my dear friend, the late Laura Tansor, I am therefore arranging for a certain object, entrusted to me on my friend's death, to be placed in your hands by my sister after my own departure from this life of sin, according to my friend's wishes. When you read this, therefore, I too will have passed beyond pain and suffering and, in the hope of being delivered of my offences by God's grace, will walk again through all eternity with her whom I served faithfully in life.

For the last years of my friend's life, her conscience was sorely troubled by an action taken by her some time before, which could be neither admitted nor undone. I – with another – was a party to that action, and my conscience, too, has been burdened, until sometimes I have thought I could stand no more. For though I tried, on several occasions, I could not dissuade my friend from the course of action she was set on taking. I once asked you never to think ill of me. I beg you now to consider what I have done, by the sin of omission, in the light of friendship and trust, in which I know you place the highest value; for I made a solemn promise, on my mother's Bible, to keep my Lady's secret safe, never to betray her while she lived, and to hold fast to that promise until such time as it pleased the Almighty to take me to His own. That I have done, as God is my witness, faithfully and unswervingly, through all these years. If I have done wrong in keeping faith with the dearest of friends, then I pray to be forgiven – by the Lord of mercy and judgment, and by those remaining whom my silence may have injured.

And so, dear Mr Carteret, I die in the hope that what now passes into your possession may perhaps be used by you to set right what was made wrong by my friend's action. I do not condemn or blame her for what she did; for who is without sin? She was mortal, and her passion – born of fierce loyalty to a beloved parent – blinded her. She repented of what she had done, truly repented, and sought to make amends. But she was consumed by the constant thought of her sin – she saw it as such; it made her mad, and drove her at last into the arms of death. I go now to meet her, and my heart is glad.

*The Lord God bless you and keep you. Pray for me, that my unrighteousness be forgiven, and my sin covered.**

J. Eames.

I laid down the letter and turned to open Lady Tansor's writing-box.

Underneath the hinged slope were a great many papers, the majority of which appeared to be a sequence of letters from Mrs Simona Glyver, sent from the village of Sandchurch in Dorset to Evenwood, and dating from the beginning of July 1819, with one or two others written by this lady from Dinan in France to an address in Paris during the summer of the following year, and yet more sent to her Ladyship from Dorset throughout the late summer and early autumn of 1820, directed first to Paris, and then, from October onwards, to Evenwood. Though not all were dated, I quickly saw that the letters in the box partially filled the fifteen-month gap that I had noticed from my earlier examination of the communications from this lady that were already in my possession. I sat down and began to read through the letters methodically.

*[A paraphrase of Psalm 32: 1. *Ed.*]

I do not have time to record here the contents of each letter in detail. Some were inconsequential and ephemeral, merely containing the usual harmless chatter and gossip characteristic of such exchanges between ladies. But others had an altogether different tone and purpose, especially the earlier communications, written throughout July 1819, which seemed indicative of some great impending crisis. A few extracts from letters written to her Ladyship by Mrs Glyver during that month (in which, I deduce, Miss Eames is referred to as 'Miss E.') will serve to illustrate the point.

[*Friday, 9th July 1819. Sandchurch*]

I beg you, dearest friend, to think again. It is not yet too late. Miss E. has, I know, more than once urged reconsideration on you. I now add my voice to hers – as one who loves you like a sister – and who will always have your best interests at heart. I know how you have suffered, after the death of yr poor father – but is not the punishment you intend out of all proportion to the offence? Even as I write the question I can anticipate yr answer – & yet still I exhort you with all my strength to stand back & consider what you are doing. I am afraid – Miss E is afraid – & you should be too, for there may be consequences – perhaps of the most terrible kind – that you can neither foresee nor control.

[*Thursday, 15th July 1819. Sandchurch*]

Your reply is as I expected – & I see you are determined to proceed. I have heard separately from Miss E, who says that you will not be persuaded, and therefore must be helped – to ensure that what is done is done well, and as privily as we may. For we cannot *let you do this alone.*

[*Saturday, 17th July 1819. Sandchurch*]

In haste. I have made my arrangements. Miss E will have told you the name of the hotel – and I have the address of yr man in London. It will be some comfort to me – though a selfish one – to have this safeguard, if such it be, for the future. God forgive us for what we are about to do – but never believe, my dearest L, that I shall fail you. That I shall never *do – though I may be called to account – in this world or the next. Sister I have called you, & sister you are, & will* always *be. There is no one more precious to me. I am with you now* unto the last.

[*Friday, 30th July 1819. Red Lion, Fareham*]

I arrived here safely this afternoon and send this on ahead to assure you that all is well. The Captain raised no objections to my leaving – he neither knows nor cares what I do, as long as I put nothing in the way of his pleasures. Indeed, he was charming enough to tell me I may go to the Devil as long as I leave him in peace. He was glad to hear that my accompanying you would not prove a drain on his purse! That was his main concern. I am to visit my aunt in Portsmouth tomorrow, as you know. She strongly suspects that the reason for my 'condition' may not be whispered, *which of course is not quite what I intended, but I shall not disabuse her – in order that the waters shall remain conveniently muddied. As she cannot abide the Captain, she will say nothing to him, and does not condemn me in the least – in fact applauds what, if it* were *true, would have been an act of the most unmitigated scandal. And so I go there as a kind of heroine – my aunt being a great admirer of Miss Wollstonecraft's disregard of social propriety and seeing me as in some sort – like Miss W – striking a blow for the rights of our sex through my transgression.* What the Captain will say when I come back with a baby in my arms, I do not know. But the calendar will now be a witness – I made sure of that (though*

*[The feminist intellectual Mary Wollstonecraft (1759–97) had an illegitimate daughter, Fanny, by the American speculator and author Gilbert Imlay (her second daughter, Mary, future wife of the poet Shelley and author of *Frankenstein*, was the product of her marriage to the novelist and social theorist William Godwin). Her *Vindication of the Rights of Women* was published in 1792. One infers that Mrs Glyver's aunt believed that her niece was pregnant by a lover, rather than by her husband. *Ed.*]

he *may not remember).* I shall be with you as planned on Tues. morning. And so the die is cast, and two husbands will go to bed tonight wifeless. I wish there was some other way – but the time for all that is past. No more words. Please to destroy this on receipt, as you have done, I hope, with the others – I have been as careful as I can & have left nothing behind.*

From a receipt dated the 3rd of August 1819, I surmise that the two friends, perhaps with Miss Eames in attendance, met together in Folkestone. They then departed for Boulogne, on or about the 5th of that month. A letter received by her Ladyship some weeks later, from an address in Torquay, confirms (what I did not know for certain before) that Miss Eames did not accompany them to the Continent. After the letter quoted above, parts of which I did not fully understand at first, there seems to have been no further communications from Mrs Glyver to her Ladyship until the 16th of June 1820, which, to my mind, strongly suggested that they remained together in France – as, indeed, proved to be the case. However, there *are* letters to her Ladyship from a Mr James Martin, an aide to Sir Charles Stuart, the Ambassador in Paris,† written in February and March of the following year – on seeing them in the writing-box, I remembered that this gentleman had been a guest at Evenwood on more than one occasion. The purpose of the exchange was to secure accommodation for her Ladyship in the French capital over the summer. I could not help but smile, despite the growing fear I felt within me, when I saw to where Mr Martin's replies had been directed: Hôtel de Québriac, Rue du Chapitre, Rennes.

*[By this rather obliquely delicate reference she appears to mean that she had recently contrived to have marital relations with Captain Glyver, the potential outcome of which would coincide with the birth of her friend's child. *Ed.*]

†[Sir Charles Stuart (1779–1845), created Baron Stuart de Rothesay in 1828, was British Ambassador to France from 1815 to 1824. I have not identified James Martin. *Ed.*]

The letter from Mrs Glyver of the 16th of June 1820, alluded to above, was written from Dinan to her friend in Paris, to a house in the Rue du Faubourg St Honoré.* The friends seem to have left Rennes together around the second week of June, taking lodgings in Dinan before her Ladyship departed alone for Paris. In her letter, Mrs Glyver begins by speaking of her imminent return to England. And then comes this extraordinary passage:

I took the little one to see the tombs in the Salle des Gisants† yesterday – he seemed much entertained by them, though the chamber was cold & damp & we did not stay long. But as we were leaving he put his little hand out – so sweetly and gently – to touch the face of one of the figures, a thin old lady. Of course it was just an accident, not deliberate at all, but yet it seemed like a conscious act & I whispered to him that these were once all fine lords and ladies – like his mamma and papa. And he gave me such a look as if he understood every word. We encountered Madame Bertrand at the Porte du Guichet & she walked with us for a time along the Promenade. It was such a beautiful day – cloudless, a delicious soft breeze, with the river sparkling below us, & I so longed for you to be with us once more. Madame B said again how like you he is, & indeed it is so, tho' he is still a mite. At least when I look into his dear face, with those great eyes gazing back, I feel you are close. I hate to think of you alone when we are here, longing for you to be with us, & I cried for us both last night. You were so brave when you left us. I could hardly bear it, for I knew how you suffered & how you wd suffer more when we were out of sight. Even now I wd bring him to you, if your resolve should falter. But I do not think it

*[The street in which the British Embassy was, and is, situated. *Ed.*]

†[Part of the so-called Château of Dinan, which is actually built into the town's ramparts. The Salle des Gisants holds seven carved medieval tombs: that of Roland de Dinan is said to be the oldest armed tomb in Western Europe. The carved figure referred to by Mrs Glyver is probably that of Renée Madeuc de Quémadeuc, second wife of Geoffroi Le Voyer, chamberlain to Duke Jean III of Brittany. *Ed.*]

will – and I weep for you, dearest sister. I kiss yr beautiful son every night & assure him that his mamma will love him for ever. And I shall love him too. Write soon.

Further letters from Mrs Glyver made the matter clear beyond peradventure: my Lady had given birth to a son in the city of Rennes. He had been born in the Hôtel de Québriac, Rue du Chapitre, in the month of March of the year 1820.

But there was a deeper matter even than this, of such consequence that I could scarce believe it; and yet the evidence was here in my hands, in these letters written to her Ladyship by her friend, Simona Glyver, and also in others she received in Paris from Miss Eames. Lady Tansor returned to England on the 25th of September, 1820 – alone. Where, then, was the child? The thought occurred to me that he might have died; but letters from Mrs Glyver received by her Ladyship after arriving back at Evenwood contained regular reports of the child's progress – the habits he was developing, the darkening of his hair, the little sounds he made and how they were interpreted, how he loved to be taken down to the shore to watch the waves crashing in and the gulls soaring above them. It also appears – astonishing as it is to think of – that the child was later brought surreptitiously to Evenwood, in the summer before Lady Tansor died, when her husband had been called away on political business, and much discussion ensued concerning the little boy's fascination with the white doves that fluttered around the spires and towers of the great house, and with the goldfish – some of great size and age – that glided silently through the dark waters of the fish-pond.

I read several of the letters over again, and then a third time, to make sure I had not deceived myself. But there was no other possible interpretation of the evidence before me. *Lady Tansor had brought her husband's rightful heir secretly into the world, only to give him away to another.*

So I come at last to my beginning. *This* was the crime to which I bear witness: the denial – by a premeditated act of determined duplicity and cruelty (I shall not go so far as to call it malice, though some might) – of paternity to my cousin, who lives only that he might pass on what he has inherited from his forefathers to his lawfully begotten son. This was badly done by my Lady, and I say so as one who loved her dearly. I aver that it was cruel beyond words to so deny my cousin that which would have completed his life; that it was an act of terrible vindictiveness, no one can deny; and to my mind, insofar as it took from Lord Tansor what was rightfully his, though he remained ignorant of his loss, this act of denial was, in its effects, criminal.

And yet, having arraigned her, having presented the evidence against her, can I now condemn her? She paid a terrible price for what she did; she did not act alone – others, one in particular, were guilty by association, though they aided her out of love and loyalty; she – and they – are now for ever beyond the reach of earthly justice, and have been judged by Him who judges all. For, as Miss Eames observed, who of us are without sin? No life is without secrets; and it may often be that the lesser evil is to keep such secrets hidden. Let me, as the accuser of Laura, Lady Tansor, therefore plead for clemency. Let her rest.

But the consequences of the crime remain, and they are not so easily remitted. For what accounts are still to be presented for settlement? Does the boy live? Does he know who he is? How can this be made right?

Since making my discovery, I have wrestled day and night with my conscience: to keep my Lady's secret, or place what I know before my cousin? I am tormented by the knowledge that I now possess, as I fear dear Miss Eames had been; but now, at last, I am impelled to take action – and not only to forestall any accusation that I am withholding what I know in order to protect my own interests.

My cousin's determination to adopt Phoebus Daunt as his heir in law, the device to which he has pledged himself in order to make good the deficit that Nature has apparently inflicted upon him, renders it imperative that I make the truth known, so that steps may immediately be taken to find the true heir, if he lives. I can no longer keep silent on this matter; for if the true-born heir be yet living, then everything must be done to discover him, and so prevent the disastrous course of action upon which my cousin is set. And there is another matter of concern to me.

Late one afternoon, in April of this present year, I had just entered the Library when I witnessed Mr Phoebus Daunt softly closing the door of my work-room, where he had no business to be, and then looking about him to make sure that he was unobserved. A man, I thought, is never more himself than when he thinks he is alone. I waited, out of sight, for him to quit the Library through one of the terrace doors. When I got to my room it was immediately clear that some of the papers on my desk had been disturbed; luckily, the door to the Muniments Room was locked and the key about my person.

Over the course of succeeding weeks, I would frequently encounter Mr Daunt in the Library, apparently engaged upon reading some volume or other, or occasionally writing at one of the tables. I suspected, however, that his real purpose was to seek an opportunity to enter my work-room, and perhaps gain access to the Muniments Room. But he never could, for I now took to locking the door to my work-room whenever I left the Library.

This was not the first occasion on which I had found reason to suspect my dear friend's son of frankly despicable behaviour. Did

I say suspect? Let me be blunt. I *know* him to have been guilty of reading Lord Tansor's private correspondence – including letters of a highly confidential nature – when he had not been given permission to do so. I should have spoken out, and it is a matter of the greatest regret that I did not do so. But the point that I wish to make most strongly is this: What action might a determined and unscrupulous person contemplate if he suspected that his expectations – his most considerable expectations – were threatened in any way? I answer that such a person would stop at nothing to preserve his position. Let me be even clearer. I do not know how Mr Phoebus Daunt can have come by his knowledge, but I am certain that he knows the nature of the documents left to me by Miss Julia Eames.

MIDNIGHT.

He is there, though I cannot see him now – he seems to melt away into the darkness, to become a shadow. But he was there – *is* there. I thought at first that it was John Brine, but it cannot be him. He stands so still, in the shadow of the cypress-tree – watching, waiting; but then when I opened the window, he was gone, taken up by the darkness.

I have seen him before – on many occasions, but always just out of sight, often at dusk when I have been returning home across the Park, and more frequently of late.

And then I am certain that there was an attempt last week to break into my study, where I am now writing, though I could find nothing missing. A ladder had been taken from one of the outbuildings, and was found discarded in the shrubbery, and the woodwork of my window had been damaged.

I feel constantly under his eyes, even when I cannot see him. What does it mean? Nothing good, I fear.

For I think I know who sets this watcher on me, and who it is that desires to know what I now know. He smiles, and asks me how I am, and he shines like the sun in the estimation of the world; but there is evil in his heart.

My candle is burning low and I must finish.

To those who may read this deposition, I say again that what I have written is the entire truth, as far as it is known to me, and that I have claimed nothing that has not been based on evidence provided by the documents in my possession, personal knowledge, and direct observation.

This I swear on everything I hold most sacred.

By my hand, the 23rd October, in the year 1853.

P. Carteret.

· 34 ·

*Quaere verum**

Overwhelmed by the experience of reading Mr Carteret's Deposition, I sank back, exhausted and bewildered, in my chair. The dead had spoken after all, and what a world of new prospects the words had revealed!

Pinned to the last page of the document was a short note:

To Mr Glapthorn

Sir,—

I have made arrangements for the preceding account to be given to you by Mr Chalmers, the manager of the George Hotel, when you leave there. Failing that, he has been instructed to send this directly to Mr Tredgold. I have thought it wise to make these arrangements in case any harm should come to me before I can place my Lady's letters in your hands. You will at least then know what I wished to tell you.

I am not a superstitious man, but I encountered a magpie this afternoon, strutting across the front lawn, and failed to raise my hat to him, as my mother always encouraged me to do. This has been on my mind all this evening, but I shall hope that the morning sun will make me rational once more.

The letters from my Lady's writing-box have been removed to a place of safety, but I shall have recovered them before our meeting. There is more I could say, but I am much fatigued and must sleep.

Only one more thing.

*['Seek the truth'. *Ed.*]

There was a slip of paper enclosed with the letter I received from Miss Eames. The following phrase – and nothing else – was written on it, in capital letters: SURSUM CORDA. *I puzzled my head at the time what it could mean, but gave up. I have only lately realized – to my shame – what the words may signify, and shall wish to present a possible course of action to you tomorrow relating to them.*

P.C.

I gave little thought to this postscript, having been deeply affected by the account of Lady Tansor's last years, and of her terrible death; and then to learn, in those carefully composed pages, of my birth in the Rue du Chapitre, and how I had been taken to the town of Dinan, and of the making of the box in which, I was sure, 'Miss Lamb' had placed her gift of two hundred sovereigns. It filled me with amazement to read these things; for, since the death of her whom I had once called Mother, I had believed these privities were mine – and mine alone – to know. But here they were, written down in another's hand, like cold universal fact. The sensation was alarming – like turning a corner and meeting oneself.

And to know that I had also been taken to Evenwood as a child! My heart danced with a kind of anguished elation at the thought. That bewitching palace-castle, with its soaring towers, which I had beheld in my dreams when young, had been real after all – no figment of fancy, but the perpetuated memory of my father's house, which would one day be mine.

Yet there were still so many unanswered questions, still so much to know. I read Mr Carteret's words over a second time, and then a third. Late into the night I sat, re-reading, thinking, wondering.

I appeared to myself like a man in a dream who rushes headlong, heart fit to burst, towards some eternally receding end; the faster I ran towards my goal, the more it remained tantalizingly out of reach, always just within sight, but never attainable. Yet again, I had been shown a fragment of the whole; but the greater truth, of which the Deposition was a part, was still hidden from me.

The truth? It is always the truth we seek, is it not? A conformity with known fact, or with some agreed standard, or with what experience tells us is the inescapable nature of existence. But there is something beyond the merely 'true'. What we commonly call 'true – that 'A' equals 'B', or that Death waits quietly for us all – is often but a shadow or replica of something greater. Only when this shadow-truth conjoins with *meaning*, and above all with meaning *experienced*, do we see the substance itself, the Truth of truth. I had no doubt that Mr Carteret's words had been those of a truthful man; yet still they were but portions of an elusive entireness.

I was sensible, of course, that I now possessed something that considerably advanced my claim to be Lord Tansor's heir; but I had seen enough clever barristers at work to know that Mr Carteret's Deposition was susceptible to serious legal objection, and so could not allow myself to believe that it provided in itself the final, incontestable validation that I had been seeking for so long. In the first place, the original documents from which Mr Carteret had quoted could not now be produced; they had been in his bag when he had been attacked. How, then, could it be proved that these letters had actually existed, and that the words cited by Mr Carteret were accurate and truthful, and had not been his own invention? His character and known probity might argue against such an assertion; but a lawyer who knew his business could still make much of the inherent doubt. Or it might be argued that Mr Carteret had produced his Deposition at my behest. I had made a little progress through this document coming into my hands; and, as far as my own position was concerned, the Deposition offered valuable circumstantial corroboration of what had been written in my foster-mother's journals. But it was not sufficient.

Though I knew at last what Mr Cartaret had wished to tell me, and what he had been carrying in the gamekeeper's bag, another terrible certainty had also risen up out of the mists of doubt and speculation and taken solid form. The reason for his anxious look as he had sat in the tap-room of the George Hotel awaiting my arrival was now clear: he had feared for his safety, and perhaps even for his life, at the hands of the person who, he believed, had set a watcher on him.

What a clod I had been! It had only been necessary to ask one question to prise out the truth: *Cui bono?**

Suppose someone comes by chance into possession of information which, if publicly known, would disbar another person from realizing an expected inheritance of immense worth. Suppose, further, that this second person is a man of overweening ambition, and also conscienceless in the pursuit of his interests. Would not such a man feel it imperative to secure this information, so that it might be put beyond human knowledge once and for all, and so secure his inheritance? Only one person stood to gain from acquiring the documents that Mr Carteret had been carrying in his bag. Only one. Who had Mr Carteret himself named as having pryed into Lord Tansor's private affairs, and as being guilty of worse, though unspecified, transgressions? Who had also shown an eager interest in the papers of the first Lady Tansor? Who desired to know what Mr Carteret knew? And at whose implied instigation had a watch been set on him?

*[A maxim of the tribune Lucius Cassius Longinus, quoted by Cicero, meaning 'For whose benefit?', often used to point a finger at someone who stands to gain most from a crime. *Ed.*]

Phoebus Daunt was that person; and by possessing himself of Lady Tansor's incriminating correspondence, he had no doubt thought to deny the lost heir, if he was still alive, of ever claiming his birthright. But premeditated murder? Was even Daunt capable of that?

I closed my eyes and saw again poor Mr Carteret's face, beaten and bloody. And in that moment I knew, with instinctive certainty, who had done it. Those terrible injuries constituted the violent signature of Josiah Pluckrose, seen first on the face of Mary Baker's sister, Agnes, and more recently, if I was not very much mistaken, on that of Lewis Pettingale. Pluckrose, for certain acting on the orders of Phoebus Daunt, had first kept watch on Mr Carteret, and had then attacked him as he entered Evenwood Park through the Western Gates. I saw it all clearly and distinctly in my mind. Whether the intention had been to murder Mr Carteret, or merely to steal his bag, might still be an open question. Of the identity of the perpetrators, however, I now had no doubt.

And then, as I further traced the logical course of my inferences and deductions, I began to conceive the possibility that I, too, might be in danger, if Daunt were to discover that Edward Glapthorn, the representative of Tredgold, Tredgold & Orr, was none other than Edward Glyver, the lost heir. For something told me that the game was afoot; that my enemy was even now trying to seek out his old school-fellow, and for only one purpose that I could divine. Edward Glyver alive was a perpetual threat. Edward Glyver dead made all secure.

Yet though he should seek through all the world for Edward Glyver, where could he be found? There was no one now at Sandchurch who could tell him. No letters were directed to him from there any more. He might look in the Post-office Directory for him, but in vain. He would not be there. No door-plate, and no headstone either, bore his name. He has vanished from the earth. And yet he lives and breathes in *me*! I *am* Edward Glapthorn, who *was* Edward Glyver, who *will be* Edward Duport. Oh Phoebus, light of the age! How will you catch this phantom, this wraith, who is now one man, now another? He is here; he is there; he is nowhere. He is behind you.

But I have another advantage. Though he does not yet know me, I know *him*. I have become his father's friend, and may walk through the front door of his house any time I please – as I did so recently. I am invisible to my enemy, as he walks to his club, or strolls through the Park at Evenwood of an evening. Only think, mighty Phoebus, what this means! The man who sits opposite you when you take the train back from the country: does he have a familiar look? There is something about him, perhaps, that stirs your memory; but only for a moment. You return to reading your news-paper, and do not see that his eye is fixed upon you. He is nothing to you, another traveller merely; but you should be more careful. There is a fog tonight, the streets are deserted; no one will hear you cry out. For where is your shield, where your armour, against a man whom you cannot see, whom you cannot name, whom you do not know? I find myself laughing out loud, laughing so much that the tears roll down my face.

And when the laughter stops, I see clearly where all this will end. But who will be the hunter, and who the hunted?

Part the Fifth

THE MEANING OF NIGHT

1853–1855

Our knowledge doth but show us our ignorance.

—Owen Felltham, *Resolves* (1623),
xxvii, 'Of Curiosity in Knowledge'

· 35 ·

*Credula res amor est**

Mr Carteret's Deposition had opened a window on many things that had previously been hidden from my view, providing important corroboration of what was recorded in my foster-mother's journals, as well as valuable circumstantial detail concerning the actions taken by Lady Tansor, and their far-reaching consequences. But I knew in my heart that the letters taken from Mr Carteret's bag would never now be recovered; and that without them, my case was still not unanswerable. I considered that it might be possible that other documents had survived of a similar character; but even granting this possibility, how could they now be found? I came to the forlorn conclusion that I was as far from my goal as ever, whilst Daunt's position grew ever stronger.

I subsided into one of my glooms. But then, three days later, a note came from Lizzie Brine, delivered to me by messenger, informing me that Miss Carteret and her friend, Mademoiselle Buisson, would be visiting the National Gallery on the following Monday afternoon, the 14th of November. My spirits instantly revived and, on the day in question, at just after two o'clock, I walked over to Trafalgar-square and stationed myself at the foot of the Gallery's steps.

At a little before half-past two, I saw her emerge into the autumn sunlight, with her friend at her side. They began to

*['Love is a credulous thing'. *Ed.*]

descend the steps as I, with an air of complete nonchalance, started to ascend them.

'Miss Carteret! What an extraordinary coincidence!'

She made me no reply, and for several moments not a scintilla of recognition was discernible in her expression. Instead, she stood regarding me through her round spectacles as though I were a complete stranger, until at last her companion spoke up.

'*Emilie, ma chère, est-ce que tu vas me présenter à ce monsieur?*'*

Only with these words did her features relax. Turning to Mademoiselle Buisson she introduced me as, 'Mr Edward Glapthorn, the gentleman I told you about'. Then, more deliberately, 'Mr Glapthorn has spent some time in Paris, and is a fluent French speaker.'

'Ah,' said Mademoiselle Buisson, raising her eyebrows in a singularly charming way, 'then we shall be unable to talk about him without his knowing what we say.'

Her English was perfectly expressed and enunciated, with barely a trace of a Gallic accent. With fetching, girlish volubility, she expressed herself delighted to make my acquaintance, and began at once, as if we already knew each other, to describe some of the exhibits they had seen, with a breathless enthusiasm that was most engaging. Mrs Rowthorn had told me that she was of an age with Miss Carteret, but she had a simple unaffected prettiness about her which made her seem younger. They made odd companions, certainly; Mademoiselle Buisson was animated, expressive, and forthcoming, dressed gaily *à la mode*, and displaying a natural exuberance of spirit. Miss Carteret, sombre and stately in her mourning black, stood silently watchful, like a tolerant older sister, as her companion flittered and giggled. Yet it was impossible not to sense the closeness of their connexion –

*['Emily, my dear, aren't you going to introduce me to this gentleman?' *Ed.*]

the way that Mademoiselle Buisson would turn to her friend as she made a particular point and place her hand on Miss Carteret's arm, with that same unthinking familiarity that I had seen her display at Evenwood after the funeral; the little complicit glances, eye meeting eye, speaking of confidences shared, and secrets kept safe.

'May I ask how long you will be staying in London, Miss Carteret?'

'With such prescience as you possess, Mr Glapthorn,' she replied, 'I imagine you can answer that question for yourself.'

'Prescience? What can you mean?'

'You wish me to suppose, then, that meeting you here is coincidental?'

'You may suppose what you wish,' I said, as genially as I could, 'or, if you cannot accept the fact of coincidence, perhaps you would be more comfortable with the notion of Fate.'

At this, she managed a contrite little smile, and asked to be excused for her ill humour.

'Your kind note of acceptance to my father's interment was received,' she went on, 'but we were disappointed not to have observed you amongst the company.'

'I am afraid I was a little late in arriving. I paid my respects to your father – as my firm's representative, as well as in a personal capacity – after the carriages had departed; and then, having an urgent engagement here in town, and not wishing to intrude on you or your family, I returned immediately.'

'We were hoping to receive you at the Dower House again,' she said, taking off her glasses and placing them in her reticule. 'You were expected, you know. But you had your own reasons for not coming, I dare say.'

'I did not wish to intrude, as I said.'

'As you said. But you put yourself to a great deal of trouble on our account in travelling all the way to Northamptonshire only to return immediately. I hope you met your engagement?'

'It was no trouble, I assure you.'

'You are kind to say so, Mr Glapthorn. And now, if you will excuse us. Perhaps coincidence – or Fate – will arrange for our paths to cross again.'

Mademoiselle Buisson gave me a curtsey and a smile; but Miss Carteret merely inclined her head a little, in the way that I had seen her do to Daunt, and passed on down the steps.

Of course I could not allow them to go and so, feigning a sudden disinclination to spend such an uncommonly fine November day looking at dull pictures, requested the honour of accompanying them a little way, if they were proceeding on foot. Mademoiselle announced brightly that they had thought of walking down to Green-park, which I agreed was a capital prospect on such an afternoon.

'Then come with us, by all means, Mr Glapthorn!' she cried. 'You don't mind, do you, Emily?'

'I do not mind, if you do not, and if Mr Glapthorn has nothing better to do,' came the reply.

'Then it is settled,' said her friend, clapping her hands. 'How delightful!'

And so off we set together across the Square, Miss Carteret on my right hand, Mademoiselle Buisson on my left.

Once in the open spaces of the Park, Miss Carteret's earlier irritation seemed to lessen. Little by little, we began to speak of things other than the late tragic events at Evenwood, and by the end of the afternoon, with the sun beginning to decline, we were talking openly and easily, as if we had all been old friends.

Towards four o'clock we walked into Piccadilly, and the ladies waited by the kerb while I secured a hansom.

'May I tell the driver where you wish to be taken?' I asked innocently.

She gave the address of her aunt's house in Wilton-crescent, and I handed her into the cab, followed by Mademoiselle Buisson, who smiled at me in a dreamy way as she settled herself into her seat.

'Miss Carteret, it is presumptuous, I know, but will you allow me to call on you – and Mademoiselle Buisson?'

To my surprise, she did not hesitate in her reply.

'I am at home – I should say at my aunt's home – every morning from eleven.'

'May I come on Friday, then, at eleven?' I confess that I asked the question, thinking she might invent some excuse for not being able to receive me; but instead, to my surprise, she leaned her head on one side and said:

'Of course you may.'

As the hansom pulled away, she pushed down the window, looked back at me, and smiled.

A simple smile. But it sealed my fate.

ON FRIDAY, AS ARRANGED, I CALLED UPON MISS CARTERET AT HER aunt's house in Wilton-crescent. I was shown into a large and elegant drawing-room, where I found Miss Carteret and her friend seated together on a little sofa by the window, each apparently engrossed in reading.

'Mr Glapthorn! How nice!'

It was Mademoiselle who spoke first, jumping up to pull a small arm-chair closer to their sofa, and begging me to sit down.

'We have been so dreadfully dull here this morning, Mr Glapthorn,' she said, resuming her place next to Miss Carteret, and tossing her book onto a nearby table. 'Like two old spinsters.

I declare I might have gone quite mad if you hadn't come to see us. Emily, of course, can sit for hours on her own and never minds it; but I must have company. Don't you love company, Mr Glapthorn?'

'Only my own,' I replied.

'Oh, but that is terrible. You are as bad as Emily. And yet you were such a lively companion the other day, in the Park, was he not, Emily?'

All through this exchange Miss Carteret had sat, book in hand, impassively regarding her friend. Then, ignoring the question, she turned towards me and took off her spectacles.

'How is your employer, Mr Glapthorn?'

'My employer?'

'Yes. Mr Christopher Tredgold. I understand from Lord Tansor that he has suffered a seizure.'

'He was very poorly when I last saw him. I'm afraid I cannot say whether his condition has since improved.'

Mademoiselle Buisson gave a little sigh and crossed her arms, as if she was piqued by the suddenly serious turn of the conversation.

I had hoped for a warmer, less restrained, reception than this from Miss Carteret, and was unsure of what to say next.

'Is your aunt at home?' I said at last, feeling it would be polite of me to ask.

'She is visiting a friend,' Miss Carteret replied, 'and will not return until this evening.'

'Mrs Manners is a person who likes company very much,' Mademoiselle Buisson observed, with a defiant toss of her head.

'I think Mr Tredgold mentioned to me that Mrs Manners was your mother's youngest sister?' My employer had once spoken of Mr Carteret's family, and of this lady, with whom Miss Carteret enjoyed a particularly close relationship.

'That is correct.'

'With whom you resided when you were in Paris?'

'You are very curious about my family, Mr Glapthorn.' The rebuke – if the remark was intended as such – was spoken in a soft, almost teasing tone, which strongly conveyed to me the notion that she was, after all, disposed to maintain the friendly relations that we had established during the course of our afternoon in Green-park. This encouraged me to take a little risk with my response.

'I am curious about your family, Miss Carteret, because I am curious about you.'

'That is a rather bold statement, and curious in itself. What possible interest can my dull life hold for someone such as you? For I conceive, Mr Glapthorn, that you are a person of wide experience and interests, with a certain largeness of view that I have observed before in men of strong intellect who have lived a good deal in the world on their own terms. You live by your wits – I am sure I am right to say this – and this gives you, if I may say so, a kind of feral character. Yes, you are an adventurer, Mr Glapthorn. I do not say that you can never be tamed, but I am sure you are not destined for domesticity. Don't you agree, Marie-Madeleine?'

Mademoiselle had been regarding Miss Carteret and me with an expression of intense interest, her eyes darting from one to the other as each of us spoke.

'I think,' she said slowly, pursing her lips in concentration, 'that Mr Glapthorn is what I have heard called in English a dark horse. Yes, that is what I think. *Vous êtes un homme de mystère.*'

'Well,' I smiled, 'I am not sure whether to be flattered or not.'

'Oh,' said Mademoiselle, 'flattered, of course. A hint of mystery in a person is always an advantageous characteristic.'

'So you think I am mysterious?'

'Assuredly.'

'And what do you think, Miss Carteret?'

'I think we are all mysterious,' she replied, opening her eyes to their fullest extent. 'It is a question of degree. Everyone has things they would prefer to hide from the view of others, even from those to whom they are close – little secret sins, frailties, fears, even hopes that dare not be spoken; yet, on the whole, these are venial mysteries and do not prevent those who love us best from knowing us as we essentially are, both for good and bad. But there are those who are not at all what they seem. Such people, I think, are wholly mysterious. Their true selves are deliberately and entirely masked, leaving only a false aspect for others to know.'

Her unwavering gaze was uncomfortable, and the ensuing silence even more so. She was speaking generally, of course; yet there was an unmistakable pointedness to her words that struck me very forcefully. Mademoiselle gave a sigh, indicative of impatience with her serious friend, whilst I smiled weakly and, in an attempt to steer the conversation in another direction, asked Miss Carteret how long she would be staying in London.

'Marie-Madeleine leaves for Paris tomorrow. I shall remain here a little longer, having nothing to draw me back to Evenwood.'

'Not even Mr Phoebus Daunt?' I asked.

At this, Mademoiselle Buisson gave out a little scream of laughter and rocked back and forth on the sofa.

'Mr Phoebus Daunt! You think she would go back for him? But you are teasing, I think, Mr Glapthorn.'

'Why would Miss Carteret not wish to see her old friend?' I asked, with an exaggeratedly uncomprehending expression.

'Ah, yes,' replied Mademoiselle, smiling, 'her old friend and playfellow.'

'Mr Glapthorn does not share the world's admiration of Mr Phoebus Daunt,' said Miss Carteret. 'Indeed, he holds quite a severe opinion of him. Isn't that right, Mr Glapthorn?'

'But Mr Phoebus Daunt is so utterly charming!' cried Mademoiselle Buisson. 'And so clever, and so handsome! Are you jealous of him, Mr Glapthorn?'

'By no means, I assure you.'

'Do you know him, then?' asked Mademoiselle, smiling.

'Mr Glapthorn knows him only by reputation,' said Miss Carteret, also smiling, 'which he believes to be sufficient grounds for disliking him.'

They looked at each other as if they were playing some sort of game, the rules of which were known only by the two of them.

'Do I infer, then, Miss Carteret,' I asked, 'that we share a similar view of Mr Daunt's character and talents after all? When we last spoke on this subject you appeared inclined to defend him.'

'As I implied then, I owe Mr Daunt the courtesy due to a long acquaintance, and to a close neighbour. But I do not seek to defend him. He is well able to defend himself, against your opinion, and against mine.'

'Well,' said Mademoiselle, 'if you wish to have *my* considered opinion of Mr Phoebus Daunt, here it is. He is insufferable. *That* is my opinion – the long and the short of it, as you say in English. So you see, Mr Glapthorn, we are all of one mind on the subject.'

I said that I was glad of it.

'But you know, Emily,' she continued, turning to her friend, 'I can think of an excellent reason for you to go back to Evenwood.'

'And what is that?' asked Miss Carteret.

'Why, Mr Phoebus Daunt is not there!'

Mademoiselle seemed excessively pleased by the cleverness of her riposte. She clapped her hands together, kissed Miss Carteret on the cheek, and leaped to her feet. Then she began to dance around the room, skipping and twirling, and singing, '*Où est le soleil? Où est le soleil?*' until she sat down once more next to Miss Carteret, flushed and bright-eyed.

'And where has the sun gone?' I asked.

'To America,' said Miss Carteret. As she spoke, she regarded her friend with a quizzical uplift of her eyebrows, and again I felt an unmistakable undercurrent of complicity. 'He has embarked upon a lecture tour.'

'And what is he to lecture on?' I asked.

'His subject, I believe, is to be "The Art of the Epic".'

I could not stop myself from letting out a contemptuous guffaw. The Art of the Epic! Of all things! Then I checked myself, thinking that I might perhaps be reprimanded by Miss Carteret for my discourtesy towards her old playfellow; but I was gratified to see that both she and Mademoiselle were also laughing, Miss Carteret quietly and discreetly, her friend more openly.

'You see, Emily,' said Mademoiselle at length, 'Mr Glapthorn is a kindred spirit. He feels things as we do. We can tell him all our secrets, and never fear that he will betray us.'

Miss Carteret rose, walked to the window, and looked out into the street.

'It's so stuffy in here,' she said. 'Shall we walk out for half an hour?'

It did not take long for the two ladies to procure shawls and bonnets, and soon we were walking through carpets of fallen leaves in Hyde-park. We rested for a while on a bench overlooking the Serpentine; but Mademoiselle Buisson was restless and, after a minute or two, she wandered off a little way, leaving Miss Carteret and me alone for the first time.

'Miss Carteret,' I ventured, after we had sat for a few moments looking out over the water, 'may I enquire whether the police are any closer to apprehending your father's attackers?'

Her eyes remained fixed on some distant point as she made her reply.

'A man from Easton – a known ruffian – was questioned, but

has since been released without charge. I have no hope at all that the police will ever identify those responsible.'

She said this in a rather pat way, as if my question had been anticipated, and the answer prepared. Her beautiful face looked strained, and I noticed that she was playing with the fringes of her shawl in a distracted manner.

'Forgive me,' I said softly. 'The question was insensitive.'

'No!' She had now turned to look at me, and I saw that her eyes were full of tears. 'No. You speak out of kindness, I know that, and I am grateful for your concern, truly I am. But my heart is so full – with grief for my father, and with uncertainty as to what I shall do now. My father's death has thrown everything into doubt. I have no way of earning my living, and do not even know whether I shall be permitted to remain in my present home.'

'Surely Lord Tansor will be sensitive to your position, and to the duty he owes to you as his relative?'

'Lord Tansor will only do what serves his own interests,' she replied, somewhat tartly. 'I do not complain that he has never shown me consideration in the past, but he is certainly under no obligation to do so in the future. He gave my father employment at the behest of his aunt, my grandmother; but he did so with some reluctance, though the appointment proved of inestimable benefit to him. My father was his cousin, yet he was sometimes treated no better than a servant. I cannot deny that our material circumstances provided compensation; but we owned nothing. Everything we had was in the gift of Lord Tansor; we lived by the grace and favour of his Lordship, not as members of the family in our own right and dignity. I could never make my father see the inequity of our situation, but I felt the shame and injustice of it greatly. How, then, can I consider my relationship to his Lordship to offer any guarantee of security and independence?'

'But perhaps his Lordship will treat you generously, after all.'

'He may. I have Duport blood in me, and that is always of the greatest consideration to Lord Tansor. But I cannot count on things turning out to my advantage, and do not wish to be perpetually beholden to Lord Tansor.'

I then made the observation that a lady always had another means at her disposal to settle herself in a comfortable way of life.

'You mean marriage, I suppose. But who would want to marry me? I have no money of my own, and my father left little enough. I am almost thirty years old – no, do not say that my age is of no account. I know very well that it is. No, Mr Glapthorn, I am a lost cause. I shall live and die a spinster.'

'There is one person, surely, who would marry you.'

'And who is that?'

'Why, Mr Phoebus Daunt, of course.'

'Really, Mr Glapthorn, you are quite obsessed by Mr Phoebus Daunt. He seems to have become a fixed idea for you.'

'But you admit that I am right?'

'I admit no such thing. Any inclinations in that direction that Mr Daunt might have harboured have long since withered away. Even if my father had approved of him, which he did not, I could never have reciprocated his feelings. I do not love Mr Daunt; and, for me, having had the example of my parents constantly before me, love is the only reason for marriage. And now, shall we agree to speak no more of Mr Daunt? He bores me in company, and it bores me even more to hear him spoken of. I am determined to find some way of settling my future, on my own terms and to my own satisfaction, without having to cast myself on Mr Daunt and his expectations. Now tell me, have you read Mr Currer Bell's *Villette*?'*

*[The pseudonym, of course, of Charlotte Brontë. *Villette* was published in January 1853. *Ed.*]

With this question she began to quiz me on my tastes and opinions. Was I an admirer of Mr Dickens? What was my estimation of the work of Mr Wilkie Collins? Was not Mr Tennyson's *In Memoriam* an incomparably fine achievement?* Had I been to any concerts or recitals lately? Did I see any merit in the work of Mr Rossetti and his associates?†

She showed an informed and discerning interest in each topic that arose in the course of our discussion, and we soon found that our views on the merits or otherwise of various authors and artists coincided most fortuitously; little by little, we began to speak like two people who had silently acknowledged a mutual liking for each other. Then Mademoiselle Buisson returned to where we were sitting.

'It is getting a little cold, *ma chère*,' she said, taking her friend by the hand to encourage her to stand up, 'and I am hungry. Shall we go back? My compliments to you, Mr Glapthorn. I can see by her face that Emily has benefited from her conversation with you. What were you talking about?'

'Nothing that would interest you, dear,' said Miss Carteret as she pulled her shawl round her. 'We have been quite serious, haven't we, Mr Glapthorn?'

'And yet it has made you happy,' observed Mademoiselle, thoughtfully. 'You must visit her again soon, Mr Glapthorn, and be serious once more, and then I shall not worry about her when I return home.'

We walked back to Wilton-crescent in high spirits, with

*[*In Memoriam A.H.H.* (i.e. Arthur Henry Hallam, 1811–33) was published by Edward Moxon (Daunt's publisher) in 1850, the year Tennyson was appointed Poet Laureate following the death of Wordsworth. *Ed.*]

†[The Pre-Raphaelite Brotherhood, founded in 1848 by Dante Gabriel Rossetti (1828–82), John Everett Millais (1829–96), William Holman Hunt (1827–1910), and others. *Ed.*]

Mademoiselle chattering and laughing, Miss Carteret smiling with quiet satisfaction, whilst I glowed inside with a new happiness.

When we reached the house, Mademoiselle skipped nimbly up the steps.

'Good-bye, Mr Glapthorn,' she called back from the front door. Then she stopped and thought for a moment. 'It is a curious name, is it not? Glapthorn. Most curious, and most suitable for a dark horse.' And with that, she disappeared into the house, laughing.

I turned to Miss Carteret.

'May I call again?'

She offered her hand to me, which I took in mine, and held for a most precious moment.

'Do you need to ask?'

· 36 ·

*Amor vincit omnia**

I PAID MY SECOND VISIT TO WILTON-CRESCENT THE FOLLOWING Friday, my heart full of bright hope that Miss Carteret would receive me with the same warmth with which our last meeting had concluded. I was more in love with her than ever; and now I was beginning to allow myself to believe that, in time, she might love me too. On this occasion, I was introduced to Mrs Fletcher Manners – a bustling, pretty looking woman, only half a dozen years or so older than her niece – and invited to take luncheon with the two ladies. Afterwards, when Mrs Manners left to pay her afternoon calls, Miss Carteret and I were left alone in the drawing-room.

'This has been most delightful, Mr Glapthorn,' she said, as soon as her aunt had gone. 'But I'm afraid I shall be returning to Evenwood tomorrow, and so will not have the pleasure of receiving you again for some time – unless . . .'

I immediately took the hint.

'It is possible that I may have occasion to visit Evenwood in the near future. Dr Daunt and I are slaves to the bibliophilic passion – I mean that we love old books, and share a number of other antiquarian and scholarly interests. He has asked me to look over the proofs of translation that he has prepared, and it will be best if I return these to him in person. When I do so, perhaps you would not mind if I called at the Dower House.'

'You would be most welcome,' she said. Then she sighed.

*['Love conquers all': Virgil, *Eclogues. Ed.*]

'Though I do not know how much longer I shall be able to call the Dower House my home. Sir Hyde Teasedale has expressed a wish to acquire the tenancy for his daughter, who is soon to be married; and I fear Lord Tansor will look upon a paying tenant with rather more favour than a dependent relative.'

'But he will not turn you out, surely?'

'No, I am sure he will not. But I have little money of my own and will be unable to match the price that Sir Hyde is willing to pay for the let of the property.'

'Then Lord Tansor must find you somewhere else. Has he spoken to you on this subject?'

'Only briefly. But let us not be gloomy. Lord Tansor will not let me starve, I am sure.'

We conversed for a little longer, and I experienced again, as I had done by the Serpentine the previous week, that luxurious sense of having her all to myself. A little of her old reserve yet remained; but I left the house that afternoon emboldened by the cordiality of her manner towards me, and feeling hope rise within me that I did not love her in vain.

I IMMEDIATELY WROTE TO DR DAUNT, AND IT WAS ARRANGED THAT I would go up to Northamptonshire with the proofs of his translation the Thursday following, being the first day of December.

The Rector and I passed a stimulating afternoon discussing Iamblichus, and Dr Daunt professed himself in my debt for the few trifling amendments to his translation and commentary that I had ventured to suggest.

'This has been most kind of you, Mr Glapthorn,' he said, 'most kind. I have given you a deal of trouble, I dare say. And a trip to the country in such weather is doubly burdensome.'

It was blowing hard outside, as it had been for a day or more, and the accompanying rain had turned the surrounding roads and tracks into quagmires.

'Pray do not mention it,' I replied. 'I am willing to endure any discomfort for the sake of learning, and for the prospect of such a conversation as we have enjoyed this afternoon.'

'You are kind to say so. But will you stay and take some tea? I am afraid my wife is not at home, and my son is abroad, on a lecture tour; so it will be just us two. But I can dangle a little temptation before you – a particularly fine copy of Quarles' *Hieroglyphikes** that I have lately acquired, on which I'd value your opinion, if you have no more pressing engagement.'

I could not refuse the good old gentleman, and so tea was called for and taken, and the work in question produced and discussed, followed by several others of a similar character. It was not until a little after four o'clock, with darkness falling, that I made my escape.

The wind was blowing in strong gusts from the east, lashing the rain against my face as I picked my way through the slippery ruts of the track that led from the Rectory to the Dower House. With the rain coming on suddenly harder, I abandoned my original intention of walking round to the front of the house and ran as fast as I could across the stable-yard to knock on the kitchen door, which was soon opened by Mrs Rowthorn.

'Mr Glapthorn, sir, come in, come in.' She ushered me inside, where I found John Brine warming his toes by the kitchen fire.

'Were you expected, sir?' asked the housekeeper.

'I've been at the Rectory and wished to pay my compliments to Miss Carteret, if she is at home, before I return to Easton.'

'Oh yes, sir, she's at home. Would you like to come up and wait?'

*[*Hieroglyphikes of the Life of Man* (1638) by the English poet Francis Quarles (1592–1644). *Ed.*]

'Perhaps I could dry myself by the fire for five minutes first,' I said, taking off my coat and walking over to stand next to where John Brine was sitting. After a minute or two, Mrs Rowthorn scuttled upstairs on some errand, giving me the opportunity to ask Brine whether he had any news.

'Nothing much to tell, sir. Miss Carteret has kept to the house these past few days, and has received only Mrs Daunt, who has been twice now since Miss came back from London. Mr Phoebus Daunt, as you know, will not return for some weeks.'

'Miss Carteret has not been out, you say?'

'No, sir – except, that is, to wait on Lord Tansor.'

'Brine, you really are a most infuriating fellow. Could you not have told me this before? When did your mistress wait on Lord Tansor?'

'On Tuesday afternoon,' came a voice, not John Brine's. Turning, I saw his sister, Lizzie, standing at the foot of the stairs.

'John took her up in the landau,' she continued. 'They were back within an hour.'

'And do you know the purpose of the visit?' I asked.

'I believe it concerned Lord Tansor's decision to let the Dower House to Sir Hyde Teasedale. Miss has been offered accommodation in the great house, in the apartments previously occupied by the first Lady Tansor. I am to go with her. John will remain here, with the others, to serve Sir Hyde's daughter and her husband.'

Just then, as I was digesting this news, Mrs Rowthorn reappeared to ask whether I was ready to be shown upstairs, whereupon I proceeded to the vestibule in the housekeeper's generous wake.

Miss Carteret was seated by the fire in the room where we had conducted our first conversation. She made no movement as we entered, as if she had not heard Mrs Rowthorn's knock, and sat with her chin resting on her hand, staring meditatively into the flames.

'Please, Miss, Mr Glapthorn is here.'

Lit by the glow of the fire on one side, and on the other by the rays from a nearby colza lamp,* her face had assumed an unearthly marmoreal pallor. It seemed for a brief moment like the carved representation of some ancient goddess, terrible and untouchable, rather than the face of a living woman. But then she smiled, rose from her chair to greet me, and apologized for her dreaminess.

'I have been thinking of Papa and Mamma,' she said, 'and of all the happy years we spent here.'

'But you are not leaving Evenwood, I think, only the Dower House.'

For a moment her face took on a guarded look; but then she inclined her head slightly and looked at me teasingly. 'How well informed you are, Mr Glapthorn, on all our little doings! I wonder how you do it?'

As I did not wish to give away the identity of my informant, I said that there was no mystery to it: a passing remark from Dr Daunt, nothing more, adding that I was glad Lord Tansor had recognized his duty towards her.

'Well then, I have my explanation,' she said. 'But perhaps I should begin to inform myself a little about *you*, if we are to be friends. Come and sit by me, and tell me all about Edward Glapthorn.'

She made room for me on the little sofa on which she was sitting and folded her hands in her lap, waiting for me to begin. I

*[Colza was a thick, viscous vegetable oil used in lamps before the invention of paraffin in 1878. *Ed.*]

remained for a second or two entranced by her beautiful face, and by the closeness of her person.

'Have you nothing to say?'

'Nothing, I'm sure, that would interest you.'

'Come, come, Mr Glapthorn, no false modesty. I sense you have a great deal to say, if you would only allow yourself to do so. Your parents, now. What of them?'

The truth was on my lips; but something held me back. Once I had declared my love for her, and should it be returned, I had resolved in my heart to tell her everything; to trust her as I had trusted no one else, not even Bella. But for now, until all was certain, I felt obliged to speak the truth only as far as I was able, and to apply a little dab of falsehood to the rest.

'My father was a Captain in the Hussars and died before I was born. My mother supported us by writing novels.'

'A novelist! How fascinating! But I cannot recall an authoress by the name of Glapthorn.'

'She wrote anonymously.'

'I see. And where were you brought up?'

'On the Somerset coast. My mother's family were West Country people.'

'Somerset, do you say? I do not know it well myself, but I have heard Lord Tansor speak of it as a beautiful county – his first wife's people came from there, you know. And do you have brothers or sisters?'

'My older sister died when she was very young. I never knew her. I was educated at home by my mother, and then at the village school. Later, after my mother died, I studied at Heidelberg and then travelled a good deal on the Continent. I came to London in 1848 and found my present employment at Tredgolds. I collect books, study photography, and generally lead a rather dull life. There you have it. Edward Glapthorn, *en tout et pour tout.*'

'Well,' she said when I had finished my *résumé*, 'I still accuse you of false modesty, for I infer from your account that you undoubtedly possess some remarkable talents to which you are not prepared to admit. Photography, for example. That is something which calls for both scientific knowledge and an artistic eye, yet you mention it almost off-handedly, as if its secrets could be mastered by any Tom, Dick or Harry. I am greatly interested by photography. Lord Tansor has an album containing some excellent views of Evenwood. I've often looked through it with admiration. The same photographer, I believe, was responsible for the portrait of Lord Tansor that stands on his Lordship's desk. Do you know, I believe that I should like to have *my* portrait taken. Yes, I think I should like that very much. Would you take my portrait, Mr Glapthorn?'

I searched her eyes, those great dark pools, infinitely deep, but they gave back no suggestion of any ulterior meaning to her question. I saw only frankness and honesty, and my heart leaped within me that she should look upon me in such a way, without the reserve that had once seemed so unyielding. I told her that I would be pleased and honoured to take her portrait, and then, recklessly perhaps, tumbled out an admission that, at Mr Tredgold's instigation, I had been responsible for producing the photographic views of Evenwood that she had admired, and for the portrait of Lord Tansor.

'But of course!' she cried. 'The portrait carries the initials EG – for Edward Glapthorn! What an extraordinary thing, that you should have come to Evenwood to take your photographs and I never knew! To think that we might have met then, or passed each other in the grounds as strangers, unaware that we were destined to meet one day.'

'So you think our meeting was destined?' I asked.

'Don't you?'

'As you know, I am a fervent believer in Fate,' I replied. 'It is the pagan in me. I have tried to argue myself out of it, but find I cannot.'

'Then it seems we are helpless,' she said quietly, turning her head towards the fire.

Silence descended on the room, a silence that seemed deepened and made almost palpable by the faint ticking of a clock, and the sound of the logs crackling and flaring, and by the roaring wind, throwing leaves and small branches against the windows.

I felt my breath quicken with the desire to draw her close to me, to feel her hair against my face, and her breast against mine. Would she push me away? Or would she instantly yield to the moment? Then I saw her head drop, and knew that she was weeping.

'Forgive me,' she said, almost in a whisper.

I was on the point of assuring her that no apology was required for her display of feeling; but then I saw that she had not addressed her remark to me, but to some other person, absent in body but present in her mind.

'You should not have died!' She was speaking now in a kind of moan, and shaking her head rapidly from side to side; then I understood that the sudden thought of her father's dreadful death must have come upon her unexpectedly, as fresh grief often will.

'Miss Carteret—'

'Oh, Mr Glapthorn, I am so sorry.'

'No, no, no. You must not be sorry. Are you quite well? Shall I call for Mrs Rowthorn?'

My heart broke to see her in such open distress, though my pity for her contended with boiling rage for what Daunt had brought her to. He might not have been an active participant in Mr Carteret's death, but the conviction remained that he had been implicated in it. And so the responsibility for one more injury was added to his account, which I swore must soon be called in for settlement.

In answer to my solicitations, Miss Carteret insisted that she required nothing and began to wipe away her tears. In a moment or two she had composed herself and was asking me, with every appearance of cheerful interest, when I was to return to London. I said that I would be staying in Easton that night and would leave in the morning.

'Oh!' she exclaimed, as a violent gust of wind rattled one of the windows. 'You cannot walk back to Easton in this weather. John Brine would take you, but one of the horses is lame. You must stay the night. I insist.'

Of course I objected that I could not possibly trespass on her kindness, but she would have none of it. She immediately rang for Mrs Rowthorn, and asked her to prepare a room and lay another place for dinner.

'You will not mind our dining *à deux*, I hope, Mr Glapthorn?' she asked. 'It is a little scandalous, I know, having no one to chaperone me; but I have little time for tiresome conventions. If a lady wishes to dine with a gentleman in her own home, then it is surely no concern of anyone else's. Besides, company is rare at the Dower House these days.'

'But I think you spoke of having friends in the neighbourhood?'

'My friends keep a respectful distance at this sad time, and I have little taste for going out. I think perhaps we are alike, Mr Glapthorn. We prefer our own company best.'

Dinner alone with Miss Emily Carteret! How extraordinary it was to find myself seated opposite her in the panelled dining-room overlooking the gardens at the back of the Dower House, and to hear myself talking to her with a degree of familiarity that

I could not have imagined possible only a few hours earlier. We began to discuss the events of the day, including, of course, the late action at Sinope,* and found ourselves in agreement that Russia needed to be taught a lesson – it rather surprised, as well as pleased, me that Miss Carteret's bellicosity was even more pronounced than mine. *The Heir of Redclyffe*† was then dissected – to its disadvantage – and Mr Ruskin's views on the Gothic style of architecture considered and commended in every respect.‡ We laughed; we disputed, now seriously, now facetiously; we discovered that we liked a great many things in common, and disliked a great many more. We found that we were both intolerant of stupidity and dullness, and equally enraged by wanton ignorance. An hour flew by; then two. Ten o'clock had just chimed when, having removed ourselves to the drawing-room, I asked my hostess whether she would be kind enough to play.

'Some Chopin, perhaps,' I suggested. 'I remember so well, on my first visit to the Dower House, hearing you play something by him – a Nocturne, I think.'

'No,' she corrected, colouring slightly. 'A Prelude. Number 15, in D flat, called "The Raindrop".§ Unfortunately, I no longer have the music. Perhaps something else. Let me sing to you instead.'

*[Turkey declared war on Russia in October 1853. The Turks defeated the Russians at Oltenitza on 4 November, but the Turkish naval squadron was destroyed by the Russian Black Sea Fleet at Sinope on the 30th of that month – an action that caused outrage in England. These were the preliminary engagements of what was to become the Crimean War. Britain and France declared war on Russia in March 1854. *Ed.*]

†[By Charlotte M. Yonge (1823–1901), published in 1853. The novel, which dramatizes the spiritual struggles of its principal character, Guy Morville, reflected its author's Tractarian beliefs and was one of the most successful novels of the century. *Ed.*]

‡[The first volume of *The Stones of Venice* by John Ruskin (1819–1900), in which he championed Gothic architecture, was published in March 1851; volume II followed in July 1853, and volume III in October 1853. *Ed.*]

§[Opus 28. Composed 1836–9, published in 1839. *Ed.*]

She hurried over to the piano-forte, as if anxious not to dwell on the memory of that evening, and began to deliver a passionate rendition of Herr Schumann's 'An meinem Herzen, an meiner Brust',* to a delicate accompaniment. Her singing voice was deep and rich, but overlaid with an enchanting softness of tone. She played and sang with closed eyes, having both the music and the words by heart. When she had finished, she shut the lid and sat for a moment looking towards the window. The blind had been drawn down, but she continued to stare at the blank fabric, as if she could see straight through it, across the lawn, and through the Plantation, to some distant object of the most intense interest.

'You sing from the heart, Miss Carteret,' I said.

She did not answer me, but continued to stare at the blind.

'Perhaps the piece holds a special meaning for you?'

She turned towards me.

'Not at all. But you appear to be asking another question.'

'Another question?'

'Yes. You ask whether the piece holds a special meaning for me, but really you wish to know something else.'

'I see you have the measure of me,' I said, pulling up a chair. 'You are right. I do wish to know something, but now I am ashamed by my presumptuousness. Please forgive me.'

She gave a little smile before replying. 'Friends are allowed to be a little presumptuous, Mr Glapthorn – even such new ones as we are. Now put your scruples aside, and tell me what you wish to know.'

'Very well. I have been curious – though it is no business of mine, no business whatsoever – as to the identity of the man I saw you talking to in the Plantation, on the evening of my first visit. I

*['At my heart, at my breast', from Schumann's song-cycle for female voice and piano, *Frauenliebe und leben* ('A Woman's Life and Love', 1840). *Ed.*]

happened to be standing by the window, you see, and observed you. But you do not need to answer. I have no right—'

She coloured, and I apologized for my forwardness; but she quickly came back.

'Do you really ask out of mere curiosity, Mr Glapthorn, or from some other motive?'

I felt trapped by her questioning stare and, as I invariably do on such occasions, resorted to bluster.

'Oh no, I am incorrigibly inquisitive, that is all. It is a strength in many respects, but in others I am keenly aware that it is a rather vulgar failing of mine.'

'I applaud your frankness,' she said, 'and you shall be rewarded for it. The gentleman you saw was Mr George Langham, the brother of one of my oldest friends, Miss Henrietta Langham. I'm afraid you witnessed the final dissolution of Mr Langham's romantic hopes. He proposed to me – secretly – some months ago, but I refused him. He came again that night, not knowing that my father—'

She stopped, closed her eyes, and took a deep breath.

'No, no,' she broke in, seeing me about to speak. 'Let me continue. I saw Mr Langham from the window, as I was playing, and went to see what he wanted. He forgot himself to such an extent, even when I told him what had happened to my father, that he begged me to reconsider my previous decision. We parted in anger, I am afraid, on both sides. I fear Henrietta is also cross with me for refusing him. But I do not love George in that way, and never will, and so could not possibly marry him. There, Mr Glapthorn, is your answer. Is your curiosity satisfied.'

'Perfectly. Except—'

'Yes?'

'The music, which I found torn to pieces— '

'It was, as I think I told you, one of my father's favourites. I played it for the last time that evening, and vowed that I would never play it again. It had nothing to do with Mr Langham, and neither did the song that I sang tonight.'

'Then I am satisfied,' I said, giving her a grave little bow, 'though I feel I have pushed our friendship too far.'

'We must all do what we feel we must, Mr Glapthorn. But perhaps you will agree to reciprocate, for friendship's sake. I, too, am curious to know something.'

'And what is that?'

'A question that you refused to answer when we first met. What was your business with my father?'

I was unprepared both for the nature and the directness of the question, and only an ingrained habit of vigilance in matters of professional and private business prevented me from laying the whole thing before her. But, whether by accident or design, she had made it harder for me to prevaricate, as I had been able to do when she had previously asked me the same question, though still I made a clumsy attempt to do so.

'As I said before,' I began, 'it is a question of professional confidence—'

'And is a professional confidence more binding than a personal one?' she asked.

I was cornered. She had answered my question concerning her meeting in the Plantation; I had no choice but to respond in kind, though I took refuge in brevity, hoping thereby to answer her as honestly as I could whilst revealing as little as possible.

'Your father wrote to Mr Tredgold on a matter pertaining to the Tansor succession. My principal felt that it would not be appropriate for him to meet Mr Carteret in person, as he had requested; and so I was sent instead.'

'A matter pertaining to the succession? Surely that is something that my father would have felt obliged to put before Lord Tansor, not Mr Tredgold.'

'I can make no comment on that,' I replied. 'I can only say that it was your father's express wish that his communication to Mr Tredgold should be kept strictly confidential.'

'But what could possibly have made him act in such a way? He was a most loyal servant to Lord Tansor. It would have been against his deepest principles to go behind his Lordship's back.'

'Miss Carteret,' I said, 'I have already revealed more of the business than my employer would have wished me to do; and, indeed, I can add nothing more to what I have already said. Your father told me nothing when we met in Stamford, and his untimely death has sealed my ignorance concerning the reason for his letter to my principal. Whatever he wished to reveal to Mr Tredgold, through me, must now remain forever unknown.'

How I hated myself for the lie. She did not deserve to be treated so, as if she were an enemy to my interests, like Phoebus Daunt, whom she appeared to detest almost as much I did. I had no reason not to trust her, and every reason to draw her into my confidence. She had declared herself my friend, and had shown me courtesy and kindness, and a degree of partiality that I flattered myself betokened incipient affection. She had a right, surely, to claim my trust. Yes, she had a right to know what her father had written in his Deposition, and to understand what it signified for me, and for her. This, however, was not the time, not quite yet; but just a little longer, and then I would put all deceit aside for ever.

Had she sensed the falsehood? I could not tell, for nothing disturbed the enigmatic serenity of her face. She appeared to be turning over what I had said. Then, as if a thought had struck her, she asked:

'Do you suppose it might concern Mr Daunt – I mean, the matter that my father wished to bring to Mr Tredgold's attention?'

'I really cannot say.'

'But you would tell me, if you knew, wouldn't you? As a friend.'

She had moved closer to me and was standing, with one hand resting on the piano-forte, looking directly into my eyes.

'It would be impossible to deny a true friend,' I said.

'Well then, we have balanced the books, Mr Glapthorn.' The smile broadened. 'Confidences have been exchanged, and our debts to each other paid. I am so glad you came. When we next meet, I shall have left here for good. It will be strange, to pass by the Dower House and know that someone else is living here. But you will come and see me again, I hope, at the great house, or in London?'

'Do you need to ask?' I repeated the question she herself had put to me after our walk in Green-park.

'No,' she said, 'I do not think I do.'

· 37 ·

*Non sum qualis eram**

I DID NOT SEE MISS CARTERET THE NEXT MORNING. WHEN MRS Rowthorn came up with my breakfast, she informed me that her mistress had gone out early, though it was a damp and gloomy day for a walk.

'But it's a good sign,' she said, 'that Miss is out in the air again. She's been cooped up in her room for days on end since she came back from London, grieving still for her poor papa, it's plain. But she seemed brighter this morning, and it fair did my heart good to see.'

I had several hours before my train was due to leave, and so I resolved on a little expedition through the Park, partly to look upon my inheritance once again, and partly in the hope that I might encounter Miss Carteret.

Downstairs, I asked the girl that I found scrubbing the front step to run and fetch John Brine.

'Brine,' I asked, 'I have a mind to see the Mausoleum. Is there a key?'

'I can get that for you, sir,' he replied, 'if you'll wait till I ride up to the great house. It won't take more than a quarter of an hour.'

He was as good as his word, and I was soon wandering contentedly along sequestered paths through dripping woods and stately avenues of bare-branched limes, stopping from time to time to look out at the great house through a veil of drizzle. From certain vantage points it lay indistinct and spectral, an undifferentiated

*['I am not what I was'. *Ed.*]

mass; from others it gained in definition, its towers and spires rearing sharply up through the mist like the petrified fingers of some titanic creature. It began to seem suddenly, and curiously, imperative to drink in every separate prospect to the brim; each detail of arch or window, each angle and nuance, appeared infinitely and urgently precious to me, as if I were a man gazing on the face of the one he loves for the last time.

At length, I found myself standing – wet and cold, and splashed with mud – before the great double doors of the Mausoleum.

It stood within a dense semi-circle of ivy-clad trees, a substantial domed building in the Graeco-Egyptian style, constructed in the year 1722 by the 21st Baron, who for his design had plundered freely – some might say uncritically – from a number of mausolea illustrated in Roland Fréart's *Parallele de l'Architecture Antique et de la Moderne.**

The building consisted of a large central chamber flanked by three smaller wings, and an entrance hall, the whole being shut off by two massive and forbidding lead-faced doors, carrying representations in relief of six inverted torches, three on each door. Two life-size stone angels on plinths – one bearing a wreath, the other an open book – guarded the entrance. Reaching into my pocket, I pulled out the key that Brine had given me and placed it in the inverted escutcheon.

In the central chamber were four or five imposing tombs, whilst set around the walls of the three wings were a succession of arcaded and gated loculi, some presently empty and awaiting their occupants, others closed off by slate panels, each bearing an inscription.

The first panel to catch my attention was that of Lord Tansor's elder brother, Vortigern, whom Mr Tredgold had told me had died of an epileptic seizure; then I turned to the panel closing off the

*[Published in 1650. *Ed.*]

loculus that contained the remains of Henry Hereward Duport, my own brother. And then, next to it, was what I had come to see.

I stood in the cold, dank stillness for some minutes contemplating the simple inscription on the slate panel; but not in a mood of reverence and regret, as I had expected, but with a pounding heart. This is what I read:

Laura Rose Duport 1796–1824 Sursum Corda

The inscription instantly brought to mind the note Mr Carteret had appended to his Deposition. SURSUM CORDA:* the words from the Latin Eucharist written on a slip of paper sent to him by my mother's friend and companion, Miss Julia Eames. SURSUM CORDA. Try as I might, I could not wrench significance from the words; and yet Mr Carteret had come to a realization about them that he wished to communicate to me.

Musing on this new puzzle, I left the Mausoleum to silence and darkness and took my way down a muddy path to a gravelled bridle-way that ran alongside the Park wall back to the South Gates. Disappointed that I had not encountered Miss Carteret on my ramblings, I arrived back at the Dower House and went into

*['Lift up your hearts'. *Ed.*]

the stable-yard to reurn the key of the Mausoleum to John Brine.

'You'll oblige me by getting a duplicate cut, Brine. Discreetly. You understand?'

'I understand, sir.'

'Very good. My compliments to your sister.'

He tipped his cap and quickly pocketed the coins that I had placed in his hand.

'Don't expect we'll be seeing you for a while, sir.'

I turned back. 'What? Why do you say that?'

'I only meant that, with Miss going away—'

'Going away? What are you talking about?'

'Beg pardon, sir, I thought you'd have known. She's going to Paris, sir. To spend Christmas with her friend, Miss Buisson. Won't be back for a month or more.'

WHY? WHY HAD SHE NOT TOLD ME? FOR A TIME, AS I WALKED BACK TO Easton to take the Peterborough coach, I felt sick with doubt and suspicion; but as the coach pulled out of the market-square, I grew more rational. She had merely forgotten, nothing more. If our paths had crossed this morning, as we had both made our separate perambulations of the Park, she would have undoubtedly have told me of her imminent departure. I was sure of it.

Back in Temple-street that afternoon, I sat at my table and took out a sheet of paper. With a beating heart, I began to write.

1, Temple-street, Whitefriars, London

2nd December 1853

Dear Miss Carteret,—

I write this short note to thank you, most sincerely, for your recent hos-

pitality, & in the hope that you will allow me to anticipate an early resumption of our friendship.

It is likely, perhaps, that you may be visiting your aunt in the near future; if so, I trust you will not consider it forward of me to entertain the further hope – however slight – that you might inform me, so that I may arrange to call on you, at the usual time. If you are expecting to remain in Northamptonshire, then perhaps I may – with your permission – find occasion to visit you in your new accommodation. I wish very much to have your opinion on the work of Monsieur de Lisle. The* Poèmes antiques *seem to me admirable in every way. Do you know them?*

I remain, your friend,
E. Glapthorn.

I waited anxiously for her reply. Would she write? What would she say? Two days passed, but no word came. I could do nothing but meditate moodily in my rooms, staring out of the window at the leaden sky, or sitting, with an unopened book on my lap, for hours on end in a state of desperate vacancy.

Then, on the third day, a letter came. Reverently, I laid it – unopened – on my work-table, transfixed by the sight of her handwriting. With my forefinger I slowly traced each letter of the direction,† and then pressed the envelope to my face, to drink in the faint residue of her perfume. At last I reached for my paper-knife to release the enclosed sheet of paper from its covering.

A wave of relief and joy swept over me as I read her words.

*[Charles-Marie-René Leconte de Lisle (1818–94), leader of the Parnassian poets. His *Poèmes antiques* were published in 1852. *Ed.*]
†[i.e. the address. *Ed.*]

The Dower House
Evenwood, Northamptonshire

5th December 1853

Dear Mr Glapthorn,—

Your kind letter reached me just in time. Tomorrow I am to leave for Paris, to visit my friend Miss Buisson. I regret very much that I failed to mention this to you when you were here – my excuse is that the pleasure of your company drove all other thoughts from my head, & I did not realize the omission until after you had gone.

You must think me a very odd friend – for friends, I believe, we have agreed to be – to have kept such a thing from you, though I did not do so wilfully. But I will hope for forgiveness, as every sinner must.

I shall not return to England until January or February, but shall think of you often, and hope you will sometimes think of me. And when I return, I promise to send word to you – that, you may be assured, will be something I shall not *forget to do. You have shown me such kindness and consideration – & provided me with unlooked-for mental solace at this dark time – that I should be careless indeed of my own well-being if I were to deny myself the pleasure of seeing you again, as soon as circumstances permit.*

I am familiar with some of the work of M. de Lisle, but not the volume you mention – I shall take especial care to seek it out while I am in France, so that I may have something sensible to say about it when next we meet. In the meantime, I remain,

Your affectionate friend,
E. Carteret.

I kissed the paper and fell back in my chair. All was well. All was wonderfully well. Even the prospect of separation from her did not appal me. For was she not my affectionate friend, and would she not be often thinking of me, as I would be thinking of her? And when she returned – well, then I trusted to see affectionate friendship blossom quickly into consuming love.

I PASS OVER THE SUCCEEDING WEEKS, FOR THEY WERE BLEAK AND featureless. I sat at my work-table for hour after hour, writing notes and memoranda to myself on the various problems that still required resolution: the death of Mr Carteret, and how best to act on what he had revealed in his Deposition; the now urgent necessity to find unimpugnable evidence to prove my true identity in law; the reason why Miss Eames had sent Mr Carteret the words SURSUM CORDA; and last, but by no means least, the means by which I was to expose my enemy's true character. If only I could have called on Mr Tredgold's counsel! But his condition had been slow to improve, and during the two or three visits that I made to Canterbury, I would sit despondently by his bedside, wondering whether the dear gentleman would ever recover from the life-in-death into which he had been so cruelly plunged. His brother, however, continued to hope – in both a professional and a personal capacity – for better things to come, and assured me that he had seen such cases as this end in complete recovery. And thus I would return to Temple-street faintly hopeful that, when I next saw my employer, he would evince some signs of restoration.

But as day succeeded day, my spirits sank lower and lower. London was cold and dismal – impenetrable, with choking fog for days on end, the streets slimy with mud and grease, the people as yellow and unwholesome-looking as the enveloping miasma. I found that I missed the beautiful face of Miss Emily Carteret most desperately, and began to convince myself that she would forget me, despite her assurances. To compound matters, I was bereft of companionship. Le Grice was away in Scotland, and Bella had been called to the bedside of a sick relative in Italy. I had seen her soon after my return from Evenwood, at a dinner given by Kitty Daley to celebrate her *protégée*'s birthday. Of course both my head and my heart were full of Miss Carteret, and yet Bella was as captivating as ever. It would have been the easiest thing in the world to fall in love with her; a man would have been mad not to do so. But I was such a man – made mad beyond recourse by Miss Carteret.

At the end of the evening, after the other guests had departed, Bella and I stood looking out into the moonlit garden. As she laid her head on my shoulder, I kissed her perfumed hair.

'You have been most gallant tonight, Eddie,' she whispered. 'Perhaps absence really does make the heart grow fonder.'

'No absence, however long, could make my heart grow fonder of you than it already is,' I replied

'I am glad of it,' said Bella, holding me closer. 'But I wish you would not go away so much. Kitty says I mope like a lovelorn schoolgirl when you are not here, and that sort of thing, you know, is very bad for business. I had to turn away Sir Toby Dancer last week, and he is considered a very fine man by all the other girls. So you see, you must not leave me as you do, or you will have Kitty to answer to.'

'But, dearest, I cannot help it if my own business takes me from you. And besides, if your moping helps me keep you to myself, then perhaps I ought to stay away more often.'

She gave me a sharp pinch on my arm for my impudence and pulled away; but I could see that her chagrin was only pretended, and soon we had retired to her room, where I was allowed to admire, and then to occupy, those sweet perfections of flesh that had been denied to fine Sir Toby Dancer.

I left Blithe Lodge early the next morning, leaving Bella

asleep. She stirred slightly as I kissed her, and I stood for a moment looking down at her dark hair spread out in tangled profusion over the pillow. 'Darling Bella,' I whispered. 'If only I could love you.' Then I turned away, and left her to her dreams.

CHRISTMAS CAME AND WENT, AND THE NEW YEAR OF 1854 WAS A month old before anything of significance occurred.

On the 2nd of February, I was called before Mr Donald Orr. A rather frosty conversation ensued. Mr Orr professed himself to be aware of the fact that I was continuing to draw a salary without, as far as he could tell, doing much to earn it. But as I worked in a personal capacity for the Senior Partner, he could do nothing but look disapprovingly down his thin Scots nose at me, and say that he expected Mr Tredgold had had his reasons for employing me. 'You are right,' I replied with a satisfied smile. 'He did.'

'But this is not a situation that can continue indefinitely.' He regarded me somewhat threateningly. 'If Mr Tredgold – Heaven forbid – should fail to recover, then certain steps will have to be taken concerning the constitution of the firm. In that sad eventuality, Mr Glapthorn, it may prove necessary, regretfully, to dispense with your services, given your then redundant association with the Senior Partner. Perhaps I need say no more.' On this friendly note, the interview was swiftly terminated.

That night I drank heavily, compounding my folly by succumbing to the temptation of my bottle of Dalby's.* In my dreams I saw Evenwood, but not as I had dreamed of it as a child, nor as I had seen it in the clear light of day; but at some future time, when a great catastrophe had laid waste its former plenteousness, and toppled its soaring towers. Only the Mausoleum remained intact

*[Dalby's Carminative, one of many patent medicines containing laudanum. *Ed.*]

amidst the disfiguration and desolation. I saw myself standing once more before the loculus containing the tomb of Laura Tansor, and beating my hands against the slate slab until they bled, desperate to gain access to where she lay; but the slab remains immovable and I turn away to see Lord Tansor, perfectly attired as ever, and smiling, standing in the gloom beside me.

He speaks:

What do you know? Nothing.

What have you achieved? Nothing.

Who are you? Nobody.

And then he throws his head back and laughs until I can stand no more. I reach into my pocket, take out a long knife secreted therein, and plunge it into his heart. When I awoke, I was drenched in sweat and my hands would not stop shaking.

Then, as dawn broke, I understood what Mr Carteret had wanted to tell me.

SURSUM CORDA. The words themselves meant nothing. But what they were graven upon was of the gravest significance. For not only did the slab of slate that carried these words shut out the living from the abode of the dead; it also shut in the truth.

· 38 ·

*Confessio amantis**

Long days followed, of uncertainty and near despair, interspersed with periods of fevered elation. Was I right? Did the final proof that I had dreamed of finding lie within the tomb of the woman who had given me life, or had I become a deluded obsessionist? And how could I prove my conviction, except by an act of the grossest violation? Backwards and forwards, round and round, hither and thither, my mental turmoil increased. One moment I was triumphantly sure of my ground, the next prostrated by confusion. Abandoning both food and exercise, and resorting more and more to my drops, I lay on my bed trapped in the coils of hideous nightmares, oblivious to both the coming of night and the breaking of the day.

I continued thus until my bottle of Dalby's stood empty by my bed. Incapable as I then was of going out to procure more, I subsided into a state of stuporous vacancy until I was roused by the gentle prodding of Mrs Grainger, who, finding me in this alarming condition and believing that I was in the throes of death, had called upon the assistance of my neighbour, Fordyce Jukes, who now stood behind her, scratching his head.

'This is rum,' I heard him say, 'very rum indeed.'

'Is the gentleman dead, sir?' asked Mrs Grainger plaintively.

'Dead?' sneered Jukes, with a contemptuous click of his fin-

*['The lover's confession'. The title of the famous fourteenth-century poem by John Gower (1325?–1408). *Ed.*]

gers. 'Dead? Why of course he's not dead, woman. Can't you see he's breathing? Is there food here? No? Well, run and get some. And strong ale. Be quick now, or we'll all have died before you get back.'

'Should I bring a doctor, sir?'

'Doctor?' Jukes appeared to consider the question at some length. 'No,' he said at last. 'No need for a doctor. No need at all. Come along, come along!'

Though I could see and hear quite clearly, I found that I was unable to speak or to move either my head or my limbs, and I remained in this curious suspended state for some time. It seemed that Jukes had left my bedside, for I could hear the familiar creaking of the floor-boards in the sitting-room. Then, some time later, though whether it was hours or minutes I cannot say, I began to find strength returning and moved my head slightly to look about me.

On the table beside my bed stood an empty plate, with the remains of a chop and a half-eaten potato; beside it was a tankard of ale, partially consumed. Of either Mrs Grainger or Jukes there was no sign.

I concluded that food had been obtained for me, and partially consumed, and that I had then fallen asleep, though I had no memory of doing either. Slowly, I pulled myself out of bed and, on unsteady feet, dragged myself to the door that led to my sitting-room.

'Mr Glapthorn, sir, so pleased to see you feeling better! Let me assist you.'

Jukes, who had been sitting in my chair reading a copy of *The Times*, sprang to his feet and ushered me over to where he had been sitting.

'That's it, take my arm, sir, take my arm. There we are. Goodness me, what a scrape you got yourself in, Mr Glapthorn! I'll tell you what, sir: you appear to have stepped up to death's very front door, sir. But all's well now. Food and rest were what you needed, and what you must take great care to provide yourself with in the future – if I may be so bold. I've been sitting with you since yesterday. Oh no, sir—.' He held up his hand and shook his head from side to side in grinning admonishment as I attempted to speak. 'Pray don't say a word. It would be like your good self to thank me for my trouble, but I beg to insist that you will do nothing of the sort. Trouble? Why, what possible trouble have I been put to? None whatsoever, I assure you. A fellow toiler in the Tredgold vineyard, and neighbour to boot, taken ill? Why, only one course of action possible. Pleasure, and the satisfaction of a duty done are ample, though undeserved, reward for the little I have been able to do. And so, Mr Glapthorn, if you are feeling better, I shall leave you to your recuperation, but on the strict understanding – strict, mind! – that you will take better care yourself hereafter, and that you will allow me to call again tomorrow morning to see how you are.'

And then, having set a cushion at my back, placed a rug over my legs, and thrown a log on the fire, he made a low bow and sidled away, leaving me aghast at the situation in which I had awoken to find myself.

I immediately threw off the rug, and stumbled over to my work-table. Everything seemed to be exactly as I remembered it; nothing had been moved, I was sure of that. The pen still lay across an unfinished letter – to Dr Shakeshaft on the merits of various English translations of Paracelsus* – precisely where I had left it; the papers tied up in their labelled stacks appeared undisturbed; and the spines of my mother's journals, each one a familiar old friend, were still ranged in the strictly undeviating line in

*[Swiss physician and alchemist (real name: Theophrastus Bombastus von Hohenheim, 1493–1541). *Ed.*]

which I always took care to leave them. I went to the cabinet next, containing all my notes and indexed abstracts; nothing was out of place, and each drawer shut tightly. I let out a small sigh of relief.

And yet the thought of Jukes having the liberty of my room continued to rankle, and I began to examine everything again with redoubled care, looking for any sign that he had been through my papers or other possessions. But then I checked myself. Odious as Jukes was, I knew that Mr Tredgold trusted him, so why should I not do the same? These sudden baseless suspicions to which I was prey only served to cloud my judgment, and divert me from my true goal. Thus did I argue myself out of unreason, though I determined that Fordyce Jukes should never again be given an opportunity to enter my rooms. To this end, when he knocked on my door the next morning, as promised, I did not open it to him, but simply told him through the key-hole that I was much improved (which I was), and that I did not require his assistance.

I ventured out the next day for the first time in more than a week, to take a restorative dinner at the Albion Tavern. The following morning I thought that I would look in at Tredgolds, and so, at a little after half past eight, I locked my door, and walked through the rain to Paternoster-row.

As I entered the clerks' room, young Birtles, the office boy, came running across, and thrust a letter into my hand. 'This came in the last post yesterday, sir.' I did not recognize the handwriting; and so, having nothing better to do, I went upstairs to my room to read it.

To my complete surprise it was from Miss Rowena Tredgold, expressing the hope, in somewhat drawn-out terms, that circumstances would allow me to pay another visit to Canterbury at my earliest convenience. It concluded by saying that this invitation had been sent at the express request of her brother, Mr

Christopher Tredgold. Deducing from this that my employer's condition had improved significantly, I joyously sent off an immediate acceptance.

A FEW DAYS LATER, I WAS ADMITTED ONCE AGAIN TO MARDEN HOUSE, and shown into the room where I had first met Dr Jonathan Tredgold.

Miss Rowena Tredgold sat, unsmiling, in an uncomfortable-looking high-backed chair, set near an ugly black-marble fireplace, the cavernous opening of which yawned darkly cold. On a low table, drawn up close to her knees, was a tumbler of barley-water, beside which lay a sealed envelope. The heavy curtains in the window behind her were partially drawn, and what remained of the soft declining light of late afternoon struggled into the room through a slash of grimy glass.

I began, naturally, by asking how her brother fared.

'I am grateful to you for your concern, Mr Glapthorn. It has been a terrible time, but I am glad to say that he is much better than he was, thank you. He knows us, and has been sitting up. And we are thankful that he can speak a few words now.' She spoke in a lingering, staccato manner, carefully voicing every syllable, which produced the odd impression that she was mentally examining each word for impropriety before it was spoken.

'There is hope, then, that there will be further improvements?'

'There is hope. Mr Glapthorn,' she said, after a short expectant pause. 'Would you say that my brother, Mr Christopher Tredgold, was a good man?'

Though taken back a little by the question, I replied immediately: 'That would certainly be my opinion. I do not think there can be any other.'

'You are right. He is a good man. And would you say that he was an honourable man?'

'Unhesitatingly.'

'You are right again. He is an honourable man. Goodness and honour are two words that perfectly describe my brother.'

She said this in a way that seemed to suggest that I had in fact taken precisely the opposite view.

'But there are many people in this world who are neither good nor honourable, and who take advantage of those who regard these virtues as the unalterable foundation of their moral character.'

I said that I could only agree with her.

'Well, then, I am glad that we are of one view. I wish you to remain steady in that view, Mr Glapthorn, and remember always what kind of man my brother is. If he has erred, it is because he has been placed in an intolerable position by those who do not aspire, and who never will aspire, to the high ideals of conduct and character that have distinguished all my brother's dealings, both personal and professional.'

I confess that I had no idea what the woman was talking about, but I smiled in a conciliatory way, which I hoped would convey my complete comprehension of the matter.

'Mr Glapthorn, I have here a letter' – she gestured towards the sealed envelope – 'written by my brother the night before he was taken ill. It is addressed to you. However, before I give it to you, my brother has asked me to preface his words with some of my own. Do I have your permission?'

'By all means. May I ask first, Miss Tredgold, if you have read your brother's letter?'

'I have not.'

'But I may presume, I suppose, that it contains matters of a confidential nature?'

'I think you may presume so.'

'And are you yourself a party to any of those confidences?'

'I am merely my brother's agent, Mr Glapthorn. If he were well, then you may take it that he would be communicating these matters to you himself. However, there is one subject on which I have been honoured with his confidence. It is on this subject that he has asked me to speak to you prior to your reading his letter. Before I do so, I hope I may depend on your absolute discretion, as you may depend on mine?'

I gave her my word that I would never divulge what was imparted to me, and begged her to proceed.

'You may wish to know first,' she began, 'that the firm of which my brother is now the Senior Partner was established by my great-grandfather, Mr Jonas Tredgold, and a junior associate, Mr James Orr, in the year 1767. In due course, my late father, Mr Anson Tredgold, joined the firm, which then became known as Tredgold, Tredgold & Orr, a name which it has since retained, along with a reputation second to none amongst London solicitors.

'It was my grandfather who first established an association between the firm and a certain noble family – of whom, I believe, you have some knowledge. I speak, of course, of the Duport family of Evenwood, holders of the Tansor Barony. Later, the management of the family's legal affairs duly fell to my father; and then to my brother Christopher.

'At the time that Christopher joined the firm, Father was in his seventy-first year, still sprightly in body and active in mind, though it must be confessed that his powers of concentration and application were perhaps not quite what they had once been. Nevertheless, as the Senior Partner, he continued to enjoy the complete confidence of the firm's principal client, the present Lord Tansor, until his death.

'And now my brother is the Senior Partner. Unfortunately, he has no son into whose hands he can place the governance of the firm, in the way that his father and grandfather had done before him. It is the tragedy of my brother's life, for he would dearly have loved to marry, and so we must now contemplate the prospect of Tredgold, Tredgold & Orr existing without the living presence of a Tredgold.'

'Could you tell me, Miss Tredgold,' I broke in, 'what has prevented Mr Tredgold from following his inclination?'

'That, Mr Glapthorn, is the particular matter on which my brother has asked me to speak, if you will be so kind as to allow me.'

Her reprimand was delivered with cold courteousness and I felt obliged to apologize for my interruption.

'It was passion, Mr Glapthorn, for an object that could never have been his – a passion that he knew to be wrong, but which he could not resist; a passion that rules him now as completely as it ever did, and which has kept him a slave to its original object for these thirty years and more. Indeed I can give you the exact date when it commenced.

'I came of age in July 1819, and on the twelfth of that month my father, Mr Anson Tredgold, was visited on a matter of business by Laura, Lady Tansor, the wife of his most distinguished client. Her reputation as a great beauty preceded her, and of course I was agog to see her – I was young and foolish then and knew no better. It was whispered, as you may perhaps know, that she had been the subject of those celebrated stanzas of Lord Byron's which begin 'There be none of Beauty's daughters',* written (so it was

*['Stanzas for Music', written 28 March 1816, and first published in *Poems* (John Murray, 1816). How widely accepted the rumour was that Laura Fairmile was the subject of thse famous stanzas is perhaps debatable, and I have seen it cited nowhere else in the literature. The poem is usally said to have been addressed to Claire Clairmont. Laura Fairmile married Julius Duport in December 1817. Byron himself had married Annabella Milbanke in January 1815. *Ed.*]

rumoured) by the poet to Miss Fairmile – as she then was of course – before her marriage to Lord Tansor. Whether that be true or no, she was constantly spoken about as being one of the loveliest and best turned-out women in England; and so, being apprised of her visit, and wishing to snatch a glimpse of this marvel, I made some excuse to be at the office when she arrived, and lingered on the stairs as she was received by the chief clerk and conducted up to my father's room on the first floor. As she passed, she paused and turned her head slowly towards me. I shall always remember the moment.'

Miss Tredgold looked distantly into the black mouth of the great fireplace.

'Her face was beautiful, certainly, but had an extraordinary impression of fragility about it, like an exquisite painting made on glass: indeed her beauty and poise seemed almost too perfect to withstand the shocks that attend all human life. In that moment, as she looked directly into my eyes before honouring me with a brief nod of salutation, I felt a kind of sadness for her – pity even – that I could not explain. All beauty must pass, even hers, I thought; and those who are blessed with unusual physical beauty must, I supposed, feel this constantly. I was plain; I knew it. Yet I did not envy her – no, indeed I did not – for she appeared to me to be suffering from some great affliction of spirit that was already beginning to cast its shadow over that perfect face.

'Lady Tansor conducted her business with my father, and was escorted by him to the front door, where they encountered my brother Christopher coming in. I had remained in the downstairs office, amongst the clerks, and was well placed to observe the scene.

'I remember very well that her Ladyship appeared impatient and ill at ease, fingering the ribbons of her bonnet, and tapping the floor with the tip of her parasol. My father asked whether she would allow him to conduct her to her carriage, but she declined and made to go. My brother, however, intervened rather forcefully, and insisted that her Ladyship could not be allowed to descend the steps and cross the pavement unassisted. I had never seen him act the gallant before, and observed his attentions towards her with some amusement. She did no more than thank him, but you would have thought from his face, when he returned to the office from helping her into her carriage, that he had been in the presence of some divinity. Of course I teased him, and he was rather short with me, telling me not to be a silly little girl, which, having just attained my majority, I much resented.

'But I did wrong to tease him, Mr Glapthorn, for it soon became apparent to me – though fortunately to no one else – that Christopher was smitten by the lady to a degree that was wholly incompatible both with his personal situation and his professional position. This infatuation, for which, as a young man, he could hardly be blamed, was to be the cause of his decision never to marry. It quickly grew, you see, into something fiercer, something all-consuming, that could not be denied, and yet which *must* be denied. It was a love of which poets sing, but which is scarcely seen in the world. He never confessed it to her, never acted upon it, and behaved at all times with the utmost propriety. There were times when I feared for his sanity, though it was only to me that he revealed the extent of his anguish. Gradually, he learned to master his situation – or seemed to – and took refuge in pursuits of a bibliographical nature, which have remained his solace during his hours of leisure. But when she died, the effect on my brother was terrible – quite terrible. Imagine, then, what he had to endure when his attendance was requested by Lord Tansor at her burial in the Mausoleum at Evenwood. He returned immediately to London and took a solemn vow in the Temple Church: that he would love her unto death, and take no one else into his heart, putting all his hope in being joined with her in eternity, when all care and suffering will be put aside for ever. He has kept that vow, and will go to his grave a bachelor because of his love for Laura Tansor.

'And so, Mr Glapthorn, I have said what my brother wished me to say, and now I give you this.'

She handed me the sealed envelope.

'Perhaps you would be more comfortable if I retired to my room for half an hour.'

She rose from her chair and left, closing the door softly behind her.

To learn that my employer had not only known my real mother, but had also loved her, and that he continued to love her, to the exclusion of all others! This extraordinary revelation thrilled and alarmed me in almost equal measure. Of all the men in the world! But when secrets are finally unlocked, there are always consequences; and so it was with shaking hands that I opened the letter and began to read. I do not intend to transcribe it in full; but certain passages must be laid before you. Here is the first.

How often, my dear Edward, have I wished to bring you into my confidence! But the difficulty of my position has been, and continues to be, acute. However, recent events – I refer particularly to the death of Mr Carteret – have forced me to take a course of action that I have long contemplated, but which hitherto I have been constrained from adopting by both duty and conscience.

When you first came to me, you did so in the capacity of confidential secretary (I believe that was the phrase you used) to Mr Edward Glyver. You were enquiring after the existence of an agreement made between Mr Glyver's mother and the late Laura, Lady Tansor. I must tell you now, and you must believe how much it pains me to confess it, that I was not completely honest with you concerning the circumstances under which that agreement had been drawn up.

In the first place, it was not my father, Mr Anson Tredgold, who drafted it; it was I. His powers were in decline then and, subsequent to her Ladyship's first brief consultation with him, he asked me to produce the draft. I then met privately with Lady Tansor – on several occasions, away from the office – to ascertain that it met with her approval. Her Ladyship later returned to Paternoster-row with Mrs Glyver to execute the document in the presence of my father.

The intention of the agreement that I had drawn up – a copy of which is now in your possession – was to give Mrs Glyver some measure of immunity from any adverse consequences of certain impending actions, which she had undertaken solely at the urgent behest of Lady Tansor. In truth, I do not know whether the document would ever have held in law – my father was too ill to approve the wording and merely, as I say, officiated at the signing. But Mrs Glyver was satisfied by it, and so matters proceeded.

I told you that I could find no record of the discussions that preceded the signing of the agreement. That was the strict truth; I destroyed everything, except for a copy of the agreement itself, which makes no mention of the circumstances that lay behind its composition. My motive? A simple but unshakeable desire to protect Lady Tansor, as far as I could, from the results of her action.

I loved her, Edward, as I believe few men have loved a woman – I cannot speak of this at length here, except to say that my affection for her has been both the bedrock and the source of all my actions. It has informed and directed everything. Her *interests, both when she was living and with respect to her posthumous reputation, have been my only care.*

My enslavement began in July 1819, when her Ladyship first came to see my father. She had embarked on a most dangerous enterprise. Unknown to her husband, Lady Tansor was with child; she intended to escape to France, in the company of her closest friend, Mrs Simona Glyver, until her time was due; the child would then be placed into the charge of Mrs Glyver, who would bring it up as her own. She did not tell my father the true character of this desperate scheme, speaking to him only in vague generalities, and she had sworn her friend to absolute secrecy. But she herself was weak in this regard and soon confided in me, sensing, I believe, my deep attachment to her – illicit, I acknowledge, but never *revealed, or confessed,* or acted upon. *I was already mesmerized by her – hopelessly infatuated. So I vowed that I would help her, in whatever way I could, and that I would tell no one her secret. 'My dear sweet St Christopher,' she said to me at our last meeting. Those were her very words. And then she kissed my cheek – such a brief, chaste kiss! Though I swear that I did not confess my love for her, I told her then that I would die rather than reveal her condition.*

It was foolish of me – no; worse, much worse, than foolish – to have exposed myself to calumny and professional disgrace; it went against every principle that I had formerly held sacred. I confess that I was greatly concerned by what I had done, and conveyed to her Ladyship as strongly as I could that discovery of her plan was probable, perhaps likely, and urged that the whole thing should be abandoned forthwith; for by this terrible act, Lady Tansor was denying her husband the thing that he desired above all others. Of course my advice was disregarded – sweetly, but firmly.

I continued to regret that I had become an accessory to her Ladyship's conspiracy. But it was done; and I would not undo it for worlds. If it was iniquitous, then I would be steadfast in my iniquity, for the sake of her whom I had sworn to serve unto death.

I thought of Mr Tredgold, suave and beaming. Mr Tredgold, polishing his eye-glass. 'You shall stay to luncheon – it is all ready.' Mr Tredgold, eagerly hospitable. 'Come again next Sunday.'

He went on to speak of the effect on his own life of his love for Lady Tansor; how it had made it impossible for him to seek the affections of any other woman, and how, in consequence, he had turned to 'other means' – by which I understood his secret interest in voluptuous literature – to assuage the natural passions and inclinations that all men must attempt to master.

And so to the next passage.

After my father died, I became Lord Tansor's legal adviser, and was often at Evenwood on his Lordship's business. His wife's remorse at what she had done was plain to see – it was remarked with sadness by poor Mr Carteret; but only I was aware of the source of her misery. We spoke sometimes, when we found ourselves alone together; and she would take my hand, and call me her true friend, for she knew that I would never betray her, despite the dereliction of my professional duty to her husband, which I felt, and continue to feel, keenly. But there are higher things than professional duty, and I found that my conscience easily submitted to the greater dictates of love, allowing me to serve Lord Tansor to the best of my ability whilst still honouring my sacred vow to his wife. I withheld the truth from him, but I never lied. It is a Jesuitical distinction, I own, and would have been a poor defence; but it served. Yet if he had asked me to my face, then, God forgive me, I would have lied, if that had been her *wish.*

I therefore deceived you further when I said that I had no knowledge of the private arrangement referred to in the agreement between Lady Tansor and Mrs Glyver, and for that I humbly ask you to forgive me.

But you have also deceived me, Edward. So let us now be honest with each other.

On reading these words, perspiration begins to bead on my forehead. I lay down the letter and walk over to the window to try to open it, but it is locked tight shut. I feel entombed in this tenebrous, dusty room, with its hideous brown-painted wainscot, its dark and elaborate furniture and heavy green-plush curtains; and so I close my eyes for a moment and dream of air and light – the open sky and sunlit woods, wind and water, sand and sea, places of peace and freedom.

A door bangs, and I open my eyes. Feet scurry down the passage, then silence. I return to the letter.

He had known me all this time, from the moment I had been shown into his drawing-room in Paternoster-row by Albert Harrigan on that Sunday morning in September 1848: despite my subterfuge, my identity had been written on my face as clearly as if I had sent up a card bearing the name 'Edward Duport (formerly Glyver)'. He had known me! I had stood before him, the son of the woman he continued to adore, and he had seen her in me. Here was the reason for his immediate and obvious regard for me, his willingness to oblige me, his alacrity in offering me employment. He had known me! During all our walks in the Temple Gardens, and our Sundays together, poring over masterpieces of the erotic imagination, and through the working out of all his 'little problems'. He had known me! As I had laboured – alone and unknown, as I had thought – to reclaim my birthright, he had known me! But he had vowed to keep my mother's secret safe – *even from me*; and so, through all the years of my employment, he had watched me, the son of the woman he had loved above all others, knowing who I was and what I had been born to, but powerless to assist me in the task that I had undertaken. He saw that I had come to him in the guise of Edward Glapthorn for no other purpose than to find some means of regaining my true self. But in this he was also helpless, for – as he had admitted – he had destroyed every trace of his dealings with Lady Tansor, and possessed nothing – no letter, no memorandum, no document of any kind – that could prove conclusively what he and I knew to be the truth about my birth. He could only watch and wait, bound as he was, both by the vow that he had made to my mother, and by the code of his profession.

But then events began to threaten the accommodation that Mr Tredgold had made with his conscience.

The first indication of an impending crisis had come when Lord Tansor had indicated to Mr Tredgold that he wished to make Phoebus Daunt the heir to his property, on the single condition that the beneficiary would then take the Duport name. Everything that should have been mine was to go to Daunt, being the step-son of Lord Tansor's second cousin, Mrs Caroline Daunt, who, by this relationship, might one day complete her triumph and inherit the title herself, as a female collateral descendant of the 1st Baron Tansor.

What should Mr Tredgold do? He could not tell Lord Tansor that he had a living heir, for that would have been to betray my mother's secret, even if he had possessed proof of the assertion; but the unworthiness of the prospective heir was to him so apparent (though not to Lord Tansor) that his professional conscience almost revolted, and more than once he had been close to laying the whole truth before his noble client in order to prevent this calamitous outcome. The following passage was of particular interest to me:

Of course I knew of your former acquaintance with Daunt, as school-fellows, and guessed what estimation you might have of his subsequent endeavours. My own was very low indeed. I had received disturbing reports of his character from Mr Paul Carteret; and, indeed, I had reasons of my own to suspect him of having inclinations of the basest kind. From an early age he had been pushed forward by his step-mother as a kind of substitute for Lord Tansor's son – his younger son, I should say. Mrs Daunt has always exhibited a tigerish concern for her step-son's future prosperity (and certainly for her own as well). With great skill and determination, she constantly deployed her influence with Lord Tansor to advance the boy in his estimation. In this she succeeded, beyond all expectation.

I did everything I could, on many occasions, to intimate to my client, as far as my professional position allowed, that he would be well advised to reconsider his decision to adopt Daunt as his heir. But I could not persuade his Lordship, and at my final attempt he told me, with some force, that the matter was closed.

But then had come Mr Carteret's letter, and all was changed. Mr Tredgold had immediately sensed a startling probability: that his old friend had discovered what he himself had striven to keep secret for so many years. And so I had been despatched to Stamford, with consequences that I have already set out. On Mr Tredgold, these had had a severe effect. To hear, in the report that I had sent from Evenwood, of the fatal attack on Mr Carteret had induced a profound shock, and probably contributed greatly to the paralytic seizure that he subsequently suffered.

Just then the door opened, and I turned to see Miss Tredgold framed in the opening. The sun had dipped behind the houses on the other side of the street, leaving the room in an even deeper condition of brown-stained gloom than before. She held a light in her hand.

'If you wish, I will take you to my brother.'

· 39 ·

*Quis separabit?**

I FOLLOWED MISS TREDGOLD INTO THE HALL AND UP THE DARK STAIRS, along a cold dark landing, and into a darkened room. Mr Tredgold sat hunched in the far corner, by a little desk on which were placed some sheets of paper and writing implements. He was wrapped in a woollen shawl; his head had dropped down over his chest, and his once immaculate feathery hair was disarranged and thin looking.

'Christopher.'

Miss Tredgold spoke softly, touching her brother gently on the shoulder and raising the candle so that he might better see her face.

'I have brought Mr Glapthorn.'

He looked up and nodded.

She motioned to me to take a seat opposite my employer and placed the candle on the desk.

'Please ring when you are ready,' she said, indicating a bell-rope just behind Mr Tredgold's chair.

As she closed the door behind her, Mr Tredgold leaned forward with surprising vigour and grasped my hand.

'Dear . . . Edward . . .' The words were slurred and came haltingly, but clear enough for me to hear what he was saying.

'Mr Tredgold, sir, I am so very glad to see you . . .'

He shook his head. 'No . . . No . . . No time. You have . . . read the . . . letter?'

*['Who shall separate us?' *Ed.*]

'I have.'

'My dear fellow . . . so very sorry . . .'

He fell back in his chair, exhausted by the effort of speaking.

I glanced at the paper and writing implements on the table by his chair.

'Mr Tredgold, perhaps if you were to write down – if you are able – what you wish to say to me?'

He nodded, and turned to take up the pen. There was no sound in the room except for the scratching of the nib and the occasional crackle from the dying fire in the grate. The task was slow and laborious, but at length, as the last embers of the fire went out, he laid down the pen and handed me the sheet of paper. It was somewhat rambling, and written in a highly abbreviated, unpunctuated manner. The following is my own more finished version of what I now read.

'My dear boy – for so I think of you, as if you were my own. It breaks my heart that I cannot speak to you as I would wish to do, or help you to regain what is rightfully yours. How you came to the knowledge of your birth is dark to me, but I thank God that you did and that He led you to me, for there is a purpose in all this. I have kept the truth hidden, for love of your mother; but the time has come to put matters right. Yet in my present condition I do not know what I can do, and the death of my poor friend has robbed us both of an invaluable ally. I am certain that Carteret must have come into the possession of documents that would have materially advanced your case – but now they are lost to us, perhaps for ever, and a good man has died because he learned the truth. I now fear for *you*, dear Edward. Your enemy will be seeking high and low for Laura Tansor's son, and will stop at nothing to protect his expectations. If he should discover your true identity, then there can be only one consequence. I beg you, therefore, to take every precaution. Be constantly vigilant. *Trust no one.*'

He looked at me with a most pitifully anxious expression. When I had finished reading, I took his hand.

'My dear sir, you must not be anxious for me. I am well able to meet whatever danger may present itself; and though the documents that Mr Carteret was carrying may be lost to the enemy, we have something nearly as good.'

I then told him of my foster-mother's journals, and the corroboration of them provided by Mr Carteret's Deposition, on hearing of which he gripped my hands and uttered a strange sort of sigh. A fierce light seemed to burn in his poor pale eyes as he reached again for his pen.

'All is not lost then' – he wrote – 'as long as these statements remain safe from Daunt. They are insufficient, as you must know, but they must be safeguarded at all costs – as must the true identity of Edward Glapthorn. And then you and I must apply ourselves to overturning Lord Tansor's folly, and so set things right at last.'

'They are safe,' I assured him, 'and so am I. I have made a copy of the Deposition, which I have brought with with me, to leave in your keeping.' I placed the document on the desk. 'Daunt can have no reason whatsoever to suspect that Edward Glapthorn is the person he seeks. And you are wrong, sir, to say that we do not have an ally. I believe we do.'

He leaned forward once more, hands shaking, and wrote the words, 'An ally?'

Thus I opened my heart to Mr Tredgold concerning Miss Emily Carteret.

'I love her to the utmost degree. To you, sir, I need say no more; for you know what it means to love in this way.'

'But does she love you, in the same way?' he wrote.

'Every instinct tells me that she does,' I replied, 'though love is undeclared on both sides as yet, and must so remain until she returns from France. But already I would trust her with my life. She has long held Daunt in contempt; only think, sir, how she will regard him once he is revealed in his true colours. I have not the slightest doubt that she will support us in all our endeavours to unmask his villainy, and so expose his true character to Lord Tansor.' And then I told him of Daunt's association with Pluckrose; of his criminal career, as described to me by Lewis Pettingale; and finally of my conviction that Mr Carteret had been set upon by Pluckrose, acting on Daunt's orders.

He made no attempt to write a response, though the pen was in his hand. Instead he leaned back in his chair and closed his eyes, apparently overcome with fatigue.

'Sir,' I said gently. 'There is one more thing I must say to you.' Mr Tredgold remained immobile. 'I believe that I know where the final proof of my identity may be found.'

He opened his eyes slowly and looked at me.

As I had spoken the words, Miss Tredgold had entered the room, preventing me from speaking further. On seeing her brother's face, she pronounced him unfit to continue with the conversation, and I had no choice but to withdraw, though it was agreed that I might come again the following Wednesday, if his condition continued to improve.

On the train back to London, I reflected that my trip to Canterbury had given me some hope that, Mr Tredgold's returning strength, and the relationship of frankness that now existed between us concerning the things that we had both kept secret from each other, might together effect some improvement in my situation. Whether such optimism was justified remained to be seen; it was a comfort, at any rate, to know that I was no longer quite alone, and that Mr Tredgold and I were united in common cause. More than this, I was now resolved that I must take my fate in my hands and declare my love to Miss Carteret at the earliest opportunity. And then, I hoped, we would be three.

When I returned to Temple-street, I found a letter waiting for me, bearing a Paris postmark. I saw immediately that the envelope had not been inscribed by Miss Carteret; but I tore it open all the same. It was a short note from Mademoiselle Buisson.

Dear Mr Dark Horse, —

I am bidden by our mutual friend to inform you that she will be returning to England on Monday next and will be most happy to receive you at the house of Mrs Manners on Wednesday. She has a slight indisposition at the present, which prevents her from writing to you herself. I may say, entre nous, *that she has been a very dull companion indeed, the blame for which I lay entirely at your door. It has been 'Mr Glapthorn this' and 'Mr Glapthorn that' these weeks past, as if there was no other topic of conversation in the world but Mr Edward Glapthorn. And then with all Paris to play in, she has done nothing but keep to the house, except for little walks alone in the Bois on fine mornings, with her nose in a book. Today she is reading a tiresome volume of poetry by M. de Lisle, which I had to go out and buy for her with my own money!* Et enfin, *Mr Glapthorn, you are welcome to her. But do not fall in love with her. I am serious now.*

Adieu, cher Monsieur,
Marie-Madeleine Buisson.

I read the note through again, smiling as I called to mind the writer's little-girlish look, and her mischievously mocking ways. Serious! Flitting, fluttering Miss Buisson could never be serious. Her admonition not to fall in love with her friend was nothing but a piece of ironic teasing; for she must know that it was already too late.

Wednesday came – the day when I should have gone back to Canterbury to see Mr Tredgold. But I did not go. Everything that had seemed so demanding of my time and mental energy had fallen away into nothingness; only one desire now commanded my waking hours, and was soon to put all other duties out of mind. Instead of keeping my appointment with Mr Tredgold, I knocked on the door of Mrs Manners' house in Wilton-crescent, at precisely eleven o'clock, and asked if Miss Emily Carteret was at home.

'She is, sir,' said the maid. 'You are expected.'

'THERE,' SHE SAID AS I ENTERED THE DRAWING-ROOM, 'I HAVE KEPT my promise, you see. I am back, and you are the first person I have seen.'

How my heart leaped to be in her dear presence once again! We quickly fell into a friendly way of conversation as Miss Carteret spoke of how she'd passed her time in Paris, and I told her of the improvement in Mr Tredgold's condition. Lord Tansor, she said, was away, gone to his West Indian estates with Lady Tansor; the great house had been shut up, and so she would be staying with her aunt in London until his Lordship returned.

'Mr Daunt has gone with him,' she added, with a little sideways look.

'Why do you tell me that?' I asked.

'Because you always seem interested in where Mr Daunt is and what he is doing.'

'I am sorry to have given that impression,' I replied. 'I can assure you that I do not find Mr Phoebus Daunt in the least bit interesting.'

'My sentiments exactly,' she said. 'So now, Mr Glapthorn, if you will be good enough to examine me, *viva voce*, on my knowledge of Monsieur de Lisle, I do not think you will find me wanting.'

Two hours passed most delightfully; but then Mrs Manners appeared in the doorway, to remind her niece of some engagement they were both obliged to fulfil. Miss Carteret accompanied me into the hall.

'Will you come next Wednesday?' she asked.

Thus my world began to contract to a single point of all-absorbing interest. I could think of nothing but Miss Carteret; everything else was driven from my mind. In between our weekly conversations in Wilton-crescent I lived in a kind of featureless dream, from which I only awoke to full consciousness every Wednesday morning at eleven o'clock. I went occasionally to Blithe Lodge of an evening, but always left early on some excuse or other. One night, Bella asked me whether anything was the matter. I smiled, and told her that I had never felt better.

'I have a great deal of work to occupy me at the moment,' I said in answer to her enquiry. 'I shall be more myself when it is all done.'

'My poor Eddie! You must not work so hard, you know. It will make you ill. Come and lay your head on my lap.' When I had settled myself at her feet, she began to run her ring-laden fingers gently through my hair as she sang an Italian lullaby, and for a few sweet minutes I was a child again, listening to the cry of sea birds, and the wind coming in from the Channel as my mother read me to sleep.

I should have resisted her tender ministrations, and told her the stark truth; but honesty continued to seem the greater evil when dissimulation spared her from pain. And as time went by, I began to perceive that my heart had not been entirely conquered by Miss Carteret; that there yet remained a place in it – small and sequestered – for Isabella Gallini, of blessed memory.

. . .

As the spring of 1854 came on, I began to suggest little outings to Miss Carteret. Would she and her aunt feel inclined to go the Opera, or to a concert at the Hanover-square Rooms? What would she think about mounting an expedition to view the Assyrian antiquities at the British Museum? All my proposals, however, were regretfully, but firmly, declined. Then one morning, just as I was despairing of ever getting her out of the confines of her aunt's house, she suddenly expressed a wish to see the snakes in the Zoological Gardens. 'I have never seen a snake in my life,' she said, 'and would very much like to do so. Can it be arranged?'

'Most certainly,' I said. 'When shall we go?'

The visit was set for the following week, the 12th of April. Mrs Manners was otherwise engaged, and so, to my joy, we went alone. The rattle-snakes, in particular, delighted her, and she stood entranced for several minutes without saying a word. Later, we walked and talked in the sunshine as if we had not a care in the world. She laughed at the hippopotamus, which suddenly plunged into its bath, liberally soaking everyone close by with cold water, and clapped her hands in amusement at the pelicans being fed. As we were leaving the Gardens, descending a short flight of steps, she lost her footing, and reached out to me to prevent herself from falling down. I grasped her hand tightly until she had regained her balance; but I did not let go, and she did not pull away, not immediately. For some moments we stood a little awkwardly, hand in hand, and then, as if it were the most natural thing in the world, she gently released herself and placed her arm through mine as we walked on.

'Where shall we go now?' she asked. 'It is such a beautiful day, and I do not wish to go home quite yet.'

'Might you like to see St Paul's?'

When we arrived at the cathedral, after observing a notice setting out the charges, she expressed an immediate determination to ascend to the Golden Gallery. I tried to dissuade her, knowing the final part of the ascent to be dirty and awkward, and unsuitable, in my view, for a lady to attempt. But she would not be put off; and so, much against my judgment, we paid our sixpences and began to mount the steps to the Whispering Gallery. Here we paused for breath.

'What shall we whisper?' she asked, placing her mouth against the cold stone.

'You have to speak, not whisper,' I said.

'Run, then. See if you can hear.'

And so I ran over to the other side of the gallery, placed my ear to the wall, and waved to indicate my readiness. At first, I could hear nothing, and signalled to her to speak again; then, gradually, her words began to percolate eerily through the very walls, indistinct, but sporadically audible: '*. . . blind fool . . . to mine eyes . . . they behold . . . not what they see*'.*

'Did you hear it?' she asked excitedly when I returned to her.

'Did you mean me to hear it?' I asked.

'Of course. Come. I wish to go up higher.'

And so up we went, past the Clock Room, higher and higher, steeper and steeper, counting out the narrow steps as we went. At length, after much puffing and laughter at our situation, stooping through low-ceilinged stair-cases, and holding ourselves close to the walls of the landings to let other visitors pass by, we emerged into hazy sunlight on the Golden Gallery, just below the Lantern. Her black dress was dirtied with dust and cobwebs, and the exertion of climbing over five hundred steps had coloured her cheeks. As we stepped outside, we were immediately buffeted by a cool wind, and she gripped my arm tightly as we approached the low iron rail.

*[Words from the first two lines of Shakespeare's Sonnet 137: 'Thou blind fool, Love, what dost thou to mine eyes,/That they behold, and see not what they see?' *Ed.*]

We stood in wondering silence. It seemed as if we were on the deck of a great ship floating across an endless ocean of dirty cloud. Great thoroughfares lay far below, crowded with ant-like people and slow-moving streams of vehicles. The eye picked out familiar steeples and towers, palaces and parks, and distant factory chimneys, belching plumes of black smoke; the sun flashed off windows and gilded finials, and laid a shimmering cloak of gold over the grey river; but beyond London-bridge it was as if a dark curtain had been brought down across the port of the capital: not a single mast of the many ships moored there could be seen. Elsewhere, too, the drifting haze rendered every detail smudged, indefinite, and dreamlike. From this point of vantage, one did not so much see the great heaving metropolis below as feel its pulsing presence. I knew it well, that sense of the living power of Great Leviathan. But to her, its terrible sublimity came as a revelation, and she stood in a kind of wordless rapture, her great black eyes open to their widest extent, breathing quickly, and gripping me so hard that I could feel her finger-nails digging into me through her gloves.

She continued thus for several minutes, holding herself close to me as she looked down into the misty vastness. The illusion of her dependence on me was thrilling, though I knew it for what it was. But I look back on that frail and fleeting moment as one of the happiest of my life, standing with the woman I loved high above the dirty deceitful world of strife and sin, alone with her on a little platform poised between earth and heaven, with the restless smoky city sprawled below us, and the infinite sky above.

'I wonder what it would be like?' she said at length, in a strange quiet voice.

'What do you mean?'

'To throw yourself out from here and fall through all this great height to the hard earth. What would you think, what would you see and feel as you fell?'

'You would have to be unhappy indeed to contemplate such an act,' I said, pulling her back a little from the rail. 'And you are not so very unhappy, are you?'

'Oh no,' she said, suddenly animated. 'I was not thinking of me. I am not unhappy at all.'

THROUGHOUT THAT SPRING, AND INTO THE MONTH OF JUNE, I continued to wait upon Miss Carteret – whom I had now been allowed to call by her first name – nearly every day. Sometimes we would sit and talk for an hour or two, or perhaps stroll round Belgrave-square six or seven times, lost in conversation; at others we would go off on little expeditions – I recall with especial pleasure taking her to see the wax-work figures at the late Madame Tussaud's Bazaar* in Baker-street (where, at Emily's insistence, we paid an extra sixpence to view the grisly exhibits in the Chamber of Horrors). We went also to the Botanic Gardens at Kew, and on another occasion took a leisurely trip by steamboat from Chelsea to Blackwall, during which of course we passed the Temple Gardens, where I had walked so often with Mr Tredgold, and the Temple Pier, where my own skiff was moored. To observe her in such proximity to these familiar places gave me a kind of guilty pleasure, making me smile inwardly with delight, and with the

*[Marie Tussaud, *née* Grosholzt (1761–1850). During the French Revolution she had assisted the wax modeller Dr Philippe Curtius to make moulds of the heads of decapitated victims of the Terror. She established her Bazaar in Baker Street in 1835. The name 'Chamber of Horrors' was coined by a contributor to *Punch* in 1845 to describe the room containing the gruesome relics of the Revolution, along with newly created figures of murderers and other criminals. *Ed.*]

hope that, one day soon, she would walk with me through those same streets and lanes, sit with me in the Temple Church, and climb the stairs to my room in the eaves, as mine and mine alone.

She appeared to take unfeigned pleasure in my company, always greeting me with a sunny smile as I entered the drawing-room of her aunt's house, slipping her arm into mine as we walked, and allowing me to kiss her hand when I arrived to see her, and when I left.

She had become the most companionable of companions, the most considerate of friends; but now I began to discern unmistakable signs of something more – certain gestures and looks; a tone of voice; my hand retained a little longer, and held a little tighter, than previously; the eager, bright-eyed greetings; the intentional brush of her body against mine as we stood waiting to cross a road. These all spoke of something more – much more – than friendship; and I was overwhelmed with joy to know that love had finally come upon her, as it had come upon me.

AND THEN, IN THE THIRD WEEK OF JUNE, LORD AND LADY TANSOR returned from the West Indies – Daunt was making his separate way home, having literary business in New York. Accordingly, Miss Carteret began to make preparations to leave her aunt's house for Evenwood. On the morning before her departure, we walked out into Hyde-park. The day was overcast, and after an hour we found ourselves in a deserted corner of the Park, running towards a large oak tree to shelter from a sudden downpour of rain.

We stood for several minutes, huddled closely together and laughing like children as the raindrops pitter-pattered through the branches. Then, away to the west, came a faint rumble of thunder, the sound of which caused her to look round anxiously.

'We are not safe here,' she said.

I told her that there was no danger, and that the storm was too far away to be of concern.

'But I am frightened nonetheless.'

'But, dearest, there is no reason.'

She paused before replying. 'Perhaps it is not the storm that frightens me,' she said softly, with her eyes to the ground, 'but the greater tumult in my heart.'

In a moment I had pulled her close to me. Her breath was sweet and warm as I pressed my lips to hers, gently at first, then more urgently. The body I had once thought immune to desire now yielded willingly, eagerly, to my touch and thrust itself so hard against mine that I almost lost my balance. And still she would not break off the embrace. Like some mighty onrush of water, irreversible and immense, she broke against me, battered me, submerged me, until, as if I were a drowning man, my life seemed to pass before my eyes, and I offered myself up to sweet oblivion.

She clung to me, panting, her bonnet fallen back on her shoulders, her hair awry and disordered, her face spattered with rain.

'I have loved you from the very first moment,' I whispered.

'And I you.'

We stood in silence, her head resting on my shoulder, her fingers gently tracing little circles on the nape of my neck, until the rain began to ease.

'Will you love me always?' she said.

'Do you need to ask?'

· 40 ·

*Nec scire fas est omnia**

FROM THAT DAY ONWARDS I FELT RENEWED, VIVIFIED, HAPPIER, AND more free of care than at any time since my student days in Heidelberg. What could I not achieve, now that I possessed my dear girl's love! It had been arranged that I would go to Evenwood as soon as she was settled, a prospect that rendered everything else dreary and uninteresting. But then I received a letter from Mr Tredgold, which shamed me back to a contemplation of all the things I had neglected.

My Dear Edward, —

I was most concerned when you did not come back to Canterbury as arranged. Many weeks have passed without word from you, & now Mr Orr has written to say that you have not been to Paternoster-row this past month, which makes me fear some harm may have come to you. I am much improved, as you see by my handwriting, & as you could observe for yourself. But as I am still unable to leave Canterbury, I beg you to write to me as speedily as you may, to put my mind at rest that all is well with you.

I shall make no mention here of the other matter that has been constantly on my mind since your last visit – I allude of course to the remark that you made as you were leaving, concerning what you have been seeking – other than to say that it is of such moment that it would be foolish, for both of us, to commit anything concerning it to paper. I hope you will

*['To know all things is not permitted' (Horace, *Odes,* IV. iv). *Ed.*]

write soon, to let me know when I might expect you here, so that we may discuss this matter face to face.

May God bless you and protect you, my dear boy.

C. Tredgold.

My employer's words roused me from my lotos-dream, and I immediately took train to Canterbury.

I found Mr Tredgold sitting in a wicker chair under a lilac-tree, in a sunny garden at the rear of Marden House. He had a rug over his knees, and was in the act of making some notes in a small leather-bound book. His face, shadowed by a wide-brimmed hat, was thin and worn, but he had regained a little of his old suavity of manner, as evidenced by the beaming smile with which he greeted me.

'Edward, my dear, dear boy! You have come. Sit down! Sit down!'

His speech was a little slurred, and I noticed that his hand was shaking slightly as he polished his eye-glass; but in all other respects he appeared to have suffered no permanent disablement. He wasted no time on idle chatter, but began at once by telling me that a deed had now been enrolled in Chancery to break the entailed portion of Lord Tansor's inheritance, and that, in anticipation of this succeeding, a new will had been drawn up that would make Phoebus Daunt his Lordship's legal heir.

'Lord Tansor has instructed all concerned that he wishes the matter to be expedited,' said Mr Tredgold, 'and though of course the law cannot be hurried, it is certain that it will feel obliged to pick up its skirts and do its best to walk a little faster. Sir John Mounteagle has been retained by Lord Tansor to see the deed through Chancery, which he will do with his customary vigour, I have no doubt. I think we may expect matters to be settled by the autumn. And so, Edward, if we are to prevent the will being signed, it will be necessary to lay our hands on some invincible instrument. Do you, as you implied, have possession of such an instrument?'

'I have nothing in my possession,' I admitted, 'except my foster-mother's journals and Mr Carteret's Deposition, which, you advised, will be insufficient to prove my case. But I have a strong conviction of where the final proof may be hidden, and I believe that Mr Carteret shared my conviction.'

'And where might this place be?'

'In the Mausoleum at Evenwood. In the tomb of Lady Tansor.'

The eye-glass dropped from Mr Tredgold's trembling fingers.

'In Lady Tansor's tomb! What possible grounds do you have for this extraordinary conviction?'

And then I told him of the words that Miss Eames had written on a slip of paper and sent to Mr Carteret – the same words that were graven on my mother's tomb.

Mr Tredgold took off his hat, and placed his head in his hands. After a little time, in which nothing was said by either of us, he turned his sad blue eyes towards me.

'What do you wish to do?'

'With your permission, I wish to put my conviction to the test.'

'And if I cannot give you my permission?'

'Then of course I shall take no further action.'

'Dear Edward,' he said, the light returning to his eyes, 'you always say the right thing. I have protected her memory for too long. Carteret was right. What she did was a crime – and I was party to it. She had no right to deny you what should have been yours, and to make you a stranger to your own family. I shall always love her, but the dead must take care of themselves. You are my care now – you, her living son. You have my permission, therefore, to do whatever is required, for the sake of the truth. Come back as soon as you can, and may God forgive us both. And now I feel a little cold. Will you help me inside?'

He leaned on me as we walked slowly down a winding gravel path towards the house, still deep in conversation as we went.

'One thing has never been clear to me,' I said, as we made our way through a tunnel of pale roses. 'It is the thing on which all else hangs, and yet my foster-mother's journals, and Mr Carteret's Deposition, are silent on the matter.'

'You refer, I suspect,' replied Mr Tredgold, 'to the reason for Lady Tansor's embarking on her extraordinary action.'

'Why, yes. That is it exactly. What could possibly have driven a woman of Lady Tansor's station to abandon her child, born in legitimate wedlock, to the care of another?'

'It was quite simple. She denied her husband the one thing he craved above all others because he had denied her something which, to her, was equally paramount. *Quid pro quo.* There you have it, in a nutshell.'

He saw my puzzled expression and proceeded to elaborate.

'It all came from Lord Tansor's treatment of her father. Miss Fairmile, as she was before her marriage, was exceedingly beautiful, and of an old and decent West Country family. But they were not the Duports, or anything like them with respect to wealth and position. She met Lord Tansor in London, soon after his Lordship had succeeded to the Barony; it was not in his nature to play the gallant, but something about Laura Fairmile inspired him to pay court to her, despite his rather low opinion of her family. Many men more handsome than Lord Tansor had found themselves in a tangle over Miss Fairmile, though none could pretend to offer her what he could. It appears, strange as it may seem, that he harboured real affection for her; though it is also the case that, ever mindful of his public position, even at that age, he also wished to provide himself with an agreeable wife and companion to accompany him tamely through life, and provide him with the heir that he so desired.

'He proposed; he was accepted. No one blamed her. The inequalities – their temperaments, their respective positions in Society – seemed of slight account compared to the advantages that both secured by the match. Her Ladyship quickly became the perfect adornment to her husband's person. Oh Edward, if you could have seen her, riding by her husband's side in Rotten-row, clad in her riding-habit of bright-green silk and violet velvet, topped by a jaunty hat with swaying plumes! She never failed to please him, she supported him in every way; and she was widely liked and admired in Society, which duly reflected back on him.

'However, there was a worm in the bud. Their characters and temperaments soon proved to be fatally at odds. His Lordship was cold and detached, whereas his wife would light up a room with her bustle and laughter; he kept his counsel, she gossiped without compunction; he was respected, sometimes feared, but not widely liked, whilst she was admired by all; he lived for politics and business, and the increasing of his inheritance, while she loved quiet pleasures and the company of friends, and valued above all the deep affection that existed between herself and her family – especially her father. In the course of quite a short time, these differences became exaggerated and entrenched, so that when disagreements occurred, truces became impossible. The attachment that had sustained their union in the early months began to wither away, to be replaced by mere civility in company, and frozen silence in private.

'Then matters came to a head. I have said that the Fairmiles were an old and respectable family, but they were almost bankrupt. In marrying Lord Tansor, Miss Fairmile had believed that an end would be made to her father's desperate financial state, reasoning that, by her union with Lord Tansor, the Fairmiles would be welcomed into the wider dynastic embrace of the Duports. But she was soon disappointed. Instead of paying off Sir Robert Fairmile's debts, as she had expected, Lord Tansor simply bought out the mortgages on his father-in-law's house and grounds at Church Langton, and set the premiums at a lower level than before; but when Sir Robert was unable to honour even these reduced payments, his Lordship took the only course of action that a man of business can take, and duly foreclosed on the loan. Lady Tansor was outraged; she cajoled, she pleaded, she threatened to leave, she wheedled – all to no avail. His Lordship could make no exception to the inviolable principles that governed his business dealings. Sir Robert had defaulted. Lord Tansor's firm principle in such cases was to foreclose. He pointed out that he had already been generous in allowing his father-in-law a year to put his affairs in order, something that he would not ordinarily have contemplated. But an end must be made. The loan must be called in.

'The business finished Sir Robert, who was forced to sell the house in which he had been born, along with the last small holdings of land he had retained, and move to cramped accommodation in Taunton, leaving nothing to pass on to his only son. The old man died not long afterwards, a broken and bitter man.

'Her Ladyship, as I have indicated, adored her father. She had behaved in all things just as her husband had wished; now she had asked him to make this one exception to his rules of business, and he had refused her. She felt powerless, and trapped by the inequality of her position. However, soon afterwards, she discovered that she was with child; and this, in the extremity of her grief and rage, gave her a weapon that she could not resist using against her husband. She therefore resolved, first, to keep Lord Tansor in ignorance of her condition, and then, to compound her revenge in the most terrible fashion: to conspire with her closest friend that the latter should bring the child up as her own.'

I objected that the punishment still appeared out of all proportion to the crime.

'Well, you may think so,' Mr Tredgold replied. 'But when a passionate nature is thwarted in its desires, the consequences can be extreme. Lady Tansor had asked this one thing of her husband. It would have been a small concession to marital harmony, for a man of his wealth, to have written off the debt, for his wife's sake. But he would not do this for her – he would not even consider it, and he managed only a conventional show of remorse when Sir Robert Fairmile died. That, perhaps, was the final straw.'

At the foot of a short flight of steps, we stopped for a moment to allow Mr Tredgold to catch his breath.

'So it was simple revenge then?' I asked.

'Revenge? Yes, but not simple. On her marriage, Lady Tansor had suppressed what might be described as somewhat Jacobinical views, for the sake of her family. She told me this herself, adding that she wished her child to escape what she called the curse of inherited wealth and privilege, which had trampled so implacably on the claims of common human feeling and family connexion. It was a fanciful notion, no doubt, but it was real enough to her, who had seen her adored father hurried to his grave by the holder of one of the most ancient peerages in England, and for no other reason than the maintenance of his public position. She told me that she did not wish her child to become like his father – and who can deny that she succeeded? Yet a beneficial outcome in that respect is no justification for what she did, and what I helped her to do. She knew that she had done wrong, but it was not in her nature to undo it, though she tried to make amends to her husband in the only way she could – by subsequently giving him the heir that he so desired. But, alas, he, too, was to be taken from him, as you know.'

It seemed curious to me that the more I learned of Lady

Tansor, the less I understood her. How unlike her quiet, dutiful friend, Simona Glyver, she had been! I reflected also that she had punished me, as well as her husband, by exiling me – through no fault of mine – from the life to which I had been born. Mr Tredgold had loved her, and was naturally minded to see her actions in a considerate light, judicially weighing them against the provocation that she had received. But though I yearned to be acknowledged as Lady Tansor's son in name and position, I felt a kind of grim relief that I had been brought up by another, and that I would never now have to discover whether I loved my true mother as I had loved her friend.

As I was helping Mr Tredgold up the steps into the house, he asked me whether I was still in love with Miss Carteret.

Yes,' I smiled, 'and likely to be for all eternity.' And then I told him of our walk in Hyde-park, and how we had each declared our love for one another.

'And have you told her the truth about yourself? Ah, I see by your hesitation that you have not. How, then, can you be sure that she loves you, when she is ignorant even of your real name?'

'She loves me for myself,' I replied, 'not for my real name, or for what I may become if I succeed in my task, because she is ignorant of both; and that is why I am now prepared to tell her everything.'

'I do not know the lady well,' said Mr Tredgold as we entered the house, 'but that she is beautiful and clever is undeniable. And if she loves you as you love her, then she will be a prize indeed. Yet I would counsel you to take care before placing the truth in another's hands. Forgive me. I am a lawyer, and cannot help myself from picturing the worst. Caution comes naturally to me.'

He was smiling broadly, but his eyes were serious.

'I am sensible, sir, that you only have my best interests at heart. But recklessness, as you well know, is not in my nature; I only proceed on a matter when I am completely sure of the outcome.'

'And you are sure of Miss Carteret's love, and that you trust her absolutely?'

'I am.'

'Well, I have done my lawyer's duty. You will not be turned from the course you are set upon, that is clear; and I have no arguments powerful enough to persuade a man in love to be prudent – God knows I have committed follies enough myself in love's name. So there it is. You will write as soon as you can, I'm sure. Go, then, with my blessing, and may you bring back the truth, for it has been hidden for too long.'

I left him at the foot of the stair-case in the gloomy hall, grasping the banister with one hand as he weakly waved me good-bye with the other. I never saw him again.

My darling girl had promised to write from Evenwood, once she had settled herself in her new apartments; but a week went by, and then another, and still no word came. At last, I could stand it no longer and sent off a brief note, enquiring whether all was well, and suggesting that I might travel up to Northamptonshire the following week. I was sure that a reply would come by return, but was again disappointed. Finally, almost a week after sending my note, I received a communication.

My Love,—

Bless you for your sweet note, which has been sent on to me here in Shrewsbury.

How horrid you must have thought me! But, dearest, I wrote to you, two weeks since, to tell you that I have been travelling with Lord and Lady Tansor in Wales whilst work is being carried out at Evenwood – his Lordship has taken it into his head to have hot-water pipes installed, with consequences that you may easily imagine to one's peace and comfort. The dust and noise are not to be spoken of. Where my letter has gone, telling you all this, I cannot imagine, but the ways are wild hereabouts, and so I suppose it was simply lost or dropped somewhere. We shall be away for some time – the work will not be completed for another month at least, and after we leave here we shall be going to some dreary place in Yorkshire, belonging to Lady Tansor's brother. How I wish I could escape! But I am a captive, and must go where my master bids, seeing that I am now entirely dependent on him for the provision of a roof over my head; and then, you know, he really seems to take pleasure in my company (Lady T is so dreadfully tiresome – never says a word, or smiles), and so I really have no choice, and must do what I can to master my feelings. They *are constantly fixed on* a certain person, *whose identity I'm sure I need not reveal! I yearn to be free of my duties and to feel myself again in the arms of the man I love above all others, and whom I will always love, world without end.*

I shall send word as soon I know when we are to return to Evenwood.

Ever yours,

E.

A month at least! But it could be borne. I kissed the words she had written: '*I yearn to be free of my duties and to feel myself again in the arms of the man I love above all others, and whom I will always love, world without end.*'

How I passed the interminable weeks, I need not recount in detail. I resumed some of my former studies – reacquainting myself with some of the more abstruse Greek philosophers, continuing my study of hermeticism, and pursuing my bibliographical passions. From Mr Nutt's shop in the Strand,* I had purchased a copy of Dr Daunt's catalogue, the *Bibliotheca Duportiana,* and spent several hours a day lost in enraptured perusal of its contents. What

*[The bookseller David Nutt, at 270 and 271 Strand. *Ed.*]

a keen and unfailing pleasure it was to contemplate my eventual possession of each item, as I gorged on the Rector's meticulous descriptions. Sometimes at night I would venture out to quell my always restless demons, but with diminishing returns of satisfaction, until soon I became quite a hermit, content with purely intellectual pleasures, save for an occasional dinner with Le Grice at the Ship and Turtle.

A letter from my dear girl arrived in the first week of August, and then another a few weeks later from Lincolnshire, whither the Tansors had decamped at the invitation of the Earl of Newark. She was all sweetness, full of anguished regret that circumstances had sundered her from the man she loved above all others; and my heart overflowed to know that she was mine. 'If I had wings,' she wrote in her second letter, 'I would fly with the speed of angels to be with my dearest love, if only for the briefest moment.'

At last the great house at Evenwood was ready to receive its noble owner once more, and in the second week of September I received a note to say that Miss Carteret would be pleased to see me in Northamptonshire at any time that I might care to propose.

On my arrival, I was shown up to the first floor and entered a long, low apartment above the Library, the chief feature of which was a series of four ancient arched windows that looked down on the terrace below. I stood for a moment, gripped by the thought that my mother, Lady Tansor, had once occupied these very rooms. At the far end, a door stood ajar, allowing a partial view of an elaborately carved bed – that same bed in which my poor misguided parent had been laid, mad with grief and remorse, by John Brine's father, and from which she never again rose. Through this door my dearest girl now swept, ran towards me, and threw her arms around me in a passionate embrace. Many tender words were exchanged, after which we sat together on a seat in one of the arched windows, from where we could see the Park stretching out beyond the formal gardens to the Temple of the Winds, the Lake, and the distant woods.

'Three long months! How I have missed you!' I cried, kissing her hand feverishly.

'To be parted from the one you love is the greatest of torments,' she said. 'I never thought I would suffer so. But there is an end to all suffering. My love is here with me once more, and I am the happiest woman alive. Dearest, will you excuse me for a moment?' Whereupon she returned to the adjoining bedchamber and closed the door. I waited, feeling a little foolish and embarrassed, for several minutes until she returned, her face a little flushed, with a book in her hand.

'I have brought you a present,' she said, handing me the book.

It was a copy of Gildon's edition of Shakespeare's poems.*

'My thoughts have been ever on love during my exile,' she said, 'and this little volume has been my constant solace. Now when we are apart, you may read it and be comforted too, knowing that my tears are on every page. I have underlined those passages that gave me especial comfort. Now tell me what you have been doing since we last met.'

And so we continued to talk until the light began to fade and my dear girl said that she must call her maid to begin dressing for dinner.

'I regret that I cannot invite you to join us,' she said as we

*[*A Collection of Poems*, edited by Charles Gildon (1665–1724) and published by Bernard Lintot in a small octavo one-volume edition in 1709 (it later appeared in two volumes). It contains *Venus and Adonis*, *The Rape of Lucrece*, *The Passionate Pilgrim*, and 'Sonnets to Sundry Notes of Musick', which are in fact the last six poems in the preceding work. *Ed.*]

walked towards the door, 'but you understand that I am Lord Tansor's guest now.'

'Of course,' I replied. 'But when may I come again?'

'Tomorrow,' she said. 'Come tomorrow.'

As I was descending the stairs to the vestibule, I came upon Lizzie Brine. As she was with another servant, she made no attempt to speak to me but only gave a little bob, along with her companion, and went on her way. But when I reached the bottom of the stair-case and looked back, I saw her standing at the top with a curious anxious look on her face that I found impossible to interpret.

I returned to the Duport Arms in Easton, though I remember nothing of the walk back, nor what I ate for dinner, nor how I occupied myself that evening.

The next afternoon, I returned to Evenwood as arranged, though this time, at my dear girl's suggestion, I made my own way up to her apartments by a little winding stair-case, which was gained through a door leading off the path that ran from the Library Terrace round the base of Hamnet's Tower. Once again we sat together in the window-seat, talking and laughing until a servant brought in candles.

'Sir Hyde Teasedale and his simpering daughter are dining tonight,' she sighed. 'She is such a ninny, and her new husband is no better. I declare that I have no idea what I shall say to either of them. But, Lady Tansor being so singularly defective as a hostess, I seem to have been given the honour of entertaining her husband's guests, and so I must away to do my Lord's bidding. Oh Edward, if only I was not so beholden to Lord Tansor! It makes me so miserable to think that I must spend my life at his beck and call. And then what will happen to me when he dies? I was not born for this, but what can I do? Now that my father has gone, I have no one.'

She bowed her head as she said the words, and I felt my heart beat a little faster. Now is the time. Now. Tell her now.

'My darling,' I said, stroking her hair. 'Put all your concerns aside. This is not your future.'

'What do you mean?'

'I am your future, and you are mine.'

'Edward, dearest, you are talking in riddles. Speak plainly, my love.'

'Plainly? Very well. Here it is, as plain as I can make it. My name is not Edward Glapthorn. It is Edward Duport, and I am Lord Tansor's son.'

· 41 ·

*Resurgam**

She listened in silence as I told her my story. I spared her no detail. Everything was laid out before her: the conspiracy devised by Lady Tansor and my foster-mother, Simona Glyver; my upbringing as Edward Glyver at Sandchurch; my first meeting with Daunt at Eton, and his subsequent betrayal of me; the discovery of the truth concerning my birth in my foster-mother's journals, and my continuing quest to find the final proof that would enable me to claim my rightful place as a member of the Duport family. I told her also of how I had first come to London as Edward Glapthorn, to seek information from Mr Tredgold on the arrangement made between Lady Tansor and my foster-mother, and how I had retained my assumed name after the Senior Partner had offered me employment. Finally, I spoke of Daunt's criminal character, and of his association with Pluckrose and Pettingale. With each truth that I revealed, I felt cleansed, with a sensation of sweet relief that the burden of deceit had been lifted at last.

When I had finished, she walked to the window, and looked out across the darkling Park. I waited expectantly.

'This is so hard for me to comprehend,' she said at length, 'though at least I now understand your interest in Mr Phoebus Daunt. Lord Tansor's son – is it possible? Oh—' She gave a little cry and placed her hand to her lips. 'Cousins! We are cousins!'

Then she turned towards me.

*['I shall rise again'. *Ed.*]

'Why did you not tell me before?'

'Dearest Emily, don't be angered. How I have wished – most desperately – to bring you into my confidence; but how could I do so until I could be sure that you felt for me as I feel for you, when so much was at stake? Now that I know beyond all doubt – by your letters, and by the sweet words that you have spoken to me, and by all the tender moments we have shared – that your love for me is as strong and as unbreakable as is mine for you, why of course the situation is entirely different. Where true love is, trust and frankness must follow. There can be no more secrets between us now. When we are married—'

'Married?' She seemed to sway a little, and I reached out to wrap her in my arms.

'It is what you wish, is it not, my love?'

She nodded slowly. There were tears in her eyes.

'Of course,' she said, in a soft low voice. 'It is what I wish above all things in the world. It is just that I have not allowed myself to hope that you might ask me.' Then she raised her beautiful tear-stained eyes towards me. 'But surely, my love, we can do nothing until you have proved your claim to be Lord Tansor's son?'

'No,' I acknowledged, 'you are right. But when that day comes – as come it must – you will be beholden to his Lordship no more, for you will have become the wife of Edward Duport, the future 26th Baron Tansor.'

'Oh, Edward,' she cried, 'let it come soon!' And then she began to weep tender tears – of joy at the prospect I had presented to her, though mixed no doubt with natural apprehension.

'You understand, of course, my love,' I said, as I held her in my arms, 'how imperative it is that that the secrets we now share must be kept safe – not a word of what I have told you must be spoken of, or hinted at, to anyone. And, for the time being, it will be best to keep my visits to you confidential. For if Daunt should discover that Edward Glapthorn is Edward Duport, then my life – and perhaps yours – will certainly be in peril.'

'Danger? From Mr Daunt?'

'Oh my love, yes, from Daunt. He is a far worse villain than you think.'

'In what way?'

'Do not make me tell you.'

'What are you saying? Why do you not speak? Tell me, tell me!'

Her eyes were wild, and she seemed once again in the grip of that strange agitation of spirit that I had witnessed in the Temple of the Winds, walking round and round distractedly in a little circle in the middle of the room. I brought her back to the window-seat and took her hand.

'I believe Daunt was responsible for the assault on your father.'

I had expected some powerful uprush of emotion in reaction to my words; but instead she fell gently towards me in a swoon. I caught her, and laid her down on the seat. She was as pale as death, and her hands made strange fluttering movements, as if under the intermittent influence of some galvanic current. I was on the point of calling for help when she opened her eyes.

By and by, her colour began to return and she was able to take a sip or two of wine, which gradually effected a revival of her faculties, though she remained deeply distressed by what I had told her, and by what I now revealed concerning the documents that her father had been carrying with him when he had been attacked, as well as the reason that Daunt had gone to such lengths to obtain them.

'I do not say that Daunt intended to murder your father,' I said. 'Indeed I believe he did not. But I am certain that he ordered the attack by Pluckrose to gain possession of the documents proving the existence of a legitimate heir.' Then she asked me how I knew what had been in her father's bag, and so I told her of the Deposition, at which she became greatly agitated.

'But what if Mr Daunt should also obtain this document? How will you then hope to prosecute your case successfully?'

'He will not find it,' I said, with a confident smile.

Before coming to Evenwood, I had realized that Mr Carteret's Deposition, together with the little black volumes containing the daily record of my foster-mother's life, must now be removed to a place of absolute safety. My rooms in Temple-street were always securely locked; but locks can be picked; and Mrs Grainger's possession of the only other key had given me further concern: suppose she should be followed, or set upon? And then there was Jukes, whom I already suspected of snooping through my private papers. And so I had determined, once I had made my confession to her, and had been forgiven for keeping so much from her, to ask my dearest girl to become the custodian of these most precious items.

'But how can you be so sure that he won't find them?' she asked, her anxiety still plainly apparent.

I told her that I had given a copy of the Deposition to Mr Tredgold, and that I intended to place the original, as well as my mother's journals, beyond Daunt's reach.

'But where, dearest?' she cried, looking most pathetically apprehensive.

'Here,' I replied. 'Here, with you.'

And then relief seemed to flood over her dear sweet face. 'Yes, yes,' she sighed. 'Of course, you are right! Here is the last place in the world that he will think of looking! He would never have a reason to come into these apartments, nor can he know that you have taken me into your confidence. But I am still fearful for you, my love, so very fearful, until you can bring the documents from London.'

I took her hand and kissed it, assuring her that I would waste no time but would return to London in the morning to collect the Deposition and the journals, and bring them back to Evenwood.

'Where shall we put them?' I asked.

She thought for a moment, and then an idea struck her. 'Here,' she said, running over to a small oval portrait of Anthony Duport,* younger brother of the 21st Baron, as a boy. Taking down the portrait, she opened a small cupboard concealed in the panelling.

'Will this do?'

I inspected the interior of the cupboard, and pronounced it ideally suited.

'Then that is settled,' she said, closing the door and putting back the portrait.

We sat together in the window, holding hands, talking quietly, as close as two hearts can be. She called me her dearest love; I told her that she was my angel. Then we kissed our good-byes.

'My sweet girl,' I whispered. 'Are you sure that you wish to become the custodian of these documents? Perhaps, after all, I should remove them to the bank. If Daunt should—'

She placed her forefinger against my lips to prevent me from saying any more.

'Dearest Edward, you have asked me to do this for you, and I have said I will. Whatever you ask of me, now and in the future, I will do my best to carry out.' She gave a little laugh. 'You know that I shall soon, I hope, commit myself to honour and obey you, in sickness and in health, and so there is no harm in beginning now. It is such a little thing to ask of me, after all, and I would do anything – *anything* – for the man I love.'

*[The picture in question, of Anthony Charles Duport (1682–1709), by Sir Godfrey Kneller (1646–1723), is now in the National Portrait Gallery. *Ed.*]

She walked with me to the door, and we kissed for one last time.

'Come back to me soon, my dearest love,' she whispered. 'I shall count the minutes till you return.'

I LEFT, UNSEEN, BY THE NEW WAY, DOWN THE LITTLE WINDING staircase and out onto the path by Hamnet's Tower.

At the South Gates of the Park, I stopped. The Dower House could just be glimpsed through the Plantation: lamps were burning in the drawing-room and in one of the upstairs rooms. On a sudden impulse, I took the track round into the stable-yard. My luck was in; the door to the tack-room stood open, throwing a pale rectangle of light onto the cobbles.

'Good evening, Brine.'

He had been binding the head of a besom broom when I had entered, and looked round in surprise at the sound of my voice.

'Mr Glapthorn, sir! I – we did not expect you.'

'And you have not seen me,' I said, closing the door behind me. 'Have you the duplicate key I asked for?'

'Yes, sir.' He opened a drawer in an old dresser and handed the key to me.

'I shall need some tools. Can you get me some? And a lantern.'

'Tools? Why, yes, of course, sir.' I told him what I required and he went into an adjoining room, returning in a few minutes with a bag of the necessary implements, and a bull's-eye lamp.*

'Remember, Brine, I was not here. You understand?' I handed over the usual consideration.

'Yes, sir. Of course, sir.'

In a few moments, with the bag across my back, I was walking

*[A lantern with a thick protuberant lens of blown glass on one side for concentrating the light. *Ed.*]

along the gravel bridle-way that skirts the Park wall and leads up to the Mausoleum. It was just at that melancholy time when the savour finally goes out of the day, and twilight begins to surrender to the onset of darkness. Somewhere ahead of me a fox barked, and a cold low wind troubled the trees that lined the path running up from the bridle-way to the clearing in front of the Mausoleum. My head had been full of my dearest girl; but as I approached the lonely building, my wildly joyous mood began to seep away as I contemplated the awful reality of what I had come here to do.

SURSUM CORDA. What else had Miss Eames intimated, in sending these words to Mr Carteret, than what they were inscribed upon covered something of crucial significance? This was the instinctive conclusion that I had reached, and on which I was now about to act. But it was a fearful prospect: to break into my mother's tomb, without the least idea of what I was looking for. I prayed that, whatever was hidden there, *if* it was hidden there, would be easily found within the loculus itself. But if it should be in the coffin! That might be a horror beyond even my ability to face.

I entered through the great double doors, using the key that Brine had provided, and went about my work.

It was past midnight when the slab that closed off my mother's burial chamber finally yielded to my chisel. I had broken open the protective gates of the loculus easily enough, but it took nearly an hour to cut out the rectangular slate slab, and all my strength to support the weight of it and lay it on the floor. But at last it was done, and I turned to see, by the light of the lamp that I had brought from the tack-room, what lay within.

A plain coffin of dark oak, placed lengthways in the space, filled most of the cavity. Lifting the lantern a little higher revealed a simple brass plate bearing the words 'LAURA ROSE DUPORT' affixed to the lid of the coffin. There was barely a foot between the lid and the vaulted roof of the little chamber, and only two or three inches between the coffin itself and the back wall of the loculus; on either side, however, there was a narrow gap, perhaps eight or nine inches wide. I kneeled down at the foot of the coffin, and reached forward into the darkness, but only cobwebs and fragments of mortar met my touch. Moving across to the other side, I reached in again.

At first I could feel nothing; but then my fingers closed round something soft and separable, almost like a lock of flattened-out hair. Quickly withdrawing my arm and reaching for the lamp, I peered in.

Protruding from the narrow space between the back wall of the chamber and the coffin was what I could now see was the edge of a fringed garment of some kind – a shawl perhaps. I extended my hand behind the rear of the coffin and began to pull, but immediately met some resistance. I pulled again, with the same result. Lying down on my side, I stretched into the space and round the edge of the coffin as far as I could. After a little more gentle tugging and grappling, I finally extracted my discovery from its resting-place, and set it down in the yellow light of the lamp to examine it, breathing out my relief that it had not been necessary to disturb the coffin.

It was indeed a fringed shawl – a Paisley shawl, which had been rolled up and wedged behind the coffin. It seemed of little interest at first, until I began to unroll it. Then it soon became apparent that there were other objects wrapped inside it. I laid the shawl out on the floor.

Within another wrapping of white linen, I was astonished to find an exquisitely embroidered christening robe, a pair of tiny silk shoes, and a small book bound in old red morocco. This last item was quickly identified: it was the first edition of Felltham's *Resolves*, printed in duodecimo for Seile in about 1623.* It bore the bookplate of William, 23rd Baron Tansor. There was no doubt in my mind that it was the copy that my mother had asked Mr Carteret to bring to her from the Library before her death in 1824. Dr Daunt's failure to locate the copy listed by Burstall when compiling his catalogue was now explained. But who had put it here, and why?

That it had been intended, with the other items, to convey some message or signification was clear. Though it had been in its hiding place for over thirty years, it was in remarkably good repair, the burial chamber being clean and dry. I examined the title-page: *Resolves: Divine, Morall, Politicall.* There was no inscription of any kind, and so I began slowly turning over the leaves one by one to scrutinize each of the hundred numbered essays. I could detect nothing out of the ordinary – no annotations or marginalia, and nothing inserted between the leaves; but as I was closing the book, I observed that it did not shut quite flat. I then saw why: a sheet of paper had been carefully pasted over the original end-leaf. On closer examination, it was possible to make out that something had been interpolated between the false and the real end-leaf.

I took out my pocket-knife, and began to prise away the false leaf. It proved to have been only lightly fixed, and soon came away to reveal two folded pieces of thin paper.

It is true, indeed, that the desire accomplished is sweet to the soul.† Behold, then, how my labours were rewarded at last. On the first piece of paper were the following words:

*[The bookseller Henry Seile (fl. 1619–61). *Ed.*]
†[Proverbs, 13: 19. *Ed.*]

To My Dearest Son, —

I write this because I cannot bear to leave you without also leaving some brief record of the truth. When you see me again it will be as a stranger. I have given you up to the care of another, and have begged God that you will never know that it was not she who brought you into the world. And yet I am compelled by my conscience to write down these few words, though keeping what I have written safe by me until I am called to a better place. Perhaps this piece of paper will one day find its way into your hands, or be discovered by strangers centuries hence, when all these things will be forever beyond recall. Perhaps it will moulder with my bones, and you will live in ignorance of your true identity. I leave its fate to God, to whose tender mercies I also commit the fate of my sinful soul.

You are fast asleep in a wicker basket belonging to Madame Bertrand, a lady who has been very kind to us here in Dinan. Today has been warm, but it is cool in the courtyard, and pleasant to hear the water splashing in the fountain.

And so, my dear sweet little boy, though you are dreaming (of what I cannot imagine), and though you hardly know what it is to live and breathe and think, and though you could not understand me even if you were to open those great black eyes of yours and hear my voice, yet I still wish to say three things to you as if you were fully conscious and comprehending of my words.

First, the person to whom you will owe your duty as a son is my oldest and dearest friend. I pray you will love her, and honour her; be always kind to her, never disparage her memory or hate her for the love she bore me; and remember that faith and friendship are never truly tried except in extremes. This was said by the author of a little book that has often brought me comfort in past weeks, and to which I know I shall often turn hereafter. I pray you may find such a friend as mine. I have had*

*[The quotation is from Felltham's *Resolves*, xi ('Of the Trial of Faith and Friendship'). *Ed.*]

many blessings in my life; but truly, her friendship has been the greatest.

Second, the name you now bear is not your own, but do not despise it. As Edward Glyver, you must find your own way through life, using the strengths and talents that God has given you, and nothing else; as Edward Duport, you would have ridden in great coaches and dined off golden platters, not through your own merit, but for no other reason than that you were the son of a man possessing great inherited wealth and power. Do not think such things bring happiness, or that contentment cannot be found in honest toil and simple pleasures. I used to think so, but I have seen my error. Fortune and plenty have made me shallow, a weightless bubble, a floating feather. I shudder now to think what I have been. But this is not what I wish for you – or what I now wish for myself. So be properly proud of your adopted name, make it prosper by your own efforts, and so make your own children properly proud of it.

Third, do not hate me. Hate only what has driven me to do this thing. And do not think that I have denied you through indifference, or worse. I have denied you because I love you too much to see you corrupted, as your father has been corrupted by the blood that he holds so dear, crippled morally by that blind and terrible pride of race, *from which, by this act, I have sought to protect you.*

Yet because I am conscious of my sin, in so depriving you of what you might have had, and my husband of the heir for which he yearns, I have placed everything in God's hands. If it is His will to lead you to the truth, then I promise before I die to provide the means for you to reclaim your true name, if that is what you desire – though I pray to Him before Whom I must be judged that it is not *what you will desire; and that you will have the strength to disown what you were born to.*

So sleep, my beautiful son. When you wake I shall be gone. You will never know me as your mother, but I shall always know you as my son.

Ever your loving Mother,
L. R. Duport
Dinan, June 1820

The second sheet of paper contained only these words, in a shaky and irregular hand:

To My Dearest Son,—

I have kept my promise, and have given you the keys to unlock your true identity. If God in His wisdom and mercy should lead you to them, use them, or destroy them, as your heart dictates.

I wept when I came to see you for the last time, playing at my feet, so strong and so handsome, as I knew you would be. But I shall never see you more, until that day when the earth gives up its dead, and we are reunited in eternity.

The light is fading. This is all I can write. My heart is full.

Your mother,
L. R. Duport

At the bottom of the page, in another hand, was written the following:

She died yesterday. The shawl that she was wearing when I closed her poor eyes encloses these letters to her lost son (the last words she ever wrote), the two mementoes of his birth, and also the little book which comforted her so greatly and which she wished he might one day have. *She placed all her trust in God to bring these things forth from the darkness of the grave into the light of day once more, if it is His will to do so. This is my last service to her. May God rest her soul.*

J.E. 1824.

The hand, of course, was that of Julia Eames, who, before her own death, had written out the two words that had been inscribed on her friend's burial place and had sent them to Mr Carteret as a hint or clue to the secret that she had kept so faithfully for so many years. How she had contrived to place the shawl and its contents in the loculus before it was sealed, I could not imagine; yet here they were. The Almighty, it seemed, with a little help from Miss Julia Eames, had made His will known.

I re-read the letters from my mother, holding them close to the lantern and poring over every word, especially the beginning of the second letter: 'I have kept my promise to you, and have given you the key to unlock your true identity.' I thought at first it was a riddle that I would never solve; then I considered again the remark that I had 'played at her feet', and in an instant all became wondrously, deliriously clear.

A picture of Miss Lamb rushes into my mind: sad, thin Miss Lamb, running her long gloved fingers down my cheek as she watched me playing on the floor beside her with the fleet of little wooden ships that Billick had made for me. Time passes, and another memory of her is called up: 'A present from an old, old friend who loved you very much, but who will never see you again.' And then a final, conclusive, recollection: a receipt for the construction of a small box made of rosewood by Mr James Beach, carpenter, Church-hill, Easton, found by Mr Carteret in my mother's papers after her death. Two hundred golden sovereigns – in a rosewood box that still stands on my mantel-piece in Temple-street. But what else did it contain?

In a state of intense excitement, exhilarated beyond words by my discovery, and jubilant that I had solved the riddle left behind by Miss Eames, I replace the slab as best I can, to close the opening of the loculus, then stand for a moment contemplating the inscription. It is a curious sensation, to feel that my mother lies only a few feet away from me, within that cold narrow space, encased in lead and wood; and yet she has spoken to me directly, in her own voice, through the letters that I now hold in my hand.

The tears course down my face, and I fall to my knees. What do I feel? Elation, certainly, at my triumph; but also anger, at the gross folly and selfishness of my mother's actions; and love for her to whose care I was consigned. I think of the portrait of her Ladyship that hung above Mr Carteret's desk, and recall her haunting, imperious beauty; and then I think of her friend, Simona Glyver, always bent over her work-table, writing her books, keeping her secrets. When I first discovered the truth about my birth, I resented her faithfulness to her reckless friend; but I was wrong to do so. I called her my mother once. What shall I call her now? She did not carry me in her womb; but she cared for me, scolded me when I was bad, protected me, comforted me, and loved me. Who was she, then, but my mother?

Yet I blessed Laura Tansor for submitting to her conscience; and I blessed Miss Eames for sending Mr Carteret the clue that had delivered me from the yoke of perpetual dissimulation. The keys to the kingdom were now in my possession, and I was free at last to face the world as Edward Duport, to marry my dearest girl, and to lay my enemy low at last.

· 42 ·

*Apparatus belli**

As soon as I enter my sitting-room in Temple-street, I walk straight over to the mantel-piece, snatch up the rosewood box, and take it to my work-table.

It seems empty, but I am now certain that it is not. I shake it, and start to pick at it with my pocket-knife. A minute goes by, then two; but, as my hands now wander over every inch of its surface, pressing, pulling and probing, I know that it will eventually yield up its secret place.

And it does. I have wriggled the tiny key in the escutcheon this way and that a dozen times; but this time, when I disengage it slightly and start to turn it a little way from the vertical position, it seems to engage with something; and then a miracle happens. With a soft click, a little drawer slides out from below an inlaid band of paler wood an inch or so from the bottom of the box. The trick is so cunningly wrought that I wonder at the country skills of Mr James Beach.

The drawer is large enough to contain two folded documents, which I now remove and, trembling, lay out on my table.

The first is an affidavit, written in my mother's hand, sworn and signed in the presence of a Rennes notary, and dated the 5th day of June 1820. It states briefly, but categorically, that the child born in the house of Madame H. de Québriac, Hôtel de Québriac, Rue du Chapitre, in the city of Rennes, on the 9th day of March

*['The materials of war'. *Ed.*]

in the year 1820, was the lawfully begotten son of Julius Verney Duport, 25th Baron Tansor, of Evenwood, in the county of Northamptonshire, and his wife, Laura Rose; and that the said child, Edward Charles Duport, had been placed in the permanent care of Mrs Simona Glyver, wife of Captain Edward Glyver, late of the 11th Regiment of Light Dragoons, of Sandchurch in the County of Dorset, at the express wish of his mother, the said Laura Rose Duport, to be brought up as her own. Beside my mother's signature – witnessed by Madame de Québriac and another person whose name I cannot make out – is a small wax seal bearing an impression of the Duport arms, taken perhaps from a signet ring. With the affidavit is a short statement signed by two witnesses to my baptism in the Church of St-Sauveur, on the 19th of March, 1820.

Together with Mr Carteret's Deposition and the letters removed from Lady Tansor's tomb, and supported by the corroboration provided in my foster-mother's journals, my hand is now full, and unbeatable. I spend the rest of the day, and most of the evening, copying out extracts of particular relevance to my case from the journals, which I paste into a note-book, along with copies of the other critical documents. Then, having written up my own journal for the day, I sit in my arm-chair and fall fast asleep.

When I awoke, cold and hungry, my first thought was that I must have dreamed the discovery that I had made in Lady Tansor's tomb, and of forcing the rosewood box to give up its secret. But there, on my work-table, lay the two letters, and the signed affidavit, palpable and present to both sight and touch. They were golden arrows, tipped with truth, waiting to be shot into the villainous heart of Phoebus Daunt. After so long, I had been given the means to destroy my enemy, and take up my true station in life. A day would soon come when I would leave behind this present sorry life of confusion and duplicity for ever, and come into the golden place prepared for me by the Iron Master, with my dearest girl by my side.

My first task of the day was to write to Mr Tredgold, telling him how my conviction had been so triumphantly vindicated, and sending him for safekeeping the copies that I had made of the new documents. That done, I went forth to take a hearty breakfast.

On the following Monday I returned to Evenwood.

Once again, making sure I was unobserved, I climbed the flight of winding stairs up to my dearest girl's apartments. In the corridor, as I emerged through the staircase door, I encountered Lizzie Brine. Stepping back, I signalled for her to follow me.

'Is there anything to tell, Lizzie?' I asked.

'I do not know, sir,' she replied.

'What do you mean?'

'Only this, sir. The day we met on the stair-case, when I was with Hannah Brown . . .'

'Yes?'

'Well, sir, I couldn't tell you to your face, but then I thought you must know anyway.'

'Lizzie, this is unlike you,' I said. 'You're sounding like your brother. For God's sake, spit it out.'

'I'm sorry, sir. Here it is, as best as I can manage. I'd seen you arrive in the Front Court from the window there, just opposite my mistress's door. But a few moments before, just as I was coming up these very stairs, I'd seen a gentleman go into her room. I was on my way to the laundry, but I knew that you'd be coming up to my mistress's sitting-room at any minute. And so I naturally supposed, when I saw you later, that you must have met the gentleman. That's as clear as I can make it, sir.'

'And yet I still do not understand,' I said. 'There was no gentleman present when I was admitted to Miss Carteret's sitting-room. Are you sure of what you saw?'

'Oh yes, sir.'

'And did you see who it was? Did you recognize him?

'I only saw his coat-tails.'

I thought for a moment. 'Perhaps it was Lord Tansor,' I suggested.

'Perhaps,' said Lizzie, somewhat hesitantly.

'No, it must have been his Lordship.' I was now breezily confident that I had hit on the identity of the mystery gentleman. 'He had some brief business with Miss Carteret, no doubt – a few words only – and then left the apartment before I arrived. That must be it.'

'Yes, sir. I'm sure you're right.'

I sent her on her way, with a little bonus to keep her up to the mark, and knocked on my darling's door.

She was sitting by one of the arched windows, busily engaged on a piece of embroidery work, when I entered the room. Only on hearing my greeting did she look up and remove her spectacles.

'Have you brought them?'

I was a little taken aback by the peremptory tone of her question, for which she quickly apologized, saying that she had been racked with worry about my safety.

'Did anyone see you come?' she asked apprehensively, getting up to open the window, and look down to the the terrace below. 'Are you sure no one saw you? Oh Edward, I have been so afraid!'

'There, there, dearest. I am here now, safe and sound. And here are the papers.' I opened my bag and took out her father's Deposition, followed by half a dozen of my mother's little black volumes, and laid them on the table. She put on her spectacles again, then sat down at the table to examine, with the most intense interest, the words of her poor late papa – the last that he ever wrote. I sat a little way off, watching her turn each page of the Deposition until she reached the end.

'You are right,' she said quietly. 'He died because of what he knew.'

'And only one person stood to gain from depriving him of the source of his knowledge.'

She nodded, in mute acknowledgement that she understood to whom I had alluded, gathered the pages together with trembling hands, and then opened one of the little black volumes.

'I cannot read this,' she said, peering at the tiny writing, 'but you are sure, are you, that Mrs Glyver's words corroborate what my father discovered in Lady Tansor's papers?'

'There is no doubt whatsoever,' I answered.

After opening one or two of the other volumes and cursorily examining their contents, she gathered them together and placed them, with the Deposition, in the concealed cupboard behind the portrait of Anthony Duport in his blue silk breeches.

'There,' she said with a smile, 'all safe now.'

'Not quite all,' I said, reaching into the bag and taking out the letters that I had removed from Lady Tansor's tomb, together with the affidavit and the statement of the witness to my baptism.

'What are these?'

'These,' I said, 'are the means by which our futures will be assured: I as Lord Tansor's son and heir, and you as my wife – mistress of Evenwood!'

She gave a little gasp.

'I don't understand—'

'I have found it at last!' I cried. 'The final proof that I have been seeking, the proof that makes my case unanswerable.'

We sat down together at the table, and she read the letters, and then the affidavit.

'But this is extraordinary!' she exclaimed. 'How did you come by these documents?'

Briefly, I recounted how the clue sent by Miss Eames to her father had led me to believe that Lady Tansor's tomb might contain something of critical importance to my case.

'Oh, Edward, how terrible! But what will you do?' she asked, her eyes bright with excitement.

'I have sent copies to Mr Tredgold, and shall consult him as soon as possible on the proper course of action. It may be that he will make an approach to Lord Tansor on my behalf, but I am happy to take whatever advice he gives me on how to proceed. Only think, my dearest Emily, nothing now can stop me claiming what is rightfully mine. We can be married by Christmas!'

She gave me a look of surprise and took off her spectacles.

'So soon?'

'Dearest, don't look so startled! Surely you must feel, as I do, that to delay any longer than necessary would be intolerable?'

'Of course I do. You silly goose, Edward!' she laughed, leaning forward to kiss my cheek. 'I only meant that I had not dared to hope it would be so soon.' Whereupon she picked up the papers from the table, and placed them with the others in the cupboard behind the portrait.

An hour passed as, blissfully oblivious to time, we laid our plans and fashioned our lovers' dreams. Where would we live? Perhaps here in the great house, she said. But surely, I countered, his Lordship would wish to provide us with a country property of our own, as well as a house in town. We might travel. We might do anything we wished, for I was Lord Tansor's only son and heir, who was lost but now was found. How could he deny me anything?

At four o'clock she said that I must go as she was dining with the Langhams.

'And is Mr George Langham's heart still broken?' I asked mischievously.

She hesitated for a moment, as if puzzled by my question. Then she gave a little shake of her head.

'Oh, that! No, no. He has made a full and complete recovery from his affliction, to the extent that he is now engaged to Miss Maria Berkeley, Sir John Berkeley's youngest. Now go, before my maid comes to dress me. I don't wish her to see you here.'

She was all smiles and playful kisses, and I stood for a moment entranced by her gaiety and beauty, until she began to usher me out of the room with many charming little expressions of mock displeasure at my refusal to go, interspersed with more snatched kisses.

At the door I wheeled round to make a sweeping stage bow, hat in hand.

'I bid you good evening, dear sweet coz, the future Lady Tansor!'

'Go, you fool!'

One last laughing kiss, and then she turned away, picked up her embroidery, and sat down, spectacles perched on the end of her beautiful nose, beneath the portrait of Anthony Duport in his blue silk breeches.

Back at the Duport Arms, I had just retired to my room after taking some supper when there was a knock at the door.

'Beggin' your pardon, sir.'

It was the sullen waiter whose acquaintance I had made during my first stay at the inn. To sullenness he had now added a perceptible degree of shiftiness.

'Messenger, sir.' *Sniff.*

'A messenger? For me?'

'Yessir. Downstairs in the parlour.' *Sniff. Sniff.*

I immediately made my way downstairs, where I found a thin young man dressed in the Duport livery.

'From Miss Carteret, sir.' He stretched out a grubby hand containing a folded piece of paper. The short note written thereon was in French, which I shall here translate:

Dearest – in haste.

Lord T told me tonight that we are to leave for Ventnor tomorrow early. Date of return unknown. Her Ladyship has been unwell this past week, & his Lordship is concerned that the damp weather is making her condition worse – despite the hot-water pipes. Oh my dear love, I am distraught! What shall I do without you?*

Please do not worry about the papers. I promise you that the place is known only to you and me. I shall write when I can, and shall think of you every minute of every day. I kiss you. And so au revoir.

Ever yr loving,
E.

This was a bitter blow, and I damned his Lordship most heartily for taking my darling away. A day without her was bad enough; not to know when she would be returning to Evenwood was an intolerable prospect. Dismayed by this unexpected turn of events, I returned to London in a deeply despondent and nervous state of mind. There I languished for three weeks, seeing hardly a soul. On my first morning back in Temple-street I wrote to Mr Tredgold, to request a further meeting; but two days later I

*[A resort on the south coast of the Isle of Wight known for its mild climate. *Ed.*]

received a note from his brother to say that my employer had contracted a slight fever and was not able to enter into any correspondence at present, though Dr Tredgold promised to place my letter before him at the earliest opportunity.

I BEGIN TO FRET, AND AM KEPT AWAKE NIGHT AFTER NIGHT BY VAGUE fears. But what is there to be fearful of? The race is won, or nearly so. Why, then, do I feel so restless and abandoned?

Then my demons start to whisper and chatter, reminding me of what is always available, just beyond the confines of my room, to blot out my fears. For a time, I resist them; but then, one night, when the fog is so thick I cannot see the roofs of the houses opposite, they finally get the better of me.

The fog, however, is no impediment: I would know my way blindfolded. The subdued throb of the great city surges all around, though nothing can be seen but dim human shapes appearing out of the gloom and immediately disappearing into it, like shuffling phantoms, their faces illuminated momentarily by the smoky flare of the link-boys' torches,* or by the feeble light of gas-lamps in houses and shop windows. These living forms I can at least see, though briefly and indistinctly, and sometimes feel them as we bump into each other; I can only hear and sense, more than see, the homegoing stream of carriages, carts, omnibuses and cabs proceeding blindly, and with painful slowness, up and down the muddy thoroughfares.

It is past midnight when I stumble down the Strand, having been pursued by nightmares all the way from Bluegate-fields. The fog is beginning to lift a little, dispersed by a stiffening breeze off

*[A link was a torch made of tow and pitch used for lighting people along the streets; thus link-boys – boys who provided this service. *Ed.*]

the river. I can now see the upper stories of the buildings, and occasionally catch sight of eaves and smoking chimneys and ragged patches of ink-black sky through the shifting pall.

Almost before I realize it, I am in the Haymarket and sway through a brilliantly lighted door. A young woman is sitting alone. She bestows an obliging smile on me.

'Hello, dearie. Fancy something?'

A little conversation ensues; but as we rise to leave, we are approached by two more females, one of whom is instantly familiar to me.

'Goodness me, if it ain't Mr Glapthorn,' she says pleasantly. 'I see you've made the acquaintance of Miss Mabel.'

It is none other than Madame Mathilde, proprietress of the Abode of Beauty. I see a look pass between her and the girl and immediately understand how things lie. 'And you have added another string to your bow, Madame.'

'Things became a little slow at the Abode after that unfortunate misunderstanding with Mrs Bonner-Childs.'

'I'm sorry to hear that.'

'Oh, I don't blame you, Mr Glapthorn. I like a man that does his duty no matter what. But there, these things are sent to try us, ain't they? Besides, as you have guessed, I have another little concern now, in Gerrard-street – quite successful, too, tho' I say so mesself. Miss Mabel is one of my protijays, along with her sister here. P'raps,' she continues, looking suggestively from Mabel to her equally comely sister, Cissie by name, 'we might discuss a discount on quantity?'

In for a penny . . . I think. And so I retire to Madame's inconspicuous house in Gerrard-street, with Miss Mabel and Miss Cissie on each arm, and spend a most satisfying evening in their company, for which their employer is recompensed handsomely.

My demons temporarily satiated, I climb the stairs to my room at first light, my senses dulled, my head aching, and my conscience racked with guilt and self-loathing. I miss my dearest girl, so dreadfully. Without her, what hope is there for me?

ANOTHER WEEK GOES BY. BUT THEN, ONE BRIGHT OCTOBER MORNING, a note comes. It is from Lizzie Brine.

Sir,—

I thought you should know that my mistress returned from Ventnor three days ago.

Hoping this finds you well.
L. Brine

I sit for a full ten minutes, stunned. Three days! And no word sent! Think, think! She has been otherwise engaged. Lord Tansor has kept her constantly by his side. She has been attending her Ladyship night and day. There are a hundred most plausible reasons for her not writing to tell me *that* she is home. Perhaps, at this very moment, she is putting pen to paper.

Instantly, I resolve that I will surprise her. My Bradshaw lies on the table. The eleven-thirty departs in just under an hour. I have plenty of time.

AT EVENWOOD, THE LEAVES ARE FALLING. THEY FLUTTER FORLORNLY across paths and terraces, and scuttle about the courtyards, almost like living things, in the suddenly cold wind that scythes up from the river. In the kitchen garden, they accumulate in sodden heaps amongst tangles of decaying mint and drooping borage, and beneath the plum trees at the north end of the orchard, they lie in thick, golden-black swathes, soft underfoot, beneath which the grass is already turning a sickly yellow.

Rain begins to sweep in dark funereal sheets across the formal gardens and pleasure-grounds. When I had last seen them, the rose-beds at the end of the Long Walk had been ablaze with colour; now their early-summer glories have been cut down; and the bare earth of Lady Hester's former Clock Garden – a pointless conceit, which she had planted up with Purslane, Crane's Bill, and other flowers that supposedly opened or closed at successive hours of the day – now seems a mute and terrible witness to human folly, and to what time will do to us all.

I push open the little white-painted door, and climb up the winding stairs to the first floor, to the apartments above the Library where my mother died, and where I hope to find my dearest girl. I have missed her so very dreadfully, and my heart is afire to see her again and to kiss her sweet face. I bound up the last few stairs, feeling my spirit surge with joy at the thought that we need never be parted again.

Her door is shut, the corridor deserted. I knock twice.

'Enter!'

She is sitting by the fire, beneath the portrait of Master Anthony Duport, reading (as I soon discover) a volume of Mrs Browning's poems.* A travelling cloak lies on the sofa.

'Emily, my dearest, what is the matter? Why have you not written?'

'Edward!' she exclaims, suddenly looking up with an expression of surprise. 'I was not expecting you.'

Her face had taken on that terrible frozen look, which had

*[As the subsequent reference to 'Mrs Browning's Portuguese sonnets' (i.e. the 'Sonnets from the Portuguese') makes clear, this is the edition of *Poems* published in two volumes by Chapman and Hall in November 1850. *Ed.*]

struck me so forcibly when I had first seen her standing in the vestibule of the Dower House. She did not smile, and made no attempt to rise from her chair. There was no trace now, in either her demeanour or her voice, of the warmth and tender partiality that she had formerly shown me. In their place was a nervous coolness that instantly put me on my guard.

'Do you know Mrs Browning's Portuguese sonnets?' she asked. The tone was flat and false, and I put my question again.

'My love, tell me what is the matter? You have not written, and you said you would.'

She closed the book and gave a short impatient sigh.

'You may as well know. I am leaving Evenwood this afternoon for London. I have a great deal to do. Phoebus and I are to be married.'

· 43 ·

*Dies irae**

THE WORLD SEEMED TO CONTRACT AND THEN FALL AWAY, LEAVING ME sundered from what had once been, and from what I had known and believed before.

I stood in that dreadful room rooted to the spot in disbelief, feeling hope and happiness drain out of me like blood from a severed vein. I must have closed my eyes momentarily, for I distinctly remember opening them again, and finding that Miss Carteret had got up from her chair, and was now standing by the sofa putting on her cloak. Perhaps she had been in jest – one of those little games that women sometimes like to play with those who adore them. Perhaps . . .

'You cannot stay here, you know. You must leave immediately.'

Cold, cold! Hard and cold! Where was my dear girl, my sweet and loving Emily? Beautiful still – so wonderfully beautiful! But it was not her. This furious simulacrum was animated by a wholly different being, unrecognizable and dreadful.

'Edward – Mr Glapthorn! Why do you not answer? Did you hear what I said?'

At last I found my tongue.

'I heard, but I did not, and do not, understand.'

'Then I shall tell you again. You must go now, or I shall call for assistance.'

Now her eyes were flashing fire, and her beautiful lips, those

*['The day of wrath'. *Ed.*]

lips I had kissed so often, had pursed to a tight little pout. As she stood there, rigid and menacing, enveloped in her long black hooded cloak, she seemed like some sorceress of legend newly risen from the infernal depths; and for a moment I was afraid – yes, afraid. The change in her was so great, and so complete, that I could not conceive how it had come about. Like a photographic negative, what should have been light was now dark – dark as hell. Was she possessed? Had she gone suddenly mad? Perhaps it was I who should have called for assistance?

In a swirl of angry black, she headed for the door; and then it was as if I had woken suddenly from a dream. Sorceress? Humbug! This was plain villainy. I smelled it, and knew it for what it was.

Her hand was almost on the door-handle when I seized it and wrenched her towards me. We were face to face now, eye to eye, will to will.

'Let me go, sir! You are hurting me!' She struggled, but I had her fast.

'A moment of your time, Miss Carteret.'

She saw the resolve in my eyes, and felt the superior strength of my grip; in a moment, she surrendered to the inevitable, and her resistance ceased.

'Well, sir?'

'Let us sit in our old seat in the window. It is such a pleasant place to talk.' I held out a shepherding arm.

She threw off her cloak and walked over to the window-seat. Before joining her, I locked the door.

'I see I am a prisoner,' she said. 'Are you going to kill me?'

'You are pretty cool if I am,' I replied, standing over her. She only gave a little shrug by way of reply, and looked out of the window at the rain-lashed gardens.

'You mentioned a marriage,' I continued. 'To Mr Daunt. I don't mind admitting that this comes as something of a surprise to me.'

'Then you are a greater fool than we thought.'

I was determined to maintain an air of unconcerned bravado; but the truth was that I felt as helpless as a baby. Of course I had the advantage of physical strength; but what use was that? She had played me for a damned fool, right enough; and, once again, Phoebus Rainsford Daunt had taken what was rightfully mine. And then I suddenly found myself laughing uncontrollably, laughing so much that I had to wipe the tears away with my sleeve; laughing at my stupidity, my utter stupidity, for trusting her. If only I had taken Mr Tredgold's advice!

She watched me for a while as I stumbled about the room, shaking with laughter like some maniac. Then she stood up, anger boiling up once more in her great black eyes.

'You must let me go, sir,' she said, 'or it will be the worse for you. Unlock the door immediately!'

Ignoring her demand, I returned to where she was standing and threw her back into the window-seat. Her eyes began to dart round the room, as if she were looking for some means of escape, or perhaps for a weapon with which to attack me. If she had only smiled then, and confessed that it had all been a silly joke! I would have instantly folded her in my arms and forgiven her. But she did not smile. She sat bolt upright, breathing hard, her furious eyes wide open, larger than I had ever seen them before.

'And may I enquire whether you love Mr Phoebus Daunt?'

'Love him?' She leaned her cheek against the glass, and a sudden calm came over her, almost as if she were in a trance.

'I simply ask because you gave me the clear impression – as did your friend, Miss Buisson – that he was repellent to you.'

'There is no word to describe what I feel for Phoebus. He is my sun, my moon, my stars. My life is his to command.' Her breath had misted the pane, and she began slowly tracing out a letter, then another, and then a third and a fourth: P-H-O-E . . .

Stung now to real anger, I snatched her hand away and rubbed out the letters.

'Why did you lie to me?'

Her reply was immediate.

'Because you are nothing to me, compared to him; and because I needed to keep you fed with lies, until you delivered up to me the evidence of your true identity.'

She glanced at the portrait of young Anthony Duport in his juvenile finery, hand on hip, a dark-blue sash across his chest. Her words were like a knife to the heart. In two strides, I was standing beneath the portrait. I took hold of it with one hand and attempted to open the cupboard it concealed with the other, but it was locked.

'Would you like the key?' She reached into her pocket. 'I said I would keep everything safe.' Smiling, she held out a little black key.

I saw her face, and knew that all was lost; yet even in the agony of my despair, I took the key, inserted it in the lock of the cupboard, and the little panelled door swung open. Snatching up a candle from a nearby table, I peered inside. But I could see nothing. I stood closer and felt all around. The cupboard, of course, was empty.

'You see,' I heard her say. 'All safe. No one will find your secrets now. No one.'

I did not have to ask where the papers were. *He* had them now. The keys that would have unlocked the gates of Paradise for me were now in my enemy's hands.

And then I knew that I had been defeated; that every hope and dream I had cherished had been turned to dust and ashes.

What do you know? Nothing.
What have you achieved? Nothing.
Who are you? Nobody.

I was still standing with my back to her, staring into the empty cavity, when she spoke. Her voice had dropped to a rapt whisper.

'I have loved him ever since I can remember. Even when I was a little girl, he was my prince, and I was his princess. We knew then that we would marry some day, and dreamed of living together in some great house, just like Evenwood. My father always disliked and distrusted Phoebus, even when we were children; but we quickly learned to feign indifference to each other in public, and grew more cunning in our ways as we grew older. No one suspected the truth; only once, at a dinner given in honour of Lord Tansor's birthday, did we forget ourselves. It was such a little thing – not much more than a glance – but my father saw it. He was angry with me – angrier than I had ever seen him; but I persuaded him that he was wrong, and that Phoebus meant nothing to me. He believed me, of course. He always believed me. Everyone did.'

'But Daunt killed your father!' I cried. 'How could you continue to love him?'

She had been looking fixedly once more through the misted pane of glass on which she had begun to write her lover's name; but now she turned her face towards me, and I shivered to see the look of rage in her great dark eyes, and to hear the hard echo of an injury long borne in her voice.

'I loved my father; but I also hated him, for hating Phoebus, and for allowing his unfounded prejudice of him to keep us apart. The loss of my sister was, I think, the cause. He wanted me always by him, to be his alone; and when my mother died, of course I became all in all to him. And so I remained ever dutiful, long after I had came of age; I submitted to his will, to please him, and to keep a promise made to my dear mother that I would not abandon him while he lived. He told me more than once that he would never again receive me as his daughter if I were to marry Phoebus, and that prospect I could not bear. But it was cruel to deny me so – to keep me from my heart's desire, when he knew that I would continue to love and esteem him, and that I would never abandon him.'

'But surely he did not deserve to die!'

'No,' she said, more softly. 'He did not, and was not meant to. Pluckrose went too far, as usual. Phoebus was wrong to have brought him into it – he acknowledges it, and we have both suffered grievously for what Pluckrose did. Afterwards, when Pluckrose brought the letters to Phoebus and told him what he'd done, Phoebus was beside himself with fury. No. He should not have died. He should not have died.'

The repeated phrase trailed off into silence. Was she weeping? Really weeping? She was not lost, then, to all decent feeling. Some humanity remained.

'You have said enough to show me how utterly I have been deceived.'

She did not look at me. Her head was now pressed against the window-pane, through which she was gazing vacantly out into the deepening gloom.

'But this I must know: how did you first discover what Lady Tansor had done?'

'Dear Edward!' Oh, her voice! So tender, so inviting, so beguiling! The cold fury had melted quite away; in its place was a look of pitying compliance, as if she wished to show me her secret side, and so spare me further anguish and uncertainty. She held out her hand, long and white. I took it, and sat down beside her.

'I did not mean you to love me, you know. But when it was clear that you did – well, it made things so much easier. I know Marie-Madeleine warned you—'

'Miss Buisson! She knew?'

'But of course. Marie-Madeleine and I had no secrets. We were the closest of friends. Sometimes I told her things that even Phoebus didn't know about me. But, I suppose, by the time that she wrote to you, things had gone too far, hadn't they? Poor sweet Edward!' She leaned forward and began to brush my hair away from my forehead; in my mesmeric state I seemed powerless to stop her.

'And, you know, I found your attentions rather pleasant. It made Marie-Madeleine terribly cross.' She gave a sly little laugh. 'On more than one occasion she told me I shouldn't encourage them – that it was unnecessarily cruel. But I found I couldn't help myself; and as time went on, well, I began to think I might be falling in love with you – just a very little bit. It was bad of me, I know, and it shocked Marie-Madeleine even more when I told her. The little minx! I think she would have liked to have had you for herself! But you were asking me how we came to learn about Lady Tansor's little escapade.

'It happened purely by chance. My father had asked me to assist him in the translation of some letters in French. It was rare for my father to allow anyone into his work-room, except of course Lord Tansor, but on this occasion he made an exception. When I had finished the task, he requested me to take the papers up to the Muniments Room. As I was about to go back down, my eye was caught by an iron-bound chest. It bore a label identifying the contents as the private papers of Lord Tansor's first wife. Now I have always been fascinated by Laura Tansor. The most beautiful woman in England, they used to say. And so of course I could not help peeping into the chest. What do you think I pulled out first? A letter, dated the sixteenth of June, 1820, to Lady Tansor in Paris, from a friend – identified only by the initial letter 'S.' – in the town of Dinan, in Brittany.'

Her look told me immediately that Fate had placed into her hands the letter written by my foster-mother to her friend, and excerpted by Mr Carteret in his Deposition, in which it was clearly intimated that Lady Tansor had given birth to a child.

'I did not have time to read the letter in its entirety,' she continued, 'for I heard my father's step on the stairs; but I had read enough to know that it contained an extraordinary possibility. Naturally, I immediately told Phoebus of my little adventure. He tried, several times, to get up to the Muniments Room, but with little success; and this vexed him greatly. By now, you see, he knew that he was to be made Lord Tansor's heir. If a child had been born legitimately to Lady Tansor – well, I do not need to tell you what Phoebus thought of *that*.'

And then she told me how she had kept watch on her father, by offering to assist him further in his work. In this way, she learned that Mr Carteret was planning to remove certain of Lady Tansor's letters to the bank in Stamford, which he later retrieved in advance of his meeting with me at the George Hotel. Daunt then conceived the plan of using Pluckrose to waylay Mr Carteret on his return to Evenwood from Stamford and take the papers, under the guise of a robbery. A note was sent to the hotel, purporting to be from Lord Tansor and requesting her father to attend his Lordship at the great house. This ensured that he would take the most direct road into the Park from Easton, through the woods on the western side.

'But', I objected, 'I was told, quite categorically that Daunt was away on Lord Tansor's business when I came to meet your father.'

'He was. But he returned a day early, unknown to his family, in order to be here when you arrived. Pluckrose had been watching you – indeed he was on the same train from London that you took. We knew you had been sent by Mr Tredgold, you see. Phoebus knows everything.'

'And did you know that I was Edward Glyver before I told you?'

She shook her head.

'Not for certain, though we suspected as much.'

'How?'

She stood up, walked over to a cabinet on the far wall, and took out a book.

'This is yours, is it not?'

It was my copy of Donne's *Devotions*, which I had been reading the night before Mr Carteret's funeral.

'It was given to Mrs Daunt by Luke Groves – the waiter at the Duport Arms in Easton. Groves thought it must be yours – it had fallen down behind the bed in your room – though it had another's name inscribed in it. Of course the name – Edward Glyver – was very familiar to Phoebus. Very familiar indeed. There might be a simple explanation – the book might have come to you quite coincidentally in a number of ways. But Phoebus distrusts coincidence. He says that there is a reason for everything. So our guard was up from that moment.'

'Well,' I said, 'it seems that I have been very nicely skewered. I congratulate you both.'

'I warned you, when we first met, not to underestimate Phoebus; and then I warned you again. But you would not listen. You thought you could outwit him; but you can't. He knows all about you – everything. He is the cleverest man I know. No one will ever get the better of him.' She gave me an arch smile. 'Don't you wonder that I'm not afraid of you?'

'I will not harm you.'

'No, I don't believe you will. Because you love me still, don't you?'

I did not answer. I had nothing left to say to her. She continued to speak, but I was barely listening. Somewhere, a half-formed thought began to crawl out of the darkness into which my mind had been plunged. It grew stronger and more distinct, until at last it filled my mind to overflowing, and I could think of nothing else.

'Edward! Edward!'

Slowly I focused my attention on her; but I felt nothing. Yet one question remained.

'Why did you do this? Once my identity had been proved, I could have offered you everything Daunt could give you – and more.'

'Dear Edward! Have you not been listening? *I love him! I love him!*'

I had no reply to make; for I, too, knew what it was to love. I would have gone to the flames for her, suffered any torment for her sweet sake. How, then, could I blame her, bitter though her betrayal was, for doing these things, when she did them for love?

In a daze, I reached for my hat. She said nothing, but watched closely as I picked up my volume of Donne and walked to the door. As I was unlocking it, my eye was caught by an open box of cigars on a nearby table. With cold satisfaction, I noted the maker's name: Ramón Allones.

Opening the door, I walked out into the corridor.

I did not look back.

I REMEMBER LITTLE OF THE JOURNEY HOME, ONLY TUMBLED IMPRESSIONS of stone towers and stars and waving trees, and the sound of water, and of walking up a long dark hill; and then of a cold journey to Peterborough, followed by lights and noise and interrupted dreams; of emerging at last into the roar and smoke of London, and of finally dragging myself up the stairs to my rooms.

I passed a fearful night contemplating the ruin of my great project. The gates of Paradise had been closed upon me, and would never be opened again. I had been played with infinite skill, until the hook had pierced my gullet; and now I must live out my life drained of all hope, tormented night and day by the loss of my true self, and of her – so beautiful, so treacherous! – whom I would love to my last breath. I have been betrayed, too, it seems, by the Iron Master. Another place has been prepared for me – not Evenwood, the dream-palace of my childhood fancies, but some modest dwelling amongst other modest dwellings, where I shall live and die, unnoticed and unremembered, in perpetual exile from the life that should have been mine.

But I shall not die unavenged.

· 44 ·

*Dictum, factum**

FOR A WEEK AFTER RETURNING FROM EVENWOOD I CONFINED MYSELF to my rooms, eating little, and sleeping less.

A note came from Le Grice proposing supper, but I pleaded indisposition; another arrived from Bella, asking why I had not called at Blithe Lodge for so long, to which I replied that I had been out of town on urgent business for Mr Tredgold but would call the following week. When Mrs Grainger came to sweep my floor and clean the grate, I told her that I had no need of her, gave her ten shillings, and asked her to go home. I had no desire to see another human face, and no wish to do anything but reflect over and over again on my ruination, and the means by which it had been accomplished. After so much labour, to have lost everything so easily! The deceiver well and truly deceived! And then, whenever I closed my eyes, night or day, I experienced a recurring vision of her room at Evenwood just as it had been on the day of my betrayal, and of her face pressed against the window-pane, and the look she wore as she had traced the letters of his name on the glass. Where was she now? What was she doing? Was he with her – kissing her, whispering into her ear, making her sigh with delight? Were they congratulating themselves once again on their triumph? Thus I added my own exquisite torments to those I was already suffering.

On the seventh day, as I was sitting in my arm-chair, idly exam-

*['Said, and done' (Terentius, *Heautontimorumenos*). *Ed.*]

ining the rosewood box in which my mother had hidden the documents that would have undone the wrong she did to me, I looked about me and saw what I had come to. Was this my kingdom? Were these my sole possessions? This narrow panelled chamber, with its faded Turkey rug laid over bare boards; this blackened grate, these grimy windows; this great work-table on which my mother wrote her life away, and on which I, too, had laboured so futilely; these little reminders of happier times – the clock from my mother's bedroom, a watercolour of the house in Church Langton where she was born that used to hang in the hall at Sandchurch, a print of School Yard at Eton? Were these things my inheritance? Poor enough, to be sure, even with the addition of the few pounds that I had left at Coutts & Co., and my modest collection of books. But it did not signify. I had no heir; nor would I ever have one. I smiled to think that Mr Tredgold and I were united in our fates: both chained to the memory of a love lost for ever; both incapable of loving again.

I walked over and pulled back the piece of patched velvet curtain behind which my photographic equipment lay unused and gathering dust. Propped up on a shelf was a single view of Evenwood, the only exposure that I had not considered good enough to put into the album that I had made up for Lord Tansor back in the summer of 1850.

It had been taken within the walled area of the grounds enclosing the fish-pond, looking across the black water to the South Front of the house. The building lay in deep shadow, with only patches here and there of pale sunlit stone. I must have knocked the camera, for one of the great cupola-topped towers was out of focus; but though the execution had been flawed, the composition, and the mood it evoked, was striking. I took it down and gazed at it. But the longer I gazed, the more furious I became that I had been shut out for ever from this wonderful place, the home of my ancestors, by a worthless usurper. *I* was a Duport; *he* was a nonentity, an atom, a nullity. How could such a nothing presume to take that ancient name as his own? He could. He would not.

And then, with my rage, came a determination to hazard one final throw of the dice. I would go to Evenwood once again, though it might be for the last time. I would present myself to Lord Tansor, telling him to his face the truth that had been kept from him for over thirty years. I had nothing to lose, and everything to gain. Eye to eye, man to man, surely he would now recognize me as his own?

I was seized by this new resolve, desperate though it might be, and instantly leaped to my feet to begin my preparations. Then I ran down the wooden stairs, boots clattering, past Fordyce Jukes's door, and out into the world for the first time in a week.

It was a raw, dull day, and a flat and depressing sky hung over the city. I pushed through the morning crowds and was soon at the terminus, where I took my seat once more in the train that had so often carried me north, to Evenwood.

ONCE SET DOWN IN THE MARKET-SQUARE AT EASTON BY THE Peterborough coach, I entered the Duport Arms to take some refreshment before commencing my walk to the great house. As I sat drinking my gin-and-water, served by my old friend, the sullen waiter Groves, who had been the unwitting means by which my identity had been confirmed to Mrs Daunt and her son, the thought struck me that Lord Tansor might not be in residence at Evenwood; that he might be in town, or away somewhere else; and then I grew angry at my impetuosity. To come all this way without establishing this one essential fact only demonstrated to me that I was not myself, and that I must take better care of matters in future. But then I saw that I must take whatever came; and so I drank back my gin, buttoned up my great-coat, and set off down the hill, under a creaking canopy of bare branches, towards Evenwood.

A thick drizzle began to come on. At first I paid no heed to it; but as I turned along the Odstock Road, towards the West Gates of the Park, I felt my trousers begin to cling to my legs and grow heavy as they soaked up the moisture in the air, and by the time I passed through the woods and into the open space of the Park itself, my hat and coat were dripping wet, my boots were muddied, and I was altogether a sorry sight.

The Library Terrace came suddenly into view. To my right was Hamnet's Tower, with the windows of the Muniments Room looking out from the first floor. And there, above the Library, running the length of the terrace, were the windows of my mother's former apartments, occupied now by my faithless love. Of course I could not help wondering if she had returned from London and was there, looking out over the misty, soaking gardens towards the woods through which her father had passed on his last journey home. What would she think, if she saw my tall dishevelled figure striding through the murk? That I had come to kill her? Or her lover? But as I drew closer, scrutinizing each of the windows in turn, there was no sign of her beautiful pale face, and so I walked on.

I decided that there was no alternative but to present myself four-square at the front door and ask to see Lord Tansor; and this is what I did. Luckily, the door was opened by my sometime informant, John Hooper, whose acquaintance I had made when photographing the house four years earlier.

'Mr Glapthorn,' he said. 'Please come in, sir. Are you expected?'

'No, Hooper, I am not. But I wish to speak with his Lordship on a matter of importance. Is he at home?'

'He is in his study, sir, if you will follow me.'

He conducted me through a series of state rooms until we reached a pair of green-painted double doors. Hooper knocked softly.

'Enter!'

The footman went in first, bowed, and said: 'Mr Glapthorn, from Tredgolds, to see you, my Lord.'

The apartment was small and dark, but richly furnished. Lord Tansor sat behind a desk facing us. Through a wide sash window behind him, I glimpsed the main carriage-road that led out across the river to descend finally past the Dower House to the South Gates, the road that I had trodden so often in past months. A green-shaded lamp illuminated the documents on which his Lordship had been working. He laid down his pen and stared at me.

'Glapthorn? The photographer?' He glanced down at a sheet of paper. 'I have no note here of an interview with anyone from Tredgolds today.'

'No, my Lord,' I replied. 'I beg your pardon, most sincerely, for calling on you unannounced. But I do so on a matter of the greatest moment.'

'That will be all, Hooper.'

The footman bowed and left, quietly closing the door behind him.

'A matter of importance, you say? Has Tredgold sent you?'

'No, my Lord. I come on my own account.'

His eyes narrowed.

'What possible business can you and I have?' His voice was hard, disdainful, and intimidating. But I had expected no less from the 25th Baron Tansor.

'It concerns your late wife, my Lord.'

At this, Lord Tansor's face grew dark, and he motioned me to a chair set before his desk.

'You have my attention, Mr Glapthorn,' he said, leaning back and throwing out a most challenging stare. 'But be brief.'

I took in a deep lungful of air and began my story: how I had discovered that Lady Tansor had kept the secret of his son's birth from him, and how the boy had been brought up by another in ignorance of his true identity. I paused.

For a moment or two he said nothing. And then, with unmistakable menace: 'You had better have proof for what you allege, Mr Glapthorn. It will go hard with you if you do not.'

'I shall come to the proof shortly, my Lord. If I may continue?' He nodded. 'The boy, as I say, grew up not knowing that he was a Duport – that he was your heir. It was only after the death of the woman who brought him up, your late wife's closest friend, that he discovered the truth. The boy was by then a man; and that man lives.'

Lord Tansor's face had now grown pale and I saw that, beneath his iron self-control, he was in the grip of mounting emotion.

'Lives?'

'Yes, my Lord.'

'And where is he now?'

'He is here before you, my Lord. *I* am your son. *I* am your heir, lawfully begotten.'

His shock at my words was now palpable; but he said nothing. Then he rose slowly from his chair, and turned towards the window behind him. He stood there, hands held stiffly behind his back, rigid, silent, looking out across the gravelled entrance court. Without turning to look at me, he uttered the single word: 'Proof!'

My mouth was dry; my body all a-tremble. For of course I had no proof. The evidence – incontrovertible, incontestable – that I could have placed before him only a week before had been taken from me, and was now beyond recovery. All I had was circumstantial and unsubstantiated assertion. I saw my future hanging by the merest thread.

'Proof!' he barked, turning now towards me. 'You claimed you had proof. Show it to me at once!'

'My Lord . . .' I hesitated, fatally, and he immediately saw my discomfort.

'Well?'

'Letters,' I replied, 'in her Ladyship's own hand, and a signed affidavit, properly executed and witnessed, confirming my true parentage. These documents corroborated the daily record of events left behind in my foster-mother's journals.'

'And you have these things with you?' he asked, though he could see that I had come empty-handed, without a bag or case of any sort. I had no choice now but to make my admission.

'They are gone, my Lord.'

'Gone? You have lost them?'

'No, my Lord. They were stolen. From me, and from Mr Carteret.'

Anger began to suffuse his face. His mouth tightened.

'What in God's name has Carteret to do with this?'

Vainly, I attempted to explain how his secretary had come across the crucial letters hidden in the writing-box left to Miss Eames, and how they had been taken from him when he had been attacked. But even as I spoke, I knew that he would not believe what I was about to tell him.

'And whom do you accuse of stealing these documents, from you and Carteret?' The question hung in the air for a brief moment as he regarded me, grimly expectant.

'I accuse Mr Phoebus Daunt.'

. . .

SECONDS PASSED. ONE, TWO, THREE . . . SECONDS? NO, A LIFETIME OF agony. Outside, the partial light of late afternoon was giving way to the encroaching darkness. The world seemed to turn with infinite slowness as I waited for Lord Tansor's reply to my assertion. On his next words, I knew, all would be won, or lost. Then he spoke.

'You are pretty cool, sir, for a damned liar. I'll give you that. You want money, I suppose, and think this cock-and-bull story of yours is a way to do it.'

'No, my Lord!' I jumped up from my chair, and we faced each other, eye to eye, across the desk; but it was not how I had imagined it would be. He recognized no evidences of consanguinity; he felt no tug of that indissoluble golden thread that should unite parent and child across time and space. He did not know me as his son.

'I'll tell you what I think, Mr Glapthorn,' he said, pulling back his shoulders. 'I think you are a rogue, sir. A common rogue. And an unemployed one, too, for you can expect to be dismissed from Tredgolds with immediate effect. I shall write to your principal this very evening. And then I shall bring charges against you, sir. What do you think of that? And I'm not sure I shan't have you horsewhipped out of my house for your damned effrontery. You accuse Mr Daunt! Are you mad? A man of agreed distinction, who enjoys universal respect! And you brand him a thief and a murderer? You'll pay for this slander, sir, most dearly. We'll have every penny off you, sir. We'll have the clothes off your back, sir. You'll rue the day you tried to get the better of me!'

He turned and pulled angrily on the bell-rope that hung just behind his desk.

I made one last effort, though I knew it was too late.

'My Lord, you must believe me. I am truly your son. I am the heir of your blood for which you have longed.'

'You! My son! Look at you. You are not my son, sir. You are barely a gentleman by the state of your appearance. My only son died when he was seven years old. But I have an heir, thank God, who is every inch a gentleman; and though he does not have my blood, he is everything I could wish for in a son, and fit in all respects to assume the ancient name that I have the honour to bear.'

At that moment a knock came at the door, and Hooper reappeared.

'Hooper, show this – gentleman – out. He is not to be admitted to this house again, under any circumstance.'

Look at me! Look at me! I cried inwardly. *Do you not see her in me? Can you not see yourself? Is there nothing in these features to convince you that it is your own son, and not some adventuring impostor, who stands before you?*

I tried to hold his gaze, willing him to see the truth. But his eyes were blank and cold. I picked up my hat, and turned away from him. As I reached the door, I gave a brief half-glance back. He was sitting at his desk again, and had taken up his pen.

· 45 ·

*Vindex**

I WALKED AWAY FROM EVENWOOD FOR THE LAST TIME, THROUGH THE drizzle and the dark, stopping only once as I reached the Western Gates to look back at the many-towered palace that I had once dreamed would be mine.

The lamps on the Library Terrace had been lit – it was Lord Tansor's inveterate habit to walk there every evening, whatever the weather, with his dog. Above, in my mother's old apartments, a light gleamed. She was there – my dearest love was there! And then I felt such a weight of sadness descend upon my spirit, crushing every vestige of hope in me. I took one final, lingering look at the place that had brought me to such despair, and then turned my back on it for ever. I had been stripped of everything due to me by right of birth. But one thing remained in my full possession: the will to bring Phoebus Daunt to account. To this new end, I would now devote myself, to the last ounce of my strength.

I began the next day.

MY FIRST TASK WAS TO OBSERVE HIS MOVEMENTS. TO ACCOMPLISH this, I dressed myself in moleskin trousers, a greasy black coat, a coarse unbuttoned shirt, and a cap and dirty muffler, all purchased from a Jew-clothesman in Holywell-street, and spent several uncomfortable hours every day, loitering in the vicinity of

*[An avenger or punisher. *Ed.*]

Mecklenburgh-square, and following my enemy when he emerged. His daily routine varied little. Usually he would leave the house at about one o'clock and, if the weather permitted, walk to the Athenaeum in Pall Mall; at three o'clock on the dot he would take a cab back to Mecklenburgh-square, emerging again between five and six to walk or take another cab somewhere for dinner – sometimes to the Divan Tavern in the Strand, or perhaps to Verrey's or Jaquet's.* He usually dined alone, and never returned home later than ten o'clock. A light would burn in one of the upper rooms for several hours – some new dreary epic, I expected, was being given to the world. I never saw any visitors come to the house; and, to my infinite relief, there was no sign of Miss Carteret.

I continued to brave cold and hunger – and the indignity of seeming to belong to that vagabond class of Londoner who live and die in the streets of the metropolis – until, on the fifth day, towards six o'clock, just as I was about to give up and return to Temple-street, I saw my quarry leave his house and make his way westwards towards Gower-street. Pulling my hat down, I followed him.

I was close now – close enough to see his black beard and the shimmer on his silk hat as he passed under a lamp. He walked with a determinedly confident air, swinging his stick, his long coat trailing out behind him like a king's train. It had been four years and more since I had seen him playing croquet with a tall dark-haired lady at Evenwood. Dear God! I stopped dead in my tracks, realizing, for the first time, that it had all been laid out before my very eyes on that hot June afternoon in 1850, and I had failed to see it: Phoebus Daunt and his beautiful croquet partner – my

*[In Regent Street (corner of Hanover Street) and Clare Court, Drury Lane, respectively. *Ed.*]

enemy and my dearest love. Seething inwardly, with my eye fixed on his retreating form, I continued shadowing him.

He swung south to Bedford-square, and thence down St Martin's-lane until he came at last to Bertolini's in St Martin's-street, Leicester-square, which he entered. I took up my position just across the street. The two pocket-pistols made for me by M. Honoré of Liège, which have accompanied me on all my midnight rambles about the city, were in readiness. There was no moon that night, and sufficient fog to make escape certain.

Two hours later, he stepped out into the street again, with another fellow. They shook hands, and his companion walked off towards Pall Mall, while Daunt took his way northwards. In Broad-street, he turned into a narrow lane, lit by a single gas-lamp at the far end.

I was no more than six or seven feet behind him, but he had no idea I was there – my years as Mr Tredgold's private agent had taught me how to pursue someone without their being at all aware of my presence, and I was confident that I remained invisible to him. The lane was deserted. I reached into my pocket and pulled out one of the pistols. A few steps more. My shoes were wrapped in rags so that my steps made no sound. He stopped, just under the lamp, to light a cigar – a perfectly illuminated target. Hidden in a doorway, I raised the pistol and brought my aim to bear on the back of his head, just above the collar of his coat.

But nothing happened. My hand was shaking. Why could I not pull the trigger? I took aim again, but by now he had moved out of the yellow arc of light, and in a moment had disappeared into the darkness.

I remained standing in the doorway, gun in hand and still trembling, for several minutes.

I had done many things in my life of which, God knows, I was ashamed; but I had never yet killed a man. Yet I had imagined, foolishly, that it would be easy for me, I who had seen violence done in the course of my work, simply to raise my pistol and blow his brains out, relying on my hate and rage to carry me through. Was I so weak after all? Had my will been overruled by conscience? I had had him where I wanted him, my hated enemy; and something had held me back, though my thirst to be revenged on him remained as sharp as ever. Then I told myself that there is little in this world that may not be mastered with study and application; and murder is perhaps the least of challenges, if the injury be great enough, and the will sufficient. Conscience, if that is what had stayed my hand, must be stamped down.

I replaced the pistol in my pocket, and began to make my way back to Temple-street. I was badly shaken. I considered again whether I was really capable of such a deed. Might not my courage fail me again when the moment came to strike the fatal blow? The mere act of mentally posing the question engendered another little thrill of doubt. Surely I would not flinch a second time? There – again: that momentary prick of apprehension.

Shocked to the core by my inability to do what I wished to do above all things, I stumbled off, arriving at last at the opium-master's door in Bluegate-fields.

Oh God, what dreams came to me that night – dreams so terrible that I cannot bear to set them down! I ended by raving wildly for an hour or more, so that a doctor had to be called, to administer a strong sleeping draught. When I awoke, it seemed as if I had been laid on a soft bed. A cold salty breeze flowed over my face, and I could hear the cry of sea birds, and the sound of water lapping. Where was I? Surely I was in my old bed at Sandchurch again, with the little round window open to let in the morning air from the Channel? Slowly, I opened my eyes.

It was no bed. I was lying in the wet, clinging mud, still in my labourer's clothes, close to the river's edge, though how I had come there I still cannot say. Gradually, consciousness began to return, and with it a voice whispering to me, softly but distinctly. I moved on my oozy matress, turning slowly round to see who was with me. But no one was there. I was entirely alone on a dismal stretch of shore beneath a line of towering dark buildings. But then the voice came again, more insistently this time, telling me what I must do.

I write this now in days of calm reflection; but I was mad then, made so by treachery, despair, and rage, and by the opium-master's pipe of dreams. I lay, in my degradation, between the worlds of men and monsters; a strange putty-coloured sky, streaked and splashed with vivid red, above me; dark shingled slime beneath me; and the sound of whispering, like rushing water, in my ears.

'I hear you,' I heard myself say. 'I will obey!'

Then I jumped up, shouting in some strange tongue at the putty-coloured sky, and began running round in the mud, like some demented Bacchic votary.* But it was not wine that made me do this. It was blessed opium, opening a great black gate, behind which stood another, more terrible, god.

Some time later – whether minutes or hours, I do not know – I was once more in the world of men, though not of them. Down Dorset-street† I tramped, covered in mud, and with a look in my eyes that made even the inhabitants of these infernal regions step aside as I approached. And still the voice whispered in my ear as I made my way westwards.

At last I climbed the stairs to my rooms, heart-sick and chilled to the bone from my sojourn on the shore. Throwing off my wet and filthy rags, I washed myself and put on clean clothes. Then I

*[i.e. a drunken devotee of the god of wine, Bacchus. *Ed.*]

†[In Spitalfields, known as one of the worst streets in London for violence and poverty. *Ed.*]

lay on my bed, breathing hard, looking up through the skylight at a single winking star that hung, like fragile hope itself, in the pale immensity of morning.

I would not fail in my next attempt to kill Phoebus Daunt. The voice had told me what I must do to make a trial of my resolve to become a murderer. Another man must die before I faced my enemy again; only then would I know for sure that my will was truly equal to the task. *Practice makes perfect,* I whispered to myself, over and over again. The god of necessary violence demands two sacrifices, so that the lesser deed may secure the success of the greater.

*Monday, 23rd October 1854**

I awoke shaking. For an hour I lay and listened to the wind, dreaming that I was in my bed at Sandchurch once again. There are shadows on the wall that I cannot explain. A woman with [tusks?]. A king wielding a great scimitar. A terrible claw-like hand that creeps over the counterpane.

I reach for my bottle of Dalby's. This is the third time tonight.

. . .

At ten o'clock, Mrs Grainger knocked at the door. I sent her away again, telling her I was unwell.

I will not go out today.

Tuesday, 24th October 1854

My bottle of Dalby's is empty. I began to weep as I tried to shake the last few remaining drops into my wineglass.

*[The following sections of the MS are composed of pasted-in strips of unlined paper. The writing on these strips is occasionally almost illegible. Conjectured readings are in square brackets. *Ed.*]

It will be tonight.

I walked down to the river and across Southwark Bridge to take my luncheon in the Borough. The Catherine Wheel Inn was dark and crowded, and no one paid me any heed. I called for two slices of [beef?] from the platter, and then observed the waiter as he went about his task. The knife he used was pitted and discoloured, but it sliced through the red flesh with ease. It would do very well. Much better than a pistol.

And so to Messrs [Corbyn*] in High Holborn. 'A persistent headache, sir? Nothing more unpleasant. We recommend [Godfrey's] Cordial. You prefer Dalby's? Certainly, sir.'

FIVE O'CLOCK BY THE TEMPLE CHURCH. ON WITH MY GREAT-COAT. Stow the knife securely. On with my gloves, a new pair, which I must take care not to spoil.

I stepped outside. A sharp night, with fog coming down.

St Paul's rose monstrously into the murk. The [lantern] was invisible, and also the Golden Gallery, where I had stood with my dear girl a lifetime ago.

East down Cheapside and into Cornhill, the City churches ringing out six o'clock. I had been wandering for an hour. Him? Or him? The fellow loitering outside St Mary-le-Bow? The old gentleman coming out of Ned's Chop-house in Finch-lane? I was bewildered. So many black coats, so many black hats. So many lives. How could I choose?

At length, I found myself in Threadneedle-street, looking across to the entrance of the Bank of England.

Then I saw him, and my heart began to thump. He was

*[Corbyn, Beaumont, Stacey & Messer, well-known chemists and druggists, situated at 300 High Holborn. *Ed.*]

[dressed] the same as all the others, but something seemed to distinguish him. He stood, looking about him. Would he cross the street? Perhaps he intended to take the omnibus that was now approaching. But then he pulled on his gloves and walked smartly off towards Poultry.

I kept him in sight as we walked westwards, back along Cheapside, past St Paul's again, and down Ludgate-hill to Fleet-street and Temple Bar. Then he turned northwards a short way, up Wych-street and across to Maiden-lane, where he took some refreshment at a coffee-house, and read the paper for half an hour. At a few minutes after seven o'clock, he left, stood for a few moments on the pavement in the [swirling] mist to adjust his muffler, and then continued on his way.

A little further we went, and then he turned into a narrow court that I had never noticed before. I stood at the entrance, taking in its high blank walls and deep shadows and watching the solitary figure of my victim as he walked towards a short flight of steps leading down to the Strand. At the head of the steps was a fizzing gas-lamp that threw out a weak smudge of dirty yellow light into the foggy dark. Where was this? I looked up.

Cain-court, W.

He was nearing the steps at the far end of the court, but I quickly and silently caught up with him.

My hand closed round the handle of the knife.

AND SO, AT LAST, I BRING MY CONFESSION BACK TO THE POINT AT which it started: the killing of Lucas Trendle, the red-haired stranger, on the 24th of October 1854. He died that night so that Phoebus Daunt might also die, as justice demanded; for without the death of guiltless Lucas Trendle, I might have failed in that greater aim. But now, by his sad death, committed swiftly and without compunction, I knew, beyond all doubt, that I was capable of this terrible extremity of action. The logic was that of the madhouse; but it did not seem so to me then. On the contrary, it made perfect sense to me, in my disordered state, to kill an innocent man in order to ensure the death of a guilty one. As I confess the deed now, for the second time, I am racked with remorse for what I did to poor Lucas Trendle; but I cannot, and will never, regret what it steeled me to do.

The events successive to that momentous night have already been laid before you: the shock that I felt when I learned my victim's name; the blackmail note received by Bella, and then the invitation to Lucas Trendle's funeral at Stoke Newington slipped under my door; my parting from Bella following our night in the Clarendon Hotel, when she rightly suspected me of withholding the truth about myself from her; my confrontation with Fordyce Jukes, whom I had suspected of being the blackmailer; and, finally, those mysterious taps on the shoulder, outside the Diorama and at Stoke Newington, and the menacing figure who had followed Le Grice and me as we rowed up to Hungerford Bridge.

It is now the 13th of November 1854. The place: Le Grice's rooms in Albany. The time: an hour after dawn.

Le Grice stood up and pulled back the curtains, allowing weak pearly light into the frowsty room. The night after our dinner at Mivart's had passed away in talk, and by the time that the new day had broken forth, I had placed the true history of Edward Glyver before my dear old friend, sparing him only the despatching of Lucas Trendle, and my resolve to do the same to Phoebus Daunt. My task now was to discover the identity of the blackmailer, and then, when I have dealt with him, turn my full attention to Phoebus Rainsford Daunt.

My old friend looked at me with an expression of such concentrated seriousness that I began to regret that I had unburdened myself to him in this way.

'Well,' he said at last, 'I thought you were in trouble, and I was right. God knows though, G, why you kept all this to yourself. I mean to say, old boy, you might have given a chap a chance to help you. But that's all past now.' He shook his head, as if some great thought had presented itself for his consideration. 'Old Lord T, now. That was hard, G. Damned hard. Don't know how I'd have taken that. Your own father.' Another shake of his head; and then, with a brighter and more determined air, 'Daunt, though – an entirely different matter. Things to be done there.'

He paused once more, apparently reflecting on a new possibility.

'What I don't understand is, why Daunt sent me that book to give to you. Wouldn't Miss Carteret have told him where he could find you?'

'I can only guess that he is playing some sort of game with me,' I replied. 'As a warning, perhaps, against trying to get back at him – to let me know that I am within his reach.'

Le Grice looked doubtful. And then he suddenly spun round, an excited glint in his eyes: 'I say! The copies! You still have the copies, of the Deposition and what not, that you sent to old Tredgold.'

'Gone,' I said.

'Gone?'

'When I got back from Evenwood, after seeing Miss Carteret, there was a letter from Mr Tredgold. There'd been a burglary – his sister and brother had taken him to the Cathedral and the house was empty. It was Pluckrose, I suppose. Nothing of value taken, only papers and documents. They were no use anyway. All in my own hand, you see. I made another copy of Mr Cartaret's Deposition, but it won't help now. I have nothing.'

Crestfallen, Le Grice threw himself back into his chair. But after a minute or two of silence, he slapped the arm.

'Breakfast, I think. That's the thing we need.'

So off we went to the London Tavern, to take our fill of eggs, bacon, and oyster-toast, supplemented by liberal doses of coffee.

'There's no point beating around the bush, old boy,' said Le Grice as we walked out into the street afterwards. 'You're sunk. And that's all about it.'

'It would seem so,' I agreed gloomily.

'And there's still our friend on the river. The jolly boatman. What I think is, he might be an associate of Daunt's, perhaps, keeping an eye on you. Now what's to be done about him, I wonder?'

It is strange how a single word or phrase from another's lips can sometimes throw light on a truth that we have been struggling unsuccessfully to uncover. Was there no end to my stupidity? An associate of Daunt's? There was only one associate of his that I knew of, and that was Josiah Pluckrose. The line of reasoning that succeeded this thought was swift and, to my mind, conclusive. If Pluckrose was the man in the boat, then Pluckrose might also be the man who had tapped me on the shoulder on leaving Abney Cemetery after the funeral of Lucas Trendle, and outside the Diorama following my walk with Bella in the Regent's Park. Miss Carteret, after all, had let slip that Pluckrose had followed me to Stamford. How long had I been marked? And then the leap. '*An end is come, the end is come: it watcheth for thee; behold, it is come.*' I heard again in my head the admonitory verse from Ezekiel, to which I had been directed by a series of pin-pricked holes on the first blackmail note. Blackmail? No; a warning, *from my enemy.* Jukes, I now saw, had nothing to do with it. *The notes were the work of Daunt.*

'What ails thee, knight-at-arms?' I hear Le Grice say as he

claps me heartily on the back. 'You look distinctly seedy, but then I'm not surprised. Mr Dark Horse indeed! But fret not. The pride of the Le Grices is by your side, come what may. No need to soldier on alone any more. There's still some time before I join my regiment, and it's yours, old boy, all yours. And then, perhaps you might go travelling till I return. What do you say?'

I took his hand and thanked him, from the bottom of my heart, though my mind was already far away, reflecting on the consequences of my belated realization.

'What now?' he asked, cheroot clamped between his teeth.

'I'm to my bed,' I said.

'I'll walk with you.'

I HAD UNMASKED MY BLACKMAILER, THOUGH IT WAS NOT BLACKMAIL my enemy intended: of that I was now certain. I had nothing left to give him, and he could go to the authorities and denounce me in a moment for the murder of Lucas Trendle if he so wished. Was he merely demonstrating his power over me? I considered this question for some time, concluding at last that it would be in character for him to do so, like the spiteful little tug that he was; but I now began to perceive another, darker, danger looming behind this pleasant little prank, which Mr Tredgold had seen, but which I had formerly made light of. Daunt had set Pluckrose to watch me, and now he knows about Lucas Trendle. The note to Bella, and the invitation to my victim's funeral, were simply diversions. But from what?

Then all became clear. He had taken everything from me, but he was not satisfied. Whilst I live, I must of course be a constant threat to him; for he cannot be certain that some other piece of evidence, conclusive to my claim to be Lord Tansor's lawful heir, might not come to light, and so sink his prospects forever. If I put myself in his place, then only one course of action presented itself. He must take my life, to make his triumph certain.

I had let matters drag on too long. Action was now needed, firm and decisive. I must now, at long last, strike the first – and final – blow against my enemy.

A LETTER ARRIVED LATE THE NEXT AFTERNOON FROM MR TREDGOLD, imploring me to come to Canterbury as soon as I was able. But what could Mr Tredgold do for me? Without the evidence that had been taken from me, my claim to be Lord Tansor's son could never be pursued. 'Your continuing silence has given me great anxiety,' he wrote.

I do not well know what I can do to assist you, if you will not inform me of your present circumstances. You will understand, of course, that I am unable to take up your cause directly with Lord Tansor. There would be consequences – of the most serious character – if my part in the conspiracy carried out by his Lordship's late wife were to become known. I care nothing now for myself, or my reputation; but the standing of the firm – well, that is a very different case. Greater than even this consideration, however, is the solemn vow I took in the Temple Church, never to betray your mother. This vow I shall never *willingly break. When the truth is known, as it may soon be, then of course I shall face whatever comes, for your sake. But I cannot, and will not, of my own volition, reveal it to Lord Tansor. That responsibility is yours, dear Edward, and yours alone. But I wish to speak to you so very badly, about these matters, and when and how you intend to communicate with his Lordship, and how I may offer what help I can, within the limits of my ability. Come soon, my dear boy.*

On the back of the letter was a postscript:

I have to thank you – as I am confident that you were responsible – for the copy of the 'C— of V—' that arrived yesterday. The accompanying note from the bookseller announced that it had been obtained for me, after much searching, on the instructions of a valued customer of his, who wished to remain anonymous. I do not need to say how grateful I am that my cabinet now contains such a fine copy of this most interesting work, or how much I miss our regular bibliographic conversations. I have no one now with whom I can share my little enthusiasms; no one, indeed, to whom I can turn in the confident anticipation of delight in their company. But these are matters that belong to a former, and happier, time.*

With a sigh, I laid the letter on my work-table. I had nothing to say in reply, and there it would remain, unanswered. Even if I had possessed the proof of my identity that had been taken from me through the perfidy of Miss Carteret, I would have been unwilling to request Mr Tredgold to intercede on my behalf. The risk of catastrophe for the firm, and of professional opprobrium and scandal for himself, would have been too great. Now that the proof had been destroyed, there was no help left. Feeling a sudden oppression of spirits, I retired to my bed.

I AWOKE SUDDENLY, AT A LITTLE BEFORE MIDNIGHT. FOR TWO NIGHTS past, I had experienced that most fearful dream of mine, in which I find myself alone in the midst of a vast columned chamber in the depths of the earth, my flickering candle revealing nothing but Stygian darkness without end on every side; but then, as always, I

*[*The Cabinet of Venus.* See p. 232. *Ed.*]

realize – with suffocating terror – that I am not alone, as I had believed. Maddened with fear, I await each time the expected soft pressure on the shoulder, and the little stream of warm breath, caressing my cheek as it extinguishes the candle's flame.

I could not face it a third time, and so I got up and tried to light the fire in my sitting-room, but it would not draw and soon puttered out. Wrapped in a blanket against the cold, I took up the third volume of the *Bibliotheca Duportiana* and sat before the dreary blank mouth of the fireplace.

I had reached the letter 'N': Nabbes's *Microcosmus: A morall maske* (1637); the works of Thomas Nashe; Pynson's *Natura Brevium* of 1494; Fridericus Nausea's *Of all Blasing Starres in Generall*, published in English by Woodcocke in 1577; Netter's *Sacramentalia* (Paris, François Regnault, 1523). I lingered for a moment over Dr Daunt's description of this rare work of doctrinal theology – an exceptionally rare work; a most improbable work for a solicitor's clerk, on eighty pounds a year, to possess.

At eight o'clock the next morning I was standing at the top of the stairs, listening. At last I heard it: the sound of Fordyce Jukes's door closing behind him. Once at the bottom, I lingered for a moment or two, smelling the cold damp air coming in from the street. The door was locked, as I expected, but I had come prepared with a large selection of skeleton keys, acquired during the course of my work for Mr Tredgold, and soon gained entry.

The apartment was as I remembered it from my last uninvited visit: neat and comfortable, swept and polished, and containing an extraordinary number of fine and valuable objects. But only one of them interested me at that moment.

The lock of the cabinet presented no difficulty. I reached in and took out what I sought: Thomas Netter, *Sacramentalia* – folio, Paris, Regnault, 1523. It bore the same bookplate as that of the first edition of Felltham's *Resolves,* secreted by Miss Eames in Lady Tansor's burial chamber. There were a dozen or so other books of rare quality in the cabinet. They all carried the same plate. The books; the paintings and prints on the walls; the *objets* in the cabinets – all of the first quality, all portable, and all undoubtedly stolen from Evenwood. I carefully replaced the book, re-locked the cabinet, and then the staircase door.

This, then, had been Daunt's 'new tack', as revealed to me by Pettingale. Like the despicable ingrate that he was, he had removed these rare and exceedingly valuable items from his patron's house, and had stowed them away here, in the rooms of his creature, Fordyce Jukes, until he should have need of them. How he came to employ Jukes in this way did not concern me; but it was now clear to me how my enemy had been apprised of all my movements. There would be no trail leading back to Daunt, that was sure. But Jukes was a different matter.

Back in my room, I composed a short letter, in capital letters and using my left hand:

DEAR LORD TANSOR, —

I WISH TO BRING TO YOUR ATTENTION A MOST SERIOUS MATTER, CONCERNING A NUMBER OF VALUABLE ITEMS THAT I BELIEVE HAVE BEEN UNLAWFULLY REMOVED FROM YOUR COUNTRY RESIDENCE. THE ITEMS IN QUESTION, WHICH INCLUDE SEVERAL BOOKS OF GREAT RARITY, MAY BE FOUND, QUITE OPEN TO VIEW, IN THE ROOMS OF F. JUKES, SOLICITOR'S CLERK, 1 TEMPLE-STREET, WHITEFRIARS, GROUND FLOOR.

I ASSURE YOU, MY LORD, THAT THIS INFORMATION IS PERFECTLY ACCURATE, AND THAT I HAVE NO OTHER MOTIVE IN SETTING IT BEFORE YOU THAN A SINCERE REGARD FOR YOUR POSITION AS THE PRESENT REPRESENTATIVE OF

AN ANCIENT AND DISTINGUISHED FAMILY, AND AN EARNEST DESIRE TO SEE JUSTICE DONE.

I AM, SIR, YOUR VERY
OBEDIENT SERVANT,
*'CHRYSAOR'**

So much for Fordyce Jukes.

WINDMILL-STREET, DUSK.

The drabs, all rouged up for business, were beginning to swarm out of the surrounding courts and into the streets. I lingered for a while in Ramsden's coffee-house, and then sauntered along to the Three Spies.† A dirty little gonoph‡ tried to pick my pocket as I stood lighting my cigar, but I turned just in time and knocked him down, to the general amusement of all around.

Several of the drabs gave me the eye, but there was nothing that took my fancy. Then, as I was about to move off, a girl came out of the Three Spies, carrying an umbrella. She looked up at the sky, and was preparing to walk past me when I stopped her.

'Excuse me. Why, of course! Mabel, is it not?'

She eyed me up and down.

'And who, may I ask, wants to know?'

And then she smiled her recognition.

'Mr Glapthorn, I think. How do you do?' Delightfully, she gave me a kiss on the cheek. She smelled of soap and eau de Cologne.

I replied that I was all the better for seeing her and asked after

*[The sword of Justice wielded by Sir Artegal in Spenser's *Faerie Queene*. *Ed.*]
†[A public-house at No. 11 Windmill Street, Haymarket. *Ed.*]
‡[An inferior, usually juvenile, street thief and pickpocket. *Ed.*]

her employer, the enterprising Madame Mathilde, and also her sister Cissie, for I had a sudden strong hankering to reacquaint myself with these most accommodating *soeurs de joie.*

Cissie was in Gerrard-street, I was informed, and so after some refreshment at the Opera Tavern, we repaired thither through the rain. Up the stairs we went, to find Miss Cissie warming her pretty toes by the fire.

'Well, ladies,' I said gaily, removing my hat and gloves, 'here we are again.'

AFTERWARDS, I WALKED DOWN TO LEICESTER-SQUARE. MINDED TO take some supper, I turned into Castle-street and entered Rouget's, having briefly inspected the offerings in Mr Quaritch's window *en route.** I took my seat by the window, and ordered up supper – Julienne soup, some *pâté d'Italie,* bread, and a bottle of red wine. For an hour or more I sat in gloomy contemplation of my desolation; then I called for another bottle.

At half past eleven, the waiter opened the door to the street for me to pass through, holding out his hand to assist me as I mounted the step, but I pushed him away with a curse. For a moment or two I was unable to remember where I was. A crowd of bravoes came rolling down the street towards me, and looked me up and down, thinking perhaps that I was ripe for picking. But I was still able to eye them back, defiantly spitting out my cigar butt as I did so. They continued on their way.

'Looking for business, sir?'

Damn it. I had nothing else to do, and Miss Mabel and Miss Cissie were already dim memories. She was young, not too dirty, and had a pretty smile.

*[The bookseller Bernard Quaritch, 16 Castle Street, Leicester Square. *Ed.*]

'Always looking for business, my dear.'

What was that? I turned as quickly as I could; but in my somewhat inebriated state, I lost my balance and fell against the girl. She tried to hold me up, but I was too heavy, and we both ended up on the muddy pavement.

''Ere, wot's your game?' she asked indignantly.

But I was no longer interested in a piece of cheap cunny. That tap on the shoulder had brought me to my senses.

I saw him reach into his pocket, and in another second the cosh was in his hand. The girl, screaming obscenities, scrambled up from the pavement and started to kick at him. As he turned to push her away, I drew out my pistol and pointed it straight into the ugly face of Josiah Pluckrose.

We stood thus, eyeball to eyeball, until he gave me an evil smile, calmly replaced the cosh in his pocket, and walked off, whistling.

MY ENCOUNTER WITH PLUCKROSE STUNG ME INTO ACTION, AND I SOON devised a plan, which, I hoped, would deprive Daunt of his formidable protector.

A man like Pluckrose, I reasoned, would have made many enemies. As I turned over this likelihood in my mind, I remembered something that Lewis Pettingale had said in passing, during our conversation in Gray's-Inn, concerning Isaac Gabb, the youngest member of the Newmarket gang to have been despatched by Pluckrose, known then as Mr Verdant.

According to Pettingale, Gabb the Younger's brother had kept a public-house in Rotherhithe; a moment's consultation of the Directory on my return to Temple-street quickly identified the establishment and its location. Knowing from my own experience the general disposition of the population of Rotherhithe, and knowing also from Pettingale that Gabb Senior had expressed a clear desire to return the favour to his brother's killer, if only he could find him, it seemed most probable that this gentleman might not be averse to knowing Mr Verdant's real name and present whereabouts.

So far, so good. But where was Pluckrose now residing? He had surely moved from Weymouth-street, where he had been living when he married poor Agnes Baker. I consulted the current issue of the Directory and, to my amazement, found him listed therein. Confirmation that Mr J. Pluckrose was the present occupier of Number 42, Weymouth-street, was soon provided by the scullery maid from Number 40; Mr Pluckrose, it seems, had not vacated the house after the death of his wife, but had brazenly remained there, in defiance of his neighbours' disapproval, ever since.

Armed with this salient fact, I set off for Rotherhithe.

MR ABRAHAM GABB WAS A SHORT, LEAN-SHANKED, GIMLET-EYED gentleman possessing the vicious aspect of a terrier perpetually on the look-out for something to sink his teeth into and shake until its back-bone cracked. The public-house in Rotherhithe of which he was lord and master was, like himself, small, dirty, and vicious by reputation. Mine host regarded me warily as I approached the bar; but I was used to such places, and to men such as Mr Gabb, and had only to look him in the eye, slap down some coins, and say but a few choice words before I had his complete attention.

As he digested the information that I put before him, his terrier eyes began to glint – no doubt in eager anticipation of renewing his acquaintance with the gentleman who had undoubtedly cut short his brother's life. My plan succeeded more easily than I could have anticipated. As he had only ever known Pluckrose by his soubriquet of 'Mr Verdant', it had hitherto been impossible for Gabb to hunt down his brother's killer. Knowing now where he lived, and under what name, the landlord was in a position to mete out the vengeance that he had long contemplated. Throwing back my brandy, I expressed myself heartily gratified that I had been able to perform this trifling service to him.

But Mr Gabb was wary, and said nothing by way of reply; then, calling over two ugly looking, bull-backed bruisers who had been leaning together, deep in conversation, at the other end of the bar, he left me alone, and the three of them engaged in a huddled conference. At length, after much whistling and pursing of lips, the landlord, nodding knowingly to his two compatriots, turned back towards me.

'You're sure Verdant is there?' Mr Gabb, still wary, fixed me with his eye as he stroked his dirty chin as an aid to comprehension.

'As sure as I'm standing here.'

'And wot's your int'rest in the matter?' he growled suspiciously.

'Hygiene!' I declaimed. 'It is a passion of mine. Filth – physical and moral – appals me. I am an eager promoter of clean water, clean thoughts, and the proper disposal of waste. The streets are awash with filth of every description. I simply wish to enlist you and your comrades in my crusade, by encouraging you to make a start on the permanent removal of filth from Number 42, Weymouth-street, at your earliest convenience.'

'You're mad,' said Mr Abraham Gabb, 'stark mad.'

Thursday, 30th November 1854

Cold, clinging fog. There was nothing to see from my window but the dim dark forms of wet roofs and smoking chimneys, and nothing to hear but the muffled sound of people and carriages passing unseen up and down the street, the wheezing cough of the law stationer who lived on the floor below, and the doleful sound of distant bells tolling out the interminable hours. Despite my earlier resolve to strike at Daunt before he struck at me, I found myself sunk again in indolence. The weeks were passing, and still I had done nothing. And this was the reason.

On the 24th of November, *The Times* had announced the engagement of the distinguished poet, Mr Phoebus Rainsford Daunt, and Miss Emily Carteret, daughter of the late Mr Paul Carteret. Every day since then I had sat for hours on end, staring at the printed words, and in particular at the conclusion of the announcement: '*The wedding will take place at St Michael and All Angels, Evenwood, on the 1st of January next. Miss Carteret will be given away by her noble relative, Lord Tansor.*' I had even fallen asleep at the table and woken to find my cheek pressed against the black print.

But today had been different. The announcement from *The Times* had been consigned to the flames, along with my irresolution. At one o'clock, I walked out in order to accomplish various errands, ending my expedition with an early dinner at the Wellington,* where I was not known.

'Will you take some beef, sir?' the waiter asked.

'Certainly,' I replied.

He picked up a heavy, ivory-handled carving-knife, which he first brought to a nice edge with a sharpening steel, before cutting away at the joint most dexterously. It was a joy to behold the succulent slices of flesh falling onto the platter. When he had laid down his knife and brought the steaming plate to my table, I asked him whether he would be good enough to fetch me some brandy-and-water. By the time he returned, I had gone; and so had his knife.

*[At 160, Piccadilly. *Ed.*]

I made my way home via Weymouth-street, where, to my delight, I encountered great excitement. A large crowd had gathered outside Number 42, and a police van was drawn up in front of the house.

'What is going forward?' I enquired of a post-man, bag on shoulder, who was standing on the pavement humming softly to himself as he observed the scene.

'Murder,' he said, matter-of-factly. 'Occupier beaten to death and thrown from first-floor window.' At which he resumed his tuneless humming.

Silently approbating Mr Abraham Gabb and his associates for their admirable promptitude and efficiency, I went on my way, rejoicing that the terrible violence meted out by Josiah Pluckrose to poor undeserving Agnes Baker, and to the equally undeserving Paul Carteret, had been turned back on the perpetrator. He had escaped a stretching* because of me; but I had finally brought him to account.

So much for Pluckrose. Now – at last – for his master.

*[i.e. being hanged. *Ed.*]

· 46 ·

*Consummatum est**

Monday, 11th December 1854

I awoke with a start at a little after six, having dozed off in my chair an hour or so earlier. It was here at last. The day of reckoning.

I had slept lightly, having taken only a small swig of Dalby's before retiring early. Today, I would need all my wits about me.

Outside, the street was curiously silent, and the morning light seemed unnaturally bright for the time of year. Then I heard the sound of a shovel being scraped on the pavement. Jumping up, I rushed to the window to find that the usual vista of sooty roofs had been magically transformed by a thick covering of snow, whose purity, dazzling even under a dense slate sky, was quite at odds with the dirt and sin that lay beneath its fleecy embrace.

My mind was clear, now that the day was finally here, and I felt an eager surge of excitement at the imminent prospect of taking my long-delayed revenge on my enemy. The loss of Pluckrose must surely have unnerved him; and this advantage had been swiftly followed by the arrest of Fordyce Jukes, as related to me in a letter, received the day before, from Mr Tredgold. I had not told him of my betrayal, nor of how everything I had laboured so long to acquire had been lost beyond recall. In a few brief notes sent down to Canterbury, I had assured him that all was going along very well, and that Miss Carteret and I had been laying our plans.

*['It is finished'. *Ed.*]

In the reply he had now sent to the last of these hastily composed communications, I detected an anxious impatience, which I much regretted; but I was determined, at all costs, to keep my employer in ignorance of the true situation, and of what I was about to do.

The letter did, however, contain the welcome news concerning Jukes.

You may or may not be aware that, following information received from an anonymous source, Jukes has been found in possession of a large number of very precious objects, every one of which appears to have been stolen, over a period of time, from Evenwood. He claims that he merely stored these items under instruction from the person actually responsible for the thefts. And the person he names? None other than Mr Phoebus Daunt! Of course no one believes him. It is too ridiculous, and a dastardly slur on the reputation of a great literary man (so goes the general view). Jukes has certainly had opportunity to carry out the thefts during the time that he has been in my employ, having often accompanied me to Evenwood on business, and at other times when he was sent there alone on various errands. I very much fear his protestations will count for little when his case comes on. Nothing, I think, can lessen Lord Tansor's exalted estimation of Mr Phoebus Daunt. Jukes has of course been dismissed from the firm, and is presently awaiting trial. I shudder to think that such a person was in my trusted employ for so long, and the anonymous informant, whoever he may be, has my sincere gratitude for thus exposing him. As a result of the police investigation, it has now also emerged that Jukes may have been implicated in the defrauding of his previous employer, Pentecost and Vizard, in the year 1841. He is said to have facilitated a burglary, during which a number of the firm's blank cheques were stolen, which, if true, makes me shudder that I placed my trust in him for so long.

On another matter, what you certainly will not know is that I have decided, in consultation with my brother and sister, that I shall formally retire from the firm on the 31st of this month. Mr Donald Orr is to become

Senior Partner (my sister's views on this promotion are extremely severe), whilst I propose to take a little house in the country, play my violincello, and tend my collections, though I confess that they do not hold the fascination that once they did. Rebecca is to come and keep house for me – Harrigan has deserted her, and it now appears that they were never married. It is an arrangement that suits both parties very well. Leaving London is for the best, I think. The world is much changed, and really I wish to have as little to do with it as possible.

Dear, kind Mr Tredgold! How I wished I could turn back from the path on which my feet were now set! But it was too late. The past had been closed off; the future was dark; I had only my present unshakeable resolve, as minute succeeded minute, and the snow began to fall.

MY FIRST TASK WAS TO REMOVE MY MOUSTACHIOS. WHEN THE OPERATION was over, I stood for some moments regarding myself in the cracked mirror above my wash-stand. I was bemused. Who was this person? The boy who dreamed of sailing away to the Country of the Houyhnhnms? Or the young man who wished to become a great scholar? No: I saw clearly who I was, and what I had become. I saw, too, that I did not have, and would never have, the strength to turn aside from visiting retribution on my enemy, and so reclaim my former innocent self. I was damned, and I knew it.

The thought of who I had once been, before I discovered the truth about myself, suddenly conjured up a vivid memory of an event that I had almost forgotten until revived by some strange unconscious mechanism on this day of vengeance.

When I was eight, and in my second year at Tom Grexby's little school, our small band of scholars, three in number by now, was augmented by the son of a corn-factor from Wareham, Rowland

Beesley by name, who had been sent to Sandchurch to live temporarily in the care of his aunt. Beesley tried Tom's patience sorely from the start, and it was not long before he took it into his head to cross me – which, even at that age, was a foolish thing to do.

After several preliminary skirmishes, in which I think it is fair to say I triumphed decisively, battle was joined in earnest on the day I brought to school, for Tom's perusal, my pride and joy – the first volume of the translation of M. Galland's *Les milles et une nuits*, from which I used to read to my mother.* I was late for school that morning and had run as fast I could go down the hill to Tom's cottage, my treasure – wrapped in an old piece of dark-green plush that I had borrowed from Beth's work-basket – tucked tightly under my arm. I arrived ten minutes past the time, panting, and hurriedly placed the book, still wrapped in its plush, on a little table by the front door.

Towards the end of the morning lesson, Beesley asked to be excused. He returned after a few minutes, took his place, and the lesson continued. When at last Tom said we could go off, I waited until the others had left and then, eager to show him my treasure, jumped up and ran out into the sitting-room.

The piece of green plush lay on the floor. Of the book there was no sign.

I let out a howl of rage, rushed towards the door, and then out into the street. I knew for sure that Beesley had taken it, and I ran about screaming 'Scheherazade! Scheherazade!' like a mad thing, trying to see where he might have hidden my most precious possession; but there was no sign of either the book or the thief. And then I happened to glance into the old stone water-trough that stood just outside the King's Head. There, floating on the dark green water, was my book, its pages sodden and torn, the

*[See note, p. 26. *Ed.*]

spine ripped off and floating separately, ruined past all remedy.

There was not a doubt who had been responsible for this outrage; and so the following Sunday, when Beesley and his aunt were in church, as I knew they would be, I made my way to the back garden of Miss Henniker's house. It was a raw, wet November morning, and through one of the windows I could see a fire burning merrily. On the floor were scattered a number of playthings, amongst them a tin box, which I knew contained my foe's much-prized army of toy soldiers. He had brought this box to school on his first day and had set out the contents proudly on Tom's parlour table: a whole encampment, carved and painted, comprising two or three dozen mounted and foot soldiers, together with tents, camp followers, cannon balls and cannon.

A little while after Miss Henniker and her nephew had left for church, I saw the maid unlock the terrace doors to shake out a duster. When she had finished her work, I crept to the terrace, and was soon inside the room.

It burned well, that little wooden army. I stood and watched the conflagration for a moment or two, warming myself by the flames that spat and darted on the hearth, and saying to myself the rhyme that my foster-mother used to sing to me in which the appearance of Bonaparte was threatened if I did not go to sleep. I smiled to myself as the words now came back to me over the waste of years:

And he'll beat you, beat you, beat you,
And he'll beat you all to pap.
And he'll eat you, eat you, eat you,
Every morsel, snap, snap, snap.

And now, like Rowland Beesley, another enemy must pay for taking what was mine.

. . .

I HAVE CALLED IN A FAVOUR AND HAVE SET SOMEONE TO WATCH OVER the house in Mecklenburgh-square, day and night. Daunt is still there. No one has called. On Thursday, he went to a dinner at the London Tavern* with a number of other literary men. Last night he stayed at home the whole evening. But I know for certain where he will be tonight.

Last Tuesday week, my spy – a certain William Blunt, of Crucifix-lane, Borough – brought word that Lord Tansor was to give a dinner in Park-lane. It is to be this very evening. The Prime Minister† is to be amongst the guests. There is so much to celebrate! His Lordship has a new heir – he has now been named, in proper legal form, in the recently signed codicil to his Lordship's will. This would be cause enough to kill the fatted calf; but to augment the general joy, the heir is to marry Miss Emily Carteret, his Lordship's cousin once removed, who, following the tragic death of her father, will herself succeed to the Tansor title in the course of time. Such an exquisitely fortuitous match! And then, to cap it all, the heir has just published a new work – the thirteenth to be offered to a grateful public – and Lord Tansor had been appointed Her Majesty's Special Envoy and Plenipotentiary to the Emporers of Brazil and Haiti and the Republics of New Granada and Venezuela. During his Lordship's absence, the newly married couple are to take up residence at Evenwood, and Lord Tansor further proposes to place the management of his estates, and of

*[In Bishopsgate Street. *Ed.*]

†[The Earl of Aberdeen (George Hamilton Gordon, 1784–1860). He became Prime Minister after the resignation of the Earl of Derby in 1852. He was widely blamed for the mismanagement of the Crimean War and resigned in February 1855. He would have gone to the dinner alone: his second wife had died in 1833. *Ed.*]

his many business interests, in the capable hands of his heir, Mr Phoebus Daunt.

The establishment in his Lordship's town-house was a relatively small one; and so, to ensure the smooth running of so large and splendid an occasion, it had been necessary for extra servants to be hired. Advertisements were placed, and Mrs Horatia Venables, proprietress of the Office for Domestic Servants, Great Coram-street, had been engaged by his Lordship's agent, Captain Tallis, to secure and evaluate applicants for the evening. Amongst those who offered themselves in Great Coram-street for the available positions was a certain Ernest Geddington – a name I had used from time to time in my work.

'I see you have lived as a footman under a butler for Lord Wilmersham,'* said Mrs Venables, looking over her spectacles at Mr Geddington.

'I had that honour,' replied Mr Geddington.

'And before that, you were a footman in the establishment of the Duke of Devonshire, at Chatsworth?'

'I was.'

'And you have a character from his Grace?'

'One can easily be secured, if it is required.'

'There is no need,' replied Mrs Venables loftily. 'Lord Wilmersham's recommendation here will suffice, though I confess I have not had the pleasure of advising his Lordship before on the hiring of servants; but as this is only a temporary appointment, for one evening only, I am content to forgo the usual formalities. The standard today has been dreadfully low. You will present yourself at Lord Tansor's residence in Park-lane on Monday morning, at ten sharp, asking for his Lordship's butler, Mr James Cranshaw.'

*[Apparently fictitious. *Ed.*]

She handed me a paper on which she had indicated my suitability for the position. 'Livery will be provided. Please to remain here a little longer for your measurements to be taken.'

I did as I was told. Before I left Mrs Venables' establishment, I learned that my principal task would be to attend the guests as they arrived and departed in their carriages, and to be on hand during the dinner to open doors and perform any other necessary duties.

It was now half past seven on the great day. I boiled my kettle to make some tea, then cut myself a slice of bread and sat at my work-table to take my breakfast. There was paper all around me. 'Note on Dr A. Daunt: Feb. 1849' – 'Description of Millhead, taken from F. Walker, *A Journey Through Lancashire*, 1833' – 'Memorandum: Information supplied by J. Hooper and others', June 1850' – 'Evenwood: Architectural and Historical Notes, Sept. 1851' – 'The Tansor Barony: Genealogical Notes, March 1852' – 'Notes on conversation with W. Le G. re: King's Coll., June 1852'. Lists, questions, letters. My life, and his. Here, spread across my work-table. Truth and lies.

Le Grice left for the war last week, fortunately too late to take part in the bloody engagement at Inkerman,* though the reports now coming back, telling of the terrible privations being suffered by our troops, have given me great concern for his immediate prospects. The night before he sailed, we had a farewell dinner at the Ship and Turtle, during which he urged me once again to leave England until he returned.

'It'll be better, old chap,' he said.

Like me, he had concluded that our friend on the river had

*[The battle took place on 5 November 1854 – the day that Florence Nightingale arrived at the hospital at Scutari. *Ed.*]

been Pluckrose. Yet although I had confided in him concerning the punitive action taken by Mr Abraham Gabb and company, Le Grice had come to the same conclusion as I: that, even without the assistance of Pluckrose, Daunt still posed a threat to my safety. But I had not wished to admit the fact, given Le Grice's impending departure for the East; and so I had given him a false assurance that he need not concern himself on that score.

'I am certain that Daunt will do no harm to me. What possible reason can he have? He is to be married soon, and I am nothing to him any more. I can never forgive him, of course, but I intend to forget him.'

'And Miss Carteret?'

'You mean, of course, the future Mrs Phoebus Duport. I have forgotten her too.'

Le Grice's face darkened.

'Forget Daunt? Forget Miss Carteret? You may as well say that you intend to forget your name.'

'But I *have* forgotten my name,' I replied. 'I have no idea who I am.'

'Damn you, G,' he growled. 'I can't talk to you when you're like this. You know as well as I do that the danger from Daunt is real, Pluckrose or no Pluckrose. For the sake of our friendship, I urge you to go travelling. Give it all up. Go away – the longer the better. If I were Daunt, I'd want you dead for what you knew about me. Even though you can't prove what you know, things might still be made jolly awkward for him if you had a mind to do so.'

'But I don't,' I said quietly. 'Really, I don't. There's nothing to fear; so now, drink up, and here's to the next time you and I sit down together over grilled fowl and gin-punch.' Of course he saw through my feeble pretence. But had he also seen what burned in my eyes, which nothing could disguise or assuage?

We parted on the pavement. A handshake, a brief 'Good-night!', and he was gone.

NOW, ON THE MORNING OF THE 11TH OF DECEMBER, I SAT FOR A WHILE at my table, wondering where Le Grice was now, and what he was doing. 'May the gods keep you safe, you old bonehead,' I whispered. Then, feeling like a boy again, I threw on my great-coat and muffler, and went out into the snow – my heart as light as a child's – to look upon Great Leviathan in his winter clothes.

London was going about its usual business, despite the beautiful inconvenience of the weather. The ice-carts were out, loaded with glistening frozen fragments from ponds and streams, instead of produce from the green-market; and the omnibuses were being pulled through the rutted accumulations of dirtied snow in the roadways by extra horses. People walked along, heads down through the biting cold, with mufflers – for those who had them – wound tight over their mouths. Hats and coats and capes were flecked and dabbed with white, and every public-house carried notices advertising the provision within of hot spiced ale or similar warming potations. It was not a day to be without coat or shoes, though there were many – hundreds, thousands – who must do so; and the misery that is ever present in the metropolis was made more wretched still by the stinging cold. And yet the wondrous sight – of roofs and towers, spires and monuments, streets and squares, painted over by snow that had been shaped and scooped by the bitter east wind – elated me as I walked down Long Acre, with the smell of baked apples and roasted chestnuts in my nose.

I was still hungry after my frugal breakfast, and the pleasant sight of a coffee-house tempted me in to take a second meal. Afterwards, I sauntered back through snow-laden streets and courts to the Strand. It was not long before I became aware that I was being followed.

In Maiden-lane, I paused by the stage-entrance to the Adelphi Theatre to light up a cigar. Out of the tail of my eye, I saw my pursuer stop a few paces behind and quickly look into the window of a butcher's shop. I threw down the cigar and walked calmly towards the hooded figure.

'Good morning, Mademoiselle Buisson.'

'*Mon Dieu,* how extraordinary!' she exclaimed. 'To meet you here! My, my!'

I smiled and offered her my arm. 'You seem to have been out in the snow for a considerable time,' I said, looking down at the soaking hem of her skirt.

'Perhaps I have,' she smiled. 'I have been looking for someone.'

'And have you found them?'

'Why yes, Mr — Glapthorn. I think perhaps I have.'

In the Norfolk Hotel, Strand, we called for coffee and she threw back the hood of her cloak and removed her snow-dusted bonnet.

'I do not think we need continue to pretend,' I said. 'I believe your friend will have informed you concerning recent events.'

'She is no friend of mine anymore,' she replied, shaking out her blonde curls. 'I consider her to be – well, I do not wish to say what I consider her to be. We were once the closest of companions, you know, but now I hate her for what she has done to you.'

She gave me a look of quiet significance.

'It was just a pleasant game at first, and I was happy to help her play it, though of course much was kept from me. But as I began to understand how things were with you, and that you truly loved her, then I told her that she must put a stop to it; but she would not. And when Mr Daunt joined us in Paris—'

'In Paris?'

'Yes. I am sorry.'

'It does not signify. Go on.'

'When Mr Daunt came to join us, my heart began to break for you, knowing that you would be thinking of her constantly, and believing that she was thinking of you. That cruel note that she made me write to you was the last straw. I tried to warn you, did I not? But I think by then that you were past all warning.'

'I am grateful to you for your kind feelings towards me, Mademoiselle. But I do not think Miss Carteret could help herself. I do not and cannot defend her – not in the least – nor can I ever absolve her for deceiving me; but I understand what drove her to treat me as she did.'

'Do you?'

'Why, yes. It was that most potent, and most plausible, of motives: love. Oh yes, I understand her very well.'

'Then I consider you to be most generous. Do you not wish to punish her?'

'Not at all. How can I blame her for being a slave to love? Love makes slaves of us all.'

'So you blame no one for what has happened to you, Mr Glapthorn?'

'Perhaps you should call me by the name I was given at birth.' She gave a little nod of understanding.

'Very well, Mr Glyver. Is no one to blame for the loss of what was rightfully yours?'

'Oh yes,' I replied. 'Someone is to blame. But not her.'

'You still love her, of course,' she said with a sigh. 'I had hoped—'

'Hoped?'

'It really does not matter. Of what interest can my hopes possibly have for you? *Eh bien,* this is what I wished to say to you, my dear Mr Dark Horse. You may think this matter is over; that, having stolen your life, your adversary is content. But he is not content. I have overheard something that gives me great concern, and which should give you concern also. He has taken grave exception – very grave exception – to what has happened to his associates, and for which he blames you. I do not know, of course, whether he is right to do so; it is enough for me to know that he does; and this being so, I urge you – as a friend – to take note. He is not a man to make idle threats, as you must know. In a word, he thinks you pose a danger to him, and this he will not tolerate.'

'You have heard him threaten me, then?'

'I have heard enough to make me walk through the snow for this past hour to speak to you. And now I have done my duty, Mr Edward Glyver, who was once dear Mr Glapthorn, and I now must go.'

She rose to leave, but I held out my hand to stop her. 'Does she ever speak of me?' I asked. 'To you?'

'We do not enjoy the familiarity we once did,' she replied, and I saw and heard the regret that she felt. 'But I believe that you have left a mark on her heart, though it pleases her to deny it. I hope that is of some comfort to you. And so good-bye, Mr Edward Glyver. You may kiss my hand, if you please.'

'With the greatest of pleasure, Mademoiselle.'

I WAS BACK IN TEMPLE-STREET BY HALF PAST NINE TO MAKE MY FINAL preparations, happy in the now confirmed knowledge that my enemy wished me dead. It would make what I was soon to do so much easier.

On with my wig – courtesy of Messrs Careless & Sons, theatrical costumiers of Finch-lane, Cornhill – and a pair of wire-framed spectacles. A decent but shabby suit, with a capacious inside pocket, completed the ensemble. Into the pocket went the knife, wrapped in a piece of cloth, that I had purloined from the Wellington. I was ready.

I proceeded first to the Adelphi Theatre, where I purchased a ticket for the evening's performance: this I then gave to my spy, William Blunt, who was to take my seat at the performance in order to provide me with an alibi. Near Stanhope Gate in Hyde-park, a little across from Lord Tansor's house in Park-lane, I next located the place that I had identified a few days earlier as being suitable for concealing a bag containing my best clothes. At last, as instructed by Mrs Venables, I presented myself to Mr Cranshaw at ten sharp with my recommendation from that lady.

I was soon directed to a small bare-boarded room where I was to don my livery and powder my hair – or, rather, my wig. 'Powder,' boomed Mr Cranshaw loftily, 'is insisted upon by his Lordship.' After I had wetted the wig with water, I rubbed soap into it, and then combed through the wet mass before applying the powder with the puff provided. Then on with the livery: a stiff, white shirt; white stockings and silver-buckled pumps; blue plush knee breeches; a claret-coloured swallow-tailed coat, with silver buttons and matching waistcoat. Once powdered and liveried, I went along to the servants' hall to be instructed, with the other temporary footmen, by Mr Cranshaw. Then I went quietly about the place, as if engaged on some errand or other, getting clear in my head the disposition of the below-stairs passages and rooms. The rest of the day was spent in undertaking various tedious duties – carrying chairs and flower arrangements into the dining-room, memorizing the order of dishes in case we were called upon to assist in bringing them up, rouging* silver, familiarizing ourselves with the guest-list and seating-order – 'there were to be

*[Rouge was a preparation of oxide of iron used to clean silver plate. *Ed.*]

some forty persons at table'; and so on until darkness began to fall, the curtains were drawn, and the candles and lamps were lit.

Lord Tansor appeared at six o'clock to assure himself that all was in order. Our little army of menials lined up in the vestibule and bowed as he passed. But of course he paid no heed to me. I was but a liveried servant.

At seven o'clock, I presented myself for carriage duty, taking up my station by the front door with two other footmen.

So far, so good. I had done what was required of me by Mr Cranshaw, and had aroused no one's suspicion. But now I must wait upon events, for I had no other plan than to insinuate myself into the establishment and, if I could, put myself close to Daunt. Beyond that, I had no immediate thought. If this last act of our lives was destined to play out in my favour, then I would be most content. If not, so be it. I would have lost nothing – for I had nothing.

And so I waited, standing mutely just inside the front door, wondering when he would come – and when *she* would come.

The carriages began to arrive. First, I handed out the famous Madame Taglioni* (for whom, though the lady was by no means in the first flush of youth, Lord Tansor cherished an uncharacteristically sentimental regard), and then the fat daughter of Lord Cotterstock (a costive old roué, with a face like weathered rock, who was already half dead from an unmentionable ailment), followed by her equally porcine mamma and brother. The carriages continued to roll in through the snow to pull up under the lantern of the *porte-cochère*. Ambassadors, Honourable Members, bankers, generals, dukes and earls, and their ladies: I opened their carriage doors and helped them to disembark, and no one

*[Marie Taglioni (1801–84), the celebrated Swedish-Italian dancer, for whom her father, Filippo Taglioni, created the ballet *La Sylphide* (1832), the first ballet in which a ballerina danced *en pointe* for the duration of the work. *Ed.*]

gave me a second glance. At last the Prime Minister himself arrived, to be greeted by Lord and Lady Tansor, followed, in the very next moment, by a sleek carriage bearing the Duport arms.

As I opened the carriage door, I was met first by her perfume; then, as I bent to fold down the step, I saw her feet, encased in delicate grey-kid pumps decorated with jet beading. She gave me her gloved hand, but I was invisible to her. As she emerged from the carriage, her warm breath misted the air; and for a passing moment, with her hand resting in mine, it was as though she belonged to me once more. The thought made me forget what I am supposed to be, and I began to close my grip gently round her fingers. She shot an angry, insulted look at me, instantly removed her hand, and swept up the steps. There she paused for a moment and looked back.

'You there! Hold the door!'

I obeyed his command, and he stepped down from the carriage – immaculate, dressed in the highest taste and quality. I made an obeisance as he passed and, as I closed the carriage door behind him, I glanced up to see him take Miss Carteret's arm at the top of the steps and lead her inside.

After the last guests had arrived, I was sent to the dining-room to take up my station by the double doors that led into the vestibule. There I remained, still unregarded by all who passed back and forth, even by my fellow servants. I stood motionless, but my eyes were busy, looking for my opportunity.

My faithless girl was seated at the head of the table, an ethereal figure in pale blue silk surmounted by a *barège* overskirt sewn with gold and silver stars, her black hair set off to perfection by a tulle and lace cap ornamented with pale pink satin ribbon. On her left sat a dessicated young gentleman whom I identified from the guest list as the Honourable John Tanker, MP; on her right was Phoebus Daunt, in all his smiling pride.

After all the guests had settled themselves at the sumptuously decorated table, which gleamed and glittered as candlelight flashed off an abundance of gold and silver and crystal, the soup was brought in. Lord Tansor had become an enthusiast for *service à la Française*, no doubt following its introduction at Evenwood when his *protégé* had come of age; and so the soup was succeeded by fish, which in turn was followed by the *entrées* – a dozen in all – and the roasts, and so on, in due order, to the sweets and desserts. It was some relief to me that I had not been required to join the band of brother footmen who were handing round the dishes, for as they bent down to each guest, they had to say aloud the name of the dish they were offering. I watched with fascinated interest as one of them brought his lips close to Miss Carteret's ear to ask if she would take some of the *Boeuf à la Flammande*.* She made the most delicate gesture of assent, and then held up her hand to prevent him placing too much of the dish on her plate. Next to her, Daunt received a much larger portion and then, just as the footman was about to turn to the next guest, called him back to request some more.

In the place of honour at the head of the board, the Prime Minister sat with Lord Tansor, engaged in close and detached conversation. Lord Aberdeen looked tired and drawn, no doubt from the increasing strain of prosecuting the campaign in the Crimea, and more than once I saw Lord Tansor place a reassuring hand on his arm. Around them conversation and laughter flowed, to a contrapuntal rhythm of tinkling glasses and the sound of the finest gold cutlery on Sèvres plates.

But now the soup and fish had come and gone, and so had the *entrées* and roasts. The sweets and ices had been cleared away to

*[A rich and expensive dish consisting of ribs of beef larded and braised, together with fresh (or forced) mushrooms, truffles, meat-balls and Madeira. *Ed.*]

make room for six huge branched epergnes,* laden with dried fruits, nuts, cakes, and sweet biscuits. Lord Tansor rose to his feet, glass in hand, and his guests began to fall silent.

'My Lords, Ladies, and Gentleman,' he began, his deep baritone voice instantly commanding attention. 'I give you a toast. To Mr Phoebus Daunt, whom I am proud to call my son, as well as my heir, and to his future wife, Miss Emily Carteret.'

Glasses were charged and raised, and the happy couple were toasted, to resounding clapping and cheers. Then, from a gallery at the far end of the room, a small military band struck up with 'See, the Conquering Hero Comes'.† After the last notes had died away, the heir himself responded with fulsome deference, loquaciously thanking his Lordship for his graciousness and generosity, and then – of all things – quoting at length, without a scintilla of shame, from one of his own poems in praise of great men. He was succeeded by Lord Cotterstock, who struggled to his feet with the help of his son to thank Lord Tansor, on behalf of himself and the other distinguished guests, for his overwhelming hospitality and to congratulate his Lordship on his plenipotentiary appointment, 'a position,' he noted, looking sternly around him, as if to defy anyone to contradict him, 'that has not often been filled with such conspicuous distinction'.

All this time, Miss Carteret sat with a quiet little smile on her face, turning now towards her noble relative, now towards her lover: a smile, not of crowing triumph at her lot, but more of wistful content, as though she had emerged from some great trouble into a haven of settled security. I had watched her all evening,

*[Large ornamental dispensers of sweets, etc. *Ed.*]

†[From Handel's oratorio *Judas Maccabeus*, with a libretto by the Revd Thomas Morell. Composed to celebrate the English victory over the Young Pretender at Culloden and the return to London of the victorious Duke of Cumberland. First performed in 1747. *Ed.*]

drinking in every movement, every gesture; marvelling at her gaiety and assurance, and at her aching beauty. Never so beautiful as tonight! So lost was I in observing her that, for a moment, I did not notice that Daunt had risen from his place and was saying something to Lord Tansor. Then he moved away, nodding greetings to several of the guests, shaking hands as he passed, and stopping occasionally to receive the congratulations of some well-wisher. He approached the door where I was standing, and I inclined my head dutifully as he passed.

'Are you quite well, sir?' I heard Cranshaw asking him. 'You look rather pale.'

'One of my headaches, I fear. I'm off to take a little air before the ladies leave.'

'Very good, sir.'

With a thrill of anticipation, I seized my chance. As soon as Cranshaw had re-entered the dining-room, I slipped away, just in time to see Daunt's figure disappearing through a door at the back of the vestibule. Heart beating, I descended the stairs, and found my way as quickly as I could to the room in which my suit was hanging. Servants were coming and going, and there was a great babble and noise. No one paid any attention to me. In a flash, I retrieved the knife, and made my way to a glazed door at the end of the passage, through which I could see a flight of steps leading up the side of a lighted conservatory. Gently, I opened the door and stepped out into the cold night air. Would he come out? Was this the moment?

It had stopped snowing, though a few fluffy flakes continued to flutter down from an impenetrably dark sky. I heard a door open just above me and smelled cigar smoke on the air. He was here. *My enemy was here.*

A dark figure descended the steps from the conservatory. At the bottom he stopped and looked up; then he slowly crossed the border of light thrown out by the lamps at the top of the steps and passed into the snowy darkness beyond. I waited until he was six or seven feet from the steps before I left the shadowed recess from where I had been observing him.

I was amazed to find that I was still completely calm, as if I were contemplating some scene of surpassing, soul-easing beauty. All fear of danger, all apprehension of discovery, all confusion of purpose, all doubt, had fallen away. I saw nothing before me but this single figure of flesh, blood, and bone. The world was suddenly silent, as if Great Leviathan himself were holding his breath.

Daunt's footsteps were marked out in the pristine snow. One–two–three–four–five–six . . . I counted them as I carefully placed my own feet in each one. And then I called out to him.

'Sir! Mr Daunt, sir!'

He turned.

'What do you want?'

'A message from Lord Tansor, sir.'

He walked back towards me – ten paces.

'Well?'

We were almost face to face – and still he did not know me! There was not the faintest glimmer of recognition in his eyes. Just a moment longer, dear Phoebus. Then you will know me.

My right hand slipped inside my jacket, and round the bone handle of the freshly sharpened knife that had last been used to carve beef at the Wellington. The smoke of his cigar curled upwards to the cold sky, the end glowing as he inhaled.

'Don't just stand there, you stupid fellow. Give me your message.'

'My message? Why, here it is.'

It was done in a moment. The long pointed blade easily penetrated his evening suit, but I was not sure the wound was fatal. So I instantly withdrew the bloodied blade and then, as he staggered forward slightly, I readied myself for a second thrust, this time at his uncovered throat. He looked up at me, blinking rapidly. The cigar fell from his lips and lay smouldering on the ground.

Still upright, though swaying a little from side to side, he blinked at me again, this time in disbelief, and opened his mouth, as if to speak; but nothing came out. I took a step towards him; as I did so, his mouth opened again. This time, with a kind of breathless gurgle, he managed three words:

'Who are you?'

'Ernest Geddington, footman, at your service, sir.'

Coughing slightly, he was now leaning his head against my shoulder. I found it rather a touching gesture. We stood there for a moment, like lovers embracing. For the first time, I noticed that his thick black hair was brushed to conceal a little bald patch around the crown of his head.

Cradling my enemy in one arm, I raised the knife and struck the second blow.

'Revenge has a long memory,' I whispered, as he slipped slowly down into the snow.

HE LAY THERE, ON A PILLOW OF WINE-RED BLOOD, HIS FACE AS WHITE as the shroud of cold snow into which his body had fallen. My breath met the bitter air, forming little spurting clouds; but my enemy breathed no more. I kneeled down and looked into his face.

Snow flecked his beard. A little trickle of blood had drained from his mouth, staining his perfectly laundered shirt. His eyes were open, staring blankly at the over-arching sky.

Our great journey was at an end. But *how* had it ended? In victory, or defeat? And for whom? The two of us, Edward Glyver and Phoebus Daunt, friends once, had been brought to this moment by a power that neither of us could control, nor understand. He would never now enjoy the things that were rightfully mine; but I, too, had been denied their possession. I had taken my revenge, and he had paid the price that I had set for the many injuries he had done to me; but I felt scant comfort, and not a trace of elation, only the dull sense of a duty done.

I reached into my pocket and took out a piece of paper, on which I had copied some lines from a poem in the volume that Daunt had given to Le Grice.

The night has come upon me.
No more the breaking day,
No more the noontide's glare,
No more the evening's ray,
Soft as lovers' sighs.

For Death is the meaning of night;
The eternal shadow
Into which all lives must fall,
All hopes expire. *

They had struck me, on first reading them, as having – unusually for the author – some small merit, and I had carried them around with me ever since, as a kind of talisman. But I would need them no more. Placing the crumpled paper in his stiffening hands, I picked up the knife, and left him alone to face eternity.

IN A LARGE EARTHENWARE BOWL, ON A TABLE OUTSIDE THE KITCHEN, were dozens of dirty knives and forks soaking in hot water.

*[The poem from which these lines were taken is 'From the Persian', printed in Daunt's *Rosa Mundi; and Other Poems* (1854). *Ed.*]

Casually, I dropped the carving knife into the bowl as I walked past, along with my blood-soaked gloves, and went back up the stairs to the vestibule.

'Geddington!'

It was Mr Cranshaw, wearing an expression of deep disapproval. 'Where are your gloves, man?'

'I'm sorry, Mr Cranshaw,' I replied. 'I'm afraid I dirtied them.'

'Then go down and get some more. At once.'

He turned away; but then a servant, white-faced, suddenly appeared, hastening into the vestibule from the door that led out to the conservatory. He signalled to Mr Cranshaw, who went over to him. Whatever was said produced an expression of immediate shock in the butler. He said a few words to the servant, and then hurried into the dining-room.

Soon there was a sudden scraping of chairs, and an anxious hush descended on the guests, followed by a scream and the sound of shouting. Lord Tansor, walking quickly, with unseeing eyes, appeared in the doorway with Cranshaw, followed by three or four gentleman, including Lord Cotterstock's son, who broke away and came towards me.

'You, fellow,' he drawled. 'Run and fetch an officer. Quick as you like. There's murder done here. Mr Daunt is dead.'

'Yes, sir.'

The young man then waddled off towards the rear of the house, thinking of course that I had gone off to do his bidding. But I had not.

The hall was crowded now with a great commotion of guests all talking at once, the women in tears, the men standing in groups, loudly discussing the extraordinary turn of events; in the hubbub and confusion, I slowly made my way through the throng until I was at the door that led below stairs, my intention being to leave by one of the side entrances to the residence. At that moment, happening to look back to assure myself that no one was taking notice of me, I saw her.

She was standing alone in the dining-room doorway, alabaster pale, the tips of her fingers placed against her lips in a pathetic gesture of shock and bewilderment. Oh my dearest girl! I am become Death because of thee! Between us was an ocean of noise and tumult; but we were two opposing islands of desperate calm.

I was rooted to the spot, though I knew that every second I delayed brought discovery closer. Then, like the moon appearing from behind a cloud, she turned her face directly towards me, and our eyes met.

For a moment, I was sure, she did not see me; then her gaze seemed to narrow and intensify. But realization was slow to form; she hesitated, and in that briefest of spaces, between doubt and certainty, I turned and headed back through the crowd to the front door, expecting at any moment to hear my name being called out and the alarm raised. I reached the door, but no one stopped me. As I passed out onto the steps, I could not help glancing behind me, to assure myself that I was not about to be apprehended. Again, our eyes locked together as people ran hither and thither. I saw that she knew what I had done, and yet she did nothing. Then a little crowd closed round her, and she was lost to my sight, for ever.

I was on the bottom step when I heard her voice.

'Stop that man!'

Hampered by my silver-buckled pumps, I feared that I would quickly be taken; but when I reached the far side of Park-lane and looked back, I saw to my relief that I had given my pursuers the slip. Shivering with cold and anxiety, I ran like a mad thing through the snow-covered grass to the place where my bag was concealed; there, under the cold sky, beneath which my enemy at last lay dead, I threw off my livery and put on my suit and coat. In the distance I could hear shouting and the sound of a police whistle.

Leaving the Park, I was soon in Piccadilly, hailing a cab.

'Temple-street, Whitefriars,' I shouted to the cabman.

'Right you are, sir!'

I HAD PREPARED MYSELF FOR DISCOVERY. MY TRAVELLING BAG WAS packed; my documents in order. I hurriedly gathered together a few remaining items: my worn copy of Donne's sermons; my journal and shorthand epitomes of various documents; the watercolour of my mother's house; the discarded photograph of Evenwood taken on that hot June afternoon in 1850; and finally, the rosewood box in which my salvation had lain for so long without my knowing, and the copy of Felltham's *Resolves* that I had removed from Lady Tansor's tomb. This done, I collectd together all the remaining papers from my work-table, with the indexed notes that I had made over the years, piled them up in the grate, and threw a match on the heap. At the door, I looked back as the blaze took hold, a crackling furnace, consuming hope and happiness.

WITH MY MUFFLER DRAWN OVER MY FACE, I ENTERED MORLEY'S Hotel, Charing-cross, and called for a brandy-and-water and a room with a fire.

That night, with the snow beginning to fall once more, swathing the city in silence, I dreamed that I was standing on the cliff-top at Sandchurch. There is our little white house, and there the chestnut-tree by the gate. No school today, so I run, exulting, towards the semi-circles of white-painted stones that edge the narrow flower-beds on either side of the gate. Billick has not yet mended the rope ladder, but it still serves; so up I clamber, into the branches, into my crow's-nest. I have my spy-glass with me, and lie down to scan the shining horizon. In my mind, every sail is transformed: to the east, a vanguard of triremes sent by Caesar himself; to the west, low in the water, a Spanish treasure-ship freighted down with Indies gold; and, coming up from the south, slow and menacing, a horde of Barbary pirates intent on ravaging our quiet Dorset coast. Then there is a clatter of plates from the kitchen. Through the parlour window I can see Mamma writing at her work-table. She looks up and smiles as I wave.

Then I awoke and began to weep: not for what I had lost, or for the times that would never come again; not even for my poor broken heart; least of all for the death of my enemy; but for Lucas Trendle, the innocent red-haired stranger, who would never again send Bibles and boots to the Africans.

By my hand,
Edward Charles Glyver, —
MDCCCLV

Finis

*Post scriptum**

Marden House
Westgate, Canterbury
Kent

10th December 1854

My dear Edward,—

A brief note, to thank you for yours of the 9th. My brother is coming to town this morning, and has undertaken to ask Birtles to deliver this to you.

As you seem disinclined, no doubt for good reason, to come here, then I shall not press you.

I have to inform you, though, that Mr Donald Orr has written to me – somewhat intemperately – concerning what he calls 'a serious and prolonged dereliction' of your duties. He has indicated to me that he wishes to terminate your employment at Tredgolds, with immediate effect. I have replied, requesting that, if you so desire, you should be allowed to retain your rooms in Temple-street, for as long as you need them.

If, however, that does not accord with your wishes, then there is a cottage hard by my new residence here, which I think would suit you very well, for as long as you needed it. And so I shall leave it in your hands, to let me know what you wish to do.

You did not respond to my offer to speak to Sir Ephraim, on a strictly

*[The following items have been bound in at this point in the manuscript. *Ed.*]

confidential and theoretical basis, concerning the presentation of the evidence to Lord T that you now hold. I make it again. Should you wish to avail yourself of it, I think we can be certain that Sir Ephraim's advocacy would carry great weight with his Lordship.

And so, in anticipation of hearing from you more fully, I wish you God speed, my dear boy, as the season of our Lord's birth approaches, and hope that all continues to go forward as you would wish, and to assure you that I am ready to advise you at any time, and give whatever help I can of a legal character. I pray for an early and successful resolution of your enterprise, regardless of the consequences for myself, to which I beg you to pay no heed. Do what must be done, and set right the injustice that you have suffered for the peace of your mother's dear soul. And may God reward your labours at last. Write when you can.

Yours, most affectionately,
C. Tredgold

The Rectory
Evenwood
Northamptonshire

22nd December 1854

Dear Mr Tredgold, —

I write in gratitude for your letter of sympathy to my wife and me. Of course I remember very well meeting you, with Mr Paul Carteret, on the occasion you mention.

It has been a most terrible time for us, made worse by the violent nature of my son's death. We were first told that a footman by the name of Geddington, temporarily engaged for the evening, was suspected, though there was no obvious reason for the attack; but then came the extraordinary news that the true culprit was Mr Glapthorn, whom I must now call by the name of Glyver. I am sensible that you, too, will have been as utterly shocked as we were to learn that so talented and remarkable a man as Mr Glyver could have committed such a deed. His motives are utterly mysterious, though I now remember (which I had completely forgotten until now) that he was at school with my son. Whether that distant relationship affords any clue to his actions, I cannot say. I have been informed by the police that they believe there may be a connexion with the recent killing of Mr Lucas Trendle, of the Bank of England, which apparently demonstrated many similarities to my son's. It is supposed that Mr Glyver is suffering from some mental affliction – indeed that he may be actually insane. Of his whereabouts, as I expect you know, there is no sign, & it is likely, I suppose, that he has left the country.

Evenwood, as you may imagine, has been thrown into turmoil. My wife, for whom Phoebus was everything, though she was his mother only by marriage, is inconsolable; and Lord Tansor also is deeply stricken. We have lost a son; he has lost his heir. And then there is poor Miss Carteret. What grief that young woman has had to bear is beyond comprehension.

First her father brutally attacked and killed, & now her intended husband. She is a most pitiful sight. I hardly recognized her when I saw her last.

As for myself, I have the comfort of my faith, and the certain knowledge that the God of Abraham and Isaac has taken Phoebus unto Himself. My son was held in such high esteem by everyone who knew him, & by the many readers of his works who did not know him, that we have been overwhelmed by kind expressions of condolence. These, too, have been a great comfort.

As so often in times of trial, I turn to Sir Thomas Browne. On opening the Religio Medici, *soon after the news was brought here of my son's death, my eyes fell on these words:*

'What is made to be immortal, nature cannot – nor will the voice of God – destroy.'

This is my faith. This is my hope.

I remain, my dear Sir,
Yours faithfully,
A. B. Daunt

Marden House
Westgate, Canterbury
Kent

9th January 1855

Dear Captain Le Grice,—

I am in receipt of your enquiry concerning Edward Glyver.

From your letter it appears that you have been the recipient of various confidences concerning Edward's history. This, I may say, came as something of a surprise to me; I had thought that I was the only person in whom he confided. But it seems that none of us can truly claim to have known Edward Glyver; to emphasize the point, I am now in correspondence with a Miss Isabella Gallini, with whom, I gather, Edward enjoyed a close relationship for some time past, but which he had never mentioned to me.

And now it has come to this. I cannot say that I did not fear it would; or to another outcome that, perhaps, we would both have regretted even more. We shall never see him again – of that I am certain. You tell me that you urged him to go abroad, and to give up the business that we both know about. If only he had taken your advice! But by then it was past all remedy – you must have seen, as I did, that fixed, haunted look in his eyes.

Miss Carteret suffers, I am told; but the business has at least cured Lord Tansor of his irrational aversion to the collateral line, and so she will have the comfort in due course of inheriting both the Tansor title, and all the property associated with it. What Edward will feel if he learns of this, I cannot imagine.

As to the deceased gentleman, the least said the better. You will infer that I did not share the world's good opinion of him – though I do not say that he deserved to die. He did great wrong – to Edward, certainly; and there are other things concerning Phoebus Daunt that may never now be told – at least until much time has passed, and no more hurt or harm can be done. But there has been enough of death and deceit; and for what purpose?

I hope this letter will find you safe and well, and I pray that God will protect you, and all our brave soldiers. We have all been appalled by Mr Russell's reports. *

Yours most sincerely,
C. Tredgold

*[William Howard Russell (1820–1907), *The Times*' correspondent in the Crimea. His reports of the conditions suffered by the British Army, and especially by the wounded in the hospital at Scutari, during the winter of 1854–5 scandalized the nation. *Ed.*]

Blithe Lodge
St John's Wood, London

18th January 1855

Dear Mr Tredgold,—

Yr letter arrived only this morning, but I hurry to send you a reply.

I have not seen him since that snowy night in December last. There had been a falling-out between us, I'm afraid, which I greatly regretted. He stood on the front step & wd not come into the house, saying only that he was leaving England for a time and that he had come to beg my forgiveness for being unable to love me as he said I deserved. Then he told me his real name & the truth about his birth – replacing the half-truths (I will not say lies) that I had formerly been given. I understand that you have been long aware of who he really is – he spoke of you most affectionately, & with gratitude for how you have tried to help him. It is a most extraordinary story, & I confess that, at first, I was inclined to think it was all fancy, if not something worse; but I soon saw in his eyes that he was at last speaking the truth. I know also about Miss C—, & how she deceived him in order to deprive him of the proof that would have delivered everything that he had dreamed of into his hands. He told me that he loved her, & that he loves her still. And this is why he can never love me.

We parted, & I asked whether he would come again – as a friend – when he returned. But he only shook his head.

'You have your kingdom now,' was all he said. 'And I have mine.' Then he turned and went. I watched him walk down the path, out into the night. He did not look back.

When my employer, Mrs Daley, brought in the report from The Times, *naming Edward as the suspected killer of Mr Daunt, I thought my heart would break. What a burden he must have carried with him! To do such a terrible, terrible thing, even though clear injury had been done to him! I saw then how far I had been from knowing him, still less of understand-*

ing him. It may be wrong of me to say so, but I shall always think of him fondly, though of course I cannot now regard him as I once did. I loved him truly – then; but he was cruel to me, though I believe not intentionally. He betrayed me, which I might have forgiven. But he did not love me as I deserved, which I cannot forgive.

Yours very sincerely,
Isabella Gallini

*Calle Espiritu Santo**

25th November 1855

My Dear Mr Tredgold,—

I can easily imagine your emotions when you open this letter. Surprise and consternation, I am sure, will be uppermost; but also, I hope, a degree of guilty pleasure, to hear again – though for the last time – from someone who esteems you more highly than any man alive, and to whom you have been a father in all but name.

I have come here, where no one will ever find me, under a name no one knows, to live out my days in a solitude of my own choosing – in a blackened and shattered landscape of extraordinary otherness, carved by a furious god, and constantly fanned by hot African winds. I deserve no sympathy for what I have done; but you, my dear sir, deserve to know how I came here, and why.

After leaving England, on the night of December 11th last, I travelled first to Copenhagen, & then to Fåborg, on the island of Funen, where I remained for nearly a month. From there I went to Germany, to revisit some of my old haunts in and around Heidelberg, before going, first, to S. Bertrand de Comminges in the Pyrenees, where there was a cathedral that I had long wished to see, & then to the island of Mallorca – my last destination until I sailed here.

I intend to say nothing concerning the reason for my exile – to spare you more pain than I have already caused you. I have not escaped punishment, as some may imagine; I am punished every hour I live for the folly of my life, and what it drove me to do. My enemy and I were mined from the same mortal seam; cast into the same furnace of creation, our images impressed on opposite sides of the same coin, separate, but not distinct, con-

*[From the small amount of internal evidence, it appears that the narrator may have written this letter from the volcanic island of Lanzarote. *Ed.*]

joined by some fatal alchemy. I killed him; but in doing so, I killed the best part of myself.

I think much of her *– I mean my mother – & of how alike we were, & how we were both destroyed by believing it was in our own hands to punish those who had done wrong to us. For myself, I felt impelled by a relentless and misguided sense of fatality, which I interpreted as justifying whatever actions I chose to take. My exile has given me more wisdom. I have been immolated by my former belief in a greater Destiny, urging me ever onwards; but now I have found respite and comfort in a re-acceptance of a sterner faith: that we are all sinners, and must all come to judgment. And in this also: that we should not strive against what we cannot mend.*

Of course I think also of my dear girl, whom I shall always love, as you loved my mother. Cruel, cruel! To betray me so, knowing that I loved her above all others for herself alone. Yet though she has tormented me almost beyond endurance, I cannot withhold my forgiveness from her. She will inherit what should have been mine, as I have heard; but she has lost more than she will ever gain; and, like me, she will be required to answer for what she has done.

I live here with few comforts, but enough for my simple needs. My only companion is a one-eyed cat, of superlative hideousness, who appeared on the very first morning of my arrival, and who has not left me since. I have enough of my old humour left to have christened him Jukes.

And so, my dear old Senior Partner, I come at last to what has been occupying me, as a preliminary to asking a final favour of you – if I can trespass on your goodness so far. Since coming here, six months since, I have been writing down all that has happened to me & have accumulated, as a result, a goodly number of large-quarto sheets, purchased for the purpose before I left Mallorca. Yesterday evening, quite late, I laid down my pen at last, and packed all the sheets into a locked wooden box. I now go to meet an English gentleman, a Mr John Lazarus, shipping agent, of Billiter-street, City, who has kindly agreed to deliver the box to you in

Canterbury. He knows me by another name, and of course I can count on you not to disabuse him. The key I shall send to you separately.

If you are so minded – as I hope you will be – I would ask you, on receipt, to arrange for the pages to be bound up (I can recommend Mr Riviere, Great Queen-street) & then, if it can be so contrived, for the volume to be placed privily in the Library at Evenwood, where it may be found, or not, at some future date. It is a great deal to ask; but I can ask it of no one else but you.

There is much I would wish to hear about – of people I have known, and how it goes with the world I have left behind; and, most of all, of you, and how you are, and whether your collection prospers, and whether you are quite recovered. I am now a man apart, and can never again put on the life I once knew. But I pray – yes, truly – for your contentment and good health, and great long life, and beg your forgiveness for what I have done.

This, then, is what I have learned, since writing my confession on this final shore:

> *Honour not the malice of thine enemy so much, as to say, thy misery comes from him: Dishonour not the complexion of the times so much, as to say, thy misery comes from them; justifie not the Deity of Fortune so much, as to say, thy misery comes from her; Finde God pleased with thee, and thou hast a hook in the nostrils of every Leviathan.**

I long for sleep, and for soft English rain. But they do not come.

E.G.

*[A passage from Donne's Sermon XX, on Psalm 38: 3, in *Fifty Sermons* (1649). *Ed.*]

· Appendix ·

P. Rainsford Daunt (1819–54)
List of Published Works

Given in order of publication. Place of publication is London in all cases.

Ithaca: A Lyrical Drama (Edward Moxon, 1841)

The Maid of Minsk: A Poem in Twenty-Two Cantos (Edward Moxon, 1842)

The Tartar-King: A Story in XII Cantos (Edward Moxon, 1843)

Agrippa; with Other Poems (David Bogue, 1845)

The Cave of Merlin: A Poem (Edward Moxon, 1846)

The Pharaoh's Child: A Romance of Ancient Aegypt (Edward Moxon, 1848)

'Memories of Eton', *Saturday Review* (10 October 1848)

Montezuma: A Drama (Edward Moxon, 1849)

The Conquest of Peru: A Dramatic Romance (Edward Moxon, 1850)

Scenes of Early Life (Chapman & Hall, 1852)

Penelope: A Tragedy, in Verse (Bell & Daldy, 1853)

American Sonnets (Longman, Brown, Green & Longman, 1853)

Rosa Mundi; and Other Poems (Edward Moxon, 1854)

The Heir: A Romance of the Modern (Edward Moxon, 1854)

Epimetheus; with other posthumous poems (2 vols., Edward Moxon, 1854 for 1855)

The Art of the Epic (John Murray, 1856)

Acknowledgements

THE LITERARY AND FACTUAL SOURCES ON WHICH I HAVE DRAWN ARE too numerous, too scattered over the years, and in many cases too obvious, to list in full. In particular, accounts of mid-Victorian London abound, and I have freely ransacked them. Thirty years ago, when I first began assembling material for this novel, such works needed to be consulted in a major copyright library. Now many of them are freely available on the Web – I direct interested readers, for example, to the excellent *Victorian Dictionary* site created and maintained by Lee Jackson (www.victorianlondon.org). Indispensable sources of background detail and ambience have of course included Henry Mayhew, whose *London Labour and the London Poor* of 1851 no one writing or fictionalizing about this period can afford to neglect, but also the less well-known works of George Augustus Sala.

Three real places have contributed, in various ways, to the making of Evenwood, Glyver's cursed obsession: Drayton House, the private home of the Stopford-Sackville family, and Deene Park, the former home of James Thomas Brudenell, 7th Earl of Cardigan (of Balaclava fame) – both in my own home county of Northamptonshire; and Burghley House, Stamford. The library of – I mean the books collected by – Lord Tansor's grandfather has been based unashamedly on that of the 2nd Earl Spencer (1758–1834) at Althorp, another of Northamptonshire's great houses. Residents of East Northamptonshire will also recognize the names of several local places in those of some of the characters – Tansor (a charming village outside Oundle) and Glapthorn (ditto), Glyver's principal pseudonym, amongst them. Needless to say, the topography of Evenwood and its environs is pure invention, though Lord Tansor's seat may be envisaged as lying in the north-east corner of Northamptonshire, in the area known as Rockingham Forest.

And so to the most important sources of help and inspiration: people.

For Natasha Fairweather, my agent at A. P. Watt, no thanks are profuse enough. By taking me on, she gave me much needed hope as I was emerging from a very dark time, and through her commitment and professionalism transformed my life – the phrase is not too strong – and that of my family. Professionally speaking, I have been lucky in so many ways, but particularly in my agent. Thanks must also go to Derek Johns at A. P. Watt, to whom I first sent some draft chapters from what became *The Meaning of Night* over a decade ago; to Linda Shaughnessy and her fantastic team, Teresa Nicholls and Madeleine Buston, for getting the book to so many foreign-language publishers; to Philippa Donovan, especially for her close reading of the book's final draft; and Rob Kraitt to everyone else at A. P. Watt who have helped, and are helping, to make it all happen.

To my British publisher, Anya Serota at John Murray, I shall always feel immense gratitude. She was the first publisher to read the book, and it was her immediate and overwhelming response that got the ball well and truly rolling. She has been an unfailing source of encouragement and good sense, and the telling of Glyver's story has benefited hugely as a result of her careful and inspired editing. Indeed she has lived in Glyver's world as intensely as I have, and it shows. A great editor needs to be part diplomat, part benign dictator, and part counsellor. Anya has been all this, and more.

I cannot possibly name and thank individually all the people at John Murray who have helped, in all their various ways, in the book's production, publication, and promotion. Everyone has shown the most remarkable passion and commitment to *The Meaning of Night*; so whoever you are, and whatever you've done, I am grateful beyond words. But I must acknowledge those with whom I have been directly involved: Roland Philipps, John Murray's Managing Director; James Spackman; Nikki Barrow; Sara Marafini; Amanda Jones; Caro Westmore; Ed Faulkner; Maisie Sather; and all those people at John Murray and in the wider Hachette group, both in the UK and overseas, whose enthusiasm and support have contributed so much.

I am immensely grateful to my two North American editors – Jill Bialosky, at W. W. Norton, and Ellen Seligman, at McClelland & Stuart – both of whom provided much-appreciated encouragement and support throughout the final phase of writing. Grateful thanks also go to Louise Brockett, Bill Rusin, Erin Sinesky, and Evan Carver at Norton; Doug Pepper and Ruta Liormonas at McCelland & Stuart; and to everyone in both companies – again too numerous to name individually – who have been involved in publishing *The Meaning of Night*. I would also like to thank my foreign-language publishers for their enthusiastic commitment to making Glyver's story available to readers from Europe, Japan, and South America, as well as acknowledging the not inconsiderable labours of the individual translators.

Amongst those who have provided me with valuable background information I must acknowledge, first of all, the advice provided by Clive Cheesman, Rouge Dragon Pursuivant, at the College of Arms, on various matters relating to the (fictitious) Tansor Barony, and to the legal intricacies of Baronies by Writ. I cannot thank him enough for the care and courtesy with which he responded to all my enquiries. Without the benefit of his expertise, I do not know what legal and genealogical howlers I might have committed. Anything of that kind that may have slipped through the net is, of course, most definitely my responsibility, not his.

Michael Meredith, Librarian of Eton College, and Penny Hatfield, the Eton Archivist, supplied help on several details concerning Glyver's and Daunt's time at the school, in particular the *Ralph Roister Doister* incident, although they should in no way be held responsible for the fictional results.

Gordon Biddle helped to establish how Glyver travelled by train from Stamford to London via Cambridge; whilst for advice on the technical aspects of Glyver's passion for photography I am grateful to Dr Robin Lenman. Further advice on early photography was kindly provided by Peter Marshall.

I tender particular and admiring thanks to Celia Levett, for her miraculously meticulous copy-editing, and to Nick de Somogyi, for his equally rigorous proof-reading. Both have saved me from much embarrassment. I am also indebted to David Young, CEO of Hachette Livre USA, for his enthusiastic and confidence-boosting verdict on a draft of Part 1, and to another old and valued friend, Owen Dudley Edwards, who gallantly undertook to read the proofs over the course of a weekend and, with his usual erudition and generosity of spirit, gently pointed out a number of places where I had fallen below his own high standards of accuracy and expression.

To [Achilles] James Daunt, proprietor of Daunt's Bookshop in London, may I also record my appreciation for not objecting to the fact that I unwittingly appropriated his name for the Rector of Evenwood.

I would like to express here, without elaboration, my gratitude, and that of my family, to a group of people who have – literally – helped give me the chance to finish what has been in my mind for so long: Professor Christer Lindquist, together with Beth McLaughlin and all the other members of the Gamma Knife team at the Cromwell Hospital, London; Mr Christopher Adams; Dr Adrian Jones; Dr Diana Brown; and Professor John Wass.

Finally, like all authors who depend on those close to them for almost daily support and understanding, what is undeniably real about this novel is the debt I owe to my family: to my darling wife Dizzy, without whom I would have no reason to write; our daughter Emily (whose name, I must emphasize, is the only link with my main female character); my stepchildren Miranda and Barnaby; my grandchildren, Eleanor, Harry, and Dizzy Junior, and my daughter-in-law Becky; my mother-in-law, Joan Crockett, in whose house portions of the novel were written, and the other members of the Crockett clan in Dorset. It is a sadness to us all that my late father-in-law, Gee Crockett, is not here to see the novel published. Last, but never least, my thanks and love go to my wonderful parents, Gordon and Eileen Cox, who have supported me through thick and thin.

MICHAEL COX